THE COMPLETE SHORT STORIES
OF
W. SOMERSET MAUGHAM
II

Books by
W. SOMERSET MAUGHAM

Novels

CATALINA
ASHENDEN
THEN AND NOW
THE RAZOR'S EDGE
THE HOUR BEFORE THE DAWN
THE MOON AND SIXPENCE
UP AT THE VILLA
MRS. CRADDOCK
CHRISTMAS HOLIDAY
CAKES AND ALE
THEATRE
THE PAINTED VEIL
THE NARROW CORNER
OF HUMAN BONDAGE
LIZA OF LAMBETH

Short Stories

ENCORE
TRIO
QUARTET
CREATURES OF CIRCUMSTANCE
THE TREMBLING OF A LEAF
THE MIXTURE AS BEFORE
AH KING
COSMOPOLITANS
THE CASUARINA TREE
FIRST PERSON SINGULAR
EAST AND WEST
THE WORLD OVER

Essays

FRANCE AT WAR
STRICTLY PERSONAL

THE SUMMING UP
BOOKS AND YOU
A WRITER'S NOTEBOOK
THE MAUGHAM READER

Travel

ON A CHINESE SCREEN
DON FERNANDO
THE GENTLEMAN IN THE
  PARLOUR
THE LAND OF THE BLESSED
  VIRGIN

Plays

FOR SERVICES RENDERED
A MAN OF HONOUR
THE BREADWINNER
PENELOPE
THE SACRED FLAME
JACK STRAW
SHEPPEY
LADY FREDERICK
THE CONSTANT WIFE
THE TENTH MAN
THE CIRCLE
LANDED GENTRY
THE EXPLORER
THE UNKNOWN MRS. DOT
  SMITH
OUR BETTERS
THE LAND OF PROMISE
SIX COMEDIES

The Complete
Short Stories of
W. SOMERSET
MAUGHAM

II
The World Over

DOUBLEDAY & COMPANY, INC.

Garden City, New York

W

Library of Congress Catalog Card Number: 52-11626

PREFACE

THIS BOOK contains all the stories I have written that are not included in *East and West*. The tales in that collection were of about the same length and written on the same scale and so it seemed convenient to publish them together in a single volume. Most of the stories which I have now gathered together are very much shorter. Some were written many years ago, others more recently. They appeared in magazines and were afterwards issued in book form. To the first lot I gave the title of *Cosmopolitans*, because they were offered to the public in the *Cosmopolitan Magazine*, and except for Ray Long, who was then its editor, would never have been written.

When I was in China in 1920 I took notes of whatever I saw that excited my interest, with the intention of making a connected narrative out of them; but when I came home and read them it seemed to me that they had a vividness which I might easily lose if I tried to elaborate them. So I changed my mind and decided to publish them as they stood under the title: *On a Chinese Screen*. Ray Long chanced to read this and it occurred to him that some of my notes might well be taken for short stories. I have included two of them, "The Taipan" and "The Consul," in this volume. The fact is that if you are a storyteller any curious person you meet has a way of suggesting a story, and incidents that to others will seem quite haphazard have a way of presenting themselves to you with the pattern your natural instinct has impressed on them.

Magazine readers do not like starting a story and, after reading for a while, being told to turn to page one hundred and something. Writers do not like it either, for they think the interruption disturbs the reader and they have besides an uneasy fear that sometimes he will not take the trouble and so leave their story unfinished. There is no help for it. Everyone should know that a magazine costs more to produce than it is sold for, and could not exist but for the advertisements. The advertisers think that their announcements are more likely to be read if they are on the same page as matter which they modestly, but often mistakenly, think of greater interest. So in the illustrated periodicals it has been found advisable to put the beginning of a story or an article, with the picture that purports to illustrate it, at the beginning and the continuation with the advertisements later on.

Neither readers nor writers should complain. Readers get something for far less than cost price and writers are paid sums for their productions which only the advertisements render possible. They should remember that they are only there as bait. Their office is to fill blank spaces and indirectly induce their readers to buy motor accessories, aids to beauty and join correspondence courses. Fortunately this need not affect them. The best story from the advertisers' standpoint (and they make their views felt on this question) is the story that gives readers most entertainment. Ray Long conceived the notion that the readers of the *Cosmopolitan* would like it if they were given at least one story that they could read without having to hunt for the continuation among the advertisements, and he commissioned me to write half a dozen sketches of the same sort as those in *On a Chinese Screen*. They were to be short enough to print on opposite pages of the magazine and leave plenty of room for illustration.

The sketches I wrote pleased and the commission was renewed. I went on writing them until my natural verbosity got the better of me and I found myself no longer able to keep my stories within the limits imposed upon me. Then I had to stop. I think I learned a good deal from the writing of them and I am glad that I did. My difficulty was to compress what I had to tell into a number of words which must not be exceeded and yet leave the reader with the impression that I had told all there was to tell. It was this that made the enterprise amusing. It was also salutary. I could not afford to waste a word. I had to be succinct. I was surprised to find how many adverbs and adjectives I could leave out without any harm to the matter or the manner. One often writes needless words because they give the phrase balance. It was very good practice to try to get it into a sentence without using a word that was not necessary to the sense.

The matter, of course, had to be chosen with discretion; it would have been futile to take a theme that demanded elaborate development. I have a natural predilection for completeness, so that even in the little space at my disposal I wanted my story to have a certain structure. I do not care for the shapeless story. To my mind it is not enough when the writer gives you the plain facts seen through his own eyes (which means of course that they are not plain facts, but facts coloured by his own idiosyncrasy) ; I think he should impose a pattern on them. Naturally these stories are anecdotes. If stories are interesting and well told they are none the worse for that. The anecdote is the basis of fiction. The restlessness of writers forces upon fiction from time to time forms that are foreign to it, but when it has been oppressed for a period by obscurity, propaganda or affectation, it reverts, and returns inevitably to the proper function of fiction, which is to tell an interesting story.

In the preface to *East and West* I said pretty well all I had to say about the short story in general. I have nothing to add to that. I have written now nearly a hundred stories and one thing I have discovered is that whether you hit upon a story or not, whether it comes off or not, is very much a matter of luck. Stories are lying about at every street corner, but the writer may not be there at the moment they are waiting to be picked up or he may be looking at a shop window and pass them unnoticed. He may write them before he has seen all there is to see in them or he may turn them over in his mind so long that they have lost their freshness. He may not have seen them from the exact standpoint at which they can be written to their best advantage. It is a rare and happy event when he conceives the idea of a story, writes it at the precise moment when it is ripe, and treats it in such a way as to get out of it all that it implicitly contains. Then it will be within its limitations perfect. But perfection is seldom achieved. I think a volume of modest dimensions would contain all the short stories which even closely approach it. The reader should be satisfied if in any collection of these short pieces of fiction he finds a general level of competence and on closing the book feels that he has been amused, interested and moved.

With one exception all the stories I have written have been published in magazines. The exception is a story called "The Book Bag." When I sent it to Ray Long he wrote to me, in sorrow rather than in anger, that he had gone further with me than with any other author, but when it came to incest he had to draw the line. I could not blame him. He published the tale later in a collection of what he thought in his long career as editor of the *Cosmopolitan* were the best short stories that had ever been offered him. I know that in admitting that my stories have been published in magazines I lay myself open to critical depreciation, for to describe a tale as a magazine story is to condemn it. But when the critics do this they show less acumen than may reasonably be expected of them. Nor do they show much knowledge of literary history. For ever since magazines became a popular form of publication authors have found them a useful medium to put their work before readers. All the greatest short-story writers have published their stories in magazines, Balzac, Flaubert and Maupassant; Chekhov, Henry James, Rudyard Kipling. I do not think it rash to say that the only short stories that have not been published in a magazine are the stories that no editor would accept. So to damn a story because it is a magazine story is absurd. The magazines doubtless publish a great many bad stories, but then more bad stories are written than good ones, and an editor, even of a magazine with literary pretensions, is often obliged to print a story of which he doesn't think highly because he can get nothing better. Some editors of popular magazines think their readers demand a certain type of story and will take nothing else; and they manage to find writers who can turn out the sort of thing they want and often make a very good job of it. This is the machine-made article that has given the magazine story a bad name. But after all, no one is obliged to read it. It gives satisfaction to many people since it allows them for a brief period to experience in fancy the romance and adventure which in the monotony of their lives they crave for.

But if I may judge from the reviews I have read of the volumes of short stories that are frequently published, where the critics to my mind err is when they dismiss stories as magazine stories because they are well constructed, dramatic and have a surprise ending. There is nothing to be condemned in a surprise

ending if it is the natural end of a story. On the contrary it is
an excellence. It is only bad when, as in some of O. Henry's
stories, it is dragged in without reason to give the reader a kick.
Nor is a story any the worse for being neatly built, with a beginning, a middle and an end. All good story writers have done
their best to achieve this. It is the fashion of today for writers,
under the influence of an inadequate acquaintance with Chekhov, to write stories that begin anywhere and end inconclu-
sively. They think it enough if they have described a mood, or
given an impression, or drawn a character. That is all very well,
but it is not a story, and I do not think it satisfies the reader.
He does not like to be left wondering. He wants to have his
questions answered. That is what I have tried to do, and when
a story was suggested to me of which I didn't know the answer
I forbore to write it. One such story I wrote about in *A Writer's
Notebook*, and since I don't expect everyone to have read everything I have written I think it may amuse the reader if I here
repeat it. When I was in India I received a letter from a man
unknown to me in which he told me the following incident in
the belief that I might be able to make use of it:

Two young fellows were working on a tea plantation in the
hills and the mail had to be fetched from a long way off so that
they only got it at rather long intervals. One of the young fellows, let us call him A, got a lot of letters by every mail, ten or
twelve and sometimes more, but the other, B, never got one. He
used to watch A enviously as he took his bundle and started to
read; he hankered to have a letter, just one letter; and one day,
when they were expecting the mail, he said to A: "Look here,
you always have a packet of letters and I never get any. I'll give
you five pounds if you'll let me have one of yours." "Right-ho,"
said A, and when the mail came in he handed B his letters and
said to him: "Take whichever you like." B gave him a five-
pound note, looked over the letters, chose one and returned the
rest. In the evening when they were having a whisky and soda
before dinner, A asked casually: "By the way, what was that
letter about?" "I'm not going to tell you," said B. A, somewhat
taken aback, said: "Well, who was it from?" "That's my business," answered B. They had a bit of an argument, but B stood
on his rights and refused to say anything about the letter he
had bought. A began to fret, and as the weeks went by he did
all he could to persuade B to let him see the letter. B continued
to refuse. At length A, anxious, worried and curious, felt he

couldn't bear it any longer, so he went to B and said: "Look here, here's your five pounds, let me have my letter back again." "Not on your life," said B. "I bought it and paid for it, it's my letter and I'm not going to give it up."

In *A Writer's Notebook* I added: "I suppose if I belonged to the modern school of story writers I should write it just as it is and leave it. It goes against the grain with me. I want a story to have form, and I don't see how you can give it that unless you can bring it to a conclusion that leaves no legitimate room for questioning. But even if you could bring yourself to leave the reader up in the air you don't want to leave yourself up in the air with him." The facts as my correspondent gave them to me intrigued a good many people, and a magazine in Canada and *The New Statesman* in England, independently of one another, offered prizes to their readers for the best conclusion to the story. I don't know that the results were particularly successful.

There are literary vogues that come and go. At present short-story writers appear to have a disinclination for anything but quite usual and commonplace incident. The result is a spate of drab stories in which nothing happens. I think the influence of Chekhov is responsible for this; on one occasion he wrote: "People do not go to the North Pole and fall off icebergs; they go to offices, quarrel with their wives and eat cabbage soup." But people *do* go to the North Pole, and if they don't fall off icebergs they undergo experiences as perilous; and there is no reason why an author should not write as good stories about them as about people who eat cabbage soup. But obviously it isn't enough that they should go to their offices, quarrel with their wives and eat cabbage soup. Chekhov certainly never thought it was. In order to make a story at all they must steal the petty cash at the office, murder or leave their wives, and when they eat their cabbage soup it must be with emotion or significance. Cabbage soup then becomes a symbol of the satisfaction of a domestic life or the anguish of a frustrated one. To eat it may thus be as catastrophic as falling off an iceberg. But it is just as unusual. The simple reason for Chekhov's statement is that he believed what writers, being human, are very apt to believe; namely, that what he was best able to do was the best thing to do.

I read once an article on how to write a short story. Certain points the author made were useful, but to my mind the central

thesis was wrong. She stated that the "focal point" of a short
story should be the building of character and that the incidents
should be invented solely to "liven" personality. Oddly enough
she remarked earlier in her article that the parables are the best
short stories that have ever been written. I think it would be
difficult to describe the characters of the Prodigal Son and his
brother or of the Good Samaritan and the Man who fell among
thieves. They are in fact not characterized and we have to guess
what sort of people they were, for we are only told about them
the essential facts necessary for the pointing of the moral. And
that, whether he has a moral to point or not, is about all the
short-story writer can do. He has no room to describe and
develop a character; at best he can only give the salient traits
that bring the character to life and so make the story he has to
tell plausible. Since the beginning of history men have gathered
around the campfire or in a group in the market place to listen
to the telling of stories. The desire to listen to them appears to
be as deeply rooted in the human animal as the sense of property. I have never pretended to be anything but a storyteller.
It has amused me to tell stories and I have told a great many.

I have been writing stories for fifty years. In that long period
I have seen a number of bright stars creep shyly over the hori-
zon, travel across the sky to burn with a more or less gem-like
flame for a while in mid-heaven, and then dwindle into an
obscurity from which there is little likelihood that they will ever
emerge. The writer has his special communication to make,
which, when you come to analyse it, is the personality with
which he is endowed by nature, and during the early years
of his activity he is groping in the dark to express it; then,
if he is fortunate, he succeeds in doing this and if there is in
his personality a certain abundance he may contrive for a
long time to produce work which is varied and characteristic;
but the time comes at last (if he is so imprudent as to live
to a ripe age) when, having given what he has to give, his
powers fail. He has fashioned all the stories he himself is capable of digging out of the inexhaustible mine which is human
nature and he has created all the characters which can possibly
be constituted out of the various sides of his own personality.
For no one, I believe, can create a character from pure observation; if it is to have life it must be at least in some degree a
representation of himself. A generation has arisen which is
strange to him and it is only by an effort of will that he can

understand the interests of a world of which he can now be only an observer. But to understand is not enough; the writer of fiction must feel, and he must not only feel with, he must feel in. It is well then if he can bring himself to cease writing stories which might just as well have remained unwritten. He is wise to watch warily for the signs which will indicate to him that, having said his say, it behoves him to resign himself to silence. I have written my last story.

CONTENTS

xiv   Contents

THE COMPLETE SHORT STORIES

OF

W. SOMERSET MAUGHAM

II

A WOMAN OF FIFTY

My friend Wyman Holt is a professor of English Literature in
one of the smaller universities of the Middle West, and hearing
that I was speaking in a near-by city—near-by as distances go
in the vastness of America—he wrote to ask me if I would come
and give a talk to his class. He suggested that I should stay
with him for a few days so that he could show me something of
the surrounding country. I accepted the invitation, but told
him that my engagements would prevent me from spending
more than a couple of nights with him. He met me at the station, drove me to his house and after we had had a drink we
walked over to the campus. I was somewhat taken aback to find
so many people in the hall in which I was to speak, for I had
not expected more than twenty at the outside and I was not
prepared to give a solemn lecture, but only an informal chat. I
was more than a little intimidated to see a number of middle-
aged and elderly persons, some of whom I suspected were members of the faculty, and I was afraid they would find what I had
to say very superficial. However, there was nothing to do but to
start and, after Wyman had introduced me to the audience in a
manner that I very well knew I couldn't live up to, that is what
I did. I said my say, I answered as best I could a number of
questions, and then I retired with Wyman into a little room at
the back of the stage from which I had spoken.

Several people came in. They said the usual kindly things to
me that are said on these occasions, and I made the usual polite

replies. I was thirsting for a drink. Then a woman came in and
held out her hand to me.

"How very nice it is to see you again," she said. "It's years
since we last met."

To the best of my belief I'd never set eyes on her before. I
forced a cordial smile to my tired, stiff lips, shook her proffered
hand effusively and wondered who the devil she was. My professor must have seen from my face that I was trying to place
her, for he said:

"Mrs. Greene is married to a member of our faculty and she
gives a course on the Renaissance and Italian literature."

"Really," I said. "Interesting."

I was no wiser than before.

"Has Wyman told you that you're dining with us to-morrow
night?"

"I'm very glad," I said.

"It's not a party. Only my husband, his brother and my sis-
ter-in-law. I suppose Florence has changed a lot since then."

"Florence?" I said to myself. "Florence?"

That was evidently where I'd known her. She was a woman
of about fifty with grey hair simply done and marcelled without
exaggeration. She was a trifle too stout and she was dressed
neatly enough, but without distinction, in a dress that I guessed
had been bought ready-made at the local branch of a big store.
She had rather large eyes of a pale blue and a poor complexion;
she wore no rouge and had used a lipstick but sparingly. She
seemed a nice creature. There was something maternal in her
demeanour, something placid and fulfilled, which I found appealing. I supposed that I had run across her on one of my frequent visits to Florence and because it was perhaps the only
time she had been there our meeting made more of an impression on her than on me. I must confess that my acquaintance
with the wives of members of a faculty is very limited, but she
was just the sort of person I should have expected the wife of a
professor to be, and picturing her life, useful but uneventful, on
scanty means, with its little social gatherings, its bickerings, its
gossip, its busy dullness, I could easily imagine that her trip to
Florence must linger with her as a thrilling and unforgettable
experience.

On the way back to his house Wyman said to me:

"You'll like Jasper Greene. He's clever."

"What's he a professor of?"

"He's not a professor; he's an instructor. A fine scholar. He's her second husband. She was married to an Italian before."

"Oh?" That didn't chime in with my ideas at all. "What was her name?"

"I haven't a notion. I don't believe it was a great success." Wyman chuckled. "That's only a deduction I draw from the fact that she hasn't a single thing in the house to suggest that she ever spent any time in Italy. I should have expected her to have at least a refectory table, an old chest or two and an embroidered cope hanging on the wall."

I laughed. I knew those rather dreary pieces that people buy when they're in Italy, the gilt wooden candlesticks, the Venetian glass mirrors and the high-backed, comfortless chairs. They look well enough when you see them in the crowded shops of the dealers in antiques, but when you bring them to another country they're too often a sad disappointment. Even if they're genuine, which they seldom are, they look ill-at-ease and out of place.

"Laura has money," Wyman went on. "When they married she furnished the house from cellar to attic in Chicago. It's quite a show place; it's a little masterpiece of hideousness and vulgarity. I never go into the living-room without marvelling at the unerring taste with which she picked out exactly what you'd expect to find in the bridal suite of a second-class hotel in Atlantic City."

To explain this irony I should state that Wyman's living-room was all chromium and glass, rough modern fabrics, with a boldly Cubist rug on the floor, and on the walls Picasso prints and drawings by Tchelicheff. However, he gave me a very good dinner. We spent the evening chatting pleasantly about things that mutually interested us and finished it with a couple of bottles of beer. I went to bed in a room of somewhat aggressive modernity. I read for a while and then putting out the light composed myself to sleep.

"Laura?" I said to myself. "Laura what?"

I tried to think back. I thought of all the people I knew in Florence, hoping that by association I might recall when and where I had come in contact with Mrs. Greene. Since I was going to dine with her I wanted to recall something that would prove that I had not forgotten her. People look upon it as a slight if you don't remember them. I suppose we all attach a sort of importance to ourselves, and it is humiliating to realise that we have left no impression at all upon the persons we have associated with. I dozed off, but before I fell into the blessedness of deep sleep, my subconscious, released from the effort of striving at recollection, I suppose, grew active and I was suddenly wide awake, for I remembered who Laura Greene was. It was no wonder that I had forgotten her, for it was twenty-five years since I had seen her, and then only haphazardly during a month I spent in Florence.

It was just after the First World War. She had been engaged to a man who was killed in it and she and her mother had managed to get over to France to see his grave. They were San Francisco people. After doing their sad errand they had come down to Italy and were spending the winter in Florence. At that time there was quite a large colony of English and Americans. I had some American friends, a Colonel Harding and his wife, colonel because he had occupied an important position in the Red Cross, who had a handsome villa in the Via Bolognese, and they asked me to stay with them. I spent most of my mornings sightseeing and met my friends at Doney's in the Via Tornabuoni round about noon to drink a cocktail. Doney's was the gathering-place of everybody one knew, Americans, English and such of the Italians as frequented their society. There you heard all the gossip of the town. There was generally a lunch-party either at a restaurant or at one or other of the villas with their fine old gardens a mile or two from the centre of the city. I had been given a card to the Florence Club, and in the afternoon Charley Harding and I used to go there to play bridge or a dangerous game of poker with a pack of thirty-two cards. In the evening there would be a dinner-party with more bridge perhaps and often dancing. One met the same people all the time, but the group was large enough, the people sufficiently various, to prevent it from being tedious. Everyone was more or less interested in the arts, as was only right and proper in Florence, so that, idle as life seemed, it was not entirely frivolous.

Laura and her mother, Mrs. Clayton, a widow, lived in one of the better boarding-houses. They appeared to be comfortably off. They had come to Florence with letters of introduction and soon made many friends. Laura's story appealed to the sympathies, and people were glad on that account to do what they could for the two women, but they were in themselves nice and quickly became liked for themselves. They were hospitable and gave frequent lunches at one or other of the restaurants where one ate macaroni and the inevitable scaloppini, and drank Chianti. Mrs. Clayton was perhaps a little lost in this cosmopolitan society, where matters that were strange to her were seriously or gaily talked about, but Laura took to it as though it were her native element. She engaged an Italian woman to teach her the language and soon was reading the *Inferno* with her; she devoured books on the art of the Renaissance and on Florentine history, and I sometimes came across her, Baedeker in hand, at the Uffizzi or in some church studiously examining works of art.

She was twenty-four or twenty-five then and I was well over forty, so that though we often met we became cordially acquainted rather than intimate. She was by no means beautiful, but she was comely in rather an unusual way; she had an oval face with bright blue eyes and very dark hair which she wore very simply, parted in the middle, drawn over her ears and tied in a chignon low on the nape of her neck. She had a good skin and a naturally high colour; her features were good without being remarkable and her teeth were even, small and white; but her chief asset was her easy grace of movement, and I was not surprised when they told me that she danced "divinely." Her figure was very good, somewhat fuller than was the fashion of the moment; and I think what made her attractive was the odd mingling in her appearance of the Madonna in an altar-piece by one of the later Italian painters and a suggestion of sensuality. It certainly made her very alluring to the Italians who gathered at Doney's in the morning or were occasionally invited to lunch or dinner in the American or English villas. She was evidently accustomed to dealing with amorous young men, for though she was charming, gracious and friendly with them she kept them at their distance. She quickly discovered that they were all looking for an American heiress who would restore the family fortunes, and with a demure amusement which I found admirable made them delicately understand that she was far from rich. They sighed a little and turned their attentions at Doney's, which was their happy hunting-ground, to more likely objects. They continued to dance with her, and to keep their hand in flirted with her, but their aspirations ceased to be matrimonial.

But there was one young man who persisted. I knew him slightly because he was one of the regular poker-players at the club. I played occasionally. It was impossible to win and the disgruntled foreigners used sometimes to say that the Italians ganged up on us, but it may be only that they knew the particular game they played better than we did. Laura's admirer, Tito di San Pietro, was a bold and even reckless player and would often lose sums he could ill afford. (That was not his real name, but I call him that since his own is famous in Florentine history.) He was a good-looking youth, neither short nor tall, with fine black eyes, thick black hair brushed back from his forehead and shining with oil, an olive skin, and features of classical regularity. He was poor and he had some vague occupation, which did not seem to interfere with his amusements, but he was always beautifully dressed. No one quite knew where he lived, in a furnished room perhaps or in the attic of some relation; and all that remained of his ancestors' great possessions was a cinquecento villa about thirty miles from the city. I never saw it, but I was told that it was of amazing beauty, with a great neglected garden of cypresses and live oaks, overgrown borders of box, terraces, artificial grottoes and crumbling statues. His widowed father, the count, lived there alone and subsisted on the wine he made from the vines of the small property he still owned and the oil from his olive trees. He seldom came to Florence, so I never met him, but Charley Harding knew him fairly well.

"He's a perfect specimen of the Tuscan nobleman of the old school," he said. "He was in the diplomatic service in his youth and he knows the world. He has beautiful manners and such an air, you almost feel he's doing you a favour when he says how d'you do to you. He's a brilliant talker. Of course he hasn't a penny, he squandered the little he inherited on gambling and women, but he bears his poverty with great dignity. He acts as though money were something beneath his notice."

"What sort of age is he?" I asked.

"Fifty, I should say, but he's still the handsomest man I've ever seen in my life."

"Oh?"

"You describe him, Bessie. When he first came here he made a pass at Bessie. I've never been quite sure how far it went."

"Don't be a fool, Charley," Mrs. Harding laughed.

She gave him the sort of look a woman gives her husband when she has been married to him many years and is quite satisfied with him.

"He's very attractive to women and he knows it," she said. "When he talks to you he gives you the impression that you're the only woman in the world and of course it's flattering. But it's only a game and a woman would have to be a perfect fool to take him seriously. He *is* very handsome. Tall and spare and he holds himself well. He has great dark liquid eyes, like the boy's; his hair is snow-white, but very thick still, and the contrast with his bronzed, young face is really breath-taking. He has a ravaged, rather battered look, but at the same time a look of such distinction, it's really quite incredibly romantic."

"He also has his great dark liquid eyes on the main chance," said Charley Harding dryly. "And he'll never let Tito marry a girl who has no more money than Laura."

"She has about five thousand dollars a year of her own," said Bessie. "And she'll get that much more when her mother dies."

"Her mother can live for another thirty years, and five thousand a year won't go far to keep a husband, a father and two or three children, and restore a ruined villa with practically not a stick of furniture in it."

"I think the boy's desperately in love with her."

"How old is he?" I asked.

"Twenty-six."

A few days after this Charley, on coming back to lunch, since for once we were lunching by ourselves, told me that he had run across Mrs. Clayton in the Via Tornabuoni and she had said that she and Laura were driving out that afternoon with Tito to meet his father and see the villa.

"What d'you suppose that means?" asked Bessie.

"My guess is that Tito is taking Laura to be inspected by his old man, and if he approves he's going to ask her to marry him."

"And will he approve?"

"Not on your life."

But Charley was wrong. After the two women had been shown over the house they were taken for a walk round the garden. Without exactly knowing how it had happened Mrs. Clayton found herself alone in an alley with the old count. She spoke no Italian, but he had been an attaché in London and his English was tolerable.

"Your daughter is charming, Mrs. Clayton," he said. "I am not surprised that my Tito has fallen in love with her."

Mrs. Clayton was no fool and it may be that she too had guessed why the young man had asked them to go and see the ancestral villa.

"Young Italians are very impressionable. Laura is sensible enough not to take their attentions too seriously."

"I was hoping she was not quite indifferent to the boy."

"I have no reason to believe that she likes him any more than any other of the young men who dance with her," Mrs. Clayton answered somewhat coldly. "I think I should tell you at once that my daughter has a very moderate income and she will have no more till I die."

"I will be frank with you. I have nothing in the world but this house and the few acres that surround it. My son could not afford to marry a penniless girl, but he is not a fortune-hunter and he loves your daughter."

The count had not only the grand manner, but a great deal of charm and Mrs. Clayton was not insensible to it. She softened a little.

"All that is neither here nor there. We don't arrange our children's marriages in America. If Tito wants to marry her, let him ask her, and if she's prepared to marry him she'll presumably say so."

"Unless I am greatly mistaken that is just what he is doing now. I hope with all my heart that he will be successful."

They strolled on and presently saw walking towards them the two young people hand in hand. It was not difficult to guess what had passed. Tito kissed Mrs. Clayton's hand and his father on both cheeks.

"Mrs. Clayton, Papa, Laura has consented to be my wife."

The engagement made something of a stir in Florentine society and a number of parties were given for the young couple. It was quite evident that Tito was very much in love, but less so that Laura was. He was good-looking, adoring, high-spirited and gay; it was likely enough that she loved him; but she was a girl who did not display emotion and she remained what she had always been, somewhat placid, amiable, serious but friendly, and easy to talk to. I wondered to what extent she had been influenced to accept Tito's offer by his great name, with its historical associations, and the sight of that beautiful house with its lovely view and the romantic garden.

"Anyhow there's no doubt about its being a love match on his side," said Bessie Harding, when we were talking it over. "Mrs. Clayton tells me that neither Tito nor his father has shown any desire to know how much Laura has."

"I'd bet a million dollars that they know to the last cent what she's got and they've calculated exactly how much it comes to in *lire*," said Harding with a grunt.

"You're a beastly old man, darling," she answered.

He gave another grunt.

Shortly after that I left Florence. The marriage took place from the Hardings' house and a vast crowd came to it, ate their food and drank their champagne. Tito and his wife took an apartment on the Lungarno and the old count returned to his lonely villa in the hills. I did not go to Florence again for three years and then only for a week. I was staying once more with the Hardings. I asked about my old friends and then remembered Laura and her mother.

"Mrs. Clayton went back to San Francisco," said Bessie, "and Laura and Tito live at the villa with the count. They're very happy."

"Any babies?"

"No."

"Go on," said Harding.

Bessie gave her husband a look.

"I cannot imagine why I've lived thirty years with a man I dislike so much," she said. "They gave up the apartment on the Lungarno. Laura spent a good deal of money doing things to the villa, there wasn't a bathroom in it, she put in central heating, and she had to buy a lot of furniture to make it habitable, and then Tito lost a small fortune playing poker and poor Laura had to pay up."

"Hadn't he got a job?"

"It didn't amount to anything and it came to an end."

"What Bessie means by that is that he was fired," Harding put in.

"Well, to cut a long story short, they thought it would be more economical to live at the villa and Laura had the idea that it would keep Tito out of mischief. She loves the garden and she's made it lovely. Tito simply worships her and the old count's taken quite a fancy to her. So really it's all turned out very well."

"It may interest you to know that Tito was in last Thursday," said Harding. "He played like a madman and I don't know how much he lost."

"Oh, Charley. He promised Laura he'd never play again."

"As if a gambler ever kept a promise like that. It'll be like last time. He'll burst into tears and say he loves her and it's a debt of honour and unless he can get the money he'll blow his brains out. And Laura will pay as she paid before."

"He's weak, poor dear, but that's his only fault. Unlike most Italian husbands he's absolutely faithful to her and he's kindness itself." She looked at Harding with a sort of humorous grimness. "I've yet to find a husband who was perfect."

"You'd better start looking around pretty soon, dear, or it'll be too late," he retorted with a grin.

I left the Hardings and returned to London. Charley Harding and I corresponded in a desultory sort of way, and about a year later I got a letter from him. He told me as usual what he had been doing in the interval, and mentioned that he had been to Montecatini for the baths and had gone with Bessie to visit friends in Rome; he spoke of the various people I knew in Florence, So and So had just bought a Bellini and Mrs. Such and Such had gone to America to divorce her husband. Then he went on: "I suppose you've heard about the San Pietros. It's shaken us all and we can talk of nothing else. Laura's terribly upset, poor thing, and she's going to have a baby. The police keep on questioning her and that doesn't make it any easier for her. Of course we brought her to stay here. Tito comes up for trial in another month."

I hadn't the faintest notion what all this was about. So I wrote at once to Harding asking him what it meant. He answered with a long letter. What he had to tell me was terrible. I will relate the bare and brutal facts as shortly as I can. I learned them partly from Harding's letter and partly from what he and Bessie told me when two years later I was with them once more.

The count and Laura took to one another at once and Tito was pleased to see how quickly they had formed an affectionate friendship, for he was as devoted to his father as he was in love with his wife. He was glad that the count began to come more often to Florence than he had been used to. They had a spare room in the apartment and on occasion he spent two or three nights with them. He and Laura would go bargain-hunting in the antique shops and buy old pieces to put in the villa. He had tact and knowledge and little by little the house, with its spacious rooms and marble floors, lost its forlorn air and became a friendly place to live in. Laura had a passion for gardening and she and the count spent long hours together planning and then supervising the workmen who were restoring the gardens to their ancient, rather stately, beauty.

Laura made light of it when Tito's financial difficulties forced them to give up the apartment in Florence; she had had enough of Florentine society by then and was not displeased to live altogether in the grand house that had belonged to his ancestors. Tito liked city life and the prospect dismayed him, but he could not complain since it was his own folly that had made it necessary for them to cut down expenses. They still had the car and he amused himself by taking long drives while his father and Laura were busy, and if they knew that now and then he went into Florence to have a flutter at the club they shut their eyes to it. So a year passed. Then, he hardly knew why, he was seized with a vague misgiving. He couldn't put his finger on anything; he had an uneasy feeling that perhaps Laura didn't care for him so much as she had at first; sometimes it seemed to him that his father was inclined to be impatient with him; they appeared to have a great deal to say to one another, but he got the impression that he was being edged out of their conversation, as though he were a child who was expected to sit still and not interrupt while his elders talked of things over his head; he had a notion that often his presence was unwelcome to them and that they were more at their ease when he was not there. He knew his father, and his reputation, but the suspicion that arose in him was so horrible that he refused to entertain it. And yet sometimes he caught a look passing between them that disconcerted him, there was a tender possessiveness in his father's eyes, a sensual complacency in Laura's, which, if he had seen it in others, would have convinced him that they were lovers. But he couldn't, he wouldn't, believe that there was anything between them. The count couldn't help making love to a woman and it was likely enough that Laura felt his extraordinary fascination, but it was shameful to suppose for a moment that they, these two people he loved, had formed a criminal, almost an incestuous, connection. He was sure that Laura had no idea that there was anything more in her feeling than the natural affection of a young, happily-married woman for her father-in-law. Notwithstanding he thought it better that she should not remain in everyday contact with his father, and one day he suggested that they should go back to live in Florence. Laura and the count were astonished that he should propose such a thing and would not hear of it. Laura said that, having spent so much money on the villa, she couldn't afford to set up another establishment, and the count that it was absurd to leave it, now that Laura had made it so comfortable, to live in a wretched apart-

ment in the city. An argument started and Tito got rather excited. He took some remark of Laura's to mean that if she lived
at the villa it was to keep him out of temptation. This reference
to his losses at the poker-table angered him.

"You always throw your money in my face," he said passionately. "If I'd wanted to marry money I'd have had the sense to
marry someone who had a great deal more than you."

Laura went very pale and glanced at the count.

"You have no right to speak to Laura like that," he said.
"You are an ill-mannered oaf."

"I shall speak to my wife exactly as I choose."

"You are mistaken. So long as you are in my house you will
treat her with the respect which is her right and your duty."

"When I want lessons in behaviour from you, Father, I will
let you know."

"You are very impertinent, Tito. You will kindly leave the
room."

He looked very stern and dignified and Tito, furious and yet
slightly intimidated, leapt to his feet and stalked out slamming
the door behind him. He took the car and drove into Florence.
He won quite a lot of money that day (lucky at cards, unlucky
in love) and to celebrate his winnings got more than a little
drunk. He did not go back to the villa till the following morning. Laura was as friendly and placid as ever, but his father
was somewhat cool. No reference was made to the scene. But
from then on things went from bad to worse. Tito was sullen
and moody, the count critical, and on occasion sharp words
passed between them. Laura did not interfere, but Tito gained
the impression that after a dispute that had been more than
acrimonious Laura interceded with his father, for the count
thenceforward, refusing to be annoyed, began to treat him with
the tolerant patience with which you would treat a wayward
child. He convinced himself that they were acting in concert
and his suspicions grew formidable. They even increased when
Laura in her good-natured way, saying that it must be very dull
for him to remain so much in the country, encouraged him to
go more often to Florence to see his friends. He jumped to the
conclusion that she said this only to be rid of him. He began to
watch them. He would enter suddenly a room in which he knew
they were, expecting to catch them in a compromising position,
or silently follow them to a secluded part of the garden. They
were chatting unconcernedly of trivial things. Laura greeted

him with a pleasant smile. He could put his finger on nothing to
confirm his torturing suspicions. He started to drink. He grew
nervous and irritable. He had no proof, no proof whatever, that
there was anything between them, and yet in his bones he was
certain that they were grossly, shockingly deceiving him. He
brooded till he felt he was going mad. A dark aching fire within
him consumed his being. On one of his visits to Florence he
bought a pistol. He made up his mind that if he could have
proof of what in his heart he was certain of, he would kill them
both.

I don't know what brought on the final catastrophe. All that
came out at the trial was that, driven beyond endurance, Tito
had gone one night to his father's room to have it out with him.
His father mocked and laughed at him. They had a furious
quarrel and Tito took out his pistol and shot the count dead.
Then he collapsed and fell, weeping hysterically, on his father's
body; the repeated shots brought Laura and the servants rush-
ing in. He jumped up and grabbed the pistol, to shoot himself
he said afterwards, but he hesitated or they were too quick for
him, and they snatched it out of his hand. The police were sent
for. He spent most of his time in prison weeping; he would not
eat and had to be forcibly fed; he told the examining magistrate
that he had killed his father because he was his wife's lover.
Laura, examined and examined again, swore that there had
never been anything between the count and herself but a natural affection. The murder filled the Florentine public with
horror. The Italians were convinced of her guilt, but her friends,
English and American, felt that she was incapable of the crime
of which she was accused. They went about saying that Tito
was neurotic and insanely jealous and in his stupid way had
mistaken her American freedom of behaviour for a criminal
passion. On the face of it Tito's charge was absurd. Carlo di San
Pietro was nearly thirty years older than she, an elderly man
with white hair; who could suppose that there would have been
anything between her and her father-in-law, when her husband
was young, handsome and in love with her?

It was in Harding's presence that she saw the examining
magistrate and the lawyers who had been engaged to defend
Tito. They had decided to plead insanity. Experts for the defence examined him and decided that he was insane, experts for
the prosecution examined him and decided that he was sane.
The fact that he had bought a pistol three months before he

committed the dreadful crime went to prove that it was pre-
meditated. It was discovered that he was deeply in debt and his
creditors were pressing him; the only means he had of settling
with them was by selling the villa, and his father's death put
him in possession of it. There is no capital punishment in Italy,
but murder with premeditation is punished by solitary confinement for life. On the approach of the trial the lawyers came to
Laura and told her that the only way in which Tito could be
saved from this was for her to admit in court that the count
had been her lover. Laura went very pale. Harding protested
violently. He said they had no right to ask her to perjure herself
and ruin her reputation to save that shiftless, drunken gambler
whom she had been so unfortunate as to marry. Laura remained
silent for a while.

"Very well," she said at last, "if that's the only way to save
him I'll do it."

Harding tried to dissuade her, but she was decided.

"I should never have a moment's peace if I knew that Tito
had to spend the rest of his life alone in a prison cell."

And that is what happened. The trial opened. She was called
and under oath stated that for more than a year her father-in-
law had been her lover. Tito was declared insane and sent to an
asylum. Laura wanted to leave Florence at once, but in Italy
the preliminaries to a trial are endless and by then she was near
her time. The Hardings insisted on her remaining with them till
she was confined. She had a child, a boy, but it only lived
twenty-four hours. Her plan was to go back to San Francisco
and live with her mother till she could find a job, for Tito's
extravagance, the money she had spent on the villa, and then
the cost of the trial had seriously impoverished her.

It was Harding who told me most of this; but one day when
he was at the club and I was having a cup of tea with Bessie
and we were again talking over these tragic happenings she said
to me:

"You know, Charley hasn't told you the whole story because
he doesn't know it. I never told him. Men are funny in some
ways; they're much more easily shocked than women."

I raised my eyebrows, but said nothing.

"Just before Laura went away we had a talk. She was very
low and I thought she was grieving over the loss of her baby.
I wanted to say something to help her. 'You mustn't take the
baby's death too hardly,' I said. 'As things are, perhaps it's

better it died.' 'Why?' she said. 'Think what the poor little
thing's future would have been with a murderer for his father.'
She looked at me for a moment in that strange quiet way of
hers. And then what d'you think she said?"

"I haven't a notion," said I.

"She said: 'What makes you think his father was a murderer?' I felt myself grow as red as a turkey-cock. I could hardly
believe my ears. 'Laura, what *do* you mean?' I said. 'You were
in court,' she said. 'You heard me say Carlo was my lover.' "

Bessie Harding stared at me as she must have stared at
Laura.

"What did you say then?" I asked.

"What was there for me to say? I said nothing. I wasn't so
much horrified, I was bewildered. Laura looked at me and,
believe it or not, I'm convinced there was a twinkle in her eyes.
I felt a perfect fool."

"Poor Bessie," I smiled.

Poor Bessie, I repeated to myself now as I thought of this
strange story. She and Charley were long since dead and by
their death I had lost good friends. I went to sleep then, and
next day Wyman Holt took me for a long drive.

We were to dine with the Greenes at seven and we reached
their house on the dot. Now that I had remembered who Laura
was I was filled with an immense curiosity to see her again.
Wyman had exaggerated nothing. The living-room into which
we went was the quintessence of commonplace. It was comfortable enough, but there was not a trace of personality in it.
It might have been furnished *en bloc* by a mail-order house. It
had the bleakness of a government office. I was introduced first
to my host Jasper Greene and then to his brother Emery and to
his brother's wife Fanny. Jasper Greene was a large, plump man
with a moon face and a shock of black, coarse, unkempt hair.
He wore large cellulose-rimmed spectacles. I was staggered by
his youth. He could not have been much over thirty and was
therefore nearly twenty years younger than Laura. His brother,
Emery, a composer and teacher in a New York school of music,
might have been seven or eight and twenty. His wife, a pretty
little thing, was an actress for the moment out of a job. Jasper
Greene mixed us some very adequate cocktails but for a trifle
too much vermouth, and we sat down to dinner. The conversation was gay and even boisterous. Jasper and his brother were
loud-voiced and all three of them, Jasper, Emery and Emery's

wife, were loquacious talkers. They chaffed one another, they
joked and laughed; they discussed art, literature, music and the
theatre. Wyman and I joined in when we had a chance, which
was not often; Laura did not try to. She sat at the head of the
table, serene, with an amused, indulgent smile on her lips as she
listened to their scatter-brained nonsense; it was not stupid
nonsense, mind you, it was intelligent and modern, but it was
nonsense all the same. There was something maternal in her
attitude, and I was reminded oddly of a sleek dachshund lying
quietly in the sun while she looks lazily, and yet watchfully, at
her litter of puppies romping round her. I wondered whether it
crossed her mind that all this chatter about art didn't amount
to much when compared with those incidents of blood and passion that she remembered. But did she remember? It had all
happened a long time ago and perhaps it seemed no more than
a bad dream. Perhaps these commonplace surroundings were
part of her deliberate effort to forget, and to be among these
young people was restful to her spirit. Perhaps Jasper's clever
stupidity was a comfort. After that searing tragedy it might be
that she wanted nothing but the security of the humdrum.

Possibly because Wyman was an authority on the Eliza-
bethan drama the conversation at one moment touched on that.
I had already discovered that Jasper Greene was prepared to lay
down the law on subjects all and sundry, and now he delivered
himself as follows:

"Our theatre has gone all to pot because the dramatists of
our day are afraid to deal with the violent emotions which are
the proper subject matter of tragedy," he boomed. "In the sixteenth century they had a wealth of melodramatic and bloody
themes to suit their purpose and so they produced great plays.
But where can our playwrights look for themes? Our Anglo-
Saxon blood is too phlegmatic, too supine, to provide them with
material they can make anything of, and so they are condemned
to occupy themselves with the trivialities of social intercourse."

I wondered what Laura thought of this, but I took care not
to catch her eye. She could have told them a story of illicit love,
jealousy and parricide which would have been meat to one of
Shakespeare's successors, but had he treated it, I suppose he
would have felt bound to finish it with at least one more corpse
strewn about the stage. The end of her story, as I knew it now,
was unexpected certainly, but sadly prosaic and a trifle grotesque. Real life more often ends things with a whimper than

with a bang. I wondered too why she had gone out of her way to renew our old acquaintance. Of course she had no reason to suppose that I knew as much as I did; perhaps with a true instinct she was confident that I would not give her away; perhaps she didn't care if I did. I stole a glance at her now and then while she was quietly listening to the excited babbling of the three young people, but her friendly, pleasant face told me nothing. If I hadn't known otherwise I would have sworn that no untoward circumstance had ever troubled the course of her uneventful life.

The evening came to an end and this is the end of my story, but for the fun of it I am going to relate a small incident that happened when Wyman and I got back to his house. We decided to have a bottle of beer before going to bed and went into the kitchen to fetch it. The clock in the hall struck eleven and at that moment the phone rang. Wyman went to answer it and when he came back was quietly chortling to himself.

"What's the joke?" I asked.

"It was one of my students. They're not supposed to call members of the faculty after ten-thirty, but he was all hot and bothered. He asked me how evil had come into the world."

"And did you tell him?"

"I told him that St. Thomas Aquinas had got hot and bothered too about that very question and he'd better worry it out for himself. I said that when he found the solution he was to call me, no matter what time it was. Two o'clock in the morning if he liked."

"I think you're pretty safe not to be disturbed for many a long night," I said.

"I won't conceal from you that I have formed pretty much the same impression myself," he grinned.

THE MAN WITH THE SCAR

It was on account of the scar that I first noticed him, for it ran, broad and red, in a great crescent from his temple to his chin. It must have been due to a formidable wound and I wondered whether this had been caused by a sabre or by a fragment of shell. It was unexpected on that round, fat and good-humoured face. He had small and undistinguished features, and his expression was artless. His face went oddly with his corpulent body. He was a powerful man of more than common height. I never saw him in anything but a very shabby grey suit, a khaki shirt and a battered sombrero. He was far from clean. He used to come into the Palace Hotel at Guatemala City every day at cocktail time and strolling leisurely round the bar offer lottery tickets for sale. If this was the way he made his living it must have been a poor one for I never saw anyone buy, but now and then I saw him offered a drink. He never refused it. He threaded his way among the tables with a sort of rolling walk as though he were accustomed to traverse long distances on foot, paused at each table, with a little smile mentioned the numbers he had for sale and then, when no notice was taken of him, with the same smile passed on. I think he was for the most part a trifle the worse for liquor.

I was standing at the bar one evening, my foot on the rail, with an acquaintance—they make a very good dry Martini at the Palace Hotel in Guatemala City—when the man with the scar came up. I shook my head as for the twentieth time since

my arrival he held out for my inspection his lottery tickets. But
my companion nodded affably.

"*Qué tal, general?* How is life?"

"Not so bad. Business is none too good, but it might be
worse."

"What will you have, general?"

"A brandy."

He tossed it down and put the glass back on the bar. He
nodded to my acquaintance.

"*Gracias. Hasta luego.*"

Then he turned away and offered his tickets to the men who
were standing next to us.

"Who is your friend?" I asked. "That's a terrific scar on his
face."

"It doesn't add to his beauty, does it? He's an exile from
Nicaragua. He's a ruffian of course and a bandit, but not a bad
fellow. I give him a few *pesos* now and then. He was a revolutionary general, and if his ammunition hadn't given out he'd
have upset the government and be Minister of War now instead
of selling lottery tickets in Guatemala. They captured him,
along with his staff, such as it was, and tried him by court-
martial. Such things are rather summary in these countries, you
know, and he was sentenced to be shot at dawn. I guess he knew
what was coming to him when he was caught. He spent the
night in gaol and he and the others, there were five of them altogether, passed the time playing poker. They used matches for
chips. He told me he'd never had such a run of bad luck in his
life; they were playing with a short pack, Jacks to open, but he
never held a card; he never improved more than half a dozen
times in the whole sitting and no sooner did he buy a new stack
than he lost it. When day broke and the soldiers came into the
cell to fetch them for execution he had lost more matches than a
reasonable man could use in a lifetime.

"They were led into the patio of the gaol and placed against a
wall, the five of them side by side, with the firing party facing
them. There was a pause and our friend asked the officer in
charge of them what the devil they were keeping him waiting
for. The officer said that the general commanding the government troops wished to attend the execution and they awaited
his arrival.

"'Then I have time to smoke another cigarette,' said our
friend. 'He was always unpunctual.'

"But he had barely lit it when the general—it was San Ignacio, by the way: I don't know whether you ever met him—followed by his A.D.C. came into the patio. The usual formalities were performed and San Ignacio asked the condemned men whether there was anything they wished before the execution took place. Four of the five shook their heads, but our friend spoke.

" 'Yes, I should like to say good-bye to my wife.'

" '*Bueno*,' said the general, 'I have no objection to that. Where is she?'

" 'She is waiting at the prison door.'

" 'Then it will not cause a delay of more than five minutes.'

" 'Hardly that, *Señor General*,' said our friend.

" 'Have him placed on one side.'

"Two soldiers advanced and between them the condemned rebel walked to the spot indicated. The officer in command of the firing squad on a nod from the general gave an order, there was a ragged report, and the four men fell. They fell strangely, not together, but one after the other, with movements that were almost grotesque, as though they were puppets in a toy theatre: The officer went up to them and into one who was still alive emptied two barrels of his revolver. Our friend finished his cigarette and threw away the stub.

"There was a little stir at the gateway. A woman came into the patio, with quick steps, and then, her hand on her heart, stopped suddenly. She gave a cry and with outstretched arms ran forward.

" '*Caramba*,' said the general.

"She was in black, with a veil over her hair, and her face was dead white. She was hardly more than a girl, a slim creature, with little regular features and enormous eyes. But they were distraught with anguish. Her loveliness was such that as she ran, her mouth slightly open and the agony of her face beautiful, a gasp of surprise was wrung from those indifferent soldiers who looked at her.

"The rebel advanced a step or two to meet her. She flung herself into his arms and with a hoarse cry of passion: *alma de mi corazón*, soul of my heart, he pressed his lips to hers. And at the same moment he drew a knife from his ragged shirt—I haven't a notion how he managed to retain possession of it—and stabbed her in the neck. The blood spurted from the cut vein and dyed his shirt. Then he flung his arms round her and once more pressed his lips to hers.

"It happened so quickly that many did not know what had occurred, but from the others burst a cry of horror; they sprang forward and seized him. They loosened his grasp and the girl would have fallen if the A.D.C. had not caught her. She was unconscious. They laid her on the ground and with dismay on their faces stood round watching her. The rebel knew where he was striking and it was impossible to staunch the blood. In a moment the A.D.C. who had been kneeling by her side rose.

" 'She's dead,' he whispered.

"The rebel crossed himself.

" 'Why did you do it?' asked the general.

" 'I loved her.'

"A sort of sigh passed through those men crowded together and they looked with strange faces at the murderer. The general stared at him for a while in silence.

" 'It was a noble gesture,' he said at last. 'I cannot execute this man. Take my car and have him led to the frontier. *Señor*, I offer you the homage which is due from one brave man to another.'

"A murmur of approbation broke from those who listened. The A.D.C. tapped the rebel on the shoulder, and between the two soldiers without a word he marched to the waiting car."

My friend stopped and for a little I was silent. I must explain that he was a Guatemaltecan and spoke to me in Spanish. I have translated what he told me as well as I could, but I have made no attempt to tone down his rather high-flown language. To tell the truth I think it suits the story.

"But how then did he get the scar?" I asked at length.

"Oh, that was due to a bottle that burst when I was opening it. A bottle of ginger ale."

"I never liked it," said I.

THE BUM

GOD knows how often I had lamented that I had not half the
time I needed to do half the things I wanted. I could not remember when last I had had a moment to myself. I had often
amused my fancy with the prospect of just one week's complete
idleness. Most of us when not busy working are busy playing;
we ride, play tennis or golf, swim or gamble; but I saw myself
doing nothing at all. I would lounge through the morning,
dawdle through the afternoon and loaf through the evening. My
mind would be a slate and each passing hour a sponge that
wiped out the scribblings written on it by the world of sense.
Time, because it is so fleeting, time, because it is beyond recall,
is the most precious of human goods and to squander it is the
most delicate form of dissipation in which man can indulge.
Cleopatra dissolved in wine a priceless pearl, but she gave it to
Antony to drink; when you waste the brief golden hours you
take the beaker in which the gem is melted and dash its contents to the ground. The gesture is grand and like all grand
gestures absurd. That of course is its excuse. In the week I
promised myself I should naturally read, for to the habitual
reader reading is a drug of which he is the slave; deprive him of
printed matter and he grows nervous, moody and restless; then,
like the alcoholic bereft of brandy who will drink shellac or
methylated spirit, he will make do with the advertisements of
a paper five years old; he will make do with a telephone direc-
tory. But the professional writer is seldom a disinterested reader.

I wished my reading to be but another form of idleness. I made up my mind that if ever the happy day arrived when I could enjoy untroubled leisure I would complete an enterprise that had always tempted me, but which hitherto, like an explorer making reconnaissances into an undiscovered country, I had done little more than enter upon: I would read the entire works of Nick Carter.

But I had always fancied myself choosing my moment with surroundings to my liking, not having it forced upon me; and when I was suddenly faced with nothing to do and had to make the best of it (like a steamship acquaintance whom in the wide waste of the Pacific Ocean you have invited to stay with you in London and who turns up without warning and with all his luggage) I was not a little taken aback. I had come to Vera Cruz from Mexico City to catch one of the Ward Company's white cool ships to Yucatan; and found to my dismay that, a dock strike having been declared over-night, my ship would not put in. I was stuck in Vera Cruz. I took a room in the Hotel Diligencias overlooking the plaza, and spent the morning looking at the sights of the town. I wandered down side streets and peeped into quaint courts. I sauntered through the parish church; it is picturesque with its gargoyles and flying buttresses, and the salt wind and the blazing sun have patined its harsh and massive walls with the mellowness of age; its cupola is covered with white and blue tiles. Then I found that I had seen all that was to be seen and I sat down in the coolness of the arcade that surrounded the square and ordered a drink. The sun beat down on the plaza with a merciless splendour. The coco-palms drooped dusty and bedraggled. Great black buzzards perched on them for a moment uneasily, swooped to the ground to gather some bit of offal, and then with lumbering wings flew up to the church tower. I watched the people crossing the square; negroes, Indians, Creoles and Spanish, the motley people of the Spanish Main; and they varied in colour from ebony to ivory. As the morning wore on, the tables around me filled up, chiefly with men, who had come to have a drink before luncheon, for the most part in white ducks, but some notwithstanding the heat in the dark clothes of professional respectability. A small band, a guitarist, a blind fiddler and a harpist, played rag-time and after every other tune the guitarist came round with a plate. I had already bought the local paper and I was adamant to the newsvendors who pertinaciously sought to sell me more copies of the same sheet. I refused, oh, twenty times at least, the solicitations of grimy urchins who wanted to shine my spotless shoes; and having come to the end of my small change I could only shake my head at the beggars who importuned me. They gave one no peace. Little Indian women, in shapeless rags, each one with a baby tied in the shawl on her back, held out skinny hands and in a whimper recited a dismal screed; blind men were led up to my table by small boys; the maimed, the halt, the deformed exhibited the sores and the monstrosities with which nature or accident had afflicted them; and half naked, underfed children whined endlessly their demand for coppers. But these kept their eyes open for the fat policeman who would suddenly dart out on them with a thong and give them a sharp cut on the back or over the head. Then they would scamper, only to return again when, exhausted by the exercise of so much energy, he relapsed into lethargy.

But suddenly my attention was attracted by a beggar who, unlike the rest of them and indeed the people sitting round me, swarthy and black-haired, had hair and beard of a red so vivid that it was startling. His beard was ragged and his long mop of hair looked as though it had not been brushed for months. He wore only a pair of trousers and a cotton singlet, but they were tatters, grimy and foul, that barely held together. I have never seen anyone so thin; his legs, his naked arms were but skin and bone and through the rents of his singlet you saw every rib of his wasted body; you could count the bones of his dust-covered feet. Of that starveling band he was easily the most abject. He was not old, he could not well have been more than forty, and I could not but ask myself what had brought him to this pass. It was absurd to think that he would not have worked if work he had been able to get. He was the only one of the beggars who did not speak. The rest of them poured forth their litany of woe and if it did not bring the alms they asked continued until an impatient word from you chased them away. He said nothing. I suppose he felt that his look of destitution was all the appeal he needed. He did not even hold out his hand, he merely looked at you, but with such wretchedness in his eyes, such despair in his attitude, it was dreadful; he stood on and on, silent and immobile, gazing steadfastly, and then, if you took no notice of him, he moved slowly to the next table. If he was given nothing he showed neither disappointment nor anger. If someone offered him a coin he stepped forward a little, stretched out his claw-like hand, took it without a word of thanks and impassively went his way. I had nothing to give him and when he came to me, so that he should not wait in vain, I shook my head.

"*Dispense Usted por Dios,*" I said, using the polite Castillian formula with which the Spaniards refuse a beggar.

But he paid no attention to what I said. He stood in front of me, for as long as he stood at the other tables, looking at me with tragic eyes. I have never seen such a wreck of humanity. There was something terrifying in his appearance. He did not look quite sane. At length he passed on.

It was one o'clock and I had lunch. When I awoke from my siesta it was still very hot, but towards evening a breath of air coming in through the windows which I had at last ventured to open tempted me into the plaza. I sat down under my arcade and ordered a long drink. Presently people in greater numbers filtered into the open space from the surrounding streets, the tables in the restaurants round it filled up, and in the kiosk in the middle the band began to play. The crowd grew thicker. On the free benches people sat huddled together like dark grapes clustered on a stalk. There was a lively hum of conversation. The big black buzzards flew screeching overhead, swooping down when they saw something to pick up, or scurrying away from under the feet of the passers-by. As twilight descended they swarmed, it seemed from all parts of the town, towards the church tower; they circled heavily about it and hoarsely crying, squabbling and jangling, settled themselves uneasily to roost. And again bootblacks begged me to have my shoes cleaned, newsboys pressed dank papers upon me, beggars whined their plaintive demand for alms. I saw once more that strange, red-bearded fellow and watched him stand motionless, with the crushed and piteous air, before one table after another. He did not stop before mine. I supposed he remembered me from the morning and having failed to get anything from me then thought it useless to try again. You do not often see a red-haired Mexican, and because it was only in Russia that I had seen men of so destitute a mien I asked myself if he was by chance a Russian. It accorded well enough with the Russian fecklessness that he should have allowed himself to sink to such a depth of degradation. Yet he had not a Russian face; his emaciated features were clear-cut, and his blue eyes were not set in the head in a Russian manner; I wondered if he could be a sailor, English, Scandina-

vian or American, who had deserted his ship and by degrees
sunk to this pitiful condition. He disappeared. Since there was
nothing else to do, I stayed on till I got hungry, and when
I had eaten came back. I sat on till the thinning crowd suggested
it was bed-time. I confess that the day had seemed long and I
wondered how many similar days I should be forced to spend
there.

But I woke after a little while and could not get to sleep again.
My room was stifling. I opened the shutters and looked out at
the church. There was no moon, but the bright stars faintly lit
its outline. The buzzards were closely packed on the cross above
the cupola and on the edges of the tower, and now and then they
moved a little. The effect was uncanny. And then, I have no
notion why, that red scarecrow recurred to my mind and I had
suddenly a strange feeling that I had seen him before. It was so
vivid that it drove away from me the possibility of sleep. I felt
sure that I had come across him, but when and where I could
not tell. I tried to picture the surroundings in which he might
take his place, but I could see no more than a dim figure against
a background of fog. As the dawn approached it grew a little
cooler and I was able to sleep.

I spent my second day at Vera Cruz as I had spent the first.
But I watched for the coming of the red-haired beggar, and as
he stood at the tables near mine I examined him with attention.
I felt certain now that I had seen him somewhere. I even felt
certain that I had known him and talked to him, but I still
could recall none of the circumstances. Once more he passed my
table without stopping and when his eyes met mine I looked in
them for some gleam of recollection. Nothing. I wondered if I
had made a mistake and thought I had seen him in the same
way as sometimes, by some queer motion of the brain, in the
act of doing something you are convinced that you are repeat-
ing an action that you have done at some past time. I could
not get out of my head the impression that at some moment he
had entered into my life. I racked my brains. I was sure now
that he was either English or American. But I was shy of addressing him. I went over in my mind the possible occasions
when I might have met him. Not to be able to place him exasperated me as it does when you try to remember a name that
is on the tip of your tongue and yet eludes you. The day wore
on.

Another day came, another morning, another evening. It was

Sunday and the plaza was more crowded than ever. The tables
under the arcade were packed. As usual the red-haired beggar
came along, a terrifying figure in his silence, his threadbare rags
and his pitiful distress. He was standing in front of a table only
two from mine, mutely beseeching, but without a gesture. Then
I saw the policeman who at intervals tried to protect the public
from the importunities of all these beggars sneak round a column
and give him a resounding whack with his thong. His thin body
winced, but he made no protest and showed no resentment; he
seemed to accept the stinging blow as in the ordinary course of
things and with his slow movements slunk away into the
gathering night of the plaza. But the cruel stripe had whipped
my memory and suddenly I remembered.

Not his name, that escaped me still, but everything else. He
must have recognised me, for I have not changed very much in
twenty years, and that was why after that first morning he had
never paused in front of my table. Yes, it was twenty years since
I had known him. I was spending a winter in Rome and every
evening I used to dine in a restaurant in the Via Sistina where
you got excellent macaroni and a good bottle of wine. It was
frequented by a little band of English and American art students, and one or two writers; and we used to stay late into
the night engaged in interminable arguments upon art and
literature. He used to come in with a young painter who was a
friend of his. He was only a boy then, he could not have been
more than twenty-two; and with his blue eyes, straight nose
and red hair he was pleasing to look at. I remembered that he
spoke a great deal of Central America, he had had a job with
the American Fruit Company, but had thrown it over because
he wanted to be a writer. He was not popular among us because
he was arrogant and we were none of us old enough to take the
arrogance of youth with tolerance. He thought us poor fish and
did not hesitate to tell us so. He would not show us his work,
because our praise meant nothing to him and he despised our
censure. His vanity was enormous. It irritated us; but some of
us were uneasily aware that it might perhaps be justified. Was
it possible that the intense consciousness of genius that he had,
rested on no grounds? He had sacrificed everything to be a
writer. He was so certain of himself that he infected some of
his friends with his own assurance.

I recalled his high spirits, his vitality, his confidence in the
future and his disinterestedness. It was impossible that it was

the same man, and yet I was sure of it. I stood up, paid for my drink and went out into the plaza to find him. My thoughts were in a turmoil. I was aghast. I had thought of him now and then and idly wondered what had become of him. I could never have imagined that he was reduced to this frightful misery. There are hundreds, thousands of youths who enter upon the hard calling of the arts with extravagant hopes; but for the most part they come to terms with their mediocrity and find somewhere in life a niche where they can escape starvation. This was awful. I asked myself what had happened. What hopes deferred had broken his spirit, what disappointments shattered him and what lost illusions ground him to the dust? I asked myself if nothing could be done. I walked round the plaza. He was not in the arcades. There was no hope of finding him in the crowd that circled round the bandstand. The light was waning and I was afraid I had lost him. Then I passed the church and saw him sitting on the steps. I cannot describe what a lamentable object he looked. Life had taken him, rent him on its racks, torn him limb from limb, and then flung him, a bleeding wreck, on the stone steps of that church. I went up to him.

"Do you remember Rome?" I said.

He did not move. He did not answer. He took no more notice of me than if I were not standing before him. He did not look at me. His vacant blue eyes rested on the buzzards that were screaming and tearing at some object at the bottom of the steps. I did not know what to do. I took a yellow-backed note out of my pocket and pressed it in his hand. He did not give it a glance. But his hand moved a little, the thin claw-like fingers closed on the note and scrunched it up; he made it into a little ball and then edging it on to his thumb flicked it into the air so that it fell among the jangling buzzards. I turned my head instinctively and saw one of them seize it in his beak and fly off followed by two others screaming behind it. When I looked back the man was gone.

I stayed three more days in Vera Cruz. I never saw him again.

THE CLOSED SHOP

NOTHING would induce me to tell the name of the happy country in which the incidents occurred that I am constrained to relate; but I see no harm in admitting that it is a free and independent state on the continent of America. This is vague enough in all conscience and can give rise to no diplomatic incident. Now the president of this free and independent state had an eye to a pretty woman and there came to his capital, a wide and sunny town with a plaza, a cathedral that was not without dignity and a few old Spanish houses, a young person from Michigan of such a pleasing aspect that his heart went out to her. He lost no time in declaring his passion and was gratified to learn that it was returned, but he was mortified to discover that the young person regarded his possession of a wife and her possession of a' husband as a bar to their union. She had a feminine weakness for marriage. Though it seemed unreasonable to the president, he was not the man to refuse a pretty woman the gratification of her whim and promised to make such arrangements as would enable him to offer her wedlock. He called his attorneys together and put the matter before them. He had long thought, he said, that for a progressive country their marriage laws were remarkably out of date and he proposed therefore radically to amend them. The attorneys retired and after a brief interval devised a divorce law that was satisfactory to the president. But the state of which I write was always careful to do things in a constitutional way, for it was a highly civilised, democratic and reputable country. A president who respects himself and his oath of office cannot promulgate a law, even if it is to his own interest, without adhering to certain forms, and these things take time; the president had barely signed the decree that made the new divorce law valid when a revolution broke out and he was very unfortunately hanged on a lamp-post in the plaza in front of the cathedral that was not without dignity. The young person of pleasing aspect left town in a hurry, but the law remained. Its terms were simple. On the payment of one hundred dollars gold and after a residence of thirty days a man could divorce his wife or a wife her husband without even apprising the other party of the intended step. Your wife might tell you that she was going to spend a month with her aged mother and one morning at breakfast when you looked through your mail you might receive a letter from her informing you that she had divorced you and was already married to another.

Now it was not long before the happy news spread here and there that at a reasonable distance from New York was a country, the capital of which had an equable climate and tolerable accommodation, where a woman could release herself, expeditiously and with economy, from the irksome bonds of matrimony. The fact that the operation could be performed without the husband's knowledge saved her from those preliminary and acrimonious discussions that are so wearing to the nerves. Every woman knows that however much a man may argue about a proposition he will generally accept a fact with resignation. Tell him you want a Rolls-Royce and he will say he can't afford it, but buy it and he will sign his cheque like a lamb. So in a very short time beautiful women in considerable numbers began to come down to the pleasant, sunny town; tired business women and women of fashion, women of pleasure and women of leisure; they came from New York, Chicago and San Francisco, they came from Georgia and they came from Dakota, they came from all the states in the Union. The passenger accommodation on the ships of the United Fruit Line was only just adequate to the demand, and if you wanted a stateroom to yourself you had to engage it six months in advance. Prosperity descended upon the capital of this enterprising state and in a very little while there was not a lawyer in it who did not own a Ford car. Don Agosto, the proprietor of the Grand Hotel, went to the expense of building several bathrooms, but he did not grudge it; he was making a fortune, and he never passed the lamp-post on which the outgoing president had been hanged without giving it a jaunty wave of his hand.

"He was a great man," he said. "One day they will erect a statue to him."

I have spoken as though it were only women who availed themselves of this convenient and reasonable law, and this might indicate that in the United States it is they rather than men who desire release from the impediment of Holy Matrimony. I have no reason to believe that this is so. Though it was women in great majority who travelled to this country to get a divorce, I ascribe this to the fact that it is always easy for them to get away for six weeks (a week there, a week back and thirty days to establish a domicile) but it is difficult for men to leave their affairs so long. It is true that they could go there during their summer holidays, but then the heat is somewhat oppressive; and besides, there are no golf links: it is reasonable enough to suppose that many a man will hesitate to divorce his wife when he can only do it at the cost of a month's golf. There were of course two or three males spending their thirty days at the Grand Hotel, but they were generally, for a reason that is obscure, commercial travellers. I can but imagine that by the nature of their avocations they were able at one and the same time to pursue freedom and profit.

Be this as it may, the fact remains that the inmates of the Grand Hotel were for the most part women, and very gay it was in the patio at luncheon and at dinner when they sat at little square tables under the arches discussing their matrimonial troubles and drinking champagne. Don Agosto did a roaring trade with the generals and colonels (there were more generals than colonels in the army of this state), the lawyers, bankers, merchants and the young sparks of the town who came to look at these beautiful creatures. But the perfect is seldom realised in this world. There is always something that is not quite right and women engaged in getting rid of their husbands are very properly in an agitated condition. It makes them at times hard to please. Now it must be confessed that this delightful little city, notwithstanding its manifold advantages, somewhat lacked places of amusement. There was but one cinema and this showed films that had been wandering too long from their happy home in Hollywood. In the daytime you could have consultations with your lawyer, polish your nails and do a little shopping, but the evenings were intolerable. There were

many complaints that thirty days was a long time and more
than one impatient young thing asked her lawyer why they
didn't put a little pep into their law and do the whole job in
eight and forty hours. Don Agosto, however, was a man of resource and presently he had an inspiration: he engaged a
troupe of wandering Guatemaltecans who played the marimba.
There is no music in the world that sets the toes so irresistibly
tingling and in a little while everyone in the patio began dancing. It is of course obvious that twenty-five beautiful women
cannot dance with three commercial travellers, but there were
all these generals and colonels and there were all the young
sparks of the town. They danced divinely and they had great
liquid black eyes. The hours flew, the days tripped one upon the
heels of the other so quickly that the month passed before you
realised it, and more than one of Don Agosto's guests when she
bade him farewell confessed that she would willingly have
stayed longer. Don Agosto was radiant. He liked to see people
enjoy themselves. The marimba band was worth twice the
money he paid for it, and it did his heart good to see his ladies
dance with the gallant officers and the young men of the town.
Since Don Agosto was thrifty he always turned off the electric
light on the stairs and in the passages at ten o'clock at night and
the gallant officers and the young men of the town improved
their English wonderfully.

Everything went as merrily as a marriage bell, if I may use a
phrase that, however hackneyed, in this connection is irresistible, till one day Madame Coralie came to the conclusion that
she had had enough of it. For one man's meat is another man's
poison. She dressed herself and went to call on her friend
Carmencita. After she had in a few voluble words stated the
purpose of her visit, Carmencita called a maid and told her to
run and fetch La Gorda. They had a matter of importance
which they wished to discuss with her. La Gorda, a woman of
ample proportions with a heavy moustache, soon joined them
and over a bottle of Malaga the three of them held a momentous
conversation. The result of it was that they indited a letter to
the president asking for an audience. The new president was a
hefty young man in the early thirties who, a few years before,
had been a stevedore in the employment of an American firm,
and he had risen to his present exalted station by a natural eloquence and an effective use of his gun when he wanted to make

a point or emphasise a statement. When one of his secretaries placed the letter before him he laughed.

"What do those three old faggots want with me?"

But he was a good-natured fellow and accessible. He did not forget that he had been elected by the people, as one of the people, to protect the people. He had also during his early youth been employed for some months by Madame Coralie to run errands. He told his secretary that he would see them at ten o'clock next morning. They went at the appointed hour to the palace and were led up a noble stairway to the audience chamber; the official who conducted them knocked softly on the door; a barred judas was opened and a suspicious eye appeared. The president had no intention of suffering the fate of his predecessor if he could help it and no matter who his visitors were did not receive them without precaution. The official gave the three ladies' names, the door was opened, but not too wide, and they slipped in. It was a handsome room and various secretaries at little tables, in their shirt-sleeves and with a revolver on each hip, were busy typing. One or two other young men, heavily armed, were lying on sofas reading the papers and smoking cigarettes. The president, also in his shirt-sleeves, with a revolver in his belt, was standing with his thumbs in the sleeveholes of his waistcoat. He was tall and stout, of a handsome and even dignified presence.

"*Qué tal?*" he cried, jovially, with a flash of his white teeth. "What brings you here, *señoras?*"

"How well you're looking, Don Manuel," said La Gorda. "You are a fine figure of a man."

He shook hands with them, and his staff, ceasing their strenuous activity, leaned back and cordially waved their hands to the three ladies. They were old friends and the greetings, if a trifle sardonic, were hearty. I must disclose the fact now (which I could without doubt do in a manner so discreet that I might be misunderstood; but if you have to say something you may just as well say it plainly as not) that these three ladies were the Madams of the three principal brothels in the capital of this free and independent state. La Gorda and Carmencita were of Spanish origin and were very decently dressed in black, with black silk shawls over their heads, but Madame Coralie was French and she wore a toque. They were all of mature age and of modest demeanour.

The president made them sit down, and offered them madeira and cigarettes, but they refused.

"No, thank you, Don Manuel," said Madame Coralie. "It is on business that we have come to see you."

"Well, what can I do for you?"

La Gorda and Carmencita looked at Madame Coralie and Madame Coralie looked at La Gorda and Carmencita. They nodded and she saw that they expected her to be their spokeswoman.

"Well, Don Manuel, it is like this. We are three women who have worked hard for many years and not a breath of scandal has ever tarnished our good names. There are not in all the Americas three more distinguished houses than ours and they are a credit to this beautiful city. Why, only last year I spent five hundred dollars to supply my *sala principal* with plate-glass mirrors. We have always been respectable and we have paid our taxes with regularity. It is hard now that the fruits of our labours should be snatched away from us. I do not hesitate to say that after so many years of honest and conscientious attention to business it is unjust that we should have to submit to such treatment."

The president was astounded.

"But, Coralie, my dear, I do not know what you mean. Has anyone dared to claim money from you that the law does not sanction or that I know nothing about?"

He gave his secretaries a suspicious glance. They tried to look innocent, but though they were, only succeeded in looking uneasy.

"It is the law we complain of. Ruin stares us in the face."

"Ruin?"

"So long as this new divorce law is in existence we can do no business and we may just as well shut up our beautiful houses."

Then Madame Coralie explained in a manner so frank that I prefer to paraphrase her speech that owing to this invasion of the town by beautiful ladies from a foreign land the three elegant houses on which she and her two friends paid rates and taxes were utterly deserted. The young men of fashion preferred to spend their evenings at the Grand Hotel where they received for soft words entertainment which at the regular establishments they could only have got for hard cash.

"You cannot blame them," said the president.

"I don't," cried Madame Coralie. "I blame the women. They

have no right to come and take the bread out of our mouths. Don Manuel, you are one of the people, you are not one of these aristocrats; what will the country say if you allow us to be driven out of business by blacklegs? I ask you is it just, is it honest?"

"But what can I do?" said the president. "I cannot lock them up in their rooms for thirty days. How am I to blame if these foreigners have no sense of decency?"

"It's different for a poor girl," said La Gorda. "She has her way to make. But that these women do that sort of thing when they're not obliged to, no, that I shall never understand."

"It is a bad and wicked law," said Carmencita.

The president sprang to his feet and threw his arms akimbo.

"You are not going to ask me to abrogate a law that has brought peace and plenty to this country. I am of the people and I was elected by the people, and the prosperity of my fatherland is very near my heart. Divorce is our staple industry and the law shall be repealed only over my dead body."

"Oh, *Maria Santissima*, that it should come to this," said Carmencita. "And me with two daughters in a convent in New Orleans. Ah, in this business one often has unpleasantness, but I always consoled myself by thinking that my daughters would marry well, and when the time came for me to retire they would inherit my business. Do you think I can keep them in a convent in New Orleans for nothing?"

"And who is going to keep my son at Harvard if I have to close my house, Don Manuel?" asked La Gorda.

"As for myself," said Madame Coralie, "I do not care. I shall return to France. My dear mother is eighty-seven years of age and she cannot live very much longer. It will be a comfort to her if I spend her last remaining years by her side. But it is the injustice of it that hurts. You have spent many happy evenings in my house, Don Manuel, and I am wounded that you should let us be treated like this. Did you not tell me yourself that it was the proudest day of your life when you entered as an honoured guest the house in which you had once been employed as errand boy?"

"I do not deny it. I stood champagne all round." Don Manuel walked up and down the large hall, shrugging his shoulders as he went, and now and then, deep in thought, he gesticulated. "I am of the people, elected by the people," he cried, "and the fact is, these women are blacklegs." He turned to his secretaries with a dramatic gesture. "It is a stain on my administration. It is against all my principles to allow unskilled foreign labour to take the bread out of the mouths of honest and industrious people. These ladies are quite right to come to me and appeal for my protection. I will not allow the scandal to continue."

It was of course a pointed and effective speech, but all who heard it knew that it left things exactly where they were. Madame Coralie powdered her nose and gave it, a commanding organ, a brief look in her pocket mirror.

"Of course I know what human nature is," she said, "and I can well understand that time hangs heavily on the hands of these creatures."

"We could build a golf-course," hazarded one of the secretaries. "It is true that this would only occupy them by day."

"If they want men why can't they bring them with them?" said La Gorda.

"*Caramba!*" cried the president, and with that stood on a sudden quite still. "There is the solution."

He had not reached his exalted station without being a man of insight and resource. He beamed.

"We will amend the law. Men shall come in as before without let or hindrance, but women only accompanied by their husbands or with their written consent." He saw the look of consternation which his secretaries gave him, and he waved his hand. "But the immigration authorities shall receive instructions to interpret the word husband with the widest latitude."

"*Maria Santissima!*" cried Madame Coralie. "If they come with a friend he will take care that no one else interferes with them and our customers will return to the houses where for so long they have been so hospitably entertained. Don Manuel, you are a great man and one of these days they will erect a statue to you."

It is often the simplest expedients that settle the most formidable difficulties. The law was briefly amended according to the terms of Don Manuel's suggestion and, whereas prosperity continued to pour its blessings on the wide and sunny capital of this free and independent state, Madame Coralie was enabled profitably to pursue her useful avocations, Carmencita's two daughters completed their expensive education in the convent at New Orleans, and La Gorda's son successfully graduated at Harvard.

AN OFFICIAL POSITION

He was a sturdy broad-shouldered fellow, of the middle height; though his bones were well covered as became his age, which was fifty, he was not fat; he had a ruddy complexion which neither the heat of the sun nor the unwholesomeness of the climate had affected. It was good rich blood that ran through his veins. His hair was brown and thick, and only at the temples touched with grey; he was very proud of his fair, handsome moustache and he kept it carefully brushed. There was a pleasant twinkle in his blue eyes. You would have said that this was a man whom life had treated well. There was in his appearance an air of good nature and in his vigour a glow of health that gave you confidence. He reminded you of one of those well-fed, rubicund burghers in an old Dutch picture, with their pink-cheeked wives, who made money and enjoyed the good things with which their industry provided them. He was, however, a widower. His name was Louis Remire, and his number 68763. He was serving a twelve-year sentence at St. Laurent de Maroni, the great penal settlement of French Guiana, for killing his wife, but partly because he had served in the police force at Lyons, his native town, and partly on account of his good character, he had been given an official position. He had been chosen among nearly two hundred applicants to be the public executioner.

That was why he was allowed to sport the handsome moustache of which he took so much care. He was the only convict who wore one. It was in a manner of speaking his badge of office. That also was why he was allowed to wear his own clothes. The convicts wear pyjamas in pink and white stripes, round straw hats and clumsy boots with wooden soles and leather tops. Louis Remire wore espadrilles on his bare feet, blue cotton trousers, and a khaki shirt the open neck of which exposed to view his hairy and virile chest. When you saw him strolling about the public garden, with a kindly eye looking at the children, black or half-caste, who played there, you would have taken him for a respectable shopkeeper who was enjoying an hour's leisure. He had his own house. That was not only one of the perquisites of his office, but it was a necessity, since if he had lodged in the prison camp the convicts would have made short work of him. One morning he would have been found with his belly ripped open. It was true that the house was small, it was just a wooden shack of one room, with a lean-to that served as a kitchen; but it was surrounded by a tiny garden, within a palisade, and in the garden grew bananas, papayas and such vegetables as the climate allowed him to raise. The garden faced the sea and was surrounded by a coconut grove. The situation was charming. It was only a quarter of a mile from the prison, which was convenient for his rations. They were fetched by his assistant, who lived with him. The assistant, a tall, gawky, ungainly fellow, with deep-set, staring eyes and cavernous jaws, was serving a life sentence for rape and murder; he was not very intelligent, but in civil life he had been a cook and it was wonderful what, with the help of the vegetables they grew and such condiments as Louis Remire could afford to buy at the Chinese grocer's, he managed to do with the soup, potatoes and cabbage, and eternal beef, beef for three hundred and sixty-five days of the year, which the prison kitchens provided. It was on this account that Louis Remire had pressed his claim on the commandant when it had been found necessary to get a new assistant. The last one's nerves had given way and, absurdly enough, thought Louis Remire with a good-natured laugh, he had developed scruples about capital punishment; now, suffering from neurasthenia, he was on the Ile St. Joseph, where the insane were confined.

His present assistant happened to be ill. He had high fever, and looked very much as if he were going to die. It had been necessary to send him to hospital. Louis Remire was sorry; he would not easily find so good a cook again. It was bad luck that

this should have happened just now, for next day there was a
job of work to be done. Six men were to be executed. Two were
Algerians, one was a Pole, another a Spaniard from the mainland, and only two were French. They had escaped from prison
in a band and gone up the river. For nearly twelve months,
stealing, raping and killing they had spread terror through the
colony. People scarcely dared move from their homesteads. Recaptured at last, they had all been sentenced to death, but the
sentence had to be confirmed by the Minister of the Colonies,
and the confirmation had only just arrived. Louis Remire could
not manage without help, and besides there was a lot to arrange
beforehand; it was particularly unfortunate that on this occasion of all others he should have to depend on an inexperienced man. The commandant had assigned to him one of the
turnkeys. The turnkeys are convicts like the others, but they
have been given their places for good behaviour and they live
in separate quarters. They are on the side of the authorities and
so are disliked by the other prisoners. Louis Remire was a conscientious fellow, and he was anxious that everything next day
should go without a hitch. He arranged that his temporary assistant should come that afternoon to the place where the guillotine was kept so that he might explain to him thoroughly how
it worked and show him exactly what he would have to do.

The guillotine, when not in use, stood in a small room which
was part of the prison building, but which was entered by a
separate door from the outside. When he sauntered along there
at the appointed hour he found the man already waiting. He
was a large-limbed, coarse-faced fellow. He was dressed in the
pink and white stripes of the prison garb, but as turnkey he
wore a felt hat instead of the straw of common convicts.

"What are you here for?"

The man shrugged his shoulders.

"I killed a farmer and his wife."

"H'm. How long have you got?"

"Life."

He looked a brute, but you could never be sure of people. He
had himself seen a warder, a big, powerful man, faint dead away
at an execution. He did not want his assistant to have an attack
of nerves at the wrong moment. He gave him a friendly smile,
and with his thumb pointed to the closed door behind which
stood the guillotine.

"This is another sort of job," he said. "There are six of them, you know. They're a bad lot. The sooner they're out of the way the better."

"Oh, that's all right. After what I've seen in this place I'm scared of nothing. It means no more to me than cutting the head off a chicken."

Louis Remire unlocked the door and walked in. His assistant followed him. The guillotine in that small room, hardly larger than a cell, seemed to take up a great deal of space. It stood grim and sinister. Louis Remire heard a slight gasp and turning round saw that the turnkey was staring at the instrument with terrified eyes. His face was sallow and drawn from the fever and the hookworm from which all the convicts intermittently suffered, but now its pallor was ghastly. The executioner smiled good-naturedly.

"Gives you a turn, does it? Have you never seen it before?"

"Never."

Louis Remire gave a little throaty chuckle.

"If you had, I suppose you wouldn't have survived to tell the tale. How did you escape it?"

"I was starving when I did my job. I'd asked for something to eat and they set the dogs on me. I was condemned to death. My lawyer went to Paris and he got the President to reprieve me."

"It's better to be alive than dead, there's no denying that," said Louis Remire, with that agreeable twinkle in his eyes.

He always kept his guillotine in perfect order. The wood, a dark hard native wood somewhat like mahogany, was highly polished; but there was a certain amount of brass, and it was Louis Remire's pride that this should be as bright and clean as the brass-work on a yacht. The knife shone as though it had just come out of the workshop. It was necessary not only to see that everything functioned properly, but to show his assistant how it functioned. It was part of the assistant's duty to refix the rope when the knife had dropped, and to do this he had to climb a short ladder.

It was with the satisfaction of a competent workman who knows his job from A to Z that Remire entered upon the necessary explanations. It gave him a certain quiet pleasure to point out the ingenuity of the apparatus. The condemned man was strapped to the bascule, a sort of shelf, and this by a simple mechanism was precipitated down and forwards so that the man's neck was conveniently under the knife. The conscientious fellow had brought with him a banana stem, about five feet long, and the turnkey had wondered why. He was now to learn. The stem was of about the same circumference and consistency as the human neck, so that it afforded a very good way, not only of showing a novice how the apparatus worked, but of making sure beforehand that it was in perfect order. Louis Remire placed the banana stem in position. He released the knife. It fell with incredible speed and with a great bang. From the time the man was attached to the bascule to the time his head was off only thirty seconds elapsed. The head fell in the basket. The executioner took it up by the ears and exhibited it to those whose duty it was to watch the execution. He uttered the solemn words:

"Au nom du peuple français justice est faite. In the name of the French people justice is done."

Then he dropped the head back into the basket. To-morrow, with six to be dispatched, the trunk would have to be un-strapped from the bascule and placed with the head on a stretcher, and the next man brought forward. They were taken in the order of their guilt. The least guilty, executed first, were spared the horror of seeing the death of their mates.

"We shall have to be careful that the right head goes with the right body," said Louis Remire, in that rather jovial manner of his, "or there may be no end of confusion at the Resurrec-tion."

He let down the knife two or three times in order to make quite sure that the assistant understood how to fix it, and then getting his cleaning-materials from the shelf on which he kept them set him to work on the brass. Though it was spotless he thought that a final polish would do no harm. He leaned against the wall and idly smoked cigarettes.

Finally everything was in order and Louis Remire dismissed the assistant till midnight. At midnight they were moving the guillotine from the room in which it stood to the prison yard. It was always a bit of a job to set it up again, but it had to be in place an hour before dawn, at which time the execution took place. Louis Remire strolled slowly home to his shack. The afternoon was drawing to its close, and as he walked along he passed a working party who were returning to the prison. They spoke to one another in undertones and he guessed that they spoke of him; some looked down, two or three threw him a glance of hatred and one spat on the ground. Louis Remire, the

end of a cigarette sticking to his lip, looked at them with irony.
He was indifferent to the loathing, mingled with fear, with
which they regarded him. It did not matter to him that not one
of them would speak to him, and it only amused him to think
that there was hardly one who would not gladly have thrust a
knife into his guts. He had a supreme contempt for them all. He
could take care of himself. He could use a knife as well as any of
them, and he had confidence in his strength. The convicts knew
that men were to be executed next day, and as always before an
execution they were depressed and nervous. They went about
their work in sullen silence, and the warders had to be more
than usually on the alert.

"They'll settle down when it's all over," said Louis Remire as
he let himself into his little compound.

The dogs barked as he came along, and brave though he was,
he listened to their uproar with satisfaction. With his own assistant ill, so that he was alone in the house, he was not sorry
that he had the protection of those two savage mongrels. They
prowled about the coconut grove outside his compound all night
and they would give him good warning if anyone lurked there.
They could be relied on to spring at the throat of any stranger
who ventured too near. If his predecessor had had these dogs he
wouldn't have come to his end.

The man who had been executioner before Louis Remire had
only held the job a couple of years when one day he disappeared. The authorities thought he had run away; he was
known to have a bit of money, and it was very probable that he
had managed to make arrangements with the captain of a
schooner to take him to Brazil. His nerves had given way. He
had gone two or three times to the governor of the prison and
told him that he feared for his life. He was convinced that the
convicts were out to kill him. The governor felt pretty sure that
his fears were groundless and paid no attention, but when the
man was nowhere to be found he concluded that his terror had
got the better of him and he had preferred to run the danger of
escape, and the danger of being recaptured and put back into
prison, rather than face the risk of an avenging convict's knife.
About three weeks later the warder in charge of a working party
in the jungle noticed a great flock of vultures clustered round a
tree. These vultures, called urubus, are large black birds, of a
horrible aspect, and they fly about the market-place of St.
Laurent, picking up the offal that is left there by the starving

liberated convicts, and flit heavily from tree to tree in the neat, well-kept streets of the town. They fly in the prison yard to remind the convicts that if they attempt an escape into the jungle their end, ten to one, will be to have their bones picked clean by these loathsome creatures. They were fighting and screaming in such a mass round the tree that the warder thought there was something strange there. He reported it and the commandant sent a party to see. They found a man hanging by the neck from one of the branches, and when they cut him down discovered that he was the executioner. It was given out that he had committed suicide, but there was a knife-thrust in his back, and the convicts knew that he had been stabbed and then, still alive, taken to the jungle and hanged.

Louis Remire had no fear that anything of that sort would happen to him. He knew how his predecessor had been caught. The job had not been done by the convicts. By the French law when a man is sentenced to hard labour for a certain number of years he has at the expiration of his sentence to remain in the colony for the same number of years. He is free, but he may not stir from the spot that is assigned to him as a residence. In certain circumstances he can get a concession and if he works hard he manages to scrape a bare living from it, but after a long term of penal servitude, during which he has lost all power of initiative, what with the debilitating effect of fever, hookworm and so on, he is unfit for heavy and continuous labour, and so most of the liberated men subsist on begging, larceny, smuggling tobacco or money to the prisoners, and loading and unloading cargoes when two or three times a month a steamer comes into the harbour. It was the wife of one of these freed men that had been the means of the undoing of Louis Remire's predecessor. She was a coloured woman, young and pretty, with a neat little figure and mischievous eyes. The plot was well-considered. The executioner was a burly, sanguine man, of ardent passions. She had thrown herself in his way, and when she caught his approving glance, had cast him a saucy look. He saw her a day or two later in the public garden. He did not venture to speak to her (no one, man, woman or child, would be seen speaking to him), but when he winked at her she smiled. One evening he met her walking through the coconut grove that surrounded his compound. No one was about. He got into conversation with her. They only exchanged a few words, for she was evidently terrified of being seen with him. But she came again to the coconut grove. She played him carefully till his suspicions were allayed; she teased his desires; she made him give her little presents, and at last on the promise of what was for both of them quite a sum of money she agreed to come one dark night to the compound. A ship had just come in and her husband would be working till dawn. It was when he opened the door for her and she hesitated to come in as though at the last moment she could not make up her mind, that he stepped outside to draw her in, and fell to the ground with the violence of the knife-thrust in his back.

"The fool," muttered Louis Remire. "He only got what he deserved. He should have smelt a rat. The eternal vanity of man."

For his part he was through with women. It was on account of women that he found himself in the situation he was in now, at least on account of one woman; and besides, at his time of life, his passions were assuaged. There were other things in life and after a certain age a man, if he was sensible, turned his attention to them. He had always been a great fisherman. In the old days, at home in France before he had had his misfortune, as soon as he came off duty, he took his rod and line and went down to the Rhone. He got a lot of fishing now. Every morning, till the sun grew hot, he sat on his favourite rock and generally managed to get enough for the prison governor's table. The governor's wife knew the value of things and beat him down on the price he asked, but he did not blame her for that; she knew that he had to take what she was prepared to give and it would have been stupid of her to pay a penny more than she had to. In any case it brought in a little money useful for tobacco and rum and other odds and ends. But this evening he was going to fish for himself. He got his bait from the lean-to, and his rod, and settled down on his rock. No fish was so good as the fish you caught yourself, and by now he knew which were those that were good to eat and which were so tough and flavourless that you could only throw them back into the sea. There was one sort that, fried in real olive oil, was as good as mullet. He had not been sitting there five minutes when his float gave a sudden jerk, and when he pulled up his line, there, like an answer to prayer, was one of those very fish wriggling on the hook. He took it off, banged its head on the rock, and putting it down, replaced his bait. Four of them would make a good supper, the best a man could have, and with a night's hard work before him he needed a hearty meal. He would not have time to fish to-morrow morning. First of all the scaffold would have to be taken down and the pieces brought back to the room in which it was kept, and there would be a lot of cleaning to do. It was a bloody business; last time he had had his pants so soaked that he had been able to do nothing with them and had had to throw them away. The brass would have to be polished, the knife would have to be honed. He was not a man to leave a job half finished, and by the time it was through he would be pretty peckish. It would be worth while to catch a few more fish and put them in a cool place so that he could have a substantial breakfast. A cup of coffee, a couple of eggs and a bit of fried fish; he could do with that. Then he would have a good sleep; after a night on his feet, the anxiety of an inexperienced assistant, and the clearing away of all the mess, God knew he would deserve it.

In front of him was spread the bay in a noble sweep, and in the distance was a little island green with trees. The afternoon was exquisitely still. Peace descended on the fisherman's soul. He watched his float idly. When you came to think of it, he reflected, he might be a great deal worse off; some of them, the convicts he meant, the convicts who swarmed in the prison a few hundred yards away from him, some of them had such a nostalgia for France that they went mad with melancholy; but he was a bit of a philosopher, so long as he could fish he was content; and did it really matter if he watched his float on the southern sea or in the Rhone? His thoughts wandered back to the past. His wife was an intolerable woman and he did not regret that he had killed her. He had never meant to marry her. She was a dressmaker, and he had taken a fancy to her because she was always neatly and smartly dressed. She seemed respectable and ladylike. He would not have been surprised if she had looked upon herself as a cut above a policeman. But he had a way with him. She soon gave him to understand that she was no snob, and when he made the customary advances he discovered to his relief, for he was not a man who considered that resistance added a flavour to conquest, that she was no prude. He liked to be seen with her when he took her out to dinner. She talked intelligently, and she was economical. She knew where they could dine well at the cheapest price. His situation was enviable. It added to his satisfaction that he could gratify the sexual desires natural to his healthy temperament at so moderate an expense. When she came to him and said she was going to have a baby it seemed natural enough that they should get

married. He was earning good wages, and it was time that he
should settle down. He often grew tired of eating, *en pension,* at
a restaurant, and he looked forward to having his own home and
home cooking. Well, it turned out that it had been a mistake
about the baby, but Louis Remire was a good-natured fellow,
and he didn't hold it up against Adèle. But he found, as many
men have found before, that the wife was a very different
woman from the mistress. She was jealous and possessive. She
seemed to think that on a Sunday afternoon he ought to take
her for a walk instead of going out fishing, and she made it a
grievance that, on coming off duty, he would go to the café.
There was one café he frequented where other fishermen went
and where he met men with whom he had a lot in common. He
found it much pleasanter to spend his free evenings there over
a glass or two of beer, whiling away the time with a game of
cards, than to sit at home with his wife. She began to make
scenes. Though sociable and jovial by nature he had a quick
temper. There was a rough crowd at Lyons, and sometimes you
could not manage them unless you were prepared to show a certain amount of firmness. When his wife began to make a nuisance of herself it never occurred to him that there was any
other way of dealing with her than that he adopted. He let her
know the strength of his hand. If she had been a sensible woman
she would have learnt her lesson, but she was not a sensible
woman. He found occasion more and more often to apply a
necessary correction; she revenged herself by screaming the
place down and by telling the neighbours—they lived in a two-
roomed apartment on the fifth floor of a big house—what a
brute he was. She told them that she was sure he would kill her
one day. And yet never was there a more good-natured man
than Louis Remire; she blamed him for the money he spent at
the café, she accused him of wasting it on other women; well, in
his position he had opportunities now and then, and as any man
would he took them, and he was easy with his money, he never
minded paying a round of drinks for his friends, and when a girl
who had been nice to him wanted a new hat or a pair of silk
stockings he wasn't the man to say no. His wife looked upon
money that he did not spend on her as money stolen from her;
she tried to make him account for every penny he spent, and
when in his jovial way he told her he had thrown it out of the
window, she was infuriated. Her tongue grew bitter and her

voice was rasping. She was in a sullen rage with him all the time. She could not speak without saying something disagreeable. They led a cat-and-dog life. Louis Remire used to tell his friends what a harridan she was, he used to tell them that he wished ten times a day that he had never married her, and sometimes he would add that if an epidemic of influenza did not carry her off he would really have to kill her.

It was these remarks, made merely in jest, and the fact that she had so often told the neighbours that she knew he would murder her, that had sent him to St. Laurent de Maroni with a twelve-year sentence. Otherwise he might very well have got off with three or four years in a French prison. The end had come one hot summer's day. He was, which was rare for him, in a bad temper. There was a strike in progress and the strikers had been violent. The police had had to make a good many arrests and the men had not submitted to this peaceably. Louis Remire had got a nasty blow on the jaw and he had had to make free use of his truncheon. To get the arrested men to the station had been a hot and tiring job. On coming off duty he had gone home to get out of his uniform and was intending to go to the café and have a glass of beer and a pleasant game of cards. His jaw was hurting him. His wife chose that moment to ask him for money and when he told her that he had none to give her she made a scene. He had plenty of money to go to the café, but none for her to buy a scrap of food with, she could starve for all he cared. He told her to shut up, and then the row began. She got in front of the door and swore that he should not pass till he gave her money. He told her to get out of the way and took a step towards her. She whipped out his service revolver which he had taken off when he removed his uniform and threatened that she would shoot him if he moved a step. He was used to dealing with dangerous criminals, and the words were hardly out of her mouth before he had sprung upon her and snatched the revolver out of her hand. She screamed and hit him in the face. She hit him exactly where his jaw most hurt him. Blind with rage and mad with pain, he fired, he fired twice and she fell to the floor. For a moment he stood and stared at her. He was dazed. She looked as if she were dead. His first feeling was one of indescribable relief. He listened. No one seemed to have heard the sound of the shot. The neighbours must be out. That was a bit of luck, for it gave him time to do what he had to do in his own way. He changed back into his uniform, went out, locking the door behind him and putting the key in his pocket; he stopped for five minutes at his familiar café to have a glass of beer and then returned to the police-station he had lately left. On account of the day's disturbances the chief inspector was still there. Louis Remire went to his room and told him what had happened. He spent the night in a cell adjoining those of the strikers he had so recently himself arrested. Even at that tragic moment he was struck by the irony of the situation.

Louis Remire had on frequent occasions appeared as a police witness in criminal cases and he knew how eager are a man's companions to give any information that may damage him when he gets into trouble. It had caused him a certain grim amusement to realise how often it happened that a conviction was obtained only by the testimony of a prisoner's best friends. But notwithstanding his experience he was amazed, when his own case came up for trial, to listen to the evidence given by the proprietor of the little café he had so much frequented, and to that of the men who for years had fished with him, played cards with him and drunk with him. They seemed to have treasured every careless word he had ever uttered, the complaints he had made about his wife and the joking threats he had from time to time made that he would get even with her. He knew that at the time they had taken them no more seriously than he meant them. If he was able to do them a small service, and a man in the force often has it in his power to do one, he never hesitated. He had never been ungenerous with his money. You would have thought as you listened to them in the witness-box that it gave them the most intense satisfaction to disclose every trivial detail that could damage him.

From what appeared at the trial you would have thought that he was a bad man, dissolute, of violent temper, extravagant, idle and corrupt. He knew that he was nothing of the kind. He was just an ordinary, good-natured, easy-going fellow, who was willing to let you go your way if you would let him go his. It was true that he liked his game of cards and his glass of beer, it was true that he liked a pretty girl, but what of it? When he looked at the jury he wondered how many of them would come out of it any better than he if all their errors, all their rash words, all their follies were thus laid bare. He did not resent the long term of penal servitude to which he was sentenced. He was an officer of the law; he had committed a crime and it was right that he should be punished. But he was not a criminal; he was the victim of an unfortunate accident.

At St. Laurent de Maroni, in the prison camp, wearing the pink and white stripe of the prison garb and the ugly straw hat, he remembered still that he had been a policeman and that the convicts with whom he must now consort had always been his natural enemies. He despised and disliked them. He had as little to do with them as he could. And he was not frightened of them. He knew them too well. Like all the rest he had a knife and he showed that he was prepared to use it. He did not want to interfere with anybody, but he was not going to allow anyone to interfere with him.

The chief of the Lyons police had liked him, his character while in the force had been exemplary, and the *fiche* which accompanied every prisoner spoke well of him. He knew that what officials like is a prisoner who gives no trouble, who accepts his position with cheerfulness and who is willing. He got a soft job; very soon he got a cell of his own and so escaped the horrible promiscuity of the dormitories; he got on well with the warders, they were decent chaps, most of them, and knowing that he had formerly been in the police they treated him more as a comrade than as a convict. The commandant of the prison trusted him. Presently he got the job of servant to one of the prison officials. He slept in the prison, but otherwise enjoyed complete freedom. He took the children of his master to school every day and fetched them at the end of their school hours. He made toys for them. He accompanied his mistress to market and carried back the provisions she bought. He spent long hours gossiping with her. The family liked him. They liked his chaffing manner and his good-natured smile. He was industrious and trustworthy. Life once more was tolerable.

But after three years his master was transferred to Cayenne. It was a blow. But it happened just then that the post of executioner fell free and he obtained it. Now once more he was in the service of the state. He was an official. However humble his residence it was his own. He need no longer wear the prison uniform. He could grow his hair and his moustache. He cared little if the convicts looked upon him with horror and contempt. That was how he looked upon them. Scum. When he took the bleeding head of an executed man from the basket and holding it by the ears pronounced those solemn words: *Au nom du peuple français justice est faite,* he felt that he did represent the Republic. He stood for law and order. He was the protector of society against that vast horde of ruthless criminals.

He got a hundred francs for each execution. That and what the governor's wife paid him for his fish provided him with many a pleasant comfort and not a few luxuries. And now as he sat on his rock in the peace of eventide he considered what he would do with the money he would earn next day. Occasionally he got a bite, now and then a fish; he drew it out of the water, took it off the hook and put on fresh bait; but he did this mechanically, and it did not disturb the current of his thoughts. Six hundred francs. It was a respectable sum. He scarcely knew what to do with it. He had everything he wanted in his little house, he had a good store of groceries, and plenty of rum for one who was as little of a drinker as he was; he needed no fishing tackle; his clothes were good enough. The only thing was to put it aside. He already had a tidy little sum hidden in the ground at the root of a papaya tree. He chuckled when he thought how Adèle would have stared had she known that he was actually saving. It would have been balm to her avaricious soul. He was saving up gradually for when he was released. That was the difficult moment for the convicts. So long as they were in prison they had a roof over their heads and food to eat, but when they were released, with the obligation of staying for so many years more in the colony, they had to shift for themselves. They all said the same thing: it was at the expiration of their term that their real punishment began. They could not get work. Employers mistrusted them. Contractors would not engage them because the prison authorities hired out convict labour at a price that defied competition. They slept in the open, in the market-place, and for food were often glad to go to the Salvation Army. But the Salvation Army made them work hard for what they gave and besides forced them to listen to their services. Sometimes they committed a violent crime merely to get back to the safety of prison. Louis Remire was not going to take any risks. He meant to amass a sufficient capital to start in business. He ought to be able to get permission to settle in Cayenne, and there he might open a bar. People might hesitate to come at first because he had been the executioner, but if he provided good liquor they would get over their prejudice, and with his jovial manner, with his experience in keeping order, he ought to be able to make a go of it. Visitors came to Cayenne now and then and they would come out of curiosity. It would

be something interesting to tell their friends when they got
home that the best rum punch they had had in Cayenne was
at the executioner's. But he had a good many years to go yet,
and if there really was something he needed there was no reason
why he shouldn't get it. He racked his brains. No, there wasn't
a thing in the world he wanted. He was surprised. He allowed
his eyes to wander from his float. The sea was wonderfully calm
and now it was rich with all the colour of the setting sun. In
the sky already a solitary star twinkled. A thought came to him
that filled him with an extraordinary sensation.

"But if there's nothing in the world you want, surely that's
happiness." He stroked his handsome moustache and his blue
eyes shone softly. "There are no two ways about it, I'm a happy
man and till this moment I never knew it."

The notion was so unexpected that he did not know what to
make of it. It was certainly a very odd one. But there it was, as
obvious to anyone with a logical mind as a proposition of Euclid.

"Happy, that's what I am. How many men can say the same?
In St. Laurent de Maroni of all places, and for the first time in
my life."

The sun was setting. He had caught enough fish for his supper
and enough for his breakfast. He drew in his line, gathered up
his fish, and went back to his house. It stood but a few yards
from the sea. It did not take him long to light his fire and in a
little while he had four little fish cheerfully frizzling in a pan.
He was always very particular about the oil he used. The best
olive oil was expensive, but it was worth the money. The prison
bread was good, and after he had fried his fish, he fried a couple
of pieces of bread in the rest of the oil. He sniffed the savoury
smell with satisfaction. He lit a lamp, washed a lettuce grown in
his own garden, and mixed himself a salad. He had a notion
that no one in the world could mix a salad better than he. He
drank a glass of rum and ate his supper with appetite. He gave
a few odds and ends to the two mongrel dogs who were lying at
his feet, and then, having washed up, for he was by nature a
tidy man and when he came in to breakfast next morning did
not want to find things in a mess, let the dogs out of the compound to wander about the coconut grove. He took the lamp
into the house, made himself comfortable in his deck-chair, and
smoking a cigar smuggled in from the neighbouring Dutch
Colony settled down to read one of the French papers that had
arrived by the last mail. Replete, his mind at ease, he could

not but feel that life, with all its disadvantages, was good to live. He was still affected by the amused surprise that had overcome him when it suddenly occurred to him that he was a happy man. When you considered that men spent their lives seeking for happiness, it seemed hardly believable that he had found it. Yet the fact stared him in the face. A man who has everything he wants is happy, he had everything he wanted; therefore he was happy. He chuckled as a new thought crossed his mind.

"There's no denying it, I owe it to Adèle."

Old Adèle. What a foul woman!

Presently he decided that he had better have a nap; he set his alarm clock for a quarter to twelve and lying down on his bed in a few minutes was fast asleep. He slept soundly and no dreams troubled him. He woke with a start when the alarm sounded, but in a moment remembered why he had set it. He yawned and stretched himself lazily.

"Ah, well, I suppose I must get to work. Every job has its inconveniences."

He slipped from under his mosquito-net and relit his lamp. To freshen himself he washed his hands and face, and then as a protection against the night air drank a glass of rum. He thought for a moment of his inexperienced assistant and wondered whether it would be wise to take some rum in a flask with him.

"It would be a pretty business if his nerves went back on him."

It was unfortunate that so many as six men had to be executed. If there had been only one, it wouldn't have mattered so much his assistant being new to the game; but with five others waiting there, it would be awkward if there were a hitch. He shrugged his shoulders. They would just have to do the best they could. He passed a comb through his tousled hair and carefully brushed his handsome moustache. He lit a cigarette. He walked through his compound, unlocked the door in the stout palisade that surrounded it, and locked it again behind him. There was no moon. He whistled for his dogs. He was surprised that they did not come. He whistled again. The brutes. They'd probably caught a rat and were fighting over it. He'd give them a good hiding for that; he'd teach them not to come when he whistled. He set out to walk in the direction of the prison. It was dark under the coconut trees and he would just as soon have had the dogs with him. Still there were only fifty yards to go and then he would be out in the open. There were lights in the governor's house, and it gave him confidence to see them. He smiled, for he guessed what those lights at that late hour meant; the governor, with the execution before him at dawn, was finding it hard to sleep. The anxiety, the malaise, that affected convicts and ex-convicts alike on the eve of an execution, had got on his nerves. It was true that there was always the chance of an outbreak then, and the warders went around with their eyes skinned and their hands ready to draw their guns at a suspicious movement.

Louis Remire whistled for his dogs once more, but they did not come. He could not understand it. It was a trifle disquieting. He was a man who habitually walked slowly, strolling along with a sort of roll, but now he hastened his pace. He spat the cigarette out of his mouth. It had struck him that it was prudent not to betray his whereabouts by the light it gave. Suddenly he stumbled against something. He stopped dead. He was a brave man, with nerves of steel, but on a sudden he felt sick with terror. It was something soft and rather large that he had stumbled against, and he was pretty sure what it was. He wore espadrilles, and with one foot he cautiously felt the object on the ground before him. Yes, he was right. It was one of his dogs. It was dead. He took a step backwards and drew his knife. He knew it was no good to shout. The only house in the neighbourhood was the prison governor's, it faced the clearing just beyond the coconut grove; but they would not hear him, or if they did would not stir. St. Laurent de Maroni was not a place where you went out in the dead of night when you heard a man calling for help. If next day one of the freed convicts was found lying dead, well, it was no great loss. Louis Remire saw in a flash what had happened.

He thought rapidly. They had killed his dogs while he was sleeping. They must have got them when he had put them out of his compound after supper. They must have thrown them some poisoned meat and the brutes had snatched at it. If the one he had stumbled over was near his house it was because it tried to crawl home to die. Louis Remire strained his eyes. He could see nothing. The night was pitch black. He could hardly see the trunks of the coconut trees a yard away from him. His first thought was to make a rush for his shack. If he got back to the safety of that he could wait till the prison people, wondering why he did not come, sent to fetch him. But he knew he could never get back. He knew they were there in the darkness, the men who had killed his dogs; he would have to fumble with the key to find the lock and before he found it he would have a knife plunged in his back. He listened intently. There was not a sound. And yet he felt that there were men there, lurking behind the trees, and they were there to kill him. They would kill him as they had killed his dogs. And he would die like a dog. There was more than one certainly. He knew them, there were three or four of them at least, there might be more, convicts in service in private houses who were not obliged to get back to the camp till a late hour, or desperate and starving freed men who had nothing to lose. For a moment he hesitated what to do. He dared not make a run for it, they might easily have put a rope across the pathway that led from his house to the open, and if he tripped he was done for. The coconut trees were loosely planted and among them his enemies would see him as little as he saw them. He stepped over the dead dog and plunged into the grove. He stood with his back to a tree to decide how he should proceed. The silence was terrifying. Suddenly he heard a whisper and the horror of it was frightful. Again a dead silence. He felt he must move on, but his feet seemed rooted to the ground. He felt that they were peering at him out of the darkness and it seemed to him that he was as visible to them as though he stood in the broad light of day. Then from the other side was a little cough. It came as such a shock that Louis Remire nearly screamed. He was conscious now that they were all round him. He could expect no mercy from those robbers and murderers. He remembered the other executioner, his predecessor, whom they had carried still alive into the jungle, whose eyes they had gouged out, and whom they had left hanging for the vultures to devour. His knees began to tremble. What a fool he had been to take on the job! There were soft jobs he could have found in which you ran no risk. It was too late to think of that. He pulled himself together. He had no chance of getting out of the coconut grove alive, he knew that; he wanted to be sure that he would be dead. He tightened his grip on his knife. The awful part was that he could hear no one, he could see no one, and yet he knew that they were lurking there waiting to strike. For one moment he had a mad idea, he would throw his knife away and shout out to them that he was unarmed and they could come and kill him in safety. But he knew them; they would never be satisfied merely to kill him. Rage seized him. He was not the man to surrender tamely to a pack of criminals. He was an honest man and an official of the state; it was his duty to defend himself. He could not stay there all night. It was better to get it over quickly. Yet that tree at his back seemed to offer a sort of security, he could not bring himself to move. He stared at the trunk of a tree in front of him and suddenly it moved and he realised with horror that it was a man. That made up his mind for him and with a huge effort he stepped forwards. He advanced slowly and cautiously. He could hear nothing, he could see nothing. But he knew that as he advanced they advanced too. It was as though he were accompanied by an invisible body-guard. He thought he could hear the sound of their naked feet on the ground. His fear had left him. He walked on, keeping as close to the trees as he could, so that they should have less chance of attacking him from behind; a wild hope sprang up in his breast that they would be afraid to strike, they knew him, they all knew him, and whoever struck the first blow would be lucky if he escaped a knife in his own guts; he had only another thirty yards to go, and once in the open, able to see, he could make a fight for it. A few yards more and then he would run for his life. Suddenly something happened that made him start out of his skin, and he stopped dead. A light was flashed and in that heavy darkness the sudden glare was terrifying. It was an electric torch. Instinctively he sprang to a tree and stood with his back to it. He could not see who held the light. He was blinded by it. He did not speak. He held his knife low, he knew that when they struck it was in the belly, and if someone flung himself at him he was prepared to strike back. He was going to sell his life dearly. For half a minute perhaps the light shone on his face, but it seemed to him an eternity. He thought now that he discerned dimly the faces of men. Then a word broke the horrible silence.

"Throw."

At the same instant a knife came flying through the air and struck him on the breast-bone. He threw up his hands and as he did so someone sprang at him and with a great sweep of the knife ripped up his belly. The light was switched off. Louis Remire sank to the ground with a groan, a terrible groan of pain. Five, six men gathered out of the gloom and stood over him. With his fall the knife that had stuck in his breast-bone was dislodged. It lay on the ground. A quick flash of the torch showed where it was. One of the men took it and with a single, swift motion cut Remire's throat from ear to ear.

"*Au nom du peuple français justice est faite,*" he said.

They vanished into the darkness and in the coconut grove was the immense silence of death.

A MAN WITH A CONSCIENCE

St. Laurent de Maroni is a pretty little place. It is neat and clean. It has an Hôtel de Ville and a Palais de Justice of which many a town in France would be proud. The streets are wide, and the fine trees that border them give a grateful shade. The houses look as though they had just had a coat of paint. Many of them nestle in little gardens, and in the gardens are palm trees and flame of the forest; cannas flaunt their bright colours and crotons their variety; the bougainvillæas, purple or red, riot profusely, and the elegant hibiscus offers its gorgeous flowers with a negligence that seems almost affected. St. Laurent de Maroni is the centre of the French penal settlements of Guiana, and a hundred yards from the quay at which you land is the great gateway of the prison camp. These pretty little houses in their tropical gardens are the residence of the prison officials, and if the streets are neat and clean it is because there is no lack of convicts to keep them so. One day, walking with a casual acquaintance, I came upon a young man, in the round straw hat and the pink and white stripes of the convict's uniform, who was standing by the road-side with a pick. He was doing nothing.

"Why are you idling?" my companion asked him.

The man gave his shoulders a scornful shrug.

"Look at the blade of grass there," he answered. "I've got twenty years to scratch it away."

St. Laurent de Maroni exists for the group of prison camps of which it is the centre. Such trade as it has depends on them; its shops, kept by Chinese, are there to satisfy the wants of the warders, the doctors and the numerous officials who are connected with the penal settlements. The streets are silent and deserted. You pass a convict with a dispatch-case under his arm; he has some job in the administration; or another with a basket; he is a servant in somebody's house. Sometimes you come upon a little group in the charge of a warder; often you see them strolling to or from the prison unguarded. The prison gates are open all day long and the prisoners freely saunter in and out. If you see a man not in the prison uniform he is probably a freed man who is condemned to spend a number of years in the colony and who, unable to get work, living on the edge of starvation, is drinking himself to death on the cheap strong rum which is called tafia.

There is an hotel at St. Laurent de Maroni and here I had my meals. I soon got to know by sight the habitual frequenters. They came in and sat each at his little table, ate their meals in silence and went out again. The hotel was kept by a coloured woman, and the man she lived with, an ex-convict, was the only waiter. But the Governor of the colony, who lives at Cayenne, had put at my disposal his own bungalow and it was there I slept. An old Arab looked after it; he was a devout Mahommedan, and at intervals during the day I heard him say his prayers. To make my bed, keep my rooms tidy and run errands for me, the commandant of the prison had assigned me another convict. Both were serving life sentences for murder; the commandant told me that I could place entire confidence in them; they were as honest as the day, and I could leave anything about without the slightest risk. But I will not conceal from the reader that when I went to bed at night I took the precaution to lock my door and to bolt my shutters. It was foolish no doubt, but I slept more comfortably.

I had come with letters of introduction, and both the governor of the prison settlements and the commandant of the camp at St. Laurent did everything they could to make my visit agreeable and instructive. I will not here narrate all I heard and saw. I am not a reporter. It is not my business to attack or to defend the system which the French have thought fit to adopt in regard to their criminals. Besides, the system is now condemned; prisoners will soon cease to be sent out to French Guiana, to suffer the illnesses incidental to the climate and the

work in malarial jungles to which so many are relegated, to endure nameless degradations, to lose hope, to rot, to die. I will
only say that I saw no physical cruelty. On the other hand I saw
no attempt to make the criminal on the expiration of his sentence a useful citizen. I saw nothing done for his spiritual welfare. I heard nothing of classes that he could attend in order to
improve his education or organised games that might distract his
mind. I saw no library where he could get books to read when
his day's work was done. I saw a condition of affairs that only
the strongest character could hope to surmount. I saw a brutish-
ness that must reduce all but a very few to apathy and despair.

All this has nothing to do with me. It is vain to torment oneself over sufferings that one cannot alleviate. My object here is
to tell a story. As I am well aware, one can never know everything there is to be known about human nature. One can be sure
only of one thing, and that is that it will never cease to have a
surprise in store for you. When I had got over the impression of
bewilderment, surprise and horror to which my first visit to the
prison camp gave rise, I bethought myself that there were certain matters that I was interested to enquire into. I should in-
form the reader that three-quarters of the convicts at St.
Laurent de Maroni are there for murder. This is not official information and it may be that I exaggerate; every prisoner has
a little book in which are set down his crime, his sentence, his
punishments, and whatever else the authorities think necessary
to keep note of; and it was from an examination of a considerable number of these that I formed my estimate. It gave me
something of a shock to realise that in England far, far the
greater number of these men whom I saw working in shops,
lounging about the verandahs of their dormitories or sauntering through the streets would have suffered capital punishment.
I found them not at all disinclined to speak of the crime for
which they had been convicted, and in pursuance of my purpose
I spent the better part of one day enquiring into crimes of passion. I wanted to know exactly what was the motive that had
made a man kill his wife or his girl. I had a notion that jealousy
and wounded honour might not perhaps tell the whole story. I
got some curious replies, and among them one that was not to
my mind lacking in humour. This was from a man working in
the carpenter's shop who had cut his wife's throat; when I asked
him why he had done it, he answered with a shrug of the
shoulders: *Manque d'entente.* His casual tone made the best

translation of this: We didn't get on very well. I could not help observing that if men in general looked upon this as an adequate reason for murdering their wives, the mortality in the female sex would be alarming. But after putting a good many questions to a good many men I arrived at the conclusion that at the bottom of nearly all these crimes was an economic motive; they had killed their wives or mistresses not only from jealousy, because they were unfaithful to them, but also because somehow it affected their pockets. A woman's infidelity was sometimes an occasion of financial loss, and it was this in the end that drove a man to his desperate act; or, himself in need of money to gratify other passions, he murdered because his victim was an obstacle to his exclusive possession of it. I do not conclude that a man never kills his woman because his love is spurned or his honour tarnished, I only offer my observation on these particular cases as a curious sidelight on human nature. I should not venture to deduce from it a general rule.

I spent another day enquiring into the matter of conscience. Moralists have sought to persuade us that it is one of the most powerful agents in human behaviour. Now that reason and pity have agreed to regard hell-fire as a hateful myth, many good men have seen in conscience the chief safeguard that shall induce the human race to walk in the way of righteousness. Shakespeare has told us that it makes cowards of us all. Novelists and playwrights have described for us the pangs that assail the wicked; they have vividly pictured the anguish of a stricken conscience and the sleepless nights it occasions; they have shown it poisoning every pleasure till life is so intolerable that discovery and punishment come as a welcome relief. I had often wondered how much of all this was true. Moralists have an axe to grind; they must draw a moral. They think that if they say a thing often enough people will believe it. They are apt to state that a thing is so when they consider it desirable that it should be. They tell us that the wages of sin is death; we know very well that it is not always. And so far as the authors of fiction are concerned, the playwrights and the novelists, when they get hold of an effective theme they are disposed to make use of it without bothering very much whether it agrees with the facts of life. Certain statements about human nature become, as it were, common property and so are accepted as self-evident. In the same way painters for ages painted shadows black, and it was not till the impressionists looked at them with unprejudiced eyes and painted what they saw that we discovered that shadows were coloured. It had sometimes struck me that perhaps conscience was the expression of a high moral development, so that its influence was strong only in those whose virtue was so shining that they were unlikely to commit any action for which they could seriously reproach themselves. It is generally accepted that murder is a shocking crime, and it is the murderer above all other criminals who is supposed to suffer remorse. His victim, we have been led to believe, haunts his dreams in horrifying nightmares, and the recollection of his dreadful deed tortures his waking hours. I could not miss the opportunity to enquire into the truth of this. I had no intention of insisting if I encountered reticence or distress, but I found in none of those with whom I talked any such thing. Some said that in the same circumstances they would do as they had done before. Determinists without knowing it, they seemed to look upon their action as ordained by a fate over which they had no control. Some appeared to think that their crime was committed by someone with whom they had no connection.

"When one's young, one's foolish," they said, with a careless gesture or a deprecating smile.

Others told me that if they had known what the punishment was they would suffer, they would certainly have held their hands. I found in none any regret for the human being they had violently bereft of life. It seemed to me that they had no more feeling for the creature they had killed than if it had been a pig whose throat they had cut in the way of business. Far from feeling pity for their victim, they were more inclined to feel anger because he had been the occasion of their imprisonment in that distant land. In only one man did I discern anything that might appropriately be called a conscience, and his story was so remarkable that I think it well worth narrating. For in this case it was, so far as I can understand, remorse that was the motive of the crime. I noticed the man's number, which was printed on the chest of the pink and white pyjamas of his prison uniform, but I have forgotten it. Anyhow it is of no consequence. I never knew his name. He did not offer to tell me and I did not like to ask it. I will call him Jean Charvin.

I met him on my first visit to the camp with the commandant. We were walking through a courtyard round which were cells, not punishment cells, but individual cells which are given to well-behaved prisoners who ask for them. They are sought after by those to whom the promiscuity of the dormitories is odious. Most of them were empty, for their occupants were engaged in their various employments. Jean Charvin was at work in his cell, writing at a small table, and the door was open. The commandant called him and he came out. I looked into the cell. It contained a fixed hammock, with a dingy mosquito-net; by the side of this was a small table on which were his bits and pieces, a shaving-mop and a razor, a hairbrush and two or three battered books. On the walls were photographs of persons of respectable appearance and illustrations from picture papers. He had been sitting on his bed to write and the table on which he had been writing was covered with papers. They looked like accounts. He was a handsome man, tall, erect and lean, with flashing dark eyes and clean-cut, strong features. The first thing I noticed about him was that he had a fine head of long, naturally-waving dark brown hair. This at once made him look different from the rest of the prisoners, whose hair is close-cropped, but cropped so badly, in ridges, that it gives them a sinister look. The commandant spoke to him of some official business, and then as we were leaving added in a friendly way:

"I see your hair is growing well."

Jean Charvin reddened and smiled. His smile was boyish and engaging.

"It'll be some time yet before I get it right again."

The commandant dismissed him and we went on.

"He's a very decent fellow," he said. "He's in the accountant's department, and he's had leave to let his hair grow. He's delighted."

"What is he here for?" I asked.

"He killed his wife. But he's only got six years. He's clever and a good worker. He'll do well. He comes from a very decent family and he's had an excellent education."

I thought no more of Jean Charvin, but by chance I met him next day on the road. He was coming towards me. He carried a black dispatch-case under his arm, and except for the pink and white stripes of his uniform and the ugly round straw hat that concealed his handsome head of hair, you might have taken him for a young lawyer on his way to court. He walked with a long, leisurely stride, and he had an easy, you might almost say a gallant, bearing. He recognised me, and taking off his hat bade me good-morning. I stopped, and for something to say asked him where he was going. He told me he was taking some papers from the governor's office to the bank. There was a pleasing frankness in his face, and his eyes, his really beautiful eyes, shone with good will. I supposed that the vigour of his youth was such that it made life, notwithstanding his position and his surroundings, more than tolerable, even pleasant. You would have said that here was a young man without a care in the world.

"I hear you're going to St. Jean to-morrow," he said.

"Yes. It appears I must start at dawn."

St. Jean is a camp seventeen kilometres from St. Laurent, and it is here that are interned the habitual criminals who have been sentenced to transportation after repeated terms of imprisonment. They are petty thieves, confidence men, forgers, tricksters and suchlike; the prisoners of St. Laurent, condemned for more serious offences, look upon them with contempt.

"You should find it an interesting experience," Jean Charvin said, with his frank and engaging smile. "But keep your pocket-book buttoned up, they'd steal the shirt off your back if they had half a chance. They're a dirty lot of scoundrels!"

That afternoon, waiting till the heat of the day was less, I sat on the verandah outside my bedroom and read: I had drawn the jalousies and it was tolerably cool. My old Arab came up the stairs on his bare feet, and in his halting French told me that there was a man from the commandant who wanted to see me.

"Send him up," I said.

In a moment the man came, and it was Jean Charvin. He told me that the commandant had sent him to give me a message about my excursion next day to St. Jean. When he had delivered it I asked him if he would not sit down and have a cigarette with me. He wore a cheap wrist-watch and he looked at it.

"I have a few minutes to spare. I should be glad to." He sat down and lit the cigarette I offered him. He gave me a smiling look of his soft eyes. "Do you know, this is the first time I've ever been asked to sit down since I was sentenced." He inhaled a long whiff of his cigarette. "Egyptian. I haven't smoked an Egyptian cigarette for three years."

The convicts make their own cigarettes out of a coarse, strong tobacco that is sold in square blue packets. Since one is not allowed to pay them for the services they may render you, but may give them tobacco, I had bought a good many packets of this.

"How does it taste?"

"One gets accustomed to everything and, to tell you the truth, my palate is so vitiated, I prefer the stuff we get here."

"I'll give you a couple of packets."

I went into my room and fetched them. When I returned he was looking at some books that were lying on the table.

"Are you fond of reading?" I asked.

"Very. I think the want of books is what I most suffer from now. The few I can get hold of I'm forced to read over and over again."

To so great a reader as myself no deprivation seems more insupportable than the lack of books.

"I have several French ones in my bag. I'll look them out and if you care to have them I'll give them to you if you can come along again."

My offer was due only in part to kindness; I wanted to have another chance of a talk with him.

"I should have to show them to the commandant. He would only let me keep them if there was no doubt they couldn't possibly corrupt my morals. But he's a good-natured man, I don't think he'll make any difficulties."

There was a hint of slyness in the smile with which he said this, and I suspected that he had taken the measure of the well-meaning, conscientious chief of the camp and knew pretty well how to get on the right side of him. It would have been unjust to blame him if he exercised tact, and even cunning, to render his lot as tolerable as might be.

"The commandant has a very good opinion of you."

"He's a fine man. I'm very grateful to him, he's done a great deal for me. I'm an accountant by profession and he's put me in the accountant's department. I love figures, it gives me an intense satisfaction to deal with them, they're living things to me, and now that I can handle them all day long I feel myself again."

"And are you glad to have a cell of your own?"

"It's made all the difference. To be herded with fifty men, the scum of the earth, and never to be alone for a minute—it was awful. That was the worst of all. At home, at Le Havre, that is where I lived, I had an apartment, modest of course, but my own, and we had a maid who came in by the day. We lived decently. It made it ten times harder for me than for the rest, most of them, who have never known anything but squalor, filth and promiscuity."

I had asked him about the cell in the hope that I could get him to talk about the life that is led in those vast dormitories in which the men are locked from five in the evening till five next morning. During these twelve hours they are their own masters. A warder can enter, they told me, only at the risk of his life. They have no light after eight o'clock, but from sardine-tins, a little oil, and a rag they make lamps by the light of which they can see enough to play cards. They gamble furiously, not for love, but for the money they keep secreted on their bodies; they are unscrupulous ruthless men, and naturally enough bitter quarrels often arise. They are settled with knives. Often in the morning, when the dormitory is opened, a man is found dead, but no threats, no promises, will induce anyone to betray the slayer. Other things Jean Charvin told me which I cannot narrate. He told me of one young fellow who had come out from France on the same ship with himself and with whom he had made friends. He was a good-looking boy. One day he went to the commandant and asked him if he could have a cell to himself. The commandant asked him why he wanted one. He explained. The commandant looked through his list and told him that at the moment all were occupied, but that as soon as there was a vacancy he should have one. Next morning when the dormitory was opened, he was found dead on his hammock with his belly ripped open to the breast-bone.

"They're savage brutes, and if one isn't a brute by the time one arrives only a miracle can save one from becoming as brutal as the rest."

Jean Charvin looked at his watch and got up. He walked away from me and then, with his charming smile, turned and faced me.

"I must go now. If the commandant gives me permission I will come and get the books you were kind enough to offer me."

In Guiana you do not shake hands with a convict, and a tactful man, taking leave of you, puts himself in such a position that there can be no question of your offering him your hand or of refusing his should he, forgetting for a moment, instinctively tender it. Heaven knows, it would have meant nothing to me to shake hands with Jean Charvin; it gave me a pang to see the care he had taken to spare me embarrassment.

I saw him twice more during my stay at St. Laurent. He told me his story, but I will tell it now in my words rather than in his, for I had to piece it together from what he said at one time and another, and what he left out I have had to supply out of my own imagination. I do not believe it has led me astray. It was as though he had given me three letters out of a number of five-letter words; the chances are that I have guessed most of the words correctly.

Jean Charvin was born and bred in the great seaport of Le Havre. His father had a good post in the Customs. Having finished his education, he did his military service, and then looked about for a job. Like a great many other young Frenchmen he was prepared to sacrifice the hazardous chance of wealth for a respectable security. His natural gift for figures made it easy for him to get a place in the accountant's department of a large exporting house. His future was assured. He could look forward to earning a sufficient income to live in the modest comfort of the class to which he belonged. He was industrious and well-behaved. Like most young Frenchmen of his generation he was athletic. He swam and played tennis in summer, and in winter he bicycled. On two evenings a week to keep himself fit he spent a couple of hours in a gymnasium. Through his childhood, his adolescence and his young manhood, he lived in the constant companionship of a boy called, shall we say for the purposes of this narrative, Henri Renard, whose father was also an official in the Customs. Jean and Riri went to school together, played together, worked for their examinations together, spent their holidays together, for the two families were intimate, had their first affairs with girls together, partnered one another in the local tennis tournaments, and did their military service together. They never quarrelled. They were never so happy as in one another's society. They were inseparable. When the time came for them to start working they decided that they would go into the same firm; but that was not so easy; Jean tried to get Riri a job in the exporting house that had engaged him, but could not manage it, and it was not till a year later that Riri got something to do. But by then trade was as bad at Le Havre as everywhere else, and in a few months he found himself once more without employment.

Riri was a light-hearted youth, and he enjoyed his leisure. He danced, bathed and played tennis. It was thus that he made the acquaintance of a girl who had recently come to live at Le Havre. Her father had been a captain in the colonial army and on his death her mother had returned to Le Havre, which was her native place. Marie-Louise was then eighteen. She had spent

almost all her life in Tonkin. This gave her an exotic attraction
for the young men who had never been out of France in their
lives, and first Riri, then Jean, fell in love with her. Perhaps that
was inevitable; it was certainly unfortunate. She was a well-
brought-up girl, an only child, and her mother, besides her pension, had a little money of her own. It was evident that she could
be pursued only with a view to marriage. Of course Riri, dependent for the while entirely on his father, could not make an
offer that there was the least chance of Madame Meurice,
Marie-Louise's mother, accepting; but having the whole day
to himself he was able to see a great deal more of Marie-Louise
than Jean could. Madame Meurice was something of an invalid,
so that Marie-Louise had more liberty than most French girls
of her age and station. She knew that both Riri and Jean were in
love with her, she liked them both and was pleased by their
attentions, but she gave no sign that she was in love with either.
It was impossible to tell which she preferred. She was well aware
that Riri was not in a position to marry her.

"What did she look like?" I asked Jean Charvin.

"She was small, with a pretty little figure, with large grey
eyes, a pale skin and soft, mouse-coloured hair. She was rather
like a little mouse. She was not beautiful, but pretty, in a quaint
demure way; there was something very appealing about her.
She was easy to get on with. She was simple and unaffected.
You couldn't help feeling that she was reliable and would make
anyone a good wife."

Jean and Riri hid nothing from one another and Jean made
no secret of the fact that he was in love with Marie-Louise, but
Riri had met her first and it was an understood thing between
them that Jean should not stand in his way. At length she made
her choice. One day Riri waited for Jean to come away from
his office and told him that Marie-Louise had consented to
marry him. They had arranged that as soon as he got a job his
father should go to her mother and make the formal offer. Jean
was hard hit. It was not easy to listen with eager sympathy to
the plans that the excitable and enchanted Riri made for the
future. But he was too much attached to Riri to feel sore with
him; he knew how lovable he was and he could not blame Marie-
Louise. He tried with all his might to accept honestly the
sacrifice he made on the altar of friendship.

"Why did she choose him rather than you?" I asked.

"He had immense vitality. He was the gayest, most amusing

lad you ever met. His high spirits were infectious. You couldn't
be dull in his company."

"He had pep," I smiled.

"And an incredible charm."

"Was he good-looking?"

"No, not very. He was shorter than me, slight and wiry; but
he had a nice, good-humoured face." Jean Charvin smiled rather
pleasantly. "I think without any vanity I can say that I was
better-looking than Riri."

But Riri did not get a job. His father, tired of keeping him in
idleness, wrote to everyone he could think of, the members of
his family and his friends in various parts of France, asking
them if they could not find something, however modest, for
Riri to do; and at last he got a letter from a cousin in Lyons who
was in the silk business to say that his firm were looking for a
young man to go out to Phnom-Penh, in Cambodia, where they
had a branch, to buy native silk for them. If Riri was willing
to take the job he could get it for him.

Though like all French parents Riri's hated him to emigrate,
there seemed no help for it, and it was determined, although the
salary was small, that he must go. He was not disinclined.
Cambodia was not so far from Tonkin, and Marie-Louise must
be familiar with the life. She had so often talked of it that he
had come to the conclusion that she would be glad to go back to
the East. To his dismay she told him that nothing would induce her to. In the first place she could not desert her mother,
whose health was obviously declining; and then, after having at
last settled down in France, she was determined never again to
leave it. She was sympathetic to Riri, but resolute. With nothing else in prospect his father would not hear of his refusing
the offer; there was no help for it, he had to go. Jean hated losing him, but from the moment Riri told him his bad news, he
had realised with an exulting heart that fate was playing into
his hands. With Riri out of his way for five years at least, and
unless he were incompetent with the probability that he would
settle in the East for good, Jean could not doubt that after a
while Marie-Louise would marry him. His circumstances, his
settled, respectable position in Le Havre, where she could be
near her mother, would make her think it very sensible; and
when she was no longer under the spell of Riri's charm there
was no reason why her great liking for him should not turn to

love. Life changed for him. After months of misery he was happy
again, and though he kept them to himself he too now made
great plans for the future. There was no need any longer to try
not to love Marie-Louise.

Suddenly his hopes were shattered. One of the shipping firms
at Le Havre had a vacancy, and it looked as though the applica-
tion that Riri had quickly made would be favourably considered. A friend in the office told him that it was a certainty.
It would settle everything. It was an old and conservative
house, and it was well known that when you once got into it
you were there for life. Jean Charvin was in despair, and the
worst of it was that he had to keep his anguish to himself. One
day the director of his own firm sent for him.

When he reached this point Jean stopped. A harassed look
came into his eyes.

"I'm going to tell you something now that I've never told to
anyone before. I'm an honest man, a man of principle; I'm
going to tell you of the only discreditable action I've ever done
in my life."

I must remind the reader here that Jean Charvin was wearing
the pink and white stripes of the convict's uniform, with his
number stencilled on his chest, and that he was serving a term
of imprisonment for the murder of his wife.

"I couldn't imagine what the director wanted with me. He
was sitting at his desk when I went into his office, and he gave
me a searching look.

" 'I want to ask you a question of great importance,' he said.
'I wish you to treat it as confidential. I shall of course treat your
answer as equally so.'

"I waited. He went on:

" 'You've been with us for a considerable time. I am very well
satisfied with you, there is no reason why you shouldn't reach a
very good position in the firm. I put implicit confidence in you.'

" 'Thank you, sir,' I said. 'I will always try to merit your good
opinion.'

" 'The question at issue is this. Monsieur Untel is proposing
to engage Henri Renard. He is very particular about the character of his employees, and in this case it is essential that he
shouldn't make a mistake. Part of Henri Renard's duties would
be to pay the crews of the firm's ships, and many hundreds of
thousand francs will pass through his hands. I know that Henri

Renard is your great friend and that your families have always been very intimate. I put you on your honour to tell me whether Monsieur Untel would be justified in engaging this young man.'

"I saw at once what the question meant. If Riri got the job he would stay and marry Marie-Louise, if he didn't he would go out to Cambodia and I should marry her. I swear to you it was not I who answered, it was someone who stood in my shoes and spoke with my voice, I had nothing to do with the words that came from my mouth.

"'*Monsieur le directeur,*' I said, 'Henri and I have been friends all our lives. We have never been separated for a week. We went to school together; we shared our pocket-money and our mistresses when we were old enough to have them; we did our military service together.'

"'I know. You know him better than anyone in the world. That is why I ask you these questions.'

"'It is not fair, *Monsieur le directeur.* You are asking me to betray my friend. I cannot, and I will not answer your questions.'

"The director gave me a shrewd smile. He thought himself much cleverer than he really was.

"'Your answer does you credit, but it has told me all I wished to know.' Then he smiled kindly. I suppose I was pale, I dare say I was trembling a little. 'Pull yourself together, my dear boy; you're upset and I can understand it. Sometimes in life one is faced by a situation where honesty stands on the one side and loyalty on the other. Of course one mustn't hesitate, but the choice is bitter. I shall not forget your behaviour in this case and on behalf of Monsieur Untel I thank you.'

"I withdrew. Next morning Riri received a letter informing him that his services were not required, and a month later he sailed for the far East."

Six months after this Jean Charvin and Marie-Louise were married. The marriage was hastened by the increasing gravity of Madame Meurice's illness. Knowing that she could not live long, she was anxious to see her daughter settled before she died. Jean wrote to Riri telling him the facts and Riri wrote back warmly congratulating him. He assured him that he need have no compunctions on his behalf; when he had left France he realised that *he* could never marry Marie-Louise, and he was glad that Jean was going to. He was finding consolation at Phnom-Penh. His letter was very cheerful. From the beginning

Jean had told himself that Riri, with his mercurial temperament, would soon forget Marie-Louise, and his letter looked as
if he had already done so. He had done him no irreparable injury. It was a justification. For if *he* had lost Marie-Louise he
would have died; with him it was a matter of life and death.

For a year Jean and Marie-Louise were extremely happy.
Madame Meurice died, and Marie-Louise inherited a couple of
hundred thousand francs; but with the depression and the un-
stable currency they decided not to have a child till the economic situation was less uncertain. Marie-Louise was a good
and frugal housekeeper. She was an affectionate, amiable and
satisfactory wife. She was placid. This before he married her had
seemed to Jean a rather charming trait, but as time wore on it
was borne in upon him that her placidity came from a certain
lack of emotional ardour. It concealed no depth. He had always
thought she was like a little mouse; there was something mouse-
like in her furtive reticences; she was oddly serious about trivial
matters and could busy herself indefinitely with things that
were of no consequence. She had her own tiny little set of interests and they left no room in her pretty sleek head for any
others. She sometimes began a novel, but seldom cared to finish
it. Jean was obliged to admit to himself that she was rather dull.
The uneasy thought came to him that perhaps it had not been
worth while to do a dirty trick for her sake. It began to worry
him. He missed Riri. He tried to persuade himself that what
was done was done and that he had really not been a free agent,
but he could not quite still the prickings of his conscience. He
wished now that when the director of his firm spoke to him he
had answered differently.

Then a terrible thing happened. Riri contracted typhoid
fever and died. It was a frightful shock for Jean. It was a shock
to Marie-Louise too; she paid Riri's parents the proper visit of
condolence, but she neither ate less heartily nor slept less
soundly. Jean was exasperated by her composure.

"Poor chap, he was always so gay," she said, "he must have
hated dying. But why did he go out there? I told him the
climate was bad; it killed my father and I knew what I was
talking about."

Jean felt that he had killed him. If he had told the director all
the good he knew of Riri, knew as no one else in the world did,
he would have got the post and would now be alive and well.

"I shall never forgive myself," he thought. "I shall never be happy again. Oh, what a fool I was, and what a cad!"

He wept for Riri. Marie-Louise sought to comfort him. She was a kind little thing and she loved him.

"You mustn't take it too hardly. After all, you wouldn't have seen him for five years, and you'd have found him so changed that there wouldn't have been anything between you any more. He would have been a stranger to you. I've seen that sort of thing happen so often. You'd have been delighted to see him, and in half an hour you'd have discovered that you had nothing to say to one another."

"I dare say you're right," he sighed.

"He was too scatter-brained ever to have amounted to anything very much. He never had your firmness of character and your clear, solid intellect."

He knew what she was thinking. What would have been her position now if she had followed Riri to Indo-China and found herself at twenty-one a widow with nothing but her own two hundred thousand francs to live on? It was a lucky escape and she congratulated herself on her good sense. Jean was a husband of whom she could be proud. He was earning good money. Jean was tortured by remorse. What he had suffered before was nothing to what he suffered now. The anguish that the recollection of his treachery caused him was worse than a physical pain gnawing at his vitals. It would assail him suddenly when he was in the middle of his work and twist his heartstrings with a violent pang. His agony was such that he craved for relief, and it was only by an effort of all his will that he prevented himself from making a full confession to Marie-Louise. But he knew how she would take it; she would not be shocked, she would think it rather a clever trick and be even subtly flattered that for her sake he had been guilty of a despicable act. She could not help him. He began to dislike her. For it was for her that he had done the shameful thing, and what was she? An ordinary, commonplace, rather calculating little woman.

"What a fool I've been," he repeated.

He did not even find her pretty any more. He knew now that she was terribly stupid. But of course she was not to blame for that, she was not to blame because he had been false to his friend; and he forced himself to be as sweet and tender to her as he had always been. He did whatever she wanted. She had only to express a wish for him to fulfil it if it was in his power. He

tried to pity her, he tried to be tolerant; he told himself that
from her own petty standpoint she was a good wife, methodical,
saving, and in her manner, dress and appearance a credit to a
respectable young man. All that was true; but it was on her
account that Riri had died, and he loathed her. She bored him
to distraction. Though he said nothing, though he was kind,
amiable and indulgent, he could often have killed her. When he
did, however, it was almost without meaning to. It was ten
months after Riri's death, and Riri's parents, Monsieur and
Madame Renard, gave a party to celebrate the engagement of
their daughter. Jean had seen little of them since Riri's death
and he did not want to go. But Marie-Louise said they must; he
had been Riri's greatest friend and it would be a grave lack of
politeness on Jean's part not to attend an important celebration
in the family. She had a keen sense of social obligation.

"Besides, it'll be a distraction for you. You've been in poor
spirits for so long, a little amusement will do you good. There'll
be champagne, won't there? Madame Renard doesn't like
spending money, but on an occasion like this she'll have to sacrifice herself."

Marie-Louise chuckled slyly when she thought what a wrench
it would be to Madame Renard to unloose her purse-strings.

The party had been very gay. It gave Jean a nasty turn when
he found that they were using Riri's old room for the women to
put their wraps in and the men their coats. There was plenty of
champagne. Jean drank a great deal to drown the bitter remorse
that tormented him. He wanted to deaden the sound in his ears
of Riri's laugh and to shut his eyes to the good-humour of his
shining glance. It was three o'clock when they got home. Next
day was Sunday, so Jean had no work to go to. They slept late.
The rest I can tell in Jean Charvin's own words.

"I had a headache when I woke. Marie-Louise was not in bed.
She was sitting at the dressing-table brushing her hair. I've always been very keen on physical culture, and I was in the habit
of doing exercises every morning. I didn't feel very much inclined to do them that morning, but after all that champagne I
thought I'd better. I got out of bed and took up my Indian
clubs. Our bedroom was fairly large and there was plenty of
room to swing them between the bed and the dressing-table
where Marie-Louise was sitting. I did my usual exercises.
Marie-Louise had started a little while before having her hair
cut differently, quite short, and I thought it repulsive. From the

back she looked like a boy, and the stubble of cropped hair on her neck made me feel rather sick. She put down her brushes and began to powder her face. She gave a nasty little laugh.

" 'What are you laughing at?' I asked.

" 'Madame Renard. That was the same dress she wore at our wedding, she'd had it dyed and done over; but it didn't deceive me. I'd have known it anywhere.'

"It was such a stupid remark, it infuriated me. I was seized with rage, and with all my might I hit her over the head with my Indian club. I broke her skull, apparently, and she died two days later in hospital without recovering consciousness."

He paused for a moment. I handed him a cigarette and lit another myself.

"I was glad she did. We could never have lived together again, and it would have been very hard to explain my action."

"Very."

"I was arrested and tried for murder. Of course I swore it was an accident, I said the club had slipped out of my hand, but the medical evidence was against me. The prosecution proved that such an injury as Marie-Louise had suffered could only have been caused by a violent and deliberate blow. Fortunately for me they could find no motive. The public prosecutor tried to make out that I had been jealous of the attentions some man had paid her at the party and that we had quarrelled on that account, but the man he mentioned swore that he had done nothing to arouse my suspicions and others at the party testified that we had left the best of friends. They found on the dressing-table an unpaid dress-maker's bill and the prosecutor suggested that we had quarrelled about that, but I was able to prove that Marie-Louise paid for her clothes out of her own money, so that the bill could not possibly have been the cause of a dispute. Witnesses came forward and said that I had always been kind to Marie-Louise. We are generally looked upon as a devoted couple. My character was excellent and my employer spoke in the highest terms of me. I was never in danger of losing my head, and at one moment I thought I had a chance of getting off altogether. In the end I was sentenced to six years. I don't regret what I did, for from that day, all the time I was in prison awaiting my trial, and since, while I've been here, I've ceased to worry about Riri. If I believed in ghosts I'd be inclined to say that Marie-Louise's death had laid Riri's. Anyhow, my conscience is at rest, and after all the torture I suffered I can assure you that everything I've gone through since is worth it; I feel I can now look the world in the face again."

I know that this is a fantastic story; I am by way of being a realist, and in the stories I write I seek verisimilitude. I eschew the bizarre as scrupulously as I avoid the whimsical. If this had been a tale that I was inventing I would certainly have made it more probable. As it is, unless I had heard it with my own ears I am not sure that I should believe it. I do not know whether Jean Charvin told me the truth, and yet the words with which he closed his final visit to me had a convincing ring. I had asked him what were his plans for the future.

"I have friends working for me in France," he answered. "A great many people thought at the time that I was the victim of a grave miscarriage of justice; the director of my firm is convinced that I was unjustly condemned; and I may get a reduction of my sentence. Even if I don't, I think I can count upon getting back to France at the end of my six years. You see, I'm making myself very useful here. The accounts were very badly kept when I took them over, and I've got them in apple-pie order. There have been leakages, and I am convinced that if they'll give me a free hand, I can stop them. The commandant likes me and I'm certain that he'll do everything he can for me. At the worst I shan't be much over thirty when I get back."

"But won't you find it rather difficult to get work?"

"A clever accountant like me, and a man who's honest and industrious, can always get work. Of course I shan't be able to live in Le Havre, but the director of my firm has business connections at Lille and Lyons and Marseilles. He's promised to do something for me. No, I look forward to the years to come with a good deal of confidence. I shall settle down somewhere, and as soon as I'm comfortably fixed up I shall marry. After what I've been through I want a home."

We were sitting in one of the corners of the verandah that surrounded my house in order to get any draught there might be, and on the north side I had left a jalousie undrawn. The strip of sky you saw with a single coconut tree on one side, its green foliage harsh against the blue, looked like an advertisement for a tropical cruise. Jean Charvin's eyes searched the distance as though he sought to see the future.

"But next time I marry," he said thoughtfully, "I shan't marry for love, I shall marry for money."

FRENCH JOE

It was Captain Bartlett who told me of him. I do not think that many people have been to Thursday Island. It is in the Torres Straits and is so called because it was discovered on a Thursday by Captain Cook. I went there since they told me in Sydney that it was the last place God ever made. They said there was nothing to see and warned me that I should probably get my throat cut. I had come up from Sydney in a Japanese tramp and they put me ashore in a small boat. It was the middle of the night and there was not a soul on the jetty. One of the sailors who landed my kit told me that if I turned to the left I should presently come to a two-storey building and this was the hotel. The boat pushed off and I was left alone. I do not much like being separated from my luggage, but I like still less to pass the night on a jetty and sleep on hard stones; so I shouldered a bag and set out. It was pitch dark. I seemed to walk much more than a few hundred yards which they had spoken of and was afraid I had missed my way, but at last saw dimly a building which seemed to be important enough to suggest that it might be the hotel. No light showed, but my eyes by now were pretty well accustomed to the darkness and I found a door. I struck a match, but could see no bell. I knocked; there was no reply; I knocked again, with my stick, as loudly as I could, then a window above me was opened and a woman's voice asked me what I wanted.

"I've just got off the *Shika Maru*," I said. "Can I have a room?"

"I'll come down."

I waited a little longer, and the door was opened by a woman in a red flannel dressing-gown. Her hair was hanging over her shoulders in long black wisps. In her hand she held a paraffin lamp. She greeted me warmly, a little stoutish woman, with keen eyes and a nose suspiciously red, and bade me come in. She took me upstairs and showed me a room.

"Now you sit down," she said, "and I'll make up the bed before you can say Jack Robinson. What will you 'ave? A drop of whisky would do you good, I should think. You won't want to be washing at this time of night, I'll bring you a towel in the morning."

And while she made the bed she asked me who I was and what I had come to Thursday Island for. She could see I wasn't a sea-faring man—all the pilots came to this hotel and had done for twenty years—and she didn't know what business could have brought me. I wasn't that fellow as was coming to inspect the Customs, was I? She'd 'eard they were sending someone from Sydney. I asked her if there were any pilots staying there then. Yes, there was one, Captain Bartlett, did I know him? A queer fish he was and no mistake. Hadn't got a hair on his head, but the way he could put his liquor away, well, it was a caution. There, the bed was ready and she expected I'd sleep like a top and one thing she could say was, the sheets were clean. She lit the end of a candle and bade me good-night.

Captain Bartlett certainly was a queer fish, but he is of no moment to my present purpose; I made his acquaintance at dinner next day—before I left Thursday Island I had eaten turtle soup so often that I have ceased to look upon it as a luxury —and it was because in the course of conversation I mentioned that I spoke French that he asked me to go and see French Joe.

"It'll be a treat to the old fellow to talk his own lingo for a bit. He's ninety-three, you know."

For the last two years, not because he was ill but because he was old and destitute, he had lived in the hospital and it was here that I visited him. He was lying in bed, in flannel pyjamas much too large for him, a little shrivelled old man with vivacious eyes, a short white beard and bushy black eyebrows. He was glad to speak French with me, which he spoke with the marked accent of his native isle, for he was a Corsican, but he had dwelt so many years among English-speaking people that he no longer spoke his mother tongue with accuracy. He used English words as though they were French, making verbs of them with French terminations. He talked very quickly, with broad gestures, and his voice for the most part was clear and strong; but now and then it seemed suddenly to fade away so that it sounded as though he spoke from the grave. The hushed and hollow sound gave me an eerie feeling. Indeed I could not look upon him still as of this world. His real name was Joseph de Paoli. He was a nobleman and a gentleman. He was of the same family as the general we have all read of in Boswell's Johnson, but he showed no interest in his famous ancestor.

"We have had so many generals in our family," he said. "You know, of course, that Napoleon Bonaparte was a connection of mine. No, I have never read Boswell. I have not read books. I have lived."

He had entered the French army in 1851. Seventy-five years ago. It is terrifying. As a lieutenant of artillery ("like my cousin Bonaparte," he said) he had fought the Russians in the Crimea and as a captain the Prussians in 1870. He showed me a scar on his bald pate from an Uhlan's lance and then with a dramatic gesture told how he had thrust his sword in the Uhlan's body with such violence that he could not withdraw it. The Uhlan fell dead and the sword remained in the body. But the Empire perished and he joined the communists. For six weeks he fought against the government troops under Monsieur Thiers. To me Thiers is but a shadowy figure, and it was startling and even a trifle comic to hear French Joe speak with passionate hatred of a man who has been dead for half a century. His voice rose into a shrill scream as he repeated the insults, Oriental in their imagery, which in the council he had flung at the head of this mediocre statesman. French Joe was tried and sentenced to five years in New Caledonia.

"They should have shot me," he said, "but, dirty cowards, they dared not."

Then came the long journey in a sailing vessel, and the antipodes, and his wrath flamed out again when he spoke of the indignity thrust upon him, a political prisoner, when they herded him with vulgar criminals. The ship put in at Melbourne and one of the officers, a fellow-Corsican, enabled him to slip over the side. He swam ashore and, taking his friend's advice, went straight to the police-station. No one there could understand a word he said, but an interpreter was sent for, his dripping papers were examined and he was told that so long as he did not set foot on a French ship he was safe.

"Freedom," he cried to me. "Freedom."

Then came a long series of adventures. He cooked, taught French, swept streets, worked in the gold mines, tramped, starved, and at last found his way to New Guinea. Here he underwent the most astonishing of his experiences, for drifting into the savage interior, and they are cannibals there still, after a hundred desperate adventures and hair-breadth escapes he made himself king of some wild tribe.

"Look at me, my friend," he said, "I who lie here on a hospital bed, the object of charity, have been monarch of all I surveyed. Yes, it is something to say that I have been a king."

But eventually he came into collision with the British and his sovereignty passed from him. He fled the country and started life once more. It is clear that he was a fellow of resource for eventually he came to own a fleet of pearling luggers on Thursday Island. It looked as though at last he had reached a haven of peace and, an elderly man now, he looked forward to a prosperous and even respectable old age. A hurricane destroyed his boats and ruin fell upon him. He never recovered. He was too old to make a fresh start, and since then had earned as best he could a precarious livelihood till at last, beaten, he had accepted the hospital's kindly shelter.

"But why did you not go back to France or Corsica? An amnesty was granted to the communists a quarter of a century ago."

"What are France and Corsica to me after fifty years? A cousin of mine seized my land. We Corsicans never forget and never forgive. If I had gone back I should have had to kill him. He had his children."

"Funny old French Joe," smiled the hospital nurse who stood at the end of the bed.

"At all events you have had a fine life," I said.

"Never. Never. I have had a frightful life. Misfortune has followed me wherever I turned my steps and look at me now: I am rotten, fit for nothing but the grave. I thank God that I had no children to inherit the curse that is upon me."

"Why, Joe, I thought you didn't believe in God," said the nurse.

"It is true. I am a sceptic. I have never seen a sign that there is in the scheme of things an intelligent purpose. If the universe is the contrivance of some being, that being can only be a criminal imbecile." He shrugged his shoulders. "Anyhow, I have not got much longer in this filthy world and then I shall go and see for myself what is the real truth of the whole business."

The nurse told me it was time to leave the old man and I took his hand to bid him farewell. I asked him if there was anything I could do for him.

"I want nothing," he said. "I only want to die." His black shining eyes twinkled. "But meanwhile I should be grateful for a packet of cigarettes."

GERMAN HARRY

I was in Thursday Island and I wanted very much to go to New Guinea. Now the only way in which I could do this was by getting a pearling lugger to take me across the Arafura Sea. The pearl fishery at that time was in a bad way and a flock of neat little craft lay anchored in the harbour. I found a skipper with nothing much to do (the journey to Merauke and back could hardly take him less than a month) and with him I made the necessary arrangements. He engaged four Torres Straits islanders as crew (the boat was but nineteen tons) and we ransacked the local store for canned goods. A day or two before I sailed a man who owned a number of pearlers came to me and asked whether on my way I would stop at the island of Trebucket and leave a sack of flour, another of rice, and some magazines for the hermit who lived there.

I pricked up my ears. It appeared that the hermit had lived by himself on this remote and tiny island for thirty years, and when opportunity occurred provisions were sent to him by kindly souls. He said that he was a Dane, but in the Torres Straits he was known as German Harry. His history went back a long way. Thirty years before, he had been an able seaman on a sailing vessel that was wrecked in those treacherous waters. Two boats managed to get away and eventually hit upon the desert island of Trebucket. This is well out of the line of traffic and it was three years before any ship sighted the castaway. Sixteen men had landed on the island, but when at last a schooner, driven from her course by stress of weather, put in for shelter, no more than five were left. When the storm abated the skipper took four of these on board and eventually landed them at Sydney. German Harry refused to go with them. He said that during those three years he had seen such terrible things that he had a horror of his fellow-men and wished never to live with them again. He would say no more. He was absolutely fixed in his determination to stay, entirely by himself, in that lonely place. Though now and then opportunity had been given him to leave he had never taken it.

A strange man and a strange story. I learned more about him as we sailed across the desolate sea. The Torres Straits are peppered with islands and at night we anchored on the lee of one or other of them. Of late new pearling grounds have been discovered near Trebucket and in the autumn pearlers, visiting it now and then, have given German Harry various necessities so that he has been able to make himself sufficiently comfortable. They bring him papers, bags of flour and rice, and canned meats. He has a whale boat and used to go fishing in it, but now he is no longer strong enough to manage its unwieldy bulk. There is abundant pearl shell on the reef that surrounds his island and this he used to collect and sell to the pearlers for tobacco, and sometimes he found a good pearl for which he got a considerable sum. It is believed that he has, hidden away somewhere, a collection of magnificent pearls. During the war no pearlers came out and for years he never saw a living soul. For all he knew, a terrible epidemic had killed off the entire human race and he was the only man alive. He was asked later what he thought.

"I thought something had happened," he said.

He ran out of matches and was afraid that his fire would go out, so he only slept in snatches, putting wood on his fire from time to time all day and all night. He came to the end of his provisions and lived on chickens, fish and coconuts. Sometimes he got a turtle.

During the last four months of the year there may be two or three pearlers about and not infrequently after the day's work they will row in and spend an evening with him. They try to make him drunk and then they ask him what happened during those three years after the two boat-loads came to the island. How was it that sixteen landed and at the end of that time only five were left? He never says a word. Drunk or sober he is equally silent on that subject and if they insist grows angry and leaves them.

I forget if it was four or five days before we sighted the hermit's little kingdom. We had been driven by bad weather to take shelter and had spent a couple of days at an island on the way. Trebucket is a low island, perhaps a mile round, covered with coconuts, just raised above the level of the sea and surrounded by a reef so that it can be approached only on one side. There is no opening in the reef and the lugger had to anchor a mile from the shore. We got into a dinghy with the provisions. It was a stiff pull and even within the reef the sea was choppy. I saw the little hut, sheltered by trees, in which German Harry lived, and as we approached he sauntered down slowly to the water's edge. We shouted a greeting, but he did not answer. He was a man of over seventy, very bald, hatchet-faced, with a grey beard, and he walked with a roll so that you could never have taken him for anything but a sea-faring man. His sunburn made his blue eyes look very pale and they were surrounded by wrinkles as though for long years he had spent interminable hours scanning the vacant sea. He wore dungarees and a singlet, patched, but neat and clean. The house to which he presently led us consisted of a single room with a roof of corrugated iron. There was a bed in it, some rough stools which he himself had made, a table, and his various household utensils. Under a tree in front of it was a table and a bench. Behind was an enclosed run for his chickens.

I cannot say that he was pleased to see us. He accepted our gifts as a right, without thanks, and grumbled a little because something or other he needed had not been brought. He was silent and morose. He was not interested in the news we had to give him, for the outside world was no concern of his: the only thing he cared about was his island. He looked upon it with a jealous, proprietary right; he called it "my health resort" and he feared that the coconuts that covered it would tempt some enterprising trader. He looked at me with suspicion. He was sombrely curious to know what I was doing in these seas. He used words with difficulty, talking to himself rather than to us, and it was a little uncanny to hear him mumble away as though we were not there. But he was moved when my skipper told him that an old man of his own age whom he had known for a long time was dead.

"Old Charlie dead—that's too bad. Old Charlie dead."

He repeated it over and over again. I asked him if he read.
"Not much," he answered indifferently.

He seemed to be occupied with nothing but his food, his dogs and his chickens. If what they tell us in books were true his long communion with nature and the sea should have taught him many subtle secrets. It hadn't. He was a savage. He was nothing but a narrow, ignorant and cantankerous sea-faring man. As I looked at the wrinkled, mean old face I wondered what was the story of those three dreadful years that had made him welcome this long imprisonment. I sought to see behind those pale blue eyes of his what secrets they were that he would carry to his grave. And then I foresaw the end. One day a pearl fisher would land on the island and German Harry would not be waiting for him, silent and suspicious, at the water's edge. He would go up to the hut and there, lying on the bed, unrecognisable, he would see all that remained of what had once been a man. Perhaps then he would hunt high and low for the great mass of pearls that has haunted the fancy of so many adventurers. But I do not believe he would find it: German Harry would have seen to it that none should discover the treasure, and the pearls would rot in their hiding place. Then the pearl fisher would go back into his dinghy and the island once more be deserted of man.

THE FOUR DUTCHMEN

THE Van Dorth Hotel at Singapore was far from grand. The bedrooms were dingy and the mosquito nets patched and darned; the bath-houses, all in a row and detached from the bedrooms, were dank and smelly. But it had character. The people who stayed there, masters of tramps whose round ended at Singapore, mining engineers out of a job and planters taking a holiday, to my mind bore a more romantic air than the smart folk, globe-trotters, government officials and their wives, wealthy merchants, who gave luncheon-parties at the Europe and played golf and danced and were fashionable. The Van Dorth had a billiard-room, with a table with a threadbare cloth, where ships' engineers and clerks in insurance offices played snooker. The dining-room was large and bare and silent. Dutch families on the way to Sumatra ate solidly through their dinner without exchanging a word with one another, and single gentlemen on a business trip from Batavia devoured a copious meal while they intently read their paper. On two days a week there was rijstafel and then a few residents of Singapore who had a fancy for this dish came for tiffin. The Van Dorth Hotel should have been a depressing place, but somehow it wasn't; its quaintness saved it. It had a faint aroma of something strange and half-forgotten. There was a scrap of garden facing the street where you could sit in the shade of trees and drink cold beer. In that crowded and busy city, though motors whizzed past and rickshaws passed continuously, the coolies' feet pattering on the road and their bells ringing, it had the remote peacefulness of a corner of Holland. It was the third time I had stayed at the Van Dorth. I had been told about it first by the skipper of a Dutch tramp, the S.S. *Utrecht,* on which I had travelled from Merauke in New Guinea to Macassar. The journey took the best part of a month, since the ship stopped at a number of islands in the Malay Archipelago, the Aru and the Kei Islands, Banda-Neira, Amboina and others of which I have even forgotten the names, sometimes for an hour or two, sometimes for a day, to take on or discharge cargo. It was a charming, monotonous and diverting trip. When we dropped anchor the agent came out in his launch, and generally the Dutch Resident, and we gathered on deck under the awning and the captain ordered beer. The news of the island was exchanged for the news of the world. We brought papers and mail. If we were staying long enough the Resident asked us to dinner and, leaving the ship in charge of the second officer, we all (the captain, the chief officer, the engineer, the supercargo and I) piled into the launch and went ashore. We spent a merry evening. These little islands, one so like another, allured my fancy just because I knew that I should never see them again. It made them strangely unreal, and as we sailed away and they vanished into the sea and sky it was only by an effort of the imagination that I could persuade myself that they did not with my last glimpse of them cease to exist.

But there was nothing illusive, mysterious or fantastic about the captain, the chief officer, the chief engineer and the supercargo. Their solidity was amazing. They were the four fattest men I ever saw. At first I had great difficulty in telling them apart, for though one, the supercargo, was dark and the others were fair, they looked astonishingly alike. They were all big, with large round bare red faces, with large fat arms and large fat legs and large fat bellies. When they went ashore they buttoned up their stengah-shifters and then their great double chins bulged over the collars and they looked as though they would choke. But generally they wore them unbuttoned. They sweated freely and wiped their shiny faces with bandanas and vigorously fanned themselves with palm-leaf fans.

It was a treat to see them at tiffin. Their appetites were enormous. They had rijstafel every day, and each seemed to vie with the other how high he could pile his plate. They loved it hot and strong.

"In dis country you can't eat a ting onless it's tasty," said the skipper.

"De only way to keep yourself up in dis country is to eat hearty," said the chief.

They were the greatest friends, all four of them; they were like schoolboys together, playing absurd little pranks with one another. They knew each other's jokes by heart and no sooner did one of them start the familiar lines than he would splutter with laughter so violently, the heavy shaking laughter of the fat man, that he could not go on, and then the others began to laugh too. They rolled about in their chairs, and grew redder and redder, hotter and hotter, till the skipper shouted for beer, and each, gasping but happy, drank his bottle in one enchanted draught. They had been on this run together for five years and when, a little time before, the chief officer had been offered a ship of his own he refused it. He would not leave his companions. They had made up their minds that when the first of them retired they would all retire.

"All friends and a good ship. Good grub and good beer. Vot can a sensible man vant more?"

At first they were a little stand-offish with me. Although the ship had accommodation for half a dozen passengers, they did not often get any, and never one whom they did not know. I was a stranger and a foreigner. They liked their bit of fun and did not want anyone to interfere with it. But they were all of them very fond of bridge, and on occasion the chief and the engineer had duties that prevented one or the other from playing. They were willing to put up with me when they discovered that I was ready to make a fourth whenever I was wanted. Their bridge was as incredibly fantastic as they were. They played for infinitesimal stakes, five cents a hundred: they did not want to win one another's money, they said, it was the game they liked. But what a game! Each was wildly determined to play the hand and hardly one was dealt without at least a small slam being declared. The rule was that if you could get a peep at somebody else's cards you did and if you could get away with a revoke you told your partner when there was no danger it could be claimed and you both roared with laughter till the tears rolled down your fat cheeks. But if your partner had insisted on taking the bid away from you and had called a grand slam on five spades to the queen, whereas you were positive on your seven little diamonds you could have made it easily, you could always score him off by redoubling without a trick in your hand. He went down two or three thousand and the glasses on the table danced with the laughter that shook your opponents.

I could never remember their difficult Dutch names, but knowing them anonymously as it were, only by the duties they performed, as one knows the characters Pantaloon, Harlequin and Punchinello, of the old Italian comedy, added grotesquely to their drollery. The mere sight of them, all four together, set you laughing, and I think they got a good deal of amusement from the astonishment they caused in strangers. They boasted that they were the four most famous Dutchmen in the East Indies. To me not the least comic part of them was their serious side. Sometimes late at night, when they had given up all pretence of still wearing their uniforms, and one or the other of them lay by my side on a long chair in a pyjama jacket and a sarong, he would grow sentimental. The chief engineer, due to retire soon, was meditating marriage with a widow whom he had met when last he was home and spending the rest of his life in a little town with old red-brick houses on the shores of the Zuyder Zee. But the captain was very susceptible to the charms of the native girls and his thick English became almost unintelligible from emotion when he described to me the effect they had on him. One of these days he would buy himself a house on the hills in Java and marry a pretty little Javanese. They were so small and so gentle and they made no noise, and he would dress her in silk sarongs and give her gold chains to wear round her neck and gold bangles to put on her arms. But the chief mocked him.

"Silly all dat is. Silly. She goes mit all your friends and de house boys and everybody. By de time you retire, my dear, vot you'll vant vill be a nurse, not a vife."

"Me?" cried the skipper. "I shall want a vife ven I'm eighty!"

He had picked up a little thing last time the ship was at Macassar and as we approached that port he began to be all of a flutter. The chief officer shrugged fat and indulgent shoulders. The captain was always losing his head over one brazen hussy after another,, but his passion never survived the interval between one stop at a port and the next, and then the chief was called in to smooth out the difficulties that ensued. And so it would be this time.

"De old man suffers from fatty degeneration of de heart. But so long as I'm dere to look after him not much harm comes of it.

He vastes his money and dat's a pity, but as long as he's got it to vaste, why shouldn't he?"

The chief officer had a philosophic soul.

At Macassar then I disembarked, and bade farewell to my four fat friends.

"Make another journey with us," they said. "Come back next year or the year after. You'll find us all here just the same as ever."

A good many months had passed since then and I had wandered through more than one strange land. I had been to Bali and Java and Sumatra; I had been to Cambodia and Annam; and now, feeling as though I were home again, I sat in the garden of the Van Dorth Hotel. It was cool in the very early morning and having had breakfast I was looking at back numbers of the *Straits Times* to find out what had been happening in the world since last I had been within reach of papers. Nothing very much. Suddenly my eyes caught a headline: *The* Utrecht *Tragedy. Supercargo and Chief Engineer. Not Guilty.* I read the paragraph carelessly and then I sat up. The *Utrecht* was the ship of my four fat Dutchmen and apparently the supercargo and the chief engineer had been on trial for murder. It couldn't be my two fat friends. The names were given, but the names meant nothing to me. The trial had taken place in Batavia. No details were given in this paragraph; it was only a brief announcement that after the judges had considered the speeches of the prosecution and of the defence their verdict was as stated. I was astounded. It was incredible that the men I knew could have committed a murder. I could not find out who had been murdered. I looked through back numbers of the paper. Nothing.

I got up and went to the manager of the hotel, a genial Dutchman, who spoke admirable English, and showed him the paragraph.

"That's the ship I sailed on. I was in her for nearly a month. Surely these fellows aren't the men I knew. The men I knew were enormously fat."

"Yes, that's right," he answered. "They were celebrated all through the Dutch East Indies, the four fattest men in the service. It's been a terrible thing. It made a great sensation. And they were friends. I knew them all. The best fellows in the world."

"But what happened?"

He told me the story and answered my horrified questions. But there were things I wanted to know that he couldn't tell me. It was all confused. It was unbelievable. What actually had happened was only conjecture. Then someone claimed the manager's attention and I went back to the garden. It was getting hot now and I went up to my room. I was strangely shattered.

It appeared that on one of the trips the captain took with him a Malay girl that he had been carrying on with and I wondered if it was the one he had been so eager to see when I was on board. The other three had been against her coming—what did they want with a woman in the ship? it would spoil everything —but the captain insisted and she came. I think they were all jealous of her. On that journey they didn't have the fun they generally had. When they wanted to play bridge the skipper was dallying with the girl in his cabin; when they touched at a port and went ashore the time seemed long to him till he could get back to her. He was crazy about her. It was the end of all their larks. The chief officer was more bitter against her than anybody: he was the captain's particular chum, they had been shipmates ever since they first came out from Holland; more than once high words passed between them on the subject of the captain's infatuation. Presently those old friends spoke to one another only when their duties demanded it. It was the end of the good fellowship that had so long obtained between the four fat men. Things went from bad to worse. There was a feeling among the junior officers that something untoward was pending. Uneasiness. Tension. Then one night the ship was aroused by the sound of a shot and the screams of the Malay girl. The supercargo and the chief engineer tumbled out of their bunks and they found the captain, a revolver in his hand, at the door of the chief officer's cabin. He pushed past them and went on deck. They entered and found the chief officer dead and the girl cowering behind the door. The captain had found them in bed together and had killed the chief. How he had discovered what was going on didn't seem to be known, nor what was the meaning of the intrigue. Had the chief induced the girl to come to his cabin in order to get back on the captain, or had she, knowing his ill-will and anxious to placate him, lured him to become her lover? It was a mystery that would never be solved. A dozen possible explanations flashed across my mind. While the engineer and the supercargo were in the cabin, horror-struck at the sight before them, another shot was heard. They knew at once what had happened. They rushed up the companion. The captain had gone to his cabin and blown his brains out. Then the story grew dark and enigmatic. Next morning the Malay girl was nowhere to be found and when the second officer, who had taken command of the ship, reported this to the supercargo, the supercargo said: "She's probably jumped overboard. It's the best thing she could have done. Good riddance to bad rubbish." But one of the sailors on the watch, just before dawn, had seen the supercargo and the chief engineer carry something up on deck, a bulky package, about the size of a native woman, look about them to see that they were unobserved, and drop it overboard; and it was said all over the ship that these two to avenge their friends had sought the girl out in her cabin and strangled her and flung her body into the sea. When the ship arrived at Macassar they were arrested and taken to Batavia to be tried for murder. The evidence was flimsy and they were acquitted. But all through the East Indies they knew that the supercargo and the chief engineer had executed justice on the trollop who had caused the death of the two men they loved.

And thus ended the comic and celebrated friendship of the four fat Dutchmen.

THE END OF THE FLIGHT

I shook hands with the skipper and he wished me luck. Then I
went down to the lower deck crowded with passengers, Malays,
Chinese and Dyaks, and made my way to the ladder. Looking
over the ship's side I saw that my luggage was already in the
boat. It was a large, clumsy-looking craft, with a great square
sail of bamboo matting, and it was crammed full of gesticulating
natives. I scrambled in and a place was made for me. We were
about three miles from the shore and a stiff breeze was blowing.
As we drew near I saw that the coconut trees in a green abundance grew to the water's edge, and among them I saw the brown
roofs of the village. A Chinese who spoke English pointed out to
me a white bungalow as the residence of the District Officer.
Though he did not know it, it was with him that I was going to
stay. I had a letter of introduction to him in my pocket.

I felt somewhat forlorn when I landed and my bags were set
down beside me on the glistening beach. This was a remote spot
to find myself in, this little town on the north coast of Borneo,
and I felt a trifle shy at the thought of presenting myself to a
total stranger with the announcement that I was going to sleep
under his roof, eat his food and drink his whisky, till another
boat came in to take me to the port for which I was bound.

But I might have spared myself these misgivings, for the
moment I reached the bungalow and sent in my letter he came
out, a sturdy, ruddy, jovial man, of thirty-five perhaps, and
greeted me with heartiness. While he held my hand he shouted

to a boy to bring drinks and to another to look after my luggage. He cut short my apologies.

"Good God, man, you have no idea how glad I am to see you. Don't think I'm doing anything for you in putting you up. The boot's on the other leg. And stay as long as you damned well like. Stay a year."

I laughed. He put away his day's work, assuring me that he had nothing to do that could not wait till the morrow, and threw himself into a long chair. We talked and drank and talked. When the heat of the day wore off we went for a long tramp in the jungle and came back wet to the skin. A bath and a change were very grateful, and then we dined. I was tired out and though my host was plainly willing to go on talking straight through the night I was obliged to beg him to allow me to go to bed.

"All right, I'll just come along to your room and see everything's all right."

It was a large room with verandahs on two sides of it, sparsely furnished, but with a huge bed protected by mosquito netting.

"The bed is rather hard. Do you mind?"

"Not a bit. I shall sleep without rocking to-night."

My host looked at the bed reflectively.

"It was a Dutchman who slept in it last. Do you want to hear a funny story?"

I wanted chiefly to go to bed, but he *was* my host, and being at times somewhat of a humorist myself I know that it is hard to have an amusing story to tell and find no listener.

"He came on the boat that brought you, on its last journey along the coast, he came into my office and asked where the dak bungalow was. I told him there wasn't one, but if he hadn't anywhere to go I didn't mind putting him up. He jumped at the invitation. I told him to have his kit sent along.

" 'This is all I've got,' he said.

"He held out a little shiny black grip. It seemed a bit scanty, but it was no business of mine, so I told him to go along to the bungalow and I'd come as soon as I was through with my work. While I was speaking the door of my office was opened and my clerk came in. The Dutchman had his back to the door and it may be that my clerk opened it a bit suddenly. Anyhow, the Dutchman gave a shout, he jumped about two feet into the air and whipped out a revolver.

" 'What the hell are you doing?' I said.

"When he saw it was the clerk he collapsed. He leaned against the desk, panting, and upon my word he was shaking as though he'd got fever.

" 'I beg your pardon,' he said. 'It's my nerves. My nerves are terrible.'

" 'It looks like it,' I said.

"I was rather short with him. To tell you the truth I wished I hadn't asked him to stop with me. He didn't look as though he'd been drinking a lot and I wondered if he was some fellow the police were after. If he were, I said to myself, he could hardly be such a fool as to walk right into the lion's den.

" 'You'd better go and lie down,' I said.

"He took himself off, and when I got back to my bungalow I found him sitting quite quietly, but bolt upright, on the verandah. He'd had a bath and shaved and put on clean things and he looked fairly presentable.

" 'Why are you sitting in the middle of the place like that?' I asked him. 'You'll be much more comfortable in one of the long chairs.'

" 'I prefer to sit up,' he said.

"Queer, I thought. But if a man in this heat would rather sit up than lie down it's his own lookout. He wasn't much to look at, tallish and heavily built, with a square head and close-cropped bristly hair. I should think he was about forty. The thing that chiefly struck me about him was his expression. There was a look in his eyes, blue eyes they were and rather small, that beat me altogether; and his face sagged as it were; it gave you the feeling he was going to cry. He had a way of looking quickly over his left shoulder as though he thought he heard something. By God, he was nervous. But we had a couple of drinks and he began to talk. He spoke English very well; except for a slight accent you'd never have known that he was a foreigner, and I'm bound to admit he was a good talker. He'd been everywhere and he'd read any amount. It was a treat to listen to him.

"We had three or four whiskies in the afternoon and a lot of gin pahits later on, so that when dinner came along we were by way of being rather hilarious and I'd come to the conclusion that he was a damned good fellow. Of course we had a lot of whisky at dinner and I happened to have a bottle of Benedictine, so we had some liqueurs afterwards. I can't help thinking we both got very tight.

"And at last he told me why he'd come. It was a rum story."

My host stopped and looked at me with his mouth slightly open as though, remembering it now, he was struck again with its rumness.

"He came from Sumatra, the Dutchman, and he'd done something to an Achinese and the Achinese had sworn to kill him. At first he made light of it, but the fellow tried two or three times and it began to be rather a nuisance, so he thought he'd better go away for a bit. He went over to Batavia and made up his mind to have a good time. But when he'd been there a week he saw the fellow slinking along a wall. By God, he'd followed him. It looked as though he meant business. The Dutchman began to think it was getting beyond a joke and he thought the best thing he could do would be to skip off to Soerabaya. Well, he was strolling about there one day, you know how crowded the streets are, when he happened to turn round and saw the Achinese walking quite quietly just behind him. It gave him a turn. It would give anyone a turn.

"The Dutchman went straight back to his hotel, packed his things, and took the next boat to Singapore. Of course he put up at the Van Wyck, all the Dutch stay there, and one day when he was having a drink in the courtyard in front of the hotel, the Achinese walked in as bold as brass, looked at him for a minute, and walked out again. The Dutchman told me he was just paralysed. The fellow could have stuck his kris into him there and then and he wouldn't have been able to move a hand to defend himself. The Dutchman knew he was just biding his time, that damned native was going to kill him, he saw it in his eyes; and he went all to pieces."

"But why didn't he go to the police?" I asked.

"I don't know. I expect it wasn't a thing he wanted the police to be mixed up in."

"But what had he done to the man?"

"I don't know that either. He wouldn't tell me. But by the look he gave when I asked him, I expect it was something pretty rotten. I have an idea he knew he deserved whatever the Achinese could do."

My host lit a cigarette.

"Go on," I said.

"The skipper of the boat that runs between Singapore and Kuching lives at the Van Wyck between trips and the boat was starting at dawn. The Dutchman thought it a grand chance to give the fellow the slip; he left his luggage at the hotel and

walked down to the ship with the skipper, as if he were just
going to see him off, and stayed on her when she sailed. His
nerves were all anyhow by then. He didn't care about anything
but getting rid of the Achinese. He felt pretty safe at Kuching.
He got a room at the rest-house and bought himself a couple
of suits and some shirts in the Chinese shops. But he told me
he couldn't sleep. He dreamt of that man and half a dozen
times he awakened just as he thought a kris was being drawn
across his throat. By God, I felt quite sorry for him. He just
shook as he talked to me and his voice was hoarse with terror.
That was the meaning of the look I had noticed. You remember,
I told you he had a funny look on his face and I couldn't tell
what it meant. Well, it was fear.

"And one day when he was in the club at Kuching he looked
out of the window and saw the Achinese sitting there. Their
eyes met. The Dutchman just crumpled up and fainted. When
he came to, his first idea was to get out. Well, you know, there's
not a hell of a lot of traffic at Kuching and this boat that
brought you was the only one that gave him a chance to get
away quickly. He got on her. He was positive the man was not
on board."

"But what made him come here?"

"Well, the old tramp stops at a dozen places on the coast and
the Achinese couldn't possibly guess he'd chosen this one because he only made up his mind to get off when he saw there
was only one boat to take the passengers ashore, and there
weren't more than a dozen people in it.

" 'I'm safe here for a bit at all events,' he said, 'and if I can
only be quiet for a while I shall get my nerve back.'

" 'Stay as long as you like,' I said. 'You're all right here, at
all events till the boat comes along next month, and if you like
we'll watch the people who come off.'

"He was all over me. I could see what a relief it was to him.

"It was pretty late and I suggested to him that we should
turn in. I took him to his room to see that it was all right. He
locked the door of the bath-house and bolted the shutters,
though I told him there was no risk, and when I left I heard him
lock the door I had just gone out of.

"Next morning when the boy brought me my tea I asked him
if he'd called the Dutchman. He said he was just going to. I
heard him knock and knock again. Funny, I thought. The boy
hammered on the door, but there was no answer. I felt a little

nervous, so I got up. I knocked too. We made enough noise to rouse the dead, but the Dutchman slept on. Then I broke down the door. The mosquito curtains were neatly tucked in round the bed. I pulled them apart. He was lying there on his back with his eyes wide open. He was as dead as mutton. A kris lay across his throat, and say I'm a liar if you like, but I swear to God it's true, there wasn't a wound about him anywhere. The room was empty.

"Funny, wasn't it?"

"Well, that all depends on your idea of humour," I replied. My host looked at me quickly.

"You don't mind sleeping in that bed, do you?"

"N-no. But I'd just as soon you'd told me the story to-morrow morning."

FLOTSAM AND JETSAM

NORMAN GRANGE was a rubber-planter. He was up before day-break to take the roll-call of his labour and then walked over the estate to see that the tapping was properly done. This duty performed, he came home, bathed and changed, and now with his wife opposite him he was eating the substantial meal, half breakfast and half luncheon, which in Borneo is called brunch. He read as he ate. The dining-room was dingy. The worn electro-plate, the shabby cruet, the chipped dishes betokened poverty, but a poverty accepted with apathy. A few flowers would have brightened the table, but there was apparently no one to care how things looked. When Grange had finished he belched, filled his pipe and lit it, rose from the table and went out on to the verandah. He took no more notice of his wife than if she had not been there. He lay down in a long rattan chair and went on reading. Mrs. Grange reached over for a tin of cigarettes and smoked while she sipped her tea. Suddenly she looked out, for the house boy came up the steps and accompanied by two men went up to her husband. One was a Dyak and the other Chinese. Strangers seldom came and she could not imagine what they wanted. She got up and went to the door to listen. Though she had lived in Borneo for so many years she knew no more Malay than was necessary to get along with the boys, and she only vaguely understood what was said. She gathered from her husband's tone that something had happened to annoy him. He seemed to be asking questions first of the Chink and then of the Dyak; it looked as though they were pressing him to do something he didn't want to do; at length, however, with a frown on his face he raised himself from his chair and followed by the men walked down the steps. Curious to see where he was going she slipped out on to the verandah. He had taken the path that led down to the river. She shrugged her thin shoulders and went to her room. Presently she gave a violent start, for she heard her husband call her.

"Vesta."

She came out.

"Get a bed ready. There's a white man in a prahu at the land-ing-stage. He's damned ill."

"Who is he?"

"How the hell should I know? They're just bringing him up."

"We can't have anyone to stay here."

"Shut up and do as I tell you."

He left her on that and again went down to the river. Mrs. Grange called the boy and told him to put sheets on the bed in the spare room. Then she stood at the top of the steps and waited. In a little while she saw her husband coming back and behind him a huddle of Dyaks carrying a man on a mattress. She stood aside to let them pass and caught a glimpse of a white face.

"What shall I do?" she asked her husband.

"Get out and keep quiet."

"Polite, aren't you?"

The sick man was taken into the room, and in two or three minutes the Dyaks and Grange came out.

"I'm going to see about his kit. I'll have it brought up. His boy's looking after him and there's no cause for you to butt in!"

"What's the matter with him?"

"Malaria. His boatmen are afraid he's going to die and won't take him on. His name's Skelton."

"He isn't going to die, is he?"

"If he does we'll bury him."

But Skelton didn't die. He woke next morning to find himself in a room, in bed and under a mosquito-net. He couldn't think where he was. It was a cheap iron bed and the mattress was hard, but to lie on it was a relief after the discomfort of the prahu. He could see nothing of the room but a chest of drawers, roughly made by a native carpenter, and a wooden chair. Op-

posite was a doorway, with a blind down, and this he guessed
led on to a verandah.

"Kong," he called.

The blind was drawn aside and his boy came in. The Chinaman's face broke into a grin when he saw that his master was
free from fever.

"You more better, Tuan. Velly glad."

"Where the devil am I?"

Kong explained.

"Luggage all right?" asked Skelton.

"Yes, him all right."

"What's the name of this fellow—the tuan whose house this
is?"

"Mr. Norman Glange."

To confirm what he said he showed Skelton a little book in
which the owner's name was written. It was Grange. Skelton
noticed that the book was Bacon's *Essays*. It was curious to
find it in a planter's house away up a river in Borneo.

"Tell him I'd be glad to see him."

"Tuan out. Him come presently."

"What about my having a wash? And by God, I want a
shave."

He tried to get out of bed, but his head swam and with a bewildered cry he sank back. But Kong shaved and washed him,
and changed the shorts and singlet in which he had been lying
ever since he fell ill for a sarong and a baju. After that he was
glad to lie still. But presently Kong came in and said that the
tuan of the house was back. There was a knock on the door and
a large stoutish man stepped in.

"I hear you're better," he said.

"Oh, much. It's terribly kind of you to have taken me in like
this. It seems awful, planting myself on you."

Grange answered a trifle harshly.

"That's all right. You were pretty bad, you know. No wonder
those Dyaks wanted to get rid of you."

"I don't want to impose myself on you longer than I need. If
I could hire a launch here, or a prahu, I could get off this afternoon."

"There's no launch to hire. You'd better stay a bit. You must
be as weak as a rat."

"I'm afraid I shall be a frightful bother."

"I don't see why. You've got your own boy and he'll look after you."

Grange had just come in from his round of the estate and wore dirty shorts, a khaki shirt open at the neck and an old, battered terai hat. He looked as shabby as a beachcomber. He took off his hat to wipe his sweating brow; he had close-cropped grey hair; his face was red, a broad, fleshy face, with a large mouth under a stubble of grey moustache, a short, pugnacious nose and small, mean eyes.

"I wonder if you could let me have something to read," said Skelton.

"What sort of thing?"

"I don't mind so long as it's lightish."

"I'm not much of a novel reader myself, but I'll send you in two or three books. My wife can provide you with novels. They'll be trash, because that's all she reads. But it may suit you."

With a nod he withdrew. Not a very likeable man. But he was obviously very poor, the room in which Skelton lay, something in Grange's appearance, indicated that; he was probably manager of an estate on a cut salary, and it was not unlikely that the expense of a guest and his servant was unwelcome. Living in that remote spot, and so seeing white men but seldom, it might be that he was ill at ease with strangers. Some people improve unbelievably on acquaintance. But his hard, shifty little eyes were disconcerting; they gave the lie to the red face and the massive frame which otherwise might have persuaded you that this was a jolly sort of fellow with whom you could quickly make friends.

After a while the house boy came in with a parcel of books. There were half a dozen novels by authors he had never heard of, and a glance told him they were slop; these must be Mrs. Grange's; and then there was a Boswell's *Johnson*, Borrow's *Lavengro* and Lamb's *Essays*. It was an odd choice. They were not the books you would have expected to find in a planter's house. In most planters' houses there is not more than a shelf or two of books and for the most part they're detective stories. Skelton had a disinterested curiosity in human creatures, and he amused himself now by trying to make out from the books Norman Grange had sent, from the look of him and from the few words they had exchanged, what sort of a man he could be. Skelton was a little surprised that his host did not come to see

him again that day; it looked as though he were going to content himself with giving his uninvited guest board and lodging,
but were not sufficiently interested in him to seek his company.
Next morning he felt well enough to get up, and with Kong's
help settled himself in a long chair on the verandah. It badly
needed a coat of paint. The bungalow stood on the brow of a
hill, about fifty yards from the river; and on the opposite bank,
looking very small across that great stretch of water, you could
see native houses on piles nestling among the greenery. Skelton
had not yet the activity of mind to read steadily, and after a
page or two, his thoughts wandering, he found himself content
to watch idly the sluggish flow of the turbid stream. Suddenly
he heard a step. He saw a little elderly woman come towards
him, and knowing that this must be Mrs. Grange tried to get
up.

"Don't move," she said. "I only came to see if you had everything you wanted."

She wore a blue cotton dress, simple enough, but more suited
to a young girl than to a woman of her age; her short hair was
tousled, as though on getting out of bed she had scarcely
troubled to pass a comb through it, and dyed a vivid yellow,
but badly, and the roots showed white. Her skin was raddled
and dry, and there was a great dab of rouge on each cheek-bone,
put on however so clumsily that you could not for a moment
take it for a natural colour, and a smear of lipstick on her
mouth. But the strangest thing about her was a tic she had that
made her jerk her head as though she were beckoning you to an
inner room. It seemed to come at regular intervals, perhaps
three times a minute, and her left hand was in almost constant
movement; it was not quite a tremble, it was a rapid twirl as
though she wanted to draw your attention to something behind
her back. Skelton was startled by her appearance and embarrassed by her tic.

"I hope I'm not making myself too great a nuisance," he said.
"I think I shall be well enough to make a move to-morrow or
the day after."

"It's not often we see anybody in a place like this, you know.
It's a treat to have someone to talk to."

"Won't you sit down? I'll tell my boy to bring you a chair."

"Norman said I was to leave you alone."

"I haven't spoken to a white person for two years. I've been
longing for a good old talk."

Her head twitched violently, more quickly than usual, and her hand gave that queer spasmodic gesture.

"He won't be back for another hour. I'll get a chair."

Skelton told her who he was and what he had been doing, but he discovered that she had questioned his boy and already knew all about him.

"You must be crazy to get back to England?" she asked.

"I shan't be sorry."

Suddenly Mrs. Grange seemed to be attacked by what one could only describe as a nerve storm. Her head twitched so madly, her hand shook with such fury, that it was disconcerting. You could only look away.

"I haven't been to England for sixteen years," she said.

"You don't mean that? Why, I thought all you planters went home every five years at the longest."

"We can't afford it; we're broke to the wide. Norman put all the money he had into this plantation, and it hasn't really paid for years. It only just brings in enough to keep us from starvation. Of course it doesn't matter to Norman. He isn't English really."

"He looks English enough."

"He was born in Sarawak. His father was in the government service. If he's anything he's a native of Borneo."

Then, without warning, she began to cry. It was horribly painful to see the tears running down the raddled, painted cheeks of that woman with the constant tic. Skelton knew neither what to say nor what to do. He did what wa⁻ probably the best thing, he kept silent. She dried her eyes.

"You must think me a silly old fool. I sometimes wonder that after all these years I can still cry. I suppose it's in my nature. I always could cry very easy when I was on the stage."

"Oh, were you on the stage?"

"Yes, before I married. That's how I met Norman. We were playing in Singapore and he was there on holiday. I don't suppose I shall ever see England any more. I shall stay here till I die and every day of my life I shall look at that beastly river. I shall never get away now. Never."

"How did you happen to find yourself in Singapore?"

"Well, it was soon after the war, I couldn't get anything to suit me in London, I'd been on the stage a good many years and I was fed up with playing small parts; the agents told me a fellow called Victor Palace was taking a company out East. His

wife was playing lead, but I could play seconds. They'd got half
a dozen plays, comedies, you know, and farces. The salary
wasn't much, but they were going to Egypt and India, the
Malay States and China and then down to Australia. It was a
chance to see the world and I accepted. We didn't do badly in
Cairo and I think we made money in India, but Burma wasn't
much good, and Siam was worse; Penang was a disaster and so
were the rest of the Malay States. Well, one day Victor called us
together and said he was bust, he hadn't got the money for our
fares on to Hong Kong, and the tour was a wash-out and he was
very sorry but we'd have to get back home as best we could. Of
course we told him he couldn't do that to us. You never heard
such a row. Well, the long and short of it was that he said we
could have the scenery and the props if we thought they was
any good to us, but as to money it was no use asking for it because he damned well hadn't got it. And next day we found out
that him and his wife, without saying a word to anybody, had
got on a French boat and skipped. I was in a rare state, I can
tell you. I had a few pounds I'd saved out of me salary, and that
was all; somebody told me if we was absolutely stranded the
government would have to send us home, but only steerage, and
I didn't much fancy that. We got the Press to put our plight before the public and someone came along with the proposition
that we should give a benefit performance. Well, we did, but it
wasn't much without Victor or his wife, and by the time we'd
paid the expenses we weren't any better off than we'd been before. I was at my wits' end, I don't mind telling you. It was
then that Norman proposed to me. The funny thing is that I
hardly knew him. He'd taken me for a drive round the island
and we'd had tea two or three times at the Europe and danced.
Men don't often do things for you without wanting something
in return, and I thought he expected to get a little bit of fun,
but I'd had a good deal of experience and I thought he'd be
clever if he got round me. But when he asked me to marry him,
well, I was so surprised, I couldn't hardly believe me own ears.
He said he'd got his own estate in Borneo and it only wanted a
little patience and he'd make a packet. And it was on the banks
of a fine river and all round was the jungle. He made it sound
very romantic. I was getting on, you know, I was thirty, it
wasn't going to be any easier to get work as time went on, and
it was tempting to have a house of me own and all that. Never
to have to hang around agents' offices no more. Never to have

to lay awake no more and wonder how you was going to pay
next week's rent. He wasn't a bad-looking chap in those days,
brown and big and virile. No one could say I was willing to
marry anybody just to . . ." Suddenly she stopped. "There he
is. Don't say you've seen me."

She picked up the chair she had been sitting in and quickly
slipped away with it into the house. Skelton was bewildered.
Her grotesque appearance, the painful tears, her story told with
that incessant twitching; and then her obvious fear when she
heard her husband's voice in the compound, and her hurried
escape; he could make nothing of it.

In a few minutes Norman Grange stumped along the verandah.

"I hear you're better," he said.

"Much, thanks."

"If you care to join us at brunch I'll have a place laid for
you."

"I'd like it very much."

"All right. I'm just going to have a bath and a change."

He walked away. Presently a boy came along and told
Skelton his tuan was waiting for him. Skelton followed him into
a small sitting-room, with the jalousies drawn to keep out the
heat, an uncomfortable, overcrowded room with a medley of
furniture, English and Chinese, and occasional tables littered
with worthless junk. It was neither cosy nor cool. Grange had
changed into a sarong and baju and in the native dress looked
coarse but powerful. He introduced Skelton to his wife. She
shook hands with him as though she had never seen him before
and uttered a few polite words of greeting. The boy announced
that their meal was ready and they went into the dining-room.

"I hear that you've been in this bloody country for some
time," said Grange.

"Two years. I'm an anthropologist and I wanted to study the
manners and customs of tribes that haven't had any contact
with civilisation."

Skelton felt that he should tell his host how it had come
about that he had been forced to accept a hospitality which he
could not but feel was grudgingly offered. After leaving the village that had been his headquarters he had journeyed by land
for ten days till he reached the river. There he had engaged a
couple of prahus, one for himself and his luggage and the other
for Kong, his Chinese servant, and the camp equipment, to take

him to the coast. The long trek across country had been hard
going and he found it very comfortable to lie on a mattress
under an awning of rattan matting and take his ease. All the
time he had been away Skelton had been in perfect health, and
as he travelled down the river he could not but think that he
was very lucky; but even as the thought passed through his
mind, it occurred to him that if he happened just then to congratulate himself on his good fortune in this respect, it was because he did not feel quite so well as usual. It was true that he
had been forced to drink a great deal of arak the night before at
the long-house where he had put up, but he was used to it and
that hardly accounted for his headache. He had a general sense
of malaise. He was wearing nothing but shorts and a singlet,
and he felt chilly; it was curious because the sun was shining
fiercely and when he put his hand on the gunwale of the prahu
the heat was hardly bearable. If he had had a coat handy he
would have put it on. He grew colder and colder and presently
his teeth began to chatter; he huddled up on his mattress,
shivering all over in a desperate effort to get warm. He could
not fail to guess what was the matter.

"Christ," he groaned. "Malaria."

He called the headman, who was steering the prahu.

"Get Kong."

The headman shouted to the second prahu and ordered his
own paddlers to stop. In a moment the two boats were side by
side and Kong stepped in.

"I've got fever, Kong," gasped Skelton. "Get me the medicine
chest and, for God's sake, blankets. I'm freezing to death."

Kong gave his master a big dose of quinine and piled on him
what coverings they had. They started off again.

Skelton was too ill to be taken ashore when they tied up for
the night and so passed it in the prahu. All next day and the
day after he was very ill. Sometimes one or other of the crew
came and looked at him, and often the headman stayed for
quite a long while staring at him thoughtfully.

"How many days to the coast?" Skelton asked the boy.

"Four, five." He paused for a minute. "Headman, he no go
coast. He say, he wantchee go home."

"Tell him to go to hell."

"Headman say, you velly sick, you die. If you die and he go
coast he catchee trouble."

"I'm not thinking of dying," said Skelton. "I shall be all right. It's just an ordinary go of malaria."

Kong did not answer. The silence irritated Skelton. He knew that the Chinese had something in mind that he did not like to say.

"Spit it out, you fool," he cried.

Skelton's heart sank when Kong told him the truth. When they reached their resting-place that night the headman was going to demand his money and slip away with the two prahus before dawn. He was too frightened to carry a dying man farther. Skelton had no strength to take the determined attitude that might have availed him; he could only hope by the offer of more money to persuade the headman to carry out his agreement. The day passed in long arguments between Kong and the headman, but when they tied up for the night the headman came to Skelton and told him sulkily that he would go no farther. There was a long-house near-by where he might get lodging till he grew better. He began to unload the baggage. Skelton refused to move. He got Kong to give him his revolver and swore to shoot anyone who came near him.

Kong, the crew and the headman went up to the long-house and Skelton was left alone. Hour after hour he lay there, the fever burning his body and his mouth parched, while muddled thoughts hammered away in his brain. Then there were lights and the sound of men talking. The Chinese boy came with the headman and another man, whom Skelton had not yet seen, from the neighbouring long-house. He did his best to understand what Kong was telling him. It appeared that a few hours down-stream there lived a white man, and to his house, if that would satisfy Skelton, the headman was willing to take him.

"More better you say yes," said Kong. "Maybe white man has launch, then we go down to coast chop-chop."

"Who is he?"

"Planter," said Kong. "This fellow say, him have rubber estate."

Skelton was too tired to argue further. All he wanted just then was to sleep. He accepted the compromise.

"To tell you the truth," he finished, "I don't remember much more till I woke up yesterday morning to find myself an uninvited guest in your house."

"I don't blame those Dyaks, you know," said Grange. "When

I came down to the prahu and saw you, I thought you were for it."

Mrs. Grange sat silent while Skelton told his story, her head and her hand twitching regularly, as though by the action of some invisible clockwork, but when her husband addressed her, asking for the Worcester Sauce, and that was the only time he spoke to her, she was seized with such a paroxysm of involuntary movement that it was horrible to see. She passed him what he asked for without a word. Skelton got an uncomfortable impression that she was terrified of Grange. It was odd, because to all appearance he was not a bad sort. He was knowledgeable and far from stupid; and though you could not have said that his manner was cordial, it was plain that he was ready to be of what service he could.

They finished their meal and separated to rest through the heat of the day.

"See you again at six for a sun-downer," said Grange.

When Skelton had had a good sleep, a bath and a read, he went out on to the verandah. Mrs. Grange came up to him. It looked as though she had been waiting.

"He's back from the office. Don't think it's funny if I don't speak to you. If he thought I liked having you here he'd turn you out to-morrow."

She said these words in a whisper and slipped back into the house. Skelton was startled. It was a strange house he had come into in a strange manner. He went into the overcrowded sitting-room and there found his host. He had been worried by the evident poverty of the establishment and he felt that the Granges could ill afford even the small expense he must be putting them to. But he had already formed the impression that Grange was a quick-tempered, susceptible man and he did not know how he would take an offer to help. He made up his mind to risk it.

"Look here," he said to him, "it looks as though I might have to inflict myself on you for several days, I'd be so much more comfortable if you'd let me pay for my board and lodging."

"Oh, that's all right, your lodging costs nothing, the house belongs to the mortgagees, and your board doesn't come to much."

"Well, there are drinks anyway and I've had to come down on your stores of tobacco and cigarettes."

"It's not more than once a year that anyone comes up here, and then it's only the D.O. or someone like that—besides, when one's as broke as I am nothing matters much."

"Well, then, will you take my camp equipment? I shan't be wanting it any more, and if you'd like one of my guns, I'd be only too glad to leave it with you."

Grange hesitated. There was a glimmer of cupidity in those small, cunning eyes of his.

"If you'd let me have one of your guns you'd pay for your board and lodging over and over again."

"That's settled, then."

They began to talk over the whisky and sparkler with which, following the Eastern habit, they celebrated the setting of the sun. Discovering that they both played chess they had a game. Mrs. Grange did not join them till dinner. The meal was dull. An insipid soup, a tasteless river fish, a tough piece of steak and a caramel pudding. Norman Grange and Skelton drank beer; Mrs. Grange water. She never of her own will uttered a word. Skelton had again the uncomfortable impression that she was scared to death of her husband. Once or twice, Skelton from common politeness sought to bring her into the conversation, addressing himself to her, telling her a story or asking her a question, but it evidently distressed her so much, her head twitched so violently, her hand was agitated by gestures so spasmodic that he thought it kinder not to insist. When the meal was over she got up.

"I'll leave you gentlemen to your port," she said.

Both the men got up as she left the room. It was rather absurd, and somehow sinister, to see this social pretence in those poverty-stricken surroundings on a Borneo river.

"I may add that there is no port. There might be a little Benedictine left."

"Oh, don't bother."

They talked for a while and Grange began to yawn. He got up every morning before sunrise and by nine o'clock at night could hardly keep his eyes open.

"Well, I'm going to turn in," he said.

He nodded to Skelton and without further ceremony left him. Skelton went to bed, but he could not sleep. Though the heat was oppressive, it was not the heat that kept him awake. There was something horrible about that house and those two people who lived in it. He didn't know what it was that affected

him with this peculiar uneasiness, but this he knew, that he
would be heartily thankful to be out of it and away from them.
Grange had talked a good deal about himself, but he knew no
more of him than he had learned at the first glance. To all appearances he was just the commonplace planter who had fallen
upon evil days. He had bought his land immediately after the
war and had planted trees; but by the time they were bearing
the slump had come and since then it had been a constant
struggle to keep going. The estate and the house were heavily
mortgaged, and now that rubber was once more selling profitably all he made went to the mortgagees. That was an old story
in Malaya. What made Grange somewhat unusual was that he
was a man without a country. Born in Borneo, he had lived
there with his parents till he was old enough to go to school in
England; at seventeen he had come back and had never left it
since except to go to Mesopotamia during the war. England
meant nothing to him. He had neither relations nor friends
there. Most planters, like civil servants, have come from England, go back on leave now and then, and look forward to settling down there when they retire. But what had England to
offer Norman Grange?

"I was born here," he said, "and I shall die here. I'm a
stranger in England. I don't like their ways over there and I
don't understand the things they talk about. And yet I'm a
stranger here too. To the Malays and the Chinese I'm a white
man, though I speak Malay as well as they do, and a white man
I shall always be." Then he said a significant thing. "Of course
if I'd had any sense I'd have married a Malay girl and had half
a dozen half-caste kids. That's the only solution really for us
chaps who were born and bred here."

Grange's bitterness was greater than could be explained by
his financial embarrassment. He had little good to say of any
of the white men in the colony. He seemed to think that they
despised him because he was native-born. He was a sour, disappointed fellow, and a conceited one. He had shown Skelton
his books. There were not many of them, but they were the best
on the whole that English iterature can show; he had read them
over and over again; but it looked as though he had learnt from
them neither charity nor loving-kindness, it looked as though
their beauty had left him unmoved; and to know them so well
had only made him self-complacent. His exterior, which was so
hearty and English, seemed to have little relation to the man

within; you could not resist the suspicion that it masked a very
sinister being.

Early next morning, to enjoy the cool of the day, Skelton,
with his pipe and a book, was sitting on the verandah outside
his room. He was still very weak, but felt much better. In a
little while Mrs. Grange joined him. She held in her hand a
large album.

"I thought I'd like to show you some of me old photos and me
notices. You mustn't think I always looked like what I do now.
He's off on his round and he won't be back for two or three
hours yet."

Mrs. Grange, in the same blue dress she had worn the day
before, her hair as untidy, appeared strangely excited.

"It's all I have to remind me of the past. Sometimes when I
can't bear life any more I look at my album."

She sat by Skelton's side as he turned the pages. The notices
were from provincial papers, and the references to Mrs. Grange,
whose stage name had been apparently Vesta Blaise, were carefully underlined. From the photographs you could see that she
had been pretty enough in an undistinguished way. She had
acted in musical comedy and revue, in farce and comedy, and
taking the photographs and the notices together it was easy
to tell that here had been the common, dreary, rather vulgar
career of the girl with no particular talent who has taken to the
stage on the strength of a pretty face and a good figure. Her
head twitching, her hand shaking, Mrs. Grange looked at the
photographs and read the notices with as much interest as if she
had never seen them before.

"You've got to have influence on the stage, and I never had
any," she said. "If I'd only had my chance I know I'd have
made good. I had bad luck, there's no doubt about that."

It was all sordid and somewhat pathetic.

"I daresay you're better off as you are," said Skelton.

She snatched the book from him and shut it with a bang. She
had a paroxysm so violent that it was really frightening to look
at her.

"What d'you mean by that? What d'you know about the life
I lead here? I'd have killed myself years ago only I know he
wants me to die. That's the only way I can get back on him, by
living, and I'm going to live; I'm going to live as long as he does.
Oh, I hate him. I've often thought I'd poison him, but I was
afraid. I didn't know how to do it really, and if he died the

Chinks would foreclose and I'd be turned out. And where should
I go then? I haven't a friend in the world."

Skelton was aghast. It flashed through his mind that she was
crazy. He hadn't a notion what to say. She gave him a keen
look.

"I suppose it surprises you to hear me talk like that. I mean
it, you know, every word of it. He'd like to kill me too, but he
daren't either. And he knows how to do it all right. He knows
how the Malays kill people. He was born here. There's nothing
he doesn't know about the country."

Skelton forced himself to speak.

"You know, Mrs. Grange, I'm a total stranger. Don't you
think it's rather unwise to tell me all sorts of things there's no
need for me to know? After all, you live a very solitary life. I
daresay you get on one another's nerves. Now that things are
looking up perhaps you'll be able to take a trip to England."

"I don't want to go to England. I'd be ashamed to let them
see me like I am now. D'you know how old I am? Forty-six. I
look sixty and I know it. That's why I showed you those photos,
so as you might see I wasn't always like what I am now. Oh,
my God, how I've wasted my life! They talk of the romance of
the East. They can have it. I'd rather be a dresser in a provincial theatre, I'd rather be one of the sweepers that keep it
clean, than what I am now. Until I came here I'd never been
alone in me life, I'd always lived in a crowd; you don't know
what it is to have nobody to talk to from year's end to year's
end. To have to keep it all bottled up. How would you like to
see no one, week in and week out, day after day for sixteen
years, except the man you hate most in the world? How would
you like to live for sixteen years with a man who hates you so
he can't bear to look at you?"

"Oh, come, it can't be as bad as that."

"I'm telling you the truth. Why should I tell you a lie? I shall
never see you again; what do I care what you think of me? And
if you tell them what I've said when you get down to the coast,
what's the odds? They'll say: 'God, you don't mean to say you
stayed with those people? I pity you. He's an outsider and she's
crazy; got a tic; they say it looks as if she was always trying to
wipe the blood off her dress. They were mixed up in a damned
funny business, but no one ever really knew the ins and outs of
it; it all happened a long time ago and the country was pretty
wild in those days.' A damned funny business and no mistake.

I'd tell you for two pins. That would be a bit of dirt for them at the club. You wouldn't have to pay for a drink for days. Damn them. Oh, Christ, how I hate this country. I hate that river. I hate this house. I hate that damned rubber. I loathe the filthy natives. And that's all I've got to look forward to till I die—till I die without a doctor to take care of me, without a friend to hold me hand."

She began to cry hysterically. Mrs. Grange had spoken with a dramatic intensity of which Skelton would never have thought her capable. Her coarse irony was as painful as her anguish. Skelton was young, he was not yet thirty, and he did not know how to deal with the difficult situation. But he could not keep silent.

"I'm terribly sorry, Mrs. Grange. I wish I could do something to help you."

"I'm not asking for your help. No one can help me."

Skelton was distressed. From what she said he could not but suspect that she had been concerned in a mysterious and perhaps dreadful occurrence, and it might be that to tell him about it without fear of the consequences was just the relief she needed.

"I don't want to butt into what's no business of mine, but, Mrs. Grange, if you think it would ease your mind to tell me— what you were referring to just now, I mean what you said was a damned funny business, I promise you on my word of honour that I'll never repeat it to a living soul."

She stopped crying quite suddenly and gave him a long, intent look. She hesitated. He had an impression that the desire to speak was almost irresistible. But she shook her head and sighed.

"It wouldn't do any good. Nothing can do me any good."

She got up and abruptly left him.

The two men sat down to brunch by themselves.

"My wife asks you to excuse her," said Grange. "She's got one of her sick headaches and she's staying in bed to-day."

"Oh, I'm sorry."

Skelton had a notion that in the searching look that Grange gave him was mistrust and animosity. It flashed through his mind that somehow he had discovered that Mrs. Grange had been talking to him and perhaps had said things that should have been left unsaid. Skelton made an effort at conversation, but his host was taciturn, and they ended the meal in a silence that was only broken by Grange when he got up.

"You seem pretty fit to-day and I don't suppose you want to stay in this God-forsaken place longer than you must. I've sent over the river to arrange for a couple of prahus to take you down to the coast. They'll be here at six to-morrow morning."

Skelton felt sure then that he was right; Grange knew or guessed that his wife had spoken too freely, and he wanted to be rid as soon as possible of the dangerous visitor.

"That's terribly kind of you," Skelton answered, smiling. "I'm as fit as a fiddle."

But in Grange's eyes was no answering smile. They were coldly hostile.

"We might have another game of chess later on," said he.

"All right. When d'you get back from your office?"

"I haven't got much to do there to-day. I shall be about the house."

Skelton wondered if it were only his fancy that there was something very like a threat in the tone in which Grange uttered these words. It looked as though he were going to make sure that his wife and Skelton should not again be left alone. Mrs. Grange did not come to dinner. They drank their coffee and smoked their cheroots. Then Grange, pushing back his chair, said:

"You've got to make an early start to-morrow. I daresay you'd like to turn in. I shall have started out on my round by the time you go, so I'll say good-bye to you now."

"Let me get my guns. I want you to take the one you like best."

"I'll tell the boy to fetch them."

The guns were brought and Grange made his choice. He gave no sign that he was pleased with the handsome gift.

"You quite understand that this gun's worth a damned sight more than what your food and drink and smoke have run me into?" he said.

"For all I know you saved my life. I don't think an old gun is an over-generous return for that."

"Oh, well, if you like to look at it that way, I suppose it's your own business. Thank you very much all the same."

They shook hands and parted.

Next morning, while the baggage was being stowed away in the prahus, Skelton asked the house boy whether, before start-

ing, he could say good-bye to Mrs. Grange. The house boy said
he would go and see. He waited a little while. Mrs. Grange came
out of her room on to the verandah. She was wearing a pink
dressing-gown, shabby, rumpled and none too clean, of Japanese
silk, heavily trimmed with cheap lace. The powder was thick on
her face, her cheeks were rouged and her lips scarlet with lipstick. Her head seemed to twitch more violently than usual and
her hand was agitated by that strange gesture. When first Skelton saw it he had thought that it suggested a wish to call attention to something behind her back, but now, after what she
had told him yesterday, it did indeed look as though she were
constantly trying to brush something off her dress. Blood, she
had said.

"I didn't want to go without thanking you for all your kindness to me," he said.

"Oh, that's all right."

"Well, good-bye."

"I'll walk down with you to the landing-stage."

They hadn't far to go. The boatmen were still arranging the
luggage. Skelton looked across the river where you could see
some native houses.

"I suppose these men come from over there. It looks quite a
village."

"No, only those few houses. There used to be a rubber estate
there, but the company went broke and it was abandoned."

"D'you ever go over there?"

"Me?" cried Mrs. Grange. Her voice rose shrill and her head,
her hand, were on a sudden convulsed by a paroxysm of involuntary movement. "No. Why should I?"

Skelton could not imagine why that simple question, asked
merely for something to say, should so greatly upset her. But
by now all was in order and he shook hands with her. He stepped
into the boat and comfortably settled down. They pushed off.
He waved to Mrs. Grange. As the boat slid into the current she
cried out with a harsh, strident scream:

"Give my regards to Leicester Square."

Skelton heaved a great sigh of relief as with their powerful
strokes the paddlers took him farther and farther away from
that dreadful house and from those two unhappy and yet re-
pellent people. He was glad now that Mrs. Grange had not told
him the story that was on the tip of her tongue to tell. He did
not want some tragic tale of sin or folly to connect him with

them in a recollection that he could not escape. He wanted to
forget them as one forgets a bad dream.

But Mrs. Grange watched the two prahus till a bend of the
river took them out of sight. She walked slowly up to the house
and went into her bedroom. The light was dim because the
blinds were drawn to keep out the heat, but she sat down at her
dressing-table and stared at herself in the glass. Norman had
had the dressing-table made for her soon after they were married. It had been made by a native carpenter, of course, and
they had had the mirror sent from Singapore, but it was made
to her own design, of the exact size and shape she wanted, with
plenty of room for all her toilet things and her make-up. It was
the dressing-table she had hankered after for donkey's years and
had never had. She remembered still how pleased she was when
first she had it. She threw her arms round her husband's neck
and kissed him.

"Oh, Norman, you are good to me," she said. "I'm a lucky
little girl to have caught a chap like you, aren't I?"

But then everything delighted her. She was amused by the
river life and the life of the jungle, the teeming growth of the
forest, the birds with their gay plumage and the brilliant butterflies. She set about giving the house a woman's touch; she put
out all her own photographs and she got vases to put flowers in;
she routed around and got a lot of knick-knacks to place here
and there. "They make a room look homey," she said. She
wasn't in love with Norman, but she liked him all right; and it
was lovely to be married; it was lovely to have nothing to do
from morning till night, except play the gramophone, or patience, and read novels. It was lovely to think one hadn't got to
bother about one's future. Of course it was a bit lonely sometimes, but Norman said she'd get used to that, and he'd promised that in a year, or two at the outside, he'd take her to England for three months. It would be a lark to show him off to her
friends. She felt that what had caught him was the glamour of
the stage and she'd made herself out a good deal more successful than she really had been. She wanted him to realise that
she'd made a sacrifice when she'd thrown up her career to become a planter's wife. She'd claimed acquaintance with a good
many stars that in point of fact she'd never even spoken to.
That would need a bit of handling when they went home, but
she'd manage it; after all, poor Norman knew no more about the
stage than a babe unborn, if she couldn't cod a simple fellow

like that, after twelve years on the stage, well, she'd wasted her
time, that's all she could say. Things went all right the first
year. At one moment she thought she was going to have a baby.
They were both disappointed when it turned out not to be true.
Then she began to grow bored. It seemed to her that she'd done
the same damned thing day after day for ever and it frightened
her to think that she'd have to go on doing the same damned
thing day after day for ever more. Norman said he couldn't
leave the plantation that year. They had a bit of a scene. It was
then that he'd said something that scared her.

"I hate England," he said. "If I had my way I'd never set
foot in the damned country again."

Living this lonely life Mrs. Grange got into the habit of talking out loud to herself. Shut up in her room she could be heard
chattering away hour after hour; and now, dipping the puff in
her powder and plastering her face with it, she addressed her
reflection in the mirror exactly as though she were talking to
another person.

"That ought to have warned me. I should have insisted on
going by myself, and who knows, I might have got a job when
I got to London. With all the experience I had and everything.
Then I'd have written to him and said I wasn't coming back."
Her thoughts turned to Skelton. "Pity I didn't tell him," she
continued. "I had half a mind to. P'raps he was right, p'raps
it would have eased me mind. I wonder what he'd have said."
She imitated his Oxford accent. "I'm so terribly sorry, Mrs.
Grange. I wish I could help you." She gave a chuckle which
was almost a sob. "I'd have liked to tell him about Jack. Oh,
Jack."

It was when they had been married for two years that they
got a neighbour. The price of rubber at that time was so high
that new estates were being put under cultivation and one of
the big companies had bought a great tract of land on the opposite bank of the river. It was a rich company and everything
was done on a lavish scale. The manager they had put in had
a launch at his disposal so that it was no trouble for him to pop
over and have a drink whenever he felt inclined. Jack Carr his
name was. He was quite a different sort of chap from Norman;
for one thing he was a gentleman, he'd been to a public school
and a university; he was about thirty-five, tall, not beefy like
Norman, but slight, he had the sort of figure that looked lovely
in evening dress; and he had crisply curling hair and a laughing

look in his eyes. Just her type. She took to him at once. It was
a treat, having someone you could talk about London to, and
the theatre. He was gay and easy. He made the sort of jokes
you could understand. In a week or two she felt more at home
with him than she did with her husband after two years. There
had always been something about Norman that she hadn't
quite been able to get to the bottom of. He was crazy about her,
of course, and he'd told her a lot about himself, but she had a
funny feeling that there was something he kept from her, not
because he wanted to, but—well, you couldn't hardly explain
it, because it was so alien, you might say, that he couldn't put
it into words. Later, when she knew Jack better, she mentioned
it to him, and Jack said it was because he was country-born;
even though he hadn't a drop of native blood in his veins,
something of the country had gone to the making of him so
that he wasn't white really; he had an Eastern streak in him.
However hard he tried he could never be quite English.

She chattered away aloud, in that empty house, for the two
boys, the cook and the house boy, were in their own quarters,
and the sound of her voice, ringing along the wooden floors,
piercing the wooden walls, was like the uncanny, unhuman
gibber of new wine fermenting in a vat. She spoke just as though
Skelton were there, but so incoherently that if he had been, he
would have had difficulty in following the story she told. It did
not take her long to discover that Jack Carr wanted her. She
was excited. She'd never been promiscuous, but in all those
years she'd been on the stage naturally there'd been episodes.
You couldn't hardly have put up with being on tour month
after month if you didn't have a bit of fun sometimes. Of course
now she wasn't going to give in too easily, she didn't want to
make herself cheap, but what with the life she led, she'd be a
fool if she missed the chance; and as far as Norman was concerned, well, what the eye didn't see the heart didn't grieve over.
They understood one another all right, Jack and her; they knew
it was bound to happen sooner or later, it was only a matter of
waiting for the opportunity; and the opportunity came. But
then something happened that they hadn't bargained for: they
fell madly in love with one another. If Mrs. Grange really had
been telling the story to Skelton it might have seemed as unlikely to him as it did to them. They were two very ordinary
people, he a jolly, good-natured, commonplace planter, and she
a small-part actress far from clever, not even very young, with

nothing to recommend her but a neat figure and a prettyish face. What started as a casual affair turned without warning into a devastating passion, and neither of them was of a texture to sustain its exorbitant compulsion. They longed to be with one another; they were restless and miserable apart. She'd been finding Norman a bore for some time, but she'd put up with him because he was her husband; now he irritated her to frenzy because he stood between her and Jack. There was no question of their going off together, Jack Carr had nothing but his salary, and he couldn't throw up a job he'd been only too glad to get. It was difficult for them to meet. They had to run awful risks. Perhaps the chances they had to take, the obstacles they had to surmount, were fuel to their love; a year passed and it was as overwhelming as at the beginning; it was a year of agony and bliss, of fear and thrill. Then she discovered that she was pregnant. She had no doubt that Jack Carr was the father and she was wildly happy. It was true life was difficult, so difficult sometimes that she felt she just couldn't cope with it, but there'd be a baby, his baby, and that would make everything easy. She was going to Kuching for her confinement. It happened about then that Jack Carr had to go to Singapore on business and was to be away for several weeks; but he promised to get back before she left and he said he'd send word by a native the moment he arrived. When at last the message came she felt sick with the anguish of her joy. She had never wanted him so badly.

"I hear that Jack is back," she told her husband at dinner. "I shall go over to-morrow morning and get the things he promised to bring me."

"I wouldn't do that. He's pretty sure to drop in towards sundown and he'll bring them himself."

"I can't wait. I'm crazy to have them."

"All right. Have it your own way."

She couldn't help talking about him. For some time now they had seemed to have little to say to one another, Norman and she, but that night, in high spirits, she chattered away as she had done during the first months of their marriage. She always rose early, at six, and next morning she went down to the river and had a bathe. There was a little dent in the bank just there, with a tiny sandy beach, and it was delicious to splash about in the cool, transparent water. A kingfisher stood on the branch of a tree overhanging the pool and its reflection was brilliantly blue in the water. Lovely. She had a cup of tea and then stepped into a dug-out. A boy paddled her across the river. It took a good half-hour. As they got near she scanned the bank; Jack knew she would come at the earliest opportunity; he must be on the lookout. Ah, there he was. The delicious pain in her heart was almost unbearable. He came down to the landing-stage and helped her to get out of the boat. They walked hand in hand up the pathway and when they were out of sight of the boy who had paddled her over and of prying eyes from the house, they stopped. He put his arms round her and she yielded with ecstasy to his embrace. She clung to him. His mouth sought hers. In that kiss was all the agony of their separation and all the bliss of their reunion. The miracle of love transfused them so that they were unconscious of time and place. They were not human any more, but two spirits united by a divine fire. No thought passed through their minds. No words issued from their lips. Suddenly there was a brutal shock, like a blow, and immediately, almost simultaneously, a deafening noise. Horrified, not understanding, she clung to Jack more tightly and his grip on her was spasmodic, so that she gasped; then she felt that he was bearing her over.

"Jack."

She tried to hold him up. His weight was too great for her and as he fell to the ground she fell with him. Then she gave a great cry, for she felt a gush of heat, and his blood sputtered over her. She began to scream. A rough hand seized her and dragged her to her feet. It was Norman. She was distraught. She could not understand.

"Norman, what have you done?"

"I've killed him."

She stared at him stupidly. She pushed him aside.

"Jack. Jack."

"Shut up. I'll go and get help. It was an accident."

He walked quickly up the pathway. She fell to her knees and took Jack's head in her arms.

"Darling," she moaned. "Oh, my darling."

Norman came back with some coolies and they carried him up to the house. That night she had a miscarriage and was so ill that for days it looked as if she would die. When she recovered she had the nervous tic that she'd had ever since. She expected that Norman would send her away; but he didn't, he had to keep her to allay suspicion. There was some talk among the natives, and after a while the District Officer came up and asked a lot of questions; but the natives were frightened of Norman, and the D.O. could get nothing out of them. The Dyak boy who paddled her over had vanished. Norman said something had gone wrong with his gun and Jack was looking at it to see what was the matter and it went off. They bury people quickly in that country and by the time they might have dug him up there wouldn't have been much left to show that Norman's story wasn't true. The D.O. hadn't been satisfied.

"It all looks damned fishy to me," he said, "but in the absence of any evidence, I suppose I must accept your version."

She would have given anything to get away, but with that nervous affliction she had no ghost of a chance any longer of earning a living. She had to stay—or starve; and Norman had to keep her—or hang. Nothing had happened since then and now nothing ever would happen. The endless years one after another dragged out their weary length.

Mrs. Grange on a sudden stopped talking. Her sharp ears had caught the sound of a footstep on the path and she knew that Norman was back from his round. Her head twitching furiously, her hand agitated by that sinister, uncontrollable gesture, she looked in the untidy mess of her dressing-table for her precious lipstick. She smeared it on her lips, and then, she didn't know why, on a freakish impulse daubed it all over her nose till she looked like a red-nose comedian in a music-hall. She looked at herself in the glass and burst out laughing.

"To hell with life!" she shouted.

A CASUAL AFFAIR

I AM telling this story in the first person, though I am in no way connected with it, because I do not want to pretend to the reader that I know more about it than I really do. The facts are as I state them, but the reasons for them I can only guess; and it may be that when the reader has read them he will think me wrong. No one can know for certain. But if you are interested in human nature there are few things more diverting than to consider the motives that have resulted in certain actions. It was only by chance that I heard anything of the unhappy circumstances at all. I was spending two or three days on an island on the north coast of Borneo and the District Officer had very kindly offered to put me up. I had been roughing it for some time and I was glad enough to have a rest. The island had been at one time a place of some consequence, with a Governor of its own, but was so no longer; and now there was nothing much to be seen of its former importance except the imposing stone house in which the Governor had once lived and which now the District Officer, grumblingly because of its unnecessary size, inhabited. But it was a comfortable house to stay in, with an immense drawing-room, a dining-room large enough to seat forty people, and lofty, spacious bedrooms. It was shabby, because the government at Singapore very wisely spent as little money on it as possible; but I rather liked this, and the heavy official furniture gave it a sort of dull stateliness that was amusing. The

garden was too large for the District Officer to keep up and it
was a wild tangle of tropical vegetation. His name was Arthur
Low; he was a quiet, smallish man in the later thirties, married,
with two young children. The Lows had not tried to make
themselves at home in this great place, but camped there, like
refugees from a stricken area, and looked forward to the time
when they would be moved to some other post where they could
settle down in surroundings more familiar to them.

I took a fancy to them at once. The D.O. had an easy manner
and a humorous way with him. I am sure he performed his various duties admirably, but he did everything he could to avoid
the official demeanour. He was slangy of speech and pleasantly
caustic. It was charming to see him play with the two children.
It was quite obvious that he had found marriage a very satisfactory state. Mrs. Low was an extremely nice little woman,
plump, with dark eyes under fine eyebrows, not very pretty, but
certainly attractive. She looked healthy and she had high
spirits. They chaffed one another continually and each one
seemed to look upon the other as immensely comic. Their jokes
were neither very good nor very new, but they thought them
so killing that you were obliged to laugh with them.

I think they were glad to see me, especially Mrs. Low, for
with nothing much to do but keep an eye on the house and the
children, she was thrown very much on her own resources.
There were so few white people on the island that the social life
was soon exhausted; and before I had been there twenty-four
hours she pressed me to stay a week, a month or a year. On the
evening of my arrival they gave a dinner-party to which the
official population, the government surveyor, the doctor, the
schoolmaster, the chief of constabulary, were invited, but on
the following evening the three of us dined by ourselves. At the
dinner-party the guests had brought their house-boys to help,
but that night we were waited on by the Lows' one boy and my
travelling servant. They brought in the coffee and left us to ourselves. Low and I lit cheroots.

"You know that I've seen you before," said Mrs. Low.

"Where?" I asked.

"In London. At a party. I heard someone point you out to
somebody else. In Carlton House Terrace at Lady Kastellan's."

"Oh? When was that?"

"Last time we were home on leave. There were Russian
dancers."

"I remember. About two or three years ago. Fancy you being there!"

"That's exactly what we said to one another at the time," said Low, with his slow, engaging smile. "We'd never been at such a party in our lives."

"It made a great splash, you know," I said. "It was *the* party of the season. Did you enjoy it?"

"I hated every minute of it," said Mrs. Low.

"Don't let's overlook the fact that you insisted on going, Bee," said Low. "I knew we'd be out of it among all those swells. My dress clothes were the same I'd had at Cambridge and they'd never been much of a fit."

"I bought a frock specially at Peter Robinson's. It looked lovely in the shop. I wished I hadn't wasted so much money when I got there; I never felt so dowdy in my life."

"Well, it didn't much matter. We weren't introduced to any-body."

I remembered the party quite well. The magnificent rooms in Carlton House Terrace had been decorated with great festoons of yellow roses and at one end of the vast drawing-room a stage had been erected. Special costumes of the Regency period had been designed for the dancers and a modern composer had written the music for the two charming ballets they danced. It was hard to look at it all and not allow the vulgar thought to cross one's mind that the affair must have cost an enormous amount of money. Lady Kastellan was a beautiful woman and a great hostess, but I do not think anyone would have ascribed to her any vast amount of kindliness, she knew too many people to care much for any one in particular, and I couldn't help wondering why she had asked to such a grand party two obscure and quite unimportant little persons from a distant colony.

"Had you known Lady Kastellan long?" I asked.

"We didn't know her at all. She sent us a card and we went because I wanted to see what she was like," said Mrs. Low.

"She's a very able woman," I said.

"I dare say she is. She hadn't an idea who we were when the butler man announced us, but she remembered at once. 'Oh, yes,' she said, 'you're poor Jack's friend. Do go and find your-selves seats where you can see. You'll adore Lifar, he's too mar-vellous.' And then she turned to say how d'you do to the next people. But she gave me a look. She wondered how much I knew and she saw at once that I knew everything."

"Don't talk such nonsense, darling," said Low. "How could she know all you think she did by just looking at you, and how could you tell what she was thinking?"

"It's true, I tell you. We said everything in that one look, and unless I'm very much mistaken I spoilt her party for her."

Low laughed and I smiled, for Mrs. Low spoke in a tone of triumphant vindictiveness.

"You are terribly indiscreet, Bee."

"Is she a great friend of yours?" Mrs. Low asked me.

"Hardly. I've met her here and there for fifteen years. I've been to a good many parties at her house. She gives very good parties and she always asks you to meet the people you want to see."

"What d'you think of her?"

"She's by way of being a considerable figure in London. She's amusing to talk to and she's nice to look at. She does a lot for art and music. What do *you* think of her?"

"I think she's a bitch," said Mrs. Low, with cheerful but decided frankness.

"That settles her," I said.

"Tell him, Arthur."

Low hesitated for a moment.

"I don't know that I ought to."

"If you don't, I shall."

"Bee's got her knife into her all right," he smiled. "It was rather a bad business really."

He made a perfect smoke-ring and watched it with absorption.

"Go on, Arthur," said Mrs. Low.

"Oh, well. It was before we went home last time. I was D.O. in Selangor and one day they came and told me that a white man was dead in a small town a couple of hours up the river. I didn't know there was a white man living there. I thought I'd better go and see about it, so I got in the launch and went up. I made enquiries when I got there. The police didn't know anything about him except that he'd been living there for a couple of years with a Chinese woman in the bazaar. It was rather a picturesque bazaar, tall houses on each side, with a board walk in between, built on piles on the river-bank, and there were awnings above to keep out the sun. I took a couple of policemen with me and they led me to the house. They sold brass-ware in the shop below and the rooms above were let out. The master of the shop took me up two flights of dark, rickety stairs, foul with every kind of Chinese stench, and called out when we got to the top. The door was opened by a middle-aged Chinese woman and I saw that her face was all bloated with weeping. She didn't say anything, but made way for us to pass. It wasn't much more than a cubby-hole under the roof; there was a small window that looked on the street, but the awning that stretched across it dimmed the light. There wasn't any furniture except a deal table and a kitchen chair with a broken back. On a mat against the wall a dead man was lying. The first thing I did was to have the window opened. The room was so frowsty that I retched, and the strongest smell was the smell of opium. There was a small oil-lamp on the table and a long needle, and of course I knew what they were there for. The pipe had been hidden. The dead man lay on his back with nothing on but a sarong and a dirty singlet. He had long brown hair, going grey, and a short beard. He was a white man all right. I examined him as best I could. I had to judge whether death was due to natural causes. There were no signs of violence. He was nothing but skin and bone. It looked to me as though he might very likely have died of starvation. I asked the man of the shop and the woman a number of questions. The policeman corroborated their statements. It appeared that the man coughed a great deal and brought up blood now and then, and his appearance suggested that he might very well have had T.B. The Chinaman said he'd been a confirmed opium smoker. It all seemed pretty obvious. Fortunately cases of that sort are rare, but they're not unheard-of—the white man who goes under and gradually sinks to the last stage of degradation. It appeared that the Chinese woman had been fond of him. She'd kept him on her own miserable earnings for the last two years. I gave the necessary instructions. Of course I wanted to know who he was. I supposed he'd been a clerk in some English firm or an assistant in an English store at Singapore or Kuala Lumpur. I asked the Chinese woman if he'd left any effects. Considering the destitution in which they'd lived it seemed a rather absurd question, but she went to a shabby suit-case that lay in a corner, opened it and showed me a square parcel about the size of two novels put together wrapped in an old newspaper. I had a look at the suit-case. It contained nothing of any value. I took the parcel."

Low's cheroot had gone out and he leaned over to relight it from one of the candles on the table.

"I opened it. Inside was another wrapping, and on this, in a neat, well-educated writing: To the District Officer, me as it happened, and the words: please deliver personally to the Viscountess Kastellan, 53 Carlton House Terrace, London, S.W. That was a bit of a surprise. Of course I had to examine the contents. I cut the string and the first thing I found was a gold and platinum cigarette case. As you can imagine I was mystified, From all I'd heard the pair of them, the dead man and the Chinese woman, had scarcely enough to eat, and the cigarette-case looked as if it had cost a packet. Besides the cigarette-case there was nothing but a bundle of letters. There were no en-velopes. They were in the same neat writing as the directions and they were signed with the initial J. There were forty or fifty of them. I couldn't read them all there, but a rapid glance showed me that they were a man's love letters to a woman. I sent for the Chinese woman to ask her the name of the dead man. Either she didn't know or wouldn't tell me. I gave orders that he should be buried and got back into the launch to go home. I told Bee."

He gave her his sweet little smile.

"I had to be rather firm with Arthur," she said. "At first he wouldn't let me read the letters, but of course I wasn't going to put up with any nonsense like that."

"It was none of our business."

"You had to find out the name if you could."

"And where exactly did you come in?"

"Oh, don't be so silly," she laughed. "I should have gone mad if you hadn't let me read them."

"And did you find out his name?" I asked.

"No."

"Was there no address?"

"Yes, there was, and a very unexpected one. Most of the letters were written on Foreign Office paper."

"That was funny."

"I didn't quite know what to do. I had half a mind to write to the Viscountess Kastellan and explain the circumstances, but I didn't know what trouble I might be starting; the directions were to deliver the parcel to her personally, so I wrapped every-thing up again and put it in the safe. We were going home on leave in the spring and I thought the best thing was to leave everything over till then. The letters were by way of being rather compromising."

"To put it mildly," giggled Mrs. Low. "The truth is they gave the whole show away."

"I don't think we need go into that," said Low.

A slight altercation ensued; but I think on his part it was more for form's sake, since he must have known that his desire to preserve an official discretion stood small chance against his wife's determination to tell me everything. She had a down on Lady Kastellan and didn't care what she said about her. Her sympathies were with the man. Low did his best to tone down her rash assertions. He corrected her exaggerations. He told her that she'd let her imagination run away with her and had read into the letters more than was there. She would have done it. They'd evidently made a deep impression on her, and from her vivid account and Low's interruptions I gained a fairly coherent impression of them. It was plain for one thing that they were very moving.

"I can't tell you how it revolted me, the way Bee gloated over them," said Low.

"They were the most wonderful letters I've ever read. You never wrote letters like that to me."

"What a damned fool you would have thought me if I had," he grinned.

She gave him a charming, affectionate smile.

"I suppose I should, and yet, God knows I was crazy about you, and I'm damned if I know why."

The story emerged clearly enough. The writer, the mysterious J., presumably a clerk in the Foreign Office, had fallen in love with Lady Kastellan and she with him. They had become lovers and the early letters were passionately lyrical. They were happy. They expected their love to last for ever. He wrote to her immediately after he had left her and told her how much he adored her and how much she meant to him. She was never for a moment absent from his thoughts. It looked as though her infatuation was equal to his, for in one letter he justified himself because she had reproached him for not coming to some place where he knew she would be. He told her what agony it had been to him that a sudden job had prevented him from being with her when he'd so eagerly looked forward to it.

Then came the catastrophe. How it came or why one could only guess. Lord Kastellan learnt the truth. He not merely suspected his wife's infidelity, he had proofs of it. There was a fearful scene between them, she left him and went to her father's.

Lord Kastellan announced his intention of divorcing her. The letters changed in character. J. wrote at once asking to see Lady Kastellan, but she begged him not to come. Her father insisted that they shouldn't meet. J. was distressed at her unhappiness and dismayed by the trouble he had brought upon her, and he was deeply sympathetic because of what she was enduring at home, for her father and mother were furious; but at the same time it was plain that he was relieved that the crisis had come. Nothing mattered except that they loved one another. He said he hated Kastellan. Let him bring his action. The sooner they could get married the better. The correspondence was one-sided, there were no letters from her, and one had to guess from his replies what she said in them. She was obviously frightened out of her wits and nothing that he could say helped. Of course he would have to leave the Foreign Office. He assured her that this meant nothing to him. He could get a job somewhere, in the colonies, where he would earn much more money. He was sure he could make her happy. Naturally there would be a scandal, but it would be forgotten, and away from England people would not bother. He besought her to have courage. Then it looked as though she had written somewhat peevishly. She hated being divorced, Kastellan refused to take the blame on himself and be made respondent, she did not want to leave London, it was her whole life, and bury herself in some God-forsaken place on the other side of nowhere. He answered unhappily. He said he would do anything she wanted. He implored her not to love him less and he was tortured by the thought that this disaster had changed her feelings for him. She reproached him for the mess they had got into; he did not try to defend himself; he was prepared to admit that he alone was to blame. Then it appeared that pressure was being brought to bear on Kastellan from some high quarter and there was even yet a chance that something might be arranged. Whatever she wrote made J., the unknown J., desperate. His letter was almost incoherent. He begged her again to see him, he implored her to have strength, he repeated that she meant everything in the world to him, he was frightened that she would let people influence her, he asked her to burn her boats behind her and bolt with him to Paris. He was frantic. Then it seemed that for some days she did not write to him. He could not understand. He did not know if she was receiving his letters. He was in an agony. The blow fell. She must have written to say that if he would resign from the Foreign

Office and leave England her husband was prepared to take her back. His answer was brokenhearted.

"He never saw through her for a moment," said Mrs. Low.

"What was there to see through?" I asked.

"Don't you know what she wrote to him? I do."

"Don't be such an ass, Bee. You can't possibly know."

"Ass yourself. Of course I do. She put it up to him. She threw herself on his mercy. She dragged in her father and mother. She brought in her children; I bet that was the first thought she'd given them since they were born. She knew that he loved her so much that he was willing to do everything in the world for her, even lose her. She knew that he was prepared to accept the sacrifice of his love, his life, his career, everything for her sake, and she let him make it. She let the offer come from him. She let him persuade her to accept it."

I listened to Mrs. Low with a smile, but with attention. She was a woman and she felt instinctively how a woman in those circumstances would act. She thought it hateful, but she felt in her bones that in just that way would she herself have acted. Of course it was pure invention, with nothing but J.'s letter as a foundation, but I had an impression that it was very likely.

That was the last letter in the bundle.

I was astonished. I had known Lady Kastellan for a good many years, but only casually; and I knew her husband even less. He was immersed in politics, he was Under-Secretary at the Home Office at the time of the great do to which the Lows and I had been invited; and I never saw him but in his own house. Lady Kastellan had the reputation of being a beauty; she was tall and her figure was good in a massive way. She had a lovely skin. Her blue eyes were large, set rather wide apart and her face was broad. It gave her a slightly cow-like look. She had pretty pale brown hair and she held herself superbly. She was a woman of great self-possession, and it amazed me to learn that she had ever surrendered to such passion as the letters suggested. She was ambitious and there was no doubt that she was very useful to Kastellan in his political life. I should have thought her incapable of indiscretion. Searching my memory I seemed to remember hearing years before that the Kastellans were not getting on very well, but I had never heard any details, and whenever I saw them it looked as though they were on very good terms with one another. Kastellan was a big, red-faced fellow with sleek black hair, jovial and loud-voiced, but with little shrewd eyes that watched and noted. He was industrious, an effective speaker, but a trifle pompous. He was a little too conscious of his own importance. He did not let you forget that he had rank and wealth. He was inclined to be patronising with people of less consequence than himself.

I could well believe that when he discovered that his wife was having an affair with a junior clerk in the Foreign Office there was a devil of a row. Lady Kastellan's father had been for many years permanent Under-Secretary for Foreign Affairs and it would have been more than usually embarrassing for his daughter to be divorced on account of one of his subordinates. For all I knew Kastellan was in love with his wife and he may have been teased by a very natural jealousy. But he was a proud man, deficient in humour. He feared ridicule. The rôle of the deceived husband is difficult to play with dignity. I do not suppose he wanted a scandal that might well jeopardise his political future. It may be that Lady Kastellan's advisers threatened to defend the case and the prospect of washing dirty linen in public horrified him. It is likely enough that pressure was brought to bear on him and the solution to forgive and take his wife back if her lover were definitely eliminated may have seemed the best to adopt. I have no doubt Lady Kastellan promised everything she was asked.

She must have had a bad fright. I didn't take such a severe view of her conduct as Mrs. Low. She was very young; she was not more than thirty-five now. Who could tell by what accident she had become J.'s mistress? I suspect that love had caught her unawares and that she was in the middle of an affair almost before she knew what she was about. She must always have been a cold, self-possessed woman, but it is just with people like that that nature at times plays strange tricks. I am prepared to believe that she lost her head completely. There is no means of knowing how Kastellan discovered what was going on, but the fact that she kept her lover's letters shows that she was too much in love to be prudent. Arthur Low had mentioned that it was strange to find in the dead man's possession his letters and not hers; but that seemed to me easily explainable. At the time of the catastrophe they were doubtless given back to him in exchange for hers. He very naturally kept them. Reading them again he could relive the love that meant everything in the world to him.

I didn't suppose that Lady Kastellan, devoured by passion,

could ever have considered what would happen if she were found out. When the blow fell it is not strange that she was scared out of her wits. She may not have had more to do with her children than most women who live the sort of life she lived, but she may for all that not have wanted to lose them. I did not even know whether she had ever cared for her husband, but from what I knew of her I guessed that she was not indifferent to his name and wealth. The future must have looked pretty grim. She was losing everything, the grand house in Carlton House Terrace, the position, the security; her father could give her no money and her lover had still to find a job. It may not have been heroic that she should yield to the entreaties of her family, but it was comprehensible.

While I was thinking all this Arthur Low went on with his story.

"I didn't quite know how to set about getting in touch with Lady Kastellan," he said. "It was awkward not knowing the chap's name. However, when we got home I wrote to her. I explained who I was and said that I'd been asked to give her some letters and a gold and platinum cigarette-case by a man who'd recently died in my district. I said I'd been asked to deliver them to her in person. I thought perhaps she wouldn't answer at all or else communicate with me through a solicitor. But she answered all right. She made an appointment for me to come to Carlton House Terrace at twelve one morning. Of course it was stupid of me, but when finally I stood on the doorstep and rang the bell I was quite nervous. The door was opened by a butler. I said I had an appointment with Lady Kastellan. A footman took my hat and coat. I was led upstairs to an enormous drawing-room.

" 'I'll tell her ladyship you're here, sir,' the butler said.

"He left me and I sat on the edge of a chair and looked round. There were huge pictures on the walls, portraits you know, I don't know who they were by, Reynolds I should think and Romney, and there was a lot of Oriental china, and gilded consoles and mirrors. It was all terribly grand and it made me feel very shabby and insignificant. My suit smelt of camphor and it was baggy at the knees. My tie felt a bit loud. The butler came in again and asked me to go with him. He opened another door from the one I'd come in by and I found myself in a further room, not so large as the drawing-room, but large all the same and very grand too. A lady was standing by the fireplace. She

looked at me as I came in and bowed slightly. I felt frightfully
awkward as I walked along the whole length of the room and I
was afraid of stumbling over the furniture. I can only hope I
didn't look such a fool as I felt. She didn't ask me to sit down.

" 'I understand you have some things that you wish to deliver
to me personally,' she said. 'It's very good of you to bother.'

"She didn't smile. She seemed perfectly self-possessed, but
I had a notion that she was sizing me up. To tell you the truth
it put my back up. I didn't much fancy being treated as if I were
a chauffeur applying for a situation.

" 'Please don't mention it,' I said, rather stiffly. 'It's all in the
day's work.'

" 'Have you got the things with you?' she asked.

"I didn't answer, but I opened the dispatch-case I'd brought
with me and took out the letters. I handed them to her. She
accepted them without a word. She gave them a glance. She was
very much made up, but I swear she went white underneath.
The expression of her face didn't change. I looked at her hands.
They were trembling a little. Then she seemed to pull herself together.

" 'Oh, I'm so sorry,' she said. 'Won't you sit down?'

"I took a chair. For a moment she didn't seem to know quite
what to do. She held the letters in her hand. I, knowing what
they were, wondered what she felt. She didn't give much away.
There was a desk beside the chimney-piece and she opened a
drawer and put them in. Then she sat down opposite me and
asked me to have a cigarette. I handed her the cigarette-case.
I'd had it in my breast pocket.

" 'I was asked to give you this too,' I said.

"She took it and looked at it. For a moment she didn't speak
and I waited. I didn't quite know if I ought to get up and go.

" 'Did you know Jack well?' she asked suddenly.

" 'I didn't know him at all,' I answered. 'I never saw him until
after his death.'

" 'I had no idea he was dead till I got your note,' she said.
'I'd lost sight of him for a long time. Of course he was a very old
friend of mine.'

"I wondered if she thought I hadn't read the letters or if she'd
forgotten what sort of letters they were. If the sight of them
had given her a shock she had quite got over it by then. She
spoke almost casually.

" 'What did he die of in point of fact?' she asked.

" 'Tuberculosis, opium and starvation,' I answered.

" 'How dreadful,' she said.

"But she said it quite conventionally. Whatever she felt she wasn't going to let me see. She was as cool as a cucumber, but I fancied, though it may have been only my fancy, that she was watching me, with all her wits about her, and wondering how much I knew. I think she'd have given a good deal to be certain of that.

" 'How did you happen to get hold of these things?' she asked me.

" 'I took possession of his effects after his death,' I explained. 'They were done up in a parcel and I was directed to give them to you.'

" 'Was there any need to undo the parcel?'

"I wish I could tell you what frigid insolence she managed to get into the question. It made me go white and I hadn't any make-up on to hide it. I answered that I thought it my duty to find out if I could who the dead man was. I should have liked to be able to communicate with his relations.

" 'I see,' she said.

"She looked at me as though that were the end of the interview and she expected me to get up and take myself off. But I didn't. I thought I'd like to get a bit of my own back. I told her how I'd been sent for and how I'd found him. I described the whole thing and I told her how, as far as I knew, there'd been no one at the end to take pity on him but a Chinese woman. Suddenly the door was opened and we both looked round. A big, middle-aged man came in and stopped when he saw me.

" 'I beg your pardon,' he said, 'I didn't know you were busy.'

" 'Come in,' she said, and when he had approached, 'This is Mr. Low. My husband.'

"Lord Kastellan gave me a nod.

" 'I just wanted to ask you,' he began, and then he stopped.

"His eyes had caught the cigarette-case that was still resting on Lady Kastellan's open hand. I don't know if she saw the look of enquiry in his eyes. She gave him a friendly little smile. She was quite amazingly mistress of herself.

" 'Mr. Low comes from the Federated Malay States. Poor Jack Almond's dead and he's left me his cigarette-case.'

" 'Really?' said Lord Kastellan. 'When did he die?'

" 'About six months ago,' I said.

"Lady Kastellan got up.

" 'Well, I won't keep you any longer. I dare say you're busy. Thank you so much for carrying out Jack's request.'

" 'Things are pretty bad just now in the F.M.S. if all I hear is true,' said Lord Kastellan.

"I shook hands with them both and Lady Kastellan rang a bell.

" 'Are you staying in London?' she asked, as I was going. 'I wonder if you'd like to come to a little party I'm giving next week.'

" 'I have my wife with me,' I said.

" 'Oh, how very nice. I'll send you a card.'

"A couple of minutes later I found myself in the street. I was glad to be alone. I'd had a bad shock. As soon as Lady Kastellan mentioned the name I remembered. It was Jack Almond, the wretched bum I'd found dead in the Chinese house, dead of starvation. I'd known him quite well. It never struck me for a moment that it was he. Why, I'd dined and played cards with him, and we'd played tennis together. It was awful to think of him dying quite near me and me never knowing. He must have known he only had to send me a message and I'd have done something. I made my way into St. James's Park and sat down. I wanted to have a good think."

I could understand that it was a shock to Arthur Low to discover who the dead wastrel had been, for it was a shock to me too. Oddly enough I also had known him. Not intimately, but as a man I met at parties and now and then at a house in the country where we were both passing the week-end. Except that it was years since I had even thought of him it would have been stupid of me not to put two and two together. With his name there flashed back into my memory all my recollections of him. So that was why he had suddenly thrown up a career he liked so much! At that time, it was just after the war, I happened to know several people in the Foreign Office; Jack Almond was thought the cleverest of all the young men attached to it, and the highest posts the Diplomatic Service had to offer were within his reach. Of course it meant waiting. But it did seem absurd for him to fling away his chances in order to go into business in the Far East. His friends did all they could to dissuade him. He said he had had losses and found it impossible to live on his salary. One would have thought he could scrape along till things grew better. I remembered very well what he looked like. He was tall and well-made, a trifle dressy, but he was young enough to carry off his faultless clothes with a dash, with dark brown hair, very neat and sleek, blue eyes with very long lashes, and a fresh brilliant colour. He looked the picture of health. He was amusing, gay and quick-witted. I never knew anyone who had more charm. It is a dangerous quality and those who have it trade on it. Often they think it enough to get them through life without any further effort. It is well to be on one's guard against it. But with Jack Almond it was the expression of a sweet and generous nature. He delighted because he was delightful. He was entirely without conceit. He had a gift for languages, he spoke French and German without a trace of accent, and his manners were admirable. You felt that when the time came he would play the part of an ambassador to a foreign power in the grand style. No one could fail to like him. It was not strange that Lady Kastellan should have fallen madly in love with him. My fancy ran away with me. What is there more moving than young love? The walks together of that handsome pair in one of the parks in the warm evenings of early summer, the dances they went to where he held her in his arms, the enchantment of the secret they shared when they exchanged glances across a dinner-table, and the passionate encounters, hurried and dangerous, but worth a thousand risks, when at some clandestine meeting-place they could give themselves to the fulfilment of their desire. They drank the milk of Paradise.

How frightful that the end of it all should have been so tragic!

"How did you know him?" I now asked Low.

"He was with Dexter and Farmilow. You know, the shipping people. He had quite a good job. He'd brought letters to the Governor and people like that. I was in Singapore at the time. I think I met him first at the club. He was damned good at games and all that sort of thing. Played polo. He was a fine tennis-player. You couldn't help liking him."

"Did he drink, or what?"

"No." Arthur Low was quite emphatic. "He was one of the best. The women were crazy about him, and you couldn't blame them. He was one of the most decent fellows I've ever met."

I turned to Mrs. Low.

"Did you know him?"

"Only just. When Arthur and I were married we went to Perak. He was sweet, I remember that. He had the longest eyelashes I've ever seen on a man."

"He was out quite a long time without going home. Five

years, I think. I don't want to use hackneyed phrases, but the
fact is I can't say it in any other way, he'd won golden opinions.
There were a certain number of fellows who'd been rather sick
at his being shoved into a damned good job by influence, but
they couldn't deny that he'd made good. We knew about his
having been in the F.O. and all that, but he never put on any
frills."

"I think what took me," Mrs. Low interrupted, "was that he
was so tremendously alive. It bucked you up just to talk to
him."

"He had a wonderful send-off when he sailed. I happened to
have run up to Singapore for a couple of days and I went to the
dinner at the Europe the night before. We all got rather tight.
It was a grand lark. There was quite a crowd to see him off. He
was only going for six months. I think everybody looked forward
to his coming back. It would have been better for him if he never
had."

"Why, what happened then?"

"I don't know exactly. I'd been moved again, and I was right
away north."

How exasperating! It is really much easier to invent a story
out of your own head than to tell one about real people, of
whom you not only must guess the motives, but whose behaviour even at crucial moments you are ignorant of.

"He was a very good chap, but he was never an intimate
friend of ours, you know how cliquey Singapore is, and he moved
in rather more exalted circles than we did; when we went
north I forgot about him. But one day at the club I heard a
couple of fellows talking. Walton and Kenning. Walton had
just come up from Singapore. There'd been a big polo match.

" 'Did Almond play?' asked Kenning.

" 'You bet your life he didn't,' said Walton. 'They kicked
him out of the team last season.'

"I interrupted.

" 'What *are* you talking about?' I said.

" 'Don't you know?' said Walton. 'He's gone all to pot, poor
devil.'

" 'How?' I asked.

" 'Drink.'

" 'They say he dopes too,' said Kenning.

" 'Yes, I've heard that,' said Walton. 'He won't last long at
that rate. Opium, isn't it?'

" 'If he doesn't look out he'll lose his job,' said Kenning.

"I couldn't make it out," Low went on. "He was the last man I should ever have expected to go that way. He was so typically English and he was a gentleman and all that. It appeared that Walton had travelled out with him on the same ship when Jack came back from leave. He joined the ship at Marseilles. He was rather low, but there was nothing funny about that; a lot of people don't feel any too good when they're leaving home and have to get back to the mill. He drank a good deal. Fellows do that sometimes too. But Walton said rather a curious thing about him. He said it looked as if the life had gone out of him. You couldn't help noticing it because he'd always had such high spirits. There'd been a general sort of idea that he was engaged to some girl in England and on the ship they jumped to the conclusion that she'd thrown him over."

"That's what I said when Arthur told me," said Mrs. Low. "After all, five years is a long time to leave a girl."

"Anyhow they thought he'd get over it when he got back to work. But he didn't, unfortunately. He went from bad to worse. A lot of people liked him and they did all they could to persuade him to pull himself together. But there was nothing doing. He just told them to mind their own business. He was snappy and rude, which was funny because he'd always been so nice to everybody. Walton said you could hardly believe it was the same man. Government House dropped him and a lot of others followed suit. Lady Ormonde, the Governor's wife, was a snob, she knew he was well-connected and all that, and she wouldn't have given him the cold shoulder unless things had got pretty bad. He was a nice chap, Jack Almond, it seemed a pity that he should make such a mess of things. I was sorry, you know, but of course it didn't impair my appetite or disturb my night's sleep. A few months later I happened to be in Singapore myself, and when I went to the club I asked about him. He'd lost his job all right, it appeared that he often didn't go to the office for two or three days at a time; and I was told that someone had made him manager of a rubber estate in Sumatra in the hope that away from the temptations of Singapore he might pull himself together. You see, everyone had liked him so much, they couldn't bear the thought of his going under without some sort of a struggle. But it was no good. The opium had got him. He didn't keep the job in Sumatra long and he was back again in Singapore. I heard afterwards that you would

hardly have recognised him. He'd always been so spruce and
smart; he was shabby and unwashed and wild-eyed. A number
of fellows at the club got together and arranged something. They
felt they had to give him one more chance and they sent him
out to Sarawak. But it wasn't any use. The fact is, I think, he
didn't want to be helped. I think he just wanted to go to hell
in his own way and be as quick as he could about it. Then he
disappeared; someone said he'd gone home; anyhow he was
forgotten. You know how people drop out in the F.M.S. I suppose that's why when I found a dead man in a sarong, with a
beard, lying in a little smelly room in a Chinese house thirty
miles from anywhere, it never occurred to me for a moment that
it might be Jack Almond. I hadn't heard his name for years."

"Just think what he must have gone through in that time,"
said Mrs. Low, and her eyes were bright with tears, for she had
a good and tender heart.

"The whole thing's inexplicable," said Low.

"Why?" I asked.

"Well, if he was going to pieces, why didn't he do it when he
first came out? His first five years he was all right. One of the
best. If this affair of his had broken him you'd have expected
him to break when it was all fresh. All that time he was as gay
as a bird. You'd have said he hadn't a care in the world. From
all I heard it was a different man who came back from leave."

"Something happened during those six months in London,"
said Mrs. Low. "That's obvious."

"We shall never know," sighed Low.

"But we can guess," I smiled. "That's where the novelist
comes in. Shall I tell you what I think happened?"

"Fire away."

"Well, I think that during those first five years he was buoyed
up by the sacrifice he'd made. He had a chivalrous soul. He had
given up everything that made life worth living to him to save
the woman he loved better than anything in the world. I think
he had an exaltation of spirit that never left him. He loved her
still, with all his heart; most of us fall in and out of love; some
men can only love once, and I think he was one of them. And
in a strange way he was happy because he'd been able to
sacrifice his happiness for the sake of someone who was worthy
of the sacrifice. I think she was always in his thoughts. Then he
went home. I think he loved her as much as ever and I don't
suppose he ever doubted that her love was as strong and endur-

ing as his. I don't know what he expected. He may have thought
she'd see it was no good fighting her inclination any more and
would run away with him. It may have been that he'd have
been satisfied to realise that she loved him still. It was inevitable that they should meet; they lived in the same world. He
saw that she didn't care a row of pins for him any longer. He
saw that the passionate girl had become a prudent, experienced
woman of the world, he saw that she'd never loved him as he
thought she loved him, and he may have suspected that she'd
lured him coldly into making the sacrifice that was to save her.
He saw her at parties, self-possessed and triumphant. He knew
that the lovely qualities he'd ascribed to her were of his own
imagining and she was just an ordinary woman who had been
carried away by a momentary infatuation and having got over
it had returned to her true life. A great name, wealth, social
distinction, worldly success: those were the things that mattered
to her. He'd sacrificed everything, his friends, his familiar surroundings, his profession, his usefulness in the world, all that
gives value to existence—for nothing. He'd been cheated, and it
broke him. Your friend Walton said the true thing, you noticed
it yourself, he said it looked as if the life had gone out of him.
It had. After that he didn't care any more, and perhaps the
worst thing was that even with it all, though he knew Lady
Kastellan for what she was, he loved her still. I know nothing
more shattering than to love with all your heart, than not to be
able however hard you try to break yourself of it, someone who
you know is worthless. Perhaps that is why he took to opium.
To forget and to remember."

It was a long speech I had made, and now I stopped.

"All that's only fancy," said Low.

"I know it is," I answered, "but it seems to fit the circumstances."

"There must have been a weak strain in him. Otherwise he
could have fought and conquered."

"Perhaps. Perhaps there is always a certain weakness attached to such great charm as he possessed. Perhaps few people
love as wholeheartedly and as devotedly as he loved. Perhaps
he didn't want to fight and conquer. I can't bring myself to
blame him."

I didn't add, because I was afraid they would think it cynical,
that maybe if only Jack Almond hadn't had those wonderfully
long eyelashes he might now have been alive and well, minister

to some foreign power and on the high road to the Embassy in
Paris.

"Let's go into the drawing-room," said Mrs. Low. "The boy
wants to clear the table."

And that was the end of Jack Almond.

MR. KNOW-ALL

I was prepared to dislike Max Kelada even before I knew him. The war had just finished and the passenger traffic in the ocean-going liners was heavy. Accommodation was very hard to get and you had to put up with whatever the agents chose to offer you. You could not hope for a cabin to yourself and I was thankful to be given one in which there were only two berths. But when I was told the name of my companion my heart sank. It suggested closed port-holes and the night air rigidly excluded. It was bad enough to share a cabin for fourteen days with anyone (I was going from San Francisco to Yokohama), but I should have looked upon it with less dismay if my fellow-passenger's name had been Smith or Brown.

When I went on board I found Mr. Kelada's luggage already below. I did not like the look of it; there were too many labels on the suitcases, and the wardrobe trunk was too big. He had unpacked his toilet things, and I observed that he was a patron of the excellent Monsieur Coty; for I saw on the washing-stand his scent, his hair-wash and his brilliantine. Mr. Kelada's brushes, ebony with his monogram in gold, would have been all the better for a scrub. I did not at all like Mr. Kelada. I made my way into the smoking-room. I called for a pack of cards and began to play patience. I had scarcely started before a man came up to me and asked me if he was right in thinking my name was so-and-so.

"I am Mr. Kelada," he added, with a smile that showed a row of flashing teeth, and sat down.

*"Oh, yes, we're sharing a cabin, I think."

"Bit of luck, I call it. You never know who you're going to be put in with. I was jolly glad when I heard you were English. I'm all for us English sticking together when we're abroad, if you understand what I mean."

I blinked.

"Are you English?" I asked, perhaps tactlessly.

"Rather. You don't think I look like an American, do you? British to the backbone, that's what I am."

To prove it, Mr. Kelada took out of his pocket a passport and airily waved it under my nose.

King George has many strange subjects. Mr. Kelada was short and of a sturdy build, clean-shaven and dark-skinned, with a fleshy, hooked nose and very large, lustrous and liquid eyes. His long black hair was sleek and curly. He spoke with a fluency in which there was nothing English and his gestures were exuberant. I felt pretty sure that a closer inspection of that British passport would have betrayed the fact that Mr. Kelada was born under a bluer sky than is generally seen in England.

"What will you have?" he asked me.

I looked at him doubtfully. Prohibition was in force and to all appearances the ship was bone-dry. When I am not thirsty I do not know which I dislike more, ginger-ale or lemon-squash. But Mr. Kelada flashed an oriental smile at me.

"Whisky and soda or a dry Martini, you have only to say the word."

From each of his hip-pockets he fished a flask and laid them on the table before me. I chose the Martini, and calling the steward he ordered a tumbler of ice and a couple of glasses.

"A very good cocktail," I said.

"Well, there are plenty more where that came from, and if you've got any friends on board, you tell them you've got a pal who's got all the liquor in the world."

Mr. Kelada was chatty. He talked of New York and of San Francisco. He discussed plays, pictures, and politics. He was patriotic. The Union Jack is an impressive piece of drapery, but when it is flourished by a gentleman from Alexandria or Beirut, I cannot but feel that it loses somewhat in dignity. Mr. Kelada was familiar. I do not wish to put on airs, but I cannot help feeling that it is seemly in a total stranger to put mister before my name when he addresses me. Mr. Kelada, doubtless to set me at my ease, used no such formality. I did not like Mr. Kelada. I had put aside the cards when he sat down, but now, thinking that for this first occasion our conversation had lasted long enough, I went on with my game.

"The three on the four," said Mr. Kelada.

There is nothing more exasperating when you are playing patience than to be told where to put the card you have turned up before you have had a chance to look for yourself.

"It's coming out, it's coming out," he cried. "The ten on the knave."

With rage and hatred in my heart I finished. Then he seized the pack.

"Do you like card tricks?"

"No, I hate card tricks," I answered.

"Well, I'll just show you this one."

He showed me three. Then I said I would go down to the dining-room and get my seat at table.

"Oh, that's all right," he said. "I've already taken a seat for you. I thought that as we were in the same state-room we might just as well sit at the same table."

I did not like Mr. Kelada.

I not only shared a cabin with him and ate three meals a day at the same table, but I could not walk round the deck without his joining me. It was impossible to snub him. It never occurred to him that he was not wanted. He was certain that you were as glad to see him as he was to see you. In your own house you might have kicked him downstairs and slammed the door in his face without the suspicion dawning on him that he was not a welcome visitor. He was a good mixer, and in three days knew everyone on board. He ran everything. He managed the sweeps, conducted the auctions, collected money for prizes at the sports, got up quoit and golf matches, organised the concert and arranged the fancy dress ball. He was everywhere and always. He was certainly the best-hated man in the ship. We called him Mr. Know-All, even to his face. He took it as a compliment. But it was at meal times that he was most intolerable. For the better part of an hour then he had us at his mercy. He was hearty, jovial, loquacious and argumentative. He knew everything better than anybody else, and it was an affront to his overweening vanity that you should disagree with him. He

would not drop a subject, however unimportant, till he had
brought you round to his way of thinking. The possibility that
he could be mistaken never occurred to him. He was the chap
who knew. We sat at the doctor's table. Mr. Kelada would certainly have had it all his own way, for the doctor was lazy and
I was frigidly indifferent, except for a man called Ramsay who
sat there also. He was as dogmatic as Mr. Kelada and resented
bitterly the Levantine's cocksureness. The discussions they had
were acrimonious and interminable.

Ramsay was in the American Consular Service, and was
stationed at Kobe. He was a great heavy fellow from the Middle
West, with loose fat under a tight skin, and he bulged out of his
ready-made clothes. He was on his way back to resume his post,
having been on a flying visit to New York to fetch his wife, who
had been spending a year at home. Mrs. Ramsay was a very
pretty little thing, with pleasant manners and a sense of humour.
The Consular Service is ill paid, and she was dressed always very
simply; but she knew how to wear her clothes. She achieved an
effect of quiet distinction. I should not have paid any particular
attention to her but that she possessed a quality that may be
common enough in women, but nowadays is not obvious in their
demeanour. You could not look at her without being struck by
her modesty. It shone in her like a flower on a coat.

One evening at dinner the conversation by chance drifted to
the subject of pearls. There had been in the papers a good deal
of talk about the culture pearls which the cunning Japanese were
making, and the doctor remarked that they must inevitably
diminish the value of real ones. They were very good already;
they would soon be perfect. Mr. Kelada, as was his habit, rushed
the new topic. He told us all that was to be known about pearls.
I do not believe Ramsay knew anything about them at all, but
he could not resist the opportunity to have a fling at the
Levantine, and in five minutes we were in the middle of a heated
argument. I had seen Mr. Kelada vehement and voluble before, but never so voluble and vehement as now. At last something that Ramsay said stung him, for he thumped the table
and shouted:

"Well, I ought to know what I am talking about. I'm going to
Japan just to look into this Japanese pearl business. I'm in the
trade and there's not a man in it who won't tell you that what I
say about pearls goes. I know all the best pearls in the world
and what I don't know about pearls isn't worth knowing."

Here was news for us, for Mr. Kelada, with all his loquacity, had never told anyone what his business was. We only knew vaguely that he was going to Japan on some commercial errand. He looked round the table triumphantly.

"They'll never be able to get a culture pearl that an expert like me can't tell with half an eye." He pointed to a chain that Mrs. Ramsay wore. "You take my word for it, Mrs. Ramsay, that chain you're wearing will never be worth a cent less than it is now."

Mrs. Ramsay in her modest way flushed a little and slipped the chain inside her dress. Ramsay leaned forward. He gave us all a look and a smile flickered in his eyes.

"That's a pretty chain of Mrs. Ramsay's, isn't it?"

"I noticed it at once," answered Mr. Kelada. "Gee, I said to myself, those are pearls all right."

"I didn't buy it myself, of course. I'd be interested to know how much you think it cost."

"Oh, in the trade somewhere round fifteen thousand dollars. But if it was bought on Fifth Avenue I shouldn't be surprised to hear that anything up to thirty thousand was paid for it."

Ramsay smiled grimly.

"You'll be surprised to hear that Mrs. Ramsay bought that string at a department store the day before we left New York, for eighteen dollars."

Mr. Kelada flushed.

"Rot. It's not only real, but it's as fine a string for its size as I've ever seen."

"Will you bet on it? I'll bet you a hundred dollars it's imitation."

"Done."

"Oh, Elmer, you can't bet on a certainty," said Mrs. Ramsay. She had a little smile on her lips and her tone was gently deprecating.

"Can't I? If I get a chance of easy money like that I should be all sorts of a fool not to take it."

"But how can it be proved?" she continued. "It's only my word against Mr. Kelada's."

"Let me look at the chain, and if it's imitation I'll tell you quickly enough. I can afford to lose a hundred dollars," said Mr. Kelada.

"Take it off, dear. Let the gentleman look at it as much as he wants."

Mrs. Ramsay hesitated a moment. She put her hands to the clasp.

"I can't undo it," she said. "Mr. Kelada will just have to take my word for it."

I had a sudden suspicion that something unfortunate was about to occur, but I could think of nothing to say.

Ramsay jumped up.

"I'll undo it."

He handed the chain to Mr. Kelada. The Levantine took a magnifying glass from his pocket and closely examined it. A smile of triumph spread over his smooth and swarthy face. He handed back the chain. He was about to speak. Suddenly he caught sight of Mrs. Ramsay's face. It was so white that she looked as though she were about to faint. She was staring at him with wide and terrified eyes. They held a desperate appeal; it was so clear that I wondered why her husband did not see it.

Mr. Kelada stopped with his mouth open. He flushed deeply. You could almost *see* the effort he was making over himself.

"I was mistaken," he said. "It's a very good imitation, but of course as soon as I looked through my glass I saw that it wasn't real. I think eighteen dollars is just about as much as the damned thing's worth."

He took out his pocket-book and from it a hundred-dollar note. He handed it to Ramsay without a word.

"Perhaps that'll teach you not to be so cocksure another time, my young friend," said Ramsay as he took the note.

I noticed that Mr. Kelada's hands were trembling.

The story spread over the ship as stories do, and he had to put up with a good deal of chaff that evening. It was a fine joke that Mr. Know-All had been caught out. But Mrs. Ramsay retired to her state-room with a headache.

Next morning I got up and began to shave. Mr. Kelada lay on his bed smoking a cigarette. Suddenly there was a small scraping sound and I saw a letter pushed under the door. I opened the door and looked out. There was nobody there. I picked up the letter and saw that it was addressed to Max Kelada. The name was written in block letters. I handed it to him.

"Who's this from?" He opened it. "Oh!"

He took out of the envelope, not a letter, but a hundred-dollar note. He looked at me and again he reddened. He tore the envelope into little bits and gave them to me.

"Do you mind just throwing them out of the port-hole?"

I did as he asked, and then I looked at him with a smile.

"No one likes being made to look a perfect damned fool," he said.

"Were the pearls real?"

"If I had a pretty little wife I shouldn't let her spend a year in New York while I stayed at Kobe," said he.

At that moment I did not entirely dislike Mr. Kelada. He reached out for his pocket-book and carefully put in it the hundred-dollar note.

STRAIGHT FLUSH

I AM not a bad sailor and when under stress of weather the game broke up I did not go below. We were in the habit of playing poker into the small hours, a mild game that could hurt nobody, but it had been blowing all day and with nightfall the wind strengthened to half a gale. One or two of our bunch admitted that they felt none too comfortable and one or two others played with unwonted detachment. But even if you are not sick dirty weather at sea is an unpleasant thing. I hate the fool who tells you he loves a storm and tramping the deck lustily vows that it can never be too rough for him. When the woodwork groans and creaks, glasses crash to the floor and you lurch in your chair as the ship heels over, when the wind howls and the waves thunder against the side, I very much prefer dry land. I think no one was sorry when one of the players said he had had enough, and the last round of jack pots was agreed to without demur. I remained alone in the smoking-room, for I knew I should not easily get to sleep in that racket and I could not read in bed with any comfort when the North Pacific kept dashing itself against my portholes. I shuffled together the two packs we had been playing with and set out a complicated patience.

I had been playing about ten minutes when the door was opened with a blast of wind that sent my cards flying, and two passengers, rather breathless, slipped into the smoking-room. We were not a full ship and we were ten days out from Hong-Kong, so that I had had time to become acquainted with pretty

well everyone on board. I had spoken on several occasions to the
pair who now entered, and seeing me by myself they came over
to my table.

They were very old men, both of them. That perhaps was
what had brought them together, for they had first met when
they got on board at Hong-Kong, and now you saw them sitting
together in the smoking-room most of the day, not talking very
much, but just comfortable to be side by side, with a bottle of
Vichy water between them. They were very rich old men too
and that was a bond between them. The rich feel at ease in one
another's company. They know that money means merit. Their
experience of the poor is that they always want something. It is
true that the poor admire the rich and it is pleasant to be admired, but they envy them as well and this prevents their admiration from being quite candid. Mr. Rosenbaum was a little
hunched-up Jew, very frail in clothes that looked too big for
him, and he gave you the impression of hanging on to mortality
only by a hair. His ancient, emaciated body looked as though it
were already attacked by the corruption of the grave. The only
expression his face ever bore was one of cunning, but it was
purely habitual, the result of ever so many years astuteness; he
was a kindly, friendly person, very free with his drinks and
cigars, and his charity was world-famous. The other was called
Donaldson. He was a Scot, but had gone to California as a little
boy and made a great deal of money mining. He was short and
stout, with a red, clean-shaven, shiny face and no hair but a
sickle of silver above his neck, and very gentle eyes. Whatever
force he had had to make his way in the world had been worn
away by the years and he was now a picture of mild beneficence.

"I thought you'd turned in long ago," I remarked.

"I should have," returned the Scot, "only Mr. Rosenbaum
kept me up talking of old times."

"What's the good of going to bed when you can't sleep?" said
Mr. Rosenbaum.

"Walk ten times round the deck with me to-morrow morning
and you'll sleep all right."

"I've never taken any exercise in my life and I'm not going to
begin now."

"That's foolishness. You'd be twice the man you are now if
you'd taken exercise. Look at me. You'd never think I was
seventy-nine, would you?"

Mr. Rosenbaum looked critically at Mr. Donaldson.

"No, I wouldn't. You're very well preserved. You look younger than me and I'm only seventy-six. But then I never had a chance to take care of myself."

At that moment the steward came up.

"The bar's just going to close, gentlemen. Is there anything I can get you?"

"It's a stormy night," said Mr. Rosenbaum. "Let's have a bottle of champagne."

"Small Vichy for me," said Mr. Donaldson.

"Oh, very well, small Vichy for me too."

The steward went away.

"But mind you," continued Mr. Rosenbaum testily, "I wouldn't have done without the things you've done without, not for all the money in the world."

Mr. Donaldson gave me his gentle smile.

"Mr. Rosenbaum can't get over it because I've never touched a card nor a drop of alcohol for fifty-seven years."

"Now I ask you, what sort of a life is that?"

"I was a very heavy drinker when I was a young fellow and a desperate gambler, but I had a very terrible experience. It was a lesson to me and I took it."

"Tell him about it," said Mr. Rosenbaum. "He's an author. He'll write it up and perhaps he'll be able to make his passage money."

"It's not a story I like telling very much even now. I'll make it as short as I can. Me and three others had staked out a claim, friends all of us, and the oldest wasn't twenty-five; there was me and my partner and a couple of brothers, McDermott their name was, but they were more like friends than brothers. What was one's was the other's, and one wouldn't go into town without the other went too, and they were always laughing and joking together. A fine clean pair of boys, over six feet high both of them, and handsome. We were a wild bunch and we had pretty good luck on the whole and when we made money we didn't hesitate to spend it. Well, one night we'd all been drinking very heavily and we started a poker game. I guess we were a good deal drunker than we realised. Anyhow suddenly a row started between the McDermotts. One of them accused the other of cheating. 'You take that back,' cried Jamie. 'I'll see you in hell first,' says Eddie. And before me and my partner could do anything Jamie had pulled out his gun and shot his brother dead."

The ship gave a huge roll and we all clung to our seats. In the steward's pantry there was a great clatter as bottles and glasses slid along a shelf. It was strange to hear that grim little story told by that mild old man. It was a story of another age and you could hardly believe that this fat, red-faced little fellow, with his silver fringe of hair, in a dinner jacket, two large pearls in his shirt-front, had really taken part in it.

"What happened then?" I asked.

"We sobered up pretty quick. At first Jamie couldn't believe Eddie was dead. He took him in his arms and kept calling him. 'Eddie,' he says, 'wake up, old boy, wake up.' He cried all night and next day we rode in with him to town, forty miles it was, me on one side of him and my partner on the other, and handed him over to the sheriff. I was crying too when we shook hands with him and said good-bye. I told my partner I'd never touch a card again or drink as long as I lived, and I never have, and I never will."

Mr. Donaldson looked down, and his lips were trembling. He seemed to see again that scene of long ago. There was one thing I should have liked to ask him about, but he was evidently so much moved I did not like to. They seem not to have hesitated, his partner and himself, but delivered up this wretched boy to justice as though it were the most natural thing in the world. It suggested that even in those rough, wild men the respect for the law had somehow the force of an instinct. A little shiver ran through me. Mr. Donaldson emptied his glass of Vichy and with a curt good-night left us.

"The old fellow's getting a bit childish," said Mr. Rosenbaum. "I don't believe he was ever very bright."

"Well, apparently he was bright enough to make an awful lot of money."

"But how? In those days in California you didn't want brains to make money, you only wanted luck. I know what I'm talking about. Johannesburg was the place where you had to have your wits about you. Joburg in the 'eighties. It was grand. We were a tough lot of guys, I can tell you. It was each for himself and the devil take the hindmost."

He took a meditative sip of his Vichy.

"You talk of your cricket and baseball, your golf and tennis and football, you can have them, they're all very well for boys; is it a reasonable thing, I ask you, for a grown man to run about and hit a ball? Poker's the only game fit for a grown man. Then your hand is against every man and every man's hand is against yours. Team-work? Who ever made a fortune by team-work? There's only one way to make a fortune and that's to down the fellow who's up against you."

"I didn't know you were a poker player," I interrupted. "Why don't you take a hand one evening?"

"I don't play any more. I've given it up too, but for the only reason a man should. I can't see myself giving it up because a friend of mine was unlucky enough to get killed. Anyway a man who's damn fool enough to get killed isn't worth having as a friend. But in the old days! If you wanted to know what poker was you ought to have been in South Africa then. It was the biggest game I've ever seen. And they were fine players; there wasn't a crooked dodge they weren't up to. It was grand. Just to give you an example, one night I was playing with some of the biggest men in Johannesburg and I was called away. There was a couple of thousand pounds in the pot! 'Deal me a hand, I won't keep you waiting,' I said. 'All right,' they said, 'don't hurry.' Well, I wasn't gone more than a minute. When I came back I picked up my cards and saw I'd got a straight flush to the queen. I didn't say a word, I just threw in my hand. I knew my company. And do you know, I was wrong."

"What do you mean? I don't understand."

"It was a perfectly straight deal and the pot was won on three sevens. But how could I tell that? Naturally I thought someone else had a straight flush to the king. It looked to me just the sort of hand I might lose a hundred thousand pounds on."

"Too bad," I said.

"I very nearly had a stroke. And it was on account of another pat straight flush that I gave up playing poker. I've only had about five in my life."

"I believe the chances are nearly sixty-six thousand to one against."

"In San Francisco it was, the year before last. I'd been playing in poor luck all the evening. I hadn't lost much money because I never had a chance to play. I'd hardly had a pair and if I got a pair I couldn't improve. Then I got a hand just as bad as the others and I didn't come in. The man next me wasn't playing either and I showed him my hand. 'That's the kind of thing I've been getting all the evening,' I said. 'How can anyone be expected to play with cards like that?' 'Well, I don't know what more you want,' he said, as he looked at them. 'Most of us would be prepared to come in on a straight flush.' 'What's that,'

I cried. I was trembling like a leaf. I looked at the cards again. I thought I had two or three little hearts and two or three little diamonds. It was a straight flush in hearts all right and I hadn't seen it. My eyes, it was. I knew what it meant. Old age. I don't cry much. I'm not that sort of man. But I couldn't help it then. I tried to control myself, but the tears just rolled down my cheeks. Then I got up. 'I'm through, gentlemen,' I said. 'When a man's eyes are so dim that he can't see a straight flush when it's dealt him he has no business to play poker. Nature's given me a hint and I'm taking it. I'll never play poker again as long as I live.' I cashed in my chips, all but one, and I left the house. I've never played since."

Mr. Rosenbaum took a chip out of his waistcoat pocket and showed it to me.

"I kept this as a souvenir. I always carry it about with me. I'm a sentimental old fool, I know that, but, you see, poker was the only thing I cared for. Now I've only got one thing left."

"What is that?" I asked.

A smile flickered across his cunning little face and behind his thick glasses his rheumy eyes twinkled with ironic glee. He looked incredibly astute and malicious. He gave the thin, high-pitched cackle of an old man amused and answered with a single word "Philanthropy."

THE PORTRAIT OF A
GENTLEMAN

I ARRIVED in Seoul towards evening and after dinner, tired by the long railway journey from Peking, to stretch my cramped legs I went for a walk. I wandered at random along a narrow and busy street. The Koreans in their long white gowns and their little white top-hats were amusing to look at and the open shops displayed wares that arrested my foreign eyes. Presently I came to a second-hand bookseller's and catching sight of shelves filled with English books went in to have a look at them. I glanced at the titles and my heart sank. They were commentaries on the Old Testament, treatises on the Epistles of St. Paul, sermons and lives of divines doubtless eminent, but whose names were unfamiliar to me; I am an ignorant person. I supposed that this was the library of some missionary whom death had claimed in the midst of his labours and whose books then had been purchased by a Japanese bookseller. The Japanese are astute, but I could not imagine who in Seoul would be found to buy a work in three volumes on the Epistle to the Corinthians. But as I was turning away, between volume two and volume three of this treatise I noticed a little book bound in paper. I do not know what induced me to take it out. It was called the *Complete Poker Player* and its cover was illustrated with a hand holding four aces. I looked at the title-page. The author was Mr. John Blackbridge, actuary and counsellor-at-law, and the preface was dated 1879. I wondered how this work happened to be among the books of a deceased missionary and I looked in one or two of them to see if I could find his name. Perhaps it was there only by accident. It may be that it was the entire library of a stranded gambler and had found its way to those shelves when his effects were sold to pay his hotel bill. But I preferred to think that it was indeed the property of the missionary and that when he was weary of reading divinity he rested his mind by the perusal of these lively pages. Perhaps somewhere in Korea, at night and alone in his mission-house, he dealt innumerable poker hands in order to see for himself whether you could really only get a straight flush once in sixty-five thousand hands. But the owner of the shop was looking at me with disfavour so I turned to him and asked the price of the book. He gave it a contemptuous glance and told me I could have it for twenty sen. I put it in my pocket.

I do not remember that for so small a sum I have ever purchased better entertainment. For Mr. John Blackbridge in these pages of his did a thing that no writer can do who deliberately tries to, but that, if done unconsciously, gives a book a rare and precious savour; he painted a complete portrait of himself. He stands before the reader so vividly that I was convinced that a wood-cut of him figured as a frontispiece and I was surprised to discover, on looking at the book again the other day, that there was nothing of the kind. I see him very distinctly as a man of middle-age, in a black frock-coat and a chimney-pot hat, wearing a black satin stock; he is clean-shaven and his jaw is square; his lips are thin and his eyes wary; his face is sallow and somewhat wrinkled. It is a countenance not without severity, but when he tells a story or makes one of his dry jokes his eyes light up and his smile is winning. He enjoyed his bottle of Burgundy, but I cannot believe that he ever drank enough to confuse his excellent faculties. He was just rather than merciful at the card-table and he was prepared to punish presumption with rigour. He had few illusions, for here are some of the things that life had taught him: "Men hate those whom they have injured; men love those whom they have benefited; men naturally avoid their benefactors; men are universally actuated by self-interest; gratitude is a lively sense of expected benefits; promises are never forgotten by those to whom they are made, usually by those who make them."

It may be presumed that he was a Southerner, for while speaking of Jack Pots, which he describes as a frivolous attempt to make the game more interesting, he remarks that they are not popular in the South. "This last fact," he says, "contains much promise, because the South is the conservative portion of the country, and may be relied on as the last resort of good sense in social matters. The revolutionary Kossuth made no progress below Richmond; neither Spiritualism, nor Free Love, nor Communism, has ever been received with the least favour by the Southern mind; and it is for this reason that we greatly respect the Southern verdict upon the Jack Pot." It was in his day an innovation and he condemned it. "The time has arrived when all additions to the present standard combinations in Draw Poker must be worthless; the game being complete. The Jack Pot," he says, "was invented (in Toledo, Ohio) by reckless players to compensate losses incurred by playing against cautious players; and the principle is the same as if a party should play whist for stakes, and all be obliged every few minutes to stop, and purchase tickets in a lottery; or raffle for a turkey; or share a deal in Keno."

Poker is a game for gentlemen (he does not hesitate to make frequent use of this abused word; he lived in a day when to be a gentleman had its obligations but also its privileges) and a straight flush is to be respected, not because you make money on it ("I have never seen anyone make much money upon a straight flush," he says) but "because it prevents any hand from being *absolutely* the winning hand, and thus relieves gentlemen from the necessity of betting on a certainty. Without the use of straights, and hence without the use of a straight flush, four aces would be a certainty and no gentleman could do more than *call* on them." This, I confess, catches me on the raw, for once in my life I had a straight flush, and bet on it till I was called.

Mr. John Blackbridge had personal dignity, rectitude, humour and common sense. "The amusements of mankind," he says, "have not as yet received proper recognition at the hands of the makers of the civil law, and of the unwritten social law," and he had no patience with the persons who condemn the most agreeable pastime that has been invented, namely gambling, because risk is attached to it. Every transaction in life is a risk, he truly observes, and involves the question of loss and gain. "To retire to rest at night is a practice that is fortified by countless precedents, and it is generally regarded as prudent and necessary. Yet it is surrounded by risks of every kind." He enumerates them and finally sums up his argument with these reasonable words: "If social circles welcome the banker and merchant who live by taking fair risks for the sake of profit, there is no apparent reason why they should not at least tolerate the man who at times employs himself in giving and taking fair risks for the sake of amusement." But here his good sense is obvious. "Twenty years of experience in the city of New York, both professionally (you must not forget that he is an actuary and counsellor-at-law) and as a student of social life, satisfy me that the average American gentleman in a large city has not over three thousand dollars a year to spend upon amusements. Will it be fair to devote more than one-third of this fund to cards? I do not think that anyone will say that one-third is not ample allowance for a single amusement. Given, therefore, a thousand dollars a year for the purpose of playing Draw Poker, what should be the limit of the stakes, in order that the average American gentleman may play the game with a contented mind, and with the certainty not only that he can pay his losses, but that his winnings will be paid to him?" Mr. Blackbridge has no doubt that the answer is two dollars and a half. "The game of Poker should be intellectual and not emotional; and it is impossible to exclude the emotions from it, if the stakes are so high that the question of loss and gain penetrates to the feelings." From this quotation it may be seen that Mr. Blackbridge looked upon poker as only on the side a game of chance. He considered that it needed as much force of character, mental ability, power of decision and insight into motive to play poker as to govern a country or to lead an army, and I have an idea that on the whole he would have thought it a more sensible use of a man's faculties.

I am tempted to quote interminably, for Mr. Blackbridge seldom writes a sentence that is other than characteristic, and his language is excellent; it is dignified as befits his subject and his condition (he does not forget that he is a gentleman), measured, clear and pointed. His phrase takes an ample sweep when he treats of mankind and its foibles, but he can be as direct and simple as you please. Could anything be better than this terse but adequate description of a card-sharper? "He was a very good-looking man of about forty years of age, having the appearance of one who had been leading a temperate and thoughtful life." But I will content myself with giving a few of his aphorisms and wise saws chosen almost at random from the wealth of his book.

"Let your chips talk for you. A silent player is so far forth, a mystery; and a mystery is always feared."

"In this game never do anything that you are not compelled to; while cheerfully responding to your obligations."

"At Draw Poker all statements not called for by the laws of the game, or supported by ocular demonstration, may be set down as fictitious; designed to enliven the path of truth throughout the game, as flowers in summer enliven the margins of the highway."

"Lost money is never recovered. After losing you may win, but the losing does not bring the winning."

"No gentleman will ever play any game of cards with the design of habitually winning and never losing."

"A gentleman is always willing to pay a fair price for recreation and amusement."

". . . that habit of mind which continually leads us to under-value the mental force of other men, while we continually over-value their good luck."

"The injury done to your capital by a loss is never compensated by the benefit done to your capital by a gain of the same amount."

"Players usually straddle when they are in bad luck, upon the principle that bad play and bad luck united will win. A slight degree of intoxication aids to perfect this intellectual deduction."

"Euchre is a contemptible game."

"The lower cards as well as the lower classes are only useful in combination or in excess, and cannot be depended upon under any other circumstances."

"It is a hard matter to hold four Aces as steadily as a pair, but the table will bear their weight with as much equanimity as a pair of deuces."

Of good luck and bad luck: "To feel emotions over such incidents is unworthy of a man; and it is much more unworthy to express them. But no words need be wasted over practices which all men despise in others; and, in their reflecting moments, lament in themselves."

"Endorsing for your friends is a bad habit, but it is nothing to playing Poker on credit. . . . Debit and credit ought never to interfere with the fine intellectual calculations of this game."

There is a grand ring in his remarks on the player who has trained his intellect to bring logic to bear upon the principles and phenomena of the game. "He will thus feel a constant sense of security amid all possible fluctuations that occur, and he will also abstain from pressing an ignorant or an intellectually weak opponent, beyond what may be necessary either for the purpose of playing the game correctly, or of punishing presumption."

I leave Mr. John Blackbridge with this last word and I can hear him saying it gently, but with a tolerant smile:

"For we must take human nature as it is."

RAW MATERIAL

I HAVE long had in mind a novel in which a card-sharper was the principal character; and, going up and down the world, I have kept my eyes open for members of this profession. Because the idea is prevalent that it is a slightly dishonourable one the persons who follow it do not openly acknowledge the fact. Their reticence is such that it is often not till you have become quite closely acquainted with them, or even have played cards with them two or three times, that you discover in what fashion they earn their living. But even then they have a disinclination to enlarge upon the mysteries of their craft. They have a weakness for passing themselves off for cavalrymen, commercial agents or landed proprietors. This snobbish attitude makes them the most difficult class in the world for the novelist to study. It has been my good fortune to meet a number of these gentlemen, and though I have found them affable, obliging and debonair, I have no sooner hinted, however discreetly, at my curiosity (after all purely professional) in the technique of their calling than they have grown shy and uncommunicative. An airy reference on my part to stacking the cards has made them assume immediately the appearance of a clam. I am not easily discouraged, and learning by experience that I could hope for no good results from a direct method, I have adopted the oblique. I have been childlike with them and bland. I have found that they gave me their attention and even their sympathy. Though

they confessed honestly that they had never read a word I had
written they were interested by the fact that I was a writer. I
suppose they felt obscurely that I too followed a calling that the
Philistine regarded without indulgence. But I have been forced
to gather my facts by a bold surmise. It has needed patience and
industry.

It may be imagined with what enthusiasm I made the acquaintance a little while ago of two gentlemen who seemed likely
to add appreciably to my small store of information. I was
travelling from Haiphong on a French liner going East, and they
joined the ship at Hong-Kong. They had gone there for the
races and were now on their way back to Shanghai. I was going
there too, and thence to Peking. I soon learned that they had
come from New York for a trip, were bound for Peking also,
and by a happy coincidence meant to return to America in the
ship in which I had myself booked a passage. I was naturally
attracted to them, for they were pleasant fellows, but it was not
till a fellow-passenger warned me that they were professional
gamblers that I settled down to complete enjoyment of their acquaintance. I had no hope that they would ever discuss with
frankness their interesting occupation, but I expected from a
hint here, from a casual remark there, to learn some very useful
things.

One—Campbell was his name—was a man in the late thirties,
small, but so well built as not to look short, slender, with large,
melancholy eyes and beautiful hands. But for a premature baldness he would have been more than commonly good-looking. He
was neatly dressed. He spoke slowly, in a low voice, and his
movements were deliberate. The other was made on another
pattern. He was a big, burly man with a red face and crisp black
hair, of powerful appearance, strong in the arm and pugnacious.
His name was Peterson.

The merits of the combination were obvious. The elegant,
exquisite Campbell had the subtle brain, the knowledge of character, and the deft hands; but the hazards of the card-sharper's
life are many, and when it came to a scrap Peterson's ready
fist must often have proved invaluable. I do not know how it
spread through the ship so quickly that a blow of Peterson's
would stretch any man out. But during the short voyage from
Hong-Kong to Shanghai they never even suggested a game of
cards. Perhaps they had done well during the race-week and
felt entitled to a holiday. They were certainly enjoying the ad-

vantages of not living for the time in a dry country and I do
not think I do them an injustice if I say that for the most part
they were far from sober. Each one talked little of himself but
willingly of the other. Campbell informed me that Peterson was
one of the most distinguished mining engineers in New York
and Peterson assured me that Campbell was an eminent banker.
He said that his wealth was fabulous. And who was I not to accept ingenuously all that was told me? But I thought it negli-
gent of Campbell not to wear jewellery of a more expensive
character. It seemed to me that to use a silver cigarette case was
rather careless.

I stayed but a day in Shanghai, and though I met the pair
again in Peking I was then so much engaged that I saw little of
them. I thought it a little odd that Campbell should spend his
entire time in the hotel. I do not think he even went to see the
Temple of Heaven. But I could quite understand that from
his point of view Peking was unsatisfactory and I was not surprised when the pair returned to Shanghai, where, I knew the
wealthy merchants played for big money. I met them again in
the ship that was to take us across the Pacific and I could not
but sympathise with my friends when I saw that the passengers
were little inclined to gamble. There were no rich people among
them. It was a dull crowd. Campbell indeed suggested a game
of poker, but no one would play more than twenty-dollar table
stakes, and Peterson, evidently not thinking it worth his while,
would not join. Although we played afternoon and evening
through the journey he sat down with us only on the last day.
I suppose he thought he might just as well make his bar chits,
and this he did very satisfactorily in a single sitting. But Campbell evidently loved the game for itself. Of course it is only if
you have a passion for the business by which you earn your
living that you can make a success of it. The stakes were nothing to him and he played all day and every day. It fascinated me
to see the way in which he dealt the cards, very slowly, with
his delicate hands. His eyes seemed to bore through the back
of each one. He drank heavily, but remained quiet and self-
controlled. His face was expressionless. I judged him to be a
perfect card-player and I wished that I could see him at work.
It increased my esteem for him to see that he could take what
was only a relaxation so seriously.

I parted with the pair at Victoria and concluded that I should
never see them again. I set about sorting my impressions and

made notes of the various points that I thought would prove useful.

When I arrived in New York I found an invitation to luncheon at the Ritz with an old friend of mine. When I went she said to me:

"It's quite a small party. A man is coming whom I think you'll like. He's a prominent banker; he's bringing a friend with him."

The words were hardly out of her mouth when I saw coming up to us Campbell and Peterson. The truth flashed across me: Campbell really was an opulent banker; Peterson really was a distinguished engineer; they were not card-sharpers at all. I flatter myself I kept my face, but as I blandly shook hands with them I muttered under my breath furiously:

"Impostors!"

A FRIEND IN NEED

FOR THIRTY YEARS now I have been studying my fellow-men. I do not know very much about them. I should certainly hesitate to engage a servant on his face, and yet I suppose it is on the face that for the most part we judge the persons we meet. We draw our conclusions from the shape of the jaw, the look in the eyes, the contour of the mouth. I wonder if we are more often right than wrong. Why novels and plays are so often untrue to life is because their authors, perhaps of necessity, make their characters all of a piece. They cannot afford to make them self-contradictory, for then they become incomprehensible, and yet self-contradictory is what most of us are. We are a haphazard bundle of inconsistent qualities. In books on logic they will tell you that it is absurd to say that yellow is tubular or gratitude heavier than air; but in that mixture of incongruities that makes up the self yellow may very well be a horse and cart and gratitude the middle of next week. I shrug my shoulders when people tell me that their first impressions of a person are always right. I think they must have small insight or great vanity. For my own part I find that the longer I know people the more they puzzle me: my oldest friends are just those of whom I can say that I don't know the first thing about them.

These reflections have occurred to me because I read in this morning's paper that Edward Hyde Burton had died at Kobe. He was a merchant and he had been in business in Japan for many years. I knew him very little, but he interested me because once he gave me a great surprise. Unless I had heard the story from his own lips I should never have believed that he was capable of such an action. It was more startling because both in appearance and manner he suggested a very definite type. Here if ever was a man all of a piece. He was a tiny little fellow, not much more than five feet four in height, and very slender, with white hair, a red face much wrinkled, and blue eyes. I suppose he was about sixty when I knew him. He was always neatly and quietly dressed in accordance with his age and station.

Though his offices were in Kobe Burton often came down to Yokohama. I happened on one occasion to be spending a few days there, waiting for a ship, and I was introduced to him at the British Club. We played bridge together. He played a good game and a generous one. He did not talk very much, either then or later when we were having drinks, but what he said was sensible. He had a quiet, dry humour. He seemed to be popular at the club and afterwards, when he had gone, they described him as one of the best. It happened that we were both staying at the Grand Hotel and next day he asked me to dine with him. I met his wife, fat, elderly and smiling, and his two daughters. It was evidently a united and affectionate family. I think the chief thing that struck me about Burton was his kindliness. There was something very pleasing in his mild blue eyes. His voice was gentle; you could not imagine that he could possibly raise it in anger; his smile was benign. Here was a man who attracted you because you felt in him a real love for his fellows. He had charm. But there was nothing mawkish in him: he liked his game of cards and his cocktail, he could tell with point a good and spicy story, and in his youth he had been something of an athlete. He was a rich man and he had made every penny himself. I suppose one thing that made you like him was that he was so small and frail; he aroused your instincts of protection. You felt that he could not bear to hurt a fly.

One afternoon I was sitting in the lounge of the Grand Hotel. This was before the earthquake and they had leather arm-chairs there. From the windows you had a spacious view of the harbour with its crowded traffic. There were great liners on their way to Vancouver and San Francisco or to Europe by way of Shanghai, Hong-Kong and Singapore; there were tramps of all nations, battered and sea-worn, junks with their high sterns and great coloured sails, and innumerable sampans. It was a busy, exhilarating scene, and yet, I know not why, restful to the spirit. Here was romance and it seemed that you had but to stretch out your hand to touch it.

Burton came into the lounge presently and caught sight of me. He seated himself in the chair next to mine.

"What do you say to a little drink?"

He clapped his hands for a boy and ordered two gin fizzes. As the boy brought them a man passed along the street outside and seeing me waved his hand.

"Do you know Turner?" said Burton as I nodded a greeting.

"I've met him at the club. I'm told he's a remittance man."

"Yes, I believe he is. We have a good many here."

"He plays bridge well."

"They generally do. There was a fellow here last year, oddly enough a namesake of mine, who was the best bridge player I ever met. I suppose you never came across him in London. Lenny Burton he called himself. I believe he'd belonged to some very good clubs."

"No, I don't believe I remember the name."

"He was quite a remarkable player. He seemed to have an instinct about the cards. It was uncanny. I used to play with him a lot. He was in Kobe for some time."

Burton sipped his gin fizz.

"It's rather a funny story," he said. "He wasn't a bad chap. I liked him. He was always well-dressed and smart-looking. He was handsome in a way with curly hair and pink-and-white cheeks. Women thought a lot of him. There was no harm in him, you know, he was only wild. Of course he drank too much. Those sort of fellows always do. A bit of money used to come in for him once a quarter and he made a bit more by card-playing. He won a good deal of mine, I know that."

Burton gave a kindly chuckle. I knew from my own experience that he could lose money at bridge with a good grace. He stroked his shaven chin with his thin hand; the veins stood out on it and it was almost transparent.

"I suppose that is why he came to me when he went broke, that and the fact that he was a namesake of mine. He came to see me in my office one day and asked me for a job. I was rather surprised. He told me that there was no more money coming from home and he wanted to work. I asked him how old he was.

" 'Thirty-five,' he said.

" 'And what have you been doing hitherto?' I asked him.

" 'Well, nothing very much,' he said.

"I couldn't help laughing.

" 'I'm afraid I can't do anything for you just yet,' I said.
'Come back and see me in another thirty-five years, and I'll see
what I can do.'

"He didn't move. He went rather pale. He hesitated for a
moment and then he told me that he had had bad luck at cards
for some time. He hadn't been willing to stick to bridge, he'd
been playing poker, and he'd got trimmed. He hadn't a penny.
He'd pawned everything he had. He couldn't pay his hotel bill
and they wouldn't give him any more credit. He was down and
out. If he couldn't get something to do he'd have to commit
suicide.

"I looked at him for a bit. I could see now that he was all to
pieces. He'd been drinking more than usual and he looked fifty.
The girls wouldn't have thought so much of him if they'd seen
him then.

" 'Well, isn't there anything you can do except play cards?'
I asked him.

" 'I can swim,' he said.

" 'Swim!'

"I could hardly believe my ears; it seemed such an insane
answer to give.

" 'I swam for my university.'

"I got some glimmering of what he was driving at. I've known
too many men who were little tin gods at their university to be
impressed by it.

" 'I was a pretty good swimmer myself when I was a young
man,' I said.

"Suddenly I had an idea."

Pausing in his story, Burton turned to me.

"Do you know Kobe?" he asked.

"No," I said, "I passed through it once, but I only spent a
night there."

"Then you don't know the Shioya Club. When I was a young
man I swam from there round the beacon and landed at the
creek of Tarumi. It's over three miles and it's rather difficult
on account of the currents round the beacon. Well, I told my
young namesake about it and I said to him that if he'd do it I'd
give him a job.

"I could see he was rather taken aback.

" 'You say you're a swimmer,' I said.

" 'I'm not in very good condition,' he answered.

"I didn't say anything. I shrugged my shoulders. He looked at me for a moment and then he nodded.

" 'All right,' he said. 'When do you want me to do it?' "

"I looked at my watch. It was just after ten.

" 'The swim shouldn't take you much over an hour and a quarter. I'll drive round to the creek at half-past twelve and meet you. I'll take you back to the club to dress and then we'll have lunch together.'

" 'Done,' he said.

"We shook hands. I wished him good luck and he left me. I had a lot of work to do that morning and I only just managed to get to the creek at Tarumi at half-past twelve. But I needn't have hurried; he never turned up."

"Did he funk it at the lost moment?" I asked.

"No, he didn't funk it. He started all right. But of course he'd ruined his constitution by drink and dissipation. The currents round the beacon were more than he could manage. We didn't get the body for about three days."

I didn't say anything for a moment or two. I was a trifle shocked. Then I asked Burton a question.

"When you made him that offer of a job, did you know he'd be drowned?"

He gave a little mild chuckle and he looked at me with those kind and candid blue eyes of his. He rubbed his chin with his hand.

"Well, I hadn't got a vacancy in my office at the moment."

THE DREAM

It chanced that in August, 1917, the work upon which I was then engaged obliged me to go from New York to Petrograd and I was instructed for safety's sake to travel by way of Vladivostok. I landed there in the morning and passed an idle day as best I could. The trans-Siberian train was due to start, so far as I remember, at about nine in the evening. I dined at the station restaurant by myself. It was crowded and I shared a small table with a man whose appearance entertained me. He was a Russian, a tall fellow, but amazingly stout, and he had so vast a paunch that he was obliged to sit well away from the table. His hands, small for his size, were buried in rolls of fat. His hair, long, dark and thin, was brushed carefully across his crown in order to conceal his baldness, and his huge sallow face, with its enormous double chin, clean-shaven, gave you an impression of indecent nakedness. His nose was small, a funny little button. upon that mass of flesh, and his black shining eyes were small too. But he had a large, red and sensual mouth. He was dressed neatly enough in a black suit. It was not worn but shabby; it looked as if it had been neither pressed nor brushed since he had had it.

The service was bad and it was almost impossible to attract the attention of a waiter. We soon got into conversation. The Russian spoke good and fluent English. His accent was marked but not tiresome. He asked me many questions about myself and my plans, which—my occupation at the time making caution necessary—I answered with a show of frankness but with dissimulation. I told him I was a journalist. He asked me whether I wrote fiction and when I confessed that in my leisure moments I did, he began to talk of the later Russian novelists. He spoke intelligently. It was plain that he was a man of education.

By this time we had persuaded the waiter to bring us some cabbage soup, and my acquaintance pulled a small bottle of vodka from his pocket which he invited me to share. I do not know whether it was the vodka or the natural loquaciousness of his race that made him communicative, but presently he told me, unasked, a good deal about himself. He was of noble birth, it appeared, a lawyer by profession, and a radical. Some trouble with the authorities had made it necessary for him to be much abroad, but now he was on his way home. Business had detained him at Vladivostok, but he expected to start for Moscow in a week and if I went there he would be charmed to see me.

"Are you married?" he asked me.

I did not see what business it was of his, but I told him that I was. He sighed a little.

"I am a widower," he said. "My wife was a Swiss, a native of Geneva. She was a very cultivated woman. She spoke English, German and Italian perfectly. French, of course, was her native tongue. Her Russian was much above the average for a foreigner. She had scarcely the trace of an accent."

He called a waiter who was passing with a tray full of dishes and asked him, I suppose—for then I knew hardly any Russian —how much longer we were going to wait for the next course. The waiter, with a rapid but presumably reassuring exclamation, hurried on, and my friend sighed.

"Since the revolution the waiting in restaurants has become abominable."

He lighted his twentieth cigarette and I, looking at my watch, wondered whether I should get a square meal before it was time for me to start.

"My wife was a very remarkable woman," he continued. "She taught languages at one of the best schools for the daughters of noblemen in Petrograd. For a good many years we lived together on perfectly friendly terms. She was, however, of a jealous temperament and unfortunately she loved me to distraction."

It was difficult for me to keep a straight face. He was one of the ugliest men I had ever seen. There is sometimes a certain charm in the rubicund and jovial fat man, but this saturnine obesity was repulsive.

"I do not pretend that I was faithful to her. She was not young when I married her and we had been married for ten years. She was small and thin, and she had a bad complexion. She had a bitter tongue. She was a woman who suffered from a fury of possession, and she could not bear me to be attracted to anyone but her. She was jealous not only of the women I knew, but of my friends, my cat and my books. On one occasion in my absence she gave away a coat of mine merely because I liked none of my coats so well. But I am of equable temperament. I will not deny that she bored me, but I accepted her acrimonious disposition as an act of God and no more thought of rebelling against it than I would against bad weather or a cold in the head. I denied her accusations as long as it was possible to deny them, and when it was impossible I shrugged my shoulders and smoked a cigarette.

"The constant scenes she made me did not very much affect me. I led my own life. Sometimes, indeed, I wondered whether it was passionate love she felt for me or passionate hate. It seemed to me that love and hate were very near allied.

"So we might have continued to the end of the chapter if one night a very curious thing had not happened. I was awakened by a piercing scream from my wife. Startled, I asked her what was the matter. She told me that she had had a fearful nightmare; she had dreamt that I was trying to kill her. We lived at the top of a large house and the well round which the stairs climbed was broad. She had dreamt that just as we had arrived at our own floor I had caught hold of her and attempted to throw her over the balusters. It was six storeys to the stone floor at the bottom and it meant certain death.

"She was much shaken. I did my best to soothe her. But next morning, and for two or three days after, she referred to the subject again and, notwithstanding my laughter, I saw that it dwelt in her mind. I could not help thinking of it either, for this dream showed me something that I had never suspected. She thought I hated her, she thought I would gladly be rid of her; she knew of course that she was insufferable, and at some time or other the idea had evidently occurred to her that I was capable of murdering her. The thoughts of men are incalculable and ideas enter our minds that we should be ashamed to confess. Sometimes I had wished that she might run away with a lover, sometimes that a painless and sudden death might give me my freedom; but never, never had the idea come to me that I might deliberately rid myself of an intolerable burden.

"The dream made an extraordinary impression upon both of us. It frightened my wife, and she became for a little less bitter and more tolerant. But when I walked up the stairs to our apartment it was impossible for me not to look over the balusters and reflect how easy it would be to do what she had dreamt. The balusters were dangerously low. A quick gesture and the thing was done. It was hard to put the thought out of my mind. Then some months later my wife awakened me one night. I was very tired and I was exasperated. She was white and trembling. She had had the dream again. She burst into tears and asked me if I hated her. I swore by all the saints of the Russian calendar that I loved her. At last she went to sleep again. It was more than I could do. I lay awake. I seemed to see her falling down the well of the stairs, and I heard her shriek and the thud as she struck the stone floor. I could not help shivering."

The Russian stopped and beads of sweat stood on his forehead. He had told the story well and fluently so that I had listened with attention. There was still some vodka in the bottle; he poured it out and swallowed it at a gulp.

"And how did your wife eventually die?" I asked after a pause.

He took out a dirty handkerchief and wiped his forehead.

"By an extraordinary coincidence she was found late one night at the bottom of the stairs with her neck broken."

"Who found her?"

"She was found by one of the lodgers who came in shortly after the catastrophe."

"And where were you?"

I cannot describe the look he gave me of malicious cunning. His little black eyes sparkled.

"I was spending the evening with a friend of mine. I did not come in till an hour later."

At that moment the waiter brought us the dish of meat that we had ordered, and the Russian fell upon it with good appetite. He shovelled the food into his mouth in enormous mouthfuls.

I was taken aback. Had he really been telling me in this hardly veiled manner that he had murdered his wife? That obese and sluggish man did not look like a murderer; I could not

believe that he would have had the courage. Or was he making a
sardonic joke at my expense?

In a few minutes it was time for me to go and catch my train.
I left him and I have not seen him since. But I have never been
able to make up my mind whether he was serious or jesting.

THE TAIPAN

No ONE knew better than he that he was an important person. He was number one in not the least important branch of the most important English firm in China. He had worked his way up through solid ability and he looked back with a faint smile at the callow clerk who had come out to China thirty years before. When he remembered the modest home he had come from, a little red house in a long row of little red houses, in Barnes, a suburb which, aiming desperately at the genteel, achieves only a sordid melancholy, and compared it with the magnificent stone mansion, with its wide verandahs and spacious rooms, which was at once the office of the company and his own residence, he chuckled with satisfaction. He had come a long way since then. He thought of the high tea to which he sat down when he came home from school (he was at St. Paul's), with his father and mother and his two sisters, a slice of cold meat, a great deal of bread and butter and plenty of milk in his tea, everybody helping himself, and then he thought of the state in which now he ate his evening meal. He always dressed and whether he was alone or not he expected the three boys to wait at table. His number one boy knew exactly what he liked and he never had to bother himself with the details of housekeeping; but he always had a set dinner with soup and fish, entrée, roast, sweet and savoury, so that if he wanted to ask anyone in at the last moment he could. He liked his food and he did not see why when he was alone he should have less good a dinner than when he had a guest.

He had indeed gone far. That was why he did not care to go home now, he had not been to England for ten years, and he took his leave in Japan or Vancouver, where he was sure of meeting old friends from the China coast. He knew no one at home. His sisters had married in their own station, their husbands were clerks and their sons were clerks; there was nothing between him and them; they bored him. He satisfied the claims of relationship by sending them every Christmas a piece of fine silk, some elaborate embroidery, or a case of tea. He was not a mean man and as long as his mother lived he had made her an allowance. But when the time came for him to retire he had no intention of going back to England, he had seen too many men do that and he knew how often it was a failure; he meant to take a house near the racecourse in Shanghai: what with bridge and his ponies and golf he expected to get through the rest of his life very comfortably. But he had a good many years before he need think of retiring. In another five or six Higgins would be going home and then he would take charge of the head office in Shanghai. Meanwhile he was very happy where he was, he could save money, which you couldn't do in Shanghai, and have a good time into the bargain. This place had another advantage over Shanghai: he was the most prominent man in the community and what he said went. Even the consul took care to keep on the right side of him. Once a consul and he had been at loggerheads and it was not he who had gone to the wall. The taipan thrust out his jaw pugnaciously as he thought of the incident.

But he smiled, for he felt in an excellent humour. He was walking back to his office from a capital luncheon at the Hong-Kong and Shanghai Bank. They did you very well there. The food was first-rate and there was plenty of liquor. He had started with a couple of cocktails, then he had some excellent sauterne and he had finished up with two glasses of port and some fine old brandy. He felt good. And when he left he did a thing that was rare with him; he walked. His bearers with his chair kept a few paces behind him in case he felt inclined to slip into it, but he enjoyed stretching his legs. He did not get enough exercise these days. Now that he was too heavy to ride it was difficult to get exercise. But if he was too heavy to ride he could still keep ponies, and as he strolled along in the balmy air he thought of the spring meeting. He had a couple of griffins that he had hopes of and one of the lads in his office had turned out a fine jockey (he must see they didn't sneak him away, old Higgins in Shanghai would give a pot of money to get him over there) and he ought to pull off two or three races. He flattered himself that he had the finest stable in the city. He pouted his broad chest like a pigeon. It was a beautiful day, and it was good to be alive.

He paused as he came to the cemetery. It stood there, neat and orderly, as an evident sign of the community's opulence. He never passed the cemetery without a little glow of pride. He was pleased to be an Englishman. For the cemetery stood in a place, valueless when it was chosen, which with the increase of the city's affluence was now worth a great deal of money. It had been suggested that the graves should be moved to another spot and the land sold for building, but the feeling of the community was against it. It gave the taipan a sense of satisfaction to think that their dead rested on the most valuable site on the island. It showed that there were things they cared for more than money. Money be blowed! When it came to "the things that mattered" (this was a favourite phrase with the taipan), well, one remembered that money wasn't everything.

And now he thought he would take a stroll through. He looked at the graves. They were neatly kept and the pathways were free from weeds. There was a look of prosperity. And as he sauntered along he read the names on the tombstones. Here were three side by side; the captain, the first mate, and the second mate of the barque *Mary Baxter,* who had all perished together in the typhoon of 1908. He remembered it well. There was a little group of two missionaries, their wives and children, who had been massacred during the Boxer troubles. Shocking thing that had been! Not that he took much stock in missionaries; but, hang it all, one couldn't have these damned Chinese massacring them. Then he came to a cross with a name on it he knew. Good chap, Edward Mulock, but he couldn't stand his liquor, drank himself to death, poor devil, at twenty-five; the taipan had known a lot of them do that; there were several more neat crosses with a man's name on them and the age, twenty-five, twenty-six, or twenty-seven; it was always the same story: they had come out to China; they had never seen so much money before, they were good fellows and they wanted to drink with the rest: they couldn't stand it, and there they were in the cemetery. You had to have a strong head and a fine constitution to drink drink for drink on the China coast. Of course it was very sad, but the taipan could hardly help a smile when he thought how many of those young fellows he had drunk underground. And there was a death that had been useful, a fellow in his own firm, senior to him and a clever chap too: if that fellow had lived he might not have been taipan now. Truly the ways of fate were inscrutable. Ah, and here was little Mrs. Turner, Violet Turner, she had been a pretty little thing, he had had quite an affair with her; he had been devilish cut up when she died. He looked at her age on the tombstone. She'd be no chicken if she were alive now. And as he thought of all those dead people a sense of satisfaction spread through him. He had beaten them all. They were dead and he was alive, and by George he'd scored them off. His eyes collected in one picture all those crowded graves and he smiled scornfully. He very nearly rubbed his hands.

"No one ever thought I was a fool," he muttered.

He had a feeling of good-natured contempt for the gibbering dead. Then, as he strolled along, he came suddenly upon two coolies digging a grave. He was astonished, for he had not heard that anyone in the community was dead.

"Who the devil's that for?" he said aloud.

The coolies did not even look at him, they went on with their work, standing in the grave, deep down, and they shovelled up heavy clods of earth. Though he had been so long in China he knew no Chinese, in his day it was not thought necessary to learn the damned language, and he asked the coolies in English whose grave they were digging. They did not understand. They answered him in Chinese and he cursed them for ignorant fools. He knew that Mrs. Broome's child was ailing and it might have died, but he would certainly have heard of it, and besides, that wasn't a child's grave, it was a man's and a big man's too. It was uncanny. He wished he hadn't gone into that cemetery; he hurried out and stepped into his chair. His good-humour had all gone and there was an uneasy frown on his face. The moment he got back to his office he called to his number two:

"I say, Peters, who's dead, d'you know?"

But Peters knew nothing. The taipan was puzzled. He called one of the native clerks and sent him to the cemetery to ask the coolies. He began to sign his letters. The clerk came back and said the coolies had gone and there was no one to ask. The taipan began to feel vaguely annoyed: he did not iike things to happen of which he knew nothing. His own boy would know, his boy always knew everything, and he sent for him; but the boy had heard of no death in the community.

"I knew no one was dead," said the taipan irritably. "But what's the grave for?"

He told the boy to go to the overseer of the cemetery and find out what the devil he had dug a grave for when no one was dead.

"Let me have a whisky and soda before you go," he added, as the boy was leaving the room.

He did not know why the sight of the grave had made him uncomfortable. But he tried to put it out of his mind. He felt better when he had drunk the whisky, and he finished his work. He went upstairs and turned over the pages of *Punch*. In a few minutes he would go to the club and play a rubber or two of bridge before dinner. But it would ease his mind to hear what his boy had to say and he waited for his return. In a little while the boy came back and he brought the overseer with him.

"What are you having a grave dug for?" he asked the overseer point-blank. "Nobody's dead."

"I no dig glave," said the man.

"What the devil do you mean by that? There were two coolies digging a grave this afternoon."

The two Chinese looked at one another. Then the boy said they had been to the cemetery together. There was no new grave there.

The taipan only just stopped himself from speaking.

"But damn it all, I saw it myself," were the words on the tip of his tongue.

But he did not say them. He grew very red as he choked them down. The two Chinese looked at him with their steady eyes. For a moment his breath failed him.

"All right. Get out," he gasped.

But as soon as they were gone he shouted for the boy again, and when he came, maddeningly impassive, he told him to bring some whisky. He rubbed his sweating face with a handkerchief. His hand trembled when he lifted the glass to his lips. They could say what they liked, but he had seen the grave. Why, he could hear still the dull thud as the coolies threw the spadefuls of earth on the ground above them. What did it mean? He could feel his heart beating. He felt strangely ill at ease. But he pulled himself together. It was all nonsense. If there was no grave there

it must have been an hallucination. The best thing he could do
was to go to the club, and if he ran across the doctor he would
ask him to give him a look over.

Everyone in the club looked just the same as ever. He did not
know why he should have expected them to look different. It
was a comfort. These men, living for many years with one another lives that were methodically regulated, had acquired a
number of little idiosyncrasies—one of them hummed incessantly while he played bridge, another insisted on drinking beer
through a straw—and these tricks which had so often irritated
the taipan now gave him a sense of security. He needed it, for
he could not get out of his head that strange sight he had seen;
he played bridge very badly; his partner was censorious, and the
taipan lost his temper. He thought the men were looking at him
oddly. He wondered what they saw in him that was unaccustomed.

Suddenly he felt he could not bear to stay in the club any
longer. As he went out he saw the doctor reading *The Times* in
the reading-room, but he could not bring himself to speak to
him. He wanted to see for himself whether that grave was really
there and stepping into his chair he told his bearers to take him
to the cemetery. You couldn't have an hallucination twice, could
you? And besides, he would take the overseer in with him and
if the grave was not there he wouldn't see it, and if it was he'd
give the overseer the soundest thrashing he'd ever had. But
the overseer was nowhere to be found. He had gone out and
taken the keys with him. When the taipan found he could not
get into the cemetery he felt suddenly exhausted. He got back
into his chair and told his bearers to take him home. He would
lie down for half an hour before dinner. He was tired out. That
was it. He had heard that people had hallucinations when they
were tired. When his boy came in to put out his clothes for
dinner it was only by an effort of will that he got up. He had a
strong inclination not to dress that evening, but he resisted it:
he made it a rule to dress, he had dressed every evening for
twenty years and it would never do to break his rule. But he
ordered a bottle of champagne with his dinner and that made
him feel more comfortable. Afterwards he told the boy to bring
him the best brandy. When he had drunk a couple of glasses
of this he felt himself again. Hallucinations be damned! He
went to the billiard-room and practised a few difficult shots.
There could not be much the matter with him when his eye was

so sure. When he went to bed he sank immediately into a sound sleep.

But suddenly he awoke. He had dreamed of that open grave and the coolies digging leisurely. He was sure he had seen them. It was absurd to say it was an hallucination when he had seen them with his own eyes. Then he heard the rattle of the night-watchman going his rounds. It broke upon the stillness of the night so harshly that it made him jump out of his skin. And then terror seized him. He felt a horror of the winding multitudinous streets of the Chinese city, and there was something ghastly and terrible in the convoluted roofs of the temples with their devils grimacing and tortured. He loathed the smells that assaulted his nostrils. And the people. Those myriads of blue-clad coolies, and the beggars in their filthy rags, and the merchants and the magistrates, sleek, smiling, and inscrutable, in their long black gowns. They seemed to press upon him with menace. He hated the country. China. Why had he ever come? He was panic-stricken now. He must get out. He would not stay another year, another month. What did he care about Shanghai?

"Oh, my God," he cried, "if I were only safely back in England."

He wanted to go home. If he had to die he wanted to die in England. He could not bear to be buried among all these yellow men, with their slanting eyes and their grinning faces. He wanted to be buried at home, not in that grave he had seen that day. He could never rest there. Never. What did it matter what people thought? Let them think what they liked. The only thing that mattered was to get away while he had the chance.

He got out of bed and wrote to the head of the firm and said he had discovered he was dangerously ill. He must be replaced. He could not stay longer than was absolutely necessary. He must go home at once.

They found the letter in the morning clenched in the taipan's hand. He had slipped down between the desk and the chair. He was stone dead.

THE CONSUL

Mr. Pete was in a state of the liveliest exasperation. He had been in the consular service for more than twenty years and he had had to deal with all manner of vexatious people, officials who would not listen to reason, merchants who took the British Government for a debt-collecting agency, missionaries who resented as gross injustice any attempt at fair play; but he never recollected a case which had left him more completely at a loss. He was a mild-mannered man, but for no reason he flew into a passion with his writer and he very nearly sacked the Eurasian clerk because he had wrongly spelt two words in a letter placed before him for his official signature. He was a conscientious man and he could not persuade himself to leave his office before the clock struck four, but the moment it did he jumped up and called for his hat and stick. Because his boy did not bring them at once he abused him roundly. They say that the consuls all grow a little odd; and the merchants who can live for thirty-five years in China without learning enough of the language to ask their way in the street say that it is because they have to study Chinese; and there was no doubt that Mr. Pete was decidedly odd. He was a bachelor and on that account had been sent to a series of posts which by reason of their isolation were thought unsuited to married men. He had lived so much alone that his natural tendency to eccentricity had developed to an extravagant degree, and he had habits which surprised the stranger. He was very absent-minded. He paid no attention to his house,

which was always in great disorder, nor to his food; his boys
gave him to eat what they liked and for everything he had made
him pay through the nose. He was untiring in his efforts to suppress the opium traffic, but he was the only person in the city
who did not know that his servants kept opium in the consulate
itself, and a busy traffic in the drug was openly conducted at the
back door of the compound. He was an ardent collector and the
house provided for him by the government was filled with the
various things which he had collected one after the other,
pewter, brass, carved wood; these were his more legitimate en-
terprises; but he also collected stamps, birds' eggs, hotel labels,
and postmarks: he boasted that he had a collection of postmarks
which was unequalled in the Empire. During his long sojourning
in lonely places he had read a great deal, and though he was no
sinologue he had a greater knowledge of China, its history,
literature, and people, than most of his colleagues; but from his
wide reading he had acquired not toleration but vanity. He was
a man of a singular appearance. His body was small and frail
and when he walked he gave you the idea of a dead leaf dancing
before the wind; and then there was something extraordinarily
odd in the small Tyrolese hat, with a cock's feather in it, very
old and shabby, which he wore perched rakishly on the side of
his large head. He was exceedingly bald. You saw that his eyes,
blue and pale, were weak behind the spectacles, and a drooping,
ragged, dingy moustache did not hide the peevishness of his
mouth. And now, turning out of the street in which was the
consulate, he made his way on to the city wall, for there only
in the multitudinous city was it possible to walk with comfort.

He was a man who took his work hardly, worrying himself to
death over every trifle, but as a rule a walk on the wall soothed
and rested him. The city stood in the midst of a great plain and
often at sundown from the wall you could see in the distance
the snow-capped mountains, the mountains of Tibet; but now
he walked quickly, looking neither to the right nor to the left,
and his fat spaniel frisked about him unobserved. He talked to
himself rapidly in a low monotone. The cause of his irritation
was a visit that he had that day received from a lady who called
herself Mrs. Yü and whom he with a consular passion for precision insisted on calling Miss Lambert. This in itself sufficed to
deprive their intercourse of amenity. She was an Englishwoman
married to a Chinese. She had arrived two years before with her
husband from England, where he had been studying at the

University of London; he had made her believe that he was a great personage in his own country and she had imagined herself to be coming to a gorgeous palace and a position of consequence. It was a bitter surprise when she found herself brought to a shabby Chinese house crowded with people: there was not even a foreign bed in it, nor a knife and fork: everything seemed to her very dirty and smelly. It was a shock to find that she had to live with her husband's father and mother and he told her that she must do exactly what his mother bade her; but in her complete ignorance of Chinese it was not till she had been two or three days in the house that she realised that she was not her husband's only wife. He had been married as a boy before he left his native city to acquire the knowledge of the barbarians. When she bitterly upbraided him for deceiving her he shrugged his shoulders. There was nothing to prevent a Chinese from having two wives if he wanted them and, he added with some disregard to truth, no Chinese woman looked upon it as a hardship. It was upon making this discovery that she paid her first visit to the consul. He had already heard of her arrival—in China everyone knows everything about everyone—and he received her without surprise. Nor had he much sympathy to show her. That a foreign woman should marry a Chinese at all filled him with indignation, but that she should do so without making proper inquiries vexed him like a personal affront. She was not at all the sort of woman whose appearance led you to imagine that she would be guilty of such a folly. She was a solid, thick-set, young person, short, plain, and matter-of-fact. She was cheaply dressed in a tailor-made suit and she wore a tam-o'-shanter. She had bad teeth and a muddy skin. Her hands were large and red and ill-cared for. You could tell that she was not unused to hard work. She spoke English with a cockney whine.

"How did you meet Mr. Yü?" asked the consul frigidly.

"Well, you see, it's like this," she answered. "Dad was in a very good position, and when he died mother said: 'Well, it seems a sinful waste to keep all these rooms empty, I'll put a card in the window.'"

The consul interrupted her.

"He had lodgings with you?"

"Well, they weren't exactly lodgings," she said.

"Shall we say apartments then?" replied the consul, with his thin, slightly vain smile.

That was generally the explanation of these marriages. Then because he thought her a very foolish vulgar woman he explained bluntly that according to English law she was not married to Yü and that the best thing she could do was to go back to England at once. She began to cry and his heart softened a little to her. He promised to put her in charge of some missionary ladies who would look after her on the long journey, and indeed, if she liked, he would see if meanwhile she could not live in one of the missions. But while he talked Miss Lambert dried her tears.

"What's the good of going back to England?" she said at last. "I 'aven't got nowhere to go to."

"You can go to your mother."

"She was all against my marrying Mr. Yü. I should never hear the last of it if I was to go back now."

The consul began to argue with her, but the more he argued the more determined she became, and at last he lost his temper.

"If you like to stay here with a man who isn't your husband it's your own look-out, but I wash my hands of all responsibility."

Her retort had often rankled.

"Then you've got no cause to worry," she said, and the look on her face returned to him whenever he thought of her.

That was two years ago and he had seen her once or twice since then. It appeared that she got on very badly both with her mother-in-law and with her husband's other wife, and she had come to the consul with preposterous questions about her rights according to Chinese law. He repeated his offer to get her away, but she remained steadfast in her refusal to go, and their interview always ended in the consul's flying into a passion. He was almost inclined to pity the rascally Yü who had to keep the peace between three warring women. According to his English wife's account he was not unkind to her. He tried to act fairly by both his wives. Miss Lambert did not improve. The consul knew that ordinarily she wore Chinese clothes, but when she came to see him she put on European dress. She was become extremely blowsy. Her health suffered from the Chinese food she ate and she was beginning to look wretchedly ill. But really he was shocked when she had been shown into his office that day. She wore no hat and her hair was dishevelled. She was in a highly hysterical state.

"They're trying to poison me," she screamed and she put before him a bowl of some foul-smelling food. "It's poisoned," she said. "I've been ill for the last ten days, it's only by a miracle I've escaped."

She gave him a long story, circumstantial and probable enough to convince him: after all, nothing was more likely than that the Chinese women should use familiar methods to get rid of an intruder who was hateful to them.

"Do they know you've come here?"

"Of course they do; I told them I was going to show them up."

Now at last was the moment for decisive action. The consul looked at her in his most official manner.

"Well, you must never go back there. I refuse to put up with your nonsense any longer. I insist on your leaving this man who isn't your husband."

But he found himself helpless against the woman's insane obstinacy. He repeated all the arguments he had used so often, but she would not listen, and as usual he lost his temper. It was then, in answer to his final, desperate question, that she had made the remark which had entirely robbed him of his calm.

"But what on earth makes you stay with the man?" he cried.

She hesitated for a moment and a curious look came into her eyes.

"There's something in the way his hair grows on his forehead that I can't help liking," she answered.

The consul had never heard anything so outrageous. It really was the last straw. And now while he strode along, trying to walk off his anger, though he was not a man who often used bad language he really could not restrain himself, and he said fiercely:

"Women are simply bloody."

MIRAGE

I HAD BEEN WANDERING about the East for months and at last reached Haiphong. It is a commercial town and a dull one, but I knew that from there I could find a ship of sorts to take me to Hong-Kong. I had some days to wait and nothing to do. It is true that from Haiphong you can visit the Bay of Along, which is one of the *sehenswürdigkeiten* of Indo-China, but I was tired of sights. I contented myself with sitting in the cafés, for here it was none too warm and I was glad to get out of tropical clothes, and reading back numbers of *L'Illustration,* or for the sake of exercise taking a brisk walk along straight, wide streets. Haiphong is traversed by canals and sometimes I got a glimpse of a scene which in its varied life, with all the native craft on the water, was multicoloured and charming. There was one canal, with tall Chinese houses on each side of it, that had a pleasant curve. The houses were whitewashed, but the whitewash was discoloured and stained; with their grey roofs they made an agreeable composition against the pale sky. The picture had the faded elegance of an old water-colour. There was nowhere an emphatic note. It was soft and a little weary and inspired one with a faint melancholy. I was reminded I scarcely know why of an old maid I knew in my youth, a relic of the Victorian age, who wore black silk mittens and made crochet shawls for the poor, black for widows and white for married women. She had suffered in her youth, but whether from ill-health or unrequited love, no one exactly knew.

But there was a local paper at Haiphong, a small dingy sheet with stubby type the ink of which came off on your fingers, and it gave you a political article, the wireless news, advertisements and local intelligence. The editor, doubtless hard pressed for matter, printed the names of the persons, Europeans, natives of the country and Chinese, who had arrived at Haiphong or left it, and mine was put in with the rest. On the morning of the day before that on which the old tub I was taking was to sail for Hong-Kong I was sitting in the café of the hotel drinking a Dubonnet before luncheon when the boy came in and said that a gentleman wished to see me. I did not know a soul in Haiphong and asked who it was. The boy said he was an Englishman and lived there, but he could not tell me his name. The boy spoke very little French and it was hard for me to understand what he said. I was mystified, but told him to show the visitor in. A moment later he came back followed by a white man and pointed me out to him. The man gave me a look and walked towards me. He was a very tall fellow, well over six feet high, rather fat and bloated, with a red, clean-shaven face and extremely pale blue eyes. He wore very shabby khaki shorts and a stengah-shifter unbuttoned at the neck, and a battered helmet. I concluded at once that he was a stranded beachcomber who was going to touch me for a loan and wondered how little I could hope to get off for.

He came up to me and held out a large red hand with broken, dirty nails.

"I don't suppose you remember me," he said. "My name's Grosely. I was at St. Thomas's Hospital with you. I recognised your name as soon as I saw it in the paper and I thought I'd look you up."

I had not the smallest recollection of him, but I asked him to sit down and offered him a drink. By his appearance I had first thought he would ask me for ten piastres and I might have given him five, but now it looked more likely that he would ask for a hundred and I should have to think myself lucky if I could content him with fifty. The habitual borrower always asks twice what he expects to get and it only dissatisfies him to give him what he has asked since then he is vexed with himself for not having asked more. He feels you have cheated him.

"Are you a doctor?" I asked.

"No, I was only at the bloody place a year."

He took off his sun-helmet and showed me a mop of grey hair,

which much needed a brush. His face was curiously mottled and
he did not look healthy. His teeth were badly decayed and at
the corners of his mouth were empty spaces. When the boy
came to take the orders he asked for brandy.

"Bring the bottle," he said. *"La bouteille.* Savvy?" He turned
to me. "I've been living here for the last five years, but I can't
get along with French somehow. I talk Tonkinese." He leaned
his chair back and looked at me. "I remember you, you know.
You used to go about with those twins. What was their name?
I expect I've changed more than you have. I've spent the best
part of my life in China. Rotten climate, you know. It plays hell
with a man."

I still had not the smallest recollection of him. I thought it
best to say so.

"Were you the same year as I was?" I asked.

"Yes. '92."

"It's a devil of a long time ago."

About sixty boys and young men entered the hospital every
year; they were most of them shy and confused by the new life
they were entering upon; many had never been in London before; and to me at least they were shadows that passed without
any particular rhyme or reason across a white sheet. During the
first year a certain number for one reason or another dropped
out, and in the second year those that remained gained by
degrees the beginnings of a personality. They were not only
themselves, but the lectures one had attended with them, the
scone and coffee one had eaten at the same table for luncheon,
the dissection one had done at the same board in the same dissecting room, and *The Belle of New York* one had seen together
from the pit of the Shaftesbury Theatre.

The boy brought the bottle of brandy and Grosely, if that
was really his name, pouring himself out a generous helping
drank it down at a gulp without water or soda.

"I couldn't stand doctoring," he said, "I chucked it. My
people got fed up with me and I went out to China. They gave
me a hundred pounds and told me to shift for myself. I was
damned glad to get out, I can tell you. I guess I was just about
as much fed up with them as they were with me. I haven't
troubled them much since."

Then from somewhere in the depths of my memory a faint
hint crept into the rim, as it were, of consciousness, as on a
rising tide the water slides up the sand and then withdraws to

advance with the next wave in a fuller volume. I had first an inkling of some shabby little scandal that had got into the papers. Then I saw a boy's face, and so gradually the facts recurred to me; I remembered him now. I didn't believe he was called Grosely then, I think he had a one-syllabled name, but that I was uncertain of. He was a very tall lad (I began to see him quite well), thin, with a slight stoop, he was only eighteen and had grown too fast for his strength, he had curly, shining brown hair, rather large features (they did not look so large now, perhaps because his face was fat and puffy) and a peculiarly fresh complexion, very pink and white, like a girl's. I imagine people, women especially, would have thought him a very handsome boy, but to us he was only a clumsy, shuffling lout. Then I remembered that he did not often come to lectures, no, it wasn't that I remembered, there were too many students in the theatre to recollect who was there and who wasn't. I remembered the dissecting room. He had a leg at the next table to the one I was working at and he hardly ever touched it; I forget why the men who had other parts of the body complained of his neglecting the work, I suppose somehow it interfered with them. In those days a good deal of gossip went on over the dissection of a "part" and out of the distance of thirty years some of it came back to me. Someone started the story that Grosely was a very gay dog. He drank like a fish and was an awful womaniser. Most of those boys were very simple, and they had brought to the hospital the notions they had acquired at home and at school. Some were prudish and they were shocked; others, those who worked hard, sneered at him and asked how he could hope to pass his exams; but a good many were excited and impressed, he was doing what they would have liked to do if they had had the courage. Grosely had his admirers and you could often see him surrounded by a little band listening open-mouthed to stories of his adventures. Recollections now were crowding upon me. In a very little while he lost his shyness and assumed the airs of a man of the world. They must have looked absurd on this smooth-cheeked boy with his pink and white skin. Men (so they called themselves) used to tell one another of his escapades. He became quite a hero. He would make caustic remarks as he passed the museum and saw a pair of earnest students going over their anatomy together. He was at home in the public-houses of the neighbourhood and was on familiar terms with the barmaids. Looking back, I imagine that, newly arrived from the

country and the tutelage of parents and schoolmasters, he was
captivated by his freedom and the thrill of London. His dissipa-
tions were harmless enough. They were due only to the urge of
youth. He lost his head.

But we were all very poor and we did not know how Grosely
managed to pay for his garish amusements. We knew his father
was a country doctor and I think we knew exactly how much he
gave his son a month. It was not enough to pay for the harlots
he picked up on the promenade at the Pavilion and for the
drinks he stood his friends in the Criterion Bar. We told one another in awe-struck tones that he must be getting fearfully into
debt. Of course he could pawn things, but we knew by experience that you could not get more than three pounds for a micro-
scope and thirty shillings for a skeleton. We said he must be
spending at least ten pounds a week. Our ideas were not very
grand and this seemed to us the wildest pitch of extravagance.
At last one of his friends disclosed the mystery: Grosely had
discovered a wonderful system for making money. It amused
and impressed us. None of us would have thought of anything
so ingenious or have had the nerve to attempt it if he had.
Grosely went to auctions, not Christie's, of course, but auctions
in the Strand and Oxford Street, and in private houses, and
bought anything portable that was going cheap. Then he took
his purchase to a pawnbroker's and pawned it for ten shillings
or a pound more than he had paid. He was making money, four
or five pounds a week, and he said he was going to give up
medicine and make a regular business of it. Not one of us had
ever made a penny in his life and we regarded Grosely with admiration.

"By Jove, he's clever," we said.

"He's just about as sharp as they make them."

"That's the sort that ends up as a millionaire."

We were all very worldly-wise and what we didn't know
about life at eighteen we were pretty sure wasn't worth knowing. It was a pity that when an examiner asked us a question we
were so nervous that the answer often flew straight out of our
head and when a nurse asked us to post a letter we blushed
scarlet. It became known that the Dean had sent for Grosely
and hauled him over the coals. He had threatened him with
sundry penalties if he continued systematically to neglect his
work. Grosely was indignant. He'd had enough of that sort of
thing at school. he said, he wasn't going to let a horse-faced

eunuch treat him like a boy. Damn it all, he was getting on for nineteen and there wasn't much you could teach him. The Dean had said he heard he was drinking more than was good for him. Damned cheek. He could carry his liquor as well as any man of his age, he'd been blind last Saturday and he meant to get blind next Saturday, and if anyone didn't like it he could do the other thing. Grosely's friends quite agreed with him that a man couldn't let himself be insulted like that.

But the blow fell at last and now I remembered quite well the shock it gave us all. I suppose we had not seen Grosely for two or three days, but he had been in the habit of coming to the hospital more and more irregularly, so if we thought anything about it, I imagine we merely said that he was off on one of his bats. He would turn up again in a day or so, rather pale, but with a wonderful story of some girl he had picked up and the time he had had with her. The anatomy lecture was at nine in the morning and it was a rush to get there in time. On this particular day little attention was paid to the lecturer, who, with a visible pleasure in his limpid English and admirable elocution, was describing I know not what part of the human skeleton, for there was much excited whispering along the benches and a newspaper was surreptitiously passed from hand to hand. Suddenly the lecturer stopped. He had a pedagogic sarcasm. He affected not to know the names of his students.

"I am afraid I am disturbing the gentleman who is reading the paper. Anatomy is a very tedious science and I regret that the regulations of the Royal College of Surgeons oblige me to ask you to give it enough of your attention to pass an examination in it. Any gentleman, however, who finds this impossible is at liberty to continue his perusal of the paper outside."

The wretched boy to whom this reproof was addressed reddened to the roots of his hair and in his embarrassment tried to stuff the newspaper in his pocket. The professor of anatomy observed him coldly.

"I'm afraid, sir, that the paper is a little too large to go into your pocket," he remarked. "Perhaps you would be good enough to hand it down to me?"

The newspaper was passed from row to row to the well of the theatre, and, not content with the confusion to which he had put the poor lad, the eminent surgeon, taking it, asked:

"May I enquire what it is in the paper that the gentleman in question found of such absorbing interest?"

The student who gave it to him without a word pointed out the paragraph that we had all been reading. The professor read it and we watched him in silence. He put the paper down and went on with his lecture. The headline ran *Arrest of a Medical Student*. Grosely had been brought before the police-court magistrate for getting goods on credit and pawning them. It appears that this is an indictable offence and the magistrate had remanded him for a week. Bail was refused. It looked as though his method of making money by buying things at auctions and pawning them had not in the long run proved as steady a source of income as he expected and he had found it more profitable to pawn things that he was not at the expense of paying for. We talked the matter over excitedly as soon as the lecture was over and I am bound to say that, having no property ourselves, so deficient was our sense of its sanctity we could none of us look upon his crime as a very serious one; but with the natural love of the young for the terrible there were few who did not think he would get anything from two years hard labour to seven years penal servitude.

I do not know why, but I did not seem to have any recollection of what happened to Grosely. I think he may have been arrested towards the end of a session and his case may have come on again when we had all separated for holidays. I did not know if it was disposed of by the police-court magistrate or whether it went up for trial. I had a sort of feeling that he was sentenced to a short term of imprisonment, six weeks perhaps, for his operations had been pretty extensive; but I knew that he had vanished from our midst and in a little while was thought of no more. It was strange to me that after all these years I should recollect so much of the incident so clearly. It was as though, turning over an album of old snapshots, I saw all at once the photograph of a scene I had quite forgotten.

But of course in that gross elderly man with grey hair and mottled red face I should never have recognised the lanky pink-cheeked boy. He looked sixty, but I knew he must be much less than that. I wondered what he had done with himself in the intervening time. It did not look as though he had excessively prospered.

"What were you doing in China?" I asked him.

"I was a tide-waiter."

"Oh, were you?"

It is not a position of great importance and I took care to

keep out of my tone any note of surprise. The tide-waiters are
employees of the Chinese Customs whose duty it is to board the
ships and junks at the various treaty ports and I think their
chief business is to prevent opium-smuggling. They are mostly
retired A.B.s from the Royal Navy and non-commissioned officers who have finished their time. I have seen them come on
board at various places up the Yangtse. They hobnob with the
pilot and the engineer, but the skipper is a trifle curt with them.
They learn to speak Chinese more fluently than most Europeans and often marry Chinese women.

"When I left England I swore I wouldn't go back till I'd
made my pile. And I never did. They were glad enough to get
anyone to be a tide-waiter in those days, any white man I mean,
and they didn't ask questions. They didn't care who you were. I
was damned glad to get the job, I can tell you, I was about
broke to the wide when they took me on. I only took it till I
could get something better, but I stayed on, it suited me, I
wanted to make money and I found out that a tide-waiter could
make a packet if he knew the right way to go about it. I was
with the Chinese Customs for the best part of twenty-five years
and when I came away I wouldn't mind betting that lots of
commissioners would have been glad to have the money I had."

He gave me a sly, mean look. I had an inkling of what he
meant. But there was a point on which I was willing to be reassured; if he was going to ask me for a hundred piastres (I was
resigned to that sum now) I thought I might just as well take
the blow at once.

"I hope you kept it," I said.

"You bet I did. I invested all my money in Shanghai and
when I left China I put it all in American railway bonds. Safety
first is my motto. I know too much about crooks to take any
risks myself."

I liked that remark, so I asked him if he wouldn't stay and
have luncheon with me.

"No, I don't think I will. I don't eat much tiffin and anyway
my chow's waiting for me at home. I think I'll be getting
along." He got up and he towered over me. "But look here, why
don't you come along this evening and see my place? I've married a Haiphong girl. Got a baby too. It's not often I get a
chance of talking to anyone about London. You'd better not
come to dinner. We only eat native food and I don't suppose
you'd care for that. Come along about nine, will you?"

"All right," I said.

I had already told him that I was leaving Haiphong next day. He asked the boy to bring him a piece of paper so that he might write down his address. He wrote laboriously in the hand of a boy of fourteen.

"Tell the porter to explain to your rickshaw boy where it is. I'm on the second floor. There's no bell. Just knock. Well, see you later."

He walked out and I went in to luncheon.

After dinner I called a rickshaw and with the porter's help made the boy understand where I wanted to go. I found presently that he was taking me along the curved canal the houses of which had looked to me so like a faded Victorian water-colour; he stopped at one of them and pointed to the door. It looked so shabby and the neighbourhood was so squalid that I hesitated, thinking he had made a mistake. It seemed unlikely that Grosely could live so far in the native quarter and in a house so bedraggled. I told the rickshaw boy to wait and pushing open the door saw a dark staircase in front of me. There was no one about and the street was empty. It might have been the small hours of the morning. I struck a match and fumbled my way upstairs; on the second floor I struck another match and saw a large brown door in front of me. I knocked and in a moment it was opened by a little Tonkinese woman holding a candle. She was dressed in the earth-brown of the poorer classes, with a tight little black turban on her head; her lips and the skin round them were stained red with betel and when she opened her mouth to speak I saw that she had the black teeth and black gums that so disfigure these people. She said something in her native language and then I heard Grosely's voice:

"Come along in. I was beginning to think you weren't going to turn up."

I passed through a little dark ante-chamber and entered a large room that evidently looked on the canal. Grosely was lying on a long chair and he raised his length from it as I came in. He was reading the Hong-Kong papers by the light of a paraffin-lamp that stood on a table by his side.

"Sit down," he said, "and put your feet up."

"There's no reason I should take your chair."

"Go on. I'll sit on this."

He took a kitchen chair and sitting on it put his feet on the end of mine.

"That's my wife," he said pointing with his thumb at the Tonkinese woman who had followed me into the room. "And over there in the corner's the kid."

I followed his eyes and against the wall, lying on bamboo mats and covered with a blanket, I saw a child sleeping.

"Lively little beggar when he's awake. I wish you could have seen him. She's going to have another soon."

I glanced at her and the truth of what he said was apparent. She was very small, with tiny hands and feet, but her face was flat and the skin muddy. She looked sullen, but may only have been shy. She went out of the room and presently came back with a bottle of whisky, two glasses and a syphon. I looked round. There was a partition at the back of dark unpainted wood, which I suppose shut off another room, and pinned against the middle of this was a portrait cut out of an illustrated paper of John Galsworthy. He looked austere, mild and gentlemanly, and I wondered what he did there. The other walls were whitewashed, but the whitewash was dingy and stained. Pinned on to them were pages of pictures from the *Graphic* or the *Illustrated London News*.

"I put them up," said Grosely, "I thought they made the place look homelike."

"What made you put up Galsworthy? Do you read his books?"

"No, I didn't know he wrote books. I liked his face."

There were one or two torn and shabby rattan mats on the floor and in a corner a great pile of the *Hong-Kong Times*. The only furniture consisted of a wash-hand stand, two or three kitchen chairs, a table or two and a large teak native bed. It was cheerless and sordid.

"Not a bad little place, is it?" said Grosely. "Suits me all right. Sometimes I've thought of moving, but I don't suppose I ever shall now." He gave a little chuckle. "I came to Haiphong for forty-eight hours and I've been here five years. I was on my way to Shanghai really."

He was silent. Having nothing to say I said nothing. Then the little Tonkinese woman made a remark to him, which I could not of course understand, and he answered her. He was silent again for a minute or two, but I thought he looked at me as though he wanted to ask me something. I did not know why he hesitated.

"Have you ever tried smoking opium on your travels in the East?" he inquired at last, casually.

"Yes, I did once, at Singapore. I thought I'd like to see what it was like."

"What happened?"

"Nothing very thrilling, to tell you the truth. I thought I was going to have the most exquisite emotions. I expected visions, like de Quincey's, you know. The only thing I felt was a kind of physical well-being, the same sort of feeling that you get when you've had a Turkish bath and are lying in the cooling room, and then a peculiar activity of mind so that everything I thought of seemed extremely clear."

"I know."

"I really felt that two and two are four and there could not be the smallest doubt about it. But next morning—oh God! My head reeled. I was as sick as a dog, I was sick all day, I vomited my soul out, and as I vomited I said to myself miserably: And there are people who call this fun."

Grosely leaned back in his chair and gave a low mirthless laugh.

"I expect it was bad stuff. Or you went at it too hard. They saw you were a mug and gave you dregs that had been smoked already. They're enough to turn anybody up. Would you like to have another try now? I've got some stuff here that I know's good."

"No, I think once was enough for me."

"D'you mind if I have a pipe or two? You want it in a climate like this. It keeps you from getting dysentery. And I generally have a bit of a smoke about this time."

"Go ahead," I said.

He spoke again to the woman and she, raising her voice, called out something in a raucous tone. An answer came from the room behind the wooden partition and after a minute or two an old woman came out carrying a little round tray. She was shrivelled and old and when she entered gave me an ingratiating smile of her stained mouth. Grosely got up and crossed over to the bed and lay on it. The old woman set the tray down on the bed; on it was a spirit-lamp, a pipe, a long needle and a little round box of opium. She squatted on the bed and Grosely's wife got on it too and sat, her feet tucked up under her, with her back against the wall. Grosely watched the old woman while she

put a little pellet of the drug on the needle, held it over the
flame till it sizzled and then plugged it into the pipe. She
handed it to him and with a great breath he inhaled it, he held
the smoke for a little while and then blew it out in a thick grey
cloud. He handed her back the pipe and she started to make another. Nobody spoke. He smoked three pipes in succession and
then sank back.

"By George, I feel better now. I was feeling all in. She makes
a wonderful pipe, this old hag. Are you sure you won't have
one?"

"Quite."

"Please yourself. Have some tea then."

He spoke to his wife, who scrambled off the bed and went out
of the room. Presently she came back with a little china pot of
tea and a couple of Chinese bowls.

"A lot of people smoke here, you know. It does you no harm
if you don't do it to excess. I never smoke more than twenty to
twenty-five pipes a day. You can go on for years if you limit
yourself to that. Some of the Frenchmen smoke as many as
forty or fifty a day. That's too much. I never do that, except
now and then when I feel I want a binge. I'm bound to say it's
never done me any harm."

We drank our tea, pale and vaguely scented and clean on the
palate. Then the old woman made him another pipe and then
another. His wife had got back on to the bed and soon curling
herself up at his feet went to sleep. Grosely smoked two or three
pipes at a time, and while he was smoking seemed intent upon
nothing else, but in the intervals he was loquacious. Several
times I suggested going, but he would not let me. The hours
wore on. Once or twice while he smoked I dozed. He told me all
about himself. He went on and on. I spoke only to give him a
cue. I cannot relate what he told me in his own words. He repeated himself. He was very long-winded and he told me his
story confusedly, first a late bit, then an early bit, so that I had
to arrange the sequence for myself; sometimes I saw that, afraid
he had said too much, he held something back; sometimes he
lied and I had to make a guess at the truth from the smile he
gave me or the look in his eyes. He had not the words to describe what he had felt, and I had to conjecture his meaning
from slangy metaphors and hackneyed, vulgar phrases. I kept
on asking myself what his real name was, it was on the tip of my
tongue and it irritated me not to be able to recall it, though why

it should in the least matter to me I did not know. He was somewhat suspicious of me at first and I saw that this escapade of his in London and his imprisonment had been all these years a tormenting secret. He had always been haunted by the fear that sooner or later someone would find out.

"It's funny that even now you shouldn't remember me at the hospital," he said, looking at me shrewdly. "You must have a rotten memory."

"Hang it all, it's nearly thirty years ago. Think of the thousands of people I've met since then. There's no reason why I should remember you any more than you remember me."

"That's right. I don't suppose there is."

It seemed to reassure him. At last he had smoked enough and the old woman made herself a pipe and smoked it. Then she went over to the mat on which the child was lying and huddled down beside it. She lay so still that I supposed she had fallen directly asleep. When at last I went I found my boy curled up on the foot-board of the rickshaw in so deep a slumber that I had to shake him. I knew where I was and I wanted air and exercise, so I gave him a couple of piastres and told him I would walk.

It was a strange story I carried away with me.

It was with a sort of horror that I had listened to Grosely, telling me of those twenty years he had spent in China. He had made money, I do not know how much, but from the way he talked I should think something between fifteen and twenty thousand pounds, and for a tide-waiter it was a fortune. He could not have come by it honestly, and little as I knew of the details of his trade, by his sudden reticences, by his leers and hints I guessed that there was no base transaction that, if it was made worth his while, he jibbed at. I suppose that nothing paid him better than smuggling opium, and his position gave him the opportunity to do this with safety and profit. I understood that his superior officers had often had their suspicions of him, but had never been able to get such proof of his malpractices as to justify them in taking any steps. They contented themselves with moving him from one port to another, but that did not disturb him; they watched him, but he was too clever for them. I saw that he was divided between the fear of telling me too much to his discredit and the desire to boast of his own astuteness. He prided himself on the confidence the Chinese had placed in him.

"They knew they could trust me," he said, "and it gave me a
pull. I never double-crossed a Chinaman once."

The thought filled him with the complacency of the honest
man. The Chinese discovered that he was keen on curios and
they got in the habit of giving him bits or bringing him things
to buy; he never made enquiries how they had come by them
and he bought them cheap. When he had got a good lot he sent
them to Peking and sold them at a handsome profit. I remembered how he had started his commercial career by buying
things at auctions and pawning them. For twenty years by
shabby shift and petty dishonesty he added pound to pound,
and everything he made he invested in Shanghai. He lived
penuriously, saving half his pay; he never went on leave because
he did not want to waste his money, he would not have anything to do with the Chinese women, he wanted to keep himself
free from any entanglement; he did not drink. He was consumed by one ambition, to save enough to be able to go back to
England and live the life from which he had been snatched as a
boy. That was the only thing he wanted. He lived in China as
though in a dream; he paid no attention to the life around him;
its colour and strangeness, its possibilities of pleasure, meant
nothing to him. There was always before him the mirage of
London, the Criterion Bar, himself standing with his foot on the
rail, the promenade at the Empire and the Pavilion, the
picked-up harlot, the serio-comic at the music-hall and the
musical comedy at the Gaiety. This was life and love and adventure. This was romance. This was what he yearned for with
all his heart. There was surely something impressive in the way
in which during all those years he had lived like an anchorite
with that one end in view of leading again a life that was so
vulgar. It showed character.

"You see," he said to me, "even if I'd been able to get back to
England on leave I wouldn't have gone. I didn't want to go till
I could go for good. And then I wanted to do the thing in style."

He saw himself putting on evening clothes every night and
going out with a gardenia in his buttonhole, and he saw himself
going to the Derby in a long coat and a brown hat and a pair of
opera glasses slung over his shoulder. He saw himself giving the
girls a look over and picking out the one he fancied. He made
up his mind that on the night he arrived in London he would
get blind, he hadn't been drunk for twenty years; he couldn't
afford to in his job, you had to keep your wits about you. He'd

take care not to get drunk on the ship on the way home. He'd
wait till he got to London. What a night he'd have! He thought
of it for twenty years.

I do not know why Grosely left the Chinese Customs,
whether the place was getting too hot for him, whether he had
reached the end of his service or whether he had amassed the
sum he had fixed. But at last he sailed. He went second class; he
did not intend to start spending money till he reached London.
He took rooms in Jermyn Street, he had always wanted to live
there, and he went straight to a tailor's and ordered himself an
outfit. Slap up. Then he had a look round the town. It was different from how he remembered it, there was much more traffic and
he felt confused and a little at sea. He went to the Criterion and
found there was no longer a bar where he had been used to
lounge and drink. There was a restaurant in Leicester Square
where he had been in the habit of dining when he was in funds,
but he could not find it; he supposed it had been torn down. He
went to the Pavilion, but there were no women there; he was
rather disgusted and went on to the Empire, he found they had
done away with the Promenade. It was rather a blow. He could
not quite make it out. Well, anyhow, he must be prepared for
changes in twenty years, and if he couldn't do anything else he
could get drunk. He had had fever several times in China and
the change of climate had brought it on again, he wasn't feeling
any too well, and after four or five drinks he was glad to go to
bed.

That first day was only a sample of many that followed it.
Everything went wrong. Grosely's voice grew peevish and bitter
as he told me how one thing and another had failed him. The
old places were gone, the people were different, he found it hard
to make friends, he was strangely lonely; he had never expected
that in a great city like London. That's what was wrong with it,
London had become too big, it wasn't the jolly, intimate place
it had been in the early nineties. It had gone to pieces. He
picked up a few girls, but they weren't as nice as the girls he had
known before, they weren't the fun they used to be, and he grew
dimly conscious that they thought him a rum sort of cove. He
was only just over forty and they looked upon him as an old
man. When he tried to cotton on to a lot of young fellows standing round a bar they gave him the cold shoulder. Anyway, these
young fellows didn't know how to drink. He'd show them. He
got soused every night, it was the only thing to do in that

damned place, but, by Jove, it made him feel rotten next day.
He supposed it was the climate of China. When he was a medical student he could drink a bottle of whisky every night and be
as fresh as a daisy in the morning. He began to think more
about China. All sorts of things that he never knew he had
noticed came back to him. It wasn't a bad life he'd led there.
Perhaps he'd been a fool to keep away from those Chinese girls,
they were pretty little things some of them, and they didn't put
on the airs these English girls did. One could have a damned
good time in China if one had the money he had. One could
keep a Chinese girl and get into the club, and there'd be a lot of
nice fellows to drink with and play bridge with and billiards. He
remembered the Chinese shops and all the row in the streets and
the coolies carrying loads and the ports with the junks in them
and the rivers with pagodas on the banks. It was funny, he
never thought much of China while he was there and now—
well, he couldn't get it out of his mind. It obsessed him. He began to think that London was no place for a white man. It had
just gone to the dogs, that was the long and short of it, and one
day the thought came to him that perhaps it would be a good
thing if he went back to China. Of course it was silly, he'd
worked like a slave for twenty years to be able to have a good
time in London, and it was absurd to go and live in China. With
his money he ought to be able to have a good time anywhere.
But somehow he couldn't think of anything else but China. One
day he went to the pictures and saw a scene at Shanghai. That
settled it. He was fed up with London. He hated it. He was going to get out and this time he'd get out for good. He had been
home a year and a half, and it seemed longer to him than all his
twenty years in the East. He took a passage on a French boat
sailing from Marseilles, and when he saw the coast of Europe
sink into the sea he heaved a great sigh of relief. When they got
to Suez and he felt the first touch of the East he knew he had
done the right thing. Europe was finished. The East was the
only place.

He went ashore at Djibouti and again at Colombo and Singapore, but though the ship stopped for two days at Saigon he
remained on board there. He'd been drinking a good deal and
he was feeling a bit under the weather. But when they reached
Haiphong, where they were staying for forty-eight hours, he
thought he might just as well have a look at it. That was the
last stopping-place before they got to China. He was bound for

Shanghai. When he got there he meant to go to a hotel and look around a bit and then get hold of a girl and a place of his own. He would buy a pony or two and race. He'd soon make friends. In the East they weren't so stiff and stand-offish as they were in London. Going ashore, he dined at the hotel and after dinner got into a richshaw and told the boy he wanted a woman. The boy took him to the shabby tenement in which I had sat for so many hours and there were the old woman and the girl who was now the mother of his child. After a while the old woman asked him if he wouldn't like to smoke. He had never tried opium, he had always been frightened of it, but now he didn't see why he shouldn't have a go. He was feeling good that night and the girl was a jolly cuddlesome little thing; she was rather like a Chinese girl, small and pretty, like an idol. Well, he had a pipe or two, and he began to feel very happy and comfortable. He stayed all night. He didn't sleep. He just lay, feeling very restful, and thought about things.

"I stopped there till my ship went on to Hong-Kong," he said. "And when she left I just stopped on."

"How about your luggage?" I asked.

For I am perhaps unworthily interested in the manner people combine practical details with the ideal aspects of life. When in a novel penniless lovers drive in a long, swift racing car over the distant hills I have always a desire to know how they managed to pay for it; and I have often asked myself how the characters of Henry James in the intervals of subtly examining their situation coped with the physiological necessities of their bodies.

"I only had a trunk full of clothes, I was never one to want much more than I stood up in, and I went down with the girl in a rickshaw to fetch it. I only meant to stay on till the next boat came through. You see, I was so near China here I thought I'd wait a bit and get used to things, if you understand what I mean, before I went on."

I did. Those last words of his revealed him to me. I knew that on the threshold of China his courage had failed him. England had been such a terrible disappointment that now he was afraid to put China to the test too. If that failed him he had nothing. For years England had been like a mirage in the desert. But when he had yielded to the attraction, those shining pools and the palm trees and the green grass were nothing but the rolling sandy dunes. He had China, and so long as he never saw it again he kept it.

"Somehow I stayed on. You know, you'd be surprised how quickly the days pass. I don't seem to have time to do half the things I want to. After all I'm comfortable here. The old woman makes a damned good pipe, and she's a jolly little girl, my girl, and then there's the kid. A lively young beggar. If you're happy somewhere what's the good of going somewhere else?"

"And are you happy here?" I asked him.

I looked round that large bare sordid room. There was no comfort in it and not one of the little personal things that one would have thought might have given him the feeling of home. Grosely had taken on this equivocal little apartment, which served as a house of assignation and as a place for Europeans to smoke opium in, with the old woman who kept it, just as it was, and he camped, rather than lived, there still as though next day he would pack his traps and go. After a little while he answered my question.

"I've never been so happy in my life. I often think I'll go on to Shanghai some day, but I don't suppose I ever shall. And God knows, I never want to see England again."

"Aren't you awfully lonely sometimes for people to talk to?"

"No. Sometimes a Chinese tramp comes in with an English skipper or a Scotch engineer, and then I go on board and we have a talk about old times. There's an old fellow here, a Frenchman who was in the Customs, and he speaks English; I go and see him sometimes. But the fact is I don't want anybody very much. I think a lot. It gets on my nerves when people come between me and my thoughts. I'm not a big smoker, you know, I just have a pipe or two in the morning to settle my stomach, but I don't really smoke till night. Then I think."

"What d'you think about?"

"Oh, all sorts of things. Sometimes about London and what it was like when I was a boy. But mostly about China. I think of the good times I had and the way I made my money, and I remember the fellows I used to know, and the Chinese. I had some narrow squeaks now and then, but I always came through all right. And I wonder what the girls would have been like that I might have had. Pretty little things. I'm sorry now I didn't keep one or two. It's a great country, China; I love those shops, with an old fellow sitting on his heels smoking a water-pipe, and all the shop-signs. And the temples. By George, that's the place for a man to live in. There's life."

Mirage

The mirage shone before his eyes. The illusion held him. He was happy. I wondered what would be his end. Well, that was not yet. For the first time in his life perhaps he held the present in his hand.

MABEL

I was at Pagan, in Burma, and from there I took the steamer to Mandalay, but a couple of days before I got there, when the boat tied up for the night at a riverside village, I made up my mind to go ashore. The skipper told me that there was there a pleasant little club in which I had only to make myself at home; they were quite used to having strangers drop off like that from the steamer, and the secretary was a very decent chap; I might even get a game of bridge. I had nothing in the world to do, so I got into one of the bullock-carts that were waiting at the landing-stage and was driven to the club. There was a man sitting on the verandah and as I walked up he nodded to me and asked whether I would have a whisky and soda or a gin and bitters. The possibility that I would have nothing at all did not even occur to him. I chose the longer drink and sat down. He was a tall, thin, bronzed man, with a big moustache, and he wore khaki shorts and a khaki shirt. I never knew his name, but when we had been chatting a little while another man came in who told me he was the secretary, and he addressed my friend as George.

"Have you heard from your wife yet?" he asked him.

The other's eyes brightened.

"Yes, I had letters by this mail. She's having no end of a time."

"Did she tell you not to fret?"

George gave a little chuckle, but was I mistaken in thinking that there was in it the shadow of a sob?

"In point of fact she did. But that's easier said than done. Of course I know she wants a holiday, and I'm glad she should have it, but it's devilish hard on a chap." He turned to me. "You see, this is the first time I've ever been separated from my missus, and I'm like a lost dog without her."

"How long have you been married?"

"Five minutes."

The secretary of the club laughed.

"Don't be a fool, George. You've been married eight years."

After we had talked for a little, George, looking at his watch, said he must go and change his clothes for dinner and left us. The secretary watched him disappear into the night with a smile of not unkindly irony.

"We all ask him as much as we can now that he's alone," he told me. "He mopes so terribly since his wife went home."

"It must be very pleasant for her to know that her husband is as devoted to her as all that."

"Mabel is a remarkable woman."

He called the boy and ordered more drinks. In this hospitable place they did not ask you if you would have anything; they took it for granted. Then he settled himself in his long chair and lit a cheroot. He told me the story of George and Mabel.

They became engaged when he was home on leave, and when he returned to Burma it was arranged that she should join him in six months. But one difficulty cropped up after another; Mabel's father died, the war came, George was sent to a district unsuitable for a white woman; so that in the end it was seven years before she was able to start. He made all arrangements for the marriage, which was to take place on the day of her arrival, and went down to Rangoon to meet her. On the morning on which the ship was due he borrowed a motor-car and drove along to the dock. He paced the quay.

Then, suddenly, without warning, his nerve failed him. He had not seen Mabel for seven years. He had forgotten what she was like. She was a total stranger. He felt a terrible sinking in the pit of his stomach and his knees began to wobble. He couldn't go through with it. He must tell Mabel that he was very sorry, but he couldn't, he really couldn't marry her. But how could a man tell a girl a thing like that when she had been engaged to him for seven years and had come six thousand miles to marry him? He hadn't the nerve for that either. George was seized with the courage of despair. There was a boat at the quay on the very point of starting for Singapore; he wrote a hurried letter to Mabel, and without a stick of luggage, just in the clothes he stood up in, leaped on board.

The letter Mabel received ran somewhat as follows:

Dearest Mabel, I have been suddenly called away on business and do not know when I shall be back. I think it would be much wiser if you returned to England. My plans are very uncertain. Your loving George.

But when he arrived at Singapore he found a cable waiting for him.

Quite understand. Don't worry. Love. Mabel.

Terror made him quick-witted.

"By Jove, I believe she's following me," he said.

He telegraphed to the shipping-office at Rangoon and sure enough her name was on the passenger list of the ship that was now on its way to Singapore. There was not a moment to lose. He jumped on the train to Bangkok. But he was uneasy; she would have no difficulty in finding out that he had gone to Bangkok and it was just as simple for her to take the train as it had been for him. Fortunately there was a French tramp sailing next day for Saigon. He took it. At Saigon he would be safe; it would never occur to her that he had gone there; and if it did, surely by now she would have taken the hint. It is five days journey from Bangkok to Saigon and the boat is dirty, cramped and uncomfortable. He was glad to arrive and took a rickshaw to the hotel. He signed his name in the visitors' book and a telegram was immediately handed to him. It contained but two words: *Love. Mabel.* They were enough to make him break into a cold sweat.

"When is the next boat for Hong-Kong?" he asked.

Now his flight grew serious. He sailed to Hong-Kong, but dared not stay there; he went to Manila; Manila was ominous; he went on to Shanghai: Shanghai was nerve-racking; every time he went out of the hotel he expected to run straight into Mabel's arms; no, Shanghai would never do. The only thing was to go to Yokohama. At the Grand Hotel at Yokohama a cable awaited him.

So sorry to have missed you at Manila. Love. Mabel.

He scanned the shipping intelligence with a fevered brow. Where was she now? He doubled back to Shanghai. This time he went straight to the club and asked for a telegram. It was handed to him.

Arriving shortly. Love. Mabel.

No, no, he was not so easy to catch as all that. He had already made his plans. The Yangtse is a long river and the Yangtse was falling. He could just about catch the last steamer that could get up to Chungking and then no one could travel till the following spring except by junk. Such a journey was out of the question for a woman alone. He went to Hankow and from Hankow to Ichang, he changed boats here and from Ichang through the rapids went to Chungking. But he was desperate now, he was not going to take any risks: there was a place called Cheng-tu, the capital of Szechuan, and it was four hundred miles away. It could only be reached by road, and the road was infested with brigands. A man would be safe there.

George collected chair-bearers and coolies and set out. It was with a sigh of relief that he saw at last the crenellated walls of the lonely Chinese city. From those walls at sunset you could see the snowy mountains of Tibet.

He could rest at last: Mabel would never find him there. The consul happened to be a friend of his and he stayed with him. He enjoyed the comfort of a luxurious house, he enjoyed his idleness after that strenuous escape across Asia, and above all he enjoyed his divine security. The weeks passed lazily one after the other.

One morning George and the consul were in the courtyard looking at some curios that a Chinese had brought for their inspection when there was a loud knocking at the great door of the Consulate. The door-man flung it open. A chair borne by four coolies entered, advanced, and was set down. Mabel stepped out. She was neat and cool and fresh. There was nothing in her appearance to suggest that she had just come in after a fortnight on the road. George was petrified. He was as pale as death. She went up to him.

"Hulloa, George, I was so afraid I'd missed you again."

"Hulloa, Mabel," he faltered.

He did not know what to say. He looked this way and that: she stood between him and the doorway. She looked at him with a smile in her blue eyes.

"You haven't altered at all," she said. "Men can go off so dreadfully in seven years and I was afraid you'd got fat and bald. I've been so nervous. It would have been terrible if after all these years I simply hadn't been able to bring myself to marry you after all."

She turned to George's host.

"Are you the consul?" she asked.

"I am."

"That's all right. I'm ready to marry him as soon as I've had a bath."

And she did.

MASTERSON

WHEN I left Colombo I had no notion of going to Keng Tung, but on the ship I met a man who told me he had spent five years there. He said it had an important market, held every five days, whither came natives of half a dozen countries and members of half a hundred tribes. It had pagodas darkly splendid and a remoteness that liberated the questing spirit from its anxiety. He said he would sooner live there than anywhere in the world. I asked him what it had offered him and he said, contentment. He was a tall, dark fellow with the aloofness of manner you often find in those who have lived much alone in unfrequented places. Men like this are a little restless in the company of others and though in the smoking-room of a ship or at the club bar they may be talkative and convivial, telling their story with the rest, joking and glad sometimes to narrate their unusual experiences, they seem always to hold something back. They have a life in themselves that they keep apart, and there is a look in their eyes, as it were turned inwards, that informs you that this hidden life is the only one that signifies to them. And now and then their eyes betray their weariness with the social round into which hazard or the fear of seeming odd has for a moment forced them. They seem then to long for the monotonous solitude of some place of their predilection where they can be once more alone with the reality they have found.

It was as much the manner of this chance acquaintance as what he told me that persuaded me to make the journey across the Shan States on which I now set out. From the rail-head in Upper Burma to the rail-head in Siam, whence I could get down to Bangkok, it was between six and seven hundred miles. Kind people had done everything possible to render the excursion easy for me and the Resident at Taunggyi had wired to me that he had made arrangements for mules and ponies to be ready for me on my arrival. I had bought in Rangoon such stores as seemed necessary, folding chairs and a table, a filter, lamps and I know not what. I took the train from Mandalay to Thazi, intending there to hire a car for Taunggyi, and a man I had met at the club at Mandalay and who lived at Thazi asked me to have brunch (the pleasant meal of Burma that combines breakfast and lunch) with him before I started. His name was Masterson. He was a man in the early thirties, with a pleasant friendly face, curling dark hair speckled with grey, and handsome dark eyes. He spoke with a singularly musical voice, very slowly, and this, I hardly know why, inspired you with confidence. You felt that a man who took such a long time to say what he had to say and had found the world with sufficient leisure to listen to him must have qualities that made him sympathetic to his fellows. He took the amiability of mankind for granted and I suppose he could only have done this because he was himself amiable. He had a nice sense of humour, without of course a quick thrust and parry, but agreeably sarcastic; it was of that agreeable type that applies common sense to the accidents of life and so sees them in a faintly ridiculous aspect. He was engaged in a business that kept him travelling up and down Burma most of the year and in his journeyings he had acquired the collector's habit. He told me that he spent all his spare money on buying Burmese curiosities and it was especially to see them that he asked me to have a meal with him.

The train got in early in the morning. He had warned me that, having to be at his office, he could not meet me; but brunch was at ten and he told me to go to his house as soon as I was finished with the one or two things I had to do in the town.

"Make yourself at home," he said, "and if you want a drink ask the boy for it. I'll get back as soon as I've got through with my business."

I found out where there was a garage and made a bargain with the owner of a very dilapidated Ford to take me and my baggage to Taunggyi. I left my Madrassi servant to see that everything was stowed in it that was possible and the rest tied on to the footboards, and strolled along to Masterson's house. It was a neat little bungalow in a road shaded by tall trees, and in the early light of a sunny day looked pretty and homelike. I walked up the steps and was hailed by Masterson.

"I got done more quickly than I expected. I shall have time to show you my things before brunch is ready. What will you have? I'm afraid I can only offer you a whisky and soda."

"Isn't it rather early for that?"

"Rather. But it's one of the rules of the house that nobody crosses the threshold without having a drink."

"What can I do but submit to the rule?"

He called the boy and in a moment a trim Burmese brought in a decanter, a syphon and glasses. I sat down and looked about the room. Though it was still so early the sun was hot outside and the jalousies were drawn. The light was pleasant and cool after the glare of the road. The room was comfortably furnished with rattan chairs and on the walls were water-colour paintings of English scenes. They were a little prim and old-fashioned and I guessed that they had been painted in her youth by the maiden and elderly aunt of my host. There were two of a cathedral I did not know, two or three of a rose garden and one of a Georgian house. When he saw my eyes for an instant rest upon this, he said:

"That was our house at Cheltenham."

"Oh, is that where you come from?"

Then there was his collection. The room was crowded with Buddhas and with figures, in bronze or wood, of the Buddha's disciples; there were boxes of all shapes, utensils of one kind and another, curiosities of every sort, and although there were far too many they were arranged with a certain taste so that the effect was pleasing. He had some lovely things. He showed them to me with pride, telling me how he had got this object and that, and how he had heard of another and hunted it down and the incredible astuteness he had employed to induce an unwilling owner to part with it. His kindly eyes shone when he described a great bargain and they flashed darkly when he inveighed against the unreasonableness of a vendor who rather than accept a fair price for a bronze dish had taken it away. There were flowers in the room, and it had not the forlorn look that so many bachelors' houses have in the East.

"You've made the place very comfortable," I said.

He gave the room a sweeping glance.

"It *was* all right. It's not much now."

I did not quite know what he meant. Then he showed me a long wooden gilt box, decorated with the glass mosaic that I had admired in the palace at Mandalay, but the workmanship was more delicate than anything I had seen there, and this with its gem-like richness had really something of the ornate exquisiteness of the Italian Renaissance.

"They tell me it's about a couple of hundred years old," he said. "They've not been able to turn out anything like this for a long time."

It was a piece made obviously for a king's palace and you wondered to what uses it had been put and what hands it had passed through. It was a jewel.

"What is the inside like?" I asked.

"Oh, nothing much. It's just lacquered."

He opened it and I saw that it contained three or four framed photographs.

"Oh, I'd forgotten those were there," he said.

His soft, musical voice had a queer sound in it, and I gave him a sidelong look. He was bronzed by the sun, but his face notwithstanding flushed a deeper red. He was about to close the box, and then he changed his mind. He took out one of the photographs and showed it to me.

"Some of these Burmese girls are rather sweet when they're young, aren't they?" he said.

The photograph showed a young girl standing somewhat self-consciously against the conventional background of a photographer's studio, a pagoda and a group of palm-trees. She was wearing her best clothes and she had a flower in her hair. But the embarrassment you saw she felt at having her picture taken did not prevent a shy smile from trembling on her lips and her large solemn eyes had nevertheless a roguish twinkle. She was very small and very slender.

"What a ravishing little thing," I said.

Then Masterson took out another photograph in which she sat with a child standing by her side, his hand timidly on her knee and a baby in her arms. The child stared straight in front of him with a look of terror on his face; he could not understand what that machine and the man behind it, his head under a black cloth, were up to.

"Are those her children?" I asked.

"And mine," said Masterson.

At that moment the boy came in to say that brunch was ready. We went into the dining-room and sat down.

"I don't know what you'll get to eat. Since my girl went away everything in the house has gone to blazes."

A sulky look came into his red honest face and I did not know what to reply.

"I'm so hungry that whatever I get will seem good," I hazarded.

He did not say anything and a plate of thin porridge was put before us. I helped myself to milk and sugar. Masterson ate a spoonful or two and pushed his plate aside.

"I wish I hadn't looked at those damned photographs," he said. "I put them away on purpose."

I did not want to be inquisitive or to force a confidence my host had no wish to give, but neither did I desire to seem so unconcerned as to prevent him from telling me something he had in his heart. Often in some lonely post in the jungle or in a stiff grand house, solitary in the midst of a teeming Chinese city, a man has told me stories about himself that I was sure he had never told to a living soul. I was a stray acquaintance whom he had never seen before and would never see again, a wanderer for a moment through his monotonous life, and some starved impulse led him to lay bare his soul. I have in this way learned more about men in a night (sitting over a syphon or two and a bottle of whisky, the hostile, inexplicable world outside the radius of an acetylene lamp) than I could have if I had known them for ten years. If you are interested in human nature it is one of the great pleasures of travel. And when you separate (for you have to be up betimes) sometimes they will say to you:

"I'm afraid I've bored you to death with all this nonsense. I haven't talked so much for six months. But it's done me good to get it off my chest."

The boy removed the porridge plates and gave each of us a piece of pale fried fish. It was rather cold.

"The fish is beastly, isn't it?" said Masterson. "I hate river fish, except trout; the only thing is to smother it with Worcester sauce."

He helped himself freely and passed me the bottle.

"She was a damned good housekeeper, my girl; I used to feed

like a fighting-cock when she was here. She'd have had the cook out of the house in a quarter of an hour if he'd sent in muck like this."

He gave me a smile, and I noticed that his smile was very sweet. It gave him a peculiarly gentle look.

"It was rather a wrench parting with her, you know."

It was quite evident now that he wished to talk and I had no hesitation in giving him a lead.

"Did you have a row?"

"No. You could hardly call it a row. She lived with me five years and we never had a tiff even. She was the best-tempered little thing that ever was. Nothing seemed to put her out. She was always as merry as a cricket. You couldn't look at her without her lips breaking into a smile. She was always happy. And there was no reason why she shouldn't be. I was very good to her."

"I'm sure you were," I answered.

"She was mistress here. I gave her everything she wanted. Perhaps if I'd been more of a brute she wouldn't have gone away."

"Don't make me say anything so obvious as that women are incalculable."

He gave me a deprecating glance and there was a trace of shyness in the smile that just flickered in his eyes.

"Would it bore you awfully if I told you about it?"

"Of course not."

"Well, I saw her one day in the street and she rather took my fancy. I showed you her photograph, but the photograph doesn't begin to do her justice. It sounds silly to say about a Burmese girl, but she was like a rose-bud, not an English rose, you know, she was as little like that as the glass flowers on that box I showed you are like real flowers, but a rose grown in an Eastern garden that had something strange and exotic about it. I don't know how to make myself plain."

"I think I understand what you mean all the same," I smiled.

"I saw her two or three times and found out where she lived. I sent my boy to make enquiries about her, and he told me that her parents were quite willing that I should have her if we could come to an arrangement. I wasn't inclined to haggle and everything was settled in no time. Her family gave a party to celebrate the occasion and she came to live here. Of course I treated her in every way as my wife and put her in charge of the house.

I told the boys that they'd got to take their orders from her and if she complained of any of them out they went. You know, some fellows keep their girls in the servants' quarters and when they go away on tour the girls have a rotten time. Well, I think that's a filthy thing to do. If you are going to have a girl to live with you the least you can do is to see that she has a good time.

"She was a great success and I was as pleased as Punch. She kept the house spotless. She saved me money. She wouldn't let the boys rob me. I taught her to play bridge and, believe me, she learned to play a damned good game."

"Did she like it?"

"Loved it. When people came here she couldn't have received them better if she'd been a duchess. You know, these Burmese have beautiful manners. Sometimes it would make me laugh to see the assurance with which she would receive my guests, government officials, you know, and soldiers who were passing through. If some young subaltern was rather shy she'd put him at his ease at once. She was never pushing or obtrusive, but just there when she was wanted and doing her best to see that everything went well and everyone had a good time. And I'll tell you what, she could mix the best cocktail you'd get anywhere between Rangoon and Bhamo. People used to say I was lucky."

"I'm bound to say I think you were," I said.

The curry was served and I piled my plate with rice and helped myself to chicken and then chose from a dozen little dishes the condiments I fancied. It was a good curry.

"Then she had her babies, three in three years, but one died when it was six weeks old. I showed you a photograph of the two that are living. Funny-looking little things, aren't they? Are you fond of children?"

"Yes. I have a strange and almost unnatural passion for new-born babies."

"I don't think I am, you know. I couldn't even feel very much about my own. I've often wondered if it showed that I was rather a rotter."

"I don't think so. I think the passion many people affect for children is merely a fashionable pose. I have a notion that children are all the better for not being burdened with too much parental love."

"Then my girl asked me to marry her, legally I mean, in the English way. I treated it as a joke. I didn't know how she'd got such an idea in her head. I thought it was only a whim and I gave her a gold bracelet to keep her quiet. But it wasn't a whim. She was quite serious about it. I told her there was nothing doing. But you know what women are, when they once set their mind on getting something they never give you a moment's peace. She wheedled and sulked, she cried, she appealed to my compassion, she tried to extract a promise out of me when I was rather tight, she was on the watch for me when I was feeling amorous, she nearly tripped me when she was ill. She watched me more carefully, I should think, than a stockbroker ever watched the market, and I knew that, however natural she seemed, however occupied with something else, she was always warily alert for the unguarded moment when she could pounce on me and gain her point."

Masterson gave me once more his slow, ingenuous smile.

"I suppose women are pretty much the same all the world over," he said.

"I expect so," I answered.

"A thing I've never been able to understand is why a woman thinks it worth while to make you do something you don't want to. She'd rather you did a thing against the grain than not do it at all. I don't see what satisfaction it can be to them."

"The satisfaction of triumph. A man convinced against his will may be of the same opinion still, but a woman doesn't mind that. She has conquered. She has proved her power."

Masterson shrugged his shoulders. He drank a cup of tea.

"You see, she said that sooner or later I was bound to marry an English girl and turn her out. I said I wasn't thinking of marrying. She said she knew all about that. And even if I didn't I should retire some day and go back to England. And where would she be then? It went on for a year. I held out. Then she said that if I wouldn't marry her she'd go and take the kids with her. I told her not to be a silly little fool. She said that if she left me now she could marry a Burman, but in a few years nobody would want her. She began to pack her things. I thought it was only a bluff and I called it: I said: 'Well, go if you want to, but if you do you won't come back.' I didn't think she'd give up a house like this, and the presents I made her, and all the pickings, to go back to her own family. They were as poor as church mice. Well, she went on packing her things. She was just as nice as ever to me, she was gay and smiling; when some fellows came to spend the night here she was just as cordial as usual, and she played bridge with us till two in the morning. I couldn't believe she meant to go and yet I was rather scared. I was very fond of her. She was a damned good sort."

"But if you were fond of her why on earth didn't you marry her? It had been a great success."

"I'll tell you. If I married her I'd have to stay in Burma for the rest of my life. Sooner or later I shall retire and then I want to go back to my old home and live there. I don't want to be buried out here, I want to be buried in an English churchyard. I'm happy enough here, but I don't want to live here always. I couldn't. I want England. Sometimes I get sick of this hot sunshine and these garish colours. I want grey skies and a soft rain falling and the smell of the country. I shall be a funny fat elderly man when I go back, too old to hunt even if I could afford it, but I can fish. I don't want to shoot tigers, I want to shoot rabbits. And I can play golf on a proper course. I know I shall be out of it, we fellows who've spent our lives out here always are, but I can potter about the local club and talk to retired Anglo-Indians. I want to feel under my feet the grey pavement of an English country town, I want to be able to go and have a row with the butcher because the steak he sent me in yesterday was tough, and I want to browse about second-hand bookshops. I want to be said how d'you do to in the street by people who knew me when I was a boy. And I want to have a walled garden at the back of my house and grow roses. I dare say it all sounds very humdrum and provincial and dull to you, but that's the sort of life my people have always lived and that's the sort of life I want to live myself. It's a dream if you like, but it's all I have, it means everything in the world to me, and I can't give it up."

He paused for a moment and looked into my eyes.

"Do you think me an awful fool?"

"No."

"Then one morning she came to me and said that she was off. She had her things put on a cart and even then I didn't think she meant it. Then she put the two children in a rickshaw and came to say good-bye to me. She began to cry. By George, that pretty well broke me up. I asked her if she really meant to go and she said yes, unless I married her. I shook my head. I very nearly yielded. I'm afraid I was crying too. Then she gave a great sob and ran out of the house. I had to drink about half a tumbler of whisky to steady my nerves."

"How long ago did this happen?"

"Four months. At first I thought she'd come back and then because I thought she was ashamed to make the first step I sent my boy to tell her that if she wanted to come I'd take her. But she refused. The house seemed awfully empty without her. At first I thought I'd get used to it, but somehow it doesn't seem to get any less empty. I didn't know how much she meant to me. She'd twined herself round my heart."

"I suppose she'll come back if you agree to marry her."

"Oh, yes, she told the boy that. Sometimes I ask myself if it's worth while to sacrifice my happiness for a dream. It is only a dream, isn't it? It's funny, one of the things that holds me back is the thought of a muddy lane I know, with great clay banks on both sides of it, and above, beech trees bending over. It's got a sort of cold, earthy smell that I can never quite get out of my nostrils. I don't blame her, you know. I rather admire her. I had no idea she had so much character. Sometimes I'm awfully inclined to give way." He hesitated for a little while. "I think, perhaps, if I thought she loved me I would. But of course, she doesn't; they never do, these girls who go and live with white men, I think she liked me, but that's all. What would you do in my place?"

"Oh, my dear fellow, how can I tell? Would you ever forget that dream?"

"Never."

At that moment the boy came in to say that my Madrassi servant with the Ford car had just come up. Masterson looked at his watch.

"You'll want to be getting off, won't you? And I must get back to my office. I'm afraid I've rather bored you with my domestic affairs."

"Not at all," I said.

We shook hands, I put on my topee, and he waved to me as the car drove off.

A MARRIAGE OF CONVENIENCE

I LEFT Bangkok on a shabby little ship of four or five hundred tons. The dingy saloon, which served also as dining-room, had two narrow tables down its length with swivel chairs on both sides of them. The cabins were in the bowels of the ship and they were extremely dirty. Cockroaches walked about on the floor and however placid your temperament it is difficult not to be startled when you go to the wash-basin to wash your hands and a huge cockroach stalks leisurely out.

We dropped down the river, broad and lazy and smiling, and its green banks were dotted with little huts on piles standing at the water's edge. We crossed the bar; and the open sea, blue and still, spread before me. The look of it and the smell of it filled me with elation.

I had gone on board early in the morning and soon discovered that I was thrown amid the oddest collection of persons I had ever encountered. There were two French traders and a Belgian colonel, an Italian tenor, the American proprietor of a circus with his wife, and a retired French official with his. The circus proprietor was what is termed a good mixer, a type which according to your mood you fly from or welcome, but I happened to be feeling much pleased with life and before I had been on board an hour we had shaken for drinks, and he had shown me his animals. He was a very short fat man and his stengah-shifter, white but none too clean, outlined the noble proportions of his abdomen, but the collar was so tight that you wondered he did not choke. He had a red, clean-shaven face, a merry blue eye and short, untidy sandy hair. He wore a battered topee well on the back of his head. His name was Wilkins and he was born in Portland, Oregon. It appears that the Oriental has a passion for the circus and Mr. Wilkins for twenty years had been travelling up and down the East from Port Said to Yokohama (Aden, Bombay, Madras, Calcutta, Rangoon, Singapore, Penang, Bangkok, Saigon, Huë, Hanoi, Hong-Kong, Shanghai, their names roll on the tongue savourily, crowding the imagination with sunshine and strange sounds and a multi-coloured activity) with his menagerie and his merry-go-rounds. It was a strange life he led, unusual and one that, one would have thought, must offer the occasion for all sorts of curious experiences, but the odd thing about him was that he was a perfectly commonplace little man and you would have been prepared to find him running a garage or keeping a third-rate hotel in a second-rate town in California. The fact is, and I have noticed it so often that I do not know why it should always surprise me, that the extraordinariness of a man's life does not make him extraordinary, but contrariwise if a man is extraordinary he will make extraordinariness out of a life as humdrum as that of a country curate. I wish I could feel it reasonable to tell here the story of the hermit I went to see on an island in the Torres Straits, a shipwrecked mariner who had lived there alone for thirty years, but when you are writing a book you are imprisoned by the four walls of your subject and though for the entertainment of my own digressing mind I set it down now I should be forced in the end, by my sense of what is fit to go between two covers and what is not, to cut it out. Anyhow, the long and short of it is that notwithstanding his long and intimate communion with nature and his thoughts the man was as dull, insensitive and vulgar an oaf at the end of this experience as he must have been at the beginning.

The Italian singer passed us and Mr. Wilkins told me that he was a Neapolitan who was on his way to Hong-Kong to rejoin his company, which he had been forced to leave owing to an attack of malaria in Bangkok. He was an enormous fellow, and very fat, and when he flung himself into a chair it creaked with dismay. He took off his topee, displayed a great head of long, curly, greasy hair, and ran podgy and beringed fingers through it.

"He ain't very sociable," said Mr. Wilkins. "He took the cigar

I gave him, but he wouldn't have a drink. I shouldn't wonder if there wasn't somethin' rather queer about him. Nasty-lookin' guy, ain't he?"

Then a little fat woman in white came on deck holding by the hand a Wa-Wa monkey. It walked solemnly by her side.

"This is Mrs. Wilkins," said the circus proprietor, "and our youngest son. Draw up a chair, Mrs. Wilkins, and meet this gentleman. I don't know his name, but he's already paid for two drinks for me and if he can't shake any better than he has yet he'll pay for one for you too."

Mrs. Wilkins sat down with an abstracted, serious look, and with her eyes on the blue sea suggested that she did not see why she shouldn't have a lemonade.

"My, it's hot," she murmured, fanning herself with the topee which she took off.

"Mrs. Wilkins feels the heat," said her husband. "She's had twenty years of it now."

"Twenty-two and a half," said Mrs. Wilkins, still looking at the sea.

"And she's never got used to it yet."

"Nor never shall and you know it," said Mrs. Wilkins.

She was just the same size as her husband and just as fat, and she had a round red face like his and the same sandy, untidy hair. I wondered if they had married because they were so exactly alike, or if in the course of years they had acquired this astonishing resemblance. She did not turn her head but continued to look absently at the sea.

"Have you shown him the animals?" she asked.

"You bet your life I have."

"What did he think of Percy?"

"Thought him fine."

I could not but feel that I was being unduly left out of a conversation of which I was at all events partly the subject, so I asked:

"Who's Percy?"

"Percy's our eldest son. There's a flyin'-fish, Elmer. He's the oran-utan. Did he eat his food well this morning?"

"Fine. He's the biggest oran-utan in captivity. I wouldn't take a thousand dollars for him."

"And what relation is the elephant?" I asked.

Mrs. Wilkins did not look at me, but with her blue eyes still gazed indifferently at the sea.

"He's no relation," she answered. "Only a friend."

The boy brought lemonade for Mrs. Wilkins, a whisky and soda for her husband and a gin and tonic for me. We shook dice and I signed the chit.

"It must come expensive if he always loses when he shakes," Mrs. Wilkins murmured to the coast-line.

"I guess Egbert would like a sip of your lemonade, my dear," said Mr. Wilkins.

Mrs. Wilkins slightly turned her head and looked at the monkey sitting on her lap.

"Would you like a sip of mother's lemonade, Egbert?"

The monkey gave a little squeak and putting her arm round him she handed him a straw. The monkey sucked up a little lemonade and having drunk enough sank back against Mrs. Wilkins' ample bosom.

"Mrs. Wilkins thinks the world of Egbert," said her husband. "You can't wonder at it, he's her youngest."

Mrs. Wilkins took another straw and thoughtfully drank her lemonade.

"Egbert's all right," she remarked. "There's nothin' wrong with Egbert."

Just then the French official, who had been sitting down, got up and began walking up and down. He had been accompanied on board by the French minister at Bangkok, one or two secretaries and a prince of the royal family. There had been a great deal of bowing and shaking of hands and as the ship slipped away from the quay much waving of hats and handkerchiefs. He was evidently a person of consequence. I had heard the captain address him as Monsieur le Gouverneur.

"That's the big noise on this boat," said Mr. Wilkins. "He was Governor of one of the French colonies and now he's makin' a tour of the world. He came to see my circus at Bangkok. I guess I'll ask him what he'll have. What shall I call him, my dear?"

Mrs. Wilkins slowly turned her head and looked at the Frenchman, with the rosette of the Legion of Honour in his buttonhole, pacing up and down.

"Don't call him anythin'," she said. "Show him a hoop and he'll jump right through it."

I could not but laugh. Monsieur le Gouverneur was a little man, well below the average height, and smally made, with a very ugly little face and thick, almost negroid features; and he had a bushy grey head, bushy grey eyebrows and a bushy grey moustache. He did look a little like a poodle and he had the poodle's soft, intelligent and shining eyes. Next time he passed us Mr. Wilkins called out:

"*Monsoo. Qu'est ce que vous prenez?*" I cannot reproduce the eccentricities of his accent. "*Une petite verre de porto.*" He turned to me. "Foreigners, they all drink porto. You're always safe with that."

"Not the Dutch," said Mrs. Wilkins, with a look at the sea. "They won't touch nothin' but Schnapps."

The distinguished Frenchman stopped and looked at Mr. Wilkins with some bewilderment. Whereupon Mr. Wilkins tapped his breast and said:

"*Moa, proprietarre Cirque. Vous avez visité.*"

Then, for a reason that escaped me, Mr. Wilkins made his arms into a hoop and outlined the gestures that represented a poodle jumping through it. Then he pointed at the Wa-Wa that Mrs. Wilkins was still holding on her lap.

"*La petit fils de mon femme,*" he said.

Light broke upon the Governor and he burst into a peculiarly musical and infectious laugh. Mr. Wilkins began laughing too.

"*Oui, oui,*" he cried. "*Moa,* circus proprietor. *Une petite verre de porto. Oui. Oui. N'est ce pas?*"

"Mr. Wilkins talks French like a Frenchman," Mrs. Wilkins informed the passing sea.

"*Mais très volontiers,*" said the Governor, still smiling. I drew him up a chair and he sat down with a bow to Mrs. Wilkins.

"Tell poodle-face his name's Egbert," she said, looking at the sea.

I called the boy and we ordered a round of drinks.

"You sign the chit, Elmer," she said. "It's not a bit of good Mr. What's-his-name shakin' if he can't shake nothin' better than a pair of treys."

"*Vous comprenez le français, madame?*" asked the Governor politely.

"He wants to know if you speak French, my dear."

"Where does he think I was raised? Naples?"

Then the Governor, with exuberant gesticulation, burst into a torrent of English so fantastic that it required all my knowledge of French to understand what he was talking about.

Presently Mr. Wilkins took him down to look at his animals and a little later we assembled in the stuffy saloon for luncheon.

The Governor's wife appeared and was put on the captain's right. The Governor explained to her who we all were and she gave us a gracious bow. She was a large woman, tall and of a robust build, of fifty-five perhaps, and she was dressed somewhat severely in black silk. On her head she wore a huge round topee. Her features were so large and regular, her form so statuesque, that you were reminded of the massive females who take part in processions. She would have admirably suited the rôle of Columbia or Britannia in a patriotic demonstration. She towered over her diminutive husband like a skyscraper over a shack. He talked incessantly, with vivacity and wit, and when he said anything amusing her heavy features relaxed into a large, fond smile.

"Que tu es bête, mon ami," she said. She turned to the captain. "You must not pay any attention to him. He is always like that."

We had indeed a very amusing meal and when it was over we separated to our various cabins to sleep away the heat of the afternoon. In such a small ship having once made the acquaintance of my fellow passengers, it would have been impossible, even had I wished it, not to pass with them every moment of the day that I was not in my cabin. The only person who held himself aloof was the Italian tenor. He spoke to no one, but sat by himself as far forward as he could get, twanging a guitar in an undertone so that you had to strain your ears to catch the notes. We remained in sight of land and the sea was like a pail of milk. Talking of one thing and another we watched the day decline, we dined, and then we sat out again on deck under the stars. The two traders played piquet in the hot saloon, but the Belgian colonel joined our little group. He was shy and fat and opened his mouth only to utter a civility. Soon, influenced perhaps by the night and encouraged by the darkness that gave him, up there in the bows, the sensation of being alone with the sea, the Italian tenor, accompanying himself on his guitar, began to sing, first in a low tone, and then a little louder, till presently, his music captivating him, he sang with all his might. He had the real Italian voice, all macaroni, olive oil and sunshine, and he sang the Neapolitan songs that I had heard in my youth in the Piazza San Ferdinando, and fragments from *La Bohème*, and *Traviata* and *Rigoletto*. He sang with emotion and false emphasis and his tremolo reminded you of every third-rate Italian tenor you had ever heard, but there in the openness of that lovely night his exaggerations only made you smile and you could not but feel in your heart a lazy sensual pleasure. He sang for an hour, perhaps, and we all fell silent; then he was still, but he did not move and we saw his huge bulk dimly outlined against the luminous sky.

I saw that the little French Governor had been holding the hand of his large wife and the sight was absurd and touching.

"Do you know that this is the anniversary of the day on which I first saw my wife?" he said, suddenly breaking the silence which had certainly weighed on him, for I had never met a more loquacious creature. "It is also the anniversary of the day on which she promised to be my wife. And, which will surprise you, they were one and the same."

"*Voyons, mon ami,*" said the lady, "you are not going to bore our friends with that old story. You are really quite insupportable."

But she spoke with a smile on her large, firm face, and in a tone that suggested that she was quite willing to hear it again.

"But it will interest them, *mon petit chou.*" It was in this way that he always addressed his wife and it was funny to hear this imposing and even majestic lady thus addressed by her small husband. "Will it not, *monsieur?*" he asked me. "It is a romance and who does not like romance, especially on such a night as this?"

I assured the Governor that we were all anxious to hear and the Belgian colonel took the opportunity once more to be polite.

"You see, ours was a marriage of convenience pure and simple."

"*C'est vrai,*" said the lady. "It would be stupid to deny it. But sometimes love comes after marriage and not before, and then it is better. It lasts longer."

I could not but notice that the Governor gave her hand an affectionate little squeeze.

"You see, I had been in the navy, and when I retired I was forty-nine. I was strong and active and I was very anxious to find an occupation. I looked about; I pulled all the strings I could. Fortunately I had a cousin who had some political importance. It is one of the advantages of democratic government that if you have sufficient influence, merit, which otherwise might pass unnoticed, generally receives its due reward."

"You are modesty itself, *mon pauvre ami,*" said she.

"And presently I was sent for by the Minister to the Colonies and offered the post of Governor in a certain colony. It was a very distant spot that they wished to send me to and a lonely one, but I had spent my life wandering from port to port, and that was not a matter that troubled me. I accepted with joy. The minister told me that I must be ready to start in a month. I told him that would be easy for an old bachelor who had nothing much in the world but a few clothes and a few books.

" '*Comment, mon lieutenant,*' he cried. 'You are a bachelor?'

" 'Certainly,' I answered. 'And I have every intention of remaining one.'

" 'In that case I am afraid I must withdraw my offer. For this position it is essential that you should be married.'

"It is too long a story to tell you, but the gist of it was that owing to the scandal my predecessor, a bachelor, had caused by having native girls to live in the Residency and the consequent complaints of the white people, planters and the wives of functionaries, it had been decided that the next Governor must be a model of respectability. I expostulated. I argued. I recapitulated my services to the country and the services my cousin could render at the next elections. Nothing would serve. The minister was adamant.

" 'But what can I do?' I cried with dismay.

" 'You can marry,' said the minister.

" '*Mais voyons, monsieur le ministre,* I do not know any women. I am not a lady's man and I am forty-nine. How do you expect me to find a wife?'

" 'Nothing is more simple. Put an advertisement in the paper.'

"I was confounded. I did not know what to say.

" 'Well, think it over,' said the minister. 'If you can find a wife in a month you can go, but no wife no job. That is my last word.' He smiled a little, to him the situation was not without humour. 'And if you think of advertising I recommend the *Figaro*.'

"I walked away from the ministry with death in my heart. I knew the place to which they desired to appoint me and I knew it would suit me very well to live there; the climate was tolerable and the Residency was spacious and comfortable. The notion of being a Governor was far from displeasing me and, having nothing much but my pension as a naval officer, the salary was not to be despised. Suddenly I made up my mind. I walked to the offices of the *Figaro*, composed an advertisement and handed it in for insertion. But I can tell you, when I walked up the Champs Elysées afterwards my heart was beating much more furiously than it had ever done when my ship was stripped for action."

The Governor leaned forward and put his hand impressively on my knee.

"*Mon cher monsieur*, you will never believe it, but I had four thousand three hundred and seventy-two replies. It was an avalanche. I had expected half-a-dozen; I had to take a cab to take the letters to my hotel. My room was swamped with them. There were four thousand three hundred and seventy-two women who were willing to share my solitude and be a Governor's lady. It was staggering. They were of all ages from seventeen to seventy. There were maidens of irreproachable ancestry and the highest culture, there were unmarried ladies who had made a little slip at one period of their career and now desired to regularise their situation; there were widows whose husbands had died in the most harrowing circumstances; and there were widows whose children would be a solace to my old age. They were blonde and dark, tall and short, fat and thin; some could speak five languages and others could play the piano. Some offered me love and some craved for it; some could only give me a solid friendship but mingled with esteem; some had a fortune and others golden prospects. I was overwhelmed. I was bewildered. At last I lost my temper, for I am a passionate man, and I got up and I stamped on all those letters and all those photographs and I cried: I will marry none of them. It was hopeless, I had less than a month now and I could not see over four thousand aspirants to my hand in that time. I felt that if I did not see them all, I should be tortured for the rest of my life by the thought that I had missed the one woman the fates had destined to make me happy. I gave it up as a bad job.

"I went out of my room hideous with all those photographs and littered papers and to drive care away went on to the boulevard and sat down at the Café de la Paix. After a time I saw a friend passing and he nodded to me and smiled. I tried to smile but my heart was sore. I realised that I must spend the years that remained to me in a cheap *pension* at Toulon or Brest as an *officier de marine en retraite*. *Zut!* My friend stopped and coming up to me sat down.

" 'What is making you look so glum, *mon cher?*' he asked me. 'You who are the gayest of mortals.'

"I was glad to have someone in whom I could confide my

troubles and told him the whole story. He laughed consumedly. I have thought since that perhaps the incident had its comic side, but at the time, I assure you, I could see in it nothing to laugh at. I mentioned the fact to my friend not without asperity and then, controlling his mirth as best he could, he said to me: 'But, my dear fellow, do you really want to marry?' At this I entirely lost my temper.

" 'You are completely idiotic,' I said. 'If I did not want to marry, and what is more marry at once, within the next fortnight, do you imagine that I should have spent three days reading love letters from women I have never set eyes on?'

" 'Calm yourself and listen to me,' he replied. 'I have a cousin who lives in Geneva. She is Swiss, *du reste*, and she belongs to a family of the greatest respectability in the republic. Her morals are without reproach, she is of a suitable age, a spinster, for she has spent the last fifteen years nursing an invalid mother who has lately died, she is well educated and *pardessus le marché* she is not ugly.'

" 'It sounds as though she were a paragon,' I said.

" 'I do not say that, but she has been well brought up and would become the position you have to offer her.'

" 'There is one thing you forget. What inducement would there be for her to give up her friends and her accustomed life to accompany in exile a man of forty-nine who is by no means a beauty?' "

Monsieur le Gouverneur broke off his narrative and shrugging his shoulders so emphatically that his head almost sank between them, turned to us.

"I am ugly. I admit it. I am of an ugliness that does not inspire terror or respect, but only ridicule, and that is the worst ugliness of all. When people see me for the first time they do not shrink with horror, there would evidently be something flattering in that, they burst out laughing. Listen, when the admirable Mr. Wilkins showed me his animals this morning, Percy, the oran-utan, held out his arms and but for the bars of the cage would have clasped me to his bosom as a long lost brother. Once indeed when I was at the Jardin des Plantes in Paris and was told that one of the anthropoid apes had escaped I made my way to the exit as quickly as I could in fear that, mistaking me for the refugee, they would seize me and, notwithstanding my expostulations, shut me up in the monkey house."

"*Voyons, mon ami,*" said Madame his wife, in her deep slow

voice, "you are talking even greater nonsense than usual. I do not say that you are an Apollo, in your position it is unnecessary that you should be, but you have dignity, you have poise, you are what any woman would call a fine man."

"I will resume my story. When I made this remark to my friend he replied: 'One can never tell with women. There is something about marriage that wonderfully attracts them. There would be no harm in asking her. After all it is regarded as a compliment by a woman to be asked in marriage. She can but refuse.'

" 'But I do not know your cousin and I do not see how I am to make her acquaintance. I cannot go to her house, ask to see her and when I am shown into the drawing-room say: *Voilà*, I have come to ask you to marry me. She would think I was a lunatic and scream for help. Besides, I am a man of an extreme timidity, and I could never take such a step.'

" 'I will tell you what to do,' said my friend. 'Go to Geneva and take her a box of chocolates from me. She will be glad to have news of me and will receive you with pleasure. You can have a little talk and then if you do not like the look of her you take your leave and no harm is done. If on the other hand you do, we can go into the matter and you can make a formal demand for her hand.'

"I was desperate. It seemed the only thing to do. We went to a shop at once and bought an enormous box of chocolates and that night I took the train to Geneva. No sooner had I arrived than I sent her a letter to say that I was the bearer of a gift from her cousin and much wished to give myself the pleasure of delivering it in person. Within an hour I received her reply to the effect that she would be pleased to receive me at four o'clock in the afternoon. I spent the interval before my mirror and seventeen times I tied and retied my tie. As the clock struck four I presented myself at the door of her house and was immediately ushered into the drawing-room. She was waiting for me. Her cousin said she was not ugly. Imagine my surprise to see a young woman, *enfin* a woman still young, of a noble presence, with the dignity of Juno, the features of Venus, and in her expression the intelligence of Minerva."

"You are too absurd," said Madame. "But by now these gentlemen know that one cannot believe all you say."

"I swear to you that I do not exaggerate. I was so taken aback that I nearly dropped the box of chocolates. But I said to myself: *La garde meurt mais ne se rend pas.* I presented the box of chocolates. I gave her news of her cousin. I found her amiable. We talked for a quarter of an hour. And then I said to myself: *Allons-y.* I said to her:

" 'Mademoiselle, I must tell you that I did not come here merely to give you a box of chocolates.'

"She smiled and remarked that evidently I must have had reasons to come to Geneva of more importance than that.

" 'I came to ask you to do me the honour of marrying me.' She gave a start.

" 'But, *monsieur,* you are mad,' she said.

" 'I beseech you not to answer till you have heard the facts,' I interrupted, and before she could say another word I told her the whole story. I told her about my advertisement in the *Figaro* and she laughed till the tears ran down her face. Then I repeated my offer.

" 'You are serious?' she asked.

" 'I have never been more serious in my life.'

" 'I will not deny that your offer has come as a surprise. I had not thought of marrying, I have passed the age; but evidently your offer is not one that a woman should refuse without consideration. I am flattered. Will you give me a few days to reflect?'

" '*Mademoiselle,* I am absolutely desolated,' I replied. 'But I have not time. If you will not marry me I must go back to Paris and resume my perusal of the fifteen or eighteen hundred letters that still await my attention.'

" 'It is quite evident that I cannot possibly give you an answer at once. I had not set eyes on you a quarter of an hour ago. I must consult my friends and my family.'

" 'What have they got to do with it? You are of full age. The matter is pressing. I cannot wait. I have told you everything. You are an intelligent woman. What can prolonged reflection add to the impulse of the moment?'

" 'You are not asking me to say yes or no this very minute? That is outrageous.'

" 'That is exactly what I am asking. My train goes back to Paris in a couple of hours.'

"She looked at me reflectively.

" 'You are quite evidently a lunatic. You ought to be shut up both for your own safety and that of the public.'

" 'Well, which is it to be?' I said. 'Yes or no?'

"She shrugged her shoulders.

" '*Mon Dieu.*' She waited a minute and I was on tenterhooks. 'Yes.' "

The Governor waved his hand towards his wife.

"And there she is. We were married in a fortnight and I became Governor of a colony. I married a jewel, my dear sirs, a woman of the most charming character, one in a thousand, a woman of a masculine intelligence and a feminine sensibility, an admirable woman."

"But hold your tongue, *mon ami*," his wife said. "You are making me as ridiculous as yourself."

He turned to the Belgian colonel.

"Are you a bachelor, *mon colonel?* If so I strongly recommend you to go to Geneva. It is a nest (*une pépinière* was the word he used) of the most adorable young women. You will find a wife there as nowhere else. Geneva is besides a charming city. Do not waste a minute, but go there and I will give you a letter to my wife's nieces."

It was she who summed up the story.

"The fact is that in a marriage of convenience you expect less and so you are less likely to be disappointed. As you do not make senseless claims on one another there is no reason for exasperation. You do not look for perfection and so you are tolerant to one another's faults. Passion is all very well, but it is not a proper foundation for marriage. *Voyez-vous,* for two people to be happy in marriage they must be able to respect one another, they must be of the same condition and their interests must be alike; then if they are decent people and are willing to give and take, to live and let live, there is no reason why their union should not be as happy as ours." She paused. "But, of course, my husband is a very, very remarkable man."

PRINCESS SEPTEMBER

FIRST the King of Siam had two daughters and he called them Night and Day. Then he had two more, so he changed the names of the first ones and called the four of them after the seasons, Spring and Autumn, Winter and Summer. But in course of time he had three others and he changed their names again and called all seven by the days of the week. But when his eighth daughter was born he did not know what to do till he suddenly thought of the months of the year. The Queen said there were only twelve and it confused her to have to remember so many new names, but the King had a methodical mind and when he made it up he never could change it if he tried. He changed the names of all his daughters and called them January, February, March (though of course in Siamese) till he came to the youngest, who was called August, and the next one was called September.

"That only leaves October, November, and December," said the Queen. "And after that we shall have to begin all over again."

"No, we shan't," said the King, "because I think twelve daughters are enough for any man and after the birth of dear little December I shall be reluctantly compelled to cut off your head."

He cried bitterly when he said this, for he was extremely fond of the Queen. Of course it made the Queen very uneasy because she knew that it would distress the King very much if he had to

cut off her head. And it would not be very nice for her. But it
so happened that there was no need for either of them to worry
because September was the last daughter they ever had. The
Queen only had sons after that and they were called by the
letters of the alphabet, so there was no cause for anxiety there
for a long time, since she had only reached the letter J.

Now the King of Siam's daughters had had their characters
permanently embittered by having to change their names in
this way, and the older ones, whose names of course had been
changed oftener than the others, had their characters more permanently embittered. But September, who had never known
what it was to be called anything but September (except of
course by her sisters, who because their characters were embittered called her all sorts of names), had a very sweet and
charming nature.

The King of Siam had a habit which I think might be usefully
imitated in Europe. Instead of receiving presents on his birthday he gave them and it looks as though he liked it, for he used
often to say he was sorry he had only been born on one day and
so only had one birthday in the year. But in this way he managed in course of time to give away all his wedding presents and
the loyal addresses which the mayors of the cities in Siam presented him with and all his own crowns which had gone out of
fashion. One year on his birthday, not having anything else
handy, he gave each of his daughters a beautiful green parrot in
a beautiful golden cage. There were nine of them and on each
cage was written the name of the month which was the name of
the princess it belonged to. The nine princesses were very proud
of their parrots and they spent an hour every day (for like their
father they were of a methodical turn of mind) in teaching
them to talk. Presently all the parrots could say God Save the
King (in Siamese, which is very difficult) and some of them
could say Pretty Polly in no less than seven oriental languages.
But one day when the Princess September went to say good-
morning to her parrot she found it lying dead at the bottom of
its golden cage. She burst into a flood of tears, and nothing that
her Maids of Honour could say comforted her. She cried so
much that the Maids of Honour, not knowing what to do, told
the Queen, and the Queen said it was stuff and nonsense and the
child had better go to bed without any supper. The Maids of
Honour wanted to go to a party, so they put the Princess September to bed as quickly as they could and left her by herself.

And while she lay in her bed, crying still even though she felt rather hungry, she saw a little bird hop into her room. She took her thumb out of her mouth and sat up. Then the little bird began to sing and he sang a beautiful song all about the lake in the King's garden and the willow trees that looked at themselves in the still water and the goldfish that glided in and out of the branches that were reflected in it. When he had finished, the Princess was not crying any more and she quite forgot that she had had no supper.

"That was a very nice song," she said.

The little bird gave her a bow, for artists have naturally good manners, and they like to be appreciated.

"Would you care to have me instead of your parrot?" said the little bird. "It's true that I'm not so pretty to look at, but on the other hand I have a much better voice."

The Princess September clapped her hands with delight and then the little bird hopped on to the end of her bed and sang her to sleep.

When she awoke next day the little bird was still sitting there, and as she opened her eyes he said good-morning. The Maids of Honour brought in her breakfast, and he ate rice out of her hand and he had his bath in her saucer. He drank out of it too. The Maids of Honour said they didn't think it was very polite to drink one's bath water, but the Princess September said that was the artistic temperament. When he had finished his breakfast he began to sing again so beautifully that the Maids of Honour were quite surprised, for they had never heard anything like it, and the Princess September was very proud and happy.

"Now I want to show you to my eight sisters," said the Princess.

She stretched out the first finger of her right hand so that it served as a perch and the little bird flew down and sat on it. Then, followed by her Maids of Honour, she went through the palace and called on each of the Princesses in turn, starting with January, for she was mindful of etiquette, and going all the way down to August. And for each of the Princesses the little bird sang a different song. But the parrots could only say God Save the King and Pretty Polly. At last she showed the little bird to the King and Queen. They were surprised and delighted.

"I knew I was right to send you to bed without any supper," said the Queen.

"This bird sings much better than the parrots," said the King.

"I should have thought you got quite tired of hearing people say God Save the King," said the Queen. "I can't think why those girls wanted to teach their parrots to say it too."

"The sentiment is admirable," said the King, "and I never mind how often I hear it. But I do get tired of hearing those parrots say Pretty Polly."

"They say it in seven different languages," said the Princesses.

"I dare say they do," said the King, "but it reminds me too much of my councillors. They say the same thing in seven different ways and it never means anything in any way they say it."

The Princesses, their characters as I have already said being naturally embittered, were vexed at this, and the parrots looked very glum indeed. But the Princess September ran through all the rooms of the palace, singing like a lark, while the little bird flew round and round her, singing like a nightingale, which indeed it was.

Things went on like this for several days and then the eight Princesses put their heads together. They went to September and sat down in a circle round her, hiding their feet as is proper for Siamese princesses to do.

"My poor September," they said. "We are sorry for the death of your beautiful parrot. It must be dreadful for you not to have a pet bird as we have. So we have all put our pocket-money together and we are going to buy you a lovely green and yellow parrot."

"Thank you for nothing," said September. (This was not very civil of her, but Siamese princesses are sometimes a little short with one another.) "I have a pet bird which sings the most charming songs to me and I don't know what on earth I should do with a green and yellow parrot."

January sniffed, then February sniffed, then March sniffed; in fact all the Princesses sniffed, but in their proper order of precedence. When they had finished September asked them:

"Why do you sniff? Have you all got colds in the head?"

"Well, my dear," they said, "it's absurd to talk of *your* bird when the little fellow flies in and out just as he likes." They looked round the room and raised their eyebrows so high that their foreheads entirely disappeared.

"You'll get dreadful wrinkles," said September.

"Do you mind our asking where your bird is now?" they said.

"He's gone to pay a visit to his father-in-law," said the Princess September.

"And what makes you think he'll come back?" asked the Princesses.

"He always does come back," said September.

"Well, my dear," said the eight Princesses, "if you'll take our advice you won't run any risks like that. If he comes back, and mind you, if he does you'll be lucky, pop him into the cage and keep him there. That's the only way you can be sure of him."

"But I like to have him fly about the room," said the Princess September.

"Safety first," said her sisters ominously.

They got up and walked out of the room, shaking their heads, and they left September very uneasy. It seemed to her that her little bird was away a long time and she could not think what he was doing. Something might have happened to him. What with hawks and men with snares you never knew what trouble he might get into. Besides, he might forget her, or he might take a fancy to somebody else; that would be dreadful; oh, she wished he were safely back again, and in the golden cage that stood there empty and ready. For when the Maids of Honour had buried the dead parrot they had left the cage in its old place.

Suddenly September heard a tweet-tweet just behind her ear and she saw the little bird sitting on her shoulder. He had come in so quietly and alighted so softly that she had not heard him.

"I wondered what on earth had become of you," said the Princess.

"I thought you'd wonder that," said the little bird. "The fact is I very nearly didn't come back to-night at all. My father-in-law was giving a party and they all wanted me to stay, but I thought you'd be anxious."

Under the circumstances this was a very unfortunate remark for the little bird to make.

September felt her heart go thump, thump against her chest, and she made up her mind to take no more risks. She put up her hand and took hold of the bird. This he was quite used to, she liked feeling his heart go pit-a-pat, so fast, in the hollow of her hand, and I think he liked the soft warmth of her little hand. So the bird suspected nothing and he was so surprised when she carried him over to the cage, popped him in, and shut the door on him for a moment he could think of nothing to say. But in a moment or two he hopped up on the ivory perch and said:

"What is the joke?"

"There's no joke," said September, "but some of mamma's cats are prowling about to-night, and I think you're much safer in there."

"I can't think why the Queen wants to have all those cats," said the little bird, rather crossly.

"Well, you see, they're very special cats," said the Princess, "they have blue eyes and a kink in their tails, and they're a speciality of the royal family, if you understand what I mean."

"Perfectly," said the little bird, "but why did you put me in this cage without saying anything about it? I don't think it's the sort of place I like."

"I shouldn't have slept a wink all night if I hadn't known you were safe."

"Well, just for this once I don't mind," said the little bird, "so long as you let me out in the morning."

He ate a very good supper and then began to sing. But in the middle of his song he stopped.

"I don't know what is the matter with me," he said, "but I don't feel like singing to-night."

"Very well," said September, "go to sleep instead."

So he put his head under his wing and in a minute' was fast asleep. September went to sleep too. But when the dawn broke she was awakened by the little bird calling her at the top of his voice:

"Wake up, wake up," he said. "Open the door of this cage and let me out. I want to have a good fly while the dew is still on the ground."

"You're much better off where you are," said September. "You have a beautiful golden cage. It was made by the best workman in my papa's kingdom, and my papa was so pleased with it that he cut off his head so that he should never make an-other."

"Let me out, let me out," said the little bird.

"You'll have three meals a day served by my Maids of Honour; you'll have nothing to worry you from morning till night, and you can sing to your heart's content."

"Let me out, let me out," said the little bird. And he tried to slip through the bars of the cage, but of course he couldn't, and he beat against the door but of course he couldn't open it. Then the eight Princesses came in and looked at him. They told September she was very wise to take their advice. They said he would soon get used to the cage and in a few days would quite forget that he had ever been free. The little bird said nothing at all while they were there, but as soon as they were gone he began to cry again: "Let me out, let me out."

"Don't be such an old silly," said September. "I've only put you in the cage because I'm so fond of you. *I* know what's good for you much better than you do yourself. Sing me a little song and I'll give you a piece of brown sugar."

But the little bird stood in the corner of his cage, looking out at the blue sky, and never sang a note. He never sang all day.

"What's the good of sulking?" said September. "Why don't you sing and forget your troubles?"

"How can I sing?" answered the bird. "I want to see the trees and the lake and the green rice growing in the fields."

"If that's all you want I'll take you for a walk," said September.

She picked up the cage and went out and she walked down to the lake round which grew the willow trees, and she stood at the edge of the rice-fields that stretched as far as the eye could see.

"I'll take you out every day," she said. "I love you and I only want to make you happy."

"It's not the same thing," said the little bird. "The rice-fields and the lake and the willow trees look quite different when you see them through the bars of a cage."

So she brought him home again and gave him his supper. But he wouldn't eat a thing. The Princess was a little anxious at this, and asked her sisters what they thought about it.

"You must be firm," they said.

"But if he won't eat, he'll die," she answered.

"That would be very ungrateful of him," they said. "He must know that you're only thinking of his own good. If he's obstinate and dies it'll serve him right and you'll be well rid of him."

September didn't see how that was going to do *her* very much good, but they were eight to one and all older than she, so she said nothing.

"Perhaps he'll have got used to his cage by to-morrow," she said.

And next day when she awoke she cried out good-morning in a cheerful voice. She got no answer. She jumped out of bed and ran to the cage. She gave a startled cry, for there the little bird lay, at the bottom, on his side, with his eyes closed, and he looked as if he were dead. She opened the door and putting her hand in lifted him out. She gave a sob of relief, for she felt that his little heart was beating still.

"Wake up, wake up, little bird," she said.

She began to cry and her tears fell on the little bird. He opened his eyes and felt that the bars of the cage were no longer round him.

"I cannot sing unless I'm free and if I cannot sing, I die," he said.

The Princess gave a great sob.

"Then take your freedom," she said, "I shut you in a golden cage because I loved you and wanted to have you all to myself. But I never knew it would kill you. Go. Fly away among the trees that are round the lake and fly over the green rice-fields. I love you enough to let you be happy in your own way."

She threw open the window and gently placed the little bird on the sill. He shook himself a little.

"Come and go as you will, little bird," she said. "I will never put you in a cage any more."

"I will come because I love you, little Princess," said the bird. "And I will sing you the loveliest songs I know. I shall go far away, but I shall always come back, and I shall never forget you." He gave himself another shake. "Good gracious me, how stiff I am," he said.

Then he opened his wings and flew right away into the blue. But the little Princess burst into tears, for it is very difficult to put the happiness of someone you love before your own, and with her little bird far out of sight she felt on a sudden very lonely. When her sisters knew what had happened they mocked her and said that the little bird would never return. But he did at last. And he sat on September's shoulder and ate out of her hand and sang her the beautiful songs he had learned while he was flying up and down the fair places of the world. September kept her window open day and night so that the little bird might come into her room whenever he felt inclined, and this was very good for her; so she grew extremely beautiful. And when she was old enough she married the King of Cambodia and was carried all the way to the city in which he lived on a white elephant. But her sisters never slept with their windows open, so they grew extremely ugly as well as disagreeable, and when the time came to marry them off they were given away to the King's councillors with a pound of tea and a Siamese cat.

IN A STRANGE LAND

I AM of a roving disposition; but I travel not to see imposing monuments, which indeed somewhat bore me, nor beautiful scenery, of which I soon tire; I travel to see men. I avoid the great. I would not cross the road to meet a president or a king; I am content to know the writer in the pages of his book and the painter in his picture; but I have journeyed a hundred leagues to see a missionary of whom I had heard a strange story and I have spent a fortnight in a vile hotel in order to improve my acquaintance with a billiard-marker. I should be inclined to say that I am not surprised to meet any sort of person were it not that there is one sort that I am constantly running against and that never fails to give me a little shock of amused astonishment. This is the elderly Englishwoman, generally of adequate means, who is to be found living alone, up and down the world, in unexpected places. You do not wonder when you hear of her living in a villa on a hill outside a small Italian town, the only Englishwoman in the neighbourhood, and you are almost prepared for it when a lonely hacienda is pointed out to you in Andalusia and you are told that there has dwelt for many years an English lady. But it is more surprising when you hear that the only white person in a Chinese city is an Englishwoman, not a missionary, who lives there none knows why; and there is another who inhabits an island in the South Seas and a third who has a bungalow on the outskirts of a large village in the centre of Java. They live solitary lives, these women, without friends, and they do not welcome the stranger. Though they may not have seen one of their own race for months they will pass you on the road as though they did not see you, and if, presuming on your nationality, you should call, as likely as not they will decline to see you; but if they do, they will give you a cup of tea from a silver teapot and on a plate of Old Worcester you will find Scotch scones. They will talk to you politely, as though they were entertaining you in a Kentish vicarage, but when you take your leave will show no particular desire to continue the acquaintance. One wonders in vain what strange instinct it is that has driven them to separate themselves from their kith and kin and thus to live apart from all their natural interests in an alien land. Is it romance they have sought or freedom?

But of all these Englishwomen whom I have met or perhaps only heard of (for as I have said they are difficult of access) the one who remains most vividly in my memory is an elderly person who lived in Asia Minor. I had arrived after a tedious journey at a little town from which I proposed to make the ascent of a celebrated mountain and I was taken to a rambling hotel that stood at its foot. I arrived late at night and signed my name in the book. I went up to my room. It was cold and I shivered as I undressed, but in a moment there was a knock at the door and the dragoman came in.

"Signora Niccolini's compliments," he said.

To my astonishment he handed me a hot-water bottle. I took it with grateful hands.

"Who is Signora Niccolini?" I asked.

"She is the proprietor of this hotel," he answered.

I sent her my thanks and he withdrew. The last thing I expected in a scrubby hotel in Asia Minor kept by an old Italian woman was a beautiful hot-water bottle. There is nothing I like more (if we were not all sick to death of the war I would tell you the story of how six men risked their lives to fetch a hot-water bottle from a château in Flanders that was being bombarded) ; and next morning, so that I might thank her in person, I asked if I might see the Signora Niccolini. While I waited for her I racked my brains to think what hot-water bottle could possibly be in Italian. In a moment she came in. She was a little stout woman, not without dignity, and she wore a black apron trimmed with lace and a small black lace cap. She stood with her hands crossed. I was astonished at her appearance for she looked exactly like a housekeeper in a great English house.

"Did you wish to speak to me, sir?"

She was an Englishwoman and in those few words I surely recognised the trace of a cockney accent.

"I wanted to thank you for the hot-water bottle," I replied in some confusion.

"I saw by the visitors' book that you were English, sir, and I always send up a 'ot-water bottle to English gentlemen."

"Believe me, it was very welcome."

"I was for many years in the service of the late Lord Ormskirk, sir. He always used to travel with a 'ot-water bottle. Is there anything else, sir?"

"Not at the moment, thank you."

She gave me a polite little nod and withdrew. I wondered how on earth it came about that a funny old Englishwoman like that should be the landlady of a hotel in Asia Minor. It was not easy to make her acquaintance, for she knew her place, as she would herself have put it, and she kept me at a distance. It was not for nothing that she had been in service in a noble English family. But I was persistent and I induced her at last to ask me to have a cup of tea in her own little parlour. I learnt that she had been lady's-maid to a certain Lady Ormskirk, and Signor Niccolini (for she never alluded to her deceased husband in any other way) had been his lordship's chef. Signor Niccolini was a very handsome man and for some years there had been an "understanding" between them. When they had both saved a certain amount of money they were married, retired from service, and looked about for a hotel. They had bought this one on an advertisement because Signor Niccolini thought he would like to see something of the world. That was nearly thirty years ago and Signor Niccolini had been dead for fifteen. His widow had not once been back to England. I asked her if she was never homesick.

"I don't say as I wouldn't like to go back on a visit, though I expect I'd find many changes. But my family didn't like the idea of me marrying a foreigner and I 'aven't spoken to them since. Of course there are many things here that are not the same as what they 'ave at 'ome, but it's surprising what you get used to. I see a lot of life. I don't know as I should care to live the 'umdrum life they do in a place like London."

I smiled. For what she said was strangely incongruous with her manner. She was a pattern of decorum. It was extraordinary that she could have lived for thirty years in this wild and almost barbaric country without its having touched her. Though I knew no Turkish and she spoke it with ease I was convinced that she spoke it most incorrectly and with a cockney accent. I suppose she had remained the precise, prim English lady's-maid, knowing her place, through all these vicissitudes because she had no faculty of surprise. She took everything that came as a matter of course. She looked upon everyone who wasn't English as a foreigner and therefore as someone, almost imbecile, for whom allowances must be made. She ruled her staff despotically—for did she not know how an upper servant in a great house should exercise his authority over the under servants?—and everything about the hotel was clean and neat.

"I do my best," she said, when I congratulated her on this, standing, as always when she spoke to me, with her hands respectfully crossed. "Of course one can't expect foreigners to 'ave the same ideas what we 'ave, but as his lordship used to say to me, what we've got to do, Parker, he said to me, what we've got to do in this life is to make the best of our raw material."

But she kept her greatest surprise for the eve of my departure.

"I'm glad you're not going before you've seen my two sons, sir."

"I didn't know you had any."

"They've been away on business, but they've just come back. You'll be surprised when you've seen them. I've trained them with me own 'ands so to speak, and when I'm gone they'll carry on the 'otel between them."

In a moment two tall, swarthy, strapping young fellows entered the hall. Her eyes lit up with pleasure. They went up to her and took her in their arms and gave her resounding kisses.

"They don't speak English, sir, but they understand a little, and of course they speak Turkish like natives, and Greek and Italian."

I shook hands with the pair and then Signora Niccolini said something to them and they went away.

"They're handsome fellows, Signora," I said. "You must be very proud of them."

"I am, sir, and they're good boys, both of them. They've never give me a moment's trouble from the day they was born and they're the very image of Signor Niccolini."

"I must say no one would think they had an English mother."

"I'm not exactly their mother, sir. I've just sent them along to say 'ow do you do to 'er."

I dare say I looked a little confused.

"They're the sons that Signor Nicolini 'ad by a Greek girl that used to work in the 'otel, and 'aving no children of me own I adopted them."

I sought for some remark to make.

"I 'ope you don't think that there's any blame attaches to Signor Niccolini," she said, drawing herself up a little. "I shouldn't like you to think that, sir." She folded her hands again and with a mixture of pride, primness and satisfaction added the final word: "Signor Niccolini was a very full-blooded man."

THE LOTUS EATER

MOST PEOPLE, the vast majority in fact, lead the lives that circumstances have thrust upon them, and though some repine, looking upon themselves as round pegs in square holes, and think that if things had been different they might have made a much better showing, the greater part accept their lot, if not with serenity, at all events with resignation. They are like tramcars travelling for ever on the selfsame rails. They go backwards and forwards, backwards and forwards, inevitably, till they can go no longer and then are sold as scrap-iron. It is not often that you find a man who has boldly taken the course of his life into his own hands. When you do, it is worth while having a good look at him.

That was why I was curious to meet Thomas Wilson. It was an interesting and a bold thing he had done. Of course the end was not yet and until the experiment was concluded it was impossible to call it successful. But from what I had heard it seemed he must be an odd sort of fellow and I thought I should like to know him. I had been told he was reserved, but I had a notion that with patience and tact I could persuade him to confide in me. I wanted to hear the facts from his own lips. People exaggerate, they love to romanticise, and I was quite prepared to discover that his story was not nearly so singular as I had been led to believe.

And this impression was confirmed when at last I made his acquaintance. It was on the Piazza in Capri, where I was spending the month of August at a friend's villa, and a little before sunset, when most of the inhabitants, native and foreign, gather together to chat with their friends in the cool of the evening. There is a terrace that overlooks the Bay of Naples, and when the sun sinks slowly into the sea the island of Ischia is silhouetted against a blaze of splendour. It is one of the most lovely sights in the world. I was standing there with my friend and host watching it, when suddenly he said:

"Look, there's Wilson."

"Where?"

"The man sitting on the parapet, with his back to us. He's got a blue shirt on."

I saw an undistinguished back and a small head of grey hair short and rather thin.

"I wish he'd turn round," I said.

"He will presently."

"Ask him to come and have a drink with us at Morgano's."

"All right."

The instant of overwhelming beauty had passed and the sun, like the top of an orange, was dipping into a wine-red sea. We turned round and leaning our backs against the parapet looked at the people who were sauntering to and fro. They were all talking their heads off and the cheerful noise was exhilarating. Then the church bell, rather cracked, but with a fine resonant note, began to ring. The Piazza at Capri, with its clock tower over the footpath that leads up from the harbour, with the church up a flight of steps, is a perfect setting for an opera by Donizetti, and you felt that the voluble crowd might at any moment break out into a rattling chorus. It was charming and unreal.

I was so intent on the scene that I had not noticed Wilson get off the parapet and come towards us. As he passed us my friend stopped him.

"Hulloa, Wilson, I haven't seen you bathing the last few days."

"I've been bathing on the other side for a change."

My friend then introduced me. Wilson shook hands with me politely, but with indifference; a great many strangers come to Capri for a few days, or a few weeks, and I had no doubt he was constantly meeting people who came and went; and then my friend asked him to come along and have a drink with us.

"I was just going back to supper," he said.

"Can't it wait?" I asked.

"I suppose it can," he smiled.

Though his teeth were not very good his smile was attractive. It was gentle and kindly. He was dressed in a blue cotton shirt and a pair of grey trousers, much creased and none too clean, of a thin canvas, and on his feet he wore a pair of very old espadrilles. The get-up was picturesque, and very suitable to the place and the weather, but it did not at all go with his face. It was a lined, long face, deeply sunburned, thin-lipped, with small grey eyes rather close together and tight, neat features. The grey hair was carefully brushed. It was not a plain face, indeed in his youth Wilson might have been good-looking, but a prim one. He wore the blue shirt, open at the neck, and the grey canvas trousers, not as though they belonged to him, but as though, shipwrecked in his pyjamas, he had been fitted out with odd garments by compassionate strangers. Notwithstanding this careless attire he looked like the manager of a branch office in an insurance company, who should by rights be wearing a black coat with pepper-and-salt trousers, a white collar and an unobjectionable tie. I could very well see myself going to him to claim the insurance money when I had lost a watch, and being rather disconcerted while I answered the questions he put to me by his obvious impression, for all his politeness, that people who made such claims were either fools or knaves.

Moving off, we strolled across the Piazza and down the street till we came to Morgano's. We sat in the garden. Around us people were talking in Russian, German, Italian and English. We ordered drinks. Donna Lucia, the host's wife, waddled up and in her low, sweet voice passed the time of day with us. Though middle-aged now and portly, she had still traces of the wonderful beauty that thirty years before had driven artists to paint so many bad portraits of her. Her eyes, large and liquid, were the eyes of Hera and her smile was affectionate and gracious. We three gossiped for a while, for there is always a scandal of one sort or another in Capri to make a topic of conversation, but nothing was said of particular interest and in a little while Wilson got up and left us. Soon afterwards we strolled up to my friend's villa to dine. On the way he asked me what I had thought of Wilson.

"Nothing," I said. "I don't believe there's a word of truth in your story."

"Why not?"

"He isn't the sort of man to do that sort of thing."

"How does anyone know what anyone is capable of?"

"I should put him down as an absolutely normal man of business who's retired on a comfortable income from gilt-edged
securities. I think your story's just the ordinary Capri tittle-
tattle."

"Have it your own way," said my friend.

We were in the habit of bathing at a beach called the Baths of
Tiberius. We took a fly down the road to a certain point and
then wandered through lemon groves and vineyards, noisy with
cicadas and heavy with the hot smell of the sun, till we came to
the top of the cliff down which a steep winding path led to the
sea. A day or two later, just before we got down my friend said:

"Oh, there's Wilson back again."

We scrunched over the beach, the only drawback to the bathing-place being that it was shingle and not sand, and as we came
along Wilson saw us and waved. He was standing up, a pipe in
his mouth, and he wore nothing but a pair of trunks. His body
was dark brown, thin but not emaciated, and, considering his
wrinkled face and grey hair, youthful. Hot from our walk, we
undressed quickly and plunged at once into the water. Six feet
from the shore it was thirty feet deep, but so clear that you
could see the bottom. It was warm, yet invigorating.

When I got out Wilson was lying on his belly, with a towel
under him reading a book. I lit a cigarette and went and sat
down beside him.

"Had a nice swim?" he asked.

He put his pipe inside his book to mark the place and closing
it put it down on the pebbles beside him. He was evidently willing to talk.

"Lovely," I said. "It's the best bathing in the world."

"Of course people think those were the Baths of Tiberius."
He waved his hand towards a shapeless mass of masonry that
stood half in the water and half out. "But that's all rot. It was
just one of his villas, you know."

I did. But it is just as well to let people tell you things when
they want to. It disposes them kindly towards you if you suffer
them to impart information. Wilson gave a chuckle.

"Funny old fellow, Tiberius. Pity they're saying now there's
not a word of truth in all those stories about him."

He began to tell me all about Tiberius. Well, I had read my
Suetonius too and I had read histories of the Early Roman Em-

pire, so there was nothing very new to me in what he said. But I observed that he was not ill-read. I remarked on it.

"Oh, well, when I settled down here I was naturally interested, and I have plenty of time for reading. When you live in a place like this, with all its associations, it seems to make history so actual. You might almost be living in historical times yourself."

I should remark here that this was in 1913. The world was an easy, comfortable place and no one could have imagined that anything might happen seriously to disturb the serenity of existence.

"How long have you been here?" I asked.

"Fifteen years." He gave the blue and placid sea a glance, and a strangely tender smile hovered on his thin lips. "I fell in love with the place at first sight. You've heard, I daresay, of the mythical German who came here on the Naples boat just for lunch and a look at the Blue Grotto and stayed forty years; well, I can't say I exactly did that, but it's come to the same thing in the end. Only it won't be forty years in my case. Twenty-five. Still, that's better than a poke in the eye with a sharp stick."

I waited for him to go on. For what he had just said looked indeed as though there might be something after all in the singular story I had heard. But at that moment my friend came dripping out of the water very proud of himself because he had swum a mile, and the conversation turned to other things.

After that I met Wilson several times, either in the Piazza or on the beach. He was amiable and polite. He was always pleased to have a talk and I found out that he not only knew every inch of the island but also the adjacent mainland. He had read a great deal on all sorts of subjects, but his speciality was the history of Rome and on this he was very well informed. He seemed to have little imagination and to be of no more than average intelligence. He laughed a good deal, but with restraint, and his sense of humour was tickled by simple jokes. A commonplace man. I did not forget the odd remark he had made during the first short chat we had had by ourselves, but he never so much as approached the topic again. One day on our return from the beach, dismissing the cab at the Piazza, my friend and I told the driver to be ready to take us up to Anacapri at five. We were going to climb Monte Solaro, dine at a tavern we favoured, and walk down in the moonlight. For it was full moon and the views by night were lovely. Wilson was standing by while we gave the cabman instructions, for we had given him a lift to save him the hot dusty walk, and more from politeness than for any other reason I asked him if he would care to join us.

"It's my party," I said.

"I'll come with pleasure," he answered.

But when the time came to set out my friend was not feeling well, he thought he had stayed too long in the water, and would not face the long and tiring walk. So I went alone with Wilson. We climbed the mountain, admired the spacious view, and got back to the inn as night was falling, hot, hungry and thirsty. We had ordered our dinner beforehand. The food was good, for Antonio was an excellent cook, and the wine came from his own vineyard. It was so light that you felt you could drink it like water and we finished the first bottle with our macaroni. By the time we had finished the second we felt that there was nothing much wrong with life. We sat in a little garden under a great vine laden with grapes. The air was exquisitely soft. The night was still and we were alone. The maid brought us *bel paese* cheese and a plate of figs. I ordered coffee and strega, which is the best liqueur they make in Italy. Wilson would not have a cigar, but lit his pipe.

"We've got plenty of time before we need start," he said, "the moon won't be over the hill for another hour."

"Moon or no moon," I said briskly, "of course we've got plenty of time. That's one of the delights of Capri, that there's never any hurry."

"Leisure," he said. "If people only knew! It's the most priceless thing a man can have and they're such fools they don't even know it's something to aim at. Work? They work for work's sake. They haven't got the brains to realise that the only object of work is to obtain leisure."

Wine has the effect on some people of making them indulge in general reflections. These remarks were true, but no one could have claimed that they were original. I did not say anything, but struck a match to light my cigar.

"It was full moon the first time I came to Capri," he went on reflectively. "It might be the same moon as to-night."

"It was, you know," I smiled.

He grinned. The only light in the garden was what came from an oil lamp that hung over our heads. It had been scanty to eat by, but it was good now for confidences.

"I didn't mean that. I mean, it might be yesterday. Fifteen years it is, and when I look back it seems like a month. I'd never been to Italy before. I came for my summer holiday. I went to Naples by boat from Marseilles and I had a look round, Pompeii, you know, and Paestum and one or two places like that; then I came here for a week. I liked the look of the place right away, from the sea, I mean, as I watched it come closer and closer; and then when we got into the little boats from the steamer and landed at the quay, with all that crowd of jabbering people who wanted to take your luggage, and the hotel touts, and the tumbledown houses on the Marina and the walk up to the hotel, and dining on the terrace—well, it just got me. That's the truth. I didn't know if I was standing on my head or my heels. I'd never drunk Capri wine before, but I'd heard of it; I think I must have got a bit tight. I sat on that terrace after they'd all gone to bed and watched the moon over the sea, and there was Vesuvius with a great red plume of smoke rising up from it. Of course I know now that wine I drank was ink, Capri wine my eye, but I thought it all right then. But it wasn't the wine that made me drunk, it was the shape of the island and those jabbering people, the moon and the sea and the oleander in the hotel garden. I'd never seen an oleander before."

It was a long speech and it had made him thirsty. He took up his glass, but it was empty. I asked him if he would have another strega.

"It's sickly stuff. Let's have a bottle of wine. That's sound, that is, pure juice of the grape and can't hurt anyone."

I ordered more wine, and when it came filled the glasses. He took a long drink and after a sigh of pleasure went on.

"Next day I found my way to the bathing-place we go to. Not bad bathing, I thought. Then I wandered about the island. As luck would have it, there was a *festa* up at the Punta di Timberio and I ran straight into the middle of it. An image of the Virgin and priests, acolytes swinging censers, and a whole crowd of jolly, laughing, excited people, a lot of them all dressed up. I ran across an Englishman there and asked him what it was all about. 'Oh, it's the feast of the Assumption,' he said, 'at least that's what the Catholic Church says it is, but that's just their hanky-panky. It's the festival of Venus. Pagan, you know. Aphrodite rising from the sea and all that.' It gave me quite a funny feeling to hear him. It seemed to take one a long way back, if you know what I mean. After that I went down one night to have a look at the Faraglioni by moonlight. If the fates had wanted me to go on being a bank manager they oughtn't to have let me take that walk."

"You were a bank manager, were you?" I asked.

I had been wrong about him, but not far wrong.

"Yes. I was manager of the Crawford Street branch of the York and City. It was convenient for me because I lived up Hendon way. I could get from door to door in thirty-seven minutes."

He puffed at his pipe and relit it.

"That was my last night, that was. I'd got to be back at the bank on Monday morning. When I looked at those two great rocks sticking out of the water, with the moon above them, and all the little lights of the fishermen in their boats catching cuttle-fish, all so peaceful and beautiful, I said to myself, well, after all, why should I go back? It wasn't as if I had anyone dependent on me. My wife had died of bronchial pneumonia four years before and the kid went to live with her grandmother, my wife's mother. She was an old fool, she didn't look after the kid properly and she got blood-poisoning, they amputated her leg, but they couldn't save her and she died, poor little thing."

"How terrible," I said.

"Yes, I was cut up at the time, though of course not so much as if the kid had been living with me, but I dare say it was a mercy. Not much chance for a girl with only one leg. I was sorry about my wife too. We got on very well together. Though I don't know if it would have continued. She was the sort of woman who was always bothering about what other people'd think. She didn't like travelling. Eastbourne was her idea of a holiday. D'you know, I'd never crossed the Channel till after her death."

"But I suppose you've got other relations, haven't you?"

"None. I was an only child. My father had a brother, but he went to Australia before I was born. I don't think anyone could easily be more alone in the world than I am. There wasn't any reason I could see why I shouldn't do exactly what I wanted. I was thirty-four at that time."

He had told me he had been on the island for fifteen years. That would make him forty-nine. Just about the age I should have given him.

"I'd been working since I was seventeen. All I had to look

forward to was doing the same old thing day after day till I retired on my pension. I said to myself, is it worth it? What's wrong with chucking it all up and spending the rest of my life down here? It was the most beautiful place I'd ever seen. But I'd had a business training, I was cautious by nature. 'No,' I said, 'I won't be carried away like this, I'll go to-morrow like I said I would and think it over. Perhaps when I get back to London I'll think quite differently.' Damned fool, wasn't I? I lost a whole year that way."

"You didn't change your mind, then?"

"You bet I didn't. All the time I was working I kept thinking of the bathing here and the vineyards and the walks over the hills and the moon and the sea, and the Piazza in the evening when everyone walks about for a bit of a chat after the day's work is over. There was only one thing that bothered me: I wasn't sure if I was justified in not working like everybody else did. Then I read a sort of history book, by a man called Marion Crawford it was, and there was a story about Sybaris and Crotona. There were two cities; and in Sybaris they just enjoyed life and had a good time, and in Crotona they were hardy and industrious and all that. And one day the men of Crotona came over and wiped Sybaris out, and then after a while a lot of other fellows came over from somewhere else and wiped Crotona out. Nothing remains of Sybaris, not a stone, and all that's left of Crotona is just one column. That settled the matter for me."

"Oh?"

"It came to the same in the end, didn't it? And when you look back now, who were the mugs?"

I did not reply and he went on.

"The money was rather a bother. The bank didn't pension one off till after thirty years' service, but if you retired before that they gave you a gratuity. With that and what I'd got for the sale of my house and the little I'd managed to save, I just hadn't enough to buy an annuity to last the rest of my life. It would have been silly to sacrifice everything so as to lead a pleasant life and not have a sufficient income to make it pleasant. I wanted to have a little place of my own, a servant to look after me, enough to buy tobacco, decent food, books now and then, and something over for emergencies. I knew pretty well how much I needed. I found I had just enough to buy an annuity for twenty-five years."

"You were thirty-five at the time?"

"Yes. It would carry me on till I was sixty. After all, no one can be certain of living longer than that, a lot of men die in their fifties, and by the time a man's sixty he's had the best of life."

"On the other hand no one can be sure of dying at sixty," I said.

"Well, I don't know. It depends on himself, doesn't it?"

"In your place I should have stayed on at the bank till I was entitled to my pension."

"I should have been forty-seven then. I shouldn't have been too old to enjoy my life here, I'm older than that now and I enjoy it as much as I ever did, but I should have been too old to experience the particular pleasure of a young man. You know, you can have just as good a time at fifty as you can at thirty, but it's not the same sort of good time. I wanted to live the perfect life while I still had the energy and the spirit to make the most of it. Twenty-five years seemed a long time to me, and twenty-five years of happiness seemed worth paying something pretty substantial for. I'd made up my mind to wait a year and I waited a year. Then I sent in my resignation and as soon as they paid me my gratuity I bought the annuity and came on here."

"An annuity for twenty-five years?"

"That's right.

"Have you never regretted?"

"Never. I've had my money's worth already. And I've got ten years more. Don't you think after twenty-five years of perfect happiness one ought to be satisfied to call it a day?"

"Perhaps."

He did not say in so many words what he would do then, but his intention was clear. It was pretty much the story my friend had told me, but it sounded different when I heard it from his own lips. I stole a glance at him. There was nothing about him that was not ordinary. No one, looking at that neat, prim face, could have thought him capable of an unconventional action. I did not blame him. It was his own life that he had arranged in this strange manner, and I did not see why he should not do what he liked with it. Still, I could not prevent the little shiver that ran down my spine.

"Getting chilly?" he smiled. "We might as well start walking down. The moon'll be up by now."

Before we parted Wilson asked me if I would like to go and see his house one day; and two or three days later, finding out where he lived, I strolled up to see him. It was a peasant's cottage, well away from the town, in a vineyard, with a view of the sea. By the side of the door grew a great oleander in full flower. There were only two small rooms, a tiny kitchen and a lean-to in which firewood could be kept. The bedroom was furnished like a monk's cell, but the sitting-room, smelling agreeably of tobacco, was comfortable enough, with two large arm-chairs that he had brought from England, a large roll-top desk, a cottage piano and crowded bookshelves. On the walls were framed engravings of pictures by G. F. Watts and Lord Leighton. Wilson told me that the house belonged to the owner of the vineyard who lived in another cottage higher up the hill, and his wife came in every day to do the rooms and the cooking. He had found the place on his first visit to Capri, and taking it on his return for good had been there ever since. Seeing the piano and music open on it, I asked him if he would play.

"I'm no good, you know, but I've always been fond of music and I get a lot of fun out of strumming."

He sat down at the piano and played one of the movements from a Beethoven sonata. He did not play very well. I looked at his music, Schumann and Schubert, Beethoven, Bach and Chopin. On the table on which he had his meals was a greasy pack of cards. I asked him if he played patience.

"A lot."

From what I saw of him then and from what I heard from other people I made for myself what I think must have been a fairly accurate picture of the life he had led for the last fifteen years. It was certainly a very harmless one. He bathed; he walked a great deal, and he seemed never to lose his sense of the beauty of the island which he knew so intimately; he played the piano and he played patience; he read. When he was asked to a party he went and, though a trifle dull, was agreeable. He was not affronted if he was neglected. He liked people, but with an aloofness that prevented intimacy. He lived thriftily, but with sufficient comfort. He never owed a penny. I imagine he had never been a man whom sex had greatly troubled, and if in his younger days he had had now and then a passing affair with a visitor to the island whose head was turned by the atmosphere, his emotion, while it lasted, remained, I am pretty sure, well under his control. I think he was determined that nothing should interfere with his independence of spirit. His only passion was for the beauty of nature, and he sought felicity in the simple and natural things that life offers to everyone. You may say that it was a grossly selfish existence. It was. He was of no use to anybody, but on the other hand he did nobody any harm. His only object was his own happiness, and it looked as though he had attained it. Very few people know where to look for happiness; fewer still find it. I don't know whether he was a fool or a wise man. He was certainly a man who knew his own mind. The odd thing about him to me was that he was so immensely commonplace. I should never have given him a second thought but for what I knew, that on a certain day, ten years from then, unless a chance illness cut the thread before, he must deliberately take leave of the world he loved so well. I wondered whether it was the thought of this, never quite absent from his mind, that gave him the peculiar zest with which he enjoyed every moment of the day.

I should do him an injustice if I omitted to state that he was not at all in the habit of talking about himself. I think the friend I was staying with was the only person in whom he had confided. I believe he only told me the story because he suspected I already knew it, and on the evening on which he told it me he had drunk a good deal of wine.

My visit drew to a close and I left the island. The year after, war broke out. A number of things happened to me, so that the course of my life was greatly altered, and it was thirteen years before I went to Capri again. My friend had been back some time, but he was no longer so well off, and had moved into a house that had no room for me; so I was putting up at the hotel. He came to meet me at the boat and we dined together. During dinner I asked him where exactly his house was.

"You know it," he answered. "It's the little place Wilson had. I've built on a room and made it quite nice."

With so many other things to occupy my mind I had not given Wilson a thought for years; but now, with a little shock, I remembered. The ten years he had before him when I made his acquaintance must have elapsed long ago.

"Did he commit suicide as he said he would?"

"It's rather a grim story."

Wilson's plan was all right. There was only one flaw in it and this, I suppose, he could not have foreseen. It had never occurred to him that after twenty-five years of complete happiness, in this quiet backwater, with nothing in the world to disturb his serenity, his character would gradually lose its strength.

The will needs obstacles in order to exercise its power; when it is never thwarted, when no effort is needed to achieve one's desires, because one has placed one's desires only in the things that can be obtained by stretching out one's hand, the will grows impotent. If you walk on a level all the time the muscles you need to climb a mountain will atrophy. These observations are trite, but there they are. When Wilson's annuity expired he had no longer the resolution to make the end which was the price he had agreed to pay for that long period of happy tranquillity. I do not think, as far as I could gather, both from what my friend told me and afterwards from others, that he wanted courage. It was just that he couldn't make up his mind. He put it off from day to day.

He had lived on the island for so long and had always settled his accounts so punctually that it was easy for him to get credit; never having borrowed money before, he found a number of people who were willing to lend him small sums when now he asked for them. He had paid his rent regularly for so many years that his landlord, whose wife Assunta still acted as his servant, was content to let things slide for several months. Everyone believed him when he said that a relative had died and that he was temporarily embarrassed because owing to legal formalities he could not for some time get the money that was due to him. He managed to hang on after this fashion for something over a year. Then he could get no more credit from the local tradesmen, and there was no one to lend him any more money. His landlord gave him notice to leave the house unless he paid up the arrears of rent before a certain date.

The day before this he went into his tiny bedroom, closed the door and the window, drew the curtain and lit a brazier of charcoal. Next morning when Assunta came to make his breakfast she found him insensible but still alive. The roof was draughty, and though he had done this and that to keep out the fresh air he had not done it very thoroughly. It almost looked as though at the last moment, and desperate though his situation was, he had suffered from a certain infirmity of purpose. Wilson was taken to the hospital, and though very ill for some time he at last recovered. But as a result either of the charcoal poisoning or of the shock he was no longer in complete possession of his faculties. He was not insane, at all events not insane enough to be put in an asylum, but he was quite obviously no longer in his right mind.

"I went to see him," said my friend. "I tried to get him to talk, but he kept looking at me in a funny sort of way, as though he couldn't quite make out where he'd seen me before. He looked rather awful lying there in bed, with a week's growth of grey beard on his chin; but except for that funny look in his eyes he seemed quite normal."

"What funny look in his eyes?"

"I don't know exactly how to describe it. Puzzled. It's an absurd comparison, but suppose you threw a stone up into the air and it didn't come down but just stayed there . . ."

"It would be rather bewildering," I smiled.

"Well, that's the sort of look he had."

It was difficult to know what to do with him. He had no money and no means of getting any. His effects were sold, but for too little to pay what he owed. He was English, and the Italian authorities did not wish to make themselves responsible for him. The British Consul in Naples had no funds to deal with the case. He could of course be sent back to England, but no one seemed to know what could be done with him when he got there. Then Assunta, the servant, said that he had been a good master and a good tenant, and as long as he had the money had paid his way; he could sleep in the woodshed in the cottage in which she and her husband lived, and he could share their meals. This was suggested to him. It was difficult to know whether he understood or not. When Assunta came to take him from the hospital he went with her without remark. He seemed to have no longer a will of his own. She had been keeping him now for two years.

"It's not very comfortable, you know," said my friend. "They've rigged him up a ramshackle bed and given him a couple of blankets, but there's no window, and it's icy cold in winter and like an oven in summer. And the food's pretty rough. You know how these peasants eat: macaroni on Sundays and meat once in a blue moon."

"What does he do with himself all the time?"

"He wanders about the hills. I've tried to see him two or three times, but it's no good; when he sees you coming he runs like a hare. Assunta comes down to have a chat with me now and then and I give her a bit of money so that she can buy him tobacco, but God knows if he ever gets it."

"Do they treat him all right?" I asked.

"I'm sure Assunta's kind enough. She treats him like a child.

I'm afraid her husband's not very nice to him. He grudges the cost of his keep. I don't believe he's cruel or anything like that, but I think he's a bit sharp with him. He makes him fetch water and clean the cow-shed and that sort of thing."

"It sounds pretty rotten," I said.

"He brought it on himself. After all, he's only got what he deserved."

"I think on the whole we all get what we deserve," I said. "But that doesn't prevent its being rather horrible."

Two or three days later my friend and I were taking a walk. We were strolling along a narrow path through an olive grove.

"There's Wilson," said my friend suddenly. "Don't look, you'll only frighten him. Go straight on."

I walked with my eyes on the path, but out of the corners of them I saw a man hiding behind an olive tree. He did not move as we approached, but I felt that he was watching us. As soon as we had passed I heard a scamper. Wilson, like a hunted animal, had made for safety. That was the last I ever saw of him.

He died last year. He had endured that life for six years. He was found one morning on the mountainside lying quite peacefully as though he had died in his sleep. From where he lay he had been able to see those two great rocks called the Faraglioni which stand out of the sea. It was full moon and he must have gone to see them by moonlight. Perhaps he died of the beauty of that sight.

SALVATORE

I wonder if I can do it.

I knew Salvatore first when he was a boy of fifteen with a pleasant, ugly face, a laughing mouth and care-free eyes. He used to spend the morning lying about the beach with next to nothing on and his brown body was as thin as a rail. He was full of grace. He was in and out of the sea all the time, swimming with the clumsy, effortless stroke common to the fisher boys. Scrambling up the jagged rocks on his hard feet, for except on Sundays he never wore shoes, he would throw himself into the deep water with a cry of delight. His father was a fisherman who owned his own little vineyard and Salvatore acted as nursemaid to his two younger brothers. He shouted to them to come in-shore when they ventured out too far and made them dress when it was time to climb the hot, vineclad hill for the frugal midday meal.

But boys in those Southern parts grow apace and in a little while he was madly in love with a pretty girl who lived on the Grande Marina. She had eyes like forest pools and held herself like a daughter of the Cæsars. They were affianced, but they could not marry till Salvatore had done his military service, and when he left the island which he had never left in his life before, to become a sailor in the navy of King Victor Emmanuel, he wept like a child. It was hard for one who had never been less free than the birds to be at the beck and call of others; it was harder still to live in a battleship with strangers instead of in a little white cottage among the vines; and when he was ashore, to walk in noisy, friendless cities with streets so crowded that he was frightened to cross them, when he had been used to silent paths and the mountains and the sea. I suppose it had never struck him that Ischia, which he looked at every evening (it was like a fairy island in the sunset) to see what the weather would be like next day, or Vesuvius, pearly in the dawn, had anything to do with him at all; but when he ceased to have them before his eyes he realised in some dim fashion that they were as much part of him as his hands and his feet. He was dreadfully homesick. But it was hardest of all to be parted from the girl he loved with all his passionate young heart. He wrote to her (in his childlike handwriting) long, ill-spelt letters in which he told her how constantly he thought of her and how much he longed to be back. He was sent here and there, to Spezzia, to Venice, to Bari and finally to China. Here he fell ill of some mysterious ailment that kept him in hospital for months. He bore it with the mute and uncomprehending patience of a dog. When he learnt that it was a form of rheumatism that made him unfit for further service his heart exulted, for he could go home; and he did not bother, in fact he scarcely listened, when the doctors told him that he would never again be quite well. What did he care when he was going back to the little island he loved so well and the girl who was waiting for him?

When he got into the rowing-boat that met the steamer from Naples and was rowed ashore he saw his father and mother standing on the jetty and his two brothers, big boys now, and he waved to them. His eyes searched among the crowd that waited there, for the girl. He could not see her. There was a great deal of kissing when he jumped up the steps and they all, emotional creatures, cried a little as they exchanged their greetings. He asked where the girl was. His mother told him that she did not know; they had not seen her for two or three weeks; so in the evening when the moon was shining over the placid sea and the lights of Naples twinkled in the distance he walked down to the Grande Marina to her house. She was sitting on the doorstep with her mother. He was a little shy because he had not seen her for so long. He asked her if she had not received the letter that he had written to her to say that he was coming home. Yes, they had received a letter, and they had been told by another of the island boys that he was ill. Yes, that was why he was back; was

it not a piece of luck? Oh, but they had heard that he would
never be quite well again. The doctors talked a lot of nonsense,
but he knew very well that now he was home again he would
recover. They were silent for a little, and then the mother
nudged the girl. She did not try to soften the blow. She told him
straight out, with the blunt directness of her race, that she could
not marry a man who would never be strong enough to work
like a man. They had made up their minds, her mother and
father and she, and her father would never give his consent.

When Salvatore went home he found that they all knew. The
girl's father had been to tell them what they had decided, but
they had lacked the courage to tell him themselves. He wept on
his mother's bosom. He was terribly unhappy, but he did not
blame the girl. A fisherman's life is hard and it needs strength
and endurance. He knew very well that a girl could not afford to
marry a man who might not be able to support her. His smile
was very sad and his eyes had the look of a dog that has been
beaten, but he did not complain, and he never said a hard word
of the girl he had loved so well. Then, a few months later, when
he had settled down to the common round, working in his
father's vineyard and fishing, his mother told him that there
was a young woman in the village who was willing to marry
him. Her name was Assunta.

"She's as ugly as the devil," he said.

She was older than he, twenty-four or twenty-five, and she
had been engaged to a man who, while doing his military service,
had been killed in Africa. She had a little money of her own and
if Salvatore married her she could buy him a boat of his own
and they could take a vineyard that by a happy chance happened at that moment to be without a tenant. His mother told
him that Assunta had seen him at the *festa* and had fallen in
love with him. Salvatore smiled his sweet smile and said he
would think about it. On the following Sunday, dressed in the
stiff black clothes in which he looked so much less well than in
the ragged shirt and trousers of every day, he went up to High
Mass at the parish church and placed himself so that he could
have a good look at the young woman. When he came down
again he told his mother that he was willing.

Well, they were married and they settled down in a tiny
whitewashed house in the middle of a handsome vineyard.
Salvatore was now a great big husky fellow, tall and broad, but
still with that ingenuous smile and those trusting, kindly eyes

that he had had as a boy. He had the most beautiful manners I have ever seen in my life. Assunta was a grim-visaged female, with decided features, and she looked old for her years. But she had a good heart and she was no fool. I used to be amused by the little smile of devotion that she gave her husband when he was being very masculine and masterful; she never ceased to be touched by his gentle sweetness. But she could not bear the girl who had thrown him over, and notwithstanding Salvatore's smiling expostulations she had nothing but harsh words for her. Presently children were born to them.

It was a hard enough life. All through the fishing season towards evening he set out in his boat with one of his brothers for the fishing grounds. It was a long pull of six or seven miles, and he spent the night catching the profitable cuttlefish. Then there was the long row back again in order to sell the catch in time for it to go on the early boat to Naples. At other times he was working in his vineyard from dawn till the heat drove him to rest and then again, when it was a trifle cooler, till dusk. Often his rheumatism prevented him from doing anything at all and then he would lie about the beach, smoking cigarettes, with a pleasant word for everyone notwithstanding the pain that racked his limbs. The foreigners who came down to bathe and saw him there said that these Italian fishermen were lazy devils.

Sometimes he used to bring his children down to give them a bath. They were both boys and at this time the elder was three and the younger less than two. They sprawled about at the water's edge stark naked and Salvatore standing on a rock would dip them in the water. The elder one bore it with stoicism, but the baby screamed lustily. Salvatore had enormous hands, like legs of mutton, coarse and hard from constant toil, but when he bathed his children, holding them so tenderly, drying them with delicate care, upon my word they were like flowers. He would seat the naked baby on the palm of his hand and hold him up, laughing a little at his smallness, and his laugh was like the laughter of an angel. His eyes then were as candid as his child's.

I started by saying that I wondered if I could do it and now I must tell you what it is that I have tried to do. I wanted to see whether I could hold your attention for a few pages while I drew for you the portrait of a man, just an ordinary fisherman who possessed nothing in the world except a quality which is the rarest, the most precious and the loveliest that anyone can have.

Heaven only knows why he should so strangely and unexpectedly have possessed it. All I know is that it shone in him with a radiance that, if it had not been so unconscious and so humble, would have been to the common run of men hardly bearable. And in case you have not guessed what the quality was, I will tell you. Goodness, just goodness.

THE WASH-TUB

Positano stands on the side of a steep hill, a disarray of huddled white houses, their tiled roofs washed pale by the suns of a hundred years; but unlike many of these Italian towns perched out of harm's way on a rocky eminence it does not offer you at one delightful glance all it has to give. It has quaint streets that zig-zag up the hill and battered, painted houses in the baroque style, but very late, in which Neapolitan noblemen led for a season lives of penurious grandeur. It is indeed almost excessively picturesque and in winter its two or three modest hotels are crowded with painters, male and female, who in their different ways acknowledge by their daily labours the emotion it has excited in them. Some take infinite pairs to place on canvas every window and every tile their peering eyes can discover and doubtless achieve the satisfaction that rewards honest industry. "At all events it's sincere," they say modestly when they show you their work. Some, rugged and dashing, in a fine frenzy attack their canvas with a pallet knife charged with a wad of paint, and they say: "You see, what I was trying to bring out was my personality." They slightly close their eyes and tentatively murmur: "I think it's rather me, don't you?" And there are some who give you highly entertaining arrangements of spheres and cubes and utter sombrely: "That's how I see it!" These for the most part are strong silent men who waste no words.

But Positano looks full south and the chances are that in

summer you will have it to yourself. The hotel is clean and cool
and there is a terrace, overhung with vines, where you can sit
at night and look at the sea bespangled with dim stars. Down at
the Marina, on the quay, is a little tavern where you can dine
under an archway off anchovies and ham, macaroni and fresh-
caught mullet, and drink cold wine. Once a day the steamer
from Naples comes in, bringing the mail, and for a quarter of an
hour gives the beach (there is no port and the passengers are
landed in small boats) an air of animation.

One August, tiring of Capri where I had been staying, I made
up my mind to spend a few days at Positano, so I hired a
fishing-boat and rowed over. I stopped on the way in a shady
cove to bathe and lunch and sleep, and did not arrive till evening. I strolled up the hill, my two bags following me on the
heads of two sturdy women, to the hotel, and was surprised to
learn that I was not its only guest. The waiter, whose name was
Giuseppe, was an old friend of mine, and at that season he was
boots, porter, chambermaid and cook as well. He told me that
an American signore had been staying there for three months.

"Is he a painter or a writer or something?" I asked.

"No, *Signore*, he's a gentleman."

Odd, I thought. No foreigners came to Positano at that time
of year but German *Wandervögel*, looking hot and dusty, with
satchels on their backs, and they only stayed overnight. I could
not imagine anyone wishing to spend three months there; unless
of course he were hiding. And since all London had been excited
by the flight earlier in the year of an eminent, but dishonest,
financier, the amusing thought occurred to me that this mysterious stranger was perhaps he. I knew him slightly and trusted
that my sudden arrival would not disconcert him.

"You'll see the *Signore* at the Marina," said Giuseppe, as I
was setting out to go down again. "He always dines there."

He was certainly not there when I arrived. I asked what there
was for dinner and drank an americano, which is by no means a
bad substitute for a cocktail. In a few minutes, however, a man
walked in who could be no other than my fellow-guest at the
hotel and I had a moment's disappointment when I saw that it
was not the absconding financier. A tall, elderly man, bronzed
after his summer on the Mediterranean, with a handsome, thin
face. He wore a very neat, even smart, suit of cream-coloured
silk and no hat. His grey hair was cut very short, but was still
thick. There was ease in his bearing, and elegance. He looked

round the half-dozen tables under the archway at which the natives of the place were playing cards or dominoes and his eyes rested on me. They smiled pleasantly. He came up.

"I hear you have just arrived at the hotel. Giuseppe suggested that as he couldn't come down here to effect an introduction you wouldn't mind if I introduced myself. Would it bore you to dine with a total stranger?"

"Of course not. Sit down."

He turned to the maid who was laying a cover for me and in beautiful Italian told her that I would eat with him. He looked at my americano.

"I have got them to stock a little gin and French vermouth for me. Would you allow me to mix you a very dry Martini?"

"Without hesitation."

"It gives an exotic note to the surroundings which brings out the local colour."

He certainly made a very good cocktail and with added appetite we ate the ham and anchovies with which our dinner began. My host had a pleasant humour and his fluent conversation was agreeable.

"You must forgive me if I talk too much," he said presently. "This is the first chance I've had to speak English for three months. I don't suppose you will stay here long and I mean to make the most of it."

"Three months is a long time to stay at Positano."

"I've hired a boat and I bathe and fish. I read a great deal. I have a good many books here and if there's anything I can lend you I shall be very glad."

"I think I have enough reading matter. But I should love to look at what you have. It's always fun looking at other people's books."

He gave me a sharp look and his eyes twinkled.

"It also tells you a good deal about them," he murmured.

When we finished dinner we went on talking. The stranger was well-read and interested in a diversity of topics. He spoke with so much knowledge of painting that I wondered if he was an art critic or a dealer. But then it appeared that he had been reading Suetonius and I came to the conclusion that he was a college professor. I asked him his name.

"Barnaby," he answered.

"That's a name that has recently acquired an amazing celebrity."

"Oh, how so?"

"Have you never heard of the celebrated Mrs. Barnaby? She's a compatriot of yours."

"I admit that I've seen her name in the papers rather frequently of late. Do you know her?"

"Yes, quite well. She gave the grandest parties all last season and I went to them whenever she asked me. Everyone did. She's an astounding woman. She came to London to do the season, and, by George, she did it. She just swept everything before her."

"I understand she's very rich?"

"Fabulously, I believe, but it's not that that has made her success. Plenty of American women have money. Mrs. Barnaby has got where she has by sheer force of character. She never pretends to be anything but what she is. She's natural. She's priceless. You know her history, of course?"

My friend smiled.

"Mrs. Barnaby may be a great celebrity in London, but to the best of my belief in America she is almost inconceivably unknown."

I smiled also, but within me; I could well imagine how shocked this distinguished and cultured man would be by the rollicking humour, the frankness, with its tang of the soil, and the rich and vital experience of the amazing Mrs. Barnaby.

"Well, I'll tell you about her. Her husband appears to be a very rough diamond; he's a great hulking fellow, she says, who could fell a steer with his fist. He's known in Arizona as One-Bullet Mike."

"Good gracious! Why?"

"Well, years ago in the old days he killed two men with a single shot. She says he's handier with his gun even now than any man West of the Rockies. He's a miner, but he's been a cowpuncher, a gun-runner and God knows what in his day."

"A thoroughly Western type," said my professor a trifle acidly, I thought.

"Something of a desperado, I imagine. Mrs. Barnaby's stories about him are a real treat. Of course everyone's been begging her to let him come over, but she says he'd never leave the wide open spaces. He struck oil a year or two ago and now he's got all the money in the world. He must be a great character. I've heard her keep the whole dinner-table spellbound when she's talked of the old days when they roughed it together. It gives you quite a thrill when you see this grey-haired woman, not at all pretty, but exquisitely dressed, with the most wonderful pearls, and hear her tell how she washed the miners' clothes and cooked for the camp. Your American women have an adaptability that's really stupendous. When you see Mrs. Barnaby sitting at the head of her table, perfectly at home with princes of the blood, ambassadors, cabinet ministers and the duke of this and the duke of that, it seems almost incredible that only a few years ago she was cooking the food of seventy miners."

"Can she read or write?"

"I suppose her invitations are written by her secretary, but she's by no means an ignorant woman. She told me she used to make a point of reading for an hour every night after the fellows in camp had gone to bed."

"Remarkable!"

"On the other hand One-Bullet Mike only learnt to write his name when he suddenly found himself under the necessity of signing cheques."

We walked up the hill to our hotel and before separating for the night arranged to take our luncheon with us next day and row over to a cove that my friend had discovered. We spent a charming day bathing, reading, eating, sleeping and talking, and we dined together in the evening. The following morning, after breakfast on the terrace, I reminded Barnaby of his promise to show me his books.

"Come right along."

I accompanied him to his bedroom, where Giuseppe, the waiter, was making his bed. The first thing I caught sight of was a photograph in a gorgeous frame of the celebrated Mrs. Barnaby. My friend caught sight of it too and suddenly turned pale with anger.

"You fool, Giuseppe. Why have you taken that photograph out of my wardrobe? Why the devil did you think I put it away?"

"I didn't know, *Signore*. That's why I put it back on the *Signore's* table. I thought he liked to see the portrait of his *signora*."

I was staggered.

"Is my Mrs. Barnaby your wife?" I cried.

"She is."

"Good Lord, are you One-Bullet Mike?"

"Do I look it?"

I began to laugh.

"I'm bound to say you don't."

I glanced at his hands. He smiled grimly and held them out.

"No, sir, I have never felled a steer with my naked fist."

For a moment we stared at one another in silence.

"She'll never forgive me," he moaned. "She wanted me to take a false name, and when I wouldn't she was quite vexed with me. She said it wasn't safe. I said it was bad enough to hide myself in Positano for three months, but I'd be damned if I'd use any other name than my own." He hesitated. "I throw myself on your mercy. I can do nothing but trust to your generosity not to disclose a secret that you have discovered by the most unlikely chance."

"I will be as silent as the grave, but honestly I don't understand. What does it all mean?"

"I am a doctor by profession and for the last thirty years my wife and I have lived in Pennsylvania. I don't know if I have struck you as a roughneck, but I venture to say that Mrs. Barnaby is one of the most cultivated women I have ever known. Then a cousin of hers died and left her a very large fortune. There's no mistake about that. My wife is a very, very rich woman. She has always read a great deal of English fiction and her one desire was to have a London season and entertain and do all the grand things she had read about in books. It was her money and although the prospect did not particularly tempt me, I was very glad that she should gratify her wish. We sailed last April. The young Duke and Duchess of Hereford happened to be on board."

"I know. It was they who first launched Mrs. Barnaby. They were crazy about her. They've boomed her like an army of press-agents."

"I was ill when we sailed, I had a carbuncle which confined me to my stateroom, and Mrs. Barnaby was left to look after herself. Her deck-chair happened to be next the duchess's, and from a remark she overheard it occurred to her that the English aristocracy were not so wrapped up in our social leaders as one might have expected. My wife is a quick little woman and she remarked to me that if you had an ancestor who signed Magna Charta perhaps you were not excessively impressed because the grandfather of one of your acquaintances sold skunks and the grandfather of another ran ferryboats. My wife has a very keen sense of humour. Getting into conversation with the duchess,

she told her a little Western anecdote, and to make it more interesting told it as having happened to herself. Its success was
immediate. The duchess begged for another and my wife ventured a little further. Twenty-four hours later she had the duke
and duchess eating out of her hand. She used to come down to
my stateroom at intervals and tell me of her progress. In the innocence of my heart I was tickled to death and since I had
nothing else to do, I sent to the library for the works of Bret
Harte and primed her with effective touches."

I slapped my forehead.

"We said she was as good as Bret Harte," I cried.

"I had a grand time thinking of the consternation of my
wife's friends when at the end of the voyage I appeared and we
told them the truth. But I reckoned without my wife. The day
before we reached Southampton Mrs. Barnaby told me that the
Herefords were arranging parties for her. The duchess was crazy
to introduce her to all sorts of wonderful people. It was a chance
in a thousand; but of course I should spoil everything, she admitted that she had been forced by the course of events to
represent me as very different from what I was. I did not know
that she had already transformed me into One-Bullet Mike, but
I had a shrewd suspicion that she had forgotten to mention that
I was on board. Well, to make a long story short, she asked me
to go to Paris for a week or two till she had consolidated her
position. I didn't mind that. I was much more inclined to do a
little work at the Sorbonne than to go to parties in Mayfair, and
so leaving her to go on to Southampton, I got off at Cherbourg.
But when I had been in Paris ten days she flew over to see me.
She told me that her success had exceeded her wildest dreams:
it was ten times more wonderful than any of the novels; but my
appearance would ruin it all. Very well, I said, I would stay in
Paris. She didn't like the idea of that; she said she'd never have
a moment's peace so long as I was so near and I might run
across someone who knew me. I suggested Vienna or Rome.
They wouldn't do either, and at last I came here and here have
I been hiding like a criminal for three interminable months."

"Do you mean to say you never killed the two gamblers,
shooting one with your right hand and the other with your left?"

"Sir, I have never fired a pistol in my life."

"And what about the attack on your log-cabin by the Mexican bandits when your wife loaded your guns for you and you

stood the siege for three days till the Federal troops rescued you?"

Mr. Barnaby smiled grimly.

"I never heard that one. Isn't it a trifle crude?"

"Crude! It was as good as any Wild West picture."

"If I may venture a guess, that is where my wife in all probability got the idea."

"But the wash-tub. Washing the miners' clothes and all that. You don't know how she made us roar with that story. Why, she swam into London Society in her wash-tub."

I began to laugh.

"She's made the most gorgeous fools of us all," I said.

"She's made a pretty considerable fool of me, I would have you observe," remarked Mr. Barnaby.

"She's a marvellous woman and you're right to be proud of her. I always said she was priceless. She realised the passion for romance that beats in every British heart and she's given us exactly what we wanted. I wouldn't betray her for worlds."

"It's all very fine for you, sir. London may have gained a wonderful hostess, but I'm beginning to think that I have lost a perfectly good wife."

"The only place for One-Bullet Mike is the great open West. My dear Mr. Barnaby, there is only one course open to you now. You must continue to disappear."

"I'm very much obliged to you."

I thought he replied with a good deal of acidity.

MAYHEW

THE lives of most men are determined by their environment. They accept the circumstances amid which fate has thrown them not only with resignation but even with good will. They are like street-cars running contentedly on their rails and they despise the sprightly flivver that dashes in and out of the traffic and speeds so jauntily across the open country. I respect them; they are good citizens, good husbands, and good fathers, and of course somebody has to pay the taxes; but I do not find them exciting. I am fascinated by the men, few enough in all conscience, who take life in their own hands and seem to mould it to their own liking. It may be that we have no such thing as free will, but at all events we have the illusion of it. At a cross-road it does seem to us that we might go either to the right or to the left and, the choice once made, it is difficult to see that the whole course of the world's history obliged us to take the turning we did.

I never met a more interesting man than Mayhew. He was a lawyer in Detroit. He was an able and a successful one. By the time he was thirty-five he had a large and a lucrative practice, he had amassed a competence, and he stood on the threshold of a distinguished career. He had an acute brain, an attractive personality, and uprightness. There was no reason why he should not become, financially or politically, a power in the land. One evening he was sitting in his club with a group of friends and they were perhaps a little the worse (or the better) for liquor. One of them had recently come from Italy and he told them of a house he had seen at Capri, a house on the hill, overlooking the Bay of Naples, with a large and shady garden. He described to them the beauty of the most beautiful island in the Mediterranean.

"It sounds fine," said Mayhew. "Is that house for sale?"

"Everything is for sale in Italy."

"Let's send 'em a cable and make an offer for it."

"What in heaven's name would you do with a house in Capri?"

"Live in it," said Mayhew.

He sent for a cable form, wrote it out, and despatched it. In a few hours the reply came back. The offer was accepted.

Mayhew was no hypocrite and he made no secret of the fact that he would never have done so wild a thing if he had been sober, but when he was he did not regret it. He was neither an impulsive nor an emotional man, but a very honest and sincere one. He would never have continued from bravado in a course that he had come to the conclusion was unwise. He made up his mind to do exactly as he had said. He did not care for wealth and he had enough money on which to live in Italy. He thought he could do more with life than spend it on composing the trivial quarrels of unimportant people. He had no definite plan. He merely wanted to get away from a life that had given him all it had to offer. I suppose his friends thought him crazy; some must have done all they could to dissuade him. He arranged his affairs, packed up his furniture and started.

Capri is a gaunt rock of austere outline, bathed in a deep blue sea; but its vineyards, green and smiling, give it a soft and easy grace. It is friendly, remote and debonair. I find it strange that Mayhew should have settled on this lovely island, for I never knew a man more insensible to beauty. I do not know what he sought there: happiness, freedom, or merely leisure; I know what he found. In this place which appeals so extravagantly to the senses he lived a life entirely of the spirit. For the island is rich with historic associations and over it broods always the enigmatic memory of Tiberius the Emperor. From his windows which overlooked the Bay of Naples, with the noble shape of Vesuvius changing colour with the changing light, Mayhew saw a hundred places that recalled the Romans and the Greeks. The past began to haunt him. All that he saw for the first time, for he had never been abroad before, excited his fancy; and in his soul stirred the creative imagination. He was a man of energy. Presently he made up his mind to write a history. For some time he looked about for a subject, and at last decided on the second century of the Roman Empire. It was little known and it seemed to him to offer problems analogous with those of our own day.

He began to collect books and soon he had an immense library. His legal training had taught him to read quickly. He settled down to work. At first he had been accustomed to fore-gather in the evening with the painters, writers and suchlike who met in the little tavern near the Piazza, but presently he withdrew himself, for his absorption in his studies became more pressing. He had been accustomed to bathe in that bland sea and to take long walks among the pleasant vineyards, but little by little, grudging the time, he ceased to do so. He worked harder than he had ever worked in Detroit. He would start at noon and work all through the night till the whistle of the steamer that goes every morning from Capri to Naples told him that it was five o'clock and time to go to bed. His subject opened out before him, vaster and more significant, and he imagined a work that would put him for ever beside the great historians of the past. As the years went by he was to be found seldom in the ways of men. He could be tempted to come out of his house only by a game of chess or the chance of an argu-ment. He loved to set his brain against another's. He was widely read now, not only in history, but in philosophy and science; and he was a skilful controversialist, quick, logical and incisive. But he had good-humour and kindliness; though he took a very human pleasure in victory, he did not exult in it to your morti-fication.

When first he came to the island he was a big, brawny fellow, with thick black hair and a black beard, of a powerful physique; but gradually his skin became pale and waxy; he grew thin and frail. It was an odd contradiction in the most logical of men that, though a convinced and impetuous materialist, he de-spised the body; he looked upon it as a vile instrument which he could force to do the spirit's bidding. Neither illness nor lassitude prevented him from going on with his work. For fourteen years he toiled unremittingly. He made thousands and thousands of notes. He sorted and classified them. He had his subject at his finger ends, and at last was ready to begin. He sat down to write. He died.

The body that he, the materialist, had treated so contumeliously took its revenge on him.

That vast accumulation of knowledge is lost for ever. Vain was that ambition, surely not an ignoble one, to set his name beside those of Gibbon and Mommsen. His memory is treasured in the hearts of a few friends, fewer, alas! as the years pass on, and to the world he is unknown in death as he was in life.

And yet to me his life was a success. The pattern is good and complete. He did what he wanted, and he died when his goal was in sight and never knew the bitterness of an end achieved.

THE HAPPY MAN

It is a dangerous thing to order the lives of others and I have often wondered at the self-confidence of politicians, reformers and suchlike who are prepared to force upon their fellows measures that must alter their manners, habits and points of view. I have always hesitated to give advice, for how can one advise another how to act unless one knows that other as well as one knows oneself? Heaven knows, I know little enough of myself: I know nothing of others. We can only guess at the thoughts and emotions of our neighbours. Each one of us is a prisoner in a solitary tower and he communicates with the other prisoners, who form mankind, by conventional signs that have not quite the same meaning for them as for himself. And life, unfortunately, is something that you can lead but once; mistakes are often irreparable, and who am I that I should tell this one and that how he should lead it? Life is a difficult business and I have found it hard enough to make my own a complete and rounded thing; I have not been tempted to teach my neighbour what he should do with his. But there are men who flounder at the journey's start, the way before them is confused and hazardous, and on occasion, however unwillingly, I have been forced to point the finger of fate. Sometimes men have said to me, what shall I do with my life? and I have seen myself for a moment wrapped in the dark cloak of Destiny.

Once I know that I advised well.

I was a young man and I lived in a modest apartment in London near Victoria Station. Late one afternoon, when I was beginning to think that I had worked enough for that day, I heard a ring at the bell. I opened the door to a total stranger. He asked me my name; I told him. He asked if he might come in.

"Certainly."

I led him into my sitting-room and begged him to sit down. He seemed a trifle embarrassed. I offered him a cigarette and he had some difficulty in lighting it without letting go of his hat. When he had satisfactorily achieved this feat I asked him if I should not put it on a chair for him. He quickly did this and while doing it dropped his umbrella.

"I hope you don't mind my coming to see you like this," he said. "My name is Stephens and I am a doctor. You're in the medical, I believe?"

"Yes, but I don't practise."

"No, I know. I've just read a book of yours about Spain and I wanted to ask you about it."

"It's not a very good book, I'm afraid."

"The fact remains that you know something about Spain and there's no one else I know who does. And I thought perhaps you wouldn't mind giving me some information."

"I shall be very glad."

He was silent for a moment. He reached out for his hat and holding it in one hand absent-mindedly stroked it with the other. I surmised that it gave him confidence.

"I hope you won't think it very odd for a perfect stranger to talk to you like this." He gave an apologetic laugh. "I'm not going to tell you the story of my life."

When people say this to me I always know that it is precisely what they are going to do. I do not mind. In fact I rather like it.

"I was brought up by two old aunts. I've never been anywhere. I've never done anything. I've been married for six years. I have no children. I'm a medical officer at the Camberwell Infirmary. I can't stick it any more."

There was something very striking in the short, sharp sentences he used. They had a forcible ring. I had not given him more than a cursory glance, but now I looked at him with curiosity. He was a little man, thick-set and stout, of thirty perhaps, with a round red face from which shone small, dark and very bright eyes. His black hair was cropped close to a bullet-shaped head. He was dressed in a blue suit a good deal the worse for wear. It was baggy at the knees and the pockets bulged untidily.

"You know what the duties are of a medical officer in an infirmary. One day is pretty much like another. And that's all I've got to look forward to for the rest of my life. Do you think it's worth it?"

"It's a means of livelihood," I answered.

"Yes, I know. The money's pretty good."

"I don't exactly know why you've come to me."

"Well, I wanted to know whether you thought there would be any chance for an English doctor in Spain?"

"Why Spain?"

"I don't know, I just have a fancy for it."

"It's not like *Carmen,* you know."

"But there's sunshine there, and there's good wine, and there's colour, and there's air you can breathe. Let me say what I have to say straight out. I heard by accident that there was no English doctor in Seville. Do you think I could earn a living there? Is it madness to give up a good safe job for an uncertainty?"

"What does your wife think about it?"

"She's willing."

"It's a great risk."

"I know. But if you say take it, I will: if you say stay where you are, I'll stay."

He was looking at me intently with those bright dark eyes of his and I knew that he meant what he said. I reflected for a moment.

"Your whole future is concerned: you must decide for yourself. But this I can tell you: if you don't want money but are content to earn just enough to keep body and soul together, then go. For you will lead a wonderful life."

He left me, I thought about him for a day or two, and then forgot. The episode passed completely from my memory.

Many years later, fifteen at least, I happened to be in Seville and having some trifling indisposition asked the hotel porter whether there was an English doctor in the town. He said there was and gave me the address. I took a cab and as I drove up to the house a little fat man came out of it. He hesitated when he caught sight of me.

"Have you come to see me?" he said. "I'm the English doctor."

I explained my errand and he asked me to come in. He lived in an ordinary Spanish house, with a patio, and his consulting room which led out of it was littered with papers, books, medical appliances, and lumber. The sight of it would have startled a squeamish patient. We did our business and then I asked the doctor what his fee was. He shook his head and smiled.

"There's no fee."

"Why on earth not?"

"Don't you remember me? Why, I'm here because of something you said to me. You changed my whole life for me. I'm Stephens."

I had not the least notion what he was talking about. He reminded me of our interview, he repeated to me what we had said, and gradually, out of the night, a dim recollection of the incident came back to me.

"I was wondering if I'd ever see you again," he said, "I was wondering if ever I'd have a chance of thanking you for all you've done for me."

"It's been a success then?"

I looked at him. He was very fat now and bald, but his eyes twinkled gaily and his fleshy, red face bore an expression of perfect good-humour. The clothes he wore, terribly shabby they were, had been made obviously by a Spanish tailor and his hat was the wide-brimmed sombrero of the Spaniard. He looked to me as though he knew a good bottle of wine when he saw it. He had a dissipated, though entirely sympathetic, appearance. You might have hesitated to let him remove your appendix, but you could not have imagined a more delightful creature to drink a glass of wine with.

"Surely you were married?" I said.

"Yes. My wife didn't like Spain, she went back to Camberwell, she was more at home there."

"Oh, I'm sorry for that."

His black eyes flashed a bacchanalian smile. He really had somewhat the look of a young Silenus.

"Life is full of compensations," he murmured.

The words were hardly out of his mouth when a Spanish woman, no longer in her first youth, but still boldly and voluptuously beautiful, appeared at the door. She spoke to him in Spanish, and I could not fail to perceive that she was the mistress of the house.

As he stood at the door to let me out he said to me:

"You told me when last I saw you that if I came here I should earn just enough money to keep body and soul together, but that I should lead a wonderful life. Well, I want to tell you that you were right. Poor I have been and poor I shall always be, but by heaven I've enjoyed myself. I wouldn't exchange the life I've had with that of any king in the world."

THE POINT OF HONOUR

SOME YEARS AGO, being engaged on writing a book about Spain in the Golden Age, I had occasion to read again the plays of Calderón. Among others I read one called *El Medico de su Honra,* which means the Physician of his Honour. It is a cruel play and you can hardly read it without a shudder. But re-reading it, I was reminded of an encounter I had had many years before which has always remained in my memory as one of the strangest I have ever known. I was quite young then and I had gone to Seville on a short visit to see the celebration of the Feast of Corpus Christi. It was the height of summer and the heat was terrific. Great sail-cloths were drawn across the narrow streets, giving a grateful shade, but in the squares the sun beat down. mercilessly. In the morning I watched the procession. It was splendid and impressive. The crowd knelt down as the Host was solemnly carried past, and the Civil Guards in full uniform stood at salute to do homage to the heavenly King. And in the after-noon I joined the dense throng which was making its way to the bull-ring. The cigarette girls and the sewing girls wore carna-tions in their dark hair and their young men were dressed in all their best. It was just after the Spanish-American war, and the short, embroidered jacket, the skin-tight trousers and the broad-brimmed, low-crowned hat were still worn. Sometimes the crowd was scattered by a picador on the wretched hack that would never survive the afternoon, and the rider, with conscious pride in his picturesque costume, exchanged pleasantries with the facetious. A long line of carriages, dilapidated and shabby, overfilled with *aficionados,* drove noisily along.

I went early, for it amused me to see the people gradually filling the vast arena. The cheaper seats in the sun were already packed, and it was a curious effect that the countless fans made, like the fluttering of a host of butterflies, as men and women restlessly fanned themselves. In the shade, where I was sitting, the places were taken more slowly, but even there, an hour before the fight began, one had to look rather carefully for a seat. Presently a man stopped in front of me and with a pleasant smile asked if I could make room for him. When he had settled down, I took a sidelong glance at him and noticed that he was well-dressed, in English clothes, and looked like a gentleman. He had beautiful hands, small but resolute, with thin, long fingers. Wanting a cigarette, I took out my case and thought it would be polite to offer him one. He accepted. He had evidently seen that I was a foreigner, for he thanked me in French.

"You are English?" he went on.

"Yes."

"How is it you haven't run away from the heat?"

I explained that I had come on purpose to see the Feast of Corpus Christi.

"After all, it's something you must come to Seville for."

Then I made some casual remark about the vast concourse of people.

"No one would imagine that Spain was bleeding from the loss of all that remained of her Empire and that her ancient glory is now nothing but a name."

"There's a great deal left."

"The sunshine, the blue sky, and the future."

He spoke dispassionately, as though the misfortunes of his fallen country were no concern of his. Not knowing what to reply, I remained silent. We waited. The boxes began to fill up. Ladies in their mantillas of black or white lace entered them and spread their Manila shawls over the balustrade so as to form a gay and many-coloured drapery. Now and then, when one of them was of particular beauty, a round of applause would greet her appearance and she would smile and bow without embarrassment. At last the president of the bull-fight made his entry, the band struck up, and the fighters, all glittering in their satin and gold and silver, marched swaggering across the ring. A minute later a great black bull charged in. Carried away by the horrible excitement of the contest, I noticed, notwithstanding, that my neighbour remained cool. When a man fell and only escaped by a miracle the horns of the furious beast, and with a gasp thousands sprang to their feet, he remained motionless. The bull was killed and the mules dragged out the huge carcass. I sank back exhausted.

"Do you like bull-fighting?" he asked me. "Most English do, though I have noticed that in their own country they say hard enough things about it."

"Can one like something that fills one with horror and loathing? Each time I come to a fight I swear I will never go to another. And yet I do."

"It's a curious passion that leads us to delight in the peril of others. Perhaps it's natural to the human race. The Romans had their gladiators and the moderns have their melodramas. It may be that it is an instinct in man to find pleasure in bloodshed and torture."

I did not answer directly.

"Don't you think that the bull-fight is the reason why human life is of so little account in Spain?"

"And do you think human life is of any great account?" he asked.

I gave him a quick look, for there was an ironical tone in his voice that no one could have missed, and I saw that his eyes were full of mockery. I flushed a little, for he made me on a sudden feel very young. I was surprised at the change of his expression. He had seemed rather an amiable man, with his large soft friendly eyes, but now his face bore a look of sardonic hauteur which was a trifle disquieting. I shrank back into my shell. We said little to one another during the rest of the afternoon, but when the last bull was killed and we all rose to our feet he shook hands with me and expressed the hope that we might meet again. It was a mere politeness and neither of us, I imagine, thought that there was even a remote possibility of it.

But quite by chance, two or three days later, we did. I was in a quarter of Seville that I did not know very well. I had been that afternoon to the palace of the Duke of Alba, which I knew had a fine garden and in one of the rooms a magnificent ceiling reputed to have been made by Moorish captives before the fall of Granada. It was not easy to gain admittance, but I wanted very much to see it and thought that now, in the height of summer when there were no tourists, with two or three pesetas

I might be allowed in. I was disappointed. The man in charge
told me that the house was under repair and no stranger could
visit it without a written permission from the Duke's agent.
So, having nothing else to do, I went to the royal garden of the
Alcazar, the old palace of Don Pedro the Cruel, whose memory
lives still among the people of Seville. It was very pleasant
among the orange trees and cypresses. I had a book with me, a
volume of Calderón, and I sat there for a while and read. Then I
went for a stroll. In the older parts of Seville the streets are
narrow and tortuous. It is delicious to wander along them under
the awnings that stretch above, but not easy to find one's way.
I lost mine. When I had just made up my mind that I had no
notion in which direction to turn I saw a man walking towards
me and recognised my acquaintance of the bull-ring. I stopped
him and asked whether he could direct me. He remembered me.

"You'll never find your way," he smiled, turning round. "I'll
walk a little with you until you can't mistake it."

I protested, but he would not listen. He assured me it was no
trouble.

"You haven't gone away then?" he said.

"I'm leaving to-morrow. I've just been to the Duke of Alba's
house. I wanted to see that Moorish ceiling of his, but they
wouldn't let me in."

"Are you interested in Arabic art?"

"Well, yes. I've heard that that ceiling is one of the finest
things in Seville."

"I think I could show you one as good."

"Where?"

He looked at me for a moment reflectively as though wondering what sort of a person I was. If he was, he evidently came
to a satisfactory decision.

"If you have ten minutes to spare I will take you to it."

I thanked him warmly and we turned back and retraced our
steps. We chatted of indifferent things till we came to a large
house, washed in pale green, with the Arabic look of a prison,
the windows on the street heavily barred, which so many houses
in Seville have. My guide clapped his hands at the gateway and
a servant looked out from a window into the patio, and pulled a
cord.

"Whose house is this?"

"Mine."

I was surprised, for I knew how jealously Spaniards guarded

their privacy and how little inclined they were to admit
strangers into their houses. The heavy iron gate swung open
and we walked into the courtyard; we crossed it and went
through a narrow passage. Then I found myself suddenly in an
enchanted garden. It was walled on three sides, with walls as
high as houses; and their old red brick, softened by time, was
covered with roses. They clad every inch in wanton, scented
luxuriance. In the garden, growing wildly, as if the gardeners
had striven in vain to curb the exuberance of nature, were palm-
trees rising high into the air in their passionate desire for the
sun, dark orange-trees and trees in flower whose names I did
not know, and among them roses and more roses. The fourth
wall was a Moorish loggia, with horseshoe arches heavily decorated with tracery, and when we entered this I saw the magnificent ceiling. It was like a little bit of the Alcazar, but it had not
suffered the restorations that have taken all the charm from
that palace, and the colours were exquisitely tender. It was a
gem.

"Believe me, you need not regret that you have not been able
to see the duke's house. Further, you can say that you have
seen something that no other foreigner has seen within living
memory."

"It's very kind of you to have shown it to me. I'm infinitely
grateful."

He looked about him with a pride with which I could sympathise.

"It was built by one of my own ancestors in the time of Don
Pedro the Cruel. It is very likely that the King himself more
than once caroused under this ceiling with my ancestor."

I held out the book I was carrying.

"I've just been reading a play in which Don Pedro is one of
the important characters."

"What is the book?"

I handed it to him and he glanced at the title. I looked about
me.

"Of course, what adds to the beauty is that wonderful garden," I said. "The whole impression is awfully romantic."

The Spaniard was evidently pleased with my enthusiasm. He
smiled. I had already noticed how grave his smile was. It hardly
dispelled the habitual melancholy of his expression.

"Would you like to sit down for a few minutes and smoke a
cigarette?"

"I should love to."

We walked out into the garden and came upon a lady sitting on a bench of Moorish tiles like those in the gardens of the Alcazar. She was working at some embroidery. She looked up quickly, evidently taken aback to see a stranger, and gave my companion an enquiring stare.

"Allow me to present you to my wife," he said.

The lady gravely bowed. She was very beautiful, with magnificent eyes, a straight nose with delicate nostrils, and a pale smooth skin. In her black hair, abundant as with most Spanish women, there was a broad white streak. Her face was quite unlined and she could not have been more than thirty.

"You have a very lovely garden, Señora," I said because I had to say something.

She gave it an indifferent glance.

"Yes, it is pretty."

I felt suddenly embarrassed. I did not expect her to show me any cordiality, and I could not blame her if she thought my intrusion merely a nuisance. There was something about her that I could not quite make out. It was not an active hostility. Absurd as it seemed, since she was a young woman and beautiful, I felt that there was something dead in her.

"Are you going to sit here?" she asked her husband.

"With your permission. Only for a few minutes."

"I won't disturb you."

She gathered her silks and the canvas on which she had been working and rose to her feet. When she stood up I saw that she was taller than Spanish women generally are. She gave me an unsmiling bow. She carried herself with a sort of royal composure and her gait was stately. I was flippant in those days, and I remember saying to myself that she was not the sort of girl you could very well think of being silly with. We sat down on the multi-coloured bench and I gave my host a cigarette. I held a match to it. He still had my volume of Calderón in his hands, and now he idly turned the pages.

"Which of the plays have you been reading?"

"*El Medico de su Honra.*"

He gave me a look, and I thought I discerned in his large eyes a sardonic glint.

"And what do you think of it?"

"I think its revolting. The fact is, of course, that the idea is so foreign to our modern notions."

"What idea?"

"The point of honour and all that sort of thing."

I should explain that the point of honour is the mainspring of much of the Spanish drama. It is the nobleman's code that impels a man to kill his wife, in cold blood, not only if she has been unfaithful to him, but even if, however little she was to blame, her conduct has given rise to scandal. In this particular play there is an example of this more deliberate than any I have ever read: the physician of his honour takes vengeance on his wife, though aware that she is innocent, simply as a matter of decorum.

"It's in the Spanish blood," said my friend. "The foreigner must just take it or leave it."

"Oh, come, a lot of water has flowed down the Guadalquivir since Calderón's day. You're not going to pretend that any man would behave like that now."

"On the contrary I pretend that even now a husband who finds himself in such a humiliating and ridiculous position can only regain his self-respect by the offender's death."

I did not answer. It seemed to me that he was pulling a romantic gesture, and within me I murmured, Bosh. He gave me an ironic smile.

"Have you ever heard of Don Pedro Aguria?"

"Never."

"The name is not unknown in Spanish history. An ancestor was Admiral of Spain under Philip II and another was bosom friend to Philip IV. By royal command he sat for his portrait to Velasquez."

My host hesitated a moment. He gave me a long, reflective stare before he went on.

"Under the Philips the Agurias were rich, but by the time my friend Don Pedro succeeded his father their circumstances were much reduced. But still he was not poor, he had estates between Cordova and Aguilar, and in Seville his house retained at least traces of its ancient splendour. The little world of Seville was astonished when he announced his engagement to Soledad, the daughter of the ruined Count of Acaba, for though her family was distinguished her father was an old scamp. He was crippled with debts, and the shifts he resorted to in order to keep his head above water were none too nice. But Soledad was beautiful and Don Pedro in love with her. They were married. He adored her with the vehement passion of which perhaps only

a Spaniard is capable. But he discovered to his dismay that she
did not love him. She was kind and gentle. She was a good wife
and a good housekeeper. She was grateful to him. But that was
all. He thought that when she had a child she would change,
but the child came, and it made no difference. The barrier between them that he had felt from the beginning was still there.
He suffered. At last he told himself that she had a character too
noble, a spirit too delicate, to descend to earthly passion, and
he resigned himself. She was too high above him for mortal
love."

I moved a little uneasily in my seat. I thought the Spaniard
was unduly rhetorical. He went on.

"You know that here in Seville the Opera House is open only
for the six weeks after Easter, and since the Sevillans don't care
very much for European music we go more to meet our friends
than to listen to the singers. The Agurias had a box, like everybody else, and they went on the opening night of the season.
Tannhaüser was being given. Don Pedro and his wife, like
typical Spaniards, with nothing to do all day but always late,
did not arrive till nearly the end of the first act. In the interval
the Count of Acaba, Soledad's father, came into the box accompanied by a young officer of artillery whom Don Pedro had
never seen before. But Soledad seemed to know him well.

" 'Here is Pepe Alvarez,' said the Count. 'He's just come back
from Cuba and I insisted on bringing him to see you.'

"Soledad smiled and held out her hand, then introduced the
newcomer to her husband.

" 'Pepe is the son of the attorney at Carmona. We used to
play together when we were children.'

"Carmona is a small town near Seville, and it was here that
the Count had retired when his creditors in the city grew too
troublesome. The house he owned there was almost all that was
left him of the fortune he had squandered. He lived in Seville
now through Don Pedro's generosity. But Don Pedro did not
like him and he bowed stiffly to the young officer. He guessed
that his father the attorney and the count had been concerned
together in transactions that were none too reputable. In a
minute he left the box to talk with his cousin, the Duchess of
Santaguador, whose box was opposite his own. A few days later
he met Pepe Alvarez at his club in the Sierpes and had a chat
with him. To his surprise he found him a very pleasant young

fellow. He was full of his exploits in Cuba and he related them with humour.

"The six weeks about Easter and the great Fair are the gayest in Seville, and the world meets to exchange gossip and laughter, at one festivity after another. Pepe Alvarez with his good nature and high spirits was in great request and the Agurias met him constantly. Don Pedro saw that he amused Soledad. She was more vivacious when he was there, and her laughter, which he had so seldom heard, was a delight to him. Like other members of the aristocracy he took a booth for the Fair, where they danced, supped and drank champagne till dawn. Pepe Alvarez was always the life and soul of the parties.

"One night Don Pedro was dancing with the Duchess of Santaguador and they passed Soledad with Pepe Alvarez.

" 'Soledad is looking very beautiful this evening,' she remarked.

" 'And happy,' he replied.

" 'Is it true that once she was engaged to be married to Pepe Alvarez?'

" 'Of course not.'

"But the question startled him. He had known that Soledad and Pepe had known one another when they were children, but it had never crossed his mind that there could have been anything between them. The Count of Acaba, though a rogue, was a gentleman by birth, and it was inconceivable that he could have thought of marrying his daughter to the son of a provincial attorney. When they got home Don Pedro told his wife what the duchess had said and what he had replied.

" 'But I was engaged to Pepe,' she said.

" 'Why did you never tell me?'

" 'It was finished and done with. He was in Cuba. I never expected to see him again.'

" 'There must be people who know you were engaged to him.'

" 'I daresay. Does it matter?'

" 'Very much. You shouldn't have renewed your acquaintance with him when he returned.'

" 'Does that mean that you have no confidence in me?'

" 'Of course not. I have every confidence in you. All the same I wish you to discontinue it now.'

" 'And if I refuse?'

" 'I shall kill him.'

"They looked long into one another's eyes. Then she gave him a little bow and went to her room. Don Pedro sighed. He wondered whether she still loved Pepe Alvarez and whether it was on account of this that she had never loved him. But he would not allow himself to give way to the unworthy emotion of jealousy. He looked into his heart and was sure that it harboured no feeling of hatred for the young artilleryman. On the contrary, he liked him. This was not an affair of love or hate, but of honour. On a sudden he remembered that a few days before when he went to his club he noticed that the conversation suddenly failed, and, looking back, he seemed to remember that several of the group who were sitting there and chatting eyed him curiously. Was it possible that he had been the subject of their conversation? He shivered a little at the thought.

"The Fair was drawing to its end, and when it was over the Agurias had arranged to go to Cordova, where Don Pedro had an estate which it was necessary for him to visit from time to time. He looked forward to the peace of a country life after the turmoil of Seville. The day after this conversation Soledad, saying she was not well, stayed in the house, and she did the same the day following. Don Pedro visited her in her room morning and evening and they talked of indifferent things. But on the third day his cousin Conchita de Santaguador was giving a ball. It was the last of the season and everyone in her exclusive set would be there. Soledad, saying she was still indisposed, announced that she would stay at home.

" 'Are you refusing to go because of our conversation of the other night?' Don Pedro asked.

" 'I have been thinking over what you said. I think your demand unreasonable, but I shall accede to it. The only way I can cease my friendship with Pepe is by not going to places where I am likely to meet him.' A tremor of pain passed over her lovely face. 'Perhaps it is best.'

" 'Do you love him still?'

" 'Yes.'

"Don Pedro felt himself go cold with anguish.

" 'Then why did you marry me?'

" 'Pepe was away, in Cuba, no one knew when he would come back. Perhaps never. My father said that I must marry you.'

" 'To save him from ruin?'

" 'From worse than ruin.'

" 'I am very sorry for you.'

" 'You have been kind to me. I have done everything in my power to prove to you that I am grateful.'

" 'And does Pepe love you?'

"She shook her head and smiled sadly.

" 'Men are different. He's young. He's too gay to love anyone very long. No, to him I'm just the friend whom he used to play with when he was a child and flirt with when he was a boy. He can make jokes about the love he once had for me.'

"He took her hand and pressed it, then kissed it and left her. He went to the ball by himself. His friends were sorry to hear of Soledad's indisposition, but after expressing a proper sympathy devoted themselves to the evening's amusement. Don Pedro drifted into the card-room. There was room at a table, and he sat down to play *chemin de fer*. He played with extraordinary luck and made a good deal of money. One of the players laughingly asked where Soledad was that evening. Don Pedro saw another give him a startled glance, but he laughed and answered that she was safely in bed and asleep. Then an unlucky incident occurred. Some young man came into the room, and addressing an artillery officer who was playing asked where Pepe Alvarez was.

" 'Isn't he here?' said the officer.

" 'No.'

"An odd silence fell upon the party. Don Pedro exercised all his self-control to prevent his face from showing what he suddenly felt. The thought flashed through his mind that those men at the table suspected that Pepe was with Soledad, his wife. Oh, the shame! The indignity! He forced himself to go on playing for another hour and still he won. He could not go wrong. The game broke up and he returned to the ballroom. He went up to his cousin.

" 'I've hardly had a word with you,' he said. 'Come into another room and let us sit down for a little.'

" 'If you like.'

"The room, Conchita's boudoir, was empty.

" 'Where is Pepe Alvarez to-night?' he asked casually.

" 'I can't think.'

" 'You were expecting him?'

" 'Of course.'

"She was smiling as he was, but he noticed that she looked at him sharply. He dropped his mask of casualness and, though they were alone, lowered his voice.

" 'Conchita, I beseech you to tell me the truth. Are they saying that he is Soledad's lover?'

" 'Pedrito, what a monstrous question to put to me!'

"But he had seen the terror in her eyes and the sudden instinctive movement of her hand to her face.

" 'You've answered it.'

"He got up and left her. He went home and looking up from the patio saw a light in his wife's room. He went upstairs and knocked at the door. There was no answer, but he went in. To his surprise, for it was late, she was sitting up working at the embroidery upon which much of her time was spent.

" 'Why are you working at this hour?'

" 'I couldn't sleep, I couldn't read. I thought it would distract my mind if I worked.'

"He did not sit down.

" 'Soledad, I have something to tell you that must cause you pain. I must ask you to be brave. Pepe Alvarez was not at Conchita's to-night.'

" 'What is that to me?'

" 'It is unfortunate that you were not there either. Everyone at the ball thought that you were together.'

" 'That's preposterous.'

" 'I know, but that doesn't help matters. You could have opened the gate for him yourself and let him out, or you could have slipped out yourself without anyone seeing you go or come.'

" 'But do you believe it?'

" 'No. I agreed with you that the thing was preposterous. Where was Pepe Alvarez?'

" 'How do I know? How should I know?'

" 'It is very strange that he should not have come to the most brilliant party, the last party, of the season.'

"She was silent for a minute.

" 'The night after you spoke to me about him I wrote and told him that in view of the circumstances I thought it would be better if in future we saw no more of one another than could be helped. It may be that he did not go to the ball for the same reason that I did not.'

"They were silent for a while. He looked down at the ground, but he felt that her eyes were fixed on him. I should have told you before that Don Pedro possessed one accomplishment which raised him above his fellows, but at the same time was a drawback. He was the best shot in Andalusia. Everyone knew this and it would have been a brave man who ventured to offend him. A few days earlier there had been pigeon-shooting at Tablada, the wide common outside Seville along the Guadal-quivir, and Don Pedro had carried all before him. Pepe Alvarez on the other hand had shown himself so indifferent a marksman that everyone had laughed at him. The young artilleryman had borne the chaff with good-humour. Cannon were his weapon, he said.

" 'What are you going to do?' Soledad asked.

" 'You know that there is only one thing I can do.'

"She understood. But she tried to treat what he said as a pleasantry.

" 'You're childish. We're not living any more in the sixteenth century.'

" 'I know. That is why I am talking to you now. If I have to challenge Pepe I shall kill him. I don't want to do that. If he will resign his commission and leave Spain I will do nothing.'

" 'How can he? Where is he to go?'

" 'He can go to South America. He may make his fortune.'

" 'Do you expect me to tell him that?'

" 'If you love him.'

" 'I love him too much to ask him to run away like a coward. How could he face life without honour?'

"Don Pedro laughed.

" 'What has Pepe Alvarez, the son of the attorney at Car-mona, to do with honour?'

"She did not answer, but in her eyes he saw the fierce hatred she bore him. That look stabbed his heart, for he loved her, he loved her as passionately as ever.

"Next day he went to his club and joined a group who were sitting at the window looking out at the crowd passing up and down the Sierpes. Pepe Alvarez was in it. They were talking of last night's party.

" 'Where were you, Pepe?' someone asked.

" 'My mother was ill. I had to go to Carmona,' he answered. 'I was dreadfully disappointed, but perhaps it was all for the best.' He turned laughingly to Don Pedro. 'I hear you were in luck and won everybody's money.'

" 'When are you going to give us our revenge, Pedrito?' asked another.

" 'I'm afraid you'll have to wait for that,' he answered. 'I have to go to Cordova. I find that my attorney has been robbing me. I know that all attorneys are thieves, but I stupidly thought this one was honest.'

"He seemed to speak quite lightly, and it was as lightly that Pepe Alvarez put in his word.

" 'I think you exaggerate, Pedrito. Don't forget that my father is an attorney and he at least is honest.'

" 'I don't believe it for a minute,' laughed Don Pedro. 'I have no doubt that your father is as big a thief as any.'

"The insult was so unexpected and so unprovoked that for a moment Pepe Alvarez was staggered. The others were startled into sudden seriousness.

" 'What do you mean, Pedrito?'

" 'Exactly what I say.'

" 'It's a lie and you know it's a lie. You must withdraw that at once.'

"Don Pedro laughed.

" 'Of course I shall not withdraw. Your father is a thief and a rascal.'

"Pepe did the only thing he could do. He sprang from his chair and with his open hand hit Don Pedro in the face. The outcome was inevitable. Next day the two men met on the frontier of Portugal. Pepe Alvarez, the attorney's son, died like a gentleman with a bullet in his heart."

The Spaniard ended his story on such a casual note that for the first moment I hardly took it in. But when I did I was profoundly shocked.

"Barbarous," I said. "It was just cold-blooded murder."

My host got up.

"You're talking nonsense, my young friend. Don Pedro did the only thing he could do in the circumstances."

I left Seville next day, and from then till now have never been able to discover the name of the man who told me this strange story. I have often wondered whether the lady I saw, the lady with the pale face and the lock of white hair, was the unhappy Soledad.

THE MOTHER

Two or three people, hearing sounds of a quarrel in the patio, came out of their rooms and listened.

"It's the new lodger," said a woman. "She's having a row with the porter who brought her things."

It was a tenement house of two storeys, built round a patio, in a back street of La Macarena, which is the roughest quarter in Seville. The rooms were let to working men and the small functionaries with whom Spain is overrun, postmen, policemen, or tram-conductors, and the place swarmed with children. There were twenty families there. They squabbled and made it up; they chattered their heads off; they helped one another when help was needed; for the Andalusians are good-natured people, and on the whole they got on well enough together. One room had been for some time unlet. A woman had taken it that morning, and an hour later had brought her bits and pieces, carrying as much as she could herself, a *gallego*—the Galicians are the general porters of Spain—laden with the rest.

But the quarrel was growing more violent, and the two women above, on the first floor, anxious not to miss a word, leant over the balcony.

They heard the newcomer's shrill voice raised in a torrent of abuse and the man's sullen interjections. The two women nudged one another.

"I shan't go till you pay me," he kept on saying.

"But I've paid you already. You said you'd do it for three reales."

"Never! You promised me four."

They were haggling over rather less than twopence half-penny.

"Four reales for moving those few things? You're crazy."

She tried to push him away.

"I shan't go till you pay me," he repeated.

"I'll give you a penny more."

"I won't take it."

The dispute grew more and more noisy. The woman screamed at the porter and cursed him. She shook her fist in his face. At last he lost patience.

"Oh, all right, give me the penny and I'll go. I'm not going to waste time on a slut like you."

She paid him, and the man, throwing down her mattress, left her. She flung a filthy word at him as he went. She came out of the room to drag the things in, and the two women in the balcony saw her face.

"*Carai*, what an evil face! She looks like a murderess."

A girl came up the stairs at that moment, and her mother called out: "Did you see her, Rosalia?"

"I asked the *gallego* where she came from, he says he brought the things from Triana. She promised him four reales and then wouldn't pay."

"Did he tell you her name?"

"He didn't know. But in Triana they called her La Cachirra."

The vixen appeared again to fetch a bundle she had forgotten. She glanced at the women in the balcony watching her unconcernedly, but said nothing. Rosalia shuddered.

"She frightens me."

La Cachirra was forty, haggard and very thin, with bony hands and fingers like a vulture's claws. Her cheeks were sunken and her skin wrinkled and yellow. When she opened her mouth, with its pale, heavy lips, she showed teeth that were pointed like those of a beast of prey. Her hair was black and coarse; she wore it in a clumsy knot, which seemed on the point of falling over her shoulders, and in front of each ear fell a straight wisp. Her eyes, deep-set in their sockets, large and black, shone fiercely. Her face bore an expression of such ferocity that no one dared come near to speak with her. She kept entirely to herself. The curiosity of the neighbours was aroused. They knew she was very poor, for her clothes were wretched. She went out every morning at six and did not return till night; but they could not even find out how she earned her living. They urged a policeman who lived in the house to make inquiries.

"As long as she doesn't break the peace, I have nothing to do with her," said he.

But in Seville scandal travels quickly and in a few days a mason who lived in an upper room brought the news that a friend in Triana knew her story. La Cachirra had only come out of prison one month before, and she had spent seven years there—for murder. She had lodged in a house in Triana, but the children, finding out what had happened, threw stones at her and called her names; and she, turning upon them with foul words and with blows, had filled the whole place with such tumult that the landlord gave her notice. Cursing him and all who had turned her out, La Cachirra one morning suddenly disappeared.

"And whom did she murder?" asked Rosalia.

"They say it was her lover," replied the mason.

"She can never have had one," said Rosalia, with a laugh of scorn.

"Santa Maria!" cried Pilar, her mother, "I hope she won't kill any of us. I said she looked like a murderess!"

Rosalia, shivering, crossed herself. At that moment La Cachirra came in from her day's work and a sudden oppression fell upon the talkers. They made a movement as if to huddle together and looked nervously at the wild-eyed woman. She seemed to see something ominous in their silence and gave them a rapid, suspicious glance. The policeman, to make conversation, bade her good-evening.

"*Buena sera*," she replied, with a scowl, and, passing quickly into her room, slammed the door.

They heard her lock it. The evil, sullen eyes had cast a gloom over them and they talked in whispers as if under a mischievous spell.

"She has the devil in her," said Rosalia.

"I'm glad you're here to protect us, Manuel," added her mother to the policeman.

But La Cachirra seemed indisposed to give trouble. She went her way, unbending, never addressing so much as a word to anyone, and brusquely cut short every attempt at friendliness. She felt that the neighbours had discovered her secret, the homicide and the long years of imprisonment; and the lines in her face grew sterner, the expression of her deep-set eyes more inhuman. But gradually the anxiety she had caused was dispelled. Even the garrulous Pilar ceased to pay attention to the silent gaunt figure who occasionally passed through the group sitting in the patio.

"I dare say the prison has sent her mad, they say it often does."

But one day an event occurred to revive the gossip. A youth came to the *reja*—the wrought-iron gate that serves as front door to the Sevillan house—and asked for Antonia Sanchez. Pilar, who was mending a skirt in the patio, looked up at her daughter and shrugged her shoulders.

"No one of that names lives here," she said.

"Yes, she does," the young man answered; then, after a pause: "They call her La Cachirra."

"Ah!" Rosalia opened the gate and pointed to the door. "She's in there."

"Thank you."

The youth gave her a smile. She was a pretty girl, with a high colour and fine bold eyes. A red carnation threw up the glossy blackness of her hair. Her breasts were full and the nipples were prominent under her blouse.

"Blessed be the mother that bore you," he said, using a hackneyed phrase.

"*Vaya Usted con Dios,* go you with God," answered Pilar.

He passed on and knocked at the door. The two women looked after him curiously.

"Who can he be?" asked Pilar. "La Cachirra's never had a visitor before."

There was no reply to his knocking, and he knocked again. They heard La Cachirra's rasping voice ask who was there.

"*Madre!*" he cried. "Mother."

There was a shriek. The door was burst open.

"Currito!"

The woman threw her arms round his neck and kissed him passionately. She fondled him and with a loving gesture stroked his face with both her hands. The girl and her mother who watched would never have thought her capable of such tenderness. At last, with little sobs of joy, she dragged him into her room.

"He's her son," said Rosalia, with surprise. "Who'd have thought it! And a fine fellow like that."

Currito had a lean face and white, even teeth; his hair was cut very close, shaved on the temples, and set on the scalp with a truly Andalusian perfection. The shadow of his precocious beard showed blue beneath his brown skin. And of course he was a dandy. He had the national love of fine clothes and his trousers were skin-tight; his short jacket and his frilled shirt were as new as new could be. He wore a broad-brimmed hat.

At last the door of La Cachirra's room was opened and she appeared, hanging on her son's arm.

"You'll come again next Sunday?" she asked.

"If nothing stops me."

He glanced at Rosalia and, having bidden his mother good-night, nodded to her also.

"*Vaya Usted con Dios!*" said she.

She gave him a smile and a flash of her dark eyes. La Cachirra intercepted the look; and the sullenness which her intense joy had driven away suddenly darkened her face like a thunder-cloud. She scowled fiercely at the handsome girl.

"Is that your son?" asked Pilar, when the youth was gone.

"Yes, he's my son," answered La Cachirra gruffly, going back to her room.

Nothing could soften her, and even when her heart was brimming over with happiness she repelled the overtures of friendship.

"He's a good-looking fellow," said Rosalia; and she thought of him more than once during the next few days.

It was a terrible love that La Cachirra had for her son. He was all she had in the world and she adored him with a fiery, jealous passion that demanded in·return impossible devotion. She wished to be all in all to him. On account of his work they could not live together and it·tortured her to imagine what he did when he was away from her. She could not bear him to look at a woman and she writhed at the bare idea that he might pay court to some girl. No amusement is more common in Seville than the long flirtation in which the maid sits at her window half the night long, guarded by iron bars, or stands at the gate, while her lover in the street pours his rapture into her willing ear. La Cachirra asked the boy if he had a *novia*, a sweetheart, aware that so attractive a youth must enjoy the smiles of women, and she knew he lied when he swore he spent his evenings at work. But his denials gave her a fierce delight.

When she saw Rosalia's provoking glance and Currito's answering smile, rage leapt to her throat. She had hated her neighbours before, because they were happy and she was wretched, because they knew her terrible secret; but now she hated them more, already fancying, half crazily, that they were conspiring to rob her of her son. On the following Sunday, in the afternoon, La Cachirra came out of her room, crossed the patio and stood at the gate. This was a proceeding so unusual that the neighbours commented upon it.

"Don't you know why she's there?" said Rosalia, with a stifled laugh. "Her precious son is coming, and she doesn't want us to see him."

"Does she think we'll eat him?"

Currito arrived and his mother took him quickly to her room.

"She's as jealous of him as if he was her lover," said Pilar.

Rosalia looked at the closed door, laughing again, and her shining eyes were filled with mischief. It occurred to her that it would be very amusing to have a word with Currito. Rosalia's white teeth gleamed at the thought of La Cachirra's anger. She stationed herself at the gate, so that the pair, when they came out, could not help crossing her; but La Cachirra, seeing the girl, moved to the other side of her son so that not even a glance should pass between them. Rosalia shrugged her shoulders.

"You won't beat me so easily as that," she thought.

The Sunday after, when La Cachirra took up her place at the gate, Rosalia went out into the street and strolled along in the direction from which she guessed he would come. In a minute she saw Currito, and walked on, elaborately ignoring him.

"Hola!" said he, stopping.

"Is it you? I thought you were afraid to speak to me."

"I'm afraid of nothing," he answered boastingly.

"Except mamma!"

She walked on, as if she wanted him to leave her; but she knew very well he would do no such thing.

"Where are you going?" he asked.

"What has that to do with you, Currito? Go to your mother, my son, or she'll beat you. You're afraid to look at me when she's with you."

"What nonsense."

"Well, *vaya Usted con Dios!* I have commissions."

He went off rather sheepishly, and Rosalia laughed to herself. She was in the courtyard once more when he passed through with La Cachirra on his way out; and this time, shamed into courage, he stopped and said good-night. La Cachirra turned red with anger.

"Come, Currito," she cried, with a rasping voice, "what are you waiting for?"

He went away, and the woman stopped a moment in front of Rosalia as if she were going to speak, but, with a visible effort, she restrained herself, and went back to her dark, silent room.

A few days later was the feast of San Isidoro, the patron saint of Seville, and to celebrate the holiday the mason and one or two others had put a string of Chinese lanterns in the patio. They glowed warmly in the clear summer night. The sky was soft against the shining stars. The people of the house were gathered in the middle of the patio, sitting on chairs; and the women, some with babies at their breasts, fanned themselves with little paper fans, interrupting their ceaseless chattering to fling a word of abuse at some older child who was making a nuisance of himself. The cool air was very pleasant after the day's breathless heat. Those who had been to the bull-fight were telling the less fortunate all about it. They described with precise detail a wonderful feat that Belmonte, the famous matador, had performed. With their vivid imaginations, the particulars gained every minute in variety and colour, so that it appeared that never in the history of Seville had there been a more excellent *corrida*. Everyone was present but La Cachirra, and in her room they saw the light of a solitary candle.

"And her son?"

"He's in there," answered Pilar. "I saw him pass an hour ago."

"He must be amusing himself," said Rosalia, with a laugh.

"Oh, don't bother about La Cachirra," said another. "Give us a dance, Rosalia."

"Yes, yes," they cried. "Go on, my girl. You dance."

In Spain they love dancing and they love to look at dancing. Years and years ago it was said that there was never a Spanish woman that was not born to dance.

The chairs were quickly set in a ring. The mason and the

tram conductor fetched their guitars. Rosalia got her castanets, and stepping forward with another girl, began.

Currito, in the poky room, pricked up his ears when he heard the music.

"They're dancing," he said, and an itching shot down his limbs.

He looked through the curtain and saw the group in the mellow light of the Chinese lanterns. He saw the two girls dancing. Rosalia wore her Sunday clothes, and, as is customary, she was heavily powdered. A splendid carnation gleamed in her hair. Currito's heart beat quickly. Love in Spain grows fast, and he had thought often of the handsome girl since that day on which he first spoke to her. He moved towards the door.

"What are you doing?" asked La Cachirra.

"I'm going to look at them dance. You never wish me to amuse myself."

"It's Rosalia you want to see."

He pushed her away as she tried to stop him, and joined the group that watched the dancers. La Cachirra followed a step or two, and then stood, half hidden by the gloom, with fury gnawing at her heart. Rosalia saw him.

"Aren't you frightened to look at me?" she whispered, as she passed him.

The dancing had made her light-headed and she felt no fear of La Cachirra. When the measure ended and her partner sank into a chair, Rosalia marched up to Currito and stood in front of him, upright, with her head thrown back and her breast heaving with the rapid motion.

"Of course, you don't know how to dance," she said.

"Yes, I do."

"Well, come then."

She smiled provokingly, but he hesitated. He looked over his shoulder at his mother, whom he divined, rather than saw, in the darkness. Rosalia caught the glance and its meaning.

"Are you afraid?"

"What should I be afraid of?" he asked with a shrug of the shoulders.

He stepped into the ring. The guitarists strummed away and the onlookers rhythmically clapped their hands, punctuating the time with an occasional cry of Olé. A girl gave Currito a pair of castanets and the pair began to dance. They heard a little hiss, as of a serpent in the darkness, and Rosalia, quite reckless now, looked with a laugh at the face, ghastly white, that gleamed from the shadows. La Cachirra did not move. She watched the movements of the dance, the swaying of the bodies, the intricate steps; she saw Rosalia lean back with a graceful gesture and smile in Currito's face as he wound about her, clapping his castanets. Her eyes glowed like coals of fire and she felt them burning in the sockets; but no one noticed her, and she gave a groan of rage. The dance came to an end, and Rosalia, smiling with pleasure at the applause, told Currito she did not know he could dance so well.

La Cachirra flung herself into her room and bolted the door. She gave no answer when Currito came and bade her open.

"Well, I shall go home," he said.

Her heart bled with pain, but she would not speak. He was all she had, all she loved in the world; and yet she hated him. She could not sleep that night, but lay thinking, half-madly, that they were robbing her of her son. In the morning she did not go to work, but lay in wait for Rosalia. The girl came out at last, rather bedraggled after the night's festivities, and she started when La Cachirra suddenly faced her.

"What do you want with my son?"

"What do you mean?" replied Rosalia, assuming an expression of surprise.

La Cachirra quivered with passion and she bit her hand to keep herself quiet.

"Oh, you know what I mean. You're stealing him from me."

"Do you think I want your son? Keep him away from me. I can't help it if he runs after me wherever I go."

"That's a lie!"

"Ask him!" And now Rosalia's voice was so scornful that La Cachirra could hardly contain herself. "He waits an hour in the street to see me. Why don't you keep him to yourself?"

"You lie, you lie! You throw yourself in his way."

"If I wanted lovers I could get them without asking. I don't want the son of a murderess."

Then everything grew confused to La Cachirra; the blood leaped to her head and choked her eyes. She sprang at Rosalia and tore her hair. The girl gave a shrill cry and sought to defend herself, but immediately a passer-by wrenched them apart.

"If you don't leave Currito alone, I'll kill you!" cried La Cachirra.

"Do you think I'm frightened? Keep him from me if you can. You fool, don't you see that he loves me better than his eyes?"

"Now then, go away," said the man. "Don't answer her, Rosalia."

La Cachirra gave a little roar of passion, like a wild beast baulked of its prey, and pushed past into the street.

But the dance had left Currito madly in love with Rosalia, and all next day he thought of her red lips; the light of her eyes shone in his heart and filled him with enchantment. He passionately desired her. At nightfall he wandered towards the Macarena and presently found himself at her house. He waited in the darkness of the porch till he saw her in the patio. At the other end burned his mother's lonely light.

"Rosalia," he called in a low voice.

She turned, stifling a cry of surprise.

"Why are you here to-day?" she whispered, going towards him.

"I couldn't keep away from you."

"Why?" she smiled.

"Because I love you."

"Do you know your mother nearly killed me this morning?"

And with the embellishments necessary to the Andalusian temperament, she related the occurrence, omitting, however, the final taunt which had enraged La Cachirra beyond endurance.

"She's got the temper of the devil," said Currito; and then. with bravado: "I shall tell her that you're my sweetheart."

"She will be pleased," said Rosalia ironically.

"Will you come to the *reja* to-morrow?"

"Perhaps," she answered.

He gave a little chuckle, for he knew by her tone that she would. He swaggered even more than usual when he walked through the Sierpes on his way home. She was waiting for him when he came next day and, as is the way with lovers in Seville, they talked for hours under their breath, with the iron gate between them, and it never even occurred to Currito that it was a needless impediment. When he asked Rosalia if she loved him she answered with a little amorous sigh. They tried to see the passion that burnt hotly in one another's eyes. Then he went every night.

But fearing that his mother knew of his visits, Currito did not go to see her on the following Sunday. The wretched woman waited for him with an aching heart. She was ready to fall on her knees and beg him to forgive her, but then, when he did not come, she hated him; she would have liked to see him dead at her feet. Her heart sank when she thought that another week must pass before she could even hope to see him.

The week passed and still he did not come. She could not bear it. Anguish, anguish! She loved him as no sweetheart could ever love him. She told herself that this was Rosalia's doing and when she thought of her, rage filled her heart. At last Currito plucked up his courage and went to see his mother; but she had waited too long. It seemed as though her love was dead. She pushed him away when he wanted to kiss her.

"Why haven't you come before?"

"You locked the door on me. I thought you didn't want me!"

"Was it only that? Had you no other reason?"

"I've been busy," he said, shrugging his shoulders.

"Busy? An idle loafer like you. What have you been doing? You wouldn't have been too busy to come and see Rosalia."

"Why did you hit her?"

"How do you know I hit her? Have you seen her?" La Cachirra strode up to her son; her eyes flashed. "She called me a murderess."

"Well, what of it?"

"What of it?" she screamed, so that they heard her in the patio. "And if I am a murderess—it was for you. Yes, I killed Pepe Santi; but it was because he was beating you. It was for your sake that I lay in prison for seven years—for seven years. Oh, you fool, you think she cares for you, and every night she spends hours at the gate."

"I know," Currito answered with a grin.

La Cachirra started violently. She shot a puzzled look at him and then she understood. She gasped with pain and wrath; she clutched at her heart as though the agony were too intense to bear.

"You've been coming every night to the *reja* and you never came near me? Oh, how cruel! I've done everything in the world for you. Do you think I loved Pepe Santi? I endured his blows so that I could give you bread; and I killed him when he beat you. Oh, God, I only lived for you. But for the thought of you I would have died rather than suffer those years of prison."

"Come, woman, be reasonable. I'm twenty. What d'you expect? If it wasn't Rosalia it would be another."

"You beast. I hate you. Get out."

She pushed him violently to the door. Currito shrugged his shoulders.

"You needn't think I want to stay."

He walked jauntily through the patio and slammed the iron gate behind him. La Cachirra stalked to and fro in her tiny room. The hours passed slowly. For a long while she remained at the window, watching with the horrible steadfastness of a savage beast ready to spring. She stood motionless, repressing the convulsive restlessness that tore at her heart-strings. There was a clapping of hands at the *reja* as a signal that someone was without, and she peered forward with panting mouth, her fiery eyes almost starting from her head. But it was only the mason. She waited longer, and Pilar, Rosalia's mother, came in and walked slowly up the stairs to her room. La Cachirra clutched at her throat to relieve the intolerable oppression of her breath. Still she waited. Now and then an extraordinary quiver travelled through all her limbs.

At last! There was a clap of light hands at the gate, and a voice above called out: "Who is it?"

"Peace!"

La Cachirra recognised Rosalia's voice. She gave a gasp of triumph. The door was opened from above, and Rosalia, entering, crossed the courtyard with a buoyant and easy step. The joy of life was in her every motion. She was about to put her foot on the stair when La Cachirra sprang forward and stopped her. She caught hold of her arm and the girl could not shake herself free.

"What do you want?" said Rosalia. "Let me pass."

"What have you been doing with my son?"

"Let me pass, or I shall call out."

"Is it true that you meet at the *reja* every night?"

"Mother, help! Antonio!" Rosalia cried out shrilly.

"Answer me."

"Well, if you want the truth, you can have it. He's going to marry me. He loves me, and I—I love him with all my heart." She turned on La Cachirra, trying to free herself from the vicious grip. "D'you think you can prevent us? D'you think he's frightened of you? He hates you, he told me so. He wishes you'd never come out of prison."

"He told you that?"

La Cachirra shrank back. Rosalia pursued the advantage.

"Yes, he told me that; and he told me much more. He told me that you murdered Pepe Santi; and that you were in prison for seven years; and he wished you were dead."

Rosalia hissed the words venomously, laughing with shrill voice when she saw the wretched woman shrink as though struck by palpable blows.

"And you ought to be proud that I don't refuse to marry the son of a murderess."

Then, giving La Cachirra a push, she leapt to the stairs; but the movement revived the woman, stunned by the horrible taunts, and with a cry of brutal rage she sprang upon Rosalia and caught her by the shoulders and dragged her down. Rosalia turned and hit her in the face. La Cachirra drew a knife from her bosom, and with an oath buried it in the girl's neck. Rosalia shrieked.

"Mother, she's killed me."

She fell to the bottom of the stairs and lay huddled up on the stones. Blood made a little pool on the ground.

Half a dozen doors were flung open at the despairing cry, and people rushed to seize La Cachirra; but she backed against the wall and faced them, with an expression of such ferocity on her face that no one dared approach her. The hesitation was momentary, but Pilar ran from the balcony shrieking, and the common attention for an instant was distracted. La Cachirra saw the opportunity and ran forward. She reached her room and locked and bolted the door behind her.

Suddenly the court was filled with people. Pilar with loud dreadful cries flung herself down on her daughter and would not let herself be dragged away. Someone rushed for a doctor and someone else went for the police. The crowd surged in from the street and collected round the door. The doctor hurried in with a black bag in his hand. When the police came a dozen people at once excitedly explained what had happened. They pointed to the door of La Cachirra's room, and the police broke in. There was a scuffle and they came out with La Cachirra handcuffed. The mob rushed forward, but the police surrounded her and with their scabbards beat the people off; but they shook their fists and hurled curses at her. She looked at them scornfully. She deigned to make no answer. Her eyes shone with tri-

312   The Mother

umph. The policemen led her through the patio and they passed by the body of Rosalia.

"Is she dead?" asked La Cachirra.

"Yes," the doctor answered gravely.

"Thanks be to God!" she said.

THE ROMANTIC YOUNG LADY

ONE of the many inconveniences of real life is that it seldom gives you a complete story. Some incident has excited your interest, the people who are concerned in it are in the devil's own muddle, and you wonder what on earth will happen next. Well, generally nothing happens. The inevitable catastrophe you foresaw wasn't inevitable after all, and high tragedy, without any regard to artistic decency, dwindles into drawing-room comedy. Now, growing old has many disadvantages, but it has this compensation (among, let us admit, not a few others), that sometimes it gives you the opportunity of seeing what was the outcome of certain events you had witnessed long ago. You had given up the hope of ever knowing what was the end of the story, and then, when you least expected it, it is handed to you on a platter.

These reflections occurred to me when, having escorted the Marquesa de San Esteban to her car, I went back into the hotel and sat down again in the lounge. I ordered a cocktail, lit a cigarette and composed myself to order my recollections. The hotel was new and splendid, it was like every other first-class hotel in Europe, and I had been regretting that for the sake of its modern plumbing I had deserted the old-fashioned, picturesque Hotel de Madrid to which I generally went when I stayed in Seville. It was true that from my hotel I had a view of the noble river, the Guadalquivir, but that did not make up for the *thés dansants* that filled the bar-lounge two or three days a week with a fashionable crowd whose exuberant conversation almost drowned the strident din of a jazz orchestra.

I had been out all the afternoon, and coming in found myself in the midst of a seething mob. I went to the desk and asked for my key so that I might go straight up to my room. But the porter, handing it to me, said that a lady had been asking for me.

"For me?"

"She wants to see you very much. It's the Marquesa de San Esteban."

I knew no one of that name.

"It must be some mistake."

As I said the words, looking rather vaguely around, a lady came up to me with outstretched hands and a bright smile on her lips. To the best of my knowledge I had never seen her before in my life. She seized my hands, both of them, and shook them warmly. She spoke in fluent French.

"How very nice to see you again after all these years. I saw by the paper that you were staying here and I said to myself: I must look him up. How many years is it since we danced together? I daren't think. Do you still dance? I do. And I'm a grandmother. I'm fat of course, I don't care, and it keeps me from getting fatter."

She talked with such a rush that it took my breath away to listen to her. She was a stout, more than middle-aged woman, very much made up, with dark red hair, obviously dyed, cut short; and she was dressed in the height of Parisian fashion, which never suits Spanish women very well. But she had a gay, fruity laugh that made you feel you wanted to laugh too. It was quite obvious that she thoroughly enjoyed life. She was a fine figure of a woman and I could well believe that in youth she had been beautiful. But I could not place her.

"Come and drink a glass of champagne with me and we will talk of old times. Or will you have a cocktail? Our dear old Seville has changed, you see. *Thés dansants* and cocktails. It's just like Paris and London now. We've caught up. We're a civilised people."

She led me to a table near the space where they were dancing and we sat down. I could not go on pretending I was at ease; I thought I should only get into a fearful mess.

"It's terribly stupid of me, I'm afraid," I said, "but I don't seem able to remember ever having known anyone of your name in the old days in Seville."

"San Esteban?" she interrupted before I could go on. "Naturally. My husband came from Salamanca. He was in the diplomatic service. I'm a widow. You knew me as Pilar Carreon. Of course having my hair red changes me a little, but otherwise I don't think I've altered much."

"Not at all," I said quickly. "It was only the name that bothered me."

Of course now I remembered her, but I was concerned at the moment only with the effort to conceal from her the mingled consternation and amusement that filled me as I realised that the Pilar Carreon I had danced with at the Countess de Marbella's parties and at the Fair had turned into this stout, flaunting dowager. I could not get over it. But I had to watch my step. I wondered if she knew how well I recollected the story that had shaken Seville to its foundations, and I was glad when after she had finally bidden me an effusive farewell I was able to recall it at ease.

In those days, forty years ago, Seville had not become a prosperous commercial city. It had quiet, white streets, paved with cobbles, with a multitude of churches on the belfries of which storks built their nests. Bull-fighters, students and loungers sauntered in the Sierpes all day long. Life was easy. This of course, was before the time of motor-cars, and the Sevillan would live in penury, practising every possible economy, in order to have a carriage. For this luxury he was willing to sacrifice the necessities of life. Everyone who had any claim to gentility drove up and down the Delicias, the park-like gardens by the Guadalquivir, every blessed afternoon from five till seven. You saw carriages of all sorts, from fashionable London victorias to old broken-down shays that seemed as though they would fall to pieces, magnificent horses and wretched hacks whose tragic end in the bull-ring was near at hand. But there was one equipage that could not fail to attract the stranger's attention. It was a victoria, very smart and new, drawn by two beautiful mules; and the coachman and the footman wore the national costume of Andalusia in pale grey. It was the most splendid turn-out Seville had ever known, and it belonged to the Countess de Marbella. She was a Frenchwoman married to a Spaniard, who had enthusiastically adopted the manners and customs of her husband's country, but with a Parisian elegance that gave them a peculiar distinction. The rest of the carriages went at a snail's pace so that their occupants could see and be seen, but the countess, behind her mules, dashed up between the two crawling lines at a fast trot, went to the end of the Delicias and back twice and then drove away. The proceeding savoured somewhat of royalty. When you looked at her gracefully seated in that swift victoria, her head handsomely poised, her hair of too brilliant a gold to be natural, you did not wonder that her French vivacity and determination had given her the position she held. She made the fashion. Her decrees were law. But the countess had too many adorers not to have as many enemies, and the most determined of these was the widowed Duchess de Dos Palos, whose birth and social consequence made her claim as a right the first place in Society which the Frenchwoman had won by grace, wit and character.

Now the duchess had an only daughter. This was Doña Pilar. She was twenty when I first knew her and she was very beautiful. She had magnificent eyes and a skin that, however hard you tried to find a less hackneyed way to describe it, you could only call peach-like. She was very slim, rather tall for a Spanish girl, with a red mouth and dazzlingly white teeth. She wore her abundant, shining black hair dressed very elaborately in the Spanish style of the period. She was infinitely alluring. The fire in her black eyes, the warmth of her smile, the seductiveness of her movements suggested so much passion that it really wasn't quite fair. She belonged to the generation which was straining to break the old conventions that had kept the Spanish girl of good family hidden away till it was time for her to be married. I often played tennis with her and I used to dance with her at the Countess de Marbella's parties. The duchess considered the Frenchwoman's parties, with champagne and a sit-down supper, ostentatious, and when she opened her own great house to Society, which was only twice a year, it was to give them lemonade and biscuits. But she bred fighting-bulls, as her husband had done, and on the occasions when the young bulls were tried out, she gave picnic luncheons to which her friends were asked, very gay and informal, but with a sort of feudal state which fascinated my romantic imagination. Once, when the duchess's bulls were to fight at a *corrida* in Seville, I rode in with them at night as one of the men escorting Doña Pilar, dressed in a costume that reminded one of a picture by Goya, who headed the cavalcade. It was a charming experience to ride through the night, on those prancing Andalusian horses, with the six bulls, surrounded by oxen, thundering along behind.

A good many men, rich or noble and sometimes both, had asked Doña Pilar's hand in marriage, but notwithstanding her mother's remonstrances, she had refused them. The duchess had been married at fifteen and it seemed to her really indecent that her daughter at twenty should be still single. The duchess asked her what she was waiting for; it was absurd to be too difficult. It was her duty to marry. But Pilar was stubborn. She found reasons to reject every one of her suitors.

Then the truth came out.

During the daily drives in the Delicias which the duchess, accompanied by her daughter, took in a great old-fashioned landau, they passed the countess as she was twice swiftly driven up and down the promenade. The ladies were on such bad terms that they pretended not to see one another, but Pilar could not keep her eyes off that smart carriage and the two beautiful grey mules and, not wishing to catch the countess's somewhat ironic glance, her own fell on the coachman who drove her. He was the handsomest man in Seville and in his beautiful uniform he was a sight to see. Of course no one knew exactly what happened, but apparently the more Pilar looked at the coachman the more she liked the look of him, and somehow or other, for all this part of the story remained a mystery, the pair met. In Spain the classes are strangely mingled and the butler may have in his veins much nobler blood than the master. Pilar learnt, not I think without satisfaction, that the coachman belonged to the ancient family of Leon, than which there is none in Andalusia more distinguished; and really so far as birth went there was little to choose between them. Only her life had been passed in a ducal mansion, while fate had forced him to earn his living on the box of a victoria. Neither could regret this, since only in that exalted place could he have attracted the attention of the most difficult young woman in Seville. They fell madly in love with one another. It so happened that just then a young man called the Marques de San Esteban, whom they had met at San Sebastian the summer before, wrote to the duchess and asked for Pilar's hand in marriage. He was extremely eligible and the two families had formed alliances from time to time ever since the reign of Philip II. The duchess was determined not to stand any more nonsense, and when she told Pilar of the proposal

added that she had shilly-shallied long enough. She must either
marry him or she should go into a convent.

"I'm not going to do either the one or the other," said Pilar.

"What are you going to do then? I have given you a home
long enough."

"I'm going to marry José Leon."

"Who is he?"

Pilar hesitated for a moment and it may be, it is indeed to be
hoped, that she blushed a little.

"He's the countess's coachman."

"What countess?"

"The Countess de Marbella."

I remembered the duchess well and I am sure that when
roused she stuck at little. She raged, she implored, she cried, she
argued. There was a terrific scene. People said that she slapped
her daughter and pulled her hair, but I have an impression that
Pilar in such a pass was capable of hitting back. She repeated
that she loved José Leon and he loved her. She was determined
to marry him. The duchess called a family council. The matter
was put before them and it was decided that to save them all
from disgrace Pilar should be taken away to the country and
kept there till she had recovered from her infatuation. Pilar got
wind of the scheme and put a stop to it by slipping out of the
window of her room one night when everyone was asleep and
going to live with her lover's parents. They were respectable
persons who inhabited a small apartment on the unfashionable
side of the Guadalquivir, in the quarter called Triana.

After that no concealment was possible. The fat was in the
fire and the clubs along the Sierpes buzzed with the scandal.
Waiters were kept busy bringing trays of little glasses of Man-
zanilla to the members from the neighbouring wine-shops. They
gossiped and laughed over the scandal and Pilar's rejected
suitors were the recipients of many congratulations. What an
escape! The duchess was in despair. She could think of nothing
better to do than go to the Archbishop, her trusted friend and
former confessor, and beg him himself to reason with the infatu-
ated girl. Pilar was summoned to the episcopal palace, and the
good old man, used to intervening in family quarrels, did his
utmost to show her the folly of her course. But she would not be
persuaded. Nothing that anyone could say would induce her to
forsake the man she loved. The duchess, waiting in an adjoining
room, was sent for and made a final appeal to her daughter. In

vain. Pilar returned to her humble lodging and the duchess in
tears was left alone with the Archbishop. The Archbishop was
no less astute than he was pious, and when he saw that the distracted woman was in a fit state to listen to him, advised her as
a last resource to go to the Countess de Marbella. She was the
cleverest woman in Seville and it might be that she could do
something.

At first the duchess indignantly refused. She would never
suffer the humiliation of appealing to her greatest enemy.
Sooner might the ancient house of Dos Palos fall in ruin. The
Archbishop was accustomed to dealing with tiresome women.
He set himself with gentle cunning to induce her to change her
mind and presently she consented to throw herself on the
Frenchwoman's mercy. With rage in her heart she sent a message asking if she might see her, and that afternoon was ushered
into her drawing-room. The countess of course had been one of
the first to hear the story, but she listened to the unhappy
mother as though she had not known a thing about it. She
relished the situation enormously. It was the crowning triumph
to have the vindictive duchess on her knees before her. But she
was at heart a good-natured woman and she had a sense of
humour.

"It's a most unfortunate situation," she said. "And I'm sorry
that one of my servants should be the occasion of it. But I don't
exactly see what I can do."

The duchess would have liked to slap her painted face and her
voice trembled a little with the effort she made to control her
anger.

"It is not for my own sake I'm asking you to help. It's for
Pilar's. I know, we all know, that you are the cleverest woman
in the city. It seemed to me, it seemed to the Archbishop, that if
there was a way out, your quick wit would find it."

The countess knew she was being grossly flattered. She did
not mind. She liked it.

"You must let me think."

"Of course, if he'd been a gentleman I could have sent for my
son and he would have killed him, but the Duke of Dos Palos
cannot fight a duel with the Countess de Marbella's coachman."

"Perhaps not."

"In the old days it would have been so simple. I should
merely have hired a couple of ruffians and had the brute's
throat cut one night in the street. But with all these laws they

have nowadays decent people have no way of protecting themselves from insult."

"I should deplore any method of settling the difficulty that deprived me of the services of an excellent coachman," murmured the countess.

"But if he marries my daughter he cannot continue to be your coachman," cried the duchess indignantly.

"Are you going to give Pilar an income for them to live on?"

"Me? Not a peseta. I told Pilar at once that she should get nothing from me. They can starve for all I care."

"Well, I should think rather than do that he will prefer to stay on as my coachman. There are very nice rooms over my stables."

The duchess went pale. The duchess went red.

"Forget all that has passed between us. Let us be friends. You can't expose me to such a humiliation. If I've ever done things to affront you I ask you on my knees to forgive me."

The duchess cried.

"Dry your eyes, Duchess," the Frenchwoman said at last. "I will do what I can."

"Is there anything you can do?"

"Perhaps. Is it true that Pilar has and will have no money of her own?"

"Not a penny if she marries without my consent."

The countess gave one of her brightest smiles.

"There is a common impression that southern people are romantic and northern people matter-of-fact. The reverse is true. It is the northerners who are incurably romantic. I have lived long enough among you Spaniards to know that you are nothing if not practical."

The duchess was too broken to resent openly these unpleasant remarks, but, oh, how she hated the woman! The Countess de Marbella rose to her feet.

"You shall hear from me in the course of the day."

She firmly dismissed her visitor.

The carriage was ordered for five o'clock and at ten minutes to, the countess, dressed for her drive, sent for José. When he came into the drawing-room, wearing his pale grey livery with such an air, she could not deny that he was very good to look upon. If he had not been her own coachman—well, it was not the moment for ideas of that sort. He stood before her, holding himself easily, but with a gallant swagger. There was nothing servile in his bearing.

"A Greek god," the countess murmured to herself. "It is only Andalusia that can produce such types." And then aloud: "I hear that you are going to marry the daughter of the Duchess of Dos Palos."

"If the countess does not object."

She shrugged her shoulders.

"Whoever you marry is a matter of complete indifference to me. You know of course that Doña Pilar will have no fortune."

"Yes, madam. I have a good place and I can keep my wife. I love her."

"I can't blame you for that. She is a beautiful girl. But I think it only right to tell you that I have a rooted objection to married coachmen. On your wedding-day you leave my service. That is all I had to say to you. You can go."

She began to look at the daily paper that had just arrived from Paris, but José, as she expected, did not stir. He stared down at the floor. Presently the countess looked up.

"What are you waiting for?"

"I never knew madam would send me away," he answered in a troubled tone.

"I have no doubt you'll find another place."

"Yes, but . . ."

"Well, what is it?" she asked sharply.

He sighed miserably.

"There's not a pair of mules in the whole of Spain to come up to ours. They're almost human beings. They understand every word I say to them."

The countess gave him a smile that would have turned the head of anyone who was not madly in love already.

"I'm afraid you must choose between me and your betrothed."

He shifted from one foot to the other. He put his hand to his pocket to get himself a cigarette, but then, remembering where he was, restrained the gesture. He glanced at the countess and that peculiar shrewd smile came over his face which those who have lived in Andalusia know so well.

"In that case, I can't hesitate. Pilar must see that this alters my position entirely. One can get a wife any day of the week, but a place like this is found only once in a lifetime. I should be a fool to throw it up for a woman."

That was the end of the adventure. José Leon continued to drive the Countess de Marbella, but she noticed when they sped up and down the Delicias that thenceforward as many eyes were turned on her handsome coachman as on her latest hat; and a year later Pilar married the Marques de San Esteban.

THE POET

I AM not much interested in the celebrated and I have never
had patience with the passion that afflicts so many to shake
hands with the great ones of the earth. When it is proposed to
me to meet some person distinguished above his fellows by his
rank or his attainments, I seek for a civil excuse that may enable me to avoid the honour; and when my friend Diego Torre
suggested giving me an introduction to Santa Aña I declined.
But for once the excuse I made was sincere; Santa Aña was not
only a great poet but also a romantic figure and it would have
amused me to see in his decrepitude a man whose adventures
(in Spain at least) were legendary; but I knew that he was old
and ill and I could not believe that it would be anything but a
nuisance to him to meet a stranger and a foreigner. Calisto de
Santa Aña was the last descendant of the Grand School; in a
world unsympathetic to Byronism he had led a Byronic existence and he had narrated his hazardous life in a series of poems
that had brought him a fame unknown to his contemporaries. I
am no judge of their value, for I read them first when I was
three-and-twenty and then was enraptured by them; they had a
passion, a heroic arrogance and a multi-coloured vitality that
swept me off my feet, and to this day, so intermingled are those
ringing lines and haunting cadences with the charming memories of my youth, I cannot read them without a beating heart.
I am inclined to think that Calisto de Santa Aña deserves the
reputation he enjoys among the Spanish-speaking peoples. In

those days his verses were on the lips of all young men and my
friends would talk to me endlessly of his wild ways, his vehement speeches (for he was a politician as well as a poet), his
incisive wit and his amours. He was a rebel and sometimes an
outlaw, daring and adventurous; but above all he was a lover.
We knew all about his passion for this great actress or that
divine singer—had we not read till we knew them by heart the
burning sonnets in which he described his love, his anguish and
his wrath?—and we were aware that an infanta of Spain, the
proudest descendant of the Bourbons, having yielded to his
entreaties, had taken the veil when he ceased to love her. When
the Philips, her royal ancestors, tired of a mistress she entered a
convent, for it was unfitting that one whom the King had loved
should be loved by another, and was not Calisto de Santa Aña
greater than any earthly king? We applauded the lady's romantic gesture; it was creditable to her and flattering to our poet.

But all this took place many years ago and for a quarter of a
century Don Calisto, disdainfully withdrawing from a world
that had nothing more to offer, had lived in seclusion in his
native town of Ecija. It was when I announced my intention of
going there (I had been spending a week or two in Seville) not
because of him, but because it is a charming little Andalusian
town with associations that endear it to me, that Diego Torre
offered me this introduction. It appeared that Don Calisto allowed the younger men of letters occasionally to visit him and
now and then would talk to them with the fire that had electri-
fied his hearers in the great days of his prime.

"What does he look like now?" I asked.

"Magnificent."

"Have you a photograph of him?"

"I wish I had. He has refused to face the camera since he was
thirty-five. He says he does not wish posterity to know him
other than young."

I confess that I found this suggestion of vanity not a little
touching. I knew that in early manhood he was of extraordinary
beauty, and that moving sonnet of his written when he grew
conscious that youth had for ever left him shows with what a
bitter and sardonic pang he must have watched the passing of
those looks that had been so fantastically admired.

But I refused my friend's offer; I was quite satisfied to read
once more the poems I had known so well and for the rest I
preferred to wander about the silent and sunswept streets of

Ecija in freedom. It was with some consternation therefore that on the evening of my arrival I received a note from the great man himself. Diego Torre had written to him of my visit, he said, and it would give him great pleasure if I would call on him at eleven next morning. In the circumstances there was nothing for me to do but to present myself at his house at the appointed hour.

My hotel was in the Plaza and on that spring morning it was animated, but as soon as I left it I might have walked in a deserted city. The streets, the tortuous white streets, were empty but for a woman in black now and then who returned with measured steps from her devotions. Ecija is a town of churches and you can seldom go far without seeing a crumbling façade or a tower in which storks have built their nests. Once I paused to watch a string of little donkeys pass by. Their red caparisons were faded and they carried I know not what in their panniers. But Ecija has been a place of consequence in its day and many of these white houses have gateways of stone surmounted by imposing coats of arms, for to this remote spot flowed the riches of the New World and adventurers who had gathered wealth in the Americas spent here their declining years. It was in one of these houses that Don Calisto lived and as I stood at the *reja* after pulling the bell, I was pleased to think that he lived in such a fitting style. There was a dilapidated grandeur about the massive gateway that suited my impression of the flamboyant poet. Though I heard the bell peal through the house no one answered it and I rang a second and then a third time: at last an old woman with a heavy moustache, came to the gate.

"What do you want?" she said.

She had fine black eyes, but a sullen look, and I supposed that it was she who took care of the old man. I gave her my card.

"I have an appointment with your master."

She opened the iron gateway and bade me enter. Asking me to wait she left me and went upstairs. The patio was pleasantly cool after the street. Its proportions were noble and you surmised that it had been built by some follower of the conquistadores; but the paint was tarnished, the tiles on the floor broken, and here and there great flakes of plaster had fallen away. There was about everything an air of poverty but not of squalor. I knew that Don Calisto was poor. Money had come to him easily at times but he had never attached any importance to it and had spent it profusely. It was plain that he lived now in a penury that he disdained to notice. In the middle of the patio was a table with a rocking-chair on each side of it, and on the table newspapers a fortnight old. I wondered what dreams occupied his fancy as he sat there on the warm summer nights, smoking cigarettes. On the walls under the colonnade were Spanish pictures, dark and bad, and here and there stood an ancient dusty *bargueño* and on it a mended lustre plate. By the side of a door hung a pair of old pistols, and I had a pleasant fancy that they were the weapons he had used when in the most celebrated of his many duels, for the sake of Pepa Montañez the dancer (now, I suppose, a toothless and raddled hag), he had killed the Duke of Dos Hermanos.

The scene, with its associations which I vaguely divined, so aptly fitted the romantic poet that I was overcome by the spirit of the place. Its noble indigence surrounded him with a glory as great as the magnificence of his youth; in him too there was the spirit of the old conquistadores, and it was becoming that he should finish his famous life in that ruined and magnificent house. Thus surely should a poet live and die. I had arrived cool enough and even somewhat bored at the prospect of my meeting, but now I began to grow a trifle nervous. I lit a cigarette. I had come at the time appointed and wondered what detained the old man. The silence was strangely disturbing. Ghosts of the past thronged the silent patio and an age dead and gone gained a sort of shadowy life for me. The men of that day had a passion and a wildness of spirit that are gone out of the world for ever. We are no longer capable of their reckless deeds or their theatrical heroics.

I heard a sound and my heart beat quickly. I was excited now and when at last I saw him coming slowly down the stairs I caught my breath. He held my card in his hand. He was a tall old man and exceedingly thin, with a skin the colour of old ivory; his hair was abundant and white, but his bushy eyebrows were dark still; they made his great eyes flash with a more sombre fire. It was wonderful that at his age those black eyes should still preserve their brilliance. His nose was aquiline, his mouth close-set. His unsmiling eyes rested on me as he approached and there was in them a look of cool appraisal. He was dressed in black and in one hand held a broad-brimmed hat. There was in his bearing assurance and dignity. He was as I should have wished him to be and as I watched him I understood how he had swayed men's minds and touched their hearts. He was every inch a poet.

He had reached the patio and came slowly towards me. He had really the eyes of an eagle. It seemed to be a tremendous moment, for there he stood, the heir of the great old Spanish poets, the magnificent Herrera, the nostalgic and moving Fray Luis, Juan de la Cruz, the mystic, and the crabbed and obscure Gongora. He was the last of that long line and he trod in their steps not unworthily. Strangely in my heart sang the lovely and tender song which is the most famous of Don Calisto's lyrics.

I was abashed. It was fortunate for me that I had prepared beforehand the phrase with which I meant to greet him.

"It is a wonderful honour, Maestro, for a foreigner such as I to make the acquaintance of so great a poet."

A flicker of amusement passed through those piercing eyes and a smile for an instant curved the lines of that stern mouth.

"I am not a poet, Señor, but a bristle merchant. You have made a mistake, Don Calisto lives next door."

I had come to the wrong house.

A MAN FROM GLASGOW

It is not often that anyone entering a great city for the first time has the luck to witness such an incident as engaged Shelley's attention when he drove into Naples. A youth ran out of a shop pursued by a man armed with a knife. The man overtook him and with one blow in the neck laid him dead on the road. Shelley had a tender heart. He didn't look upon it as a bit of local colour; he was seized with horror and indignation. But when he expressed his emotions to a Calabrian priest who was travelling with him, a fellow of gigantic strength and stature, the priest laughed heartily and attempted to quiz him. Shelley says he never felt such an inclination to beat anyone.

I have never seen anything so exciting as that, but the first time I went to Algeciras I had an experience that seemed to me far from ordinary. Algeciras was then an untidy, neglected town. I arrived somewhat late at night and went to an inn on the quay. It was rather shabby, but it had a fine view of Gibraltar, solid and matter-of-fact, across the bay. The moon was full. The office was on the first floor, and a slatternly maid, when I asked for a room, took me upstairs. The landlord was playing cards. He seemed little pleased to see me. He looked me up and down, curtly gave me a number, and then, taking no further notice of me, went on with his game.

When the maid had shown me to my room I asked her what I could have to eat.

"What you like," she answered.

I knew well enough the unreality of the seeming profusion.
"What have you got in the house?"
"You can have eggs and ham."

The look of the hotel had led me to guess that I should get
little else. The maid led me to a narrow room with white-washed
walls and a low ceiling in which was a long table laid already for
the next day's luncheon. With his back to the door sat a tall
man, huddled over a *brasero*, the round brass dish of hot ashes
which is erroneously supposed to give sufficient warmth for the
temperate winter of Andalusia. I sat down at table and waited
for my scanty meal. I gave the stranger an idle glance. He was
looking at me, but meeting my eyes he quickly turned away. I
waited for my eggs. When at last the maid brought them he
looked up again.

"I want you to wake me in time for the first boat," he said.
"*Sì, señor.*"

His accent told me that English was his native tongue, and
the breadth of his build, his strongly marked features, led me to
suppose him a northerner. The hardy Scot is far more often
found in Spain than the Englishman. Whether you go to the
rich mines of Rio Tinto, or to the bodegas of Jerez, to Seville or
to Cadiz, it is the leisurely speech of beyond the Tweed that you
hear. You will meet Scotsmen in the olive groves of Carmona,
on the railway between Algeciras and Bobadilla, and even in the
remote cork woods of Merida.

I finished eating and went over to the dish of burning ashes.
It was midwinter and the windy passage across the bay had
chilled my blood. The man pushed his chair away as I drew
mine forwards.

"Don't move," I said. "There's heaps of room for two."

I lit a cigar and offered one to him. In Spain the Havana from
Gib is never unwelcome.

"I don't mind if I do," he said, stretching out his hand.

I recognised the singing speech of Glasgow. But the stranger
was not talkative, and my efforts at conversation broke down
before his monosyllables. We smoked in silence. He was even
bigger than I had thought, with great broad shoulders and ungainly limbs; his face was sunburned, his hair short and grizzled.
His features were hard; mouth, ears and nose were large and
heavy and his skin much wrinkled. His blue eyes were pale. He
was constantly pulling his ragged, grey moustache. It was a
nervous gesture that I found faintly irritating. Presently I felt

that he was looking at me, and the intensity of his stare grew so irksome that I glanced up expecting him, as before, to drop his eyes. He did, indeed, for a moment, but then raised them again. He inspected me from under his long, bushy eyebrows.

"Just come from Gib?" he asked suddenly.

"Yes."

"I'm going to-morrow—on my way home. Thank God."

He said the last two words so fiercely that I smiled.

"Don't you like Spain?"

"Oh, Spain's all right."

"Have you been here long?"

"Too long. Too long."

He spoke with a kind of gasp. I was surprised at the emotion my casual inquiry seemed to excite in him. He sprang to his feet and walked backwards and forwards. He stamped to and fro like a caged beast, pushing aside a chair that stood in his way, and now and again repeated the words in a groan. "Too long. Too long." I sat still. I was embarrassed. To give myself countenance I stirred the *brasero* to bring the hotter ashes to the top, and he stood suddenly still, towering over me, as though my movement had brought back my existence to his notice. Then he sat down heavily in his chair.

"D'you think I'm queer?" he asked.

"Not more than most people," I smiled.

"You don't see anything strange in me?"

He leant forward as he spoke so that I might see him well.

"No."

"You'd say so if you did, wouldn't you?"

"I would."

I couldn't quite understand what all this meant. I wondered if he was drunk. For two or three minutes he didn't say anything and I had no wish to interrupt the silence.

"What's your name?" he asked suddenly. I told him.

"Mine's Robert Morrison."

"Scotch?"

"Glasgow. I've been in this blasted country for years. Got any baccy?"

I gave him my pouch and he filled his pipe. He lit it from a piece of burning charcoal.

"I can't stay any longer. I've stayed too long. Too long."

He had an impulse to jump up again and walk up and down, but he resisted it, clinging to his chair. I saw on his face the

effort he was making. I judged that his restlessness was due to
chronic alcoholism. I find drunks very boring, and I made up
my mind to take an early opportunity of slipping off to bed.

"I've been managing some olive groves," he went on. "I'm
here working for the Glasgow and South of Spain Olive Oil
Company Limited."

"Oh yes."

"We've got a new process for refining oil, you know. Properly
treated, Spanish oil is every bit as good as Lucca. And we can
sell it cheaper."

He spoke in a dry, matter-of-fact, business-like way. He chose
his words with Scotch precision. He seemed perfectly sober.

"You know, Ecija is more or less the centre of the olive trade,
and we had a Spaniard there to look after the business. But I
found he was robbing us right and left, so I had to turn him out.
I used to live in Seville; it was more convenient for shipping the
oil. However, I found I couldn't get a trustworthy man to be at
Ecija, so last year I went there myself. D'you know it?"

"No."

"The firm has got a big estate two miles from the town, just
outside the village of San Lorenzo, and it's got a fine house on
it. It's on the crest of a hill, rather pretty to look at, all white,
you know, and straggling, with a couple of storks perched on
the roof. No one lived there, and I thought it would save the
rent of a place in town if I did."

"It must have been a bit lonely," I remarked.

"It was."

Robert Morrison smoked on for a minute or two in silence.
I wondered whether there was any point in what he was telling
me.

I looked at my watch.

"In a hurry?" he asked sharply.

"Not particularly. It's getting late."

"Well, what of it?"

"I suppose you didn't see many people?" I said, going back.

"Not many. I lived there with an old man and his wife who
looked after me, and sometimes I used to go down to the village
and play *tresillo* with Fernandez, the chemist, and one or two
men who met at his shop. I used to shoot a bit and ride."

"It doesn't sound such a bad life to me."

"I'd been there two years last spring. By God, I've never
known such heat as we had in May. No one could do a thing.

The labourers just lay about in the shade and slept. Sheep died
and some of the animals went mad. Even the oxen couldn't
work. They stood around with their backs all humped up and
gasped for breath. That blasted sun beat down and the glare was
so awful, you felt your eyes would shoot out of your head. The
earth cracked and crumbled, and the crops frizzled. The olives
went to rack and ruin. It was simply hell. One couldn't get a
wink of sleep. I went from room to room, trying to get a breath
of air. Of course I kept the windows shut and had the floors
watered, but that didn't do any good. The nights were just as
hot as the days. It was like living in an oven.

"At last I thought I'd have a bed made up for me downstairs
on the north side of the house in a room that was never used
because in ordinary weather it was damp. I had an idea that I
might get a few hours' sleep there at all events. Anyhow it was
worth trying. But it was no damned good; it was a washout. I
turned and tossed and my bed was so hot that I couldn't stand
it. I got up and opened the doors that led to the verandah and
walked out. It was a glorious night. The moon was so bright
that I swear you could read a book by it. Did I tell you the
house was on the crest of a hill? I leant against the parapet and
looked at the olive-trees. It was like the sea. I suppose that's
what made me think of home. I thought of the cool breeze in
the fir-trees and the racket of the streets in Glasgow. Believe
it or not, I could smell them, and I could smell the sea. By God,
I'd have given every bob I had in the world for an hour of that
air. They say it's a foul climate in Glasgow. Don't you believe
it. I like the rain and the grey sky and that yellow sea and the
waves. I forgot that I was in Spain, in the middle of the olive
country, and I opened my mouth and took a long breath as
though I were breathing-in the sea-fog.

"And then all of a sudden I heard a sound. It was a man's
voice. Not loud, you know, low. It seemed to creep through the
silence like—well, I don't know what it was like. It surprised
me. I couldn't think who could be down there in the olives at
that hour. It was past midnight. It was a chap laughing. A
funny sort of laugh. I suppose you'd call it a chuckle. It seemed
to crawl up the hill—disjointedly."

Morrison looked at me to see how I took the odd word he used
to express a sensation that he didn't know how to describe.

"I mean, it seemed to shoot up in little jerks, something like
shooting stones out of a pail. I leant forward and stared. With

the full moon it was almost as light as day, but I'm dashed if I could see a thing. The sound stopped, but I kept on looking at where it had come from in case somebody moved. And in a minute it started off again, but louder. You couldn't have called it a chuckle any more, it was a real belly laugh. It just rang through the night. I wondered it didn't wake my servants. It sounded like someone who was roaring drunk.

" 'Who's there?' I shouted.

"The only answer I got was a roar of laughter. I don't mind telling you I was getting a bit annoyed. I had half a mind to go down and see what it was all about. I wasn't going to let some drunken swine kick up a row like that on my place in the middle of the night. And then suddenly there was a yell. By God, I was startled. Then cries. The man had laughed with a deep bass voice, but his cries were—shrill, like a pig having his throat cut.

" 'My God,' I cried.

"I jumped over the parapet and ran down towards the sound. I thought somebody was being killed. There was silence and then one piercing shriek. After that sobbing and moaning. I'll tell you what it sounded like, it sounded like someone at the point of death. There was a long groan and then nothing. Silence. I ran from place to place. I couldn't find anyone. At last I climbed the hill again and went back to my room.

"You can imagine how much sleep I got that night. As soon as it was light, I looked out of the window in the direction from which the row had come and I was surprised to see a little white house in a sort of dale among the olives. The ground on that side didn't belong to us and I'd never been through it. I hardly ever went to that part of the house and so I'd never seen the house before. I asked José who lived there. He told me that a madman had inhabited it, with his brother and a servant."

"Oh, was that the explanation?" I said. "Not a very nice neighbour."

The Scot bent over quickly and seized my wrist. He thrust his face into mine and his eyes were starting out of his head with terror.

"The madman had been dead for twenty years," he whispered.

He let go my wrist and leant back in his chair panting.

"I went down to the house and walked all round it. The windows were barred and shuttered and the door was locked. I knocked. I shook the handle and rang the bell. I heard it tinkle, but no one came. It was a two-storey house and I looked up. The shutters were tight closed, and there wasn't a sign of life anywhere."

"Well, what sort of condition was the house in?" I asked.

"Oh, rotten. The whitewash had worn off the walls and there was practically no paint left on the door or the shutters. Some of the tiles off the roof were lying on the ground. They looked as though they'd been blown away in a gale."

"Queer," I said.

"I went to my friend Fernandez, the chemist, and he told me the same story as José. I asked about the madman and Fernandez said that no one ever saw him. He was more or less comatose ordinarily, but now and then he had an attack of acute mania and then he could be heard from ever so far laughing his head off and then crying. It used to scare people. He died in one of his attacks and his keepers cleared out at once. No one had ever dared to live in the house since.

"I didn't tell Fernandez what I'd heard. I thought he'd only laugh at me. I stayed up that night and kept watch. But nothing happened. There wasn't a sound. I waited about till dawn and then I went to bed."

"And you never heard anything more?"

"Not for a month. The drought continued and I went on sleeping in the lumber-room at the back. One night I was fast asleep, when something seemed to happen to me; I don't exactly know how to describe it, it was a funny feeling as though someone had given me a little nudge, to warn me, and suddenly I was wide awake. I lay there in my bed and then in the same way as before I heard a long, low gurgle, like a man enjoying an old joke. It came from away down in the valley and it got louder. It was a great bellow of laughter. I jumped out of bed and went to the window. My legs began to tremble. It was horrible to stand there and listen to the shouts of laughter that rang through the night. Then there was the pause, and after that a shriek of pain and that ghastly sobbing. It didn't sound human. I mean, you might have thought it was an animal being tortured. I don't mind telling you I was scared stiff. I couldn't have moved if I'd wanted to. After a time the sounds stopped, not suddenly, but dying away little by little. I strained my ears, but I couldn't hear a thing. I crept back to bed and hid my face.

"I remembered then that Fernandez had told me that the madman's attacks only came at intervals. The rest of the time he was quite quiet. Apathetic, Fernandez said. I wondered if the

fits of mania came regularly. I reckoned out how long it had
been between the two attacks I'd heard. Twenty-eight days. It
didn't take me long to put two and two together; it was quite
obvious that it was the full moon that set him off. I'm not a
nervous man really and I made up my mind to get to the bottom
of it, so I looked out in the calendar which day the moon would
be full next and that night I didn't go to bed. I cleaned my revolver and loaded it. I prepared a lantern and sat down on the
parapet of my house to wait. I felt perfectly cool. To tell you
the truth, I was rather pleased with myself because I didn't
feel scared. There was a bit of a wind, and it whistled about the
roof. It rustled over the leaves of the olive trees like waves
swishing on the pebbles of the beach. The moon shone on the
white walls of the house in the hollow. I felt particularly cheery.

"At last I heard a little sound, the sound I knew, and I almost
laughed. I was right; it was the full moon and the attacks came
as regular as clockwork. That was all to the good. I threw myself over the wall into the olive grove and ran straight to the
house. The chuckling grew louder as I came near. I got to the
house and looked up. There was no light anywhere. I put my
ear to the door and listened. I heard the madman simply laughing his bloody head off. I beat on the door with my fist and I
pulled the bell. The sound of it seemed to amuse him. He roared
with laughter. I knocked again, louder and louder, and the more
I knocked the more he laughed. Then I shouted at the top of
my voice.

" 'Open the blasted door, or I'll break it down.'

"I stepped back and kicked the latch with all my might. I
flung myself at the door with the whole weight of my body. It
cracked. Then I put all my strength into it and the damned
thing smashed open.

"I took the revolver out of my pocket and held my lantern in
the other hand. The laughter sounded louder now that the door
was opened. I stepped in. The stink nearly knocked me down.
I mean, just think, the windows hadn't been opened for twenty
years. The row was enough to raise the dead, but for a moment
I didn't know where it was coming from. The walls seemed to
throw the sound backwards and forwards. I pushed open a door
by my side and went into a room. It was bare and white and
there wasn't a stick of furniture in it. The sound was louder and
I followed it. I went into another room, but there was nothing
there. I opened a door and found myself at the foot of a stair-

case. The madman was laughing just over my head. I walked up, cautiously, you know, I wasn't taking any risks, and at the top of the stairs there was a passage. I walked along it, throwing my light ahead of me, and I came to a room at the end. I stopped. He was in there. I was only separated from the sound by a thin door.

"It was awful to hear it. A shiver passed through me and I cursed myself because I began to tremble. It wasn't like a human being at all. By Jove, I very nearly took to my heels and ran. I had to clench my teeth to force myself to stay. But I simply couldn't bring myself to turn the handle. And then the laughter was cut, cut with a knife you'd have said, and I heard a hiss of pain. I hadn't heard that before, it was too low to carry to my place, and then a gasp.

" 'Ay!' I heard the man speak in Spanish. 'You're killing me. Take it away. O God, help me!'

"He screamed. The brutes were torturing him. I flung open the door and burst in. The draught blew a shutter back and the moon streamed in so bright that it dimmed my lantern. In my ears, as clearly as I hear you speak and as close, I heard the wretched chap's groans. It was awful, moaning and sobbing, and frightful gasps. No one could survive that. He was at the point of death. I tell you I heard his broken, choking cries right in my ears. And the room was empty."

Robert Morrison sank back in his chair. That huge solid man had strangely the look of a lay figure in a studio. You felt that if you pushed him he would fall over in a heap on to the floor.

"And then?" I asked.

He took a rather dirty handkerchief out of his pocket and wiped his forehead.

"I felt I didn't much want to sleep in that room on the north side, so, heat or no heat, I moved back to my own quarters. Well, exactly four weeks later, about two in the morning, I was waked up by the madman's chuckle. It was almost at my elbow. I don't mind telling you that my nerve was a bit shaken by then, so next time the blighter was due to have an attack, next time the moon was full, I mean, I got Fernandez to come and spend the night with me. I didn't tell him anything. I kept him up playing cards till two in the morning, and then I heard it again. I asked him if he heard anything. 'Nothing,' he said. 'There's somebody laughing,' I said. 'You're drunk, man,' he said, and he began laughing too. That was too much. 'Shut up, you fool,' I

said. The laughter grew louder and louder. I cried out. I tried
to shut it out by putting my hands to my ears, but it wasn't a
damned bit of good. I heard it and I heard the scream of pain.
Fernandez thought I was mad. He didn't dare say so, because
he knew I'd have killed him. He said he'd go to bed, and in the
morning I found he'd slunk away. His bed hadn't been slept in.
He'd taken himself off when he left me.

"After that I couldn't stop in Ecija. I put a factor there and
went back to Seville. I felt myself pretty safe there, but as the
time came near I began to get scared. Of course I told myself
not to be a damned fool, but, you know, I damned well couldn't
help myself. The fact is, I was afraid the sounds had followed
me, and I knew if I heard them in Seville I'd go on hearing them
all my life. I've got as much courage as any man, but damn it
all, there are limits to everything. Flesh and blood couldn't
stand it. I knew I'd go stark staring mad. I got in such a state
that I began drinking, the suspense was so awful, and I used
to lie awake counting the days. And at last I knew it'd come.
And it came. I heard those sounds in Seville—sixty miles away
from Ecija."

I didn't know what to say. I was silent for a while.

"When did you hear the sounds last?" I asked.

"Four weeks ago."

I looked up quickly. I was startled.

"What d'you mean by that? It's not full moon to-night?"

He gave me a dark, angry look. He opened his mouth to speak
and then stopped as though he couldn't. You would have said
his vocal cords were paralysed, and it was with a strange croak
that at last he answered.

"Yes, it is."

He stared at me and his pale blue eyes seemed to shine red.
I have never seen in a man's face a look of such terror. He got up
quickly and stalked out of the room, slamming the door behind
him.

I must admit that I didn't sleep any too well that night myself.

THE LION'S SKIN

A GOOD MANY PEOPLE were shocked when they read that Captain Forestier had met his death in a forest fire when trying to save his wife's dog, which had been accidentally shut up in the house. Some said they never knew he had it in him; others said it was exactly what they would have expected of him, but of these some meant it in one way and some in another. After the tragic occurrence Mrs. Forestier found shelter in the villa of some people called Hardy, whose acquaintance she and her husband had but lately made. Captain Forestier had not liked them, at any rate he had not liked Fred Hardy, but she felt that if he had lived through that terrible night he would have changed his mind. He would have realised how much good there was in Hardy notwithstanding his reputation, and like the great gentleman he was he would not have hesitated to admit that he had been mistaken. Mrs. Forestier did not know how she could ever have kept her reason after the loss of the man who was everything in the world to her but for the Hardys' wonderful kindness. In her immense distress their unfailing sympathy had been her only consolation. They, who had been almost eye-witnesses of her husband's great sacrifice, knew as did no one else how wonderful he had been. She could never forget the words dear Fred Hardy had used when he was breaking the dreadful news to her. It was these words that had enabled her not only to bear the frightful disaster, but to face the desolate future with the courage with which she well knew that brave man, that gallant gentleman, whom she had loved so well, would have wished her to face it.

Mrs. Forestier was a very nice woman. Kindly people often say that of a woman when they can say nothing about her, and it has come to be looked upon as cold praise. I do not mean it as such. Mrs. Forestier was neither charming, beautiful nor intelligent; on the contrary she was absurd, homely and foolish; yet the more you knew her, the more you liked her, and when asked why, you found yourself forced to repeat that she was a very nice woman. She was as tall as the average man; she had a large mouth and a great hooked nose, pale-blue short-sighted eyes and big ugly hands. Her skin was lined and weather-beaten, but she made up heavily, and her hair, which she wore long, was dyed golden, tightly marcelled and elaborately dressed. She did everything she could to counteract the aggressive masculinity of her appearance, and succeeded only in looking like a vaudeville artist doing a female impersonation. Her voice was a woman's voice, but you were always expecting her, at the end of the number as it were, to break into a deep bass, and tearing off that golden wig, discover a man's bald pate. She spent a great deal of money on her clothes, which she got from the most fashionable dressmakers in Paris, but though a woman of fifty she had an unfortunate taste for choosing dresses that looked exquisite on pretty little mannequins in the flower of their youth. She always wore a great quantity of rich jewels. Her movements were awkward and her gestures clumsy. If she went into a drawing-room where there was a valuable piece of jade she managed to sweep it on the floor; if she lunched with you and you had a set of glasses you treasured she was almost certain to smash one of them to atoms.

Yet this ungainly exterior sheltered a tender, romantic and idealistic soul. It took you some time to discover this, for when first you knew her you took her for a figure of fun, and then when you knew her better (and had suffered from her clumsiness) she exasperated you; but when you did discover it, you thought yourself very stupid not to have known it all the time, for then it looked out at you through those pale-blue, near-sighted eyes, rather shyly, but with a sincerity that only a fool could miss. Those dainty muslins and spring-like organdies, those virginal silks, clothed not the uncouth body but the fresh, girlish spirit. You forgot that she broke your china and looked like a man dressed up as a woman, you saw her as she saw herself, as indeed she really was if reality were visible, as a dear little thing with a heart of gold. When you came to know her you found her as simple as a child; she was touchingly grateful for any attention you paid her; her own kindness was infinite, you could ask her to do anything for you, however tiresome, and she would do it as though by giving her the opportunity to put herself out you rendered her a service. She had a rare capacity for disinterested love. You knew that never an unkind nor a malicious thought had once passed through her head. And having granted all that you said over again that Mrs. Forestier was a very nice woman.

Unfortunately she was also a damned fool. This you discovered when you met her husband. Mrs. Forestier was American and Captain Forestier was English. Mrs. Forestier was born in Portland, Oregon, and had never been to Europe till the war of 1914, when, her first husband having recently died, she joined a hospital unit and came to France. She was not rich by American standards, but by our English ones in affluent circumstances. From the way the Forestiers lived I should guess that she had something like thirty thousand dollars a year. Except that she undoubtedly gave the wrong medicines to the wrong men, put on their bandages so that they were worse than useless, and broke every utensil that was breakable, I am sure that she was an admirable nurse. I do not think she ever found work too revolting for her to do it without hesitation; she certainly never spared herself and was surely never out of temper; I have a notion that many a poor wretch had cause to bless the tenderness of her heart, and it may be that not a few took the last bitter step into the unknown with more courage because of the loving-kindness of her golden soul. It was during the last year of the war that Captain Forestier came under her care, and soon after peace was declared they married. They settled down in a handsome villa on the hills behind Cannes, and in a short time became conspicuous in the social life of the Riviera. Captain Forestier played bridge well and was a keen golfer. He was not a bad tennis player either. He had a sailing boat, and in the summer the Forestiers gave very nice parties between the islands. After seventeen years of marriage Mrs. Forestier still adored her good-looking husband, and you were unlikely to know her long without being told in that slow Western drawl of hers the full story of their courtship.

"It was a case of love at first sight," she said. "He was brought in when I happened to be off duty, and when I came on and found him lying in one of my beds, oh, my dear, I felt such a pang in my heart, for a moment I thought I'd been overworking and had strained it. He was the handsomest man I'd ever seen in my life."

"Was he badly wounded?"

"Well, he wasn't exactly wounded. You know, it's a most extraordinary thing, he went all through the war, he was under fire for months at a time, and of course he risked his life twenty times a day, he's one of those men who simply doesn't know what fear is; but he never even got a scratch. He had carbuncles."

It seemed an unromantic ailment on which to start a passionate attachment. Mrs. Forestier was a trifle prudish, and though Captain Forestier's carbuncles greatly interested her she always found it a little difficult to tell you exactly where they were.

"They were right down at the bottom of his back, even farther really, and he hated to have me dress them. Englishmen are curiously modest, I've noticed that over and over again, and it mortified him terribly. You'd have thought being on those terms, if you know what I mean, from our first acquaintance it would have made us more intimate. But somehow it didn't. He was very stand-offish with me. When I used to get to his bed on my round I was so breathless and my heart beat so I couldn't make out what was the matter with me. I'm not naturally a clumsy woman, I never drop things or break anything; but you wouldn't believe it, when I had to give Robert his medicine I used to drop the spoon and break the glass, I couldn't imagine what he must be thinking of me."

It was almost impossible not to laugh when Mrs. Forestier told you this. She smiled rather sweetly.

"I suppose it sounds very absurd to you, but you see I'd never felt that way before. When I married my first husband— well, he was a widower with grown-up children, he was a fine man and one of the most prominent citizens in the state, but somehow it was different."

"And how did you eventually discover that you were in love with Captain Forestier?"

"Well, I don't ask you to believe me, I know it sounds funny, but the fact is that one of the other nurses told me, and as soon as she did of course I knew it was true. I was terribly upset at first. You see, I knew nothing about him. Like all Englishmen he was very reserved and for all I knew he had a wife and half a dozen children."

"How did you find out he hadn't?"

"I asked him. The moment he told me he was a bachelor I made up my mind that by hook or by crook I was going to marry him. He suffered agonies, poor darling; you see, he had to lie on his face almost all the time, lying on his back was torture, and as to sitting down—well, of course he couldn't even think of that. But I don't believe his agonies were worse than mine. Men like clinging silks and soft, fluffy things, you know what I mean, and I was at such a disadvantage in my nurse's uniform. The matron, one of those New England spinsters, couldn't bear make-up, and in those days I didn't make-up anyway; my first husband never liked it; and then my hair wasn't as pretty as it is now. He used to look at me with those wonderful blue eyes of his, and I felt he must be thinking I looked a perfect sight. He was very low and I thought I ought to do all I could to cheer him up, so whenever I had a few minutes to spare I'd go and talk to him. He said he couldn't bear the thought of a strong, husky chap like he was lying in bed week after week while all his pals were in the trenches. You couldn't talk to him without realising that he was one of those men who never feel the joy of life so intensely as when the bullets are whistling all round them, and the next moment may be their last. Danger was a stimulant to him. I don't mind telling you that when I used to write down his temperature on the chart I added a point or two so that the doctors should think him a little worse than he was. I knew he was doing his damnedest to get them to discharge him, and I thought it only fair to him to make sure that they wouldn't. He used to look at me thoughtfully while I talked away and I know he looked forward to our little chats. I told him that I was a widow and had no one dependent on me, and I told him that I was thinking of settling down in Europe after the war. Gradually he thawed a little. He didn't say much about himself, but he began to chaff me, he has a great sense of humour, you know, and sometimes I really began to think he rather liked me. At last they reported him fit for duty. To my surprise he asked me to dine with him on his last evening. I managed to get leave from the matron and we drove in to Paris You can't imagine how handsome he looked in his uniform. I've never seen anyone look so distinguished. Aristocratic to his finger-tips. Somehow or other he wasn't in such good spirits as I'd expected. He'd been crazy to get back to the front.

" 'Why are you so down to-night?' I asked him. 'After all, you've got your wish at last.'

" 'I know I have,' he said. 'If for all that I'm a bit blue, can't you guess why?'

"I simply dared not think what he meant. I thought I'd better make a little joke.

" 'I'm not very good at guessing,' I said, with a laugh. 'If you want me to know you'd better tell me.'

"He looked down and I could see he was nervous.

" 'You've been most awfully good to me,' he said. 'I can never begin to thank you for all your kindness. You're the grandest woman I've ever known.'

"It upset me terribly to hear him say that. You know how funny Englishmen are; he'd never paid me a compliment before.

" 'I've only done what any competent nurse would have,' I said.

" 'Shall I ever see you again?' he said.

" 'That's up to you,' I said.

"I hoped he didn't hear the tremble in my voice.

" 'I hate leaving you,' he said.

"I really could hardly speak.

" 'Need you?' I said.

" 'So long as my King and Country want me I am at their service.' "

When Mrs. Forestier reached this point her pale blue eyes filled with tears.

" 'But the war can't last for ever,' I said.

" 'When the war ends,' he answered, 'supposing a bullet hasn't put an end to me, I shan't have a penny. I don't even know how I shall set about earning my living. You're a very rich woman; I'm a pauper.'

" 'You're an English gentleman,' I said.

" 'Will that matter very much when the world has been made safe for democracy?' he said bitterly.

"I was just crying my eyes out by then. Everything he said was so beautiful. Of course I saw what he meant. He didn't think it honourable to ask me to marry him. I felt he'd sooner die than let me think he was after my money. He was a fine man. I knew that I wasn't worthy of him, but I saw that if I wanted him I must go out and get him myself.

" 'It's no good pretending I'm not crazy about you, because I am,' I said.

" 'Don't make it harder for me,' he said hoarsely.

"I thought I should die, I loved him so much when he said that. It told me all I wanted to know. I stretched out my hand.

" 'Will you marry me, Robert?' I said, very simply.

" 'Eleanor,' he said.

"It was then he told me that he'd loved me from the first day he ever saw me. At first he hadn't taken it seriously, he thought I was just a nurse and perhaps he'd have an affair with me, and then when he found out that I wasn't that sort of woman and had a certain amount of money, he made up his mind that he must conquer his love. You see, he thought that marriage was quite out of the question."

Probably nothing flattered Mrs. Forestier more than the idea that Captain Forestier had wanted to have a slap and tickle with her. It was certain that no one else had ever made dishonourable proposals to her, and though Forestier hadn't either, the conviction that he had entertained the notion was a never-failing source of satisfaction to her. When they were married Eleanor's relations, hard-bitten Western people, had suggested that her husband should go to work rather than live on her money, and Captain Forestier was all for it. The only stipulation he made was this:

"There are some things a gentleman can't do, Eleanor. Anything else I'll do gladly. God knows, I don't attach any importance to that sort of thing, but if one's a sahib one can't help it, and damn it all, especially in these days, one does owe something to one's class."

Eleanor thought he had done enough in risking his life for his country in one bloody battle after another during four long years, but she was too proud of him to let it be said that he was a fortune-hunter who had married her for her money, and she made up her mind not to object if he found something to do that was worth his while. Unfortunately, the only jobs that offered were not very important. But he did not turn them down on his own responsibility.

"It's up to you, Eleanor," he told her. "You've only got to say the word and I'll take it. It would make my poor old governor turn in his grave to see me do it, but that can't be helped. My first duty is to you."

Eleanor wouldn't hear of it, and gradually the idea of his working was dropped. The Forestiers lived most of the year in their villa on the Riviera. They seldom went to England; Robert said it was no place for a gentleman since the war, and all the good fellows, white men every one of them, that he used to go about with when he was "one of the boys," had been killed. He would have liked to spend his winters in England, three days a week with the Quorn, that was the life for a man, but poor Eleanor, she would be so out of it in that hunting set, he couldn't ask her to make the sacrifice. Eleanor was prepared to make any sacrifice, but Captain Forestier shook his head. He wasn't as young as he had been, and his hunting days were over. He was quite satisfied to breed Sealyhams and raise Buff Orpingtons. They had a good deal of land; the house stood on the top of a hill, on a plateau, surrounded on three sides by forest, and in front they had a garden. Eleanor said he was never so happy as when he was walking round the estate in an old tweed suit with the kennel-man, who also looked after the chickens. It was then you saw in him all those generations of country squires that he had behind him. It touched and amused Eleanor to see the long talks he had with the kennel-man about the Buff Orpingtons; it was for all the world as if he were discussing the pheasants with his head keeper: and he fussed over the Sealyhams as much as if they had been the pack of hounds you couldn't help feeling he would have been so much more at home with. Captain Forestier's great-grandfather had been one of the bucks of the Regency. It was he who had ruined the family so that the estates had to be sold. They had a wonderful old place in Shropshire, they'd had it for centuries, and Eleanor, even though it no longer belonged to them, would have liked to go and see it; but Captain Forestier said it would be too painful to him and would never take her.

The Forestiers entertained a good deal. Captain Forestier was a connoisseur of wines and was proud of his cellar.

"His father was well known to have the best palate in England," said Eleanor, "and he's inherited it."

Most of their friends were Americans, French and Russians. Robert found them on the whole more interesting than the English, and Eleanor liked everybody he liked. Robert did not think the English quite up to their mark. Most of the people he had known in the old days belonged to the shooting, hunting, and fishing set; they, poor devils, were all broke now, and though, thank God, he wasn't a snob, he didn't half like the idea of his wife getting herself mixed up with a lot of *nouveaux riches* no one had ever heard of. Mrs. Forestier was not nearly so particular, but she respected his prejudices and admired his exclusiveness.

"Of course he has his whims and fancies," she said, "but I think it's only loyal on my part to defer to them. When you know the sort of people he comes from you can't help seeing how natural it is he should have them. The only time I've ever seen him vexed in all the years we've been married was when once a gigolo came up to me in the Casino and asked me to dance. Robert nearly knocked him down. I told him the poor little thing was only doing his job, but he said he wasn't going to have a damned swine like that even asking his wife to dance."

Captain Forestier had high moral standards. He thanked God that he wasn't narrow-minded, but one had to draw the line somewhere; and just because he lived on the Riviera he didn't see why he should hob-nob with drunks, wastrels and perverts. He had no indulgence for sexual irregularities and would not allow Eleanor to frequent women of doubtful reputation.

"You see," said Eleanor, "he's a man of complete integrity; he's the cleanest man I've ever known; and if sometimes he seems a little intolerant you must always remember that he never asks of others what he isn't prepared to do himself. After all, one can't help admiring a man whose principles are so high and who's prepared to stick to them at any cost."

When Captain Forestier told Eleanor that such and such a man, whom you met everywhere, and who you thought was rather pleasant, wasn't a pukkah sahib, she knew it was no good insisting. She knew that in her husband's judgment that finished him, and she was prepared to abide by it. After nearly twenty years of marriage she was sure of one thing, if of no other, and this was that Robert Forestier was the perfect type of an English gentleman.

"And I don't know that God has ever created anything finer than that," she said.

The trouble was that Captain Forestier was almost too perfect a type of the English gentleman. He was at forty-five (he was two or three years younger than Eleanor) still a very handsome man, with his wavy, abundant grey hair and his handsome moustache; he had the weather-beaten, healthy, tanned skin of a man who is much in the open air. He was tall, lean and broad-shouldered. He looked every inch a soldier. He had a bluff, hearty way with him and a loud, frank laugh. In his conversation, in his manner, in his dress he was so typical that you could hardly believe it. He was so much of a country gentleman that he made you think rather of an actor giving a marvellous performance of the part. When you saw him walking along the Croisette, a pipe in his mouth, in plus-fours and just the sort of tweed coat he would have worn on the moors, he looked so like an English sportsman that it gave you quite a shock. And his conversation, the way he dogmatised, the platitudinous inanity of his statements, his amiable, well-bred stupidity, were all so characteristic of the retired officer that you could hardly help thinking he was putting it on.

When Eleanor heard that the house at the bottom of their hill had been taken by a Sir Frederick and Lady Hardy she was much pleased. It would be nice for Robert to have as a near neighbour someone of his own class. She made enquiries about them from her friends in Cannes. It appeared that Sir Frederick had lately come into the baronetcy on the death of an uncle and was come to the Riviera for two or three years while he was paying off the death duties. He was said to have been very wild in his youth, he was well on in the fifties when he came to Cannes, but now he was respectably married, to a very nice little woman, and had two small boys. It was a pity that Lady Hardy had been an actress, for Robert was apt to be a little stuffy about actresses, but everyone said that she was very well-mannered and ladylike, and you would never have guessed she had been on the stage. The Forestiers met her first at a tea-party to which Sir Frederick did not go, and Robert acknowledged that she seemed a very decent sort of person; so Eleanor, wishing to be neighbourly, invited them both to luncheon. A day was arranged. The Forestiers had asked a good many people to meet them, and the Hardys were rather late. Eleanor took an immediate fancy to Sir Frederick. He looked much younger than she expected, he hadn't a white hair on his close-cropped head; indeed there was about him something boyish that was rather attractive. He was slightly built, not as tall as she was; and he had bright friendly eyes and a ready smile. She noticed that he wore the same Guards tie that Robert sometimes wore; he was not nearly so well-dressed as Robert, who always looked as though he had stepped out of a show-window, but he wore his old clothes as though it didn't much matter what one wore. Eleanor could quite believe he had been a trifle wild as a young man. She was not inclined to blame him.

"I must introduce my husband to you," she said.

She called him. Robert was talking to some of the other guests on the terrace, and hadn't noticed the Hardys come in. He came forward and in his affable, hearty way, with a grace that always charmed Eleanor, shook hands with Lady Hardy. Then he turned to Sir Frederick. Sir Frederick gave him a puzzled look.

"Haven't we met before?" he said.

Robert looked at him coolly.

"I don't think so."

"I could have sworn I knew your face."

Eleanor felt her husband stiffen and at once realised that something was going wrong. Robert laughed.

"It sounds terribly rude, but to the best of my belief I've never set eyes on you in my life. We may have run across one another in the war. One met such hosts of fellers, then, didn't one? Will you have a cocktail, Lady Hardy?"

During luncheon Eleanor noticed that Hardy kept looking at Robert. He was evidently trying to place him. Robert was busy with the women on either side of him and did not catch the glances. He was making efforts to entertain his neighbours; and his loud, ringing laugh rang through the room. He was a wonderful host. Eleanor had always admired his sense of social duty; however dull the women were he was sitting next to he gave them of his best. But when their guests had gone Robert's gaiety dropped from him like a cloak from his shoulders. She had a feeling that he was upset.

"Was the princess very boring?" she asked kindly.

"She's a malignant old cat, but otherwise she was all right."

"Funny that Sir Frederick thought he knew you."

"I've never set eyes on him in my life. But I know all about him. I wouldn't have more to do with him than you can help if I were you, Eleanor. I don't think he's quite our mark."

"But it's one of the oldest baronetcies in England. We looked it out in *Who's Who*."

"He's a disreputable scamp. I didn't dream that the Captain Hardy," Robert corrected himself, "the Fred Hardy I used to know about in the old days was now Sir Frederick. I would never have allowed you to ask him to my house."

"Why, Robert? I'm bound to tell you that I thought him very attractive."

For once Eleanor thought her husband rather unreasonable.

"A great many women have found him so, and a pretty penny it's cost them."

"You know how people talk. One really can't believe everything one hears."

He took one of her hands in his and looked earnestly into her eyes.

"Eleanor, you know I'm not the sort of chap to say anything against another chap behind his back, and I'd rather not tell you what I know about Hardy; I can only ask you to take my word for it that he isn't a proper person for you to know."

This was an appeal to which Eleanor was incapable of turning a deaf ear. It thrilled her to know that Robert placed such confidence in her; he knew that in a crisis he had only to call on her loyalty and she would not fail him.

"No one can be better aware than I, Robert," she answered gravely, "of your perfect integrity; I know that if you could tell me you would, but even if you wanted to now I wouldn't let you; it would look as if I had less confidence in you than you have in me. I am willing to abide by your judgment. I promise you that the Hardys shall never darken these doors again."

But Eleanor often lunched out without Robert, when he was playing golf, and so frequently met the Hardys. She was very stiff with Sir Frederick, because if Robert disapproved of him, she must too; but he either did not notice or did not care. He went out of his way to be nice to her and she found him easy to get on with. It was difficult to dislike a man who plainly thought that no woman was better than she should be, but very sweet for all that, and who had such delightful manners. It might be that he was an improper man for her to know, but she couldn't help liking the look in his brown eyes. It was a mocking look, which put you on your guard, and yet so caressing that you could not think he meant you harm. But the more Eleanor heard about him, the more she realised how right Robert was. He was an unprincipled rascal. They mentioned the names of women who had sacrificed everything for his sake and whom he had thrown aside without ceremony the moment he was tired of them. He seemed to have settled down now, and to be devoted to his wife and children; but can the leopard change his spots? It was only too probable that Lady Hardy had more to put up with than anyone suspected.

Fred Hardy was a bad lot. Pretty women, *chemin de fer*, and an unlucky knack for backing the wrong horse had landed him in the bankruptcy court by the time he was twenty-five, and he had been forced to resign his commission. He had seen no shame then in allowing women no longer in their first youth, who found his charm irresistible, to supply his wants. But the war came, he rejoined his regiment, and got a D.S.O. Then he went out to Kenya, where he found occasion to become co-respondent in a notorious divorce case; he left Kenya over some trouble with a cheque. His ideas of honesty were lax. It was unsafe to buy a car or a horse off him, and you did much better to keep away from the champagnes he warmly recommended to you. When with his persuasive charm he put before you a speculation by which you and he would make a fortune, you could only be sure that whatever he made out of it you would make nothing. He was in turn a motor-salesman, an outside broker, a commission agent and an actor. Were there any justice in the world he should have ended if not in gaol at least in the gutter. But by one of fate's monstrous tricks, having at last inherited his baronetcy and an adequate income, having married when well over forty a pretty, clever wife to whom were in due course born two healthy and handsome children, the future offered him affluence, position and respectability. He had never taken life any more seriously than he took women, and life had been as kind to him as women. If he thought of his past it was with complacency; he had had a good time, he had enjoyed his ups and downs; and now, with good health and a clear conscience, he was prepared to settle down as a country gentleman, damn it, bring up the kids as kids should be brought up; and when the old buffer who sat for his constituency pegged out, by George, go into Parliament himself.

"I could tell them a thing or two they don't know," he said.

He was probably right, but he did not stop to reflect that perhaps they were not things they much wanted to know.

One afternoon, about sunset, Fred Hardy went into one of the bars on the Croisette. He was a sociable creature and did not care to drink alone, so he looked around to see if there were anyone he knew. He caught sight of Robert, who had been playing golf and was waiting there for Eleanor.

"Hulloa, Bob, what about having a tiddly?"

Robert gave a start. No one on the Riviera called him Bob. When he saw who it was he answered stiffly:

"I've got a drink, thanks."

"Have another. My old lady don't approve of my drinking between meals, but when I can manage to get away from her I generally slip in and have one about this time. I don't know what you think about it, but my feeling is that God made six o'clock for man to have a drink at."

He flung himself into a great leather arm-chair next to the one Robert was sitting in and called a waiter. He gave Robert his good-natured, engaging smile.

"A lot of water has passed under the bridges since first we met, old boy, hasn't it?"

Robert, frowning a little, shot a look at him which an observer might have described as wary.

"I don't know exactly what you mean. To the best of my belief we met for the first time three or four weeks ago when you and your wife were good enough to come and have lunch with us."

"Come off it, Bob. I knew I'd seen you before. I was puzzled at first and then it flashed across me. You were the car-washer at that garage off Bruton Street where I used to keep my car."

Captain Forestier gave a hearty laugh.

"I'm sorry, but you've made a mistake. I never heard anything so ridiculous."

"I've got a damned good memory and I never forget a face. I bet you haven't forgotten me either. Many's the half-crown I've given you for fetching the car away from my flat when I didn't want to be bothered to bring it round to the garage myself."

"You're talking absolute rot. I'd never seen you in my life till you came to my house."

Hardy grinned cheerfully.

"You know I've always been a Kodak-fiend. I've got albums of snaps that I've taken at one time and another. Would it surprise you to learn that I've found a snap of you standing by a two-seater I'd just bought? A damned good-looking fellow you were in those days even though you had overalls on and your face was none too clean. Of course you've broadened out, your hair's grey and you've got a moustache, but it's the same chap. Unmistakably."

Captain Forestier looked at him coolly.

"You must have been misled by an accidental resemblance. It was somebody else you gave your half-crowns to."

"Well, where were you then, if you weren't a car-washer at the Bruton Garage between 1913 and 1914?"

"I was in India."

"With your regiment?" asked Fred Hardy with another grin.

"I was shooting."

"You liar."

Robert flushed deeply.

"This isn't quite the place to choose for a scrap, but if you think I'm going to stay here to be insulted by a drunken swine like you, you're mistaken."

"Wouldn't you like to hear what else I know about you? You know how things come back to one, and I've remembered quite a lot."

"I'm not in the least interested. I tell you that you're making an absolute mistake. You're confusing me with somebody else."

But he made no attempt to go.

"You were a bit of a slacker even in those days. I remember once, when I was going into the country early, I'd told you to have my car washed by nine and it wasn't ready, so I kicked up a row and old Thompson told me then your father had been a pal of his and he'd taken you on out of charity because you were down and out. Your father had been a wine waiter at one of the clubs, White's or Brooks's, I forget which, and you'd been a page-boy there yourself. You enlisted in the Coldstream Guards, if I remember right, and some chap bought you out and made you his valet."

"It's too fantastic," said Robert scornfully.

"And I remember, when I was home on leave once and went to the garage, old Thompson told me you'd enlisted in the A.S.C. You weren't going to take any more risks than you could help, were you? You've been drawing the long bow a bit, haven't you, with all those stories I hear of your gallantry in the trenches? I suppose you did get a commission, or is that a fake too?"

"Of course I got a commission."

"Well, a lot of funny people did in those days, but you know, old boy, if it was in the A.S.C. I wouldn't wear a Guards tie if I were you."

Captain Forestier instinctively put his hand up to his tie, and Fred Hardy, watching him with his mocking eyes, was pretty sure that notwithstanding his tan he went white.

"It's no business of yours what tie I wear."

"Don't get snotty, old boy. There's no reason to get up on your hind legs. I've got the goods on you, but I'm not going to give you away, so why don't you come clean?"

"I've got nothing to come clean about. I tell you it's all an absurd mistake. And I should tell you that if I find that you've been spreading these lying stories about me, I shall immediately start proceedings for slander."

"Stow it, Bob. I'm not going to spread any stories. You don't think I care? I think the whole thing's rather a lark. I've got no ill-feeling towards you. I've been a bit of an adventurer myself; I admire you for carrying off such a stupendous bluff. Starting as a page-boy and then being a trooper, a valet and a car-washer; and there you are, a fine gentleman, with a grand house, entertaining all the big bugs of the Riviera, winning golf tournaments, vice-president of the Sailing Club, and I don't know what all. You're It in Cannes and no mistake. It's stupendous. I've done some pretty rum things in my day, but the nerve you must have; old boy, I take off my hat to you."

"I wish I deserved your compliments. I don't. My father was in the Indian cavalry and I was at least born a gentleman. I may not have had a very distinguished career, but I certainly have nothing to be ashamed of."

"Oh, come off it, Bob. I shan't split, you know, not even to my old lady. I never tell women anything that they don't know already. Believe me, I'd have got into even worse scrapes than I have if I hadn't made a rule of that. I should have thought you'd be glad to have someone around that you could be yourself with. Isn't it a strain never to let up? Silly of you to keep me at arm's length. I haven't got anything on you, old boy. It's true I'm a bart and a landed proprietor now, but I've been in some pretty tight places in my time, and it's a wonder to me that I've kept out of gaol."

"It's a wonder to a good many other people."

Fred Hardy broke into a guffaw.

"That's one on me, old boy. All the same, if you don't mind my saying so, I think it was a bit thick your telling your wife I wasn't a proper person for her to associate with."

"I never said anything of the sort."

"Oh yes, you did. She's a grand old girl, but a bit garrulous, or am I mistaken?"

"I'm not prepared to discuss my wife with a man like you," said Captain Forestier, coldly.

"Oh, don't be so damned gentlemanly with me, Bob. We're a couple of bums and that's all there is to it. We could have some grand times together if you'd only have a little sense. You're a liar, a humbug and a cheat, but you seem to be very decent to your wife, and that's something in your favour. She just dotes upon you, doesn't she? Funny, women are. She's a very nice woman, Bob."

Robert's face grew red, he clenched his fist and half rose from his chair.

"Damn you, stop talking about my wife. If you mention her name again I swear I'll knock you down."

"Oh no, you won't. You're too great a gentleman to hit a feller smaller than yourself."

Hardy had said these words mockingly, watching Robert, and quite ready to dodge if that great fist struck out; he was astounded at their effect. Robert sank back into his chair and unclenched his fist.

"You're right. But only a mean hound would trade on it."

The reply was so theatrical that Fred Hardy began to chuckle, but then he saw that the man meant it. He was deadly serious. Fred Hardy was no fool; he could hardly have lived for twenty-five years on his wits in tolerable comfort unless he had had them all about him. And now, in amazement, staring at that heavy, powerful man, who looked so like the typical English sportsman, sunk back in the chair, he had a sudden flash of comprehension. He was no common swindler who had got hold of a silly woman to keep him in luxury and idleness. She was only a means to a greater end. He had been captivated by an ideal and in pursuit of it had stuck at nothing. Perhaps the notion had come to him when he was a page-boy in a smart club; the members, with their lounging ease, their casual manner, may have seemed very wonderful to him; and afterwards as a trooper, as a valet, as a car-washer, the many men he ran across, belonging to a different world and seen through a haze of hero-worship, had filled him perhaps with admiration and envy. He wanted to be like them. He wanted to be one of them. That was the ideal that haunted his dreams. He wanted—it was grotesque, it was pathetic—he wanted to be a gentleman. The war, with the commission it brought him, gave him his chance. Eleanor's money provided the means. That wretched fellow had spent twenty years pretending to be something the only value of which was that it wasn't a pretence. That was grotesque too; that was pathetic. Without meaning to, Fred Hardy uttered the thought that passed through his head.

"Poor old chap," he said.

Forestier looked at him quickly. He could not understand what those words meant nor the tone in which they were said. He flushed.

"What d'you mean by that?"

"Nothing. Nothing."

"I don't think we need continue this conversation. Apparently there's nothing I can say to persuade you that you're mistaken. I can only repeat that there's not a word of truth in it. I am not the fellow you think I am."

"All right, old boy, have it your own way."

Forestier called the waiter.

"D'you want me to pay for your drink?" he asked icily.

"Yes, old boy."

Forestier somewhat grandly gave the waiter a note and told him to keep the change, then without a word, without giving Fred Hardy another look, stalked out of the bar.

They did not meet again till the night on which Robert Forestier lost his life.

The winter passed into spring, and the gardens on the Riviera were ablaze with colour. The hillsides were primly gay with wild flowers. The spring passed into summer. In the towns along the Riviera the streets were hot with a bright, eager heat that made the blood run faster; and women walked about in great straw hats and pyjamas. The beaches were crowded. Men in trunks and women almost naked lay in the sun. In the evening the bars on the Croisette were thronged by a restless, chattering crowd as many-coloured as the flowers of spring. It had not rained for weeks. There had been several forest fires along the coast, and Robert Forestier in his hearty, joking way had several times said that they would stand a pretty thin chance if they had a fire in their woods. One or two people had advised him to cut down some of the trees at the back of his house; but he couldn't bear to: they had been in poor condition when the Forestiers bought the place, but now that the dead wood had been cut away year by year, that they had been given air and kept clean of pests, they were magnificent.

"Why, it would be like having my leg chopped off to cut one of 'em down. They must be the best part of a hundred years old."

On the fourteenth of July the Forestiers went over to a gala dinner at Monte Carlo, and they gave their staff leave to go to Cannes. It was the national holiday, and in Cannes they danced in the open air under the plane trees, there were fireworks, and from far and near the people came in to have a good time. The Hardys had sent their servants out too, but they were sitting at home, and their two little boys were in bed. Fred was playing patience and Lady Hardy was working at a piece of tapestry to cover a chair. Suddenly there was a ring of the bell and a loud knocking on the door.

"Who the devil's that?"

Hardy went to the door and found a boy who told him that fire had broken out in the Forestiers' woods. Some men had gone up from the village and were fighting it, but they needed all the help they could get, and would he come.

"Of course I'll come." He hurried back to his wife and told her. "Wake the kids and let them come up and see the fun. By George, after all this drought it'll be a blaze."

He bolted out. The boy told him they had telephoned to the police station and they were going to send along the soldiers. Someone was trying to get through to Monte Carlo and let Captain Forestier know.

"It'll take him an hour to get here," said Hardy.

As they ran they saw the glow in the sky, and when they came to the top of the hill, the leaping flames. There was no water and the only thing was to try to beat them out. Already a number of men were at work. Hardy joined them. But you had no sooner beat out the flames in one bush than another began to crackle and before you could look had turned into a fiery torch. The heat was terrific, and the workers, unable to support it, were slowly driven back. A breeze was blowing, and the sparks were carried from tree to bush. After weeks of drought everything was as dry as tinder, and the moment a spark fell the tree, the bush, went up in flames. If it had not been terrifying, it would have been awe-inspiring to see a great fir-tree, sixty feet high, blazing like matchwood. The fire roared like the fire in a factory furnace. The best way to put a stop to it was by cutting down trees and brushwood, but the men were few, and but two or three had axes. The only hope was in the troops, who were used to dealing with the forest fires, and the troops did not come.

"Unless they get here soon we shall never save the house," said Hardy.

He caught sight of his wife, who had come up with the two boys, and waved to them. Already he was black with grime, and the sweat was pouring down his face. Lady Hardy ran up.

"Oh, Fred, the dogs and the chickens."

"By George, yes."

The kennels and the chicken-run were at the back of the house, in a clearing that had been cut in the woods, and the wretched animals were already frantic with terror. Hardy let them out and they rushed to safety. They could only be left to shift for themselves. They must be rounded up later. The blaze could be seen now from far away. But the troops did not come, and the small body of helpers were powerless against the advancing flames.

"If those damned soldiers don't get here soon the house is for it," said Hardy. "I think we'd better get what we can out of it."

It was a stone house, but there were wooden verandahs all round it, and they would burn like kindling. The Forestiers' servants had come by now. He got them together, his wife gave a hand, and the two boys; they carried out on to the lawn in front such things as were portable, linen and silver, clothes, ornaments, pictures, pieces of furniture. At last the troops came, two lorry-loads of them, and set about systematically digging trenches and felling trees. There was an officer in charge and Hardy, pointing out the danger to the house, begged him first of all to cut down the trees that surrounded it.

"The house must look after itself," he said. "I've got to prevent the fire spreading beyond the hill."

The lights of a car were seen speeding along the winding road, and a few minutes later Forestier and his wife sprang out of it.

"Where are the dogs?" he cried.

"I've let them out," said Hardy.

"Oh, it's you."

At first in that filthy fellow, his face begrimed with soot and sweat, he had not recognized Fred Hardy. He frowned angrily.

"I thought the house might catch. I've got everything out I could."

Forestier looked at the blazing forest.

"Well, that's the end of my trees," he said.

"The soldiers are working on the side of the hill. They're trying to save the next property. We'd better go along and see if we can save anything."

"I'll go. You needn't," Forestier cried irritably.

On a sudden Eleanor gave an anguished cry

"Oh, look. The house."

From where they stood they could see a verandah at the back suddenly burst into flames.

"That's all right, Eleanor. The house can't burn. It'll only get the woodwork. Take my coat; I'm going along to help the soldiers."

He took off his dinner jacket and handed it to his wife.

"I'll come with you," said Hardy. "Mrs. Forestier, you'd better go along to where your things are. I think we've got everything out that's valuable."

"Thank heaven, I was wearing most of my jewellery."

Lady Hardy was a woman of sense.

"Mrs. Forestier, let's get the servants together and carry what we can down to our house."

The two men walked towards where the soldiers were at work.

"It's very decent of you to have got that stuff out of my house," said Robert, stiffly.

"Not at all," answered Fred Hardy.

They had not gone far when they heard somebody calling. They looked round and vaguely saw a woman running after them.

"*Monsieur, Monsieur.*"

They stopped and the woman, her arms outstretched, rushed up. It was Eleanor's maid. She was distraught.

"*La petite Judy*. Judy. I shut her up when we went out. She's on heat. I put her in the servants' bathroom."

"My God!" cried Forestier.

"What is it?"

"Eleanor's dog. I must save her at any cost."

He turned round and started to run back to the house. Hardy caught hold of his arm to hold him.

"Don't be a damned fool, Bob. The house is burning. You can't go into it."

Forestier struggled to release himself.

"Let me go, damn you. D'you think I'm going to let a dog be burned alive?"

"Oh, shut up. This is no time for play-acting!"

Forestier shook Hardy off, but Hardy sprang on him and seized him round the middle. Forestier with his clenched fist hit Hardy in the face as hard as he could. Hardy staggered, releasing his hold, and Forestier hit him again; Hardy fell to the ground.

"You rotten bounder. I'll show you how a gentleman behaves."

Fred Hardy picked himself up slowly and felt his face. It hurt him.

"God, the black eye I'm going to have to-morrow." He was shaken and a trifle dazed. The maid suddenly broke into a storm of hysterical tears. "Shut up, you slut," he cried crossly. "And don't say a word to your mistress."

Forestier was nowhere to be seen. It was more than an hour before they were able to get at him. They found him lying on the landing outside the bathroom, dead, with the dead Sealyham in his arms. Hardy looked at him for a long time before speaking.

"You fool," he muttered between his teeth, angrily. "You damned fool!"

That imposture of his had paid him out at last. Like a man who cherishes a vice till it gets a stranglehold on him so that he is its helpless slave, he had lied so long that he had come to believe his own lies. Bob Forestier had pretended for so many years to be a gentleman that in the end, forgetting that it was all a fake, he had found himself driven to act as in that stupid, conventional brain of his he thought a gentleman must act. No longer knowing the difference between sham and real, he had sacrificed his life to a spurious heroism. But Fred Hardy had to break the news to Mrs. Forestier. She was with his wife, in their villa at the bottom of the hill, and she still thought that Robert was with the soldiers cutting down trees and clearing the brushwood. He told her as gently as he could, but he had to tell her, and he had to tell her everything. At first it seemed as though she could not grasp the sense of what he said.

"Dead?" she cried. "Dead? My Robert?"

Then Fred Hardy, the rip, the cynic, the unscrupulous ruffian, took her hands in his and said the words that alone enabled her to bear her anguish.

"Mrs. Forestier, he was a very gallant gentleman."

THE THREE FAT WOMEN
OF ANTIBES

ONE was called Mrs. Richman and she was a widow. The second was called Mrs. Sutcliffe; she was American and she had divorced two husbands. The third was called Miss Hickson and she was a spinster. They were all in the comfortable forties and they were all well off. Mrs. Sutcliffe had the odd first name of Arrow. When she was young and slender she had liked it well enough. It suited her and the jests it occasioned though too often repeated were very flattering; she was not disinclined to believe that it suited her character too: it suggested directness, speed and purpose. She liked it less now that her delicate features had grown muzzy with fat, that her arms and shoulders were so substantial and her hips so massive. It was increasingly difficult to find dresses to make her look as she liked to look. The jests her name gave rise to now were made behind her back and she very well knew that they were far from obliging. But she was by no means resigned to middle age. She still wore blue to bring out the colour of her eyes and, with the help of art, her fair hair had kept its lustre. What she liked about Beatrice Richman and Frances Hickson was that they were both so much fatter than she, it made her look quite slim; they were both of them older and much inclined to treat her as a little young thing. It was not disagreeable. They were good-natured women and they chaffed her pleasantly about her beaux; they had both given up the thought of that kind of nonsense, indeed

Miss Hickson had never given it a moment's consideration, but they were sympathetic to her flirtations. It was understood that one of these days Arrow would make a third man happy.

"Only you mustn't get any heavier, darling," said Mrs. Rich-man.

"And for goodness' sake make certain of his bridge," said Miss Hickson.

They saw for her a man of about fifty, but well-preserved and of distinguished carriage, an admiral on the retired list and a good golfer, or a widower without encumbrances, but in any case with a substantial income. Arrow listened to them amiably, and kept to herself that fact that this was not at all her idea. It was true that she would have liked to marry again, but her fancy turned to a dark slim Italian with flashing eyes and a sonorous title or to a Spanish don of noble lineage; and not a day more than thirty. There were times when, looking at herself in her mirror, she was certain she did not look any more than that herself.

They were great friends, Miss Hickson, Mrs. Richman and Arrow Sutcliffe. It was their fat that had brought them together and bridge that had cemented their alliance. They had met first at Carlsbad, where they were staying at the same hotel and were treated by the same doctor who used them with the same ruthlessness. Beatrice Richman was enormous. She was a handsome woman, with fine eyes, rouged cheeks and painted lips. She was very well content to be a widow with a handsome fortune. She adored her food. She liked bread and butter, cream, potatoes and suet puddings, and for eleven months of the year ate pretty well everything she had a mind to, and for one month went to Carlsbad to reduce. But every year she grew fatter. She upbraided the doctor, but got no sympathy from him. He pointed out to her various plain and simple facts.

"But if I'm never to eat a thing I like, life isn't worth living," she expostulated.

He shrugged his disapproving shoulders. Afterwards she told Miss Hickson that she was beginning to suspect he wasn't so clever as she had thought. Miss Hickson gave a great guffaw. She was that sort of woman. She had a deep bass voice, a large flat sallow face from which twinkled little bright eyes; she walked with a slouch, her hands in her pockets, and when she could do so without exciting attention smoked a long cigar. She dressed as like a man as she could.

"What the deuce should I look like in frills and furbelows?" she said. "When you're as fat as I am you may just as well be comfortable."

She wore tweeds and heavy boots and whenever she could went about bareheaded. But she was as strong as an ox and boasted that few men could drive a longer ball than she. She was plain of speech, and she could swear more variously than a stevedore. Though her name was Frances she preferred to be called Frank. Masterful, but with tact, it was her jovial strength of character that held the three together. They drank their waters together, had their baths at the same hour, they took their strenuous walks together, pounded about the tennis court with a professional to make them run, and ate at the same table their sparse and regulated meals. Nothing impaired their good humour but the scales, and when one or other of them weighed as much on one day as she had the day before neither Frank's coarse jokes, the *bonhomie* of Beatrice nor Arrow's pretty kittenish ways sufficed to dispel the gloom. Then drastic measures were resorted to, the culprit went to bed for twenty-four hours and nothing passed her lips but the doctor's famous vegetable soup which tasted like hot water in which a cabbage had been well rinsed.

Never were three women greater friends. They would have been independent of anyone else if they had not needed a fourth at bridge. They were fierce, enthusiastic players and the moment the day's cure was over they sat down at the bridge table. Arrow, feminine as she was, played the best game of the three, a hard, brilliant game, in which she showed no mercy and never conceded a point or failed to take advantage of a mistake. Beatrice was solid and reliable. Frank was dashing; she was a great theorist, and had all the authorities at the tip of her tongue. They had long arguments over the rival systems. They bombarded one another with Culbertson and Sims. It was obvious that not one of them ever played a card without fifteen good reasons, but it was also obvious from the subsequent conversation that there were fifteen equally good reasons why she should not have played it. Life would have been perfect, even with the prospect of twenty-four hours of that filthy soup when the doctor's rotten (Beatrice) bloody (Frank) lousy (Arrow) scales pretended one hadn't lost an ounce in two days, if only there had not been this constant difficulty of finding someone to play with them who was in their class.

It was for this reason that on the occasion with which this narrative deals Frank invited Lena Finch to come and stay with them at Antibes. They were spending some weeks there on Frank's suggestion. It seemed absurd to her, with her common sense, that immediately the cure was over Beatrice who always lost twenty pounds should by giving way to her ungovernable appetite put it all on again. Beatrice was weak. She needed a person of strong will to watch her diet. She proposed then that on leaving Carlsbad they should take a house at Antibes, where they could get plenty of exercise—everyone knew that nothing slimmed you like swimming—and as far as possible could go on with the cure. With a cook of their own they could at least avoid things that were obviously fattening. There was no reason why they should not all lose several pounds more. It seemed a very good idea. Beatrice knew what was good for her, and she could resist temptation well enough if temptation was not put right under her nose. Besides, she liked gambling, and a flutter at the Casino two or three times a week would pass the time very pleasantly. Arrow adored Antibes, and she would be looking her best after a month at Carlsbad. She could just pick and choose among the young Italians, the passionate Spaniards, the gallant Frenchmen, and the long-limbed English who sauntered about all day in bathing trunks and gay-coloured dressing-gowns. The plan worked very well. They had a grand time. Two days a week they ate nothing but hard-boiled eggs and raw tomatoes and they mounted the scales every morning with light hearts. Arrow got down to eleven stone and felt just like a girl; Beatrice and Frank by standing in a certain way just avoided the thirteen. The machine they had bought registered kilogrammes, and they got extraordinarily clever at translating these in the twinkling of an eye to pounds and ounces.

But the fourth at bridge continued to be the difficulty. This person played like a foot, the other was so slow that it drove you frantic, one was quarrelsome, another was a bad loser, a third was next door to a crook. It was strange how hard it was to find exactly the player you wanted.

One morning when they were sitting in pyjamas on the terrace overlooking the sea, drinking their tea (without milk or sugar) and eating a rusk prepared by Dr. Hudebert and guaranteed not to be fattening, Frank looked up from her letters.

"Lena Finch is coming down to the Riviera," she said.

"Who's she?" asked Arrow.

"She married a cousin of mine. He died a couple of months ago and she's just recovering from a nervous breakdown. What about asking her to come here for a fortnight?"

"Does she play bridge?" asked Beatrice.

"You bet your life she does," boomed Frank in her deep voice. "And a damned good game too. We should be absolutely independent of outsiders."

"How old is she?" asked Arrow.

"Same age as I am."

"That sounds all right."

It was settled. Frank, with her usual decisiveness, stalked out as soon as she had finished her breakfast to send a wire, and three days later Lena Finch arrived. Frank met her at the station. She was in deep but not obtrusive mourning for the recent death of her husband. Frank had not seen her for two years. She kissed her warmly and took a good look at her.

"You're very thin, darling," she said.

Lena smiled bravely.

"I've been through a good deal lately. I've lost a lot of weight."

Frank sighed, but whether from sympathy with her cousin's sad loss, or from envy, was not obvious.

Lena was not, however, unduly depressed, and after a quick bath was quite ready to accompany Frank to Eden Roc. Frank introduced the stranger to her two friends and they sat down in what was known as the Monkey House. It was an enclosure covered with glass overlooking the sea, with a bar at the back, and it was crowded with chattering people in bathing costumes, pyjamas or dressing-gowns, who were seated at the tables having drinks. Beatrice's soft heart went out to the lorn widow, and Arrow, seeing that she was pale, quite ordinary to look at and probably forty-eight, was prepared to like her very much. A waiter approached them.

"What will you have, Lena dear?" Frank asked.

"Oh, I don't know, what you all have, a dry Martini or a White Lady."

Arrow and Beatrice gave her a quick look. Everyone knows how fattening cocktails are.

"I daresay you're tired after your journey," said Frank kindly.

She ordered a dry Martini for Lena and a mixed lemon and orange juice for herself and her two friends.

"We find alcohol isn't very good in all this heat," she explained.

"Oh, it never affects me at all," Lena answered airily. "I like cocktails."

Arrow went very slightly pale under her rouge (neither she nor Beatrice ever wet their faces when they bathed and they thought it absurd of Frank, a woman of her size, to pretend she liked diving) but she said nothing. The conversation was gay and easy, they all said the obvious things with gusto, and presently they strolled back to the villa for luncheon.

In each napkin were two little antifat rusks. Lena gave a bright smile as she put them by the side of her plate.

"May I have some bread?" she asked.

The grossest indecency would not have fallen on the ears of those three women with such a shock. Not one of them had eaten bread for ten years. Even Beatrice, greedy as she was, drew the line there. Frank, the good hostess, recovered herself first.

"Of course, darling," she said and turning to the butler asked him to bring some.

"And some butter," said Lena in that pleasant easy way of hers.

There was a moment's embarrassed silence.

"I don't know if there's any in the house," said Frank, "but I'll enquire. There may be some in the kitchen."

"I adore bread and butter, don't you?" said Lena, turning to Beatrice.

Beatrice gave a sickly smile and an evasive reply. The butler brought a long crisp roll of French bread. Lena slit it in two and plastered it with the butter which was miraculously produced. A grilled sole was served.

"We eat very simply here," said Frank. "I hope you won't mind."

"Oh, no, I like my food very plain," said Lena as she took some butter and spread it over her fish. "As long as I can have bread and butter and potatoes and cream I'm quite happy."

The three friends exchanged a glance. Frank's great sallow face sagged a little and she looked with distaste at the dry, insipid sole on her plate. Beatrice came to the rescue.

"It's such a bore, we can't get cream here," she said. "It's one of the things one has to do without on the Riviera."

"What a pity," said Lena.

The rest of the luncheon consisted of lamb cutlets, with the fat carefully removed so that Beatrice should not be led astray, and spinach boiled in water, with stewed pears to end up with. Lena tasted her pears and gave the butler a look of enquiry. That resourceful man understood her at once and though powdered sugar had never been served at that table before handed her without a moment's hesitation a bowl of it. She helped herself liberally. The other three pretended not to notice. Coffee was served and Lena took three lumps of sugar in hers.

"You have a very sweet tooth," said Arrow in a tone which she struggled to keep friendly.

"We think saccharine so much more sweetening," said Frank, as she put a tiny tablet of it into her coffee.

"Disgusting stuff," said Lena.

Beatrice's mouth drooped at the corners, and she gave the lump sugar a yearning look.

"Beatrice," boomed Frank sternly.

Beatrice stifled a sigh, and reached for the saccharine.

Frank was relieved when they could sit down to the bridge table. It was plain to her that Arrow and Beatrice were upset. She wanted them to like Lena and she was anxious that Lena should enjoy her fortnight with them. For the first rubber Arrow cut with the newcomer.

"Do you play Vanderbilt or Culbertson?" she asked her.

"I have no conventions," Lena answered in a happy-go-lucky way, "I play by the light of nature."

"I play strict Culbertson," said Arrow acidly.

The three fat women braced themselves to the fray. No conventions indeed! They'd learn her. When it came to bridge even Frank's family feeling was forgotten and she settled down with the same determination as the others to trim the stranger in their midst. But the light of nature served Lena very well. She had a natural gift for the game and great experience. She played with imagination, quickly, boldly, and with assurance. The other players were in too high a class not to realise very soon that Lena knew what she was about, and since they were all thoroughly good-natured, generous women, they were gradually mollified. This was real bridge. They all enjoyed themselves.

Arrow and Beatrice began to feel more kindly towards Lena, and Frank, noticing this, heaved a fat sigh of relief. It was going to be a success.

After a couple of hours they parted, Frank and Beatrice to have a round of golf, and Arrow to take a brisk walk with a young Prince Roccamare whose acquaintance she had lately made. He was very sweet and young and good-looking. Lena said she would rest.

They met again just before dinner.

"I hope you've been all right, Lena dear," said Frank. "I was rather conscience-striken at leaving you with nothing to do all this time."

"Oh, don't apologise. I had a lovely sleep and then I went down to Juan and had a cocktail. And d'you know what I discovered? You'll be so pleased. I found a dear little tea-shop where they've got the most beautiful thick fresh cream. I've ordered half a pint to be sent every day. I thought it would be my little contribution to the household."

Her eyes were shining. She was evidently expecting them to be delighted.

"How very kind of you," said Frank, with a look that sought to quell the indignation that she saw on the faces of her two friends. "But we never eat cream. In this climate it makes one so bilious."

"I shall have to eat it all myself then," said Lena cheerfully.

"Don't you ever think of your figure?" Arrow asked with icy deliberation.

"The doctor said I must eat."

"Did he say you must eat bread and butter and potatoes and cream?"

"Yes. That's what I thought you meant when you said you had simple food."

"You'll get simply enormous," said Beatrice.

Lena laughed gaily.

"No, I shan't. You see, nothing ever makes me fat. I've always eaten everything I wanted to and it's never had the slightest effect on me."

The stony silence that followed this speech was only broken by the entrance of the butler.

"*Mademoiselle est servie,*" he announced.

They talked the matter over late that night, after Lena had gone to bed, in Frank's room. During the evening they had been furiously cheerful, and they had chaffed one another with a friendliness that would have taken in the keenest observer. But now they dropped the mask. Beatrice was sullen, Arrow was spiteful and Frank was unmanned.

"It's not very nice for me to sit there and see her eat all the things I particularly like," said Beatrice plaintively.

"It's not very nice for any of us," Frank snapped back.

"You should never have asked her here," said Arrow.

"How was I to know?" cried Frank.

"I can't help thinking that if she really cared for her husband she would hardly eat so much," said Beatrice. "He's only been buried two months. I mean, I think you ought to show some respect for the dead."

"Why can't she eat the same as we do?" asked Arrow viciously. "She's a guest."

"Well, you heard what she said. The doctor told her she must eat."

"Then she ought to go to a sanatorium."

"It's more than flesh and blood can stand, Frank," moaned Beatrice.

"If I can stand it you can stand it."

"She's your cousin, she's not our cousin," said Arrow. "I'm not going to sit there for fourteen days and watch that woman make a hog of herself."

"It's so vulgar to attach all this importance to food," Frank boomed, and her voice was deeper than ever. "After all the only thing that counts really is spirit."

"Are you calling *me* vulgar, Frank?" asked Arrow with flashing eyes.

"No, of course she isn't," interrupted Beatrice.

"I wouldn't put it past you to go down in the kitchen when we're all in bed and have a good square meal on the sly."

Frank sprang to her feet.

"How dare you say that, Arrow! I'd never ask anybody to do what I'm not prepared to do myself. Have you known me all these years and do you think me capable of such a mean thing?"

"How is it you never take off any weight then?"

Frank gave a gasp and burst into a flood of tears.

"What a cruel thing to say! I've lost pounds and pounds."

She wept like a child. Her vast body shook and great tears splashed on her mountainous bosom.

"Darling, I didn't mean it," cried Arrow.

She threw herself on her knees and enveloped what she could of Frank in her own plump arms. She wept and the mascara ran down her cheeks.

"D'you mean to say I don't look thinner?" Frank sobbed. "After all I've gone through."

"Yes, dear, of course you do," cried Arrow through her tears. "Everybody's noticed it."

Beatrice, though naturally of a placid disposition, began to cry gently. It was very pathetic. Indeed, it would have been a hard heart that failed to be moved by the sight of Frank, that lion-hearted woman, crying her eyes out. Presently, however, they dried their tears and had a little brandy and water, which every doctor had told them was the least fattening thing they could drink, and then they felt much better. They decided that Lena should have the nourishing food that had been ordered her and they made a solemn resolution not to let it disturb their equanimity. She was certainly a first-rate bridge player and after all it was only for a fortnight. They would do whatever they could to make her stay enjoyable. They kissed one another warmly and separated for the night feeling strangely uplifted. Nothing should interfere with the wonderful friendship that had brought so much happiness into their three lives.

But human nature is weak. You must not ask too much of it. They ate grilled fish while Lena ate macaroni sizzling with cheese and butter; they ate grilled cutlets and boiled spinach while Lena ate *pâté de foie gras;* twice a week they ate hard-boiled eggs and raw tomatoes, while Lena ate peas swimming in cream and potatoes cooked in all sorts of delicious ways. The chef was a good chef and he leapt at the opportunity afforded him to send up one dish more rich, tasty and succulent than the other.

"Poor Jim," sighed Lena, thinking of her husband, "he loved French cooking."

The butler disclosed the fact that he could make half a dozen kinds of cocktail and Lena informed them that the doctor had recommended her to drink burgundy at luncheon and champagne at dinner. The three fat women persevered. They were gay, chatty and even hilarious (such is the natural gift that women have for deception) but Beatrice grew limp and forlorn, and Arrow's tender blue eyes acquired a steely glint. Frank's deep voice grew more raucous. It was when they played bridge

that the strain showed itself. They had always been fond of
talking over their hands, but their discussions had been friendly.
Now a distinct bitterness crept in and sometimes one pointed
out a mistake to another with quite unnecessary frankness. Discussion turned to argument and argument to altercation. Sometimes the session ended in angry silence. Once Frank accused
Arrow of deliberately letting her down. Two or three times Beatrice, the softest of the three, was reduced to tears. On another
occasion Arrow flung down her cards and swept out of the room
in a pet. Their tempers were getting frayed. Lena was the peace-
maker.

"I think it's such a pity to quarrel over bridge," she said.
"After all, it's only a game."

It was all very well for her. She had had a square meal and
half a bottle of champagne. Besides, she had phenomenal luck.
She was winning all their money. The score was put down in a
book after each session, and hers mounted up day after day
with unfailing regularity. Was there no justice in the world?
They began to hate one another. And though they hated her too
they could not resist confiding in her. Each of them went to her
separately and told her how detestable the others were. Arrow
said she was sure it was bad for her to see so much of women so
much older than herself. She had a good mind to sacrifice her
share of the lease and go to Venice for the rest of the summer.
Frank told Lena that with her masculine mind it was too much
to expect that she could be satisfied with anyone so frivolous as
Arrow and so frankly stupid as Beatrice.

"I must have intellectual conversation," she boomed. "When
you have a brain like mine you've got to consort with your intellectual equals."

Beatrice only wanted peace and quiet.

"Really I hate women," she said. "They're so unreliable;
they're so malicious."

By the time Lena's fortnight drew to its close the three fat
women were barely on speaking terms. They kept up appearances before Lena, but when she was not there made no pre-
tences. They had got past quarrelling. They ignored one another, and when this was not possible treated each other with
icy politeness.

Lena was going to stay with friends on the Italian Riviera
and Frank saw her off by the same train as that by which she

had arrived. She was taking away with her a lot of their money.

"I don't know how to thank you," she said, as she got into the carriage. "I've had a wonderful visit."

If there was one thing that Frank Hickson prided herself on more than on being a match for any man it was that she was a gentlewoman, and her reply was perfect in its combination of majesty and graciousness.

"We've all enjoyed having you here, Lena," she said. "It's been a real treat."

But when she turned away from the departing train she heaved such a vast sigh of relief that the platform shook beneath her. She flung back her massive shoulders and strode home to the villa.

"Ouf!" she roared at intervals. "Ouf!"

She changed into her one-piece bathing-suit, put on her espadrilles and a man's dressing-gown (no nonsense about it) and went to Eden Roc. There was still time for a bathe before luncheon. She passed through the Monkey House, looking about her to say good morning to anyone she knew, for she felt on a sudden at peace with mankind, and then stopped dead still. She could not believe her eyes. Beatrice was sitting at one of the tables, by herself; she wore the pyjamas she had bought at Molyneux's a day or two before, she had a string of pearls round her neck, and Frank's quick eyes saw that she had just had her hair waved; her cheeks, her eyes, her lips were made up. Fat, nay vast, as she was, none could deny that she was an extremely handsome woman. But what was she doing? With the slouching gait of the Neanderthal man which was Frank's characteristic walk she went up to Beatrice. In her black bathing-dress Frank looked like the huge cetacean which the Japanese catch in the Torres Straits and which the vulgar call a sea-cow.

"Beatrice, what are you doing?" she cried in her deep voice.

It was like the roll of thunder in the distant mountains. Beatrice looked at her coolly.

"Eating," she answered.

"Damn it, I can see you're eating."

In front of Beatrice was a plate of *croissants* and a plate of butter, a pot of strawberry jam, coffee and a jug of cream. Beatrice was spreading butter thick on the delicious hot bread, covering this with jam, and then pouring the thick cream over all.

"You'll kill yourself," said Frank.

"I don't care," mumbled Beatrice with her mouth full.

"You'll put on pounds and pounds."

"Go to hell!"

She actually laughed in Frank's face. My God, how good those *croissants* smelt!

"I'm disappointed in you, Beatrice. I thought you had more character."

"It's your fault. That blasted woman. You would have her down. For a fortnight I've watched her gorge like a hog. It's more than flesh and blood can stand. I'm going to have one square meal if I bust."

The tears welled up to Frank's eyes. Suddenly she felt very weak and womanly. She would have liked a strong man to take her on his knee and pet her and cuddle her and call her little baby names. Speechless she sank down on a chair by Beatrice's side. A waiter came up. With a pathetic gesture she waved towards the coffee and *croissants.*

"I'll have the same," she sighed.

She listlessly reached out her hand to take a roll, but Beatrice snatched away the plate.

"No, you don't," she said. "You wait till you get your own."

Frank called her a name which ladies seldom apply to one another in affection. In a moment the waiter brought her *croissants,* butter, jam and coffee.

"Where's the cream, you fool?" she roared like a lioness at bay.

She began to eat. She ate gluttonously. The place was beginning to fill up with bathers coming to enjoy a cocktail or two after having done their duty by the sun and the sea. Presently Arrow strolled along with Prince Roccamare. She had on a beautiful silk wrap which she held tightly round her with one hand in order to look as slim as possible and she bore her head high so that he should not see her double chin. She was laughing gaily. She felt like a girl. He had just told her (in Italian) that her eyes made the blue of the Mediterranean look like pea-soup. He left her to go into the men's room to brush his sleek black hair and they arranged to meet in five minutes for a drink. Arrow walked on to the women's room to put a little more rouge on her cheeks and a little more red on her lips. On her way she caught sight of Frank and Beatrice. She stopped. She could hardly believe her eyes.

"My God!" she cried. "You beasts. You hogs." She seized a chair. "Waiter."

Her appointment went clean out of her head. In the twinkling of an eye the waiter was at her side.

"Bring me what these ladies are having," she ordered.

Frank lifted her great heavy head from her plate.

"Bring me some *pâté de foie gras*," she boomed.

"Frank!" cried Beatrice.

"Shut up."

"All right. I'll have some too."

The coffee was brought and the hot rolls and cream and the *pâté de foie gras* and they set to. They spread the cream on the *pâté* and they ate it. They devoured great spoonfuls of jam. They crunched the delicious crisp bread voluptuously. What was love to Arrow then? Let the Prince keep his palace in Rome and his castle in the Apennines. They did not speak. What they were about was much too serious. They ate with solemn, ecstatic fervour.

"I haven't eaten potatoes for twenty-five years," said Frank in a far-off brooding tone.

"Waiter," cried Beatrice, "bring fried potatoes for three."

"*Très bien, Madame.*"

The potatoes were brought. Not all the perfumes of Arabia smelt so sweet. They ate them with their fingers.

"Bring me a dry Martini," said Arrow.

"You can't have a dry Martini in the middle of a meal, Arrow," said Frank.

"Can't I? You wait and see."

"All right then. Bring me a double dry Martini," said Frank.

"Bring three double dry Martinis," said Beatrice.

They were brought and drunk at a gulp. The women looked at one another and sighed. The misunderstandings of the last fortnight dissolved and the sincere affection each had for the other welled up again in their hearts. They could hardly believe that they had ever contemplated the possibility of severing a friendship that had brought them so much solid satisfaction. They finished the potatoes.

"I wonder if they've got any chocolate éclairs," said Beatrice.

"Of course they have."

And of course they had. Frank thrust one whole into her huge mouth, swallowed it and seized another, but before she ate it she looked at the other two and plunged a vindictive dagger into the heart of the monstrous Lena.

"You can say what you like, but the truth is she played a damned rotten game of bridge, really."

"Lousy," agreed Arrow.

But Beatrice suddenly thought she would like a meringue.

THE HAPPY COUPLE

I DON'T KNOW that I very much liked Landon. He was a member of a club I belonged to, and I had often sat next to him at lunch. He was a judge at the Old Bailey, and it was through him I was able to get a privileged seat in court when there was an interesting trial that I wanted to attend. He was an imposing figure on the bench in his great full-bottomed wig, his red robes and his ermine tippet; and with his long, white face, thin lips and pale blue eyes, a somewhat terrifying one. He was just, but harsh; and sometimes it made me uncomfortable to hear the bitter scolding he gave a convicted prisoner whom he was about to sentence to a long term of imprisonment. But his acid humour at the lunch-table and his willingness to discuss the cases he had tried made him sufficiently good company for me to disregard the slight malaise I felt in his presence. I asked him once whether he did not feel a certain uneasiness of mind after he had sent a man to the gallows. He smiled as he sipped his glass of port.

"Not at all. The man's had a fair trial; I've summed up as fairly as I could, and the jury has found him guilty. When I condemn him to death, I sentence him to a punishment he richly deserves; and when the court rises, I put the case out of my head. Nobody but a sentimental fool would do anything else."

I knew he liked to talk to me, but I never thought he looked upon me as anything but a club acquaintance, so I was not a little surprised when one day I received a telegram from him saying that he was spending his vacation in the Riviera, and would like to stay with me for two or three days on his way to Italy. I wired that I should be glad to see him. But it was with a certain trepidation that I met him at the station.

On the day of his arrival, to help me out, I asked Miss Gray, a neighbour and an old friend of mine, to dinner. She was of mature age, but charming, and she had a flow of lively conversation which I knew nothing could discourage. I gave them a very good dinner, and though I had no port to offer the judge, I was able to provide him with a good bottle of Montrachet and an even better bottle of Mouton Rothschild. He enjoyed them both; and I was glad of that, because when I had offered him a cocktail, he had refused with indignation.

"I have never understood," he said, "how people presumably civilised can indulge in a habit that is not only barbarous but disgusting."

I may state that this did not deter Miss Gray and me from having a couple of dry Martinis, though it was with impatience and distaste that he watched us drink them.

But the dinner was a success. The good wine and Miss Gray's sprightly chatter combined to give Landon a geniality I had never before seen in him. It was plain to me that notwithstanding his austere appearance he liked feminine society; and Miss Gray in a becoming dress, with her neat head only just touched with grey and her delicate features, her sparkling eyes, was still alluring. After dinner the judge, with some old brandy still further to mellow him, let himself go, and for a couple of hours held us entranced while he told us of celebrated trials in which he had been concerned. I was not surprised therefore that when Miss Gray asked us to lunch with her next day, Landon, even before I could answer, accepted with alacrity.

"A very nice woman," he said when she had left us. "And a head on her shoulders. She must have been very pretty as a girl. She's not bad now. Why isn't she married?"

"She always says nobody asked her."

"Stuff and nonsense! Women ought to marry. Too many of these women about who want their independence. I have no patience with them."

Miss Gray lived in a little house facing the sea at St. Jean, which is a couple of miles from my own house at Cap Ferrat. We drove down next day at one and were shown into her sitting-room.

"I have a surprise for you," she said to me, as we shook hands. "The Craigs are coming."

"You've got to know them at last."

"Well, I thought it was too absurd that we should live next door to one another, and bathe from the same beach every day and not speak. So I forced myself on them, and they've promised to come to lunch to-day. I wanted you to meet them, to see what you make of them." She turned to Landon. "I hope you don't mind."

But he was on his best behaviour.

"I'm sure I shall be delighted to meet any friends of yours, Miss Gray," he said.

"But they're not friends of mine. I've seen a lot of them, but I never spoke to them till yesterday. It'll be a treat for them to meet an author and a celebrated judge."

I had heard a good deal of the Craigs from Miss Gray during the previous three weeks. They had taken the cottage next to hers, and at first she feared they would be a nuisance. She liked her own company and did not want to be bothered with the trivialities of social intercourse. But she very quickly discovered that the Craigs were as plainly disinclined to strike up an acquaintance with her as she with them. Though in that little place they could not but meet two or three times a day, the Craigs never by so much a glance gave an indication that they had ever seen her before. Miss Gray told me she thought it very tactful of them to make no attempt to intrude upon her privacy, but I had an idea that she was not affronted, a little puzzled rather, that they apparently wanted to know her as little as she wanted to know them. I had guessed some time before that she would not be able to resist making the first advance. On one occasion, while we were walking, we passed them, and I was able to have a good look at them. Craig was a handsome man, with a red, honest face, a grey moustache and thick strong grey hair. He held himself well, and there was a bluff heartiness of manner about him that suggested a broker who had retired on a handsome fortune. His wife was a woman hard of visage, tall and of masculine appearance, with dull, fair hair too elaborately dressed, a large nose, a large mouth and a weather-beaten skin. She was not only plain but grim. Her clothes, pretty, flimsy and graceful, sat oddly upon her, for they would better have suited a girl of eighteen, and Mrs. Craig was certainly forty. Miss Gray told me they were well cut and expensive. I thought he looked commonplace and she looked disagreeable, and I told Miss Gray she was lucky that they were obviously disposed to keep themselves to themselves.

"There's something rather sweet about them," she answered.

"What?"

"They love one another. And they adore the baby."

For they had a child that was not more than a year old; and from this Miss Gray had concluded that they had not long been married. She liked to watch them with their baby. A nurse took it out every morning in a pram, but before this, father and mother spent an ecstatic quarter of an hour teaching it to walk. They stood a few yards apart and urged the child to flounder from one to the other; and each time it tumbled into the parental arms it was lifted up and rapturously embraced. And when finally it was tucked up in the smart pram, they hung over it with charming baby talk and watched it out of sight as though they couldn't bear to let it go.

Miss Gray used often to see them walking up and down the lawn of their garden arm in arm; they did not talk, as though they were so happy to be together that conversation was unnecessary; and it warmed her heart to observe the affection which that dour, unsympathetic woman so obviously felt for her tall, handsome husband. It was a pretty sight to see Mrs. Craig brush an invisible speck of dust off his coat, and Miss Gray was convinced that she purposely made holes in his socks in order to have the pleasure of darning them. And it looked as though he loved her as much as she loved him. Every now and then he would give her a glance, and she would look up at him and smile, and he gave her cheek a little pat. Because they were no longer young, their mutual devotion was peculiarly touching.

I never knew why Miss Gray had never married; I felt as certain as the judge that she had had plenty of chances; and I asked myself when she talked to me about the Craigs, whether the sight of this matrimonial felicity didn't give her a slight pang. I suppose complete happiness is very rare in this world, but these two people seemed to enjoy it, and it may be that Miss Gray was so strangely interested in them only because she could not quite suppress the feeling in her heart that by remaining single she had missed something.

Because she didn't know what their first names were, she

called them Edwin and Angelina. She made up a story about them. She told it to me one day; and when I ridiculed it, she was quite short with me. This, as far as I can remember, is how it went: They had fallen in love with one another years before—perhaps twenty years—when Angelina, a young girl then, had the fresh grace of her teens and Edwin was a brave youth setting out joyously on the journey of life. And since the gods, who are said to look upon young love with kindliness, nevertheless do not bother their heads with practical matters, neither Edwin nor Angelina had a penny. It was impossible for them to marry, but they had courage, hope and confidence. Edwin made up his mind to go out to South America or Malaya or where you like, make his fortune and return to marry the girl who had patiently waited for him. It couldn't take more than two or three years, five at the utmost; and what is that, when you're twenty and the whole of life is before you? Meanwhile of course Angelina would live with her widowed mother.

But things didn't pan out according to schedule. Edwin found it more difficult than he had expected to make a fortune; in fact, he found it hard to earn enough money to keep body and soul together, and only Angelina's love and her tender letters gave him the heart to continue the struggle. At the end of five years he was not much better off than when he started. Angelina would willingly have joined him and shared his poverty, but it was impossible for her to leave her mother, bed-ridden as she was, poor thing, and there was nothing for them to do but have patience. And so the years passed slowly, and Edwin's hair grew grey, and Angelina became grim and haggard. Hers was the harder lot, for she could do nothing but wait. The cruel glass showed such charms as she had possessed slipping away from her one by one; and at last she discovered that youth, with a mocking laugh and a pirouette, had left her for good. Her sweetness turned sour from long tending of a querulous invalid; her mind was narrowed by the society of the small town in which she lived. Her friends married and had children, but she remained a prisoner to duty.

She wondered if Edwin still loved her. She wondered if he would ever come back. She often despaired. Ten years went by, and fifteen, and twenty. Then Edwin wrote to say that his affairs were settled, and he had made enough money for them to live upon in comfort, and if she were still willing to marry him, he would return at once. By a merciful interposition of provi-

dence, Angelina's mother chose that very moment to abandon a
world in which she had made herself a thorough nuisance. But
when after so long a separation they met, Angelina saw with
dismay that Edwin was as young as ever. It's true his hair was
grey, but it infinitely became him. He had always been good-
looking, but now he was a very handsome man in the flower of
his age. She felt as old as the hills. She was conscious of her
narrowness, her terrible provincialism, compared with the
breadth he had acquired by his long sojourn in foreign countries. He was gay and breezy as of old, but her spirit was
crushed. The bitterness of life had warped her soul. It seemed
monstrous to bind that alert and active man to her by a promise
twenty years old, and she offered him his release. He went
deathly pale.

"Don't you care for me any more?" he cried brokenly.

And she realised on a sudden—oh, the rapture, oh, the relief!
—that to him she was just the same as she had ever been. He
had thought of her always as she was; her portrait had been, as
it were, stamped on his heart, so that now, when the real woman
stood before him, she was, to him, still eighteen.

So they were married.

"I don't believe a word of it," I said when Miss Gray had
brought her story to its happy ending.

"I insist on your believing it," she said. "I'm convinced it's
true, and I haven't the smallest doubt that they'll live happily
together to a ripe old age." Then she made a remark that I
thought rather shrewd. "Their love is founded on an illusion,
perhaps; but since it has to them all the appearance of reality,
what does it matter?"

While I have told you this idyllic story of Miss Gray's invention, the three of us, our hostess, Landon and myself, waited for
the Craigs to come.

"Have you ever noticed that if people live next door to you,
they're invariably late?" Miss Gray asked the judge.

"No, I haven't," he answered acidly. "I'm always punctual
myself, and I expect other people to be punctual."

"I suppose it's no good offering you a cocktail?"

"None whatever, madam."

"But I have some sherry that they tell me isn't bad."

The judge took the bottle out of her hands and looked at the
label. A faint smile broke on his thin lips.

"This is a civilised drink, Miss Gray. With your permission I

will help myself. I never knew a woman yet who knew how to
pour out a glass of wine. One should hold a woman by the waist,
but a bottle by the neck."

While he was sipping the old sherry with every sign of satisfaction, Miss Gray glanced out of the window.

"Oh, that's why the Craigs are late. They were waiting for the
baby to come back."

I followed her eyes and saw that the nurse had just pushed
the pram past Miss Gray's house on her way home. Craig took
the baby out of the pram and lifted it high in the air. The baby,
trying to tug at his moustache, crowed gleefully. Mrs. Craig
stood by, watching, and the smile on her face made her harsh
features almost pleasant. The window was open, and we heard
her speak.

"Come along, darling," she said, "we're late."

He put the baby back in the pram, and they came up to the
door of Miss Gray's house and rang the bell. The maid showed
them in. They shook hands with Miss Gray, and because I was
standing near, she introduced me to them. Then she turned to
the judge.

"And this is Sir Edward Landon—Mr. and Mrs. Craig."

One would have expected the judge to move forward with an
outstretched hand, but he remained stock-still. He put his eyeglass up to his eye, that eyeglass that I had on more than one
occasion seen him use with devastating effect in court, and
stared at the newcomers.

"Gosh, what a dirty customer," I said to myself.

He let the glass drop from his eye.

"How do you do," he said. "Am I mistaken in thinking that
we've met before?"

The question turned my eyes to the Craigs. They stood side
by side close to one another, as though they had drawn together
for mutual protection. They did not speak. Mrs. Craig looked
terrified. Craig's red face was darkened by a purple flush, and
his eyes appeared almost to start out of his head. But that only
lasted a second.

"I don't think so," he said in a rich, deep voice. "Of course
I've heard of you, Sir Edward."

"More people know Tom Fool than Tom Fool knows,"
said he.

Miss Gray meanwhile had been giving the cocktail-shaker a
shake, and now she handed cocktails to her two guests. She had

noticed nothing. I didn't know what it all meant; in fact, I wasn't sure it meant anything. The incident, if incident there was, passed so quickly that I was half inclined to think that I had read into the strangers' momentary embarrassment on being introduced to a celebrated man something for which there was no foundation. I set about making myself pleasant. I asked them how they liked the Riviera and if they were comfortable in their house. Miss Gray joined in, and we chatted, as one does with strangers, of commonplace things. They talked easily and pleasantly. Mrs. Craig said how much they enjoyed the bathing and complained of the difficulty of getting fish at the seaside. I was aware that the judge did not join in the conversation, but looked down at his feet as though he were unconscious of the company.

Lunch was announced. We went into the dining-room. We were only five, and it was a small round table, so the conversation could not be anything but general. I must confess that it was carried on chiefly by Miss Gray and myself. The judge was silent, but he often was, for he was a moody creature, and I paid no attention. I noticed that he ate the omelette with good appetite, and when it was passed round again took a second helping. The Craigs struck me as a little shy, but that didn't surprise me, and as the second course was produced they began to talk more freely. It didn't strike me that they were very amusing people; they didn't seem interested in very much besides their baby, the vagaries of the two Italian maids they had, and an occasional flutter at Monte Carlo; and I couldn't help thinking that Miss Gray had erred in making their acquaintance. Then suddenly something happened: Craig rose abruptly from his chair and fell headlong to the floor. We jumped up. Mrs. Craig threw herself down, over her husband, and took his head in her hands.

"It's all right, George," she cried in an agonised tone. "It's all right!"

"Put his head down," I said. "He's only fainted."

I felt his pulse and could feel nothing. I said he had fainted, but I wasn't sure it wasn't a stroke. He was the sort of heavy, plethoric man who might easily have one. Miss Gray dipped her napkin into water and dabbed his forehead. Mrs. Craig seemed distraught. Then I noticed that Landon had remained quietly sitting in his chair.

"If he's fainted, you're not helping him to recover by crowding round him," he said acidly.

Mrs. Craig turned her head and gave him a look of bitter hatred.

"I'll ring up the doctor," said Miss Gray.

"No, I don't think that's necessary," I said. "He's coming to."

I could feel his pulse growing stronger, and in a minute or two he opened his eyes. He gasped when he realised what had happened, and tried to struggle to his feet.

"Don't move," I said. "Lie still a little longer."

I got him to drink a glass of brandy, and the colour came back to his face.

"I feel all right now," he said.

"We'll get you into the next room, and you can lie on the sofa for a bit."

"No, I'd sooner go home. It's only a step."

He got up from the floor.

"Yes, let's go back," said Mrs. Craig. She turned to Miss Gray. "I'm so sorry; he's never done anything like this before."

They were determined to go, and I thought myself it was the best thing for them to do.

"Put him to bed and keep him there, and he'll be as right as rain to-morrow."

Mrs. Craig took one of his arms and I took the other; Miss Gray opened the door, and though still a bit shaky, he was able to walk. When we arrived at the Craig's home, I offered to go in and help undress him; but they would neither of them hear of it. I went back to Miss Gray's and found them at dessert.

"I wonder why he fainted," Miss Gray was saying. "All the windows are open, and it's not particularly hot to-day."

"I wonder," said the judge.

I noticed that his thin pale face bore an expression of some complacency. We had our coffee; and then, since the judge and I were going to play golf, we got into the car and drove up the hill to my house.

"How did Miss Gray get to know those people?" Landon asked me. "They struck me as rather second-rate. I shouldn't have thought they were very much her mark."

"You know women. She likes her privacy, and when they settled in next door, she was quite decided that she wouldn't have anything to do with them; but when she discovered that they didn't want to have anything to do with her, she couldn't rest till she'd made their acquaintance."

I told him the story she had invented about her neighbours. He listened with an expressionless face.

"I'm afraid your friend Miss Gray is a sentimental donkey, my dear fellow," he said when I had come to an end. "I tell you, women ought to marry. She'd soon have had all that nonsense knocked out of her if she'd had half a dozen brats."

"What do you know about the Craigs?" I asked.

He gave me a frigid glance.

"I? Why should I know anything about them? I thought they were very ordinary people."

I wish I knew how to describe the strong impression he gave me, both by the glacial austerity of his look and by the rasping finality of his tone, that he was not prepared to say anything more. We finished the drive in silence.

Landon was well on in his sixties, and he was the kind of golfer who never hits a long ball but is never off the straight, and he was a deadly putter, so, though he gave me strokes, he beat me handsomely. After dinner I took him in to Monte Carlo, where he finished the evening by winning a couple of thousand francs at the roulette table. These successive events put him into a remarkably good humour.

"A very pleasant day," he said when we parted for the night. "I've thoroughly enjoyed it."

I spent the next morning at work, and we did not meet till lunch. We were just finishing when I was called to the telephone.

When I came back, my guest was drinking a second cup of coffee.

"That was Miss Gray," I said.

"Oh? What had she to say?"

"The Craigs have done a bolt. They disappeared last night. The maids live in the village; and when they came this morning, they found the house empty. They'd skipped—the Craigs, the nurse and the baby—and taken their luggage with them. They left money on the table for the maids' wages, the rent to the end of their tenancy and the tradesmen's bills."

The judge said nothing. He took a cigar from the box, examined it carefully and then lit it with deliberation.

"What have you got to say about that?" I asked.

"My dear fellow, are you obliged to use these American phrases? Isn't English good enough for you?"

"Is that an American phrase? It expresses exactly what I mean. You can't imagine I'm such a fool as not to have noticed that you and the Craigs had met before; and if they've vanished into thin air like figments of the imagination, it's a fairly reasonable conclusion that the circumstances under which you met were not altogether pleasant."

The judge gave a little chuckle, and there was a twinkle in his cold blue eyes.

"That was a very good brandy you gave me last night," he said. "It's against my principles to drink liqueurs after lunch, but it's a very dull man who allows his principles to enslave him, and for once I think I should enjoy one."

I sent for the brandy and watched the judge while he poured himself out a generous measure. He took a sip with obvious satisfaction.

"Do you remember the Wingford murder?" he asked me.

"No."

"Perhaps you weren't in England at the time. Pity—you might have come to the trial. You'd have enjoyed it. It caused a lot of excitement; the papers were full of it.

"Miss Wingford was a rich spinster of mature age who lived in the country with a companion. She was a healthy woman for her age; and when she died rather suddenly, her friends were surprised. Her physician, a fellow called Brandon, signed the certificate and she was duly buried. The will was read, and it appeared that she had left everything she had, something between sixty and seventy thousand pounds, to her companion. The relations were very sore, but there was nothing they could do about it. The will had been drawn up by her lawyer and witnessed by his clerk and Dr. Brandon.

"But Miss Wingford had a maid who had been with her for thirty years and had always understood that she would be remembered in the will; she claimed that Miss Wingford had promised to leave her well provided for, and when she found that she wasn't even mentioned, she flew into a passion. She told the nephew and the two nieces who had come down for the funeral that she was sure Miss Wingford had been poisoned, and she said that if they didn't go to the police, she'd go herself. Well, they didn't do that, but they went to see Dr. Brandon. He laughed. He said that Miss Wingford had had a weak heart and he'd been treating her for years. She died just as he had always expected her to die, peacefully in her sleep; and he advised them not to pay any attention to what the maid said. She had always hated the companion, a Miss Starling, and been jealous of her. Dr. Brandon was highly respected; he had been Miss Wingford's doctor for a long time, and the two nieces, who'd stayed with her often, knew him well. He was not profiting by the will, and there seemed no reason to doubt his word, so the family thought there was nothing to do but make the best of a bad job and went back to London.

"But the maid went on talking; she talked so much that at last the police, much against their will, I must admit, were obliged to take notice, and an order to exhume the body was made. There was an inquest, and it was found that Miss Wingford had died from an overdose of veronal. The coroner's jury found that it had been administered by Miss Starling, and she was arrested. A detective was sent down from Scotland Yard, and he got together some unexpected evidence. It appeared that there'd been a good deal of gossip about Miss Starling and Dr. Brandon. They'd been seen a lot together in places in which there was no reason for them to be except that they wanted to be together, and the general impression in the village was that they were only waiting for Miss Wingford to die to get married. That put a very different complexion on the case. To make a long story short, the police got enough evidence in their opinion to justify them in arresting the doctor and charging him and Miss Starling with the murder of the old lady."

The judge took another sip of brandy.

"The case came up for trial before me. The case for the prosecution was that the accused were madly in love with one another and had done the poor old lady to death so that they could carry on the fortune Miss Starling had wheedled her employer into leaving her. Miss Wingford always had a cup of cocoa when she went to bed, which Miss Starling prepared for her; and the counsel for the prosecution claimed that it was in this that Miss Starling had dissolved the tablets that caused Miss Wingford's death. The accused elected to give evidence on their own behalf, and they made a miserable showing in the witness-box. They lied their heads off. Though witnesses testified they had seen them walking together at night with their arms round one another's waists, though Brandon's maid testified she had seen them kissing one another in the doctor's house, they swore they were no more than friends. And oddly enough, medical evidence proved that Miss Starling was *virgo intacta*.

"Brandon admitted that he had given Miss Wingford a bottle of veronal tablets because she complained of sleeplessness, but declared he had warned her never to take more than one, and then only when absolutely necessary. The defence sought to prove that she had taken the tablets either by accident or because she wanted to commit suicide. That didn't hold water for a moment. Miss Wingford was a jolly, normal old lady who thoroughly enjoyed life; and her death occurred two days before the expected arrival of an old friend for a week's visit. She hadn't complained to the maid of sleeping badly—in fact, her maid had always thought her a very good sleeper. It was impossible to believe that she had accidentally taken a sufficient number of tablets to kill herself. Personally, I had no doubt that it was a put-up job between the doctor and the companion. The motive was obvious and sufficient. I summed up and I hope summed up fairly; but it was my duty to put the facts before the jury, and to my mind the facts were damning. The jury filed out. I don't suppose you know that when you are sitting on the bench, you somehow get the feeling of the court. You have to be on your guard against it, to be sure it doesn't influence you. I never had it more strongly than on that day that there wasn't a soul in court who wasn't convinced that those two people had committed the crime with which they were charged. I hadn't the shadow of a doubt that the jury would bring in a verdict of guilty. Juries are incalculable. They were out for three hours, and when they came back I knew at once that I was mistaken. In a murder case, when a jury is going to bring in a verdict of guilty they won't look at the prisoner; they look away. I noticed that three or four of the jurymen glanced at the two prisoners in the dock. They brought in a verdict of not guilty. The real names of Mr. and Mrs. Craig are Dr. and Mrs. Brandon. I'm just as certain as I am that I'm sitting here that they committed between them a cruel and heartless murder and richly deserved to be hanged."

"What do you think made the jury find them not guilty?"

"I've asked myself that; and do you know the only explanation I can give? The fact that it was conclusively proved that they had never been lovers. And if you come to think of it, that's one of the most curious features of the whole case. That woman was prepared to commit murder to get the man she loved, but she wasn't prepared to have an illicit love-affair with him."

"Human nature is very odd, isn't it?"

"Very," said Landon, helping himself to another glass of brandy.

THE VOICE OF THE TURTLE

FOR SOME TIME I could not make up my mind if I liked Peter Melrose or not. He had had a novel published that had caused some stir among the rather dreary but worthy people who are always on the lookout for new talent. Elderly gentlemen with nothing much to do but go to luncheon parties praised it with girlish enthusiasm, and wiry little women who didn't get on with their husbands thought it showed promise. I read a few reviews. They contradicted one another freely. Some of the critics claimed that with this first novel the author had sprung into the front rank of English novelists: others reviled it. I did not read it. I have learnt by experience that when a book makes a sensation it is just as well to wait a year before you read it. It is astonishing how many books then you need not read at all. But it chanced that one day I met Peter Melrose. With some misgiving I had accepted an invitation to a sherry party. It was in the top flat of a converted house in Bloomsbury, and I was a trifle out of breath when I had climbed four flights of stairs. My hostesses were two women, much over life-size, in early middle life, the sort of women who know all about the insides of motor-cars and like a good tramp in the rain, but very feminine for all that, fond of eating out of paper bags. The drawing-room, which they called "our work-shop," though being of independent means neither had ever done a stroke of work in her life, was large and bare, furnished with rustless-steel chairs, which looked as though they could with difficulty support the very substantial weight of their owners, glass-topped tables and a vast divan covered with zebra-skin. On the walls were book-shelves, and pictures by the better-known English imitators of Cézanne, Braque and Picasso. In the shelves, besides a number of "curious" books of the eighteenth century (for pornography is age-less) there were only the works of living authors, mostly first editions, and it was indeed to sign some of my own that I had been asked to the party.

It was quite small. There was but one other woman, who might have been a younger sister of my hostesses, for, though stout, she was not quite so stout, though tall, not quite so tall, and though hearty, not quite so hearty. I did not catch her name, but she answered to that of Boofuls. The only man be-sides myself was Peter Melrose. He was quite young, twenty-two or twenty-three, of the middle height, but with an ungainly figure that made him look squat. He had a reddish skin that seemed to fit over the bones of his face too tightly, a rather large Semitic nose, though he was not a Jew, and alert green eyes under bushy eyebrows. His brown hair, cut very short, was scurfy. He was dressed in the brown Norfolk jacket and grey flannel trousers that are worn by the art students who wander hatless along King's Road, Chelsea. An uncouth young man. Nor was there must to attract in his manner. He was self-assertive, disputatious and intolerant. He had a hearty con-tempt for his fellow-writers which he expressed with zest. The satisfaction he gave me by his breezy attacks on reputations which for my part I considered exaggerated, but prudently held my tongue about, was only lessened by the conviction that no sooner was my back turned than he would tear my own to shreds. He talked well. He was amusing and sometimes witty. I should have laughed at his sallies more easily if those three ladies had not been so unreasonably convulsed by them. They roared with laughter at what he said, whether it was funny or whether it was inept. He said many silly things, for he talked without stopping, but he also said some very clever ones. He had a point of view, crude and not so original as he thought, but sincere. But the most striking thing about him was his eager, impetuous vitality; it was like a hot flame that burnt him with an unendurable fury. It even shed a glow on those about him. He had something, if only that, and when I left it was with a slight sense of curiosity at what would come of him. I did not know if he had talent; so many young things can write a clever novel—that means nothing; but it seemed to me that as a man he was not quite like everybody else. He was the sort of person who at thirty, when time had softened his asperity and experience had taught him that he was not quite so intelligent as he thought, would turn into an interesting and agreeable fellow. But I never expected to see him again.

It was with surprise that I received two or three days later a copy of his novel with a very flattering dedication. I read it. It was obviously autobiographical. The scene was a small town in Sussex, and the characters of the upper middle class that strives to keep up appearances on an inadequate income. The humour was rather brutal and rather vulgar. It grated on me, for it consisted chiefly of mockery at people because they were old and poor. Peter Melrose did not know how hard those misfortunes are to bear, and that the efforts made to cope with them are more deserving of sympathy than of derision. But there were descriptions of places, little pictures of a room or impressions of the countryside, which were excellently done. They showed tenderness and a sense of the spiritual beauty of material things. The book was written easily, without affectation, and with a pleasant feeling for the sound of words. But what made it indeed somewhat remarkable, so that I understood why it had attracted attention, was the passion that quivered in the love story of which the plot, such as it was, consisted. It was, as is the modern fashion, more than a trifle coarse and, again in the modern fashion, it tailed off vaguely, without any particular result, so that everything was left in the end pretty much as it had been in the beginning; but you did get the impression of young love, idealistic and yet vehemently sexual; it was so vivid and so deeply felt that it took your breath away. It seemed to throb on the printed page like the pulse of life. It had no reticence. It was absurd, scandalous and beautiful. It was like a force of nature. That was passion all right. There is nothing, anywhere, so moving and so awe-inspiring.

I wrote to Peter Melrose and told him what I thought of his book, then suggested that we might lunch together. He rang me up next day and we made a date.

I found him unaccountably shy when we sat down opposite one another at a table in a restaurant. I gave him a cocktail. He talked glibly enough, but I could not help seeing that he was ill at ease. I gained the impression that his self-assurance was a pose assumed to conceal, from himself, maybe, a diffidence that tortured him. His manners were brusque and awkward. He would say a rude thing and then laugh nervously to cover his own embarrassment. Though he pretended to be so sure of himself he wanted all the time to be reassured by you. By irritating you, by saying the things he thought would annoy, he tried to force from you some admission, tacit it might be, that he was as wonderful as he longed to think himself. He wanted to despise the opinion of his fellows, and nothing was more important to him. I thought him rather an odious young man, but I did not mind that. It is very natural that clever young men should be rather odious. They are conscious of gifts that they do not know how to use. They are exasperated with the world that will not recognise their merit. They have something to give, and no hand is stretched out to receive it. They are impatient for the fame they regard as their due. No, I do not mind odious young men; it is when they are charming that I button up the pockets of my sympathy.

Peter Melrose was extremely modest about his book. He blushed through his reddish skin when I praised what I liked in it, and accepted my strictures with a humility that was almost embarrassing. He had made very little money out of it, and his publishers were giving him a small monthly allowance in advance of royalties on the next one. This he had just started, but he wanted to get away to write it in peace, and knowing I lived on the Riviera he asked me if I could tell him of a quiet place where he could bathe and live cheaply. I suggested that he should come and spend a few days with me so that he could look about till he found something to suit him. His green eyes sparkled when I proposed this and he flushed.

"Shouldn't I be an awful nuisance?"

"No. I shall be working. All I can offer you is three meals a day and a room to sleep in. It'll be very dull, but you can do exactly what you like."

"It sounds grand. May I let you know if I decide to come?"

"Of course."

We separated, and a week or two later I went home. This was in May. Early in June I received a letter from Peter Melrose asking, if I had really meant what I said when I invited him to spend a few days with me, whether he might arrive on such and such a date. Well, at the time I had meant it, but now, a month later, I remembered that he was an arrogant and ill-bred youth, whom I had seen but twice and wasn't in the least interested in, and I didn't mean it any longer. It seemed to me very likely that he would be bored stiff. I lived a very quiet life and saw few people. And I thought it would be a great strain on my nerves if he were as rude as I knew he could be, and I as his host felt it behoved me to keep my temper. I saw myself driven beyond endurance, and ringing the bell to have his clothes packed and the car brought round to take him away within half an hour. But there was nothing to do about it. It would save him the cost of board and lodging to spend a short period with me, and if he was tired and unhappy as he said in his letter it might be that it would do him good. I sent him a wire and shortly afterwards he arrived.

He looked very hot and grubby in his grey flannel trousers and brown tweed coat when I met him at the station, but after a swim in the pool he changed into white shorts and a Cochet shirt. He looked then quite absurdly young. He had never been out of England before. He was excited. It was touching to see his delight. He seemed, amid those unaccustomed surroundings, to lose his sense of himself, and he was simple, boyish and modest. I was agreeably surprised. In the evening, after dinner, sitting in the garden, with only the croaking of the little green frogs to break the silence, he began talking to me of his novel. It was a romantic story about a young writer and a celebrated prima donna. The theme was reminiscent of Ouida, the last thing I should have expected this hard-boiled youth to write, and I was tickled; it was odd how the fashion completed the circle and returned generation after generation to the same themes. I had no doubt that Peter Melrose would treat it in a very modern way, but there it was, the same old story as had entranced sentimental readers in the three-volume novels of the eighties. He proposed to set it in the beginning of the Edwardian era, which to the young has already acquired the fantastic, far-away feeling of a past age. He talked and talked. He was not unpleasant to listen to. He had no notion that he was putting into fiction his own day-dreams, the comic and touching day-dreams of a rather unattractive, obscure young man who sees himself beloved, to the admiration of the whole world, by an incredibly beautiful, celebrated and magnificent woman. I always enjoyed the novels of Ouida and Peter's idea did not at all displease me. With his charming gift of description, his vivid, ingenuous way of looking at material things, fabrics, pieces of furniture, walls, trees, flowers, and his power of representing the

passion of life, the passion of love, that thrilled every fibre of
his own uncouth body, I had a notion that he might well produce something exuberant, absurd and poetical. But I asked
him a question.

"Have you ever known a prima donna?"

"No, but I've read all the autobiographies and memoirs that
I could find. I've gone into it pretty thoroughly. Not only the
obvious things, you know, but I've hunted around in all sorts of
byways to get the revealing touch or the suggestive anecdote."

"And have you got what you wanted?"

"I think so."

He began to describe his heroine to me. She was young and
beautiful, wilful it is true and with a quick temper, but mag-
nanimous. A woman on the grand scale. Music was her passion;
there was music not only in her voice, but in her gestures and
in her inmost thoughts. She was devoid of envy, and her appreciation of art was such that when another singer had done her
an injury she forgave her when she heard her sing a role beautifully. She was of a wonderful generosity, and would give away
everything she possessed when a story of misfortune touched
her soft heart. She was a great lover, prepared to sacrifice the
world for the man she loved. She was intelligent and well-read.
She was tender, unselfish and disinterested. In fact she was
much too good to be true.

"I think you'd better meet a prima donna," I said at last.

"How can I?"

"Have you ever heard of La Falterona?"

"Of course I have. I've read her memoirs."

"She lives just along the coast. I'll ring her up and ask her to
dinner."

"Will you really? It would be wonderful."

"Don't blame me if you don't find her quite what you
expect."

"It's the truth I want."

Everyone has heard of La Falterona. Not even Melba had a
greater reputation. She had ceased now to sing in opera, but her
voice was still lovely, and she could fill a concert hall in any
part of the world. She went for long tours every winter, and in
summer rested in a villa by the sea. On the Riviera people are
neighbours if they live thirty miles from one another, and for
some years I had seen a good deal of La Falterona. She was a
woman of ardent temperament, and she was celebrated not only

for her singing, but for her love affairs: she never minded talking about them, and I had often sat entranced for hours while with the humour which to me was her most astonishing characteristic she regaled me with lurid tales of royal or very opulent adorers. I was satisfied that there was at least a measure of truth in them. She had been married, for short periods, three or four times, and in one of these unions had annexed a Neapolitan prince. Thinking that to be known as La Falterona was grander than any title, she did not use his name (to which indeed she had no right, since after divorcing him she had married somebody else); but her silver, her cutlery and her dinner-service were heavily decorated with a coat of arms and a crown, and her servants invariably addressed her as *madame la princesse*. She claimed to be a Hungarian, but her English was perfect; she spoke it with a slight accent (when she remembered), but with an intonation suggestive, I had been told, of Kansas City. This she explained by saying that her father was a political exile who had fled to America when she was no more than a child; but she did not seem quite sure whether he was a distinguished scientist who had got into trouble for his liberal views, or a Magyar of high rank who had brought down on his head the imperial wrath because he had had a love affair with an Archduchess. It depended on whether she was just an artist among artists, or a great lady among persons of noble birth.

With me she was not natural, for that she could never have been if she had tried, but franker than with anyone else. She had a natural and healthy contempt for the arts. She genuinely looked upon the whole thing as a gigantic bluff, and deep down in her heart was an amused sympathy for all the people who were able to put it over on the public. I will admit that I looked forward to the encounter between Peter Melrose and La Falterona with a good deal of sardonic amusement.

She liked coming to dine with me because she knew the food was good. It was the only meal she ate in the day, for she took great care of her figure, but she liked that one to be succulent and ample. I asked her to come at nine, knowing that was the earliest hour she dreamt of eating, and ordered dinner for half past. She turned up at a quarter to ten. She was dressed in apple-green satin, cut very low in front, with no back at all, and she wore a string of huge pearls, a number of expensive-looking rings, and on her left arm diamond and emerald bracelets from the wrist to the elbow. Two or three of them were certainly real.

On her raven-black hair was a thin circlet of diamonds. She could not have looked more splendid if she had been going to a ball at Stafford House in the old days. We were in white ducks.

"How grand you are," I said. "I told you it wasn't a party."

She flashed a look of her magnificent black eyes at Peter.

"Of course it's a party. You told me your friend was a writer of talent. I am only an interpreter." She ran one finger down her flashing bracelets. "This is the homage I pay to the creative artist."

I did not utter the vulgar monosyllable that rose to my lips, but offered her what I knew was her favourite cocktail. I was privileged to call her Maria, and she always called me Master. This she did, first because she knew it made me feel a perfect fool, and secondly because, though she was in point of fact not more than two or three years younger than I, it made it quite clear that we belonged to different generations. Sometimes, however, she also called me you dirty swine. This evening she certainly might very well have passed for thirty-five. She had those rather large features which somehow do not seem to be-tray age. On the stage she was a beautiful woman, and even in private life, notwithstanding her big nose, large mouth and fleshy face, a good-looking one. She wore a brown make-up, with dark rouge, and her lips were vividly scarlet. She looked very Spanish and, I suspected, felt it, for her accent at the beginning of dinner was quite Sevillian. I wanted her to talk so that Peter should get his money's worth, and I knew there was but one subject in the world that she could talk about. She was in point of fact a stupid woman who had acquired a line of glib chatter which made people on first meeting her think she was as brilliant as she looked; but it was merely a performance she gave, and you soon discovered that she not only did not know what she was talking about, but was not in the least interested in it. I do not think she had ever read a book in her life. Her knowledge of what was going on in the world was confined to what she was able to gather by looking at the pictures in the illustrated press. Her passion for music was complete bunkum. Once at a concert to which I went with her she slept all through the Fifth Symphony, and I was charmed to hear her during the interval telling people that Beethoven stirred her so much that she hesitated to come and hear him, for with those glorious themes singing through her head, it meant that she wouldn't sleep a wink all night. I could well believe she would lie awake, for she had had so sound a nap during the Symphony that it could not but interfere with her night's rest.

But there was one subject in which her interest never failed. She pursued it with indefatigable energy. No obstacle prevented her from returning to it; no chance word was so remote that she could not use it as a stepping-stone to come back to it, and in effecting this she displayed a cleverness of which one would never have thought her capable. On this subject she could be witty, vivacious, philosophic, tragic and inventive. It enabled her to exhibit all the resources of her ingenuity. There was no end to its ramifications, and no limit to its variety. This subject was herself. I gave her an opening at once and then all I had to do was to make suitable interjections. She was in great form. We were dining on the terrace and a full moon was obligingly shining on the sea in front of us. Nature, as though she knew what was proper to the occasion, had set just the right scene. The view was framed by two tall black cypresses, and all round us on the terrace the orange trees in full flower exhaled their heady perfume. There was no wind, and the candles on the table flamed with a steady softness. It was a light that exactly suited La Falterona. She sat between us, eating heartily and thoroughly appreciating the champagne, and she was enjoying herself. She gave the moon a glance. On the sea was a broad pathway of silver.

"How beautiful nature is," she said. "My God, the scenery one has to play in. How can they expect one to sing? You know, really, the sets at Covent Garden are a disgrace. The last time I sang Juliet I just told them I wouldn't go on unless they did something about the moon."

Peter listened to her in silence. He ate her words. She was better value than I had dared to hope. She got a little tight not only on the champagne but on her own loquaciousness. To listen to her you would have thought she was a meek and docile creature against whom the whole world was in conspiracy. Her life had been one long bitter struggle against desperate odds. Managers treated her vilely, impresarios played foul tricks on her, singers combined to ruin her, critics bought by the money of her enemies wrote scandalous things about her, lovers for whom she had sacrificed everything used her with base ingratitude; and yet, by the miracle of her genius and her quick wits, she had discomfited them all. With joyous glee, her eyes flashing, she told us how she had defeated their machinations and what disaster had befallen the wretches who had stood in her way. I wondered how she had the nerve to tell the disgraceful stories she told. Without the smallest consciousness of what she was doing she showed herself vindictive and envious, hard as nails, incredibly vain, cruel, selfish, scheming and mercenary. I stole a glance now and then at Peter. I was tickled at the confusion he must be experiencing when he compared his ideal picture of the prima donna with the ruthless reality. She was a woman without a heart. When at last she left us I turned to Peter with a smile.

"Well," I said, "at all events you've got some good material."

"I know, and it all fits in so beautifully," he said with enthusiasm.

"Does it?" I exclaimed, taken aback.

"She's exactly like my woman. She'll never believe that I'd sketched out the main lines of the character before I'd ever seen her."

I stared at him in amazement.

"The passion for art. The disinterestedness. She has that same nobility of soul that I saw in my mind's eye. The small-minded, the curious, the vulgar put every obstacle in her way and she sweeps them all aside by the greatness of her purpose and the purity of her ends." He gave a little happy laugh. "Isn't it wonderful how nature copies art? I swear to you, I've got her to the life."

I was about to speak; I held my tongue; though I shrugged a spiritual shoulder I was touched. Peter had seen in her what he was determined to see. There was something very like beauty in his illusion. In his own way he was a poet. We went to bed, and two or three days later, having found a pension to his liking, he left me.

In course of time his book appeared, and like most second novels by young people it had but a very moderate success. The critics had overpraised his first effort and now were unduly censorious. It is of course a very different thing to write a novel about yourself and the people you have known from childhood and to write one about persons of your own invention. Peter's was too long. He had allowed his gift for word-painting to run away with him, the humour was still rather vulgar; but he had reconstructed the period with skill, and the romantic story had that same thrill of real passion which in his first book had so much impressed me.

After dinner at my house I did not see La Falterona for more than a year. She went for a long tour in South America and did not come down to the Riviera till late in the summer. One night she asked me to dine with her. We were alone but for her companion-secretary, an Englishwoman, Miss Glaser by name, whom La Falterona bullied and ill-treated, hit and swore at, but whom she could not do without. Miss Glaser was a haggard person of fifty, with grey hair and a sallow, wrinkled face. She was a queer creature. She knew everything there was to be known about La Falterona. She both adored and hated her. Behind her back she could be extremely funny at her expense, and the imitation she gave in secret of the great singer with her admirers was the most richly comic thing I have ever heard. But she watched over her like a mother. It was she who, sometimes by wheedling, sometimes by sheer plainness of speech, caused La Falterona to behave herself something like a human being. It was she who had written the singer's exceedingly inaccurate memoirs.

La Falterona wore pale-blue satin pyjamas (she liked satin) and, presumably to rest her hair, a green silk wig; except for a few rings, a pearl necklace, a couple of bracelets and a diamond brooch at her waist, she wore no jewellery. She had much to tell me of her triumphs in South America. She talked on and on. She had never been in more superb voice and the ovations she had received were unparalleled. The concert halls were sold out for every performance, and she had made a packet.

"Is it true or is it not true, Glaser?" cried Maria with a strong South American accent.

"Most of it," said Miss Glaser.

La Falterona had the objectionable habit of addressing her companion by her surname. But it must long since have ceased to annoy the poor woman, so there was not much point in it.

"Who was that man we met in Buenos Aires?"

"Which man?"

"You fool, Glaser. You remember perfectly. The man I was married to once."

"Pepe Zapata," Miss Glaser replied without a smile.

"He was broke. He had the impudence to ask me to give him back a diamond necklace he'd given me. He said it had belonged to his mother."

"It wouldn't have hurt you to give it him," said Miss Glaser. "You never wear it."

"Give it him back?" cried La Falterona, and her astonishment was such that she spoke the purest English. "Give it him back? You're crazy."

She looked at Miss Glaser as though she expected her there and then to have an attack of acute mania. She got up from the table, for we had finished our dinner.

"Let us go outside," she said. "If I hadn't the patience of an angel I'd have sacked that woman long ago."

La Falterona and I went out, but Miss Glaser did not come with us. We sat on the verandah. There was a magnificent cedar in the garden, and its dark branches were silhouetted against the starry sky. The sea, almost at our feet, was marvellously still. Suddenly La Falterona gave a start.

"I almost forgot. Glaser, you fool," she shouted, "why didn't you remind me?" And then again to me: "I'm furious with you."

"I'm glad you didn't remember till after dinner," I answered.

"That friend of yours and his book."

I didn't immediately grasp what she was talking about.

"What friend and what book?"

"Don't be so stupid. An ugly little man with a shiny face and a bad figure. He wrote a book about me."

"Oh! Peter Melrose. But it's not about you."

"Of course it is. Do you take me for a fool? He had the impudence to send it me."

"I hope you had the decency to acknowledge it."

"Do you think I have the time to acknowledge all the books twopenny-halfpenny authors send me? I expect Glaser wrote to him. You had no right to ask me to dinner to meet him. I came to oblige you, because I thought you liked me for myself, I didn't know I was just being made use of. It's awful that one can't trust one's oldest friends to behave like gentlemen. I'll never dine with you again so long as I live. Never, never, never."

She was working herself into one of her tantrums, so I interrupted her before it was too late.

"Come off it, my dear," I said. "In the first place the character of the singer in that book, which I suppose is the one you're referring to . . ."

"You don't suppose I'm referring to the charwoman, do you?"

"Well, the character of the singer was roughed out before he'd even seen you, and besides, it isn't in the least like you."

"How d'you mean, it's not like me? All my friends have recognised me. I mean, it's the most obvious portrait."

"Mary," I expostulated.

"My name is Maria and no one knows it better than you, and if you can't call me Maria you can call me Madame Falterona or Princess."

I paid no attention to this.

"Did you read the book?"

"Of course I read it. When everyone told me it was about me."

"But the boy's heroine, the prima donna, is twenty-five."

"A woman like me is ageless."

"She's musical to her finger-tips, gentle as a dove, and a miracle of unselfishness; she's frank, loyal and disinterested. Is that the opinion you have of yourself?"

"And what is *your* opinion of me?"

"Hard as nails, absolutely ruthless, a born intriguer and as self-centred as they make 'em."

She then called me a name which a lady does not habitually apply to a gentleman who, whatever his faults, has never had his legitimacy called in question. But though her eyes flashed I could see that she was not in the least angry. She accepted my description of her as complimentary.

"And what about the emerald ring? Are you going to deny that I told him that?"

The story of the emerald ring was this: La Falterona was having a passionate love-affair with the Crown Prince of a powerful state and he had made her a present of an emerald of immense value. One night they had a quarrel, high words passed, and some reference being made to the ring she tore it off her finger and flung it in the fire. The Crown Prince, being a man of thrifty habit, with a cry of consternation, threw himself on his knees and began raking out the coals till he recovered the ring. The Falterona watched him scornfully as he grovelled on the floor. She didn't give much away herself, but she could not bear economy in others. She finished the story with these splendid words:

"After that I *couldn't* love him."

The incident was picturesque and had taken Peter's fancy. He had used it very neatly.

"I told you both about that in the greatest confidence and I've never told it to a soul before. It's a scandalous breach of confidence to have put it into a book. There are no excuses either for him or for you."

"But I've heard you tell the story dozens of times. And it was told me by Florence Montgomerie about herself and the Crown Prince Rudolf. It was one of her favourite stories too. Lola Montez used to tell it about herself and the King of Bavaria. I have little doubt that Nell Gwyn told it about herself and Charles II. It's one of the oldest stories in the world."

She was taken aback, but only for an instant.

"I don't see anything strange in its having happened more than once. Everyone knows that women are passionate and that men are as mean as cat's-meat. I could show you the emerald if you liked. I had to have it reset, of course."

"With Lola Montez it was pearls," I said ironically. "I believe they were considerably damaged."

"Pearls?" She gave that brilliant smile of hers. "Have I ever told you about Benjy Riesenbaum and the pearls? You might make a story out of it."

Benjy Riesenbaum was a person of great wealth, and it was common knowledge that for a long time he had been the Falterona's lover. In fact it was he who had bought her the luxurious little villa in which we were now sitting.

"He'd given me a very handsome string in New York. I was singing at the Metropolitan, and at the end of the season we travelled back to Europe together. You never knew him, did you?"

"No."

"Well, he wasn't bad in some ways, but he was insanely jealous. We had a row on the boat because a young Italian officer was paying me a good deal of attention. Heaven knows, I'm the easiest woman in the world to get on with, but I will not be bullied by any man. After all, I have my self-respect to think of. I told him where he got off, if you understand what I mean, and he slapped my face. On deck if you please. I don't mind telling you I was mad. I tore the string of pearls off my neck and flung it in the sea. 'They cost fifty thousand dollars,' he gasped. He went white. I drew myself up to my full height. 'I only valued them because I loved you,' I said. And I turned on my heel."

"You were a fool," I said.

"I wouldn't speak to him for twenty-four hours. At the end of that time I had him eating out of my hand. When we got to Paris the first thing he did was to go to Cartier's and buy me another just as good."

She began to giggle.

"Did you say I was a fool? I'd left the real string in the bank in New York, because I knew I was going back next season. It was an imitation one that I threw in the sea."

She started to laugh, and her laugh was rich and joyous and like a child's. That was the sort of trick that thoroughly appealed to her. She chortled with glee.

"What fools men are," she gasped. "And you, you thought I'd throw a real string into the sea."

She laughed and laughed. At last she stopped. She was excited.

"I want to sing. Glaser, play an accompaniment."

A voice came from the drawing-room.

"You can't sing after all that food you walloped down."

"Shut up, you old cow. Play something, I tell you."

There was no reply, but in a moment Miss Glaser began to play the opening bars of one of Schumann's songs. It was no strain on the voice, and I guessed that Miss Glaser knew what she was doing when she chose it. La Falterona began to sing, in an undertone, but as she heard the sounds come from her lips and found that they were clear and pure she let herself go. The song finished. There was silence. Miss Glaser had heard that La Falterona was in magnificent voice, and she sensed that she wished to sing again. The prima donna was standing in the window, with her back to the lighted room, and she looked out at the darkly shining sea. The cedar made a lovely pattern against the sky. The night was soft and balmy. Miss Glaser played a couple of bars. A cold shiver ran down my spine. La Falterona gave a little start as she recognised the music, and I felt her gather herself together.

> "*Mild und leise wie er lächelt*
> *Wie das Auge er öffnet.*"

It was Isolde's death song. She had never sung in Wagner, fearing the strain on her voice, but this, I suppose, she had often sung in concerts. It did not matter now that instead of an orchestral accompaniment she had only the thin tinkle of a piano. The notes of the heavenly melody fell upon the still air and travelled over the water. In that too romantic scene, in that starry night, the effect was shattering. La Falterona's voice, even now, was exquisite in its quality, mellow and crystalline; and she sang with wonderful emotion, so tenderly, with such tragic, beautiful anguish that my heart melted within me. I had a most awkward lump in my throat when she finished, and looking at her I saw that tears were streaming down her face. I did not want to speak. She stood quite still looking out at that ageless sea.

What a strange woman! I thought then that I would sooner have her as she was, with her monstrous faults, than as Peter Melrose saw her, a pattern of all the virtues. But then people blame me because I rather like people who are a little worse than is reasonable. She was hateful, of course, but she was irresistible.

THE FACTS OF LIFE

It was Henry Garnet's habit on leaving the city of an afternoon to drop in at his club and play bridge before going home to dinner. He was a pleasant man to play with. He knew the game well and you could be sure that he would make the best of his cards. He was a good loser; and when he won was more inclined to ascribe his success to his luck than to his skill. He was indulgent, and if his partner made a mistake could be trusted to find an excuse for him. It was surprising then on this occasion to hear him telling his partner with unnecessary sharpness that he had never seen a hand worse played; and it was more surprising still to see him not only make a grave error himself, an error of which you would never have thought him capable, but when his partner, not unwilling to get a little of his own back, pointed it out, insist against all reason and with considerable heat that he was perfectly right. But they were all old friends, the men he was playing with, and none of them took his ill-humour very seriously. Henry Garnet was a broker, a partner in a firm of repute, and it occurred to one of them that something had gone wrong with some stock he was interested in.

"How's the market to-day?" he asked.

"Booming. Even the suckers are making money."

It was evident that stocks and shares had nothing to do with Henry Garnet's vexation; but something was the matter; that was evident too. He was a hearty fellow, who enjoyed excellent health; he had plenty of money; he was fond of his wife and de-

voted to his children. As a rule he had high spirits, and he
laughed easily at the nonsense they were apt to talk while they
played; but to-day he sat glum and silent. His brows were
crossly puckered and there was a sulky look about his mouth.
Presently, to ease the tension, one of the others mentioned a
subject upon which they all knew Henry Garnet was glad to
speak.

"How's your boy, Henry? I see he's done pretty well in the
tournament."

Henry Garnet's frown grew darker.

"He's done no better than I expected him to."

"When does he come back from Monte?"

"He got back last night."

"Did he enjoy himself?"

"I suppose so; all I know is that he made a damned fool of
himself."

"Oh. How?"

"I'd rather not talk about it if you don't mind."

The three men looked at him with curiosity. Henry Garnet
scowled at the green baize.

"Sorry, old boy. Your call."

The game proceeded in a strained silence. Garnet got his bid,
and when he played his cards so badly that he went three down
not a word was said. Another rubber was begun and in the
second game Garnet denied a suit.

"Having none?" his partner asked him.

Garnet's irritability was such that he did not even reply, and
when at the end of the hand it appeared that he had revoked,
and that his revoke cost the rubber, it was not to be expected
that his partner should let his carelessness go without remark.

"What the devil's the matter with you, Henry?" he said.
"You're playing like a fool."

Garnet was disconcerted. He did not so much mind losing a
big rubber himself, but he was sore that his inattention should
have made his partner lose too. He pulled himself together.

"I'd better not play any more. I thought a few rubbers would
calm me, but the fact is I can't give my mind to the game. To
tell you the truth I'm in a hell of a temper."

They all burst out laughing.

"You don't have to tell us that, old boy. It's obvious."

Garnet gave them a rueful smile.

"Well, I bet you'd be in a temper if what's happened to me

had happened to you. As a matter of fact I'm in a damned awkward situation, and if any of you fellows can give me any advice
how to deal with it I'd be grateful."

"Let's have a drink and you tell us all about it. With a K.C.,
a Home Office official and an eminent surgeon—if we can't tell
you how to deal with a situation, nobody can."

The K.C. got up and rang the bell for a waiter.

"It's about that damned boy of mine," said Henry Garnet.

Drinks were ordered and brought. And this is the story that
Henry Garnet told them.

The boy of whom he spoke was his only son. His name was
Nicholas and of course he was called Nicky. He was eighteen.
The Garnets had two daughters besides, one of sixteen and the
other of twelve, but however unreasonable it seemed, for a
father in generally supposed to like his daughters best, and
though he did all he could not to show his preference, there was
no doubt that the greater share of Henry Garnet's affection was
given to his son. He was kind, in a chaffing, casual way, to his
daughters, and gave them handsome presents on their birthdays
and at Christmas; but he doted on Nicky. Nothing was too good
for him. He thought the world of him. He could hardly take his
eyes off him. You could not blame him, for Nicky was a son that
any parent might have been proud of. He was six foot two, lithe
but muscular, with broad shoulders and a slim waist, and he
held himself gallantly erect; he had a charming head, well
placed on the shoulders, with pale brown hair that waved
slightly, blue eyes with long dark lashes under well-marked eyebrows, a full red mouth and a tanned, clean skin. When he
smiled he showed very regular and very white teeth. He was not
shy, but there was a modesty in his demeanour that was attractive. In social intercourse he was easy, polite and quietly gay.
He was the offspring of nice, healthy, decent parents, he had
been well brought up in a good home, he had been sent to a
good school, and the general result was as engaging a specimen
of young manhood as you were likely to find in a long time. You
felt that he was as honest, open and virtuous as he looked. He
had never given his parents a moment's uneasiness. As a child
he was seldom ill and never naughty. As a boy he did everything that was expected of him. His school reports were excellent. He was wonderfully popular, and he ended his career, with
a creditable number of prizes, as head of the school and captain
of the football team. But this was not all. At the age of fourteen

Nicky had developed an unexpected gift for lawn tennis. This was a game that his father not only was fond of, but played very well, and when he discerned in the boy the promise of a tennis-player he fostered it. During the holidays he had him taught by the best professionals and by the time he was sixteen he had won a number of tournaments for boys of his age. He could beat his father so badly that only parental affection reconciled the older player to the poor show he put up. At eighteen Nicky went to Cambridge and Henry Garnet conceived the ambition that before he was through with the university he should play for it. Nicky had all the qualifications for becoming a great tennis-player. He was tall, he had a long reach, he was quick on his feet and his timing was perfect. He realised instinctively where the ball was coming and, seemingly without hurry, was there to take it. He had a powerful serve, with a nasty break that made it difficult to return, and his forehand drive, low, long and accurate, was deadly. He was not so good on the backhand and his volleying was wild, but all through the summer before he went to Cambridge Henry Garnet made him work on these points under the best teacher in England. At the back of his mind, though he did not even mention it to Nicky, he cherished a further ambition, to see his son play at Wimbledon, and who could tell, perhaps be chosen to represent his country in the Davis Cup. A great lump came into Henry Garnet's throat as he saw in fancy his son leap over the net to shake hands with the American champion whom he had just defeated, and walk off the court to the deafening plaudits of the multitude.

As an assiduous frequenter of Wimbledon Henry Garnet had a good many friends in the tennis world, and one evening he found himself at a City dinner sitting next to one of them, a Colonel Brabazon, and in due course began talking to him of Nicky and what chance there might be of his being chosen to play for his university during the following season.

"Why don't you let him go down to Monte Carlo and play in the spring tournament there?" said the Colonel suddenly.

"Oh, I don't think he's good enough for that. He's not nineteen yet, he only went up to Cambridge last October; he wouldn't stand a chance against all those cracks."

"Of course, Austin and von Cramm and so on would knock spots off him, but he might snatch a game or two; and if he got up against some of the smaller fry there's no reason why he shouldn't win two or three matches. He's never been up against any of the first-rate players and it would be wonderful practice for him. He'd learn a lot more than he'll ever learn in the seaside tournaments you enter him for."

"I wouldn't dream of it. I'm not going to let him leave Cambridge in the middle of a term. I've always impressed upon him that tennis is only a game and it mustn't interfere with work."

Colonel Brabazon asked Garnet when the term ended.

"That's all right. He'd only have to cut about three days. Surely that could be arranged. You see, two of the men we were depending on have let us down, and we're in a hole. We want to send as good a team as we can. The Germans are sending their best players and so are the Americans."

"Nothing doing, old boy. In the first place Nicky's not good enough, and secondly, I don't fancy the idea of sending a kid like that to Monte Carlo without anyone to look after him. If I could get away myself I might think of it, but that's out of the question."

"I shall be there. I'm going as the non-playing captain of the English team. I'll keep an eye on him."

"You'll be busy, and besides, it's not a responsibility I'd like to ask you to take. He's never been abroad in his life, and to tell you the truth, I shouldn't have a moment's peace all the time he was there."

They left it at that and presently Henry Garnet went home. He was so flattered by Colonel Brabazon's suggestion that he could not help telling his wife.

"Fancy his thinking Nicky's as good as that. He told me he'd seen him play and his style was fine. He only wants more practice to get into the first flight. We shall see the kid playing in the semi-finals at Wimbledon yet, old girl."

To his surprise Mrs. Garnet was not so much opposed to the notion as he would have expected.

"After all the boy's eighteen. Nicky's never got into mischief yet and there's no reason to suppose he will now."

"There's his work to be considered; don't forget that. I think it would be a very bad precedent to let him cut the end of term."

"But what can three days matter? It seems a shame to rob him of a chance like that. I'm sure he'd jump at it if you asked him."

"Well, I'm not going to. I haven't sent him to Cambridge just to play tennis. I know he's steady, but it's silly to put temptation in his way. He's much too young to go to Monte Carlo by himself."

"You say he won't have a chance against these crack players, but you can't tell."

Henry Garnet sighed a little. On the way home in the car it had struck him that Austin's health was uncertain and that von Cramm had his off-days. Supposing, just for the sake of argument, that Nicky had a bit of luck like that—then there would be no doubt that he would be chosen to play for Cambridge. But of course that was all nonsense.

"Nothing doing, my dear. I've made up my mind and I'm not going to change it."

Mrs. Garnet held her peace. But next day she wrote to Nicky, telling him what had happened, and suggested to him what she would do in his place if, wanting to go, he wished to get his father's consent. A day or two later Henry Garnet received a letter from his son. He was bubbling over with excitement. He had seen his tutor, who was a tennis-player himself, and the Provost of his college, who happened to know Colonel Brabazon, and no objection would be made to his leaving before the end of term; they both thought it an opportunity that shouldn't be missed. He didn't see what harm he could come to, and if only, just this once, his father would stretch a point, well, next term, he promised faithfully, he'd work like blazes. It was a very pretty letter. Mrs. Garnet watched her husband read it at the breakfast table; she was undisturbed by the frown on his face. He threw it over to her.

"I don't know why you thought it necessary to tell Nicky something I told you in confidence. It's too bad of you. Now you've thoroughly unsettled him."

"I'm sorry. I thought it would please him to know that Colonel Brabazon had such a high opinion of him. I don't see why one should only tell people the disagreeable things that are said about them. Of course I made it quite clear that there could be no question of his going."

"You've put me in an odious position. If there's anything I hate it's for the boy to look upon me as a spoil-sport and a tyrant."

"Oh, he'll never do that. He may think you rather silly and unreasonable, but I'm sure he'll understand that it's only for his own good that you're being so unkind."

"Christ," said Henry Garnet.

His wife had a great inclination to laugh. She knew the battle was won. Dear, oh dear, how easy it was to get men to do what you wanted. For appearance sake Henry Garnet held out for forty-eight hours, but then he yielded, and a fortnight later Nicky came to London. He was to start for Monte Carlo next morning, and after dinner, when Mrs. Garnet and her elder daughter had left them, Henry took the opportunity to give his son some good advice.

"I don't feel quite comfortable about letting you go off to a place like Monte Carlo at your age practically by yourself," he finished, "but there it is and I can only hope you'll be sensible. I don't want to play the heavy father, but there are three things especially that I want to warn you against: one is gambling, don't gamble; the second is money, don't lend anyone money; and the third is women, don't have anything to do with women. If you don't do any of those three things you can't come to much harm, so remember them well."

"All right, father," Nicky smiled.

"That's my last word to you. I know the world pretty well and believe me, my advice is sound."

"I won't forget it. I promise you."

"That's a good chap. Now let's go up and join the ladies."

Nicky beat neither Austin nor von Cramm in the Monte Carlo tournament, but he did not disgrace himself. He snatched an unexpected victory over a Spanish player and gave one of the Austrians a closer match than anyone had thought possible. In the mixed doubles he got into the semi-finals. His charm conquered everyone and he vastly enjoyed himself. It was generally allowed that he showed promise, and Colonel Brabazon told him that when he was a little older and had had more practice with first-class players he would be a credit to his father. The tournament came to an end and the day following he was to fly back to London. Anxious to play his best he had lived very carefully, smoking little and drinking nothing, and going to bed early; but on his last evening he thought he would like to see something of the life in Monte Carlo of which he had heard so much. An official dinner was given to the tennis-players and after dinner with the rest of them he went into the Sporting Club. It was the first time he had been there. Monte Carlo was very full and the rooms were crowded. Nicky had never before seen roulette played except in the pictures; in a maze he stopped at the first table he came to; chips of different sizes were scattered over the green cloth in what looked like a hopeless muddle; the croupier gave the wheel a sharp turn and with a flick threw in the little white ball. After what seemed an endless time the ball stopped and another croupier with a broad, indifferent gesture raked in the chips of those who had lost.

Presently Nicky wandered over to where they were playing *trente et quarante*, but he couldn't understand what it was all about and he thought it dull. He saw a crowd in another room and sauntered in. A big game of baccara was in progress and he was immediately conscious of the tension. The players were protected from the thronging bystanders by a brass rail; they sat round the table, nine on each side, with the dealer in the middle and the croupier facing him. Big money was changing hands. The dealer was a member of the Greek Syndicate. Nicky looked at his impassive face. His eyes were watchful, but his expression never changed whether he won or lost. It was a terrifying, strangely impressive sight. It gave Nicky, who had been thriftily brought up, a peculiar thrill to see someone risk a thousand pounds on the turn of a card and when he lost make a little joke and laugh. It was all terribly exciting. An acquaintance came up to him.

"Been doing any good?" he asked.

"I haven't been playing."

"Wise of you. Rotten game. Come and have a drink."

"All right."

While they were having it Nicky told his friends that this was the first time he had ever been in the rooms.

"Oh, but you must have one little flutter before you go. It's idiotic to leave Monte without having tried your luck. After all it won't hurt you to lose a hundred francs or so."

"I don't suppose it will, but my father wasn't any too keen on my coming at all and one of the three things he particularly advised me not to do was to gamble."

But when Nicky left his companion he strolled back to one of the tables where they were playing roulette. He stood for a while looking at the losers' money being raked-in by the croupier and the money that was won paid out to the winners. It was impossible to deny that it was thrilling. His friend was right, it did seem silly to leave Monte without putting something on the table just once. It would be an experience, and at

his age you had to have all the experience you could get. He reflected that he hadn't promised his father not to gamble, he'd
promised him not to forget his advice. It wasn't quite the same,
was it? He took a hundred-franc note out of his pocket and
rather shyly put it on number eighteen. He chose it because
that was his age. With a wildly beating heart he watched the
wheel turn; the little white ball whizzed about like a small
demon of mischief; the wheel went round more slowly, the little
white ball hesitated, it seemed about to stop, it went on again;
Nicky could hardly believe his eyes when it fell into number
eighteen. A lot of chips were passed over to him and his hands
trembled as he took them. It seemed to amount to a lot of
money. He was so confused that he never thought of putting
anything on the following round; in fact he had no intention of
playing any more, once was enough; and he was surprised when
eighteen again came up. There was only one chip on it.

"By George, you've won again," said a man who was standing near to him.

"Me? I hadn't got anything on."

"Yes, you had. Your original stake. They always leave it on
unless you ask for it back. Didn't you know?"

Another packet of chips was handed over to him. Nicky's
head reeled. He counted his gains: seven thousand francs. A
queer sense of power seized him; he felt wonderfully clever. This
was the easiest way of making money that he had ever heard of.
His frank, charming face was wreathed in smiles. His bright eyes
met those of a woman standing by his side. She smiled.

"You're in luck," she said.

She spoke English, but with a foreign accent.

"I can hardly believe it. It's the first time I've ever played."

"That explains it. Lend me a thousand francs, will you? I've
lost everything I've got. I'll give it you back in half an hour."

"All right."

She took a large red chip from his pile and with a word of
thanks disappeared. The man who had spoken to him before
grunted.

"You'll never see that again."

Nicky was dashed. His father had particularly advised him
not to lend anyone money. What a silly thing to do! And to
somebody he'd never seen in his life. But the fact was, he felt at
that moment such a love for the human race that it had never
occurred to him to refuse. And that big red chip, it was almost

impossible to realise that it had any value. Oh well, it didn't matter, he still had six thousand francs, he'd just try his luck once or twice more and if he didn't win he'd go home. He put a chip on sixteen, which was his elder sister's age, but it didn't come up; then on twelve, which was his younger sister's, and that didn't come up either; he tried various numbers at random, but without success. It was funny, he seemed to have lost his knack. He thought he would try just once more and then stop; he won. He had made up all his losses and had something over. At the end of an hour, after various ups and downs, having experienced such thrills as he had never known in his life, he found himself with so many chips that they would hardly go in his pockets. He decided to go. He went to the changers' office and he gasped when twenty thousand-franc notes were spread out before him. He had never had so much money in his life. He put it in his pocket and was turning away when the woman to whom he had lent the thousand francs came up to him.

"I've been looking for you everywhere," she said. "I was afraid you'd gone. I was in a fever, I didn't know what you'd think of me. Here's your thousand francs and thank you so much for the loan."

Nicky, blushing scarlet, stared at her with amazement. How he had misjudged her! His father had said, don't gamble; well, he had, and he'd made twenty thousand francs; and his father had said, don't lend anyone money; well, he had, he'd lent quite a lot to a total stranger, and she'd returned it. The fact was that he wasn't nearly such a fool as his father thought: he'd had an instinct that he could lend her the money with safety, and you see, his instinct was right. But he was so obviously taken aback that the little lady was forced to laugh.

"What is the matter with you?" she asked.

"To tell you the truth I never expected to see the money back."

"What did you take me for? Did you think I was a—cocotte?"

Nicky reddened to the roots of his wavy hair.

"No, of course not."

"Do I look like one?"

"Not a bit."

She was dressed very quietly, in black, with a string of gold beads round her neck; her simple frock showed off a neat, slight figure; she had a pretty little face and a trim head. She was made up, but not excessively, and Nicky supposed that she was not

more than three or four years older than himself. She gave him
a friendly smile.

"My husband is in the administration in Morocco, and I've
come to Monte Carlo for a few weeks because he thought I
wanted a change."

"I was just going," said Nicky because he couldn't think of
anything else to say.

"Already!"

"Well, I've got to get up early to-morrow. I'm going back to
London by air."

"Of course. The tournament ended to-day, didn't it? I saw you
play, you know, two or three times."

"Did you? I don't know why you should have noticed me."

"You've got a beautiful style. And you looked very sweet in
your shorts."

Nicky was not an immodest youth, but it did cross his mind
that perhaps she had borrowed that thousand francs in order to
scrape acquaintance with him.

"Do you ever go to the Knickerbocker?" she asked.

"No. I never have."

"Oh, but you mustn't leave Monte Carlo without having
been there. Why don't you come and dance a little? To tell you
the truth, I'm starving with hunger and I should adore some
bacon and eggs."

Nicky remembered his father's advice not to have anything
to do with women, but this was different; you had only to look
at the pretty little thing to know at once that she was perfectly
respectable. Her husband was in what corresponded, he supposed, to the Civil Service. His father and mother had friends
who were Civil Servants and they and their wives sometimes
came to dinner. It was true that the wives were neither so young
nor so pretty as this one, but she was just as ladylike as they
were. And after winning twenty thousand francs he thought it
wouldn't be a bad idea to have a little fun.

"I'd love to go with you," he said. "But you won't mind if I
don't stay very long. I've left instructions at my hotel that I'm
to be called at seven."

"We'll leave as soon as ever you like."

Nicky found it very pleasant at the Knickerbocker. He ate his
bacon and eggs with appetite. They shared a bottle of champagne. They danced, and the little lady told him he danced
beautifully. He knew he danced pretty well, and of course she

was easy to dance with. As light as a feather. She laid her cheek
against his and when their eyes met there was in hers a smile
that made his heart go pit-a-pat. A coloured woman sang in a
throaty, sensual voice. The floor was crowded.

"Have you ever been told that you're very good-looking?" she
asked.

"I don't think so," he laughed. "Gosh," he thought, "I believe she's fallen for me."

Nicky was not such a fool as to be unaware that women often
liked him, and when she made that remark he pressed her to him
a little more closely. She closed her eyes and a faint sigh escaped
her lips.

"I suppose it wouldn't be quite nice if I kissed you before all
these people," he said.

"What do you think they would take me for?"

It began to grow late and Nicky said that really he thought he
ought to be going.

"I shall go too," she said. "Will you drop me at my hotel on
your way?"

Nicky paid the bill. He was rather surprised at its amount,
but with all that money he had in his pocket he could afford not
to care, and they got into a taxi. She snuggled up to him and he
kissed her. She seemed to like it.

"By Jove," he thought, "I wonder if there's anything doing."

It was true that she was a married woman, but her husband
was in Morocco, and it certainly did look as if she'd fallen for
him. Good and proper. It was true also that his father had
warned him to have nothing to do with women, but, he reflected
again, he hadn't actually promised he wouldn't, he'd only promised not to forget his advice. Well, he hadn't; he was bearing it in
mind that very minute. But circumstances alter cases. She was
a sweet little thing; it seemed silly to miss the chance of an adventure when it was handed to you like that on a tray. When
they reached the hotel he paid off the taxi.

"I'll walk home," he said. "The air will do me good after the
stuffy atmosphere of that place."

"Come up a moment," she said. "I'd like to show you the
photo of my little boy."

"Oh, have you got a little boy?" he exclaimed, a trifle dashed.

"Yes, a sweet little boy."

He walked upstairs after her. He didn't in the least want to
see the photograph of her little boy, but he thought it only civil

to pretend he did. He was afraid he'd made a fool of himself; it occurred to him that she was taking him up to look at the photograph in order to show him in a nice way that he'd made a mistake. He'd told her he was eighteen.

"I suppose she thinks I'm just a kid."

He began to wish he hadn't spent all that money on champagne at the night-club.

But she didn't show him the photograph of her little boy after all. They had no sooner got into her room than she turned to him, flung her arms round his neck, and kissed him full on the lips. He had never in all his life been kissed so passionately.

"Darling," she said.

For a brief moment his father's advice once more crossed Nicky's mind and then he forgot it.

Nicky was a light sleeper and the least sound was apt to wake him. Two or three hours later he awoke and for a moment could not imagine where he was. The room was not quite dark, for the door of the bathroom was ajar, and the light in it had been left on. Suddenly he was conscious that someone was moving about the room. Then he remembered. He saw that it was his little friend, and he was on the point of speaking when something in the way she was behaving stopped him. She was walking very cautiously, as though she were afraid of waking him; she stopped once or twice and looked over at the bed. He wondered what she was after. He soon saw. She went over to the chair on which he had placed his clothes and once more looked in his direction. She waited for what seemed to him an interminable time. The silence was so intense that Nicky thought he could hear his own heart beating. Then, very slowly, very quietly, she took up his coat, slipped her hand into the inside pocket and drew out all those beautiful thousand-franc notes that Nicky had been so proud to win. She put the coat back and placed some other clothes on it so that it should look as though it had not been disturbed, then, with the bundle of notes in her hand, for an appreciable time stood once more stock-still. Nicky had repressed an instinctive impulse to jump up and grab her, it was partly surprise that had kept him quiet, partly the notion that he was in a strange hotel, in a foreign country, and if he made a row he didn't know what might happen. She looked at him. His eyes were partly closed and he was sure that she thought he was asleep. In the silence she could hardly fail to hear his regular breathing. When she had reassured herself that her movements had not disturbed him she stepped, with infinite caution, across the room. On a small table in the window a cineraria was growing in a pot. Nicky watched her now with his eyes wide open. The plant was evidently placed quite loosely in the pot, for taking it by the stalks she lifted it out; she put the banknotes in the bottom of the pot and replaced the plant. It was an excellent hiding-place. No one could have guessed that anything was concealed under that richly-flowering plant. She pressed the earth down with her fingers and then, very slowly, taking care not to make the smallest noise, crept across the room, and slipped back into bed.

"Chéri," she said, in a caressing voice.

Nicky breathed steadily, like a man immersed in deep sleep. The little lady turned over on her side and disposed herself to slumber. But though Nicky lay so still his thoughts worked busily. He was extremely indignant at the scene he had just witnessed, and to himself he spoke his thoughts with vigour.

"She's nothing but a damned tart. She and her dear little boy and her husband in Morocco. My eye! She's a rotten thief, that's what she is. Took me for a mug. If she thinks she's going to get away with anything like that, she's mistaken."

He had already made up his mind what he was going to do with the money he had so cleverly won. He had long wanted a car of his own, and had thought it rather mean of his father not to have given him one. After all, a feller doesn't always want to drive about in the family bus. Well, he'd just teach the old man a lesson and buy one himself. For twenty thousand francs, two hundred pounds roughly, he could get a very decent second-hand car. He meant to get the money back, but just then he didn't quite know how. He didn't like the idea of kicking up a row, he was a stranger, in an hotel he knew nothing of; it might very well be that the beastly woman had friends there, he didn't mind facing anyone in a fair fight, but he'd look pretty foolish if someone pulled a gun on him. He reflected besides, very sensibly, that he had no proof the money was his. If it came to a showdown and she swore it was hers, he might very easily find himself hauled off to a police-station. He really didn't know what to do. Presently by her regular breathing he knew that the little lady was asleep. She must have fallen asleep with an easy mind, for she had done her job without a hitch. It infuriated Nicky that she should rest so peacefully while he lay awake worried to death. Suddenly an idea occurred to him. It was such a good one that it was only by the exercise of all his self-control that he prevented himself from jumping out of bed and carrying it out at once. Two could play at her game. She'd stolen his money; well, he'd steal it back again, and they'd be all square. He made up his mind to wait quite quietly until he was sure that deceitful woman was sound asleep. He waited for what seemed to him a very long time. She did not stir. Her breathing was as regular as a child's.

"Darling," he said at last.

No answer. No movement. She was dead to the world. Very slowly, pausing after every movement, very silently, he slipped out of bed. He stood still for a while, looking at her to see whether he had disturbed her. Her breathing was as regular as before. During the time he was waiting he had taken note carefully of the furniture in the room so that in crossing it he should not knock against a chair or a table and make a noise. He took a couple of steps and waited, he took a couple of steps more; he was very light on his feet and made no sound as he walked; he took fully five minutes to get to the window, and here he waited again. He started, for the bed slightly creaked, but it was only because the sleeper turned in her sleep. He forced himself to wait till he had counted one hundred. She was sleeping like a log. With infinite care he seized the cineraria by the stalks and gently pulled it out of the pot; he put his other hand in, his heart beat nineteen to the dozen as his fingers touched the notes, his hand closed on them and he slowly drew them out. He replaced the plant and in his turn carefully pressed down the earth. While he was doing all this he had kept one eye on the form lying in the bed. It remained still. After another pause he crept softly to the chair on which his clothes were lying. He first put the bundle of notes in his coat pocket and then proceeded to dress. It took him a good quarter of an hour, because he could afford to make no sound. He had been wearing a soft shirt with his dinner jacket, and he congratulated himself on this, because it was easier to put on silently than a stiff one. He had some difficulty in tying his tie without a looking-glass, but he very wisely reflected that it didn't really matter if it wasn't tied very well. His spirits were rising. The whole thing now began to seem rather a lark. At length he was completely dressed except for his shoes, which he took in his hand; he thought he would put them on when he got into the passage. Now he had to cross the room to get to the door. He reached it so quietly that he could not have disturbed the lightest sleeper. But the door had to be unlocked. He turned the key very slowly; it creaked.

"Who's that?"

The little woman suddenly sat up in bed. Nicky's heart jumped to his mouth. He made a great effort to keep his head.

"It's only me. It's six o'clock and I've got to go. I was trying not to wake you."

"Oh, I forgot."

She sank back on to the pillow.

"Now that you're awake I'll put on my shoes."

He sat down on the edge of the bed and did this.

"Don't make a noise when you go out. The hotel people don't like it. Oh, I'm so sleepy."

"You go right off to sleep again."

"Kiss me before you go." He bent down and kissed her. "You're a sweet boy and a wonderful lover. *Bon voyage.*"

Nicky did not feel quite safe till he got out of the hotel. The dawn had broken. The sky was unclouded, and in the harbour the yachts and the fishing-boats lay motionless on the still water. On the quay fishermen were getting ready to start on their day's work. The streets were deserted. Nicky took a long breath of the sweet morning air. He felt alert and well. He also felt as pleased as Punch. With a swinging stride, his shoulders well thrown back, he walked up the hill and along the gardens in front of the Casino—the flowers in that clear light had a dewy brilliance that was delicious—till he came to his hotel. Here the day had already begun. In the hall porters with mufflers round their necks and berets on their heads were busy sweeping. Nicky went up to his room and had a hot bath. He lay in it and thought with satisfaction that he was not such a mug as some people might think. After his bath he did his exercises, dressed, packed and went down to breakfast. He had a grand appetite. No continental breakfast for him! He had grapefruit, porridge, bacon and eggs, rolls fresh from the oven, so crisp and delicious they melted in your mouth, marmalade and three cups of coffee. Though feeling perfectly well before, he felt better after that. He lit the pipe he had recently learnt to smoke, paid his bill and stepped into the car that was waiting to take him to the aerodrome on the other side of Cannes. The road as far as Nice ran over the hills and below him was the blue sea and the coast-line. He couldn't help thinking it damned pretty. They passed through Nice, so gay and friendly in the early morning, and presently they came to a long stretch of straight road that ran by the sea. Nicky had paid his bill, not with the money he had won the night before, but with the money his father had given him; he had changed a thousand francs to pay for supper at the Knickerbocker, but that deceitful little woman had returned him the thousand francs he had lent her, so that he still had twenty thousand-franc notes in his pocket. He thought he would like to have a look at them. He had so nearly lost them that they had a double value for him. He took them out of his hip-pocket into which for safety's sake he had stuffed them when he put on the suit he was travelling in, and counted them one by one. Something very strange had happened to them. Instead of there being twenty notes as there should have been there were twenty-six. He couldn't understand it at all. He counted them twice more. There was no doubt about it; somehow or other he had twenty-six thousand francs instead of the twenty he should have had. He couldn't make it out. He asked himself if it was possible that he had won more at the Sporting Club than he had realised. But no, that was out of the question; he distinctly remembered the man at the desk laying the notes out in four rows of five, and he had counted them himself. Suddenly the explanation occurred to him; when he had put his hand into the flower-pot, after taking out the cineraria, he had grabbed everything he felt there. The flower-pot was the little hussy's money-box and he had taken out not only his own money, but her savings as well. Nicky leant back in the car and burst into a roar of laughter. It was the funniest thing he had ever heard in his life. And when he thought of her going to the flower-pot some time later in the morning when she awoke, expecting to find the money she had so cleverly got away with, and finding, not only that it wasn't there, but that her own had gone too, he laughed more than ever. And so far as he was concerned there was nothing to do about it; he neither knew her name, nor the name of the hotel to which she had taken him. He couldn't return her money even if he wanted to.

"It serves her damned well right," he said.

This then was the story that Henry Garnet told his friends over the bridge-table, for the night before, after dinner when his wife and daughter had left them to their port, Nicky had narrated it in full.

"And you know what infuriated me is that he's so damned pleased with himself. Talk of a cat swallowing a canary. And d'you know what he said to me when he'd finished? He looked at me with those innocent eyes of his and said: 'You know, father, I can't help thinking there was something wrong about the advice you gave me. You said, don't gamble; well, I did, and I made a packet; you said, don't lend money; well, I did, and I got it back; and you said, don't have anything to do with women; well, I did, and I made six thousand francs on the deal.'"

It didn't make it any better for Henry Garnet that his three companions burst out laughing.

"It's all very well for you fellows to laugh, but you know, I'm in a damned awkward position. The boy looked up to me, he respected me, he took whatever I said as gospel truth, and now, I saw it in his eyes, he just looks upon me as a drivelling old fool. It's no good my saying one swallow doesn't make a summer; he doesn't see that it was just a fluke, he thinks the whole thing was due to his own cleverness. It may ruin him."

"You do look a bit of a damned fool, old man," said one of the others. "There's no denying that, is there?"

"I know I do, and I don't like it. It's so dashed unfair. Fate has no right to play one tricks like that. After all, you must admit that my advice was good."

"Very good."

"And the wretched boy ought to have burnt his fingers. Well, he hasn't. You're all men of the world, you tell me how I'm to deal with the situation now."

But they none of them could.

"Well, Henry, if I were you I wouldn't worry," said the lawyer. "My belief is that your boy's born lucky, and in the long run that's better than to be born clever or rich."

GIGOLO AND GIGOLETTE

THE BAR was crowded. Sandy Westcott had had a couple of cocktails and he was beginning to feel hungry. He looked at his watch. He had been asked to dinner at half-past nine and it was nearly ten. Eva Barrett was always late and he would be lucky if he got anything to eat by ten-thirty. He turned to the barman to order another cocktail and caught sight of a man who at that moment came up to the bar.

"Hullo, Cotman," he said. "Have a drink?"

"I don't mind if I do, sir."

Cotman was a nice-looking fellow, of thirty perhaps, short, but with so good a figure that he did not look it, very smartly dressed in a double-breasted dinner jacket, a little too much waisted, and a butterfly tie a good deal too large. He had a thick mat of black, wavy hair, very sleek and shiny, brushed straight back from his forehead, and large flashing eyes. He spoke with great refinement, but with a Cockney accent.

"How's Stella?" asked Sandy.

"Oh, she's all right. Likes to have a lay-down before the show, you know. Steadies the old nerves, she says."

"I wouldn't do that stunt of hers for a thousand pounds."

"I don't suppose you would. No one can do it but her, not from that height, I mean, and only five foot of water."

"It's the most sick-making thing I've ever seen."

Cotman gave a little laugh. He took this as a compliment.

Stella was his wife. Of course she did the trick and took the risk, but it was he who had thought of the flames, and it was the flames that had taken the public fancy and made the turn the huge success it was. Stella dived into a tank from the top of a ladder sixty feet high, and as he said, there were only five feet of water in the tank. Just before she dived they poured enough petrol on to cover the surface and he set it alight; the flames soared up and she dived straight into them.

"Paco Espinel tells me it's the biggest draw the Casino has ever had," said Sandy.

"I know. He told me they'd served as many dinners in July as they generally do in August. And that's you, he says to me."

"Well, I hope you're making a packet."

"Well, I can't exactly say that. You see, we've got our contract and naturally we didn't know it was going to be a riot, but Mr. Espinel's talking of booking us for next month, and I don't mind telling you he's not going to get us on the same terms or anything like it. Why, I had a letter from an agent only this morning saying they wanted us to go to Deauville."

"Here are my people," said Sandy.

He nodded to Cotman and left him. Eva Barrett sailed in with the rest of her guests. She had gathered them together downstairs. It was a party of eight.

"I knew we should find you here, Sandy," she said. "I'm not late, am I?"

"Only half an hour."

"Ask them what cocktails they want and then we'll dine."

While they were standing at the bar, emptying now, for nearly everyone had gone down to the terrace for dinner, Paco Espinel passed through and stopped to shake hands with Eva Barrett. Paco Espinel was a young man who had run through his money and now made his living by arranging the turns with which the Casino sought to attract visitors. It was his duty to be civil to the rich and great. Mrs. Chaloner Barrett was an American widow of vast wealth; she not only entertained expensively, but also gambled. And after all, the dinners and suppers and the two cabaret shows that accompanied them were only provided to induce people to lose their money at the tables.

"Got a good table for me, Paco?" said Eva Barrett.

"The best." His eyes, fine, dark Argentine eyes, expressed his admiration of Mrs. Barrett's opulent, ageing charms. This also was business. "You've seen Stella?"

"Of course. Three times. It's the most terrifying thing I've ever seen."

"Sandy comes every night."

"I want to be in at the death. She's bound to kill herself one of these nights and I don't want to miss that if I can help it."

Paco laughed.

"She's been such a success, we're going to keep her on another month. All I ask is that she shouldn't kill herself till the end of August. After that she can do as she likes."

"Oh, God, have I got to go on eating trout and roast chicken every night till the end of August?" cried Sandy.

"You brute, Sandy," said Eva Barrett. "Come on, let's go in to dinner. I'm starving."

Paco Espinel asked the barman if he'd seen Cotman. The barman said he'd had a drink with Mr. Westcott.

"Oh, well, if he comes in here again, tell him I want a word with him."

Mrs. Barrett paused at the top of the steps that led down to the terrace long enough for the Press representative, a little haggard woman with an untidy head, to come up with her notebook. Sandy whispered the names of the guests. It was a representative Riviera party. There was an English lord and his lady, long and lean both of them, who were prepared to dine with anyone who would give them a free meal. They were certain to be as tight as drums before midnight. There was a gaunt Scotch woman, with a face like a Peruvian mask that has been battered by the storms of ten centuries, and her English husband. Though a broker by profession, he was bluff, military and hearty. He gave you an impression of such integrity that you were almost more sorry for him than for yourself when the good thing he had put you on to as a special favour turned out to be a dud. There was an Italian countess who was neither Italian nor a countess, but played a beautiful game of bridge, and there was a Russian prince who was ready to make Mrs. Barrett a princess and in the meantime sold champagne, motorcars and Old Masters on commission. A dance was in progress and Mrs. Barrett, waiting for it to end, surveyed with a look which her short upper lip made scornful the serried throng on the dance floor. It was a gala night and the dining tables were crowded together. Beyond the terrace the sea was calm and silent. The music stopped and the head waiter, affably smiling, came up to guide her to her table. She swept down the steps with majestic gait.

"We shall have quite a good view of the dive," she said as she sat down.

"I like to be next door to the tank," said Sandy, "so that I can see her face."

"Is she pretty?" asked the Countess.

"It's not that. It's the expression of her eyes. She's scared to death every time she does it."

"Oh, I don't believe that," said the City gentleman, Colonel Goodhart by name, though no one had ever discovered how he came by the title. "I mean, the whole bally stunt's only a trick. There's no danger really, I mean."

"You don't know what you're talking about. Diving from that height in as little water as that, she's got to turn like a flash the moment she touches the water. And if she doesn't do it right she's bound to bash her head against the bottom and break her back."

"That's just what I'm telling you, old boy," said the Colonel, "it's a trick. I mean, there's no argument."

"If there's no danger there's nothing to it, anyway," said Eva Barrett. "It's over in a minute. Unless she's risking her life it's the biggest fraud of modern times. Don't say we've come to see this over and over again and it's only a fake."

"Pretty well everything is. You can take my word for that."

"Well, you ought to know," said Sandy.

If it occurred to the Colonel that this might be a nasty dig he admirably concealed it. He laughed.

"I don't mind saying I know a thing or two," he admitted. "I mean, I've got my eyes peeled all right. You can't put much over on me."

The tank was on the far left of the terrace, and behind it, supported by stays, was an immensely tall ladder at the top of which was a tiny platform. After two or three dances more, when Eva Barrett's party were eating asparagus, the music stopped and the lights were lowered. A spot was turned on the tank. Cotman was visible in the brilliance. He ascended half a dozen steps so that he was on a level with the top of the tank.

"Ladies and gentlemen," he cried out, in a loud clear voice, "you are now going to see the most marvellous feat of the century. Madam Stella, the greatest diver in the world, is about to dive from a height of sixty feet into a lake of flames five foot

deep. This is a feat that has never been performed before, and
Madam Stella is prepared to give one hundred pounds to anyone who will attempt it. Ladies and gentlemen, I have the
honour to present Madam Stella."

A little figure appeared at the top of the steps that led on to
the terrace, ran quickly up to the tank, and bowed to the ap-
plauding audience. She wore a man's silk dressing-gown and on
her head a bathing-cap. Her thin face was made up as if for the
stage. The Italian countess looked at her through her *face-à-
main*.

"Not pretty," she said.

"Good figure," said Eva Barrett. "You'll see."

Stella slipped out of her dressing-gown and gave it to Cotman.
He went down the steps. She stood for a moment and looked at
the crowd. They were in darkness and she could only see vague
white faces and white shirt-fronts. She was small, beautifully
made, with legs long for her body and slim hips. Her bathing
costume was very scanty.

"You're quite right about the figure, Eva," said the Colonel.
"Bit undeveloped, of course, but I know you girls think that's
quite the thing."

Stella began to climb the ladder and the spot-light followed
her. It seemed an incredible height. An attendant poured petrol
on the surface of the water. Cotman was handed a flaming
torch. He watched Stella reach the top of the ladder and settle
herself on the platform.

"Ready?" he cried.

"Yes."

"Go," he shouted.

And as he shouted he seemed to plunge the burning torch into
the water. The flames sprang up, leaping high, and really terrifying to look at. At the same moment Stella dived. She came
down like a streak of lightning and plunged through the flames,
which subsided a moment after she had reached the water. A
second later she was at the surface and jumped out to a roar, a
storm of applause. Cotman wrapped the dressing-gown round
her. She bowed and bowed. The applause went on. Music struck
up. With a final wave of the hand she ran down the steps and
between the tables to the door. The lights went up and the
waiters hurried along with their neglected service.

Sandy Westcott gave a sigh. He did not know whether he was
disappointed or relieved.

"Top hole," said the English peer.

"It's a bally fake," said the Colonel, with his British pertinacity. "I bet you anything you like."

"It's over so quickly," said her English ladyship. "I mean, you don't get your money's worth really."

Anyhow it wasn't her money. That it never was. The Italian countess leaned forward. She spoke fluent English, but with a strong accent.

"Eva, my darling, who are those extraordinary people at the table near the door under the balcony?"

"Packet of fun, aren't they?" said Sandy. "I simply haven't been able to take my eyes off them."

Eva Barrett glanced at the table the Countess indicated, and the Prince, who sat with his back to it, turned round to look.

"They can't be true," cried Eva. "I must ask Angelo who they are."

Mrs. Barrett was the sort of woman who knew the head waiters of all the principal restaurants in Europe by their first names. She told the waiter who was at that moment filling her glass to send Angelo to her.

It was certainly an odd pair. They were sitting by themselves at a small table. They were very old. The man was big and stout, with a mass of white hair, great bushy white eyebrows and an enormous white moustache. He looked like the late King Humbert of Italy, but much more like a king. He sat bolt upright. He wore full evening dress, with a white tie and a collar that has been out of fashion for hard on thirty years. His companion was a little old lady in a black satin ball dress, cut very low and tight at the waist. Round her neck were several chains of coloured beads. She wore what was obviously a wig, and a very ill-fitting one at that; it was very elaborate, all curls and sausages, and raven black. She was outrageously made-up, bright blue under the eyes and on the eyelids, the eyebrows heavily black, a great patch of very pink rouge on each cheek and the lips a livid scarlet. The skin hung loosely on her face in deep wrinkles. She had large bold eyes and they darted eagerly from table to table. She was taking everything in, and every other minute called the old man's attention to someone or other. The appearance of the couple was so fantastic in that fashionable crowd, the men in dinner jackets, the women in thin, pale-coloured frocks, that many eyes were turned on them. The staring did not seem to incommode the old lady. When she felt certain persons were looking at her she raised her eyebrows archly, smiled and rolled her eyes. She seemed on the point of acknowledging applause.

Angelo hurried up to the good customer that Eva Barrett was. "You wished to see me, my lady?"

"Oh, Angelo, we're simply dying to know who those absolutely marvellous people are at the next table to the door."

Angelo gave a look and then assumed a deprecating air. The expression of his face, the movement of his shoulders, the turn of his spine, the gesture of his hands, probably even the twiddle of his toes, all indicated a half-humorous apology.

"You must overlook them, my lady." He knew of course that Mrs. Barrett had no right to be thus addressed, just as he knew that the Italian countess was neither Italian nor a countess and that the English lord never paid for a drink if anyone else would pay for it, but he also knew that to be thus addressed did not displease her. "They begged me to give them a table because they wanted to see Madam Stella do her dive. They were in the profession themselves once. I know they're not the sort of people one expects to see dining here, but they made such a point of it I simply hadn't the heart to refuse."

"But I think they're a perfect scream. I adore them."

"I've known them for many years. The man indeed is a compatriot of mine." The head waiter gave a condescending little laugh. "I told them I'd give them a table on the condition that they didn't dance. I wasn't taking any risks, my lady."

"Oh, but I should have loved to see them dance."

"One has to draw the line somewhere, my lady," said Angelo gravely.

He smiled, bowed again and withdrew.

"Look," cried Sandy, "they're going."

The funny old couple were paying their bill. The old man got up and put round his wife's neck a large white, but not too clean, feather boa. She rose. He gave her his arm, holding himself very erect, and she, small in comparison, tripped out beside him. Her black satin dress had a long train, and Eva Barrett (who was well over fifty) screamed with joy.

"Look, I remember my mother wearing a dress like that when I was in the school-room."

The comic pair walked, still arm in arm, through the spacious rooms of the Casino till they came to the door. The old man addressed a commissionaire.

"Be so good as to direct me to the artistes' dressing-rooms. We wish to pay our respects to Madam Stella."

The commissionaire gave them a look and summed them up. They were not people with whom it was necessary to be very polite.

"You won't find her there."

"She has not gone? I thought she gave a second performance at two?"

"That's true. They might be in the bar."

"It won't 'urt us just to go an' 'ave a look, Carlo," said the old lady.

"Right-o, my love," he answered with a great roll of the R.

They walked slowly up the great stairs and entered the bar. It was empty but for the deputy-barman and a couple sitting in two arm-chairs in the corner. The old lady released her husband's arm and tripped up with outstretched hands.

" 'Ow are you, dear? I felt I just 'ad to come and congratulate you, bein' English same as you are. And in the profession meself. It's a grand turn, my dear, it deserves to be a success." She turned to Cotman. "And this is your 'usband?"

Stella got out of her arm-chair and a shy smile broke on her lips as she listened with some confusion to the voluble old lady.

"Yes, that's Syd."

"Pleased to meet you," he said.

"And this is mine," said the old lady, with a little dig of the elbow in the direction of the tall white-haired man. "Mr. Penezzi. 'E's a count really, and I'm the Countess Penezzi by rights, but when we retired from the profession we dropped the title."

"Will you have a drink?" said Cotman.

"No, you 'ave one with us," said Mrs. Penezzi, sinking into an arm-chair. "Carlo, you order."

The barman came, and after some discussion three bottles of beer were ordered. Stella would not have anything.

"She never has anything till after the second show," explained Cotman.

Stella was slight and small, about twenty-six, with light brown hair, cut short and waved, and grey eyes. She had reddened her lips, but wore little rouge on her face. Her skin was pale. She was not very pretty, but she had a neat little face. She wore a very simple evening frock of white silk. The beer was brought and Mr. Penezzi, evidently not very talkative, took a long swig.

"What was your line?" asked Syd Cotman, politely.

Mrs. Penezzi gave him a rolling glance of her flashing, made-up eyes and turned to her husband.

"Tell 'em who I am, Carlo," she said.

"The 'uman cannon-ball," he announced.

Mrs. Penezzi smiled brightly and with a quick, birdlike glance looked from one to the other. They stared at her in dismay.

"Flora," she said. "The 'uman cannon-ball."

She so obviously expected them to be impressed that they did not quite know what to do. Stella gave her Syd a puzzled look. He came to the rescue.

"It must have been before our time."

"Naturally it was before your time. Why, we retired from the profession definitely the year poor Queen Victoria died. It made quite a sensation when we did too. But you've 'eard of me, of course." She saw the blank look on their faces; her tone changed a little. "But I was the biggest draw in London. At the Old Aquarium, that was. All the swells came to see me. The Prince of Wales and I don't know who all. I was the talk of the town. Isn't that true, Carlo?"

"She crowded the Aquarium for a year."

"It was the most spectacular turn they'd ever 'ad there. Why, only a few years ago I went up and introduced meself to Lady de Bathe. Lily Langtry, you know. She used to live down 'ere. She remembered me perfectly. She told me she'd seen me ten times."

"What did you do?" asked Stella.

"I was fired out of a cannon. Believe me, it was a sensation. And after London I went all over the world with it. Yes, my dear, I'm an old woman now and I won't deny it. Seventy-eight Mr. Penezzi is and I shall never see seventy again, but I've 'ad me portrait on every 'oardin' in London. Lady de Bathe said to me: My dear, you was as celebrated as I was. But you know what the public is, give 'em a good thing and they go mad over it, only they want change; 'owever good it is, they get sick of it and then they won't go and see it any more. It'll 'appen to you, my dear, same as it 'appened to me. It comes to all of us. But Mr. Penezzi always 'ad 'is 'ead screwed on 'is shoulders the right way. Been in the business since 'e was so 'igh. Circus, you know.

Ringmaster. That's 'ow I first knew 'im. I was in a troupe of acrobacks. Trapeze act, you know. 'E's a fine-lookin' man now, but you should 'ave seen 'im then, in 'is Russian boots, and ridin' breeches, and a tight-fittin' coat with frogs all down the front of it, crackin' 'is long whip as 'is 'orses galloped round the ring, the 'andsomest man I ever see in my life."

Mr. Penezzi did not make any remark, but thoughtfully twisted his immense white moustache.

"Well, as I was tellin' you, 'e was never one to throw money about and when the agents couldn't get us bookin's any more 'e said, let's retire. An 'e was quite right, after 'avin' been the biggest star in London, we couldn't go back to circus work any more, I mean, Mr. Penezzi bein' a count really, 'e 'ad 'is dignity to think of, so we come down 'ere and we bought a 'ouse and started a pension. It always 'ad been Mr. Penezzi's ambition to do something like that. Thirty-five years we been 'ere now. We 'aven't done so badly not until the last two or three years, and the slump came, though visitors are very different from what they was when we first started, the things they want, electric-light and runnin' water in their bedrooms and I don't know what all. Give them a card, Carlo. Mr. Penezzi does the cookin' 'imself, and if ever you want a real 'ome from 'ome, you'll know where to find it. I like professional people and we'd 'ave a rare lot to talk about, you and me, dearie. Once a professional always a professional, I say."

At that moment the head barman came back from his supper. He caught sight of Syd.

"Oh, Mr. Cotman, Mr. Espinel was looking for you, wants to see you particularly."

"Oh, where is he?"

"You'll find him around somewhere."

"We'll be going," said Mrs. Penezzi, getting up. "Come and 'ave lunch with us one day, will you? I'd like to show you my old photographs and me press cuttin's. Fancy you not 'avin' 'eard of the 'uman cannon-ball. Why, I was as well known as the Tower of London."

Mrs. Penezzi was not vexed at finding that these young people had never even heard of her. She was simply amused.

They bade one another good-bye, and Stella sank back again into her chair.

"I'll just finish my beer," said Syd, "and then I'll go and see what Paco wants. Will you stay here, ducky, or would you like to go to your dressing-room?"

Stella's hands were tightly clenched. She did not answer. Syd gave her a look and then quickly glanced away.

"Perfect riot, that old girl," he went on, in his hearty way. "Real figure of fun. I suppose it's true what she said. It's difficult to believe, I must say. Fancy 'er drawing all London, what, forty year ago? And the funny thing is, her thinking anybody remembered. Seemed as though she simply couldn't understand us not having heard of her even."

He gave Stella another glance, from the corner of his eye so that she should not see he was looking at her, and he saw she was crying. He faltered. The tears were rolling down her pale face. She made no sound.

"What's the matter, darling?"

"Syd, I can't do it again to-night," she sobbed.

"Why on earth not?"

"I'm afraid."

He took her hand.

"I know you better than that," he said. "You're the bravest little woman in the world. Have a brandy, that'll pull you together."

"No, that'd only make it worse."

"You can't disappoint your public like that."

"That filthy public. Swine who eat too much and drink too much. A pack of chattering fools with more money than they know what to do with. I can't stick them. What do they care if I risk my life?"

"Of course, it's the thrill they come for, there's no denying that," he replied uneasily. "But you know and I know, there's no risk, not if you keep your nerve."

"But I've lost my nerve, Syd. I shall kill myself."

She had raised her voice a little, and he looked round quickly at the barman. But the barman was reading the *Eclaireur de Nice* and paying no attention.

"You don't know what it looks like from up there, the top of the ladder, when I look down at the tank. I give you my word, to-night I thought I was going to faint. I tell you I can't do it again to-night, you've got to get me out of it, Syd."

"If you funk it to-night it'll be worse to-morrow."

"No, it won't. It's having to do it twice kills me. The long wait and all that. You go and see Mr. Espinel and tell him I can't give two shows a night. It's more than my nerves'll stand."

"He'll never stand for that. The whole supper trade depends on you. It's only to see you they come in then at all."

"I can't help it, I tell you I can't go on."

He was silent for a moment. The tears still streamed down her pale little face, and he saw that she was quickly losing control of herself. He had felt for some days that something was up and he had been anxious. He had tried not to give her an opportunity to talk. He knew obscurely that it was better for her not to put into words what she felt. But he had been worried. For he loved her.

"Anyhow Espinel wants to see me," he said.

"What about?"

"I don't know. I'll tell him you can't give the show more than once a night and see what he says. Will you wait here?"

"No, I'll go along to the dressing-room."

Ten minutes later he found her there. He was in great spirits and his step was jaunty. He burst open the door.

"I've got grand news for you, honey. They're keeping us on next month at twice the money."

He sprang forward to take her in his arms and kiss her, but she pushed him away.

"Have I got to go on again to-night?"

"I'm afraid you must. I tried to make it only one show a night, but he wouldn't hear of it. He says it's quite essential you should do the supper turn. And after all, for double the money, it's worth it."

She flung herself down on the floor and this time burst into a storm of tears.

"I can't Syd, I can't. I shall kill myself."

He sat down on the floor and raised her head and took her in his arms and petted her.

"Buck up, darling. You can't refuse a sum like that. Why, it'll keep us all the winter and we shan't have to do a thing. After all there are only four more days to the end of July and then it's only August."

"No, no, no. I'm frightened. I don't want to die, Syd. I love you."

"I know you do, darling, and I love you. Why, since we married I've never looked at another woman. We've never had money like this before and we shall never get it again. You know what these things are, we're a riot now, but we can't expect it to go on for ever. We've got to strike while the iron's hot."

"D'you want me to die, Syd?"

"Don't talk so silly. Why, where should I be without you? You mustn't give way like this. You've got your self-respect to think of. You're famous all over the world."

"Like the human cannon-ball was," she cried with a laugh of fury.

"That damned old woman," he thought.

He knew that was the last straw. Bad luck, Stella taking it like that.

"That was an eye-opener to me," she went on. "What do they come and see me over and over again for? On the chance they'll see me kill myself. And a week after I'm dead they'll have forgotten even my name. That's what the public is. When I looked at that painted old hag I saw it all. Oh, Syd, I'm so miserable." She threw her arms round his neck and pressed her face to his. "Syd, it's no good, I can't do it again."

"To-night, d'you mean? If you really feel like that about it, I'll tell Espinel you've had a fainting fit. I daresay it'll be all right just for once."

"I don't mean to-night, I mean never."

She felt him stiffen a little.

"Syd dear, don't think I'm being silly. It's not just to-day, it's been growing on me. I can't sleep at night thinking of it, and when I do drop off I see myself standing at the top of the ladder and looking down. To-night I could hardly get up it, I was trembling so, and when you lit the flames and said go, something seemed to be holding me back. I didn't even know I'd jumped. My mind was a blank till I found myself on the platform and heard them clapping. Syd, if you loved me you wouldn't want me to go through such torture."

He sighed. His own eyes were wet with tears. For he loved her devotedly.

"You know what it means," he said. "The old life. Marathons and all."

"Anything's better than this."

The old life. They both remembered it. Syd had been a dancing gigolo since he was eighteen, he was very good-looking in his dark Spanish way and full of life, old women and middle-aged women were glad to pay to dance with him, and he was never out of work. He had drifted from England to the Continent and there he had stayed, going from hotel to hotel, to the Riviera in the winter, to watering-places in France in the summer. It wasn't a bad life they led, there were generally two or three of them together, the men, and they shared a room in cheap lodgings. They didn't have to get up till late and they only dressed in time to go to the hotel at twelve to dance with stout women who wanted to get their weight down. Then they were free till five, when they went to the hotel again and sat at a table, the three of them together, keeping a sharp eye open for anyone who looked a likely client. They had their regular customers. At night they went to the restaurant and the house provided them with quite a decent meal. Between the courses they danced. It was good money. They generally got fifty or a hundred francs from anyone they danced with. Sometimes a rich woman, after dancing a good deal with one of them for two or three nights, would give him as much as a thousand francs. Sometimes a middle-aged woman would ask one to spend a night with her, and he would get two hundred and fifty francs for that. There was always the chance of a silly old fool losing her head, and then there were platinum and sapphire rings, cigarette-cases, clothes and a wrist-watch to be got. One of Syd's friends had married one of them, who was old enough to be his mother, but she gave him a car and money to gamble with, and they lived in a beautiful villa at Biarritz. Those were the good days when everybody had money to burn. The slump came and hit the gigolos hard. The hotels were empty, and the clients didn't seem to want to pay for the pleasure of dancing with a nice-looking young fellow. Often and often Syd passed a whole day without earning the price of a drink, and more than once a fat old girl who weighed a ton had had the nerve to give him ten francs. His expenses didn't go down, for he had to be smartly dressed or the manager of the hotel made remarks, washing cost a packet, and you'd be surprised the amount of linen he needed; then shoes, those floors were terribly hard on shoes, and they had to look new. He had his room to pay for and his lunch.

It was then he met Stella. It was at Evian, and the season was disastrous. She was a swimming instructress. She was Australian, and a beautiful diver. She gave exhibitions every morning and afternoon. At night she was engaged to dance at the hotel. They dined together at a little table in the restaurant

apart from the guests, and when the band began to play they
danced together to induce the customers to come on to the floor.
But often no one followed them and they danced by themselves.
Neither of them got anything much in the way of paying part-
ners. They fell in love with one another, and at the end of the
season got married.

They had never regretted it. They had gone through hard
times. Even though for business reasons (elderly ladies didn't
so much like the idea of dancing with a married man when his
wife was there) they concealed their marriage, it was not so
easy to get an hotel job for the pair of them and Syd was far
from being able to earn enough to keep Stella, even in the most
modest pension, without working. The gigolo business had gone
to pot. They went to Paris and learnt a dancing act, but the
competition was fearful and cabaret engagements were very
hard to get. Stella was a good ballroom dancer, but the rage was
for acrobatics, and however much they practised she never
managed to do anything startling. The public was sick of the
apache turn. They were out of a job for weeks at a time. Syd's
wrist-watch, his gold cigarette-case, his platinum ring, all went
up the spout. At last they found themselves in Nice reduced to
such straits that Syd had to pawn his evening clothes. It was a
catastrophe. They were forced to enter for the Marathon that
an enterprising manager was starting. Twenty-four hours a day
they danced, resting every hour for fifteen minutes. It was
frightful. Their legs ached, their feet were numb. For long
periods they were unconscious of what they were doing. They
just kept time to the music, exerting themselves as little as possible. They made a little money, people gave them sums of a
hundred francs, or two hundred, to encourage them, and sometimes to attract attention they roused themselves to give an
exhibition dance. If the public was in a good humour this might
bring in a decent sum. They grew terribly tired. On the eleventh
day Stella fainted and had to give up. Syd went on by himself,
moving without pause, grotesquely, without a partner. That
was the worst time they had ever had. It was the final degradation. It had left with them a recollection of horror and misery.

But it was then that Syd had his inspiration. It had come to
him while he was slowly going round the hall by himself. Stella
always said she could dive in a saucer. It was just a trick.

"Funny how ideas come," he said afterwards. "Like a flash of
lightning."

He suddenly remembered having seen a boy set fire to some petrol that had been spilt on the pavement, and the sudden blaze-up. For of course it was the flames on the water and the spectacular dive into them that had caught the public fancy. He stopped dancing there and then; he was too excited to go on. He talked it over with Stella, and she was enthusiastic. He wrote to an agent who was a friend of his; everyone liked Syd, he was a nice little man, and the agent put up the money for the apparatus. He got them an engagement at a circus in Paris, and the turn was a success. They were made. Engagements followed here and there, Syd bought himself an entire outfit of new clothes, and the climax came when they got a booking for the summer casino on the coast. It was no exaggeration of Syd's when he said that Stella was a riot.

"All our troubles are over, old girl," he said fondly. "We can put a bit by now for a rainy day, and when the public's sick of this I'll just think of something else."

And now, without warning, at the top of their boom, Stella wanted to chuck it. He didn't know what to say to her. It broke his heart to see her so unhappy. He loved her more now even than when he had married her. He loved her because of all they'd gone through together; after all, for five days once they'd had nothing to eat but a hunk of bread each and a glass of milk, and he loved her because she'd taken him out of all that; he had good clothes to wear again and his three meals a day. He couldn't look at her; the anguish in her dear grey eyes was more than he could bear. Timidly she stretched out her hand and touched his. He gave a deep sigh.

"You know what it means, honey. Our connection in the hotels has gone west, and the business is finished, anyway. What there is'll go to people younger than us. You know what these old women are as well as I do; it's a boy they want, and besides, I'm not tall enough really. It didn't matter so much when I was a kid. It's no good saying I don't look my age because I do."

"Perhaps we can get into pictures."

He shrugged his shoulders. They'd tried that before when they were down and out.

"I wouldn't mind what I did. I'd serve in a shop."

"D'you think jobs can be had for the asking?"

She began to cry again.

"Don't, honey. It breaks my heart."

"We've got a bit put by."

"I know we have. Enough to last us six months. And then it'll mean starvation. First popping the bits and pieces, and then the clothes'll have to go, same as they did before. And then dancing in lowdown joints for our supper and fifty francs a night. Out of a job for weeks together. And Marathons whenever we hear of one. And how long will the public stand for them?"

"I know you think I'm unreasonable, Syd."

He turned and looked at her now. There were tears in her eyes. He smiled, and the smile he gave her was charming and tender.

"No, I don't, ducky. I want to make you happy. After all, you're all I've got. I love you."

He took her in his arms and held her. He could feel the beating of her heart. If Stella felt like that about it, well, he must just make the best of it. After all, supposing she were killed? No, no, let her chuck it and be damned to the money. She made a little movement.

"What is it, honey?"

She released herself and stood up. She went over to the dressing-table.

"I expect it's about time for me to be getting ready," she said.

He started to his feet.

"You're not going to do a show to-night?"

"To-night, and every night till I kill myself. What else is there? I know you're right, Syd. I can't go back to all that other, stinking rooms in fifth-rate hotels and not enough to eat. Oh, that Marathon. Why did you bring that up? Being tired and dirty for days at a time and then having to give up because flesh and blood just couldn't stand it. Perhaps I can go on another month and then there'll be enough to give you a chance of looking round."

"No, darling. I can't stand for that. Chuck it. We'll manage somehow. We starved before; we can starve again."

She slipped out of her clothes, and for a moment stood naked but for her stockings, looking at herself in the glass. She gave her reflection a hard smile.

"I mustn't disappoint my public," she sniggered.

APPEARANCE AND REALITY

I DO NOT VOUCH for the truth of this story, but it was told me by a professor of French literature at an English university, and he was a man of too high a character, I think, to have told it to me unless it were true. His practice was to draw the attention of his students to three French writers who in his opinion combined the qualities that are the mainsprings of the French character. By reading them, he said, you could learn so much about the French people that, if he had the power, he would not trust such of our rulers as have to deal with the French nation to enter upon their offices till they had passed a pretty stiff examination on their works. They are Rabelais, with his *gauloiserie*, which may be described as the ribaldry that likes to call a spade something more than a bloody shovel; La Fontaine, with his *bon sens*, which is just horse sense; and finally Corneille, with his *panache*. This is translated in the dictionaries as the plume, the plume the knight at arms wore on his helmet, but metaphorically it seems to signify dignity and bravado, display and heroism, vainglory and pride. It was *le panache* that made the French gentlemen at Fontenoy say to the officers of King George II, fire first, gentlemen; it was *le panache* that wrung from Cambronne's bawdy lips at Waterloo the phrase: the guard dies but never surrenders; and it is *le panache* that urges an indigent French poet, awarded the Nobel prize, with a splendid gesture to give it all away. My professor was not a frivolous man and to his mind the story I am about to tell brought out so distinctly the three master qualities of the French that it had a high educational value.

I have called it Appearance and Reality. This is the title of what I suppose may be looked upon as the most important philosophical work that my country (right or wrong) produced in the nineteenth century. It is stiff, but stimulating reading. It is written in excellent English, with considerable humour, and even though the lay reader is unlikely to follow with understanding some of its very subtle arguments he has nevertheless the thrilling sensation of walking a spiritual tight-rope over a metaphysical abyss, and he ends the book with a comfortable feeling that nothing matters a hang anyway. There is no excuse for my making use of the title of so celebrated a book except that it so admirably suits my story. Though Lisette was a philosopher only in the sense in which we are all philosophers, that she exercised thought in dealing with the problems of existence, her feeling for reality was so strong and her sympathy for appearance so genuine that she might almost claim to have established that reconciliation of irreconcilables at which the philosophers have for so many centuries been aiming. Lisette was French, and she passed several hours of every working day dressing and undressing herself at one of the most expensive and fashionable establishments in Paris. A pleasant occupation for a young woman who was well aware that she had a lovely figure. She was in short a mannequin. She was tall enough to be able to wear a train with elegance and her hips were so slim that in sports clothes she could bring the scent of heather to your nostrils. Her long legs enabled her to wear pyjamas with distinction, and her slim waist, her little breasts, made the simplest bathing dress a ravishment. She could wear anything. She had a way of huddling herself in a chinchilla coat that made the most sensible persons admit that chinchilla was worth all the money it cost. Fat women, gross women, stumpy women, bony women, shapeless women, old women, plain women, sat in the spacious arm-chairs and because Lisette looked so sweet bought the clothes that so admirably suited her. She had large brown eyes, a large red mouth and a very clear but slightly freckled skin. It was difficult for her to preserve that haughty, sullen and coldly indifferent demeanour that appears to be essential to the mannequin as she sails in with deliberate steps, turns round slowly and, with an air of contempt for the universe equalled only by the camel's, sails out. There was the suspicion

of a twinkle in Lisette's large brown eyes and her red lips seemed
to tremble as though on the smallest provocation they would
break into a smile. It was the twinkle that attracted the attention of Monsieur Raymond Le Sueur.

He was sitting in a spurious Louis XVI chair by the side of
his wife (in another) who had induced him to come with her to
see the private view of the spring fashions. This was a proof of
Monsieur Le Sueur's amiable disposition, for he was an extremely busy man who, one would have thought, had many
more important things to do than to sit for an hour and watch
a dozen beautiful young women parade themselves in a bewildering variety of costumes. He could not have thought that
any of them could possibly make his wife other than she was,
and she was a tall, angular woman of fifty, with features considerably larger than life-size. He had not indeed married her
for her looks, and she had never, even in the first delirious days
of their honeymoon, imagined that he had. He had married her
in order to combine the flourishing steel works of which she
was the heiress with his equally flourishing manufactory of loco-
motives. The marriage had been a success. She had provided
him with a son who could play tennis nearly as well as a professional, dance quite as well as a gigolo, and hold his own at
bridge with any of the experts; and a daughter whom he had
been able to dower sufficiently to marry to a very nearly au-
thentic prince. He had reason to be proud of his children. By
perseverance and a reasonable integrity he had prospered sufficiently to gain the controlling interest in a sugar refinery, a
movie company, a firm that built motor-cars and a newspaper;
and finally he had been able to spend enough money to persuade the free and independent electorate of a certain district
to send him to the Senate. He was a man of a dignified presence,
a pleasing corpulence and a sanguine complexion, with a neat
grey beard cut square, a bald head and a roll of fat at the back
of his neck. You had no need to look at the red button that
adorned his black coat to surmise that he was a person of consequence. He was a man who made up his mind quickly and
when his wife left the dressmaker's to go and play bridge he
parted from her, saying that for the sake of exercise he would
walk to the Senate, where his duty to his country called him. He
did not however go as far as this, but contented himself with
taking his exercise up and down a back street into which he
rightly surmised the young ladies of the dressmaker's establish-

ment would emerge at the close of business hours. He had barely waited for a quarter of an hour when the appearance of a number of women in groups, some young and pretty, some not so young and far from pretty, apprised him that the moment for which he had been waiting was come, and in two or three minutes Lisette tripped into the street. The Senator was well aware that his appearance and his age made it unlikely that young women would find him attractive at first sight, but he had found that his wealth and his position counterbalanced these disadvantages. Lisette had a companion with her, which would possibly have embarrassed a man of less importance, but did not cause the Senator to hesitate for an instant; he went up to her, raising his hat politely but not so much as to show how bald he was, and bade her good evening.

"Bon soir, Mademoiselle," he said with an ingratiating smile.

She gave him the shortest possible look and, her full red lips just trembling with a smile, stiffened; she turned her head away and breaking into conversation with her friend, walked on with a very good assumption of supreme indifference. Far from disconcerted, the Senator turned round and followed the two girls at a distance of a few yards. They walked along the little back street, turned into the boulevard and at the Place de la Madeleine took a bus. The Senator was well satisfied. He had drawn a number of correct conclusions. The fact that she was obviously going home with a girl friend proved that she had no accredited admirer. The fact that she had turned away when he had accosted her showed that she was discreet and modest and well behaved, which he liked young women to be when they were pretty; and her coat and skirt, the plain black hat and the rayon stockings proclaimed that she was poor and therefore virtuous. In those clothes she looked just as attractive as in the splendid garments he had seen her wearing before. He had a funny little feeling in his heart. He had not had that peculiar sensation, pleasurable and yet oddly painful, for several years, but he recognised it at once.

"It's love, by blue," he muttered.

He had never expected to feel it again, and squaring his shoulders he walked on with a confident step. He walked to the offices of a private detective and there left instructions that inquiries should be made about a young person called Lisette, who worked as a mannequin at such and such an address; and then, remembering that at the Senate they were discussing the American Debt, took a cab to the impressive building, entered the library, where there was an arm-chair he very much liked, and had a pleasant nap. The information he had asked for reached him three days later. It was cheap at the price. Mademoiselle Lisette Larion lived with a widowed aunt in a two-room apartment in the district of Paris known as the Batignolles. Her father, a wounded hero of the great war, had a *bureau de tabac* in a small country town in the southwest of France. The rent of the flat was two thousand francs. She led a regular life, but was fond of going to the pictures, was not known to have a lover, and was nineteen years old. She was well spoken of by the concierge of the apartments and well liked by her companions at the shop. Obviously she was a very respectable young woman and the Senator could not but think that she was eminently suited to solace the leisure moments of a man who wanted relaxation from the cares of state and the exacting pressure of Big Business.

It is unnecessary to relate in detail the steps that Monsieur Le Sueur took to achieve the end he had in view. He was too important and too busy to occupy himself with the matter personally, but he had a confidential secretary who was very clever at dealing with electors who had not made up their minds how to vote, and who certainly knew how to put before a young woman who was honest but poor the advantages that might ensue if she were lucky enough to secure the friendship of such a man as his employer. The confidential secretary paid the widowed aunt, Madame Saladin by name, a visit and told her that Monsieur Le Sueur, always abreast of the time, had lately begun to take an interest in films and was indeed about to engage in the production of a picture. (This shows how much a clever brain can make use of a fact that an ordinary person would have passed over as insignificant.) Monsieur Le Sueur had been struck by the appearance of Mademoiselle Lisette at the dressmaker's and the brilliant way she wore her clothes, and it had occurred to him that she might very well suit a part he had it in mind for her to play. (Like all intelligent people the Senator always stuck as close to the truth as he could.) The confidential secretary then invited Madame Saladin and her niece to a dinner where they could make one another's further acquaintance and the Senator could judge whether Made-

moiselle Lisette had the aptitude for the screen that he suspected. Madame Saladin said she would ask her niece, but for
her part seemed to think the suggestion quite reasonable.

When Madame Saladin put the proposition before Lisette
and explained the rank, dignity and importance of their generous host, that young person shrugged her pretty shoulders
disdainfully.

"*Cette vieille carpe,*" she said, of which the not quite literal
translation is: that old trout.

"What does it matter if he's an old trout if he gives you a
part?" said Madame Saladin.

"*Et ta sœur,*" said Lisette.

This phrase, which of course means: and your sister, and
sounds harmless enough, and even pointless, is a trifle vulgar
and is used by well-brought-up young women, I think, only if
they want to shock. It expresses the most forcible unbelief, and
the only correct translation into the vernacular is too coarse for
my chaste pen.

"Anyhow we should get a slap-up dinner," said Madame
Saladin. "After all, you're not a child any more."

"Where did he say we should dine?"

"The Château de Madrid. Everyone knows it's the most expensive restaurant in the world."

There is no reason why it should not be. The food is very
good, the cellar is famous, and its situation makes it on a fine
evening of early summer an enchanting place to eat at. A very
pretty dimple appeared on Lisette's cheek and a smile on her
large red mouth. She had perfect teeth.

"I can borrow a dress from the shop," she murmured.

A few days later the Senator's confidential secretary fetched
them in a taxi and drove Madame Saladin and her engaging
niece to the Bois de Boulogne. Lisette looked ravishing in one
of the firm's most successful models and Madame Saladin extremely respectable in her own black satin and a hat that
Lisette had made for the occasion. The secretary introduced the
ladies to Monsieur Le Sueur, who greeted them with the benign
dignity of the politician who is behaving graciously to the wife
and daughter of a valued constituent; and this is exactly what
in his astute way he thought people at adjacent tables who
knew him would imagine his guests to be. The dinner passed off
very agreeably, and less than a month later Lisette moved into
a charming little flat at a convenient distance both from her

place of business and from the Senate. It was decorated in the modern style by a fashionable upholsterer. Monsieur Le Sueur wished Lisette to continue to work. It suited him very well that she should have something to do during the hours that he was obliged to devote to affairs, for it would keep her out of mischief, and he very well knew that a woman who has nothing to do all day spends much more money than one who has an occupation. An intelligent man thinks of these things.

But extravagance was a vice to which Lisette was strange. The Senator was fond and generous. It was a source of satisfaction to him that Lisette began very soon to save money. She ran her apartment with thrift and bought her clothes at trade prices, and every month sent a certain sum home to her heroic father, who purchased little plots of land with it. She continued to lead a quiet and modest life and Monsieur Le Sueur was pleased to learn from the concierge, who had a son she wanted to place in a government office, that Lisette's only visitors were her aunt and one or two girls from the shop.

The Senator had never been happier in his life. It was very satisfactory to him to think that even in this world a good action had its reward, for was it not from pure kindness that he had accompanied his wife to the dressmaker's on that afternoon when they were discussing the American Debt at the Senate and thus seen for the first time the charming Lisette? The more he knew her the more he doted on her. She was a delightful companion. She was gay and debonair. Her intelligence was respectable and she could listen cleverly when he discussed business matters or affairs of state with her. She rested him when he was weary and cheered him when he was depressed. She was glad to see him when he came, and he came frequently, generally from five till seven, and sorry when he went away. She gave him the impression that he was not only her lover but her friend. Sometimes they dined together in her apartment, and the well-appointed meal, the genial comfort, gave him a keen appreciation of the charm of domesticity. His friends told the Senator he looked twenty years younger. He felt it. He was conscious of his good fortune. He could not but feel, however, that after a life of honest toil and public service it was only his due.

It was thus a shock to him, after things had been proceeding so happily for nearly two years, on coming back to Paris early one Sunday morning unexpectedly after a visit to his constituency which was to last over the week-end, when he let himself into the apartment with his latchkey, thinking since it was the day of rest to find Lisette in bed, to discover her having breakfast in her bedroom *tête-à-tête* with a young gentleman he had never seen before who was wearing his (the Senator's) brand new pyjamas. Lisette was surprised to see him. Indeed she gave a distinct start.

"*Tiens,*" she said. "Where have you sprung from? I didn't expect you till to-morrow."

"The Ministry has fallen," he answered mechanically. "I have been sent for. I am to be offered the Ministry of the Interior." But that was not what he wanted to say at all. He gave the gentleman who was wearing his pyjamas a furious look. "Who is that young man?" he cried.

Lisette's large red mouth broke into a most alluring smile.

"My lover," she answered.

"Do you think I'm a fool?" shouted the Senator. "I know he's your lover."

"Why do you ask then?"

Monsieur Le Sueur was a man of action. He went straight up to Lisette and smacked her hard on her right cheek with his left hand and then smacked her hard on the left cheek with his right hand.

"Brute," screamed Lisette.

He turned to the young man, who had watched this scene of violence with some embarrassment, and, drawing himself to his full height, flung out his arm and with a dramatic finger pointed to the door.

"Get out," he cried. "Get out."

One would have thought, such was the commanding aspect of a man who was accustomed to sway a crowd of angry taxpayers and who could dominate with his frown an annual meeting of disappointed shareholders, that the young man would have made a bolt for the door; but he stood his ground, irresolutely it is true, but he stood his ground; he gave Lisette an appealing look and slightly shrugged his shoulders.

"What are you waiting for?" shouted the Senator. "Do you want me to use force?"

"He can't go out in his pyjamas," said Lisette.

"They're not his pyjamas, they're my pyjamas."

"He's waiting for his clothes."

Monsieur Le Sueur looked round and on the chair behind

him, flung down in a disorderly fashion, was a variety of masculine garments. The Senator gave the young man a look of contempt.

"You may take your clothes, Monsieur," he said with cold disdain.

The young man picked them up in his arms, gathered up the shoes that were lying about the floor, and quickly left the room. Monsieur Le Sueur had a considerable gift of oratory. Never had he made better use of it than now. He told Lisette what he thought of her. It was not flattering. He painted her ingratitude in the blackest colours. He ransacked an extensive vocabulary in order to find opprobrious names to call her. He called all the powers of heaven to witness that never had a woman repaid with such gross deception an honest man's belief in her. In short he said everything that anger, wounded vanity and disappointment suggested to him. Lisette did not seek to defend herself. She listened in silence, looking down and mechanically crumbling the roll which the Senator's appearance had prevented her from finishing. He flung an irritated glance at her plate.

"I was so anxious that you should be the first to hear my great news that I came straight here from the station. I was expecting to have my *petit déjeuner* with you, sitting at the end of your bed."

"My poor dear, haven't you had your breakfast? I'll order some for you at once."

"I don't want any."

"Nonsense. With the great responsibility you are about to assume you must keep up your strength."

She rang and when the maid came told her to bring in hot coffee. It was brought and Lisette poured it out. He would not touch it. She buttered a roll. He shrugged his shoulders and began to eat. Meanwhile he uttered a few remarks on the perfidy of women. She remained silent.

"At all events it is something," he said, "that you have not the effrontery to attempt to excuse yourself. You know that I am not a man who can be ill-used with impunity. The soul of generosity when people behave well to me I am pitiless when they behave badly. The very moment I have drunk my coffee I shall leave this apartment for ever."

Lisette sighed.

"I will tell you now that I had prepared a surprise for you. I had made up my mind to celebrate the second anniversary of our union by settling a sum of money on you sufficient to give you a modest independence if anything happened to me."

"How much?" asked Lisette sombrely.

"A million francs."

She sighed again. Suddenly something soft hit the Senator on the back of the head and he gave a start.

"What is that?" he cried.

"He's returning your pyjamas."

The young man had opened the door, flung the pyjamas at the Senator's head, and quickly closed it again. The Senator disengaged himself from the silk trousers that clung round his neck.

"What a way to return them! It is obvious that your friend has no education."

"Of course he has not your distinction," murmured Lisette.

"And has he my intelligence?"

"Oh, no."

"Is he rich?"

"Penniless."

"Then, name of a name, what is it you see in him?"

"He's young," smiled Lisette.

The Senator looked down at his plate and a tear rose in his eyes and rolled down his cheek into the coffee. Lisette gave him a kindly look.

"My poor friend, one can't have everything in this life," she said.

"I knew I was not young. But my situation, my fortune, my vitality. I thought it made up. There are women who only like men of a certain age. There are celebrated actresses who look upon it as an honour to be the little friend of a Minister. I am too well brought up to throw your origins in your face, but the fact remains that you are a mannequin and I took you out of an apartment of which the rent is only two thousand francs a year. It was a step up for you."

"The daughter of poor but honest parents, I have no reason to be ashamed of my origins, and it is not because I have earned my living in a humble sphere that you have the right to reproach me."

"Do you love this boy?"

"Yes."

"And not me?"

"You too. I love you both, but I love you differently. I love you because you are so distinguished and your conversation is instructive and interesting. I love you because you are kind and generous. I love him because his eyes are so big and his hair waves and he dances divinely. It's very natural."

"You know that in my position I cannot take you to places where they dance and I daresay when he's as old as I am he'll have no more hair than I have."

"That may well be true," Lisette agreed, but she did not think it much mattered.

"What will your aunt, the respectable Madame Saladin, say to you when she hears what you have done?"

"It will not be exactly a surprise to her."

"Do you mean to say that worthy woman countenances your conduct? *O tempora, o mores!* How long then has this been going on?"

"Since I first went to the shop. He travels for a big silk firm in Lyons. He came in one day with his samples. We liked the look of one another."

"But your aunt was there to defend you from the temptations to which a young girl is exposed in Paris. She should never have allowed you to have anything to do with this young man."

"I did not ask her permission."

"It is enough to bring the grey hairs of your poor father to the grave. Had you no thought of that wounded hero whose services to his country have been rewarded with a licence to sell tobacco? Do you forget that as Minister of the Interior the department is under my control? I should be within my rights if I revoked the licence on account of your flagrant immorality."

"I know you are too great a gentleman to do a dastardly thing like that."

He waved his hand in an impressive, though perhaps too dramatic a manner.

"Don't be afraid, I will never stoop so low as to revenge myself on one who has deserved well of his country for the misdeeds of a creature my sense of dignity forces me to despise."

He went on with his interrupted breakfast. Lisette did not speak and there was silence between them. But his appetite satisfied, his mood changed; he began to feel sorry for himself rather than angry with her, and with a strange ignorance of woman's heart he thought to arouse Lisette's remorse by exhibiting himself as an object of pity.

"It is hard to break a habit to which one has grown accus-

tomed. It was a relief and a solace to me to come here when I
could snatch a moment from my many occupations. Will you
regret me a little, Lisette?"

"Of course."

He gave a deep sigh.

"I should never have thought you capable of so much
deception."

"It is the deception that rankles," she murmured thoughtfully. "Men are funny in that way. They cannot forgive being
made fools of. It is because they are so vain. They attach importance to things that are of no consequence."

"Do you call it a matter of no consequence that I should find
you having breakfast with a young man wearing my pyjamas?"

"If he were my husband and you were my lover you would
think it perfectly natural."

"Obviously. For then I should be deceiving him and my honour would be secure."

"In short, I have only to marry him to make the situation
perfectly regular."

For a moment he did not understand. Then her meaning
flashed across his clever brain and he gave her a quick look. Her
lovely eyes had the twinkle he always found so alluring and on
her large red mouth was the suspicion of a roguish smile.

"Do not forget that as a member of the Senate I am by all
the traditions of the Republic the authorized mainstay of
morality and good behaviour."

"Does that weigh very heavily with you?"

He stroked his handsome square beard with a composed and
dignified gesture.

"Not a row of beans," he replied, but the expression he used
had a Gallic breadth that would perhaps have given his more
conservative supporters something of a shock.

"Would he marry you?" he asked.

"He adores me. Of course he would marry me. If I told him I
had a *dot* of a million francs he would ask nothing better."

Monsieur Le Sueur gave her another look. When in a moment
of anger he told her it had been his intention to settle a million
francs on her he had exaggerated a good deal in the desire to
make her see how much her treachery was costing her. But he
was not the man to draw back when his dignity was concerned.

"It is much more than a young man in his position of life

could aspire to. But if he adores you he would be always at your side."

"Didn't I tell you that he was a commercial traveller? He can only come to Paris for the week-end."

"That of course is a horse of another colour," said the Senator. "It would naturally be a satisfaction to him to know that during his absence I should be there to keep an eye on you."

"A considerable satisfaction," said Lisette.

To facilitate the conversation she rose from her seat and made herself comfortable on the Senator's knees. He pressed her hand tenderly.

"I am very fond of you, Lisette," he said. "I should not like you to make a mistake. Are you sure he will make you happy?"

"I think so."

"I will have proper enquiries made. I would never consent to you marrying anyone not of exemplary character and unimpeachable morality. For all our sakes we must make quite sure about this young man whom we are preparing to bring into our lives."

Lisette raised no objection. She was aware that the Senator liked to do things with order and method. He now prepared to leave her. He wanted to break his important news to Madame Le Sueur, and he had to get in touch with various persons in the parliamentary group to which he belonged.

"There is only one more thing," he said, as he bade Lisette an affectionate farewell, "if you marry I must insist on your giving up your work. The place of a wife is the home, and it is against all my principles that a married woman should take the bread out of a man's mouth."

Lisette reflected that a strapping young man would look rather funny walking round the room, with his hips swaying, to show off the latest models, but she respected the Senator's principles.

"It shall be as you wish, darling," she said.

The enquiries he made were satisfactory and the marriage took place on a Saturday morning as soon as the legal formalities were completed. Monsieur Le Sueur, Minister of the Interior, and Madame Saladin were witnesses. The bridegroom was a slim young man with a straight nose, fine eyes and black waving hair brushed straight back from his forehead. He looked more like a tennis-player than a traveller in silk. The Mayor, impressed by the august presence of the Minister of the Interior, made according to French practice a speech which he sought to render eloquent. He began by telling the married couple what presumably they knew already. He informed the bridegroom that he was the son of worthy parents and was engaged in an honourable profession. He congratulated him on entering the bonds of matrimony at an age when many young men thought only of their pleasures. He reminded the bride that her father was a hero of the great war, whose glorious wounds had been rewarded by a concession to sell tobacco, and he told her that she had earned a decent living since her arrival in Paris in an establishment that was one of the glories of French taste and luxury. The Mayor was of a literary turn and he briefly mentioned various celebrated lovers of fiction, Romeo and Juliet whose short but legitimate union had been interrupted by a regrettable misunderstanding, Paul and Virginia who had met her death at sea rather than sacrifice her modesty by taking off her clothes, and finally Daphnis and Chloe who had not consummated their marriage till it was sanctioned by the legitimate authority. He was so moving that Lisette shed a few tears. He paid a compliment to Madame Saladin whose example and precept had preserved her young and beautiful niece from the dangers that are likely to befall a young girl alone in a great city, and finally he congratulated the happy pair on the honour that the Minister of the Interior had done them in consenting to be a witness at the ceremony. It was a testimony to their own probity that this captain of industry and eminent statesman should find time to perform a humble office to persons in their modest sphere, and it proved not only the excellence of his heart but his lively sense of duty. His action showed that he appreciated the importance of early marriage, affirmed the security of the family and emphasised the desirability of producing offspring to increase the power, influence and consequence of the fair land of France. A very good speech indeed.

The wedding breakfast was held at the Château de Madrid, which had sentimental associations for Monsieur Le Sueur. It has been mentioned already that among his many interests the Minister (as we must now call him) was interested in a firm of motor-cars. His wedding present to the bridegroom was a very nice two-seater of his own manufacture, and in this, when lunch was over, the young couple started off for their honeymoon. This could only last over the week-end since the young man had to get back to his work, which would take him to Marseilles,

Toulon and Nice. Lisette kissed her aunt and she kissed Monsieur Le Sueur.

"I shall expect you at five on Monday," she whispered to him.

"I shall be there," he answered.

They drove away and for a moment Monsieur Le Sueur and Madame Saladin looked at the smart yellow roadster.

"As long as he makes her happy," sighed Madame Saladin, who was not used to champagne at lunch and felt unreasonably melancholy.

"If he does not make her happy he will have me to count with," said Monsieur Le Sueur impressively.

His car drove up.

"*Au revoir, chère Madame.* You will get a bus at the Avenue de Neuilly."

He stepped into his car and as he thought of the affairs of state that awaited his attention he sighed with content. It was evidently much more fitting to his situation that his mistress should be, not just a little mannequin in a dressmaker's shop, but a respectable married woman.

THE LUNCHEON

I CAUGHT sight of her at the play and in answer to her beckoning I went over during the interval and sat down beside her. It was long since I had last seen her and if someone had not mentioned her name I hardly think I would have recognised her. She addressed me brightly.

"Well, it's many years since we first met. How time does fly! We're none of us getting any younger. Do you remember the first time I saw you? You asked me to luncheon."

Did I remember?

It was twenty years ago and I was living in Paris. I had a tiny apartment in the Latin Quarter overlooking a cemetery and I was earning barely enough money to keep body and soul together. She had read a book of mine and had written to me about it. I answered, thanking her, and presently I received from her another letter saying that she was passing through Paris and would like to have a chat with me; but her time was limited and the only free moment she had was on the following Thursday; she was spending the morning at the Luxembourg and would I give her a little luncheon at Foyot's afterwards? Foyot's is a restaurant at which the French senators eat and it was so far beyond my means that I had never even thought of going there. But I was flattered and I was too young to have learned to say no to a woman. (Few men, I may add, learn this until they are too old to make it of any consequence to a woman what they say.) I had eighty francs (gold francs) to last me the rest of the month and a modest luncheon should not cost more than fifteen. If I cut out coffee for the next two weeks I could manage well enough.

I answered that I would meet my friend—by correspondence —at Foyot's on Thursday at half-past twelve. She was not so young as I expected and in appearance imposing rather than at-tractive. She was in fact a woman of forty (a charming age, but not one that excites a sudden and devastating passion at first sight), and she gave me the impression of having more teeth, white and large and even, than were necessary for any practical purpose. She was talkative, but since she seemed inclined to talk about me I was prepared to be an attentive listener.

I was startled when the bill of fare was brought, for the prices were a great deal higher than I had anticipated. But she reas-sured me.

"I never eat anything for luncheon," she said.

"Oh, don't say that!" I answered generously.

"I never eat more than one thing. I think people eat far too much nowadays. A little fish, perhaps. I wonder if they have any salmon."

Well, it was early in the year for salmon and it was not on the bill of fare, but I asked the waiter if there was any. Yes, a beau-tiful salmon had just come in, it was the first they had had. I ordered it for my guest. The waiter asked her if she would have something while it was being cooked.

"No," she answered, "I never eat more than one thing. Unless you had a little caviare. I never mind caviare."

My heart sank a little. I knew I could not afford caviare, but I could not very well tell her that. I told the waiter by all means to bring caviare. For myself I chose the cheapest dish on the menu and that was a mutton chop.

"I think you're unwise to eat meat," she said. "I don't know how you can expect to work after eating heavy things like chops. I don't believe in overloading my stomach."

Then came the question of drink.

"I never drink anything for luncheon," she said.

"Neither do I," I answered promptly.

"Except white wine," she proceeded as though I had not spoken. "These French white wines are so light. They're won-derful for the digestion."

"What would you like?" I asked, hospitable still, but not ex-actly effusive.

She gave me a bright and amicable flash of her white teeth.

"My doctor won't let me drink anything but champagne."

I fancy I turned a trifle pale. I ordered half a bottle. I mentioned casually that my doctor had absolutely forbidden me to drink champagne.

"What are you going to drink, then?"

"Water."

She ate the caviare and she ate the salmon. She talked gaily of art and literature and music. But I wondered what the bill would come to. When my mutton chop arrived she took me quite seriously to task.

"I see that you're in the habit of eating a heavy luncheon. I'm sure it's a mistake. Why don't you follow my example and just eat one thing? I'm sure you'd feel ever so much better for it."

"I *am* only going to eat one thing," I said, as the waiter came again with the bill of fare.

She waved him aside with an airy gesture.

"No, no, I never eat anything for luncheon. Just a bite, I never want more than that, and I eat that more as an excuse for conversation than anything else. I couldn't possibly eat anything more—unless they had some of those giant asparagus. I should be sorry to leave Paris without having some of them."

My heart sank. I had seen them in the shops and I knew that they were horribly expensive. My mouth had often watered at the sight of them.

"Madame wants to know if you have any of those giant asparagus," I asked the waiter.

I tried with all my might to will him to say no. A happy smile spread over his broad, priest-like face, and he assured me that they had some so large, so splendid, so tender, that it was a marvel.

"I'm not in the least hungry," my guest sighed, "but if you insist I don't mind having some asparagus."

I ordered them.

"Aren't you going to have any?"

"No, I never eat asparagus."

"I know there are people who don't like them. The fact is, you ruin your palate by all the meat you eat."

We waited for the asparagus to be cooked. Panic seized me. It was not a question now how much money I should have left over for the rest of the month, but whether I had enough to pay the bill. It would be mortifying to find myself ten francs short and be obliged to borrow from my guest. I could not bring myself to do that. I knew exactly how much I had and if the bill came to more I made up my mind that I would put my hand in my pocket and with a dramatic cry start up and say it had been picked. Of course it would be awkward if she had not money enough either to pay the bill. Then the only thing would be to leave my watch and say I would come back and pay later.

The asparagus appeared. They were enormous, succulent and appetising. The smell of the melted butter tickled my nostrils as the nostrils of Jehovah were tickled by the burned offerings of the virtuous Semites. I watched the abandoned woman thrust them down her throat in large voluptuous mouthfuls and in my polite way I discoursed on the condition of the drama in the Balkans. At last she finished.

"Coffee?" I said.

"Yes, just an ice-cream and coffee," she answered.

I was past caring now, so I ordered coffee for myself and an ice-cream and coffee for her.

"You know, there's one thing I thoroughly believe in," she said, as she ate the ice-cream. "One should always get up from a meal feeling one could eat a little more."

"Are you still hungry?" I asked faintly.

"Oh, no, I'm not hungry; you see, I don't eat luncheon. I have a cup of coffee in the morning and then dinner, but I never eat more than one thing for luncheon. I was speaking for you."

"Oh, I see!"

Then a terrible thing happened. While we were waiting for the coffee, the head waiter, with an ingratiating smile on his false face, came up to us bearing a large basket full of huge peaches. They had the blush of an innocent girl; they had the rich tone of an Italian landscape. But surely peaches were not in season then? Lord knew what they cost. I knew too—a little later, for my guest, going on with her conversation, absent-mindedly took one.

"You see, you've filled your stomach with a lot of meat"—my one miserable little chop—"and you can't eat any more. But I've just had a snack and I shall enjoy a peach."

The bill came and when I paid it I found that I had only enough for a quite inadequate tip. Her eyes rested for an instant on the three francs I left for the waiter and I knew that she thought me mean. But when I walked out of the restaurant I had the whole month before me and not a penny in my pocket.

"Follow my example," she said as we shook hands, "and never eat more than one thing for luncheon."

"I'll do better than that," I retorted. "I'll eat nothing for dinner to-night."

"Humorist!" she cried gaily, jumping into a cab. "You're quite a humorist!"

But I have had my revenge at last. I do not believe that I am a vindictive man, but when the immortal gods take a hand in the matter it is pardonable to observe the result with com‧ placency. To-day she weighs twenty-one stone.

THE UNCONQUERED

He came back into the kitchen. The man was still on the floor, lying where he had hit him, and his face was bloody. He was moaning. The woman had backed against the wall and was staring with terrified eyes at Willi, his friend, and when he came in she gave a gasp and broke into loud sobbing. Willi was sitting at the table, his revolver in his hand, with a half empty glass of wine beside him. Hans went up to the table, filled his glass and emptied it at a gulp.

"You look as though you'd had trouble, young fellow," said Willi with a grin.

Hans's face was blood-stained and you could see the gashes of five sharp finger-nails. He put his hand gingerly to his cheek.

"She'd have scratched my eyes out if she could, the bitch. I shall have to put some iodine on. But she's all right now. You go along."

"I don't know. Shall I? It's getting late."

"Don't be a fool. You're a man, aren't you? What if it is getting late? We lost our way."

It was still light and the westering sun streamed into the kitchen windows of the farm-house. Willi hesitated a moment. He was a little fellow, dark and thin-faced, a dress designer in civil life, and he didn't want Hans to think him a sissy. He got up and went towards the door through which Hans had come. When the woman saw what he was going to do she gave a shriek and sprang forwards.

"Non, Non," she cried.

With one step Hans was in front of her. He seized her by the shoulders and flung her violently back. She tottered and fell. He took Willi's revolver.

"Stop still, both of you," he rasped in French, but with his guttural German accent. He nodded his head towards the door. "Go on. I'll look after them."

Willi went out, but in a moment was back again.

"She's unconscious."

"Well, what of it?"

"I can't. It's no good."

"Stupid, that's what you are. *Ein Weibchen.* A woman."

Willi flushed.

"We'd better be getting on our way."

Hans shrugged a scornful shoulder.

"I'll just finish the bottle of wine and then we'll go."

He was feeling at ease and it would have been pleasant to linger. He had been on the job since morning and after so many hours on his motor-cycle his limbs ached. Luckily they hadn't far to go, only to Soissons—ten or fifteen kilometres. He wondered if he'd have the luck to get a bed to sleep in. Of course all this wouldn't have happened if the girl hadn't been a fool. They had lost their way, he and Willi, they had stopped a peasant working in a field and he had deliberately misled them, and they found themselves on a side road. When they came to the farm they stopped to ask for a direction. They'd asked very politely, for orders were to treat the French population well as long as they behaved themselves. The door was opened for them by the girl and she said she didn't know the way to Soissons, so they pushed in; then the woman, her mother, Hans guessed, told them. The three of them, the farmer, his wife and daughter, had just finished supper and there was a bottle of wine on the table. It reminded Hans that he was as thirsty as the devil. The day had been sweltering and he hadn't had a drink since noon. He asked them for a bottle of wine and Willi had added that they would pay them well for it. Willi was a good little chap, but soft. After all, they were the victors. Where was the French army? In headlong flight. And the English, leaving everything behind, had scuttled like rabbits back to their island. The conquerors took what they wanted, didn't they? But Willi had worked at a Paris dressmaker's for two years. It's true he spoke French well, that's why he had

his present job, but it had done something to him. A decadent
people. It did a German no good to live among them.

The farmer's wife put a couple of bottles of wine on the table
and Willi took twenty francs out of his pocket and gave it to
her. She didn't even say thank you. Hans's French wasn't as
good as Willi's, but he could make himself understood, and he
and Willi spoke it together all the time. Willi corrected his
mistakes. It was because Willi was so useful to him in this way
that he had made him his friend, and he knew that Willi
admired him. He admired him because he was so tall, slim and
broad-shouldered, because his curly hair was so fair and his
eyes so blue. He never lost an opportunity to practise his
French, and he tried to talk now, but those three French people
wouldn't meet him half-way. He told them that he was a farmer's son himself and when the war was over was going back to
the farm. He had been sent to school in Munich because his
mother wanted him to go into business, but his heart wasn't in
it, and so after matriculating he had gone to an agricultural
college.

"You came here to ask your way and now you know it," said
the girl. "Drink up your wine and go."

He had hardly looked at her before. She wasn't pretty, but
she had fine dark eyes and a straight nose. Her face was very
pale. She was plainly dressed, but somehow she didn't look
quite like what she evidently was. There was a sort of distinction
about her. Ever since the war started he'd heard fellows talk
about the French girls. They had something the German girls
hadn't. Chic, Willi said it was, but when he asked him just
what he meant by that Willi could only say that you had to see
it to understand. Of course he'd heard others say that they were
mercenary and hard as nails. Well, they'd be in Paris in a week
and he'd find out for himself. They said the High Command
had already arranged for houses for the men to go to.

"Finish your wine and let's go," said Willi.

But Hans was feeling comfortable and didn't want to be
hurried.

"You don't look like a farmer's daughter," he said to the girl.
"And so what?" she answered.
"She's a teacher," said her mother.
"Then you've had a good education." She shrugged her
shoulders, but he went on good-humouredly in his bad French.
"You ought to understand that this is the best thing that has

ever happened to the French people. We didn't declare war. You declared war. And now we're going to make France a decent country. We're going to put order into it. We're going to teach you to work. You'll learn obedience and discipline."

She clenched her fists and looked at him, her eyes black with hatred. But she did not speak.

"You're drunk, Hans," said Willi.

"I'm as sober as a judge. I'm only telling them the truth and they may just as well know it at once."

"He's right," she cried out, unable any longer to contain herself. "You're drunk. Now go. Go."

"Oh, you understand German, do you? All right, I'll go. But you must give me a kiss first."

She took a step back to avoid him, but he seized her wrist.

"Father," she cried. "Father."

The farmer flung himself on the German. Hans let go of her and with all his might hit him in the face. He crumpled up on the floor. Then, before she could escape him, he caught the girl in his arms. She gave him a swinging blow on the cheek. . . . He chuckled grimly.

"Is that how you take it when a German soldier wants to kiss you? You'll pay for this."

With his great strength he pinioned her arms and was dragging her out of the door, but her mother rushed at him and catching him by the clothes tried to pull him away. With one arm holding the girl close to him, with the flat of his other hand he gave the woman a great push and she staggered back to the wall.

"Hans, Hans," cried Willi.

"Shut up, damn you."

He put his hands over the girl's mouth to stop her shrieking and carried her out of the room. That was how it had happened and you had to admit that she'd brought it on herself. She shouldn't have slapped him. If she'd given him the kiss he'd asked for he'd have gone away. He gave a glance at the farmer still lying where he had fallen and he could hardly help laughing at his funny face. There was a smile in his eyes when he looked at the woman cowering against the wall. Was she afraid it was her turn next? Not likely. He remembered a French proverb.

"*C'est le premier pas qui coûte.* There's nothing to cry about, old woman. It had to come sooner or later." He put his hand to his hip pocket and pulled out a wallet. "Look, here's a hundred francs so that mademoiselle can buy herself a new dress. There's not much left of that one." He placed the note on the table and put his helmet back on his head. "Let's go."

They slammed the door behind them and got on their motorcycles. The woman went into the parlour. Her daughter was lying on the divan. She was lying as he had left her and she was weeping bitterly.

Three months later Hans found himself in Soissons again. He had been in Paris with the conquering army and had ridden through the Arc de Triomphe on his motor-cycle. He had advanced with the army first to Tours and then to Bordeaux. He'd seen very little fighting. The only French soldiers he'd seen were prisoners. The campaign had been the greatest spree he could ever have imagined. After the armistice he had spent a month in Paris. He'd sent picture postcards to his family in Bavaria and bought them all presents. Willi, because he knew the city like the palm of his hand, had stayed on, but he and the rest of his unit were sent to Soissons to join the force that was holding it. It was a nice little town and he was comfortably billeted. Plenty to eat and champagne for less than a mark a bottle in German money. When he was ordered to proceed there it had occurred to him that it would be fun to go and have a look at the girl he'd had. He'd take her a pair of silk stockings to show there was no ill-feeling. He had a good bump of locality and he thought he would be able to find the farm without difficulty. So one afternoon, when he had nothing to do, he put the silk stockings in his pocket and got on his machine. It was a lovely autumn day, with hardly a cloud in the sky, and it was pretty, undulating country that he rode through. It had been fine and dry for so long that, though it was September, not even the restless poplars gave sign that the summer was drawing to an end. He took one wrong turning, which delayed him, but for all that he got to the place he sought in less than half an hour. A mongrel dog barked at him as he walked up to the door. He did not knock, but turned the handle and stepped in. The girl was sitting at the table peeling potatoes. She sprang to her feet when she saw the uniformed man.

"What d'you want?" Then she recognised him. She backed to the wall, clutching the knife in her hands. "It's you. *Cochon*."

"Don't get excited. I'm not going to hurt you. Look. I've brought you some silk stockings."

"Take them away and take yourself off with them."

"Don't be silly. Drop that knife. You'll only get hurt if you try to be nasty. You needn't be afraid of me."

"I'm not afraid of you," she said.

She let the knife fall to the floor. He took off his helmet and sat down. He reached out with his foot and drew the knife towards him.

"Shall I peel some of your potatoes for you?" She did not answer. He bent down for the knife and then took a potato out of the bowl and went to work on it. Her face hard, her eyes hostile, she stood against the wall and watched him. He smiled at her disarmingly. "Why do you look so cross? I didn't do you much harm, you know. I was excited, we all were, they'd talked of the invincible French army and the Maginot line . . ." he finished the sentence with a chuckle. "And the wine went to my head. You might have fared worse. Women have told me that I'm not a bad-looking fellow."

She looked him up and down scornfully.

"Get out of here."

"Not until I choose."

"If you don't go my father will go to Soissons and complain to the general."

"Much he'll care. Our orders are to make friends with the population. What's your name?"

"That's not your business."

There was a flush in her cheeks now and her angry eyes were blazing. She was prettier than he remembered her. He hadn't done so badly. She had a refinement that suggested the city-dweller rather than the peasant. He remembered her mother saying she was a teacher. Because she was almost a lady it amused him to torment her. He felt strong and healthy. He passed his hand through his curly blond hair, and giggled when he thought that many girls would have jumped at the chance she had had. His face was so deeply tanned by the summer that his eyes were startlingly blue.

"Where are your father and mother?"

"Working in the fields."

"I'm hungry. Give me a bit of bread and cheese and a glass of wine. I'll pay."

She gave a harsh laugh.

"We haven't seen cheese for three months. We haven't enough bread to stay our hunger. The French took our horses a year ago and now the Boches have taken our cows, our pigs, our chickens, everything."

"Well, they paid you for them."

"Can we eat the worthless paper they gave us?"

She began to cry.

"Are you hungry?"

"Oh, no," she answered bitterly, "we can eat like kings on potatoes and bread and turnips and lettuce. To-morrow my father's going to Soissons to see if he can buy some horse meat."

"Listen, Miss. I'm not a bad fellow. I'll bring you a cheese, and I think I can get hold of a bit of ham."

"I don't want your presents. I'll starve before I touch the food you swine have stolen from us."

"We'll see," he said good-humouredly.

He put on his hat, got up, and with an *Au revoir, mademoiselle,* walked out.

He wasn't supposed to go joy-riding round the country and he had to wait to be sent on an errand before he was able to get to the farm again. It was ten days later. He walked in as unceremoniously as before and this time he found the farmer and his wife in the kitchen. It was round about noon and the woman was stirring a pot on the stove. The man was seated at table. They gave him a glance when he came in, but there was no surprise in it. Their daughter had evidently told them of his visit. They did not speak. The woman went on with her cooking, and the man, a surly look on his face, stared at the oil-cloth on the table. But it required more than this to disconcert the good-humoured Hans.

"Bonjour, la compagnie," he said cheerfully. "I've brought you a present."

He undid the package he had with him and set out a sizable piece of gruyère cheese, a piece of pork and a couple of tins of sardines. The woman turned round and he smiled when he saw the light of greed in her eyes. The man looked at the foodstuff sullenly. Hans gave him his sunny grin.

"I'm sorry we had a misunderstanding the first time I came here. But you shouldn't have interfered."

At that moment the girl came in.

"What are you doing here?" she cried harshly. Then her eyes fell on the things he had brought. She swept them together and flung them at him. "Take them away. Take them."

But her mother sprang forward.

"Annette, you're crazy."

"I won't take his presents."

"It's our own food that they've stolen from us. Look at the sardines. They're Bordeaux sardines."

She picked the things up. Hans looked at the girl with a mocking smile in his light blue eyes.

"Annette's your name, is it? A pretty name. Do you grudge your parents a little food? You said you hadn't had cheese for three months. I couldn't get any ham; I did the best I could."

The farmer's wife took the lump of meat in her hands and pressed it to her bosom. You felt that she could have kissed it. Tears ran down Annette's cheeks.

"The shame of it," she groaned.

"Oh, come now, there's no shame in a bit of gruyère and a piece of pork."

Hans sat down and lit a cigarette. Then he passed the packet over to the old man. The farmer hesitated for a moment, but the temptation was too strong for him; he took one and handed back the packet.

"Keep it," said Hans. "I can get plenty more." He inhaled the smoke and blew a cloud of it from his nostrils. "Why can't we be friends? What's done can't be undone. War is war, and, well, you know what I mean. I know Annette's an educated girl and I want her to think well of me. I expect we shall be in Soissons for quite a while and I can bring you something now and then to help out. You know, we do all we can to make friends with the townspeople, but they won't let us. They won't even look at us when we pass them in the street. After all, it was an accident, what happened that time I came here with Willi. You needn't be afraid of me. I'll respect Annette as if she was my own sister."

"Why do you want to come here? Why can't you leave us alone?" asked Annette.

He really didn't know. He didn't like to say that he wanted a little human friendship. The silent hostility that surrounded them all at Soissons got on his nerves so that sometimes he wanted to go up to a Frenchman who looked at him as if he wasn't there and knock him down, and sometimes it affected him so that he was almost inclined to cry. It would be nice if he had some place to go where he was welcome. He spoke the truth when he said he had no desire for Annette. She wasn't the sort of woman he fancied. He liked women to be tall and

full-breasted, blue-eyed and fair-haired like himself; he liked
them to be strong and hefty and well-covered. That refinement
which he couldn't account for, that thin fine nose and those
dark eyes, the long pale face—there was something intimidating
about the girl, so that if he hadn't been excited by the great
victories of the German armies, if he hadn't been so tired and
yet so elated, if he hadn't drunk all that wine on an empty
stomach, it would never have crossed his mind that he could
have anything to do with her.

For a fortnight after that Hans couldn't get away. He'd left
the food at the farm and he had no doubt that the old people
had wolfed it. He wondered if Annette had eaten it too; he
wouldn't have been surprised to discover that the moment his
back was turned she had set to with the others. These French
people, they couldn't resist getting something for nothing. They
were weak and decadent. She hated him, yes, God, how she
hated him, but pork was pork and cheese was cheese. He thought
of her quite a lot. It tantalised him that she should have such
a loathing for him. He was used to being liked by women. It
would be funny if one of these days she fell in love with him.
He'd been her first lover and he'd heard the students at Munich
over their beer saying that it was her first lover a woman loved,
after that it was love. When he'd set his mind on getting a girl
he'd never failed yet. Hans laughed to himself and a sly look
came into his eyes.

At last he got his chance to go to the farm. He got hold of
cheese and butter, sugar, a tin of sausages, and some coffee, and
set off on his motor-cycle. But that time he didn't see Annette.
She and her father were at work in the fields. The old woman
was in the yard and her face lit up when she saw the parcel he
was bringing. She led him into the kitchen. Her hands trembled
a little as she untied the string and when she saw what he had
brought her eyes filled with tears.

"You're very good," she said.

"May I sit down?" he asked politely.

"Of course." She looked out of the window and Hans guessed
that she wanted to make sure that Annette was not coming.
"Can I offer you a glass of wine."

"I'd be glad of it."

He was sharp enough to see that her greed for food had made
her, if not friendly to him, at least willing to come to terms with

him. That look out of the window made them almost fellow conspirators."

"Did you like the pork?" he asked.

"It was a treat."

"I'll try to bring you some more next time I come. Did Annette like it?"

"She wouldn't touch a thing you'd left. She said she'd rather starve."

"Silly."

"That's what I said to her. As long as the food is there, I said, there's nothing to be gained by not eating it."

They chatted quite amicably while Hans sipped his wine. He discovered that she was called Madame Périer. He asked her whether there were any other members of the family. She sighed. No, they'd had a son, but he'd been mobilised at the beginning of the war and he'd died. He hadn't been killed, he'd got pneumonia and died in the hospital at Nancy.

"I'm sorry," said Hans.

"Perhaps he's better off than if he'd lived. He was like Annette in many ways. He could never have borne the shame of defeat." She sighed again. "Oh, my poor friend, we've been betrayed."

"Why did you want to fight for the Poles? What were they to you?"

"You're right. If we had let your Hitler take Poland he would have left us alone."

When Hans got up to go he said he would come again soon.

"I shan't forget the pork."

Then Hans had a lucky break; he was given a job that took him twice a week to a town in the vicinity so that he was able to get to the farm much oftener. He took care never to come without bringing something. But he made no headway with Annette. Seeking to ingratiate himself with her, he used the simple wiles that he had discovered went down with women; but they only excited her derision. Thin-lipped and hard, she looked at him as though he were dirt. On more than one occasion she made him so angry that he would have liked to take her by the shoulders and shake the life out of her. Once he found her alone, and when she got up to go he barred her passage.

"Stop where you are. I want to talk to you."

"Talk. I am a woman and defenceless."

"What I want to say is this: for all I know I may be here for a long time. Things aren't going to get easier for you French, they're going to get harder. I can be useful to you. Why don't you be reasonable like your father and mother?"

It was true that old Périer had come round. You couldn't say that he was cordial, he was indeed cold and gruff, but he was civil. He had even asked Hans to bring him some tobacco, and when he wouldn't accept payment for it had thanked him. He was pleased to hear the news of Soissons and grabbed the paper that Hans brought him. Hans, a farmer's son, could talk about the farm as one who knew. It was a good farm, not too big and not too small, well watered, for a sizable brook ran through it, and well wooded, with arable land and pasture. Hans listened with understanding sympathy when the old man bewailed himself because without labour, without fertilisers, his stock taken from him, it was all going to rack and ruin.

"You ask me why I can't be reasonable like my father and mother," said Annette.

She pulled her dress tight and showed herself to him. He couldn't believe his eyes. What he saw caused such a convulsion in his soul as he had never known. The blood rushed to his cheeks.

"You're pregnant."

She sank back on her chair and leaning her head on her hands began to weep as though her heart would break.

"The shame of it. The shame."

He sprang towards her to take her in his arms.

"My sweet," he cried.

But she sprang to her feet and pushed him away.

"Don't touch me. Go away. Go away. Haven't you done me enough harm already?"

She flung out of the room. He waited by himself for a few minutes. He was bewildered. His thoughts in a whirl, he rode slowly back to Soissons, and when he went to bed he couldn't get to sleep for hours. He could think of nothing but Annette and her swollen body. She had been unbearably pathetic as she sat there at the table crying her eyes out. It was his child she bore in her womb. He began to feel drowsy, and then with a start he was once more wide awake, for suddenly it came to him, it came to him with the shattering suddenness of gun-fire: he was in love with her. It was such a surprise, such a shock that he couldn't cope with it. Of course he'd thought of her a lot, but never in that way, he'd thought it would be a great joke if he made her fall in love with him, it would be a triumph if the

time came when she offered what he had taken by force; but
not for a moment had it occurred to him that she was anything
to him but a woman like another. She wasn't his type. She
wasn't very pretty. There was nothing to her. Why should he
have all of a sudden this funny feeling for her? It wasn't a
pleasant feeling either, it was a pain. But he knew what it was
all right; it was love, and it made him feel happier than he had
ever felt in his life. He wanted to take her in his arms, he wanted
to pet her, he wanted to kiss those tear-stained eyes of hers.
He didn't desire her, he thought, as a man desires a woman,
he wanted to comfort her, he wanted her to smile at him—
strange, he had never seen her smile, he wanted to see her eyes
—fine eyes they were, beautiful eyes—soft with tenderness.

For three days he could not leave Soissons and for three days,
three days and three nights, he thought of Annette and the
child she would bear. Then he was able to go to the farm. He
wanted to see Madame Périer by herself, and luck was with him,
for he met her on the road some way from the house. She had
been gathering sticks in the wood and was going home with a
great bundle on her back. He stopped his motor-cycle. He knew
that the friendliness she showed him was due only to the provisions he brought with him, but he didn't care; it was enough
that she was mannerly, and that she was prepared to be so as
long as she could get something out of him. He told her he
wanted to talk to her and asked her to put her bundle down. She
did as he bade. It was a grey, cloudy day, but not cold.

"I know about Annette," he said.

She started.

"How did you find out? She was set on your not knowing."

"She told me."

"That was a pretty job of work you did that evening."

"I didn't know. Why didn't you tell me sooner?"

She began to talk, not bitterly, not blaming him even, but as
though it were a misfortune of nature, like a cow dying in giving
birth to a calf or a sharp spring frost nipping the fruit trees and
ruining the crop, a misfortune that human kind must accept
with resignation and humility. After that dreadful night Annette had been in bed for days with a high fever. They thought
she was going out of her mind. She would scream for hours on
end. There were no doctors to be got. The village doctor had
been called to the colours. Even in Soissons there were only two
doctors left, old men both of them, and how could they get to

the farm even if it had been possible to send for them? They weren't allowed to leave the town. Even when the fever went down Annette was too ill to leave her bed, and when she got up she was so weak, so pale, it was pitiful. The shock had been terrible, and when a month went by, and another month, without her being unwell she paid no attention. She had always been irregular. It was Madame Périer who first suspected that something was wrong. She questioned Annette. They were terrified, both of them, but they weren't certain and they said nothing to Périer. When the third month came it was impossible to doubt any longer. Annette was pregnant.

They had an old Citroën in which before the war Madame Périer had taken the farm produce into the market at Soissons two mornings a week, but since the German occupation they had had nothing to sell that made the journey worth while. Petrol was almost unobtainable. But now they got it out and drove into town. The only cars to be seen were the military cars of the Germans. German soldiers lounged about. There were German signs in the streets, and on public buildings proclamations in French signed by the Officer Commanding. Many shops were closed. They went to the old doctor they knew, and he confirmed their suspicions. But he was a devout Catholic and would not help them. When they wept he shrugged his shoulders.

"You're not the only one," he said. *"Il faut souffrir."*

They knew about the other doctor too and went to see him. They rang the bell and for a long time no one answered. At last the door was opened by a sad-faced woman in black, but when they asked to see the doctor she began to cry. He had been arrested by the Germans because he was a freemason, and was held as a hostage. A bomb had exploded in a café frequented by German officers and two had been killed and several wounded. If the guilty were not handed over before a certain date he was to be shot. The woman seemed kindly and Madame Périer told her of their trouble.

"The brutes," she said. She looked at Annette with compassion. "My poor child."

She gave them the address of a midwife in the town and told them to say that they had come from her. The midwife gave them some medicine. It made Annette so ill that she thought she was going to die, but it had no further effect. Annette was still pregnant.

That was the story that Madame Périer told Hans. For a while he was silent.

"It's Sunday to-morrow," he said then. "I shall have nothing to do. I'll come and we'll talk. I'll bring something nice."

"We have no needles. Can you bring some?"

"I'll try."

She hoisted the bundle of sticks on her back and trudged down the road. Hans went back to Soissons. He dared not use his motor-cycle, so next day he hired a push-bike. He tied his parcel of food on the carrier. It was a larger parcel than usual because he had put a bottle of champagne into it. He got to the farm when the gathering darkness made it certain that they would all be home from work. It was warm and cosy in the kitchen when he walked in. Madame Périer was cooking and her husband was reading a *Paris-Soir*. Annette was darning stockings.

"Look, I've brought you some needles," he said, as he undid his parcel. "And here's some material for you, Annette."

"I don't want it."

"Don't you?" he grinned. "You'll have to begin making things for the baby."

"That's true, Annette," said her mother, "and we have nothing." Annette did not look up from her sewing. Madame Périer's greedy eyes ran over the contents of the parcel. "A bottle of champagne."

Hans chuckled.

"I'll tell you what that's for presently. I've had an idea." He hesitated for a moment, then drew up a chair and sat down facing Annette. "I don't know quite how to begin. I'm sorry for what I did that night, Annette. It wasn't my fault, it was the circumstances. Can't you forgive me?"

She threw him a look of hatred.

"Never. Why don't you leave me alone? Isn't it enough that you've ruined my life?"

"Well, that's just it. Perhaps I haven't. When I knew you were going to have a baby it had a funny effect on me. It's all different now. It's made me so proud."

"Proud?" she flung at him viciously.

"I want you to have the baby, Annette. I'm glad you couldn't get rid of it."

"How dare you say that?"

"But listen to me. I've been thinking of nothing else since I

knew. The war will be over in six months. We shall bring the
English to their knees in the spring. They haven't got a chance.
And then I shall be demobilised and I'll marry you."

"You? Why?"

He blushed under his tan. He could not bring himself to say it
in French, so he said it in German. He knew she understood it.
"Ich liebe dich."

"What does he say?" asked Madame Périer.

"He says he loves me."

Annette threw back her head and broke into a peal of harsh
laughter. She laughed louder and louder and she couldn't stop
and tears streamed from her eyes. Madame Périer slapped her
sharply on both cheeks.

"Don't pay any attention," she said to Hans. "It's hysteria.
Her condition, you know."

Annette gasped. She gained control over herself.

"I brought the bottle of champagne to celebrate our engagement," said Hans.

"That's the bitterest thing of all," said Annette, "that we
were beaten by fools, by such fools."

Hans went on speaking in German.

"I didn't know I loved you till that day when I found out
that you were going to have a baby. It came like a clap of
thunder, but I think I've loved you all the time."

"What does he say?" asked Madame Périer.

"Nothing of importance."

He fell back into French. He wanted Annette's parents to
hear what he had to say.

"I'd marry you now, only they wouldn't let me. And don't
think I'm nothing at all. My father's well-to-do and we're well
thought of in our commune. I'm the eldest son and you'd want
for nothing."

"Are you a Catholic?" asked Madame Périer.

"Yes, I'm a Catholic."

"That's something."

"It's pretty, the country where we live and the soil's good.
There's not better farming land between Munich and Inns-
bruck, and it's our own. My grandfather bought it after the
war of '70. And we've got a car and a radio, and we're on the
telephone."

Annette turned to her father.

"He has all the tact in the world, this gentleman," she cried ironically. She eyed Hans. "It would be a nice position for me, the foreigner from the conquered country with a child born out of wedlock. It offers me a chance of happiness, doesn't it? A fine chance."

Périer, a man of few words, spoke for the first time.

"No. I don't deny that it's a fine gesture you're making. I went through the last war and we all did things we wouldn't have done in peace time. Human nature is human nature. But now that our son is dead, Annette is all we have. We can't let her go."

"I thought you might feel that way," said Hans, "and I've got my answer to that. I'll stay here."

Annette gave him a quick look.

"What do you mean?" asked Madame Périer.

"I've got another brother. He can stay and help my father. I like this country. With energy and initiative a man could make a good thing of your farm. When the war's over a lot of Germans will be settling here. It's well known that you haven't got enough men in France to work the land you've got. A fellow gave us a lecture the other day at Soissons. He said that a third of the farms were left uncultivated because there aren't the men to work them."

Périer and his wife exchanged glances and Annette saw that they were wavering. That was what they'd wanted since their son had died, a son-in-law who was strong and hefty and could take over when they grew too old to do more than potter about.

"That changes the case," said Madame Périer. "It's a proposition to consider."

"Hold your tongue," cried Annette roughly. She leant forward and fixed her burning eyes on the German. "I'm engaged to a teacher who worked in the boys' school in the town where I taught, we were to be married after the war. He's not strong and big like you, or handsome; he's small and frail. His only beauty is the intelligence that shines in his face, his only strength is the greatness of his soul. He's not a barbarian, he's civilised; he has a thousand years of civilisation behind him. I love him. I love him with all my heart and soul."

Hans's face grew sullen. It had never occurred to him that Annette might care for anyone else.

"Where is he now?"

"Where do you suppose he is? In Germany. A prisoner and starving. While you eat the fat of our land. How many times have I got to tell you that I hate you? You ask me to forgive you. Never. You want to make reparation. You fool." She threw her head back and there was a look of intolerable anguish on her face. "Ruined. Oh, he'll forgive me. He's tender. But I'm tortured by the thought that one day the suspicion may come to him that perhaps I hadn't been forced—that perhaps I'd given myself to you for butter and cheese and silk stockings. I shouldn't be the only one. And what would our life be with that child between us, your child, a German child? Big like you, and blond like you, and blue-eyed like you. Oh, my God, why do I have to suffer this?"

She got up and went swiftly out of the kitchen. For a minute the three were left in silence. Hans looked ruefully at his bottle of champagne. He sighed and rose to his feet. When he went out Madame Périer accompanied him.

"Did you mean it when you said you would marry her?" she asked him, speaking in a low voice.

"Yes. Every word. I love her."

"And you wouldn't take her away? You'd stay here and work on the farm?"

"I promise you."

"Evidently my old man can't last for ever. At home you'd have to share with your brother. Here you'd share with nobody."

"There's that too."

"We never were in favour of Annette marrying that teacher, but our son was alive then and he said, if she wants to marry him, why shouldn't she? Annette was crazy about him. But now that our son's dead, poor boy, it's different. Even if she wanted to, how could she work the farm alone?"

"It would be a shame if it was sold. I know how one feels about one's own land."

They had reached the road. She took his hand and gave it a little squeeze.

"Come again soon."

Hans knew that she was on his side. It was a comfort to him to think that as he rode back to Soissons. It was a bother that Annette was in love with somebody else. Fortunately he was a prisoner; long before he was likely to be released the baby would be born. That might change her: you could never tell with a woman. Why, in his village there'd been a woman who was so much in love with her husband that it had been a joke, and then she had a baby and after that she couldn't bear the sight of him. Well, why shouldn't the contrary happen too? And now that he'd offered to marry her she must see that he was a decent sort of fellow. God, how pathetic she'd looked with her head flung back, and how well she'd spoken! What language! An actress on the stage couldn't have expressed herself better, and yet it had all sounded so natural. You had to admit that, these French people knew how to talk. Oh, she was clever. Even when she lashed him with that bitter tongue it was a joy to listen to her. He hadn't had a bad education himself, but he couldn't hold a candle to her. Culture, that's what she had.

"I'm a donkey," he said out loud as he rode along. She'd said he was big and strong and handsome. Would she have said that if it hadn't meant something to her? And she'd talked of the baby having fair hair and blue eyes like his own. If that didn't mean that his colouring had made an impression on her he was a Dutchman. He chuckled. "Give me time. Patience, and let nature go to work."

The weeks went by. The C.O. at Soissons was an elderly, easy-going fellow and in view of what the spring had in store for them he was content not to drive his men too hard. The German papers told them that England was being wrecked by the Luft-waffe and the people were in a panic. Submarines were sinking British ships by the score and the country was starving. Revolution was imminent. Before summer it would be all over and the Germans would be masters of the world. Hans wrote home and told his parents that he was going to marry a French girl and with her a fine farm. He proposed that his brother should borrow money to buy him out of his share of the family property so that he could increase the size of his own holding while land, owing to the war and the exchange, could still be bought for a song. He went over the farm with Périer. The old man listened quietly when Hans told him his ideas: the farm would have to be restocked and as a German he would have a pull; the motor tractor was old, he would get a fine new one from Germany, and a motor plough. To make a farm pay you had to take advantage of modern inventions. Madame Périer told him afterwards that her husband had said he wasn't a bad lad and seemed to know a lot. She was very friendly with him now and insisted that he should share their midday meal with them on Sundays. She translated his name into French and called him Jean. He was always ready to give a hand, and as time went on and Annette could do less and less it was useful to have a man about who didn't mind doing a job of work.

Annette remained fiercely hostile. She never spoke to him except to answer his direct questions and as soon as it was possible went to her own room. When it was so cold that she couldn't stay there she sat by the side of the kitchen stove, sewing or reading, and took no more notice of him than if he hadn't been there. She was in radiant health. There was colour in her cheeks and in Hans's eyes she was beautiful. Her approaching maternity had given her a strange dignity and he was filled with exultation when he gazed upon her. Then one day when he was on his way to the farm he saw Madame Périer in the road waving to him to stop. He put his brakes on hard.

"I've been waiting for an hour. I thought you'd never come. You must go back. Pierre is dead."

"Who's Pierre?"

"Pierre Gavin. The teacher Annette was going to marry."

Hans's heart leapt. What luck! Now he'd have his chance.

"Is she upset?"

"She's not crying. When I tried to say something she bit my head off. If she saw you to-day she's capable of sticking a knife into you."

"It's not my fault if he died. How did you hear?"

"A prisoner, a friend of his, escaped through Switzerland and he wrote to Annette. We got the letter this morning. There was a mutiny in the camp because they weren't given enough to eat, and the ringleaders were shot. Pierre was one of them."

Hans was silent. He could only think it served the man right. What did they think that a prison camp was—the Ritz?

"Give her time to get over the shock," said Madame Périer. "When she's calmer I'll talk to her. I'll write you a letter when you can come again."

"All right. You will help me, won't you?"

"You can be sure of that. My husband and I, we're agreed. We talked it over and we came to the conclusion that the only thing to do was to accept the situation. He's no fool, my husband, and he says the best chance for France now is to collaborate. And take it all in all I don't dislike you. I shouldn't wonder if you didn't make Annette a better husband than that teacher. And with the baby coming and all."

"I want it to be a boy," said Hans.

"It's going to be a boy. I know for certain. I've seen it in the coffee grounds and I've put out the cards. The answer is a boy every time."

"I almost forgot, here are some papers for you," said Hans, as he turned his cycle and prepared to mount.

He handed her three numbers of *Paris-Soir*. Old Périer read every evening. He read that the French must be realistic and accept the new order that Hitler was going to create in Europe. He read that the German submarines were sweeping the sea. He read that the General Staff had organised to the last detail the campaign that would bring England to her knees and that the Americans were too unprepared, too soft and too divided to come to her help. He read that France must take the heaven-sent opportunity and by loyal collaboration with the Reich regain her honoured position in the new Europe. And it wasn't Germans who wrote it all; it was Frenchmen. He nodded his head with approval when he read that the plutocrats and the Jews would be destroyed and the poor man in France would at last come into his own. They were quite right, the clever fellows who said that France was essentially an agricultural country and its backbone was its industrious farmers. Good sense, that was.

One evening, when they were finishing their supper, ten days after the news had come of Pierre Gavin's death, Madame Périer, by arrangement with her husband, said to Annette:

"I wrote a letter to Hans a few days ago telling him to come here to-morrow."

"Thank you for the warning. I shall stay in my room."

"Oh, come, daughter, the time has passed for foolishness. You must be realistic. Pierre is dead. Hans loves you and wants to marry you. He's a fine-looking fellow. Any girl would be proud of him as a husband. How can we restock the farm without his help? He's going to buy a tractor and a plough with his own money. You must let bygones be bygones."

"You're wasting your breath, Mother. I earned my living before, I can earn my living again. I hate him. I hate his vanity and his arrogance. I could kill him: his death wouldn't satisfy me. I should like to torture him as he's tortured me. I think I should die happy if I could find a way to wound him as he's wounded me."

"You're being very silly, my poor child."

"Your mother's right, my girl," said Périer. "We've been defeated and we must accept the consequences. We've got to make the best arrangement we can with the conquerors. We're cleverer than they are and if we play our cards well we shall come out on top. France was rotten. It's the Jews and the plutocrats who ruined the country. Read the papers and you'll see for yourself!"

"Do you think I believe a word in that paper? Why do you think he brings it to you except that it's sold to the Germans? The men who write in it—traitors, traitors. Oh God, may I live to see them torn to pieces by the mob. Bought, bought every one of them—bought with German money. The swine."

Madame Périer was getting exasperated.

"What have you got against the boy? He took you by force— yes, he was drunk at the time. It's not the first time that's happened to a woman and it won't be the last time. He hit your father and he bled like a pig, but does your father bear him malice?"

"It was an unpleasant incident, but I've forgotten it," said Périer.

Annette burst into harsh laughter.

"You should have been a priest. You forgive injuries with a spirit truly Christian."

"And what is there wrong about that?" asked Madame Périer angrily. "Hasn't he done everything he could to make amends? Where would your father have got his tobacco all these months if it hadn't been for him. If we haven't gone hungry it's owing to him."

"If you'd had any pride, if you'd had any sense of decency, you'd have thrown his presents in his face."

"You've profited by them, haven't you?"

"Never. Never."

"It's a lie and you know it. You've refused to eat the cheese he brought and the butter and the sardines. But the soup you've eaten, you know I put the meat in it that he brought; and the salad you ate to-night, if you didn't have to eat it dry, it's because he brought me oil."

Annette sighed deeply. She passed her hand over her eyes.

"I know. I tried not to, I couldn't help myself, I was so hungry. Yes, I knew his meat went into the soup and I ate it. I knew the salad was made with his oil. I wanted to refuse it; I had such a longing for it, it wasn't I that ate it, it was a ravenous beast within me."

"That's neither here nor there. You ate it."

"With shame. With despair. They broke our strength first with their tanks and their planes, and now when we're defenceless they're breaking our spirit by starving us."

"You get nowhere by being theatrical, my girl. For an educated woman you have really no sense. Forget the past and give a father to your child, to say nothing of a good workman for the farm who'll be worth two hired men. That is sense."

Annette shrugged her shoulders wearily and they lapsed into silence. Next day Hans came. Annette give him a sullen look, but neither spoke nor moved. Hans smiled.

"Thank you for not running away," he said.

"My parents asked you to come and they've gone down to the village. It suits me because I want to have a definite talk with you. Sit down."

He took off his coat and his helmet and drew a chair to the table.

"My parents want me to marry you. You've been clever; with your presents, with your promises, you've got round them. They believe all they read in the papers you bring them. I want to tell you that I will never marry you. I wouldn't have thought it possible that I could hate a human being as I hate you."

"Let me speak in German. You understand enough to know what I'm saying."

"I ought to. I taught it. For two years I was governess to two little girls in Stuttgart."

He broke into German, but she went on speaking French.

"It's not only that I love you, I admire you. I admire your distinction and your grace. There's something about you I don't understand. I respect you. Oh, I can see that you don't want to marry me now even if it were possible. But Pierre is dead."

"Don't speak of him," she cried violently. "That would be the last straw."

"I only want to tell you that for your sake I'm sorry he died."

"Shot in cold blood by his German jailers."

"Perhaps in time you'll grieve for him less. You know, when someone you love dies, you think you'll never get over it, but you do. Won't it be better then to have a father for your child?"

"Even if there were nothing else do you think I could ever forget that you are a German and I'm a Frenchwoman? If you weren't as stupid as only a German can be you'd see that that child must be a reproach to me as long as I live. Do you think I have no friends? How could I ever look them in the face with the child I had with a German soldier? There's only one thing I ask you; leave me alone with my disgrace. Go, go—for God's sake go and never come again."

"But he's my child too. I want him."

"You?" she cried in astonishment. "What can a by-blow that you got in a moment of savage drunkenness mean to you?"

"You don't understand. I'm so proud and so happy. It was when I knew you were going to have a baby that I knew I loved you. At first I couldn't believe it; it was such a surprise to me. Don't you see what I mean? That child that's going to be born means everything in the world to me. Oh, I don't know how to put it; it's put feelings in my heart that I don't understand myself."

She looked at him intently and there was a strange gleam in her eyes. You would have said it was a look of triumph. She gave a short laugh.

"I don't know whether I more loathe the brutality of you Germans or despise your sentimentality."

He seemed not to have heard what she said.

"I think of him all the time."

"You've made up your mind it'll be a boy?"

"I know it'll be a boy. I want to hold him in my arms and I want to teach him to walk. And then when he grows older I'll teach him all I know. I'll teach him to ride and I'll teach him to shoot. Are there fish in your brook? I'll teach him to fish. I'm going to be the proudest father in the world."

She stared at him with hard, hard eyes. Her face was set and stern. An idea, a terrible idea was forming itself in her mind. He gave her a disarming smile.

"Perhaps when you see how much I love our boy, you'll come to love me too. I'll make you a good husband, my pretty."

She said nothing. She merely kept on gazing at him sullenly.

"Haven't you one kind word for me?" he said.

She flushed. She clasped her hands tightly together.

"Others may despise me. I will never do anything that can make me despise myself. You are my enemy and you will always be my enemy. I only live to see the deliverance of France. It'll come, perhaps not next year or the year after, perhaps not for thirty years, but it'll come. The rest of them can do what they like, I will never come to terms with the invaders of my country. I hate you and I hate this child that you've given me. Yes, we've been defeated. Before the end comes you'll see that we haven't been conquered. Now go. My mind's made up and nothing on God's earth can change it."

He was silent for a minute or two.

"Have you made arrangements for a doctor? I'll pay all the expenses."

"Do you suppose we want to spread our shame through the whole countryside? My mother will do all that's necessary."

"But supposing there's an accident?"

"And supposing you mind your own business!"

He sighed and rose to his feet. When he closed the door behind him she watched him walk down the pathway that led to the road. She realised with rage that some of the things he said had aroused in her heart a feeling that she had never felt for him before.

"O God, give me strength," she cried.

Then, as he walked along, the dog, an old dog they'd had for years, ran up to him barking angrily. He had tried for months to make friends with the dog, but it had never responded to his advances; when he tried to pat it, it backed away growling and showing its teeth. And now as the dog ran towards him, irritably giving way to his feeling of frustration, Hans gave it a savage, brutal kick and the dog was flung into the bushes and limped yelping away.

"The beast," she cried. "Lies, lies, lies. And I was weak enough to be almost sorry for him."

There was a looking-glass hanging by the side of the dooɪ and she looked at herself in it. She drew herself up and smiled at her reflection. But rather than a smile it was a fiendish grimace.

It was now March. There was a bustle of activity in the garrison at Soissons. There were inspections and there was intensive training. Rumour was rife. There was no doubt they were going somewhere, but the rank and file could only guess where. Some thought they were being got ready at last for the invasion of England, others were of opinion that they would be sent to the Balkans, and others again talked of the Ukraine. Hans was kept busy. It was not till the second Sunday afternoon that he was able to get out to the farm. It was a cold grey day, with sleet that looked as though it might turn to snow falling in sudden windy flurries. The country was grim and cheerless.

"You!" cried Madame Périer when he went in. "We thought you were dead."

"I couldn't come before. We're off any day now. We don't know when."

"The baby was born this morning. It's a boy."

Hans's heart gave a great leap in his breast. He hung his arms round the old woman and kissed her on both cheeks.

"A Sunday child, he ought to be lucky. Let's open the bottle of champagne. How's Annette?"

"She's as well as can be expected. She had a very easy time. She began to have pains last night and by five o'clock this morning it was all over."

Old Périer was smoking his pipe sitting as near the stove as he could get. He smiled quietly at the boy's enthusiasm.

"One's first child, it has an effect on one," he said.

"He has quite a lot of hair and it's as fair as yours; and blue eyes just like you said he'd have," said Madame Périer. "I've never seen a lovelier baby. He'll be just like his papa."

"Oh, my God, I'm so happy," cried Hans. "How beautiful the world is! I want to see Annette."

"I don't know if she'll see you. I don't want to upset her on account of the milk."

"No, no, don't upset her on my account. If she doesn't want to see me it doesn't matter. But let me see the baby just for a minute."

"I'll see what I can do. I'll try to bring it down."

Madame Périer went out and they heard her heavy tread clumping up the stairs. But in a moment they heard her clattering down again. She burst into the kitchen.

"They're not there. She isn't in her room. The baby's gone."

Périer and Hans cried out and without thinking what they were doing all three of them scampered upstairs. The harsh light of the winter afternoon cast over the shabby furniture, the iron bed, the cheap wardrobe, the chest of drawers, a dismal squalor. There was no one in the room.

"Where is she?" screamed Madame Périer. She ran into the narrow passage, opening doors, and called the girl's name. "Annette, Annette. Oh, what madness!"

"Perhaps in the sitting-room."

They ran downstairs to the unused parlour. An icy air met them as they opened the door. They opened the door of a store-room.

"She's gone out. Something awful has happened."

"How could she have got out?" asked Hans sick with anxiety.

"Through the front door, you fool."

Périer went up to it and looked.

"That's right. The bolt's drawn back."

"Oh, my God, my God, what madness," cried Madame Périer. "It'll kill her."

"We must look for her," said Hans. Instinctively, because that was the way he always went in and out, he ran back into the kitchen and the others followed him "Which way?"

"The brook," the old woman gasped.

He stopped as though turned to stone with horror. He stared at the old woman aghast.

"I'm frightened," she cried. "I'm frightened."

Hans flung open the door, and as he did so Annette walked in. She had nothing on but her nightdress and a flimsy rayon dressing-gown. It was pink, with pale blue flowers. She was soaked, and her hair, dishevelled, clung damply to her head and hung down her shoulders in bedraggled wisps. She was deathly white. Madame Périer sprang towards her and took her in her arms.

"Where have you been? Oh, my poor child, you're wet through. What madness!"

But Annette pushed her away. She looked at Hans.

"You've come at the right moment, you."

"Where's the baby?" cried Madame Périer.

"I had to do it at once. I was afraid if I waited I shouldn't have the courage."

"Annette, what have you done?"

"I've done what I had to do. I took it down to the brook and held it under water till it was dead."

Hans gave a great cry, the cry of an animal wounded to death; he covered his face with his hands, and staggering like a drunken man flung out of the door. Annette sank into a chair, and leaning her forehead on her two fists burst into passionate weeping.

THE ANT AND THE
GRASSHOPPER

WHEN I was a very small boy I was made to learn by heart certain of the fables of La Fontaine, and the moral of each was carefully explained to me. Among those I learnt was *The Ant and The Grasshopper,* which is devised to bring home to the young the useful lesson that in an imperfect world industry is rewarded and giddiness punished. In this admirable fable (I apologise for telling something which everyone is politely, but inexactly, supposed to know) the ant spends a laborious summer gathering its winter store, while the grasshopper sits on a blade of grass singing to the sun. Winter comes and the ant is comfortably provided for, but the grasshopper has an empty larder: he goes to the ant and begs for a little food. Then the ant gives him her classic answer:

"What were you doing in the summer time?"

"Saving your presence, I sang, I sang all day, all night."

"You sang. Why, then go and dance."

I do not ascribe it to perversity on my part, but rather to the inconsequence of childhood, which is deficient in moral sense, that I could never quite reconcile myself to the lesson. My sympathies were with the grasshopper and for some time I never saw an ant without putting my foot on it. In this summary (and as I have discovered since, entirely human) fashion I sought to express my disapproval of prudence and common-sense.

I could not help thinking of this fable when the other day I saw George Ramsay lunching by himself in a restaurant. I never saw anyone wear an expression of such deep gloom. He was staring into space. He looked as though the burden of the whole world sat on his shouders. I was sorry for him: I suspected at once that his unfortunate brother had been causing trouble again. I went up to him and held out my hand.

"How are you?" I asked.

"I'm not in hilarious spirits," he answered.

"Is it Tom again?"

He sighed.

"Yes, it's Tom again."

"Why don't you chuck him? You've done everything in the world for him. You must know by now that he's quite hopeless."

I suppose every family has a black sheep. Tom had been a sore trial to his for twenty years. He had begun life decently enough: he went into business, married and had two children. The Ramsays were perfectly respectable people and there was every reason to suppose that Tom Ramsay would have a useful and honourable career. But one day, without warning, he announced that he didn't like work and that he wasn't suited for marriage. He wanted to enjoy himself. He would listen to no expostulations. He left his wife and his office. He had a little money and he spent two happy years in the various capitals of Europe. Rumours of his doings reached his relations from time to time and they were profoundly shocked. He certainly had a very good time. They shook their heads and asked what would happen when his money was spent. They soon found out: he borrowed. He was charming and unscrupulous. I have never met anyone to whom it was more difficult to refuse a loan. He made a steady income from his friends and he made friends easily. But he always said that the money you spent on necessities was boring; the money that was amusing to spend was the money you spent on luxuries. For this he depended on his brother George. He did not waste his charm on him. George was a serious man and insensible to such enticements. George was respectable. Once or twice he fell to Tom's promises of amendment and gave him considerable sums in order that he might make a fresh start. On these Tom bought a motorcar and some very nice jewellery. But when circumstances forced George to realise that his brother would never settle down and he washed his hands of him, Tom, without a qualm, began to blackmail him. It was not very nice for a respectable lawyer to find his brother shaking cocktails behind the bar of his favourite restaurant or to see him waiting on the box-seat of a taxi outside his club. Tom said that to serve in a bar or to drive a taxi was a perfectly decent occupation, but if George could oblige him with a couple of hundred pounds he didn't mind for the honour of the family giving it up. George paid.

Once Tom nearly went to prison. George was terribly upset. He went into the whole discreditable affair. Really Tom had gone too far. He had been wild, thoughtless and selfish, but he had never before done anything dishonest, by which George meant illegal; and if he were prosecuted he would assuredly be convicted. But you cannot allow your only brother to go to gaol. The man Tom had cheated, a man called Cronshaw, was vindictive. He was determined to take the matter into court; he said Tom was a scoundrel and should be punished. It cost George an infinite deal of trouble and five hundred pounds to settle the affair. I have never seen him in such a rage as when he heard that Tom and Cronshaw had gone off together to Monte Carlo the moment they cashed the cheque. They spent a happy month there.

For twenty years Tom raced and gambled, philandered with the prettiest girls, danced, ate in the most expensive restaurants, and dressed beautifully. He always looked as if he had just stepped out of a bandbox. Though he was forty-six you would never have taken him for more than thirty-five. He was a most amusing companion and though you knew he was perfectly worthless you could not but enjoy his society. He had high spirits, an unfailing gaiety and incredible charm. I never grudged the contributions he regularly levied on me for the necessities of his existence. I never lent him fifty pounds without feeling that I was in his debt. Tom Ramsay knew everyone and everyone knew Tom Ramsay. You could not approve of him, but you could not help liking him.

Poor George, only a year older than his scapegrace brother, looked sixty. He had never taken more than a fortnight's holiday in the year for a quarter of a century. He was in his office every morning at nine-thirty and never left it till six. He was honest, industrious and worthy. He had a good wife, to whom he had never been unfaithful even in thought, and four daughters to whom he was the best of fathers. He made a point of saving a third of his income and his plan was to retire at fifty-five to a little house in the country where he proposed to cultivate his garden and play golf. His life was blameless. He was glad that he was growing old because Tom was growing old too. He rubbed his hands and said:

"It was all very well when Tom was young and good-looking, but he's only a year younger than I am. In four years he'll be fifty. He won't find life so easy then. I shall have thirty thousand pounds by the time I'm fifty. For twenty-five years I've said that Tom would end in the gutter. And we shall see how he likes that. We shall see if it really pays best to work or be idle."

Poor George! I sympathised with him. I wondered now as I sat down beside him what infamous thing Tom had done. George was evidently very much upset.

"Do you know what's happened now?" he asked me.

I was prepared for the worst. I wondered if Tom had got into the hands of the police at last. George could hardly bring himself to speak.

"You're not going to deny that all my life I've been hardworking, decent, respectable and straightforward. After a life of industry and thrift I can look forward to retiring on a small income in gilt-edged securities. I've always done my duty in that state of life in which it has pleased Providence to place me."

"True."

"And you can't deny that Tom has been an idle, worthless, dissolute and dishonourable rogue. If there were any justice he'd be in the workhouse."

"True."

George grew red in the face.

"A few weeks ago he became engaged to a woman old enough to be his mother. And now she's died and left him everything she had. Half a million pounds, a yacht, a house in London and a house in the country."

George Ramsay beat his clenched fist on the table.

"It's not fair, I tell you, it's not fair. Damn it, it's not fair."

I could not help it. I burst into a shout of laughter as I looked at George's wrathful face, I rolled in my chair, I very nearly fell on the floor. George never forgave me. But Tom often asks me to excellent dinners in his charming house in Mayfair, and if he occasionally borrows a trifle from me, that is merely from force of habit. It is never more than a sovereign.

HOME

THE FARM lay in a hollow among the Somersetshire hills, an old-fashioned stone house surrounded by barns and pens and outhouses. Over the doorway the date when it was built had been carved in the elegant figures of the period, 1673, and the house, grey and weather-beaten, looked as much a part of the landscape as the trees that sheltered it. An avenue of splendid elms that would have been the pride of many a squire's mansion led from the road to the trim garden. The people who lived here were as stolid, sturdy and unpretentious as the house; their only boast was that ever since it was built from father to son in one unbroken line they had been born and died in it. For three hundred years they had farmed the surrounding land. George Meadows was now a man of fifty, and his wife was a year or two younger. They were both fine, upstanding people in the prime of life; and their children, two sons and three girls, were handsome and strong. They had no new-fangled notions about being gentlemen and ladies; they knew their place and were proud of it. I have never seen a more united household. They were merry, industrious and kindly. Their life was patriarchal. It had a completeness that gave it a beauty as definite as that of a symphony by Beethoven or a picture by Titian. They were happy and they deserved their happiness. But the master of the house was not George Meadows (not by a long chalk, they said n the village); it was his mother. She was twice the man her son vas, they said.

She was a woman of seventy, tall, upright and dignified, with grey hair, and though her face was much wrinkled, her eyes were bright and shrewd. Her word was law in the house and on the farm; but she had humour, and if her rule was despotic it was also kindly. People laughed at her jokes and repeated them. She was a good business woman and you had to get up very early in the morning to best her in a bargain. She was a character. She combined in a rare degree good will with an alert sense of the ridiculous.

One day Mrs. George stopped me on my way home. She was all in a flutter. (Her mother-in-law was the only Mrs. Meadows we knew; George's wife was only known as Mrs. George.)

"Whoever do you think is coming here to-day?" she asked me. "Uncle George Meadows. You know, him as was in China."

"Why, I thought he was dead."

"We all thought he was dead."

I had heard the story of Uncle George Meadows a dozen times, and it had amused me because it had the savour of an old ballad: it was oddly touching to come across it in real life. For Uncle George Meadows and Tom, his younger brother, had both courted Mrs. Meadows when she was Emily Green, fifty years and more ago, and when she married Tom, George had gone away to sea.

They heard of him on the China coast. For twenty years now and then he sent them presents; then there was no more news of him; when Tom Meadows died his widow wrote and told him, but received no answer; and at last they came to the conclusion that he must be dead. But two or three days ago to their astonishment they had received a letter from the matron of the sailors' home at Portsmouth. It appeared that for the last ten years George Meadows, crippled with rheumatism, had been an inmate and now, feeling that he had not much longer to live, wanted to see once more the house in which he was born. Albert Meadows, his great-nephew, had gone over to Portsmouth in the Ford to fetch him and he was to arrive that afternoon.

"Just fancy," said Mrs. George, "he's not been here for more than fifty years. He's never even seen my George, who's fifty-one next birthday."

"And what does Mrs. Meadows think of it?" I asked.

"Well, you know what she is. She sits there and smiles to herself. All she says is, 'He was a good-looking young fellow when he left, but not so steady as his brother.' That's why she chose my George's father. 'But he's probably quietened down by now,' she says."

Mrs. George asked me to look in and see him. With the simplicity of a country woman who had never been further from her home than London, she thought that because we had both been in China we must have something in common. Of course I accepted. I found the whole family assembled when I arrived: they were sitting in the great old kitchen, with its stone floor, Mrs. Meadows in her usual chair by the fire, very upright, and I was amused to see that she had put on her best silk dress, while her son and his wife sat at the table with their children. On the other side of the fireplace sat an old man, bunched up in a chair. He was very thin and his skin hung on his bones like an old suit much too large for him; his face was wrinkled and yellow and he had lost nearly all his teeth.

I shook hands with him.

"Well, I'm glad to see you've got here safely, Mr. Meadows," I said.

"Captain," he corrected.

"He walked here," Albert, his great-nephew, told me. "When he got to the gate he made me stop the car and said he wanted to walk."

"And mind you, I've not been out of my bed for two years. They carried me down and put me in the car. I thought I'd never walk again, but when I see them elm trees, I remember my father set a lot of store by them elm trees, I felt I could walk. I walked down that drive fifty-two years ago when I went away and now I've walked back again."

"Silly, I call it," said Mrs. Meadows.

"It's done me good. I feel better and stronger than I have for ten years. I'll see you out yet, Emily."

"Don't you be too sure," she answered.

I suppose no one had called Mrs. Meadows by her first name for a generation. It gave me a little shock, as though the old man were taking a liberty with her. She looked at him with a shrewd smile in her eyes and he, talking to her, grinned with his toothless gums. It was strange to look at them, these two old people who had not seen one another for half a century, and to think that all that long time ago he had loved her and she had loved another. I wondered if they remembered what they had felt then and what they had said to one another. I wondered if it seemed to him strange now that for that old woman he had left the home of his fathers, his lawful inheritance, and lived an exile's life.

"Have you ever been married, Captain Meadows?" I asked.

"Not me," he said, in his quavering voice, with a grin. "I know too much about women for that."

"That's what you say," retorted Mrs. Meadows. "If the truth was known I shouldn't be surprised to hear as how you'd had half a dozen black wives in your day."

"They're not black in China, Emily, you ought to know better than that, they're yellow."

"Perhaps that's why you've got so yellow yourself. When I saw you, I said to myself, why, he's got jaundice."

"I said I'd never marry anyone but you, Emily, and I never have."

He said this not with pathos or resentment, but as a mere statement of fact, as a man might say, "I said I'd walk twenty miles and I've done it." There was a trace of satisfaction in the speech.

"Well, you might have regretted it if you had," she answered.

I talked a little with the old man about China.

"There's not a port in China that I don't know better than you know your coat pocket. Where a ship can go I've been. I could keep you sitting here all day long for six months and not tell you half the things I've seen in my day."

"Well, one thing you've not done, George, as far as I can see," said Mrs. Meadows, the mocking but not unkindly smile still in her eyes, "and that's to make a fortune."

"I'm not one to save money. Make it and spend it; that's my motto. But one thing I can say for myself: if I had the chance of going through my life again I'd take it. And there's not many as'll say that."

"No, indeed," I said.

I looked at him with admiration and respect. He was a toothless, crippled, penniless old man, but he had made a success of life, for he had enjoyed it. When I left him he asked me to come and see him again next day. If I was interested in China he would tell me all the stories I wanted to hear.

Next morning I thought I would go and ask if the old man would like to see me. I strolled down the magnificent avenue of elm trees and when I came to the garden saw Mrs. Meadows picking flowers. I bade her good-morning and she raised herself. She had a huge armful of white flowers. I glanced at the house and I saw that the blinds were drawn: I was surprised, for Mrs. Meadows liked the sunshine.

"Time enough to live in the dark when you're buried," she always said.

"How's Captain Meadows?" I asked her.

"He always was a harum-scarum fellow," she answered. "When Lizzie took him a cup of tea this morning she found he was dead."

"Dead?"

"Yes. Died in his sleep. I was just picking these flowers to put in the room. Well, I'm glad he died in that old house. It always means a lot to them Meadows to do that."

They had had a good deal of difficulty in persuading him to go to bed. He had talked to them of all the things that had happened to him in his long life. He was happy to be back in his old home. He was proud that he had walked up the drive without assistance, and he boasted that he would live for another twenty years. But fate had been kind: death had written the full-stop in the right place.

Mrs. Meadows smelt the white flowers that she held in her arms.

"Well, I'm glad he came back," she said. "After I married Tom Meadows and George went away, the fact is I was never quite sure that I'd married the right one."

THE ESCAPE

I HAVE always been convinced that if a woman once made up
her mind to marry a man nothing but instant flight could save
him. Not always that; for once a friend of mine, seeing the inevitable loom menacingly before him, took ship from a certain
port (with a tooth-brush for all his luggage, so conscious was
he of his danger and the necessity for immediate action) and
spent a year travelling round the world; but when, thinking
himself safe (women are fickle, he said, and in twelve months
she will have forgotten all about me), he landed at the selfsame
port the first person he saw gaily waving to him from the quay
was the little lady from whom he had fled. I have only once
known a man who in such circumstances managed to extricate
himself. His name was Roger Charing. He was no longer young
when he fell in love with Ruth Barlow and he had had sufficient
experience to make him careful; but Ruth Barlow had a gift (or
should I call it a quality?) that renders most men defenceless,
and it was this that dispossessed Roger of his commonsense,
his prudence and his worldly wisdom. He went down like a row
of ninepins. This was the gift of pathos. Mrs. Barlow, for she
was twice a widow, had splendid dark eyes and they were the
most moving I ever saw; they seemed to be ever on the point
of filling with tears; they suggested that the world was too
much for her, and you felt that, poor dear, her sufferings had
been more than anyone should be asked to bear. If, like Roger
Charing, you were a strong, hefty fellow with plenty of money,

it was almost inevitable that you should say to yourself: I must stand between the hazards of life and this helpless little thing, oh, how wonderful it would be to take the sadness out of those big and lovely eyes! I gathered from Roger that everyone had treated Mrs. Barlow very badly. She was apparently one of those unfortunate persons with whom nothing by any chance goes right. If she married a husband he beat her; if she employed a broker he cheated her; if she engaged a cook she drank. She never had a little lamb but it was sure to die.

When Roger told me that he had at last persuaded her to marry him, I wished him joy.

"I hope you'll be good friends," he said. "She's a little afraid of you, you know; she thinks you're callous."

"Upon my word I don't know why she should think that."

"You do like her, don't you?"

"Very much."

"She's had a rotten time, poor dear. I feel so dreadfully sorry for her."

"Yes," I said.

I couldn't say less. I knew she was stupid and I thought she was scheming. My own belief was that she was as hard as nails.

The first time I met her we had played bridge together and when she was my partner she twice trumped my best card. I behaved like an angel, but I confess that I thought if the tears were going to well up into anybody's eyes they should have been mine rather than hers. And when, having by the end of the evening lost a good deal of money to me, she said she would send me a cheque and never did, I could not but think that I and not she should have worn a pathetic expression when next we met.

Roger introduced her to his friends. He gave her lovely jewels. He took her here, there, and everywhere. Their marriage was announced for the immediate future. Roger was very happy. He was committing a good action and at the same time doing something he had very much a mind to. It is an uncommon situation and it is not surprising if he was a trifle more pleased with himself than was altogether becoming.

Then, on a sudden, he fell out of love. I do not know why. It could hardly have been that he grew tired of her conversation, for she had never had any conversation. Perhaps it was merely that this pathetic look of hers ceased to wring his heart-strings. His eyes were opened and he was once more the shrewd man of the world he had been. He became acutely conscious that Ruth Barlow had made up her mind to marry him and he swore a solemn oath that nothing would induce him to marry Ruth Barlow. But he was in a quandary. Now that he was in possession of his senses he saw with clearness the sort of woman he had to deal with and he was aware that, if he asked her to release him, she would (in her appealing way) assess her wounded feelings at an immoderately high figure. Besides, it is always awkward for a man to jilt a woman. People are apt to think he has behaved badly.

Roger kept his own counsel. He gave neither by word nor gesture an indication that his feelings towards Ruth Barlow had changed. He remained attentive to all her wishes; he took her to dine at restaurants, they went to the play together, he sent her flowers; he was sympathetic and charming. They had made up their minds that they would be married as soon as they found a house that suited them, for he lived in chambers and she in furnished rooms; and they set about looking at desirable residences. The agents sent Roger orders to view and he took Ruth to see a number of houses. It was very hard to find anything that was quite satisfactory. Roger applied to more agents. They visited house after house. They went over them thoroughly, examining them from the cellars in the basement to the attics under the roof. Sometimes they were too large and sometimes they were too small; sometimes they were too far from the centre of things and sometimes they were too close; sometimes they were too expensive and sometimes they wanted too many repairs; sometimes they were too stuffy and sometimes they were too airy; sometimes they were too dark and sometimes they were too bleak. Roger always found a fault that made the house unsuitable. Of course he was hard to please; he could not bear to ask his dear Ruth to live in any but the perfect house, and the perfect house wanted finding. House-hunting is a tiring and a tiresome business and presently Ruth began to grow peevish. Roger begged her to have patience; somewhere, surely, existed the very house they were looking for, and it only needed a little perseverance and they would find it. They looked at hundreds of houses; they climbed thousands of stairs; they inspected innumerable kitchens. Ruth was exhausted and more than once lost her temper.

"If you don't find a house soon," she said, "I shall have to reconsider my position. Why, if you go on like this we shan't be married for years."

"Don't say that," he answered, "I beseech you to have patience. I've just received some entirely new lists from agents I've only just heard of. There must be at least sixty houses on them."

They set out on the chase again. They looked at more houses and more houses. For two years they looked at houses. Ruth grew silent and scornful: her pathetic, beautiful eyes acquired an expression that was almost sullen. There are limits to human endurance. Mrs. Barlow had the patience of an angel, but at last she revolted.

"Do you want to marry me or do you not?" she asked him.

There was an unaccustomed hardness in her voice, but it did not affect the gentleness of his reply.

"Of course I do. We'll be married the very moment we find a house. By the way, I've just heard of something that might suit us."

"I don't feel well enough to look at any more houses just yet."

"Poor dear, I was afraid you were looking rather tired."

Ruth Barlow took to her bed. She would not see Roger and he had to content himself with calling at her lodgings to enquire and sending her flowers. He was as ever assiduous and gallant. Every day he wrote and told her that he had heard of another house for them to look at. A week passed and then he received the following letter:

Roger,

I do not think you really love me. I have found someone who is anxious to take care of me and I am going to be married to him to-day.

Ruth.

He sent back his reply by special messenger:

Ruth,

Your news shatters me. I shall never get over the blow, but of course your happiness must be my first consideration. I send you herewith seven orders to view; they arrived by this morning's post and I am quite sure you will find among them a house that will exactly suit you.

Roger.

THE JUDGMENT SEAT

THEY awaited their turn patiently, but patience was no new thing to them; they had practised it, all three of them, with grim determination, for thirty years. Their lives had been a long preparation for this moment and they looked forward to the issue now, if not with self-confidence, for that on so awful an occasion would have been misplaced, at all events with hope and courage. They had taken the strait and narrow path when the flowery meads of sin stretched all too invitingly before them; with heads held high, though with breaking hearts, they had resisted temptation; and now, their arduous journey done, they expected their reward. There was no need for them to speak, since each knew the others' thoughts, and they felt that in all three of them the same emotion of relief filled their bodiless souls with thanksgiving. With what anguish now would they have been wrung if they had yielded to the passion which then had seemed so nearly irresistible and what a madness it would have been if for a few short years of bliss they had sacrificed that Life Everlasting which with so bright a light at long last shone before them! They felt like men who with the skin of their teeth have escaped a sudden and violent death and touch their feet and hands and, scarce able to believe that they are still alive, look about them in amazement. They had done nothing with which they could reproach themselves and when presently their angels came and told them that the moment was come, they would advance, as they had passed through the world that was now so far behind, happily conscious that they had done their duty. They stood a little on one side, for the press was great. A terrible war was in progress and for years the soldiers of all nations, men in the full flush of their gallant youth, had marched in an interminable procession to the Judgment Seat; women and children too, their lives brought to a wretched end by violence or, more unhappily, by grief, disease and starvation; and there was in the courts of heaven not a little confusion.

It was on account of this war, too, that these three wan, shivering ghosts stood in expectation of their doom. For John and Mary had been passengers on a ship which was sunk by the torpedo of a submarine; and Ruth, broken in health by the arduous work to which she had so nobly devoted herself, hearing of the death of the man whom she had loved with all her heart, sank beneath the blow and died. John, indeed, might have saved himself if he had not tried to save his wife; he hated her; he had hated her to the depths of his soul for thirty years; but he had always done his duty by her and now, in the moment of dreadful peril, it never occurred to him that he could do otherwise.

At last their angels took them by the hand and led them to the Presence. For a little while the Eternal took not the slightest notice of them. If the truth must be told he was in a bad humour. A moment before there had come up for judgment a philosopher, deceased full of years and honours, who had told the Eternal to his face that he did not believe in him. It was not this that would have disturbed the serenity of the Kings of Kings, this could only have made him smile; but the philosopher, taking perhaps an unfair advantage of the regrettable happenings just then upon Earth, had asked him how, considering them dispassionately, it was possible to reconcile his All-Power with his All-Goodness.

"No one can deny the fact of Evil," said the philosopher, sententiously. "Now, if God cannot prevent Evil he is not all-powerful, and if he can prevent it and will not, he is not all-good."

This argument was of course not new to the Omniscient, but he had always refused to consider the matter; for the fact is, though he knew everything, he did not know the answer to this. Even God cannot make two and two five. But the philosopher, pressing his advantage, and, as philosophers often will,

drawing from a reasonable premise an unjustifiable inference—
the philosopher had finished with a statement that in the circumstances was surely preposterous.

"I will not believe," he said, "in a God who is not All-Powerful
and All-Good."

It was not then perhaps without relief that the Eternal turned
his attention to the three shades who stood humbly and yet
hopefully before him. The quick, with so short a time to live,
when they talk of themselves, talk too much; but the dead, with
eternity before them, are so verbose that only angels could
listen to them with civility. But this in brief is the story that
these three recounted. John and Mary had been happily married for five years and till John met Ruth they loved each other,
as married couples for the most part do, with sincere affection
and mutual respect. Ruth was eighteen, ten years younger than
he was, a charming, graceful animal, with a sudden and all-
conquering loveliness; she was as healthy in mind as she was
in body, and, eager for the natural happiness of life, was capable of achieving that greatness which is beauty of soul. John
fell in love with her and she with him. But it was no ordinary
passion that seized them; it was something so overwhelming
that they felt as if the whole long history of the world signified
only because it had led to the time and place that had brought
them together. They loved as Daphnis and Chloe or as Paolo
and Francesca. But after that first moment of ecstasy when each
discovered the other's love they were seized with dismay. They
were decent people and they respected themselves, the beliefs in
which they had been bred, and the society in which they lived.
How could he betray an innocent girl, and what had she to do
with a married man? Then they grew conscious that Mary was
aware of their love. The confident affection with which she had
regarded her husband was shaken; and there arose in her feelings
of which she would never have thought herself capable, jealousy
and the fear that he would desert her, anger because her possession of his heart was threatened, and a strange hunger of the
soul which was more painful than love. She felt that she would
die if he left her; and yet she knew that if he loved it was because love had come to him, not because he had sought it. She
did not blame him. She prayed for strength; she wept silent,
bitter tears. John and Ruth saw her pine away before their eyes.
The struggle was long and bitter. Sometimes their hearts failed
them and they felt that they could not resist the passion that

burned the marrow of their bones. They resisted. They wrestled
with evil as Jacob wrestled with the angel of God and at last
they conquered. With breaking hearts, but proud in their innocence, they parted. They offered up to God, as it were a sacrifice, their hopes of happiness, the joy of life and the beauty of
the world.

Ruth had loved too passionately ever to love again and with
a stony heart she turned to God and to good works. She was
indefatigable. She tended the sick and assisted the poor. She
founded orphanages and managed charitable institutions. And
little by little her beauty which she cared for no longer left her
and her face grew as hard as her heart. Her religion was fierce
and narrow; her very kindness was cruel because it was founded
not on love but on reason; she became domineering, intolerant
and vindictive. And John resigned, but sullen and angry,
dragged himself along the weary years waiting for the release
of death. Life lost its meaning to him; he had made his effort
and in conquering was conquered; the only emotion that remained with him was the unceasing, secret hatred with which
he looked upon his wife. He used her with kindness and consideration; he did everything that could be expected of a man
who was a Christian and a gentleman. He did his duty. Mary,
a good, faithful and (it must be confessed) exceptional wife,
never thought to reproach her husband for the madness that
had seized him; but all the same she could not forgive him for
the sacrifice he had made for her sake. She grew acid and
querulous. Though she hated herself for it, she could not refrain
from saying the things that she knew would wound him. She
would willingly have sacrificed her life for him, but she could
not bear that he should enjoy a moment's happiness when she
was so wretched that a hundred times she had wished she was
dead. Well, now she was and so were they; grey and drab had
life been, but that was passed; they had not sinned and now
their reward was at hand.

They finished and there was silence. There was silence in all
the courts of heaven. Go to hell were the words that came to
the Eternal's lips, but he did not utter them, for they had a
colloquial association that he rightly thought unfitting to the
solemnity of the occasion. Nor indeed would such a decree have
met the merits of the case. But his brows darkened. He asked
himself if it was for this that he had made the rising sun shine
on the boundless sea and the snow glitter on the mountain tops;

was it for this that the brooks sang blithely as they hastened down the hillsides and the golden corn waved in the evening breeze?

"I sometimes think," said the Eternal, "that the stars never shine more brightly than when reflected in the muddy waters of a wayside ditch."

But the three shades stood before him and now that they had unfolded their unhappy story they could not but feel a certain satisfaction. It had been a bitter struggle, but they had done their duty. The Eternal blew lightly, he blew as a man might blow out a lighted match, and, behold! where the three poor souls had stood—was nothing. The Eternal annihilated them.

"I have often wondered why men think I attach so much importance to sexual irregularity," he said. "If they read my works more attentively they would see that I have always been sympathetic to that particular form of human frailty."

Then he turned to the philosopher, who was still waiting for a reply to his remarks.

"You cannot but allow," said the Eternal, "that on this occasion I have very happily combined my All-Power with my All-Goodness."

SANATORIUM

For the first six weeks that Ashenden was at the sanatorium he stayed in bed. He saw nobody but the doctor who visited him morning and evening, the nurses who looked after him and the maid who brought him his meals. He had contracted tuberculosis of the lungs and since at the time there were reasons that made it difficult for him to go to Switzerland the specialist he saw in London had sent him up to a sanatorium in the north of Scotland. At last the day came that he had been patiently looking forward to when the doctor told him he could get up; and in the afternoon his nurse, having helped him to dress, took him down to the verandah, placed cushions behind him, wrapped him up in rugs and left him to enjoy the sun that was streaming down from a cloudless sky. It was mid-winter. The sanatorium stood on the top of a hill and from it you had a spacious view of the snow-clad country. There were people lying all along the verandah in deck-chairs, some chatting with their neighbours and some reading. Every now and then one would have a fit of coughing and you noticed that at the end of it he looked anxiously at his handkerchief. Before the nurse left Ashenden she turned with a kind of professional briskness to the man who was lying in the next chair.

"I want to introduce Mr. Ashenden to you," she said. And then to Ashenden: "This is Mr. McLeod. He and Mr. Campbell have been here longer than anyone else."

On the other side of Ashenden was lying a pretty girl, with

red hair and bright blue eyes; she had on no make-up, but her lips were very red and the colour on her cheeks was high. It emphasised the astonishing whiteness of her skin. It was lovely even when you realised that its delicate texture was due to illness. She wore a fur coat and was wrapped up in rugs, so that you could see nothing of her body, but her face was extremely thin, so thin that it made her nose, which wasn't really large, look a trifle prominent. She gave Ashenden a friendly look, but did not speak, and Ashenden, feeling rather shy among all those strange people, waited to be spoken to.

"First time they've let you get up, is it?" said McLeod.

"Yes."

"Where's your room?"

Ashenden told him.

"Small. I know every room in the place. I've been here for seventeen years. I've got the best room here and so I damned well ought to have. Campbell's been trying to get me out of it, he wants it himself, but I'm not going to budge; I've got a right to it, I came here six months before he did."

McLeod, lying there, gave you the impression that he was immensely tall; his skin was stretched tight over his bones, his cheeks and temples hollow, so that you could see the formation of his skull under it; and in that emaciated face, with its great bony nose, the eyes were preternaturally large.

"Seventeen years is a long time," said Ashenden, because he could think of nothing else to say.

"Time passes very quickly. I like it here. At first, after a year or two, I went away in the summer, but I don't any more. It's my home now. I've got a brother and two sisters; but they're married and now they've got families; they don't want me. When you've been here a few years and you go back to ordinary life, you feel a bit out of it, you know. Your pals have gone their own ways and you've got nothing in common with them any more. It all seems an awful rush. Much ado about nothing, that's what it is. It's noisy and stuffy. No, one's better off here. I shan't stir again till they carry me out feet first in my coffin."

The specialist had told Ashenden that if he took care of himself for a reasonable time he would get well, and he looked at McLeod with curiosity.

"What do you do with yourself all day long?" he asked.

"Do? Having T.B. is a whole time job, my boy. There's my temperature to take and then I weigh myself. I don't hurry over

my dressing. I have breakfast, I read the papers and go for a
walk. Then I have my rest. I lunch and play bridge. I have another rest and then I dine. I play a bit more bridge and I go to
bed. They've got quite a decent library here, we get all the new
books, but I don't really have much time for reading. I talk to
people. You meet all sorts here, you know. They come and they
go. Sometimes they go because they think they're cured, but a
lot of them come back, and sometimes they go because they die.
I've seen a lot of people out and before I go I expect to see a lot
more."

The girl sitting on Ashenden's other side suddenly spoke.

"I should tell you that few persons can get a heartier laugh
out of a hearse than Mr. McLeod," she said.

McLeod chuckled.

"I don't know about that, but it wouldn't be human nature if
I didn't say to myself: Well, I'm just as glad it's him and not
me they're taking for a ride."

It occurred to him that Ashenden didn't know the pretty girl,
so he introduced him.

"By the way, I don't think you've met Mr. Ashenden—Miss
Bishop. She's English, but not a bad girl."

"How long have *you* been here?" asked Ashenden.

"Only two years. This is my last winter. Dr. Lennox says I
shall be all right in a few months and there's no reason why I
shouldn't go home."

"Silly, I call it," said McLeod. "Stay where you're well off,
that's what I say."

At that moment a man, leaning on a stick, came walking
slowly along the verandah.

"Oh, look, there's Major Templeton," said Miss Bishop, a
smile lighting up her blue eyes; and then, as he came up: "I'm
glad to see you up again."

"Oh, it was nothing. Only a bit of a cold. I'm quite all right
now."

The words were hardly out of his mouth when he began to
cough. He leaned heavily on his stick. But when the attack was
over he smiled gaily.

"Can't get rid of this damned cough," he said. "Smoking too
much. Dr. Lennox says I ought to give it up, but it's no good—
I can't."

He was a tall fellow, good-looking in a slightly theatrical way,
with a dusky, sallow face, fine very dark eyes and a neat black

moustache. He was wearing a fur coat with an Astrakhan collar. His appearance was smart and perhaps a trifle showy. Miss Bishop made Ashenden known to him. Major Templeton said a few civil words in an easy, cordial way, and then asked the girl to go for a stroll with him; he had been ordered to walk to a certain place in the wood behind the sanatorium and back again. McLeod watched them as they sauntered off.

"I wonder if there's anything between those two," he said. "They do say Templeton was a devil with the girls before he got ill."

"He doesn't look up to much in that line just now," said Ashenden.

"You never can tell. I've seen a lot of rum things here in my day. I could tell you no end of stories if I wanted to."

"You evidently do, so why don't you?"

McLeod grinned.

"Well, I'll tell you one. Three or four years ago there was a woman here who was pretty hot stuff. Her husband used to come and see her every other week-end, he was crazy about her, used to fly up from London; but Dr. Lennox was pretty sure she was carrying on with somebody here, but he couldn't find out who. So one night when we'd all gone to bed he had a thin coat of paint put down just outside her room and next day he had everyone's slippers examined. Neat, wasn't it? The fellow whose slippers had paint on them got the push. Dr. Lennox has to be particular, you know. He doesn't want the place to get a bad name."

"How long has Templeton been here?"

"Three or four months. He's been in bed most of the time. He's for it all right. Ivy Bishop'll be a damned fool if she gets stuck on him. She's got a good chance of getting well. I've seen so many of them, you know, I can tell. When I look at a fellow I make up my mind at once whether he'll get well or whether he won't, and if he won't I can make a pretty shrewd guess how long he'll last. I'm very seldom mistaken. I give Templeton about two years myself."

McLeod gave Ashenden a speculative look and Ashenden, knowing what he was thinking, though he tried to be amused, could not help feeling somewhat concerned. There was a twinkle in McLeod's eyes. He plainly knew what was passing through Ashenden's mind.

"You'll get all right. I wouldn't have mentioned it if I hadn't been pretty sure of that. I don't want Dr. Lennox to hoof me out for putting the fear of God into his bloody patients."

Then Ashenden's nurse came to take him back to bed. Even though he had only sat out for an hour, he was tired, and was glad to find himself once more between the sheets. Dr. Lennox came in to see him in the course of the evening. He looked at his temperature chart.

"That's not so bad," he said.

Dr. Lennox was small, brisk and genial. He was a good enough doctor, an excellent business man, and an enthusiastic fisherman. When the fishing season began he was inclined to leave the care of his patients to his assistants; the patients grumbled a little, but were glad enough to eat the young salmon he brought back to vary their meals. He was fond of talking, and now, standing at the end of Ashenden's bed, he asked him, in his broad Scots, whether he had got into conversation with any of the patients that afternoon. Ashenden told him the nurse had introduced him to McLeod. Dr. Lennox laughed.

"The oldest living inhabitant. He knows more about the sanatorium and its inmates than I do. How he gets his information I haven't an idea, but there's not a thing about the private lives of anyone under this roof that he doesn't know. There's not an old maid in the place with a keener nose for a bit of scandal. Did he tell you about Campbell?"

"He mentioned him."

"He hates Campbell, and Campbell hates him. Funny, when you come to think of it, those two men, they've been here for seventeen years and they've got about one sound lung between them. They loathe the sight of one another. I've had to refuse to listen to the complaints about one another that they come to me with. Campbell's room is just below McLeod's and Campbell plays the fiddle. It drives McLeod wild. He says he's been listening to the same tunes for fifteen years, but Campbell says McLeod doesn't know one tune from another. McLeod wants me to stop Campbell playing, but I can't do that, he's got a perfect right to play so long as he doesn't play in the silence hours. I've offered to change McLeod's room, but he won't do that. He says Campbell only plays to drive him out of the room because it's the best in the house, and he's damned if he's going to have it. It's queer, isn't it, that two middle-aged men should think it worth while to make life hell for one another. Neither can leave the other alone. They have their meals at the same table, they play bridge together; and not a day passes without a row. Sometimes I've threatened to turn them both out if they don't behave like sensible fellows. That keeps them quiet for a bit. They don't want to go. They've been here so long, they've got no one any more who gives a damn for them, and they can't cope with the world outside. Campbell went away for a couple of months' holiday some years ago. He came back after a week; he said he couldn't stand the racket, and the sight of so many people in the streets scared him."

It was a strange world into which Ashenden found himself thrown when, his health gradually improving, he was able to mix with his fellow patients. One morning Dr. Lennox told him he could thenceforward lunch in the dining-room. This was a large, low room, with great window space; the windows were always wide open and on fine days the sun streamed in. There seemed to be a great many people and it took him some time to sort them out. They were of all kinds, young, middle-aged and old. There were some, like McLeod and Campbell, who had been at the sanatorium for years and expected to die there. Others had only been there for a few months. There was one middle-aged spinster called Miss Atkin who had been coming every winter for a long time and in the summer went to stay with friends and relations. She had nothing much the matter with her any more, and might just as well have stayed away altogether, but she liked the life. Her long residence had given her a sort of position, she was honorary librarian and hand in glove with the matron. She was always ready to gossip with you, but you were soon warned that everything you said was passed on. It was useful to Dr. Lennox to know that his patients were getting on well together and were happy, that they did nothing imprudent and followed his instructions. Little escaped Miss Atkin's sharp eyes, and from her it went to the matron and so to Dr. Lennox. Because she had been coming for so many years, she sat at the same table as McLeod and Campbell, together with an old general who had been put there on account of his rank. The table was in no way different from any other, and it was not more advantageously placed, but because the oldest residents sat there it was looked upon as the most desirable place to sit, and several elderly women were bitterly resentful because Miss Atkin, who went away for four or five months every summer, should be given a place there while they who spent the whole year in the sanatorium sat at other tables. There was an old Indian Civilian who had been at the santorium longer than anyone but McLeod and Campbell; he was a man who in his day had ruled a province, and he was waiting irascibly for either McLeod or Campbell to die so that he might take his place at the first table. Ashenden made the acquaintance of Campbell. He was a long, big-boned fellow with a bald head, so thin that you wondered how his limbs held together; and when he sat crumpled in an arm-chair he gave you the uncanny impression of a mannikin in a puppet-show. He was brusque, touchy and bad-tempered. The first thing he asked Ashenden was:

"Are you fond of music?"

"Yes."

"No one here cares a damn for it. I play the violin. But if you like it, come to my room one day and I'll play to you."

"Don't you go," said McLeod, who heard him. "It's torture."

"How can you be so rude?" cried Miss Atkin. "Mr. Campbell plays very nicely."

"There's no one in this beastly place that knows one note from another," said Campbell.

With a derisive chuckle McLeod walked off. Miss Atkin tried to smooth things down.

"You mustn't mind what McLeod said."

"Oh, I don't. I'll get back on him all right."

He played the same tune over and over again all that afternoon. McLeod banged on the floor, but Campbell went on. He sent a message by a maid to say that he had a headache and would Mr. Campbell mind not playing; Campbell replied that he had a perfect right to play and if Mr. McLeod didn't like it he could lump it. When next they met high words passed.

Ashenden was put at a table with the pretty Miss Bishop, with Templeton, and with a London man, an accountant, called Henry Chester. He was a stocky, broad-shouldered, wiry little fellow, and the last person you would ever have thought would be attacked by T.B. It had come upon him as a sudden and unexpected blow. He was a perfectly ordinary man, somewhere between thirty and forty, married, with two children. He lived in a decent suburb. He went up to the City every morning and read the morning paper; he came down from the City every evening and read the evening paper. He had no interests except his business and his family. He liked his work; he made enough money to live in comfort, he put by a reasonable sum every year, he played golf on Saturday afternoon and on Sunday, he

went every August for a three weeks' holiday to the same place
on the east coast; his children would grow up and marry, then
he would turn his business over to his son and retire with his
wife to a little house in the country where he could potter about
till death claimed him at a ripe old age. He asked nothing more
from life than that, and it was a life that thousands upon thousands of his fellow-men lived with satisfaction. He was the average citizen. Then this thing happened. He had caught cold
playing golf, it had gone to his chest, and he had had a cough
that he couldn't shake off. He had always been strong and
healthy, and had no opinion of doctors; but at last at his wife's
persuasion he had consented to see one. It was a shock to him,
a fearful shock, to learn that there was tubercle in both his
lungs and that his only chance of life was to go immediately to a
sanatorium. The specialist he saw then told him that he might
be able to go back to work in a couple of years, but two years
had passed and Dr. Lennox advised him not to think of it for at
least a year more. He showed him the bacilli in his sputum, and
in an X-ray photograph the actively-diseased patches in his
lungs. He lost heart. It seemed to him a cruel and unjust trick
that fate had played upon him. He could have understood it if
he had led a wild life, if he had drunk too much, played around
with women or kept late hours. He would have deserved it then.
But he had done none of these things. It was monstrously unfair. Having no resources in himself, no interest in books, he
had nothing to do but think of his health. It became an ob-
session. He watched his symptoms anxiously. They had to deprive him of a thermometer because he took his temperature
a dozen times a day. He got it into his head that the doctors
were taking his case too indifferently, and in order to force their
attention used every method he could devise to make the
thermometer register a temperature that would alarm; and
when his tricks were foiled he grew sulky and querulous. But he
was by nature a jovial, friendly creature, and when he forgot
himself he talked and laughed gaily; then on a sudden he remembered that he was a sick man and you would see in his eyes
the fear of death.

At the end of every month his wife came up to spend a day or
two in a lodging-house near-by. Dr. Lennox did not much like
the visits that relatives paid the patients, it excited and unsettled them. It was moving to see the eagerness with which
Henry Chester looked forward to his wife's arrival; but it was

strange to notice that once she had come he seemed less pleased than one would have expected. Mrs. Chester was a pleasant, cheerful little woman, not pretty, but neat, as commonplace as her husband, and you only had to look at her to know that she was a good wife and mother, a careful housekeeper, a nice, quiet body who did her duty and interfered with nobody. She had been quite happy in the dull, domestic life they had led for so many years, her only dissipation a visit to the pictures, her great thrill the sales in the big London shops; and it had never occurred to her that it was monotonous. It completely satisfied her. Ashenden liked her. He listened with interest while she prattled about her children and her house in the suburbs, her neighbours and her trivial occupations. On one occasion he met her in the road. Chester for some reason connected with his treatment had stayed in and she was alone. Ashenden suggested that they should walk together. They talked for a little of indifferent things. Then she suddenly asked him how he thought her husband was.

"I think he seems to be getting on all right."

"I'm so terribly worried."

"You must remember it's a slow, long business. One has to have patience."

They walked on a little and then he saw she was crying.

"You mustn't be unhappy about him," said Ashenden gently.

"Oh, you don't know what I have to put up with when I come here. I know I ought not to speak about it, but I must. I can trust you, can't I?"

"Of course."

"I love him. I'm devoted to him. I'd do anything in the world I could for him. We've never quarrelled, we've never even differed about a single thing. He's beginning to hate me and it breaks my heart."

"Oh, I can't believe that. Why, when you're not here he talks of you all the time. He couldn't talk more nicely. He's devoted to you."

"Yes, that's when I'm not here. It's when I'm here, when he sees me well and strong, that it comes over him. You see, he resents it so terribly that he's ill and I'm well. He's afraid he's going to die and he hates me because I'm going to live. I have to be on my guard all the time; almost everything I say, if I speak of the children, if I speak of the future, exasperates him, and he says bitter, wounding things. When I speak of something I've had to do to the house or a servant I've had to change it irritates him beyond endurance. He complains that I treat him as if he didn't count any more. We used to be so united, and now I feel there's a great wall of antagonism between us. I know I shouldn't blame him, I know it's only his illness, he's a dear good man really, and kindness itself, normally he's the easiest man in the world to get on with; and now I simply dread coming here and I go with relief. He'd be terribly sorry if I had T.B. but I know that in his heart of hearts it would be a relief. He could forgive me, he could forgive fate, if he thought I was going to die too. Sometimes he tortures me by talking about what I shall do when he's dead, and when I get hysterical and cry out to him to stop, he says I needn't grudge him a little pleasure when he'll be dead so soon and I can go on living for years and years and have a good time. Oh, it's so frightful to think that this love we've had for one another all these years should die in this sordid, miserable way."

Mrs. Chester sat down on a stone by the roadside and gave way to passionate weeping. Ashenden looked at her with pity, but could find nothing to say that might comfort her. What she had told him did not come quite as a surprise.

"Give me a cigarette," she said at last. "I mustn't let my eyes get all red and swollen, or Henry'll know I've been crying and he'll think I've had bad news about him. Is death so horrible? Do we all fear death like that?"

"I don't know," said Ashenden.

"When my mother was dying she didn't seem to mind a bit. She knew it was coming and she even made little jokes about it. But she was an old woman."

Mrs. Chester pulled herself together and they set off again. They walked for a while in silence.

"You won't think any the worse of Henry for what I've told you?" she said at last.

"Of course not."

"He's been a good husband and a good father. I've never known a better man in my life. Until this illness I don't think an unkind or ungenerous thought ever passed through his head."

The conversation left Ashenden pensive. People often said he had a low opinion of human nature. It was because he did not always judge his fellows by the usual standards. He accepted, with a smile, a tear or a shrug of the shoulders, much that filled others with dismay. It was true that you would never have expected that good-natured, commonplace little chap to harbour such bitter and unworthy thoughts; but who has ever been able to tell to what depths man may fall or to what heights rise? The fault lay in the poverty of his ideals. Henry Chester was born and bred to lead an average life, exposed to the normal vicissitudes of existence, and when an unforeseeable accident befell him he had no means of coping with it. He was like a brick made to take its place with a million others in a huge factory, but by chance with a flaw in it so that it is inadequate to its purpose. And the brick too, if it had a mind, might cry: What have I done that I cannot fulfil my modest end, but must be taken away from all these other bricks that support me and thrown on the dust-heap? It was no fault of Henry Chester's that he was incapable of the conceptions that might have enabled him to bear his calamity with resignation. It is not everyone who can find solace in art or thought. It is the tragedy of our day that these humble souls have lost their faith in God, in whom lay hope, and their belief in a resurrection that might bring them the happiness that has been denied them on earth; and have found nothing to put in their place.

There are people who say that suffering ennobles. It is not true. As a general rule it makes man petty, querulous and self-ish; but here in this sanatorium there was not much suffering. In certain stages of tuberculosis the slight fever that accompanies it excites rather than depresses, so that the patient feels alert and, upborne by hope, faces the future blithely; but for all that the idea of death haunts the subconscious. It is a sardonic theme song that runs through a sprightly operetta. Now and again the gay, melodious arias, the dance measures, deviate strangely into tragic strains that throb menacingly down the nerves; the petty interests of every day, the small jealousies and trivial concerns are as nothing; pity and terror make the heart on a sudden stand still and the awfulness of death broods as the silence that precedes a tropical storm broods over the tropical jungle. After Ashenden had been for some time at the sanatorium there came a boy of twenty. He was in the navy, a sub-lieutenant in a submarine, and he had what they used to call in novels galloping consumption. He was a tall, good-looking youth, with curly brown hair, blue eyes and a very sweet smile. Ashenden saw him two or three times lying on the terrace in the sun and passed the time of day with him. He was a cheerful lad. He talked of musical shows and film stars; and he read the paper for the football results and the boxing news. Then he was put to bed and Ashenden saw him no more. His relations were sent for and in two months he was dead. He died uncomplaining. He understood what was happening to him as little as an animal. For a day or two there was the same malaise in the sanatorium as there is in a prison when a man has been hanged; and then, as though by universal consent, in obedience to an instinct of self-preservation, the boy was put out of mind: life, with its three meals a day, its golf on the miniature course, its regulated exercise, its prescribed rests, its quarrels and jealousies, its scandal-mongering and petty vexations, went on as before. Campbell, to the exasperation of McLeod, continued to play the prize-song and "Annie Laurie" on his fiddle. McLeod continued to boast of his bridge and gossip about other people's health and morals. Miss Atkin continued to backbite. Henry Chester continued to complain that the doctors gave him insufficient attention and railed against fate because, after the model life he had led, it had played him such a dirty trick. Ashenden continued to read, and with amused tolerance to watch the vagaries of his fellow-creatures.

He became intimate with Major Templeton. Templeton was perhaps a little more than forty years of age. He had been in the Grenadier Guards, but had resigned his commission after the war. A man of ample means, he had since then devoted himself entirely to pleasure. He raced in the racing season, shot in the shooting season and hunted in the hunting season. When this was over he went to Monte Carlo. He told Ashenden of the large sums he had made and lost at baccarat. He was very fond of women and if his stories could be believed they were very fond of him. He loved good food and good drink. He knew by their first names the head waiters of every restaurant in London where you ate well. He belonged to half a dozen clubs. He had led for years a useless, selfish, worthless life, the sort of life which maybe it will be impossible for anyone to live in the future, but he had lived it without misgiving and had enjoyed it. Ashenden asked him once what he would do if he had his time over again and he answered that he would do exactly what he had done. He was an amusing talker, gay and pleasantly ironic, and he dealt with the surface of things, which was all he knew, with a light, easy and assured touch. He always had a pleasant word for the dowdy spinsters in the sanatorium and a joking one for the peppery old gentlemen, for he combined

good manners with a natural kindliness. He knew his way about
the superficial world of the people who have more money than
they know what to do with as well as he knew his way about
Mayfair. He was the kind of man who would always have been
willing to take a bet, to help a friend and to give a tenner to a
rogue. If he had never done much good in the world he had
never done much harm. He amounted to nothing. But he was
a more agreeable companion than many of more sterling character and of more admirable qualities. He was very ill now.
He was dying and he knew it. He took it with the same easy,
laughing nonchalance as he had taken all the rest. He'd had a
thundering good time, he regretted nothing, it was rotten tough
luck getting T.B. but to hell with it, no one can live for ever,
and when you came to think of it, he might have been killed in
the war or broken his bloody neck in a point-to-point. His principle all through life had been, when you've made a bad bet,
pay up and forget about it. He'd had a good run for his money
and he was ready to call it a day. It had been a damned good
party while it lasted, but every party's got to come to an end,
and next day it doesn't matter much if you went home with the
milk or if you left while the fun was in full swing.

Of all those people in the sanatorium he was probably from
the moral standpoint the least worthy, but he was the only one
who genuinely accepted the inevitable with unconcern. He
snapped his fingers in the face of death, and you could choose
whether to call his levity unbecoming or his insouciance gallant.

The last thing that ever occurred to him when he came to the
sanatorium was that he might fall more deeply in love there
than he had ever done before. His amours had been numerous,
but they had been light; he had been content with the politely
mercenary love of chorus girls and with ephemeral unions with
women of easy virtue whom he met at house parties. He had
always taken care to avoid any attachment that might en-
danger his freedom. His only aim in life had been to get as much
fun out of it as possible, and where sex was concerned he found
every advantage and no inconvenience in ceaseless variety. But
he liked women. Even when they were quite old he could not
talk to them without a caress in his eyes and a tenderness in his
voice. He was prepared to do anything to please them. They
were conscious of his interest in them and were agreeably
flattered, and they felt, quite mistakenly, that they could trust

him never to let them down. He once said a thing that Ashenden thought showed insight:

"You know, any man can get any woman he wants if he tries hard enough, there's nothing in that, but once he's got her, only a man who thinks the world of women can get rid of her without humiliating her."

It was simply from habit that he began to make love to Ivy Bishop. She was the prettiest and the youngest girl in the sanatorium. She was in point of fact not so young as Ashenden had first thought her, she was twenty-nine, but for the last eight years she had been wandering from one sanatorium to another, in Switzerland, England and Scotland, and the sheltered invalid life had preserved her youthful appearance so that you might easily have taken her for twenty. All she knew of the world she had learnt in these establishments, so that she combined rather curiously extreme innocence with extreme sophistication. She had seen a number of love affairs run their course. A good many men, of various nationalities, had made love to her; she accepted their attentions with self-possession and humour, but she had at her disposal plenty of firmness when they showed an inclination to go too far. She had a force of character unexpected in anyone who looked so flower-like and when it came to a show-down knew how to express her meaning in plain, cool and decisive words. She was quite ready to have a flirtation with George Templeton. It was a game she understood, and though always charming to him, it was with a bantering lightness that showed quite clearly that she had summed him up and had no mind to take the affair more seriously than he did. Like Ashenden, Templeton went to bed every evening at six and dined in his room, so that he saw Ivy only by day. They went for little walks together, but otherwise were seldom alone. At lunch the conversation between the four of them, Ivy, Templeton, Henry Chester and Ashenden, was general, but it was obvious that it was for neither of the two men that Templeton took so much trouble to be entertaining. It seemed to Ashenden that he was ceasing to flirt with Ivy to pass the time, and that his feeling for her was growing deeper and more sincere; but he could not tell whether she was conscious of it nor whether it meant anything to her. Whenever Templeton hazarded a remark that was more intimate than the occasion warranted she countered it with an ironic one that made them all laugh. But Templeton's laugh was rueful. He was no longer content to have her take him as a play-boy. The more Ashenden knew Ivy Bishop the more he liked her. There was something pathetic in her sick beauty, with that lovely transparent skin, the thin face in which the eyes were so large and so wonderfully blue; and there was something pathetic in her plight, for like so many others in the sanatorium she seemed to be alone in the world. Her mother led a busy social life, her sisters were married; they took but a perfunctory interest in the young woman from whom they had been separated now for eight years. They corresponded, they came to see her occasionally, but there was no longer very much between them. She accepted the situation without bitterness. She was friendly with everyone and prepared always to listen with sympathy to the complaints and the distress of all and sundry. She went out of her way to be nice to Henry Chester and did what she could to cheer him.

"Well, Mr. Chester," she said to him one day at lunch, "it's the end of the month, your wife will be coming to-morrow. That's something to look forward to."

"No, she's not coming this month," he said quietly, looking down at his plate.

"Oh, I am sorry. Why not? The children are all right, aren't they?"

"Dr. Lennox thinks it's better for me that she shouldn't come."

There was a silence. Ivy looked at him with troubled eyes.

"That's tough luck, old man," said Templeton in his hearty way. "Why didn't you tell Lennox to go to hell?"

"He must know best," said Chester.

Ivy gave him another look and began to talk of something else.

Looking back, Ashenden realised that she had at once suspected the truth. For next day he happened to walk with Chester.

"I'm awfully sorry your wife isn't coming," he said. "You'll miss her visit dreadfully."

"Dreadfully."

He gave Ashenden a sidelong glance. Ashenden felt that he had something he wanted to say, but could not bring himself to say it. He gave his shoulders an angry shrug.

"It's my fault if she's not coming. I asked Lennox to write and tell her not to. I couldn't stick it any more. I spend the whole month looking forward to her coming and then when she's here I hate her. You see, I resent so awfully having this filthy disease. She's strong and well and full of beans. It maddens me when I see the pain in her eyes. What does it matter to her really? Who cares if you're ill? They pretend to care, but they're jolly glad it's you and not them. I'm a swine, aren't I?"

Ashenden remembered how Mrs. Chester had sat on a stone by the side of the road and wept.

"Aren't you afraid you'll make her very unhappy, not letting her come?"

"She must put up with that. I've got enough with my own unhappiness without bothering with hers."

Ashenden did not know what to say and they walked on in silence. Suddenly Chester broke out irritably.

"It's all very well for you to be disinterested and unselfish, you're going to live. I'm going to die, and God damn it, I don't want to die. Why should I? It's not fair."

Time passed. In a place like the sanatorium where there was little to occupy the mind it was inevitable that soon everyone should know that George Templeton was in love with Ivy Bishop. But it was not so easy to tell what her feelings were. It was plain that she liked his company, but she did not seek it, and indeed it looked as though she took pains not to be alone with him. One or two of the middle-aged ladies tried to trap her into some compromising admission, but ingenuous as she was, she was easily a match for them. She ignored their hints and met their straight questions with incredulous laughter. She succeeded in exasperating them.

"She can't be so stupid as not to see that he's mad about her."

"She has no right to play with him like that."

"I believe she's just as much in love with him as he is with her."

"Dr. Lennox ought to tell her mother."

No one was more incensed than McLeod.

"Too ridiculous. After all, nothing can come of it. He's riddled with T.B. and she's not much better."

Campbell on the other hand was sardonic and gross.

"I'm all for their having a good time while they can. I bet there's a bit of hanky-panky going on if one only knew, and I don't blame 'em."

"You cad," said McLeod.

"Oh, come off it. Templeton isn't the sort of chap to play bumble-puppy bridge with a girl like that unless he's getting something out of it, and she knows a thing or two, I bet."

Ashenden, who saw most of them, knew them better than any of the others. Templeton at last had taken him into his confidence. He was rather amused at himself.

"Rum thing at my time of life, falling in love with a decent girl. Last thing I'd ever expected of myself. And it's no good denying it, I'm in it up to the neck; if I were a well man I'd ask her to marry me to-morrow. I never knew a girl could be as nice as that. I've always thought girls, decent girls, I mean, damned bores. But she isn't a bore, she's as clever as she can stick. And pretty too. My God, what a skin! And that hair: but it isn't any of that that's bowled me over like a row of ninepins. D'you know what's got me? Damned ridiculous when you come to think of it. An old rip like me. Virtue. Makes me laugh like a hyena. Last thing I've ever wanted in a woman, but there it is, no getting away from it, she's good, and it makes me feel like a worm. Surprises you, I suppose?"

"Not a bit," said Ashenden. "You're not the first rake who's fallen to innocence. It's merely the sentimentality of middle age."

"Dirty dog," laughed Templeton.

"What does she say to it?"

"Good God, you don't suppose I've told her. I've never said a word to her that I wouldn't have said before anyone else. I may be dead in six months, and besides, what have I got to offer a girl like that?"

Ashenden by now was pretty sure that she was just as much in love with Templeton as he was with her. He had seen the flush that coloured her cheeks when Templeton came into the dining-room and he had noticed the soft glance she gave him now and then when he was not looking at her. There was a peculiar sweetness in her smile when she listened to him telling some of his old experiences. Ashenden had the impression that she basked comfortably in his love as the patients on the terrace, facing the snow, basked in the hot sunshine; but it might very well be that she was content to leave it at that, and it was certainly no business of his to tell Templeton what perhaps she had no wish that he should know.

Then an incident occurred to disturb the monotony of life.
Though McLeod and Campbell were always at odds they
played bridge together because, till Templeton came, they were
the best players in the sanatorium. They bickered incessantly,
their post-mortems were endless, but after so many years each
knew the other's game perfectly and they took a keen delight
in scoring off one another. As a rule Templeton refused to play
with them; though a fine player he preferred to play with Ivy
Bishop, and McLeod and Campbell were agreed on this, that
she ruined the game. She was the kind of player who, having
made a mistake that lost the rubber, would laugh and say: Well,
it only made the difference of a trick. But one afternoon, since
Ivy was staying in her room with a headache, Templeton consented to play with Campbell and McLeod. Ashenden was the
fourth. Though it was the end of March there had been heavy
snow for several days, and they played, in a verandah open
on three sides to the wintry air, in fur coats and caps, with
mittens on their hands. The stakes were too small for a gambler
like Templeton to take the game seriously and his bidding was
overbold, but he played so much better than the other three
that he generally managed to make his contract or at least to
come near it. But there was much doubling and redoubling.
The cards ran high, so that an inordinate number of small slams
were bid; it was a tempestuous game, and McLeod and Campbell lashed one another with their tongues. Half-past five arrived and the last rubber was started, for at six the bell rang
to send everyone to rest. It was a hard-fought rubber, with sets
on both sides, for McLeod and Campbell were opponents and
each was determined that the other should not win. At ten
minutes to six it was game all and the last hand was dealt.
Templeton was McLeod's partner and Ashenden Campbell's.
The bidding started with two clubs from McLeod; Ashenden
said nothing; Templeton showed that he had substantial help,
and finally McLeod called a grand slam. Campbell doubled and
McLeod redoubled. Hearing this, the players at other tables
who had broken off gathered round and the hands were played
in deadly silence to a little crowd of onlookers. McLeod's face
was white with excitement and there were beads of sweat on his
brow. His hands trembled. Campbell was very grim. McLeod
had to take two finesses and they both came off. He finished
with a squeeze and got the last of the thirteen tricks. There
was a burst of applause from the onlookers. McLeod, arrogant

in victory, sprang to his feet. He shook his clenched fist at Campbell.

"Play that off on your blasted fiddle," he shouted. "Grand slam doubled and redoubled. I've wanted to get it all my life and now I've got it. By God. By God."

He gasped. He staggered forward and fell across the table. A stream of blood poured from his mouth. The doctor was sent for. Attendants came. He was dead.

He was buried two days later, early in the morning so that the patients should not be disturbed by the sight of a funeral. A relation in black came from Glasgow to attend it. No one had liked him. No one regretted him. At the end of a week so far as one could tell, he was forgotten. The Indian Civilian took his place at the principal table and Campbell moved into the room he had so long wanted.

"Now we shall have peace," said Dr. Lennox to Ashenden. "When you think that I've had to put up with the quarrels and complaints of those two men for years and years . . . Believe me, one has to have patience to run a sanatorium. And to think that after all the trouble he's given me he had to end up like that and scare all those people out of their wits."

"It was a bit of a shock, you know," said Ashenden.

"He was a worthless fellow and yet some of the women have been quite upset about it. Poor little Miss Bishop cried her eyes out."

"I suspect that she was the only one who cried for him and not for herself."

But presently it appeared that there was one person who had not forgotten him. Campbell went about like a lost dog. He wouldn't play bridge. He wouldn't talk. There was no doubt about it, he was moping for McLeod. For several days he remained in his room, having his meals brought to him, and then went to Dr. Lennox and said he didn't like it as well as his old one and wanted to be moved back. Dr. Lennox lost his temper, which he rarely did, and told him he had been pestering him to give him that room for years and now he could stay there or get out of the sanatorium. He returned to it and sat gloomily brooding.

"Why don't you play your violin?" the matron asked him at length. "I haven't heard you play for a fortnight."

"I haven't."

"Why not?"

"It's no fun any more. I used to get a kick out of playing be-cause I knew it maddened McLeod. But now nobody cares if I play or not. I shall never play again."

Nor did he for all the rest of the time that Ashenden was at the sanatorium. It was strange, now that McLeod was dead life had lost its savour for him. With no one to quarrel with, no one to infuriate, he had lost his incentive and it was plain that it would not be long before he followed his enemy to the grave.

But on Templeton McLeod's death had another effect, and one which was soon to have unexpected consequences. He talked to Ashenden about it in his cool, detached way.

"Grand, passing out like that in his moment of triumph. I can't make out why everyone got in such a state about it. He'd been here for years, hadn't he?"

"Eighteen, I believe."

"I wonder if it's worth it. I wonder if it's not better to have one's fling and take the consequences."

"I suppose it depends on how much you value life."

"But is this life?"

Ashenden had no answer. In a few months he could count on being well, but you only had to look at Templeton to know that he was not going to recover. The death-look was on his face.

"D'you know what I've done?" asked Templeton. "I've asked Ivy to marry me."

Ashenden was startled.

"What did she say?"

"Bless her little heart, she said it was the most ridiculous idea she'd ever heard in her life and I was crazy to think of such a thing."

"You must admit she was right."

"Quite. But she's going to marry me."

"It's madness."

"I dare say it is; but anyhow, we're going to see Lennox and ask him what he thinks about it."

The winter had broken at last; there was still snow on the hills, but in the valleys it was melted and on the lower slopes the birch-trees were in bud all ready to burst into delicate leaf. The enchantment of spring was in the air. The sun was hot. Everyone felt alert and some felt happy. The old stagers who came only for the winter were making their plans to go south. Templeton and Ivy went to see Dr. Lennox together. They told him what they had in mind. He examined them; they were

X-rayed and various tests were taken. Dr. Lennox fixed a day when he would tell them the results and in the light of this discuss their proposal. Ashenden saw them just before they went to keep the appointment. They were anxious, but did their best to make a joke of it. Dr. Lennox showed them the results of his examinations and explained to them in plain language what their condition was.

"All that's very fine and large," said Templeton then, "but what we want to know is whether we can get married."

"It would be highly imprudent."

"We know that, but does it matter?"

"And criminal if you had a child."

"We weren't thinking of having one," said Ivy.

"Well, then I'll tell you in very few words how the matter stands. Then you must decide for yourselves."

Templeton gave Ivy a little smile and took her hand. The doctor went on.

"I don't think Miss Bishop will ever be strong enough to lead a normal life, but if she continues to live as she has been doing for the last eight years . . ."

"In sanatoriums?"

"Yes. There's no reason why she shouldn't live very comfortably, if not to a ripe old age, as long as any sensible person wants to live. The disease is quiescent. If she marries, if she attempts to live an ordinary life, the foci of infection may very well light up again, and what the results of that may be no one can foretell. So far as you are concerned, Templeton, I can put it even more shortly. You've seen the X-ray photos yourself. Your lungs are riddled with tubercle. If you marry you'll be dead in six months."

"And if I don't how long can I live?"

The doctor hesitated.

"Don't be afraid. You can tell me the truth."

"Two or three years."

"Thank you, that's all we wanted to know."

They went as they had come, hand in hand; Ivy was crying softly. No one knew what they said to one another; but when they came into luncheon they were radiant. They told Ashenden and Chester that they were going to be married as soon as they could get a licence. Then Ivy turned to Chester.

"I should so much like your wife to come up for my wedding. D'you think she would?"

"You're not going to be married here?"

"Yes. Our respective relations will only disapprove, so we're not going to tell them until it's all over. We shall ask Dr. Lennox to give me away."

She looked mildly at Chester, waiting for him to speak, for he had not answered her. The other two men watched him. His voice shook a little when he spoke.

"It's very kind of you to want her. I'll write and ask her."

When the news spread among the patients, though everyone congratulated them, most of them privately told one another that it was very injudicious; but when they learnt, as sooner or later everything that happened in the sanatorium was learnt, that Dr. Lennox had told Templeton that if he married he would be dead in six months, they were awed to silence. Even the dullest were moved at the thought of these two persons who loved one another so much that they were prepared to sacrifice their lives. A spirit of kindliness and good will descended on the sanatorium: people who hadn't been speaking spoke to one another again; others forgot for a brief space their own anxieties. Everyone seemed to share in the happiness of the happy pair. And it was not only the spring that filled those sick hearts with new hope, the great love that had taken posession of the man and the girl seemed to spread its effulgence on all that came near them. Ivy was quietly blissful; the excitement became her and she looked younger and prettier. Templeton seemed to walk on air. He laughed and joked as if he hadn't a care in the world. You would have said that he looked forward to long years of uninterrupted felicity. But one day he confided in Ashenden.

"This isn't a bad place, you know," he said. "Ivy's promised me that when I hand in my checks she'll come back here. She knows the people and she won't be so lonely."

"Doctors are often mistaken," said Ashenden. "If you live reasonably I don't see why you shouldn't go on for a long time yet."

"I'm only asking for three months. If I can only have that it'll be worth it."

Mrs. Chester came up two days before the wedding. She had not seen her husband for several months and they were shy with one another. It was easy to guess that when they were alone they felt awkward and constrained. Yet Chester did his best to shake off the depression that was now habitual and at all events at mealtimes showed himself the jolly, hearty little fellow that he must have been before he fell ill. On the eve of the wedding day they all dined together, Templeton and Ashenden both sitting up for dinner; they drank champagne and stayed up till ten joking, laughing and enjoying themselves. The wedding took place next morning in the kirk. Ashenden was best man. Everyone in the sanatorium who could stand on his feet attended it. The newly married couple were setting out by car immediately after lunch. Patients, doctors and nurses assembled to see them off. Someone had tied an old shoe on the back of the car, and as Templeton and his wife came out of the door of the sanatorium rice was flung over them. A cheer was raised as they drove away, as they drove away to love and death. The crowd separated slowly. Chester and his wife went silently side by side. After they had gone a little way he shyly took her hand. Her heart seemed to miss a beat. With a sidelong glance she saw that his eyes were wet with tears.

"Forgive me, dear," he said. "I've been very unkind to you."

"I knew you didn't mean it," she faltered.

"Yes, I did. I wanted you to suffer because I was suffering. But not any more. All this about Templeton and Ivy Bishop— I don't know how to put it, it's made me see everything differently. I don't mind dying any more. I don't think death's very important, not so important as love. And I want you to live and be happy. I don't grudge you anything any more and I don't resent anything. I'm glad now it's me that must die and not you. I wish for you everything that's good in the world. I love you."

LOUISE

I COULD never understand why Louise bothered with me. She disliked me and I knew that behind my back, in that gentle way of hers, she seldom lost the opportunity of saying a disagreeable thing about me. She had too much delicacy ever to make a direct statement, but with a hint and a sigh and a little flutter of her beautiful hands she was able to make her meaning plain. She was a mistress of cold praise. It was true that we had known one another almost intimately, for five-and-twenty years, but it was impossible for me to believe that she could be affected by the claims of old association. She thought me a coarse, brutal, cynical and vulgar fellow. I was puzzled at her not taking the obvious course and dropping me. She did nothing of the kind; indeed, she would not leave me alone; she was constantly asking me to lunch and dine with her and once or twice a year invited me to spend a week-end at her house in the country. At last I thought that I had discovered her motive. She had an uneasy suspicion that I did not believe in her; and if that was why she did not like me, it was also why she sought my acquaintance: it galled her that I alone should look upon her as a comic figure and she could not rest till I acknowledged myself mistaken and defeated. Perhaps she had an inkling that I saw the face behind the mask and because I alone held out was determined that sooner or later I too should take the mask for the face. I was never quite certain that she was a complete humbug. I won-

dered whether she fooled herself as thoroughly as she fooled the
world or whether there was some spark of humour at the bottom
of her heart. If there was it might be that she was attracted to
me, as a pair of crooks might be attracted to one another, by
the knowledge that we shared a secret that was hidden from
everybody else.

I knew Louise before she married. She was then a frail, delicate girl with large and melancholy eyes. Her father and mother
worshipped her with an anxious adoration, for some illness,
scarlet fever I think, had left her with a weak heart and she had
to take the greatest care of herself. When Tom Maitland proposed to her they were dismayed, for they were convinced that
she was much too delicate for the strenuous state of marriage.
But they were not too well off and Tom Maitland was rich. He
promised to do everything in the world for Louise and finally
they entrusted her to him as a sacred charge. Tom Maitland
was a big, husky fellow, very good-looking and a fine athlete. He
doted on Louise. With her weak heart he could not hope to keep
her with him long and he made up his mind to do everything he
could to make her few years on earth happy. He gave up the
games he excelled in, not because she wished him to, she was
glad that he should play golf and hunt, but because by a coincidence she had a heart attack whenever he proposed to leave her
for a day. If they had a difference of opinion she gave in to him
at once, for she was the most submissive wife a man could have,
but her heart failed her and she would be laid up, sweet and uncomplaining, for a week. He could not be such a brute as to cross
her. Then they would have quite a little tussle about which
should yield and it was only with difficulty that at last he persuaded her to have her own way. On one occasion seeing her
walk eight miles on an expedition that she particularly wanted
to make, I suggested to Tom Maitland that she was stronger
than one would have thought. He shook his head and sighed.

"No, no, she's dreadfully delicate. She's been to all the best
heart specialists in the world and they all say that her life hangs
on a thread. But she has an unconquerable spirit."

He told her that I had remarked on her endurance.

"I shall pay for it to-morrow," she said to me in her plaintive
way. "I shall be at death's door."

"I sometimes think that you're quite strong enough to do the
things you want to," I murmured.

I had noticed that if a party was amusing she could dance till five in the morning, but if it was dull she felt very poorly and Tom had to take her home early. I am afraid she did not like my reply, for though she gave me a pathetic little smile I saw no amusement in her large blue eyes.

"You can't very well expect me to fall down dead just to please you," she answered.

Louise outlived her husband. He caught his death of cold one day when they were sailing and Louise needed all the rugs there were to keep her warm. He left her a comfortable fortune and a daughter. Louise was inconsolable. It was wonderful that she managed to survive the shock. Her friends expected her speedily to follow poor Tom Maitland to the grave. Indeed they already felt dreadfully sorry for Iris, her daughter, who would be left an orphan. They redoubled their attentions towards Louise. They would not let her stir a finger; they insisted on doing everything in the world to save her trouble. They had to, because if she was called upon to do anything tiresome or inconvenient her heart went back on her and there she was at death's door. She was entirely lost without a man to take care of her, she said, and she did not know how, with her delicate health, she was going to bring up her dear Iris. Her friends asked why she did not marry again. Oh, with her heart it was out of the question, though of course she knew that dear Tom would have wished her to, and perhaps it would be the best thing for Iris if she did; but who would want to be bothered with a wretched invalid like herself? Oddly enough more than one young man showed himself quite ready to undertake the charge and a year after Tom's death she allowed George Hobhouse to lead her to the altar. He was a fine, upstanding fellow and he was not at all badly off. I never saw anyone so grateful as he for the privilege of being allowed to take care of this frail little thing.

"I shan't live to trouble you long," she said.

He was a soldier and an ambitious one, but he resigned his commission. Louise's health forced her to spend the winter at Monte Carlo and the summer at Deauville. He hesitated a little at throwing up his career, and Louise at first would not hear of it; but at last she yielded as she always yielded, and he prepared to make his wife's last few years as happy as might be.

"It can't be very long now," she said. "I'll try not to be troublesome."

For the next two or three years Louise managed, notwithstanding her weak heart, to go beautifully dressed to all the most lively parties, to gamble very heavily, to dance and even to flirt with tall slim young men. But George Hobhouse had not the stamina of Louise's first husband and he had to brace himself now and then with a stiff drink for his day's work as Louise's second husband. It is possible that the habit would have grown on him, which Louise would not have liked at all, but very fortunately (for her) the war broke out. He rejoined his regiment and three months later was killed. It was a great shock to Louise. She felt, however, that in such a crisis she must not give way to a private grief; and if she had a heart attack nobody heard of it. In order to distract her mind she turned her villa at Monte Carlo into a hospital for convalescent officers. Her friends told her that she would never survive the strain.

"Of course it will kill me," she said, "I know that. But what does it matter? I must do my bit."

It didn't kill her. She had the time of her life. There was no convalescent home in France that was more popular. I met her by chance in Paris. She was lunching at the Ritz with a tall and very handsome young Frenchman. She explained that she was there on business connected with the hospital. She told me that the officers were too charming to her. They knew how delicate she was and they wouldn't let her do a single thing. They took care of her, well—as though they were all her husbands. She sighed.

"Poor George, who would ever have thought that I with my heart should survive him?"

"And poor Tom!" I said.

I don't know why she didn't like my saying that. She gave me her plaintive smile and her beautiful eyes filled with tears.

"You always speak as though you grudged me the few years that I can expect to live."

"By the way, your heart's much better, isn't it?"

"I'll never be better. I saw a specialist this morning and he said I must be prepared for the worst."

"Oh, well, you've been prepared for that for nearly twenty years now, haven't you?"

When the war came to an end Louise settled in London. She was now a woman of over forty, thin and frail still, with large eyes and pale cheeks, but she did not look a day more than twenty-five. Iris, who had been at school and was now grown up, came to live with her.

"She'll take care of me," said Louise. "Of course it'll be hard on her to live with such a great invalid as I am, but it can only be for such a little while, I'm sure she won't mind."

Iris was a nice girl. She had been brought up with the knowledge that her mother's health was precarious. As a child she had never been allowed to make a noise. She had always realised that her mother must on no account be upset. And though Louise told her now that she would not hear of her sacrificing herself for a tiresome old woman the girl simply would not listen. It wasn't a question of sacrificing herself, it was a happiness to do what she could for her poor dear mother. With a sigh her mother let her do a great deal.

"It pleases the child to think she's making herself useful," she said.

"Don't you think she ought to go out and about more?" I asked.

"That's what I'm always telling her. I can't get her to enjoy herself. Heaven knows, I never want anyone to put themselves out on my account."

And Iris, when I remonstrated with her, said: "Poor dear mother, she wants me to go and stay with friends and go to parties, but the moment I start off anywhere she has one of her heart attacks, so I much prefer to stay at home."

But presently she fell in love. A young friend of mine, a very good lad, asked her to marry him and she consented. I liked the child and was glad that she was to be given at last the chance to lead a life of her own. She had never seemed to suspect that such a thing was possible. But one day the young man came to me in great distress and told me that his marriage was indefinitely postponed. Iris felt that she could not desert her mother. Of course it was really no business of mine, but I made the opportunity to go and see Louise. She was always glad to receive her friends at tea-time and now that she was older she cultivated the society of painters and writers.

"Well, I hear that Iris isn't going to be married," I said after a little.

"I don't know about that. She's not going to be married quite as soon as I could have wished. I've begged her on my bended knees not to consider me, but she absolutely refuses to leave me."

"Don't you think it's rather hard on her?"

"Dreadfully. Of course it can only be for a few months, but I hate the thought of anyone sacrificing themselves for me."

"My dear Louise, you've buried two husbands, I can't see the least reason why you shouldn't bury at least two more."

"Do you think that's funny?" she asked me in a tone that she made as offensive as she could.

"I suppose it's never struck you as strange that you're always strong enough to do anything you want to and that your weak heart only prevents you from doing things that bore you?"

"Oh, I know, I know what you've always thought of me. You've never believed that I had anything the matter with me, have you?"

I looked at her full and square.

"Never. I think you've carried out for twenty-five years a stupendous bluff. I think you're the most selfish and monstrous woman I have ever known. You ruined the lives of those two wretched men you married and now you're going to ruin the life of your daughter."

I should not have been surprised if Louise had had a heart attack then. I fully expected her to fly into a passion. She merely gave me a gentle smile.

"My poor friend, one of these days you'll be so dreadfully sorry you said this to me."

"Have you quite determined that Iris shall not marry this boy?"

"I've begged her to marry him. I know it'll kill me, but I don't mind. Nobody cares for me. I'm just a burden to everybody."

"Did you tell her it would kill you?"

"She made me."

"As if anyone ever made you do anything that you were not yourself quite determined to do."

"She can marry her young man to-morrow if she likes. If it kills me, it kills me."

"Well, let's risk it, shall we?"

"Haven't you got any compassion for me?"

"One can't pity anyone who amuses one as much as you amuse me," I answered.

A faint spot of colour appeared on Louise's pale cheeks and though she smiled still her eyes were hard and angry.

"Iris shall marry in a month's time," she said, "and if anything happens to me I hope you and she will be able to forgive yourselves."

Louise was as good as her word. A date was fixed, a trousseau of great magnificence was ordered, and invitations were issued. Iris and the very good lad were radiant. On the wedding-day, at ten o'clock in the morning, Louise, that devilish woman, had one of her heart attacks—and died. She died gently forgiving Iris for having killed her.

LORD MOUNTDRAGO

DR. AUDLIN looked at the clock on his desk. It was twenty minutes to six. He was surprised that his patient was late, for Lord Mountdrago prided himself on his punctuality; he had a sententious way of expressing himself which gave the air of an epigram to a commonplace remark, and he was in the habit of saying that punctuality is a compliment you pay to the intelligent and a rebuke you administer to the stupid. Lord Mountdrago's appointment was for five-thirty.

There was in Dr. Audlin's appearance nothing to attract attention. He was tall and spare, with narrow shoulders and something of a stoop; his hair was grey and thin; his long, sallow face deeply lined. He was not more than fifty, but he looked older. His eyes, pale-blue and rather large, were weary. When you had been with him for a while you noticed that they moved very little; they remained fixed on your face, but so empty of expression were they that it was no discomfort. They seldom lit up. They gave no clue to his thoughts nor changed with the words he spoke. If you were of an observant turn it might have struck you that he blinked much less often than most of us. His hands were on the large side, with long, tapering fingers; they were soft, but firm, cool but not clammy. You could never have said what Dr. Audlin wore unless you had made a point of looking. His clothes were dark. His tie was black. His dress made his sallow lined face paler, and his pale eyes more wan. He gave you the impression of a very sick man.

Dr. Audlin was a psycho-analyst. He had adopted the profession by accident and practised it with misgiving. When the
war broke out he had not been long qualified and was getting
experience at various hospitals; he offered his services to the
authorities, and after a time was sent out to France. It was then
that he discovered his singular gift. He could allay certain pains
by the touch of his cool, firm hands, and by talking to them
often induce sleep in men who were suffering from sleeplessness.
He spoke slowly. His voice had no particular colour, and its
tone did not alter with the words he uttered, but it was musical,
soft and lulling. He told the men that they must rest, that they
mustn't worry, that they must sleep; and rest stole into their
jaded bones, tranquillity pushed their anxieties away, like a
man finding a place for himself on a crowded bench, and slumber
fell on their tired eyelids like the light rain of spring upon the
fresh-turned earth. Dr. Audlin found that by speaking to men
with that low, monotonous voice of his, by looking at them with
his pale, quiet eyes, by stroking their weary foreheads with his
long firm hands, he could soothe their perturbations, resolve the
conflicts that distracted them and banish the phobias that made
their lives a torment. Sometimes he effected cures that seemed
miraculous. He restored speech to a man who, after being buried
under the earth by a bursting shell, had been struck dumb, and
he gave back the use of his limbs to another who had been
paralysed after a crash in a plane. He could not understand his
powers; he was of a sceptical turn, and though they say that in
circumstances of this kind the first thing is to believe in yourself, he never quite succeeded in doing that; and it was only the
outcome of his activities, patent to the most incredulous observer, that obliged him to admit that he had some faculty, coming from he knew not where, obscure and uncertain, that
enabled him to do things for which he could offer no explanation. When the war was over he went to Vienna and studied
there, and afterwards to Zurich; and then settled down in London to practise the art he had so strangely acquired. He had
been practising now for fifteen years, and had attained, in the
speciality he followed, a distinguished reputation. People told
one another of the amazing things he had done, and though his
fees were high, he had as many patients as he had time to see.
Dr. Audlin knew that he had achieved some very extraordinary
results; he had saved men from suicide, others from the lunatic
asylum, he had assuaged griefs that embittered useful lives, he

had turned unhappy marriages into happy ones, he had eradicated abnormal instincts and thus delivered not a few from a hateful bondage, he had given health to the sick in spirit; he had done all this, and yet at the back of his mind remained the suspicion that he was little more than a quack.

It went against his grain to exercise a power that he could not understand, and it offended his honesty to trade on the faith of the people he treated when he had no faith in himself. He was rich enough now to live without working, and the work exhausted him; a dozen times he had been on the point of giving up practice. He knew all that Freud and Jung and the rest of them had written. He was not satisfied; he had an intimate conviction that all their theory was hocus-pocus, and yet there the results were, incomprehensible, but manifest. And what had he not seen of human nature during the fifteen years that patients had been coming to his dingy back room in Wimpole Street? The revelations that had been poured into his ears, sometimes only too willingly, sometimes with shame, with reservations, with anger, had long ceased to surprise him. Nothing could shock him any longer. He knew by now that men were liars, he knew how extravagant was their vanity; he knew far worse than that about them; but he knew that it was not for him to judge or to condemn. But year by year as these terrible confidences were imparted to him his face grew a little greyer, its lines a little more marked and his pale eyes more weary. He seldom laughed, but now and again when for relaxation he read a novel he smiled. Did their authors really think the men and women they wrote of were like that? If they only knew how much more complicated they were, how much more unexpected, what irreconcilable elements co-existed within their souls and what dark and sinister contentions afflicted them!

It was a quarter to six. Of all the strange cases he had been called upon to deal with Dr. Audlin could remember none stranger than that of Lord Mountdrago. For one thing the personality of his patient made it singular. Lord Mountdrago was an able and a distinguished man. Appointed Secretary for Foreign Affairs when still under forty, now after three years in office he had seen his policy prevail. It was generally acknowledged that he was the ablest politician in the Conservative Party and only the fact that his father was a peer, on whose death he would no longer be able to sit in the House of Commons, made it impossible for him to aim at the premiership. But if in these democratic times it is out of the question for a Prime Minister of England to be in the House of Lords, there was nothing to prevent Lord Mountdrago from continuing to be Secretary for Foreign Affairs in successive Conservative administrations and so for long directing the foreign policy of his country.

Lord Mountdrago had many good qualities. He had intelligence and industry. He was widely travelled, and spoke several languages fluently. From early youth he had specialised in foreign affairs, and had conscientiously made himself acquainted with the political and economic circumstances of other countries. He had courage, insight and determination. He was a good speaker, both on the platform and in the House, clear, precise and often witty. He was a brilliant debater and his gift of repartee was celebrated. He had a fine presence: he was a tall, handsome man, rather bald and somewhat too stout, but this gave him solidity and an air of maturity that were of service to him. As a young man he had been something of an athlete and had rowed in the Oxford boat, and he was known to be one of the best shots in England. At twenty-four he had married a girl of eighteen whose father was a duke and her mother a great American heiress, so that she had both position and wealth, and by her he had had two sons. For several years they had lived privately apart, but in public united, so that appearances were saved, and no other attachment on either side had given the gossips occasion to whisper. Lord Mountdrago indeed was too ambitious, too hard-working, and it must be added too patriotic, to be tempted by any pleasures that might interfere with his career. He had, in short, a great deal to make him a popular and successful figure. He had unfortunately great defects.

He was a fearful snob. You would not have been surprised at this if his father had been the first holder of the title. That the son of an ennobled lawyer, a manufacturer or a distiller should attach an inordinate importance to his rank is understandable. The earldom held by Lord Mountdrago's father was created by Charles II, and the barony held by the first Earl dated from the Wars of the Roses. For three hundred years the successive holders of the title had allied themselves with the noblest families of England. But Lord Mountdrago was as conscious of his birth as a *nouveau riche* is conscious of his money. He never missed an opportunity of impressing it upon others. He had beautiful manners when he chose to display them, but this he did only with people whom he regarded as his equals. He was coldly insolent to those whom he looked upon as his social inferiors. He was rude to his servants and insulting to his secretaries. The subordinate officials in the government offices to which he had been successively attached feared and hated him. His arrogance was horrible. He knew that he was a great deal cleverer than most of the persons he had to do with, and never hesitated to apprise them of the fact. He had no patience with the infirmities of human nature. He felt himself born to command and was irritated with people who expected him to listen to their arguments or wished to hear the reasons for his decisions. He was immeasurably selfish. He looked upon any service that was rendered him as a right due to his rank and intelligence and therefore deserving of no gratitude. It never entered his head that he was called upon to do anything for others. He had many enemies: he despised them. He knew no one who merited his assistance, his sympathy or his compassion. He had no friends. He was distrusted by his chiefs, because they doubted his loyalty; he was unpopular with his party, because he was over-bearing and discourteous; and yet his merit was so great, his patriotism so evident, his intelligence so solid and his management of affairs so brilliant that they had to put up with him. And what made it possible to do this was that on occasion he could be enchanting: when he was with persons whom he considered his equals, or whom he wished to captivate, in the company of foreign dignitaries or women of distinction, he could be gay, witty and debonair; his manners then reminded you that in his veins ran the same blood as had run in the veins of Lord Chesterfield; he could tell a story with point, he could be natural, sensible and even profound. You were surprised at the extent of his knowledge and the sensitiveness of his taste. You thought him the best company in the world; you forgot that he had insulted you the day before and was quite capable of cutting you dead the next.

Lord Mountdrago almost failed to become Dr. Audlin's patient. A secretary rang up the doctor and told him that his lordship, wishing to consult him, would be glad if he would come to his house at ten o'clock on the following morning. Dr. Audlin answered that he was unable to go to Lord Mountdrago's house, but would be pleased to give him an appointment at his consulting-room at five o'clock on the next day but one. The secretary took the message and presently rang back to say that Lord Mountdrago insisted on seeing Dr. Audlin in his own house and the doctor could fix his own fee. Dr. Audlin replied that he only saw patients in his consulting-room and expressed his regret that unless Lord Mountdrago was prepared to come to him he could not give him his attention. In a quarter of an hour a brief message was delivered to him that his lordship would come not next day but one, but next day, at five.

When Lord Mountdrago was then shown in he did not come forward, but stood at the door and insolently looked the doctor up and down. Dr. Audlin perceived that he was in a rage; he gazed at him, silently, with still eyes. He saw a big heavy man, with greying hair, receding on the forehead so that it gave nobility to his brow, a puffy face with bold regular features and an expression of haughtiness. He had somewhat the look of one of the Bourbon sovereigns of the eighteenth century.

"It seems that it is as difficult to see you as a Prime Minister, Dr. Audlin. I'm an extremely busy man."

"Won't you sit down?" said the doctor.

His face showed no sign that Lord Mountdrago's speech in any way affected him. Dr. Audlin sat in his chair at the desk. Lord Mountdrago still stood and his frown darkened.

"I think I should tell you that I am His Majesty's Secretary for Foreign Affairs," he said acidly.

"Won't you sit down?" the doctor repeated.

Lord Mountdrago made a gesture, which might have suggested that he was about to turn on his heel and stalk out of the room; but if that was his intention he apparently thought better of it. He seated himself. Dr. Audlin opened a large book and took up his pen. He wrote without looking at his patient.

"How old are you?"

"Forty-two."

"Are you married?"

"Yes."

"How long have you been married?"

"Eighteen years."

"Have you any children?"

"I have two sons."

Dr. Audlin noted down the facts as Lord Mountdrago abruptly answered his questions. Then he leaned back in his chair and looked at him. He did not speak; he just looked, gravely, with pale eyes that did not move.

"Why have you come to see me?" he asked at length.

"I've heard about you. Lady Canute is a patient of yours, I

understand. She tells me you've done her a certain amount of good."

Dr. Audlin did not reply. His eyes remained fixed on the other's face, but they were so empty of expression that you might have thought he did not even see him.

"I can't do miracles," he said at length. Not a smile, but the shadow of a smile flickered in his eyes. "The Royal College of Physicians would not approve of it if I did."

Lord Mountdrago gave a brief chuckle. It seemed to lessen his hostility. He spoke more amiably.

"You have a very remarkable reputation. People seem to believe in you."

"Why have you come to me?" repeated Dr. Audlin.

Now it was Lord Mountdrago's turn to be silent. It looked as though he found it hard to answer. Dr. Audlin waited. At last Lord Mountdrago seemed to make an effort. He spoke.

"I'm in perfect health. Just as a matter of routine I had myself examined by my own doctor the other day, Sir Augustus Fitzherbert, I daresay you've heard of him, and he tells me I have the physique of a man of thirty. I work hard, but I'm never tired, and I enjoy my work. I smoke very little and I'm an extremely moderate drinker. I take a sufficiency of exercise and I lead a regular life. I am a perfectly sound, normal, healthy man. I quite expect you to think it very silly and childish of me to consult you."

Dr. Audlin saw that he must help him.

"I don't know if I can do anything to help you. I'll try. You're distressed?"

Lord Mountdrago frowned.

"The work that I'm engaged in is important. The decisions I am called upon to make can easily affect the welfare of the country and even the peace of the world. It is essential that my judgment should be balanced and my brain clear. I look upon it as my duty to eliminate any cause of worry that may interfere with my usefulness."

Dr. Audlin had never taken his eyes off him. He saw a great deal. He saw behind his patient's pompous manner and arrogant pride an anxiety that he could not dispel.

"I asked you to be good enough to come here because I know by experience that it's easier for someone to speak openly in the dingy surroundings of a doctor's consulting-room than in his accustomed environment."

"They're certainly dingy," said Lord Mountdrago acidly. He paused. It was evident that this man who had so much self-assurance, so quick and decided a mind that he was never at a loss, at this moment was embarrassed. He smiled in order to show the doctor that he was at his ease, but his eyes betrayed his disquiet. When he spoke again it was with unnatural heartiness.

"The whole thing's so trivial that I can hardly bring myself to bother you with it. I'm afraid you'll just tell me not to be a fool and waste your valuable time."

"Even things that seem very trivial may have their importance. They can be a symptom of a deep-seated derangement. And my time is entirely at your disposal."

Dr. Audlin's voice was low and grave. The monotone in which he spoke was strangely soothing. Lord Mountdrago at length made up his mind to be frank.

"The fact is I've been having some very tiresome dreams lately. I know it's silly to pay any attention to them, but—well, the honest truth is that I'm afraid they've got on my nerves."

"Can you describe any of them to me?"

Lord Mountdrago smiled, but the smile that tried to be careless was only rueful.

"They're so idiotic, I can hardly bring myself to narrate them."

"Never mind."

"Well, the first I had was about a month ago. I dreamt that I was at a party at Connemara House. It was an official party. The King and Queen were to be there and of course decorations were worn. I was wearing my ribbon and my star. I went into a sort of cloakroom they have to take off my coat. There was a little man there called Owen Griffiths, who's a Welsh Member of Parliament, and to tell you the truth, I was surprised to see him. He's very common, and I said to myself: 'Really, Lydia Connemara is going too far, whom will she ask next?' I thought he looked at me rather curiously, but I didn't take any notice of him; in fact I cut the little bounder and walked upstairs. I suppose you've never been there?"

"Never."

"No, it's not the sort of house you'd ever be likely to go to. It's a rather vulgar house, but it's got a very fine marble staircase, and the Connemaras were at the top receiving their guests. Lady Connemara gave me a look of surprise when I shook

hands with her, and began to giggle; I didn't pay much attention, she's a very silly, ill-bred woman and her manners are no
better than those of her ancestors whom King Charles II made
a duchess. I must say the reception rooms at Connemara House
are stately. I walked through, nodding to a number of people
and shaking hands; then I saw the German Ambassador talking
with one of the Austrian Archdukes. I particularly wanted to
have a word with him, so I went up and held out my hand. The
moment the Archduke saw me he burst into a roar of laughter.
I was deeply affronted. I looked him up and down sternly, but
he only laughed the more. I was about to speak to him rather
sharply, when there was a sudden hush and I realised that the
King and Queen had come. Turning my back on the Archduke,
I stepped forward, and then, quite suddenly, I noticed that I
hadn't got any trousers on. I was in short silk drawers, and I
wore scarlet sock-suspenders. No wonder Lady Connemara
had giggled; no wonder the Archduke had laughed! I can't tell
you what that moment was. An agony of shame. I awoke in a
cold sweat. Oh, you don't know the relief I felt to find it was
only a dream."

"It's the kind of dream that's not so very uncommon," said
Dr. Audlin.

"I dare say not. But an odd thing happened next day. I was in
the lobby of the House of Commons, when that fellow Griffiths
walked slowly past me. He deliberately looked down at my legs
and then he looked me full in the face and I was almost certain
he winked. A ridiculous thought came to me. He'd been there
the night before and seen me make that ghastly exhibition of
myself and was enjoying the joke. But of course I knew that
was impossible because it was only a dream. I gave him an icy
glare and he walked on. But he was grinning his head off."

Lord Mountdrago took his handkerchief out of his pocket and
wiped the palms of his hands. He was making no attempt now
to conceal his perturbation. Dr. Audlin never took his eyes off
him.

"Tell me another dream."

"It was the night after, and it was even more absurd than the
first one. I dreamt that I was in the House. There was a debate
on foreign affairs which not only the country, but the world, had
been looking forward to with the gravest concern. The government had decided on a change in their policy which vitally
affected the future of the Empire. The occasion was historic. Of

course the House was crowded. All the ambassadors were there.
The galleries were packed. It fell to me to make the important
speech of the evening. I had prepared it carefully. A man like
me has enemies, there are a lot of people who resent my having
achieved the position I have at an age when even the cleverest
men are content with situations of relative obscurity, and I was
determined that my speech should not only be worthy of the
occasion, but should silence my detractors. It excited me to
think that the whole world was hanging on my lips. I rose to my
feet. If you've ever been in the House you'll know how members
chat to one another during a debate, rustle papers and turn over
reports. The silence was the silence of the grave when I began
to speak. Suddenly I caught sight of that odious little bounder
on one of the benches opposite, Griffiths the Welsh member; he
put out his tongue at me. I don't know if you've ever heard a
vulgar music-hall song called *A Bicycle Made for Two*. It was
very popular a great many years ago. To show Griffiths how
completely I despised him I began to sing it. I sang the first
verse right through. There was a moment's surprise, and when
I finished they cried 'Hear, hear,' on the opposite benches. I put
up my hand to silence them and sang the second verse. The
House listened to me in stony silence and I felt the song wasn't
going down very well. I was vexed, for I have a good baritone
voice, and I was determined that they should do me justice.
When I started the third verse the members began to laugh; in
an instant the laughter spread; the ambassadors, the strangers
in the Distinguished Strangers' Gallery, the ladies in the Ladies'
Gallery, the reporters, they shook, they bellowed, they held their
sides, they rolled in their seats; everyone was overcome with
laughter except the ministers on the Front Bench immediately
behind me. In that incredible, in that unprecedented uproar,
they sat petrified. I gave them a glance, and suddenly the
enormity of what I had done fell upon me. I had made myself
the laughing-stock of the whole world. With misery I realised
that I should have to resign. I woke and knew it was only a
dream."

Lord Mountdrago's grand manner had deserted him as he
narrated this, and now having finished he was pale and trembling. But with an effort he pulled himself together. He forced
a laugh to his shaking lips.

"The whole thing was so fantastic that I couldn't help being
amused. I didn't give it another thought, and when I went into

the House on the following afternoon I was feeling in very good form. The debate was dull, but I had to be there, and I read some documents that required my attention. For some reason I chanced to look up and I saw that Griffiths was speaking. He has an unpleasant Welsh accent and an unprepossessing appearance. I couldn't imagine that he had anything to say that it was worth my while to listen to, and I was about to return to my papers when he quoted two lines from *A Bicycle Made for Two*. I couldn't help glancing at him and I saw that his eyes were fixed on me with a grin of bitter mockery. I faintly shrugged my shoulders. It was comic that a scrubby little Welsh member should look at me like that. It was an odd coincidence that he should quote two lines from that disastrous song that I'd sung all through in my dream. I began to read my papers again, but I don't mind telling you that I found it difficult to concentrate on them. I was a little puzzled. Owen Griffiths had been in my first dream, the one at Connemara House, and I'd received a very definite impression afterwards that he knew the sorry figure I'd cut. Was it a mere coincidence that he had just quoted those two lines? I asked myself if it was possible that he was dreaming the same dreams as I was. But of course the idea was preposterous and I determined not to give it a second thought."

There was a silence. Dr. Audlin looked at Lord Mountdrago and Lord Mountdrago looked at Dr. Audlin.

"Other people's dreams are very boring. My wife used to dream occasionally and insist on telling me her dreams next day with circumstantial detail. I found it maddening."

Dr. Audlin faintly smiled.

"You're not boring me."

"I'll tell you one more dream I had a few days later. I dreamt that I went into a public-house at Limehouse. I've never been to Limehouse in my life and I don't think I've ever been in a public-house since I was at Oxford, and yet I saw the street and the place I went into as exactly as if I were at home there. I went into a room, I don't know whether they call it the saloon bar or the private bar; there was a fireplace and a large leather arm-chair on one side of it, and on the other a small sofa; a bar ran the whole length of the room and over it you could see into the public bar. Near the door was a round marble-topped table and two arm-chairs beside it. It was a Saturday night and the place was packed. It was brightly lit, but the smoke was so thick that it made my eyes smart. I was dressed like a rough, with a cap on my head and a handkerchief round my neck. It seemed to me that most of the people there were drunk. I thought it rather amusing. There was a gramophone going, or the radio, I don't know which, and in front of the fireplace two women were doing a grotesque dance. There was a little crowd round them, laughing, cheering and singing. I went up to have a look and some man said to me: ' 'Ave a drink, Bill?' There were glasses on the table full of a dark liquid which I understand is called brown ale. He gave me a glass and not wishing to be conspicuous I drank it. One of the women who were dancing broke away from the other and took hold of the glass. ' 'Ere, what's the idea?' she said. 'That's my beer you're putting away.' 'Oh, I'm so sorry,' I said, 'this gentleman offered it me and I very naturally thought it was his to offer.' 'All right, mate,' she said, 'I don't mind. You come an' 'ave a dance with me.' Before I could protest she'd caught hold of me and we were dancing together. And then I found myself sitting in the arm-chair with the woman on my lap and we were sharing a glass of beer. I should tell you that sex has never played any great part in my life. I married young because in my position it was desirable that I should marry, but also in order to settle once for all the question of sex. I had the two sons I had made up my mind to have, and then I put the whole matter on one side. I've always been too busy to give much thought to that kind of thing, and living so much in the public eye as I do it would have been madness to do anything that might give rise to scandal. The greatest asset a politician can have is a blameless record as far as women are concerned. I have no patience with the men who smash up their careers for women. I only despise them. The woman I had on my knees was drunk; she wasn't pretty and she wasn't young: in fact, she was just a blowsy old prostitute. She filled me with disgust, and yet when she put her mouth to mine and kissed me, though her breath stank of beer and her teeth were decayed, though I loathed myself, I wanted her—I wanted her with all my soul. Suddenly I heard a voice. 'That's right, old boy, have a good time.' I looked up and there was Owen Griffiths. I tried to spring out of the chair, but that horrible woman wouldn't let me. 'Don't you pay no attention to 'im,' she said, ' 'e's only one of them nosy-parkers.' 'You go to it,' he said. 'I know Moll. She'll give you your money's worth all right.' You know, I wasn't so much annoyed at his seeing me in that absurd situation as angry that he should address me as 'old boy.' I pushed the woman aside and stood up and faced him. 'I don't know you and I don't want to know you,' I said. 'I know you all right,' he said. 'And my advice to you, Molly, is, see that you get your money, he'll bilk you if he can.' There was a bottle of beer standing on the table close by. Without a word I seized it by the neck and hit him over the head with it as hard as I could. I made such a violent gesture that it woke me up."

"A dream of that sort is not incomprehensible," said Dr. Audlin. "It is the revenge nature takes on persons of unimpeachable character."

"The story's idiotic. I haven't told it you for its own sake. I've told it you for what happened next day. I wanted to look up something in a hurry and I went into the library of the House. I got the book and began reading. I hadn't noticed when I sat down that Griffiths was sitting in a chair close by me. Another of the Labour Members came in and went up to him. 'Hullo, Owen,' he said to him, 'you're looking pretty dicky today.' 'I've got an awful headache,' he answered. 'I feel as if I'd been cracked over the head with a bottle.' "

Now Lord Mountdrago's face was grey with anguish.

"I knew then that the idea I'd had and dismissed as preposterous was true. I knew that Griffiths was dreaming my dreams and that he remembered them as well as I did."

"It may also have been a coincidence."

"When he spoke he didn't speak to his friend, he deliberately spoke to me. He looked at me with sullen resentment."

"Can you offer any suggestion why this same man should come into your dreams?"

"None."

Dr. Audlin's eyes had not left his patient's face and he saw that he lied. He had a pencil in his hand and he drew a straggling line or two on his blotting-paper. It often took a long time to get people to tell the truth, and yet they knew that unless they told it he could do nothing for them.

"The dream you've just described to me took place just over three weeks ago. Have you had any since?"

"Every night."

"And does this man Griffiths come into them all?"

"Yes."

The doctor drew more lines on his blotting-paper. He wanted

the silence, the drabness, the dull light of that little room to have its effect on Lord Mountdrago's sensibility. Lord Mountdrago threw himself back in his chair and turned his head away so that he should not see the other's grave eyes.

"Dr. Audlin, you must do something for me. I'm at the end of my tether. I shall go mad if this goes on. I'm afraid to go to sleep. Two or three nights I haven't. I've sat up reading and when I felt drowsy put on my coat and walked till I was exhausted. But I must have sleep. With all the work I have to do I must be at concert pitch; I must be in complete control of all my faculties. I need rest; sleep brings me none. I no sooner fall asleep than my dreams begin, and he's always there, that vulgar little cad, grinning at me, mocking me, despising me. It's a monstrous persecution. I tell you, doctor, I'm not the man of my dreams; it's not fair to judge me by them. Ask anyone you like. I'm an honest, upright, decent man. No one can say anything against my moral character either private or public. My whole ambition is to serve my country and maintain its greatness. I have money, I have rank, I'm not exposed to many of the temptations of lesser men, so that it's no credit to me to be incorruptible; but this I can claim, that no honour, no personal advantage, no thought of self would induce me to swerve by a hair's breadth from my duty. I've sacrificed everything to become the man I am. Greatness is my aim. Greatness is within my reach and I'm losing my nerve. I'm not that mean, despicable, cowardly, lewd creature that horrible little man sees. I've told you three of my dreams; they're nothing; that man has seen me do things that are so beastly, so horrible, so shameful, that even if my life depended on it I wouldn't tell them. And he remembers them. I can hardly meet the derision and disgust I see in his eyes and I even hesitate to speak because I know my words can seem to him nothing but utter humbug. He's seen me do things that no man with any self-respect would do, things for which men are driven out of the society of their fellows and sentenced to long terms of imprisonment; he's heard the foulness of my speech; he's seen me not only ridiculous, but revolting. He despises me and he no longer pretends to conceal it. I tell you that if you can't do something to help me I shall either kill myself or kill him."

"I wouldn't kill him if I were you," said Dr. Audlin, coolly, in that soothing voice of his. "In this country the consequences of killing a fellow-creature are awkward."

"I shouldn't be hanged for it, if that's what you mean. Who would know that I'd killed him? That dream of mine has shown me how. I told you, the day after I'd hit him over the head with a beer-bottle he had such a headache that he couldn't see straight. He said so himself. That shows that he can feel with his waking body what happens to his body asleep. It's not with a bottle I shall hit him next time. One night, when I'm dreaming, I shall find myself with a knife in my hand or a revolver in my pocket, I must because I want to so intensely, and then I shall seize my opportunity. I'll stick him like a pig; I'll shoot him like a dog. In the heart. And then I shall be free of this fiendish persecution."

Some people might have thought that Lord Mountdrago was mad; after all the years during which Dr. Audlin had been treating the diseased souls of men he knew how thin a line divides those whom we call sane from those whom we call insane. He knew how often in men who to all appearance were healthy and normal, who were seemingly devoid of imagination, and who fulfilled the duties of common life with credit to themselves and with benefit to their fellows, when you gained their confidence, when you tore away the mask they wore to the world, you found not only hideous abnormality, but kinks so strange, mental extravagances so fantastic, that in that respect you could only call them lunatic. If you put them in an asylum not all the asylums in the world would be large enough. Anyhow, a man was not certifiable because he had strange dreams and they had shattered his nerve. The case was singular, but it was only an exaggeration of others that had come under Dr. Audlin's observation; he was doubtful, however, whether the methods of treatment that he had so often found efficacious would here avail.

"Have you consulted any other member of my profession?" he asked.

"Only Sir Augustus. I merely told him that I suffered from nightmares. He said I was overworked and recommended me to go for a cruise. That's absurd. I can't leave the Foreign Office just now when the international situation needs constant attention. I'm indispensable, and I know it. On my conduct at the present juncture my whole future depends. He gave me sedatives. They had no effect. He gave me tonics. They were worse than useless. He's an old fool."

"Can you give any reason why it should be this particular man who persists in coming into your dreams?"

"You asked me that question before. I answered it."

That was true. But Dr. Audlin had not been satisfied with the answer.

"Just now you talked of persecution. Why should Owen Griffiths want to persecute you?"

"I don't know."

Lord Mountdrago's eyes shifted a little. Dr. Audlin was sure that he was not speaking the truth.

"Have you ever done him an injury?"

"Never."

Lord Mountdrago made no movement, but Dr. Audlin had a queer feeling that he shrank into his skin. He saw before him a large, proud man who gave the impression that the questions put to him were an insolence, and yet for all that, behind that façade, was something shifting and startled that made you think of a frightened animal in a trap. Dr. Audlin leaned forward and by the power of his eyes forced Lord Mountdrago to meet them.

"Are you quite sure?"

"Quite sure. You don't seem to understand that our ways lead along different paths. I don't wish to harp on it, but I must remind you that I am a Minister of the Crown and Griffiths is an obscure member of the Labour Party. Naturally there's no social connection between us; he's a man of very humble origin, he's not the sort of person I should be likely to meet at any of the houses I go to; and politically our respective stations are so far separated that we could not possibly have anything in common."

"I can do nothing for you unless you tell me the complete truth."

Lord Mountdrago raised his eyebrows. His voice was rasping.

"I'm not accustomed to having my word doubted, Dr. Audlin. If you're going to do that I think to take up any more of your time can only be a waste of mine. If you will kindly let my secretary know what your fee is he will see that a cheque is sent to you."

For all the expression that was to be seen on Dr. Audlin's face you might have thought that he simply had not heard what Lord Mountdrago said. He continued to look steadily into his eyes and his voice was grave and low.

"Have you done anything to this man that *he* might look upon as an injury?"

Lord Mountdrago hesitated. He looked away, and then, as though there were in Dr. Audlin's eyes a compelling force that he could not resist, looked back. He answered sulkily:

"Only if he was a dirty, second-rate little cad."

"But that is exactly what you've described him to be."

Lord Mountdrago sighed. He was beaten. Dr. Audlin knew that the sigh meant he was going at last to say what he had till then held back. Now he had no longer to insist. He dropped his eyes and began again drawing vague geometrical figures on his blotting-paper. The silence lasted two or three minutes.

"I'm anxious to tell you everything that can be of any use to you. If I didn't mention this before, it's only because it was so unimportant that I didn't see how it could possibly have anything to do with the case. Griffiths won a seat at the last election and he began to make a nuisance of himself almost at once. His father's a miner, and he worked in a mine himself when he was a boy; he's been a schoolmaster in the board schools and a journalist. He's that half-baked, conceited intellectual, with inadequate knowledge, ill-considered ideas and impracticable plans, that compulsory education has brought forth from the working-classes. He's a scrawny, grey-faced man, who looks half-starved, and he's always very slovenly in appearance; heaven knows members nowadays don't bother much about their dress, but his clothes are an outrage to the dignity of the House. They're ostentatiously shabby, his collar's never clean and his tie's never tied properly; he looks as if he hadn't had a bath for a month and his hands are filthy. The Labour Party have two or three fellows on the Front Bench who've got a certain ability, but the rest of them don't amount to much. In the kingdom of the blind the one-eyed man is king: because Griffiths is glib and has a lot of superficial information on a number of subjects, the Whips on his side began to put him up to speak whenever there was a chance. It appeared that he fancied himself on foreign affairs, and he was continually asking me silly, tiresome questions. I don't mind telling you that I made a point of snubbing him as soundly as I thought he deserved. From the beginning I hated the way he talked, his whining voice and his vulgar accent; he had nervous mannerisms that intensely irritated me. He talked rather shyly, hesitatingly, as though it were torture to him to speak and yet he was forced to by some inner passion, and often he used to say some very disconcerting things. I'll admit that now and again he had a sort of tub-thumping eloquence. It had a certain influence over the ill-regulated minds of the members of his party. They were impressed by his earnestness and they weren't, as I was, nauseated by his sentimentality. A certain sentimentality is the common coin of political debate. Nations are governed by self-interest, but they prefer to believe that their aims are altruistic, and the politician is justified if with fair words and fine phrases he can persuade the electorate that the hard bargain he is driving for his country's advantage tends to the good of humanity. The mistake people like Griffiths make is to take these fair words and fine phrases at their face value. He's a crank, and a noxious crank. He calls himself an idealist. He has at his tongue's end all the tedious blather that the intelligentsia have been boring us with for years. Non-resistance. The brotherhood of man. You know the hopeless rubbish. The worst of it was that it impressed not only his own party, it even shook some of the sillier, more sloppy-minded members of ours. I heard rumours that Griffiths was likely to get office when a Labour Government came in; I even heard it suggested that he might get the Foreign Office. The notion was grotesque but not impossible. One day I had occasion to wind up a debate on foreign affairs which Griffiths had opened. He'd spoken for an hour. I thought it a very good opportunity to cook his goose, and by God, sir, I cooked it. I tore his speech to pieces. I pointed out the faultiness of his reasoning and emphasised the deficiency of his knowledge. In the House of Commons the most devastating weapon is ridicule: I mocked him; I bantered him; I was in good form that day and the House rocked with laughter. Their laughter excited me and I excelled myself. The Opposition sat glum and silent, but even some of them couldn't help laughing once or twice; it's not intolerable, you know, to see a colleague, perhaps a rival, made a fool of. And if ever a man was made a fool of I made a fool of Griffiths. He shrank down in a seat, I saw his face go white, and presently he buried it in his hands. When I sat down I'd killed him. I'd destroyed his prestige for ever; he had no more chance of getting office when a Labour Government came in than the policeman at the door. I heard afterwards that his father, the old miner, and his mother had come up from Wales, with various supporters of his in the constituency, to watch the triumph they expected him to have.

They had seen only his utter humiliation. He'd won the constituency by the narrowest margin. An incident like that might very easily lose him his seat. But that was no business of mine."

"Should I be putting it too strongly if I said you had ruined his career?" asked Dr. Audlin.

"I don't suppose you would."

"That is a very serious injury you've done him."

"He brought it on himself."

"Have you never felt any qualms about it?"

"I think perhaps if I'd known that his father and mother were there I might have let him down a little more gently."

There was nothing further for Dr. Audlin to say, and he set about treating his patient in such a manner as he thought might avail. He sought by suggestion to make him forget his dreams when he awoke; he sought to make him sleep so deeply that he would not dream. He found Lord Mountdrago's resistance impossible to break down. At the end of an hour he dismissed him. Since then he had seen Lord Mountdrago half a dozen times. He had done him no good. The frightful dreams continued every night to harass the unfortunate man, and it was clear that his general condition was growing rapidly worse. He was worn out. His irritability was uncontrollable. Lord Mountdrago was angry because he received no benefit from his treatment, and yet continued it, not only because it seemed his only hope, but because it was a relief to him to have someone with whom he could talk openly. Dr. Audlin came to the conclusion at last that there was only one way in which Lord Mountdrago could achieve deliverance, but he knew him well enough to be assured that of his own free will he would never, never take it. If Lord Mountdrago was to be saved from the breakdown that was threatening he must be induced to take a step that must be abhorrent to his pride of birth and his self-complacency. Dr. Audlin was convinced that to delay was impossible. He was treating his patient by suggestion, and after several visits found him more susceptible to it. At length he managed to get him into a condition of somnolence. With his low, soft, monotonous voice he soothed his tortured nerves. He repeated the same words over and over again. Lord Mountdrago lay quite still, his eyes closed; his breathing was regular, and his limbs were relaxed. Then Dr. Audlin in the same quiet tone spoke the words he had prepared.

"You will go to Owen Griffiths and say that you are sorry that you caused him that great injury. You will say that you

will do whatever lies in your power to undo the harm that you
have done him."

The words acted on Lord Mountdrago like the blow of a whip
across his face. He shook himself out of his hypnotic state and
sprang to his feet. His eyes blazed with passion and he poured
forth upon Dr. Audlin a stream of angry vituperation such as
even he had never heard. He swore at him. He cursed him. He
used language of such obscenity that Dr. Audlin, who had heard
every sort of foul word, sometimes from the lips of chaste and
distinguished women, was surprised that he knew it.

"Apologise to that filthy little Welshman? I'd rather kill myself."

"I believe it to be the only way in which you can regain your
balance."

Dr. Audlin had not often seen a man presumably sane in such
a condition of uncontrollable fury. He grew red in the face and
his eyes bulged out of his head. He did really foam at the
mouth. Dr. Audlin watched him coolly, waiting for the storm to
wear itself out, and presently he saw that Lord Mountdrago,
weakened by the strain to which he had been subjected for so
many weeks, was exhausted.

"Sit down," he said then, sharply.

Lord Mountdrago crumpled up into a chair.

"Christ, I feel all in. I must rest a minute and then I'll go."

For five minutes perhaps they sat in complete silence. Lord
Mountdrago was a gross, blustering bully, but he was also a
gentleman. When he broke the silence he had recovered his self-
control.

"I'm afraid I've been very rude to you. I'm ashamed of the
things I've said to you and I can only say you'd be justified if
you refused to have anything more to do with me. I hope you
won't do that. I feel that my visits to you do help me. I think
you're my only chance."

"You mustn't give another thought to what you said. It was
of no consequence."

"But there's one thing you mustn't ask me to do, and that is
to make excuses to Griffiths."

"I've thought a great deal about your case. I don't pretend to
understand it, but I believe that your only chance of release is
to do what I proposed. I have a notion that we're none of us one
self, but many, and one of the selves in you has risen up against
the injury you did Griffiths and has taken on the form of Grif-

fiths in your mind and is punishing you for what you cruelly did. If I were a priest I should tell you that it is your conscience that has adopted the shape and lineaments of this man to scourge you to repentance and persuade you to reparation."

"My conscience is clear. It's not my fault if I smashed the man's career. I crushed him like a slug in my garden. I regret nothing."

It was on these words that Lord Mountdrago had left him. Reading through his notes, while he waited, Dr. Audlin considered how best he could bring his patient to the state of mind that, now that his usual methods of treatment had failed, he thought alone could help him. He glanced at his clock. It was six. It was strange that Lord Mountdrago did not come. He knew he had intended to because a secretary had rung up that morning to say that he would be with him at the usual hour. He must have been detained by pressing work. This notion gave Dr. Audlin something else to think of: Lord Mountdrago was quite unfit to work and in no condition to deal with important matters of state. Dr. Audlin wondered whether it behoved him to get in touch with someone in authority, the Prime Minister or the Permanent Under-Secretary for Foreign Affairs, and impart to him his conviction that Lord Mountdrago's mind was so unbalanced that it was dangerous to leave affairs of moment in his hands. It was a ticklish thing to do. He might cause needless trouble and get roundly snubbed for his pains. He shrugged his shoulders.

"After all," he reflected, "the politicians have made such a mess of the world during the last five-and-twenty years, I don't suppose it makes much odds if they're mad or sane."

He rang the bell.

"If Lord Mountdrago comes now will you tell him that I have another appointment at six-fifteen and so I'm afraid I can't see him."

"Very good, sir."

"Has the evening paper come yet?"

"I'll go and see."

In a moment the servant brought it in. A huge headline ran across the front page: Tragic Death of Foreign Minister.

"My God!" cried Dr. Audlin.

For once he was wrenched out of his wonted calm. He was shocked, horribly shocked, and yet he was not altogether surprised. The possibility that Lord Mountdrago might commit suicide had occurred to him several times, for that it was suicide he could not doubt. The paper said that Lord Mountdrago had been waiting in a Tube station, standing on the edge of the platform, and as the train came in was seen to fall on the rail. It was supposed that he had had a sudden attack of faintness. The paper went on to say that Lord Mountdrago had been suffering for some weeks from the effects of overwork, but had felt it impossible to absent himself while the foreign situation demanded his unremitting attention. Lord Mountdrago was another victim of the strain that modern politics placed upon those who played the more important parts in it. There was a neat little piece about the talents and industry, the patriotism and vision, of the deceased statesman, followed by various surmises upon the Prime Minister's choice of his successor. Dr. Audlin read all this. He had not liked Lord Mountdrago. The chief emotion that his death caused in him was dissatisfaction with himself because he had been able to do nothing for him.

Perhaps he had done wrong in not getting into touch with Lord Mountdrago's doctor. He was discouraged, as always when failure frustrated his conscientious efforts, and repulsion seized him for the theory and practice of this empiric doctrine by which he earned his living. He was dealing with dark and mysterious forces that it was perhaps beyond the powers of the human mind to understand. He was like a man blindfold trying to feel his way to he knew not whither. Listlessly he turned the pages of the paper. Suddenly he gave a great start, and an exclamation once more was forced from his lips. His eyes had fallen on a small paragraph near the bottom of a column. Sudden Death of an M.P., he read. Mr. Owen Griffiths, member for so-and-so, had been taken ill in Fleet Street that afternoon and when he was brought to Charing Cross Hospital life was found to be extinct. It was supposed that death was due to natural causes, but an inquest would be held. Dr. Audlin could hardly believe his eyes. Was it possible that the night before Lord Mountdrago had at last in his dream found himself possessed of the weapon, knife or gun, that he had wanted, and had killed his tormentor, and had that ghostly murder, in the same way as the blow with the bottle had given him a racking headache on the following day, taken effect a certain number of hours later on the waking man? Or was it, more mysterious and more frightful, that when Lord Mountdrago sought relief in death, the enemy he had so cruelly wronged, unappeased, escaping from his own mortality, had pursued him to some other sphere there to torment him still? It was strange. The sensible thing was to look upon it merely as an odd coincidence. Dr. Audlin rang the bell.

"Tell Mrs. Milton that I'm sorry I can't see her this evening. I'm not well."

It was true; he shivered as though of an ague. With some kind of spiritual sense he seemed to envisage a bleak, a horrible void. The dark night of the soul engulfed him, and he felt a strange, primeval terror of he knew not what.

A STRING OF BEADS

WHAT a bit of luck that I'm placed next to you," said Laura, as we sat down to dinner.

"For me," I replied politely.

"That remains to be seen. I particularly wanted to have the chance of talking to you. I've got a story to tell you."

At this my heart sank a little.

"I'd sooner you talked about yourself," I answered. "Or even about me."

"Oh, but I must tell you the story. I think you'll be able to use it."

"If you must, you must. But let's look at the menu first."

"Don't you want me to?" she said, somewhat aggrieved. "I thought you'd be pleased."

"I am. You might have written a play and wanted to read me that."

"It happened to some friends of mine. It's perfectly true."

"That's no recommendation. A true story is never quite so true as an invented one."

"What does that mean?"

"Nothing very much," I admitted. "But I thought it sounded well."

"I wish you'd let me get on with it."

"I'm all attention. I'm not going to eat the soup. It's fattening."

She gave me a pinched look and then glanced at the menu.
She uttered a little sigh.

"Oh, well, if you're going to deny yourself I suppose I must
too. Heaven knows, I can't afford to take liberties with my
figure."

"And yet is there any soup more heavenly than the sort of
soup in which you put a great dollop of cream?"

"Bortsch," she sighed. "It's the only soup I really like."

"Never mind. Tell me your story and we'll forget about food
till the fish comes."

"Well, I was actually there when it happened. I was dining
with the Livingstones. Do you know the Livingstones?"

"No, I don't think I do."

"Well, you can ask them and they'll confirm every word I say.
They'd asked their governess to come in to dinner because some
woman had thrown them over at the last moment—you know
how inconsiderate people are—and they would have been thirteen at table. Their governess was a Miss Robinson, quite a nice
girl, young, you know, twenty or twenty-one, and rather pretty.
Personally I would never engage a governess who was young
and pretty. One never knows."

"But one hopes for the best."

Laura paid no attention to my remark.

"The chances are that she'll be thinking of young men instead
of attending to her duties and then, just when she's got used to
your ways, she'll want to go and get married. But Miss Robinson had excellent references, and I must allow that she was a
very nice, respectable person. I believe in point of fact she was
a clergyman's daughter.

"There was a man at dinner whom I don't suppose you've ever
heard of, but who's quite a celebrity in his way. He's a Count
Borselli and he knows more about precious stones than anyone
in the world. He was sitting next to Mary Lyngate, who rather
fancies herself on her pearls, and in the course of conversation
she asked him what he thought of the string she was wearing.
He said it was very pretty. She was rather piqued at this and
told him it was valued at eight thousand pounds.

" 'Yes, it's worth that,' he said.

"Miss Robinson was sitting opposite to him. She was looking
rather nice that evening. Of course I recognised her dress, it was
one of Sophie's old ones; but if you hadn't known Miss Robinson was the governess you would never have suspected it.

" 'That's a very beautiful necklace that young lady has on,' said Borselli.

" 'Oh, but that's Mrs. Livingstone's governess,' said Mary Lyngate.

" 'I can't help that,' he said. 'She's wearing one of the finest strings of pearls for its size that I've ever seen in my life. It must be worth fifty thousand pounds.'

" 'Nonsense.'

" 'I give you my word it is.'

"Mary Lyngate leant over. She has rather a shrill voice.

" 'Miss Robinson, do you know what Count Borselli says?' she exclaimed. 'He says that string of pearls you're wearing is worth fifty thousand pounds.'

"Just at that moment there was a sort of pause in the conversation so that everybody heard. We all turned and looked at Miss Robinson. She flushed a little and laughed.

" 'Well, I made a very good bargain,' she said, 'because I paid fifteen shillings for it.'

" 'You certainly did.'

"We all laughed. It was of course absurd. We've all heard of wives palming off on their husbands as false a string of pearls that was real and expensive. That story is as old as the hills."

"Thank you," I said, thinking of a little narrative of my own.

"But it was too ridiculous to suppose that a governess would remain a governess if she owned a string of pearls worth fifty thousand pounds. It was obvious that the Count had made a bloomer. Then an extraordinary thing happened. The long arm of coincidence came in."

"It shouldn't," I retorted. "It's had too much exercise. Haven't you seen that charming book called *A Dictionary of English Usage?*"

"I wish you wouldn't interrupt just when I'm really getting to the exciting point."

But I had to do so again, for just then a young grilled salmon was insinuated round my left elbow.

"Mrs. Livingstone is giving us a heavenly dinner," I said.

"Is salmon fattening?" asked Laura.

"Very," I answered as I took a large helping.

"Bunk," she said.

"Go on," I begged her. "The long arm of coincidence was about to make a gesture."

"Well, at that very moment the butler bent over Miss Robinson and whispered something in her ear. I thought she turned a trifle pale. It's such a mistake not to wear rouge; you never know what tricks nature will play on you. She certainly looked startled. She leant forwards.

" 'Mrs. Livingstone, Dawson says there are two men in the hall who want to speak to me at once.'

" 'Well, you'd better go,' said Sophie Livingstone.

"Miss Robinson got up and left the room. Of course the same thought flashed through all our minds, but I said it first.

" 'I hope they haven't come to arrest her,' I said to Sophie. 'It would be too dreadful for you, my dear.'

" 'Are you sure it was a real necklace, Borselli?' she asked.

" 'Oh, quite.'

" 'She could hardly have had the nerve to wear it to-night if it were stolen,' I said.

"Sophie Livingstone turned as pale as death under her make-up, and I saw she was wondering if everything was all right in her jewel case. I only had on a little chain of diamonds, but instinctively I put my hand up to my neck to feel if it was still there.

" 'Don't talk nonsense,' said Mr. Livingstone. 'How on earth would Miss Robinson have had the chance of sneaking a valuable string of pearls?'

" 'She may be a receiver,' I said.

" 'Oh, but she had such wonderful references,' said Sophie.

" 'They always do,' I said."

I was positively forced to interrupt Laura once more.

"You don't seem to have been determined to take a very bright view of the case," I remarked.

"Of course I knew nothing against Miss Robinson, and I had every reason to think her a very nice girl, but it would have been rather thrilling to find out that she was a notorious thief and a well-known member of a gang of international crooks."

"Just like a film. I'm dreadfully afraid that it's only in films that exciting things like that happen."

"Well, we waited in breathless suspense. There was not a sound. I expected to hear a scuffle in the hall or at least a smothered shriek. I thought the silence very ominous. Then the door opened and Miss Robinson walked in. I noticed at once that the necklace was gone. I could see that she was pale and excited. She came back to the table, sat down and with a smile threw on it . . ."

"On what?"

"On the table, you fool. A string of pearls."

" 'There's my necklace,' she said.

"Count Borselli leant forwards.

" 'Oh, but those are false,' he said.

" 'I told you they were,' she laughed.

" 'That's not the same string that you had on a few moments ago,' he said.

"She shook her head and smiled mysteriously. We were all intrigued. I don't know that Sophie Livingstone was so very much pleased at her governess making herself the centre of interest like that and I thought there was a suspicion of tartness in her manner when she suggested that Miss Robinson had better explain. Well, Miss Robinson said that when she went into the hall she found two men who said they'd come from Jarrot's Stores. She'd bought her string there, as she said, for fifteen shillings, and she'd taken it back because the clasp was loose and had only fetched it that afternoon. The men said they had given her the wrong string. Someone had left a string of real pearls to be re-strung and the assistant had made a mistake. Of course I can't understand how anyone could be so stupid as to take a really valuable string to Jarrot's, they aren't used to dealing with that sort of thing, and they wouldn't know real pearls from false; but you know what fools some women are. Anyhow, it was the string Miss Robinson was wearing, and it was valued at fifty thousand pounds. She naturally gave it back to them—she couldn't do anything else, I suppose, though it must have been a wrench—and they returned her own string to her; then they said that although of course they were under no obligation—you know the silly, pompous way men talk when they're trying to be businesslike—they were instructed, as a solatium or whatever you call it, to offer her a cheque for three hundred pounds. Miss Robinson actually showed it to us. She was as pleased as Punch."

"Well, it was a piece of luck, wasn't it?"

"You'd have thought so. As it turned out it was the ruin of her."

"Oh, how was that?"

"Well, when the time came for her to go on her holiday she told Sophie Livingstone that she'd made up her mind to go to Deauville for a month and blow the whole three hundred pounds. Of course Sophie tried to dissuade her, and begged her to put the money in the savings bank, but she wouldn't hear of it. She said she'd never had such a chance before and would never have it again and she meant for at least four weeks to live like a duchess. Sophie couldn't really do anything and so she gave way. She sold Miss Robinson a lot of clothes that she didn't want; she'd been wearing them all through the season and was sick to death of them; she says she gave them to her, but I don't suppose she quite did that—I dare say she sold them very cheap—and Miss Robinson started off, entirely alone, for Deauville. What do you think happened then?"

"I haven't a notion," I replied. "I hope she had the time of her life."

"Well, a week before she was due to come back she wrote to Sophie and said that she'd changed her plans and had entered another profession, and hoped that Mrs. Livingstone would forgive her if she didn't return. Of course poor Sophie was furious. What had actually happened was that Miss Robinson had picked up a rich Argentine in Deauville and had gone off to Paris with him. She's been in Paris ever since. I've seen her myself at Florence's, with bracelets right up to her elbow and ropes of pearls round her neck. Of course I cut her dead. They say she has a house in the Bois de Boulogne and I know she has a Rolls. She threw over the Argentine in a few months and then got hold of a Greek; I don't know who she's with now, but the long and short of it is that she's far and away the smartest cocotte in Paris."

"When you say she was ruined you use the word in a purely technical sense, I conclude," said I.

"I don't know what you mean by that," said Laura. "But don't you think you could make a story out of it?"

"Unfortunately I've already written a story about a pearl necklace. One can't go on writing stories about pearl necklaces."

"I've got half a mind to write it myself. Only, of course, I should change the end."

"Oh, how would you end it?"

"Well, I should have had her engaged to a bank clerk who had been badly knocked about in the war, with only one leg, say, or half his face shot away; and they'd be dreadfully poor and there would be no prospect of their marriage for years, and he would be putting all his savings into buying a little house in the suburbs, and they'd have arranged to marry when he had saved the last instalment. And then she takes him the three hundred pounds and they can hardly believe it, they're so happy, and he cries on her shoulder. He just cries like a child. And they get the little house in the suburbs and they marry, and they have his old mother to live with them, and he goes to the bank every day, and if she's careful not to have babies she can still go out as a daily governess, and he's often ill—with his wound, you know—and she nurses him, and it's all very pathetic and sweet and lovely."

"It sounds rather dull to me," I ventured.

"Yes, but moral," said Laura.

THE PROMISE

MY WIFE is a very unpunctual woman, so when, having arranged to lunch with her at Claridge's, I arrived there ten minutes late and did not find her I was not surprised. I ordered a cocktail. It was the height of the season and there were but two or three vacant tables in the lounge. Some of the people after an early meal were drinking their coffee, others like myself were toying with a dry Martini; the women in their summer frocks looked gay and charming and the men debonair; but I could see no one whose appearance sufficiently interested me to occupy the quarter of an hour I was expecting to wait. They were slim and pleasant to look upon, well dressed and carelessly at ease, but they were for the most part of a pattern and I observed them with tolerance rather than with curiosity. But it was two o'clock and I felt hungry. My wife tells me that she can neither wear a turquoise nor a watch, for the turquoise turns green and the watch stops; and this she attributes to the malignity of fate. I have nothing to say about the turquoise, but I sometimes think the watch might go if she wound it. I was engaged with these reflections when an attendant came up and with that hushed significance that hotel attendants affect (as though their message held a more sinister meaning than their words suggested) told me that a lady had just telephoned to say that she had been detained and could not lunch with me.

I hesitated. It is not very amusing to eat in a crowded restaurant by oneself, but it was late to go to a club and I decided that I had better stay where I was. I strolled into the dining-room. It has never given me any particular satisfaction (as it appears to do to so many elegant persons) to be known by name to the head waiters of fashionable restaurants, but on this occasion I should certainly have been glad to be greeted by less stony an eye. The *maître d'hôtel* with a set and hostile face told me that every table was occupied. I looked helplessly round the large and stately room and on a sudden to my pleasure caught sight of someone I knew. Lady Elizabeth Vermont was an old friend. She smiled and noticing that she was alone I went up to her.

"Will you take pity on a hungry man and let me sit with you?" I asked.

"Oh, do. But I've nearly finished."

She was at a little table by the side of a massive column and when I took my place I found that notwithstanding the crowd we sat almost in privacy.

"This is a bit of luck for me," I said. "I was on the point of fainting from hunger."

She had a very agreeable smile; it did not light up her face suddenly, but seemed rather to suffuse it by degrees with charm. It hesitated for a moment about her lips and then slowly travelled to those great shining eyes of hers and there softly lingered. No one surely could say that Elizabeth Vermont was cast in the common mould. I never knew her when she was a girl, but many have told me that then she was so lovely, it brought the tears to one's eyes, and I could well believe it; for now, though fifty, she was still incomparable. Her ravaged beauty made the fresh and blooming comeliness of youth a trifle insipid. I do not like these painted faces that look all alike; and I think women are foolish to dull their expression and obscure their personality with powder, rouge and lipstick. But Elizabeth Vermont painted not to imitate nature, but to improve it; you did not question the means but applauded the result. The flaunting boldness with which she used cosmetics increased rather than diminished the character of that perfect face. I suppose her hair was dyed; it was black and sleek and shining. She held herself upright as though she had never learned to loll and she was very slim. She wore a dress of black satin, the lines and simplicity of which were admirable, and about her neck was a long rope of pearls. Her only other jewel was an enormous emerald which guarded her wedding-ring, and its sombre fire emphasised the whiteness of her hand. But it was in her hands with their reddened nails that she most clearly betrayed her age; they had none of a girl's soft and dimpled roundness; and you could not but look at them with a certain dismay. Before very long they would look like the talons of a bird of prey.

Elizabeth Vermont was a remarkable woman. Of great birth, for she was the daughter of the seventh Duke of St. Erth, she married at the age of eighteen a very rich man and started at once upon a career of astounding extravagance, lewdness and dissipation. She was too proud to be cautious, too reckless to think of consequences, and within two years her husband in circumstances of appalling scandal divorced her. She married then one of the three co-respondents named in the case and eighteen months later ran away from him. Then followed a succession of lovers. She became notorious for her profligacy. Her startling beauty and her scandalous conduct held her in the public eye and it was never very long but that she gave the gossips something to talk about. Her name stank in the nostrils of decent people. She was a gambler, a spendthrift and a wanton. But though unfaithful to her lovers she was constant to her friends and there always remained a few who would never allow, whatever she did, that she was anything but a very nice woman. She had candour, high spirits and courage. She was never a hypocrite. She was generous and sincere. It was at this period of her life that I came to know her; for great ladies, now that religion is out of fashion, when they are very much blown upon take a flattering interest in the arts. When they receive the cold shoulder from members of their own class they condescend sometimes to the society of writers, painters and musicians. I found her an agreeable companion. She was one of those blessed persons who say quite fearlessly what they think (thus saving much useful time) and she had a ready wit. She was always willing to talk (with a diverting humour) of her lurid past. Her conversation, though uninstructed, was good, because, notwithstanding everything, she was an honest woman.

Then she did a very surprising thing. At the age of forty she married a boy of twenty-one. Her friends said it was the maddest act of all her life, and some who had stuck to her through thick and thin, now for the boy's sake, because he was nice and it seemed shameful thus to take advantage of his inexperience, refused to have anything more to do with her. It really was the limit. They prophesied disaster, for Elizabeth Vermont was incapable of sticking to any man for more than six months, nay, they hoped for it, since it seemed the only chance for the wretched youth that his wife should behave so scandalously that he must leave her. They were all wrong. I do not know whether time was responsible for a change of heart in her, or whether Peter Vermont's innocence and simple love touched her, but the fact remains that she made him an admirable wife. They were poor, and she was extravagant, but she became a thrifty housewife; she grew on a sudden so careful of her reputation that the tongue of scandal was silenced. His happiness seemed her only concern. No one could doubt that she loved him devotedly. After being the subject of so much conversation for so long Elizabeth Vermont ceased to be talked about. It looked as though her story were told. She was a changed woman, and I amused myself with the notion that when she was a very old lady, with many years of perfect respectability behind her, the past, the lurid past, would seem to belong not to her but to someone long since dead whom once she had vaguely known. For women have an enviable faculty of forgetting.

But who can tell what the fates have in store? In the twinkling of an eye all was changed. Peter Vermont, after ten years of an ideal marriage, fell madly in love with a girl called Barbara Canton. She was a nice girl, the youngest daughter of Lord Robert Canton who was at one time Under-Secretary for Foreign Affairs, and she was pretty in a fair and fluffy way. Of course she was not for a moment to be compared with Lady Elizabeth. Many people knew what had happened, but no one could tell whether Elizabeth Vermont had any inkling of it, and they wondered how she would meet a situation that was so foreign to her experience. It was always she who had discarded her lovers; none had deserted her. For my part I thought she would make short work of little Miss Canton; I knew her courage and her adroitness. All this was in my mind now while we chatted over our luncheon. There was nothing in her demeanour, as gay, charming and frank as usual, to suggest that anything troubled her. She talked as she always talked, lightly but with good sense and a lively perception of the ridiculous, of the various topics which the course of conversation brought forward. I enjoyed myself. I came to the conclusion that by some miracle she had no notion of Peter's changed feelings and I explained this to myself by the supposition that her love for him was so great, she could not conceive that his for her might be less.

We drank our coffee and smoked a couple of cigarettes, and she asked me the time.

"A quarter to three."

"I must ask for my bill."

"Won't you let me stand you lunch?"

"Of course," she smiled.

"Are you in a hurry?"

"I'm meeting Peter at three."

"Oh, how is he?"

"He's very well."

She gave a little smile, that tardy and delightful smile of hers, but I seemed to discern in it a certain mockery. For an instant she hesitated and she looked at me with deliberation.

"You like curious situations, don't you?" she said. "You'd never guess the errand I'm bound on. I rang up Peter this morning and asked him to meet me at three. I'm going to ask him to divorce me."

"You're not," I cried. I felt myself flush and did not know what to say. "I thought you got on so well together."

"Do you think it's likely that I shouldn't know what all the world knows? I'm really not such a fool as all that."

She was not a woman to whom it was possible to say what one did not believe and I could not pretend that I did not know what she meant. I remained silent for a second or two.

"Why should you allow yourself to be divorced?"

"Robert Canton is a stuffy old thing. I very much doubt if he'd let Barbara marry Peter if I divorced him. And for me, you know, it isn't of the smallest consequence: one divorce more or less . . ."

She shrugged her pretty shoulders.

"How do you know he wants to marry her?"

"He's head over ears in love with her."

"Has he told you so?"

"No. He doesn't even know that I know. He's been so wretched, poor darling. He's been trying so hard not to hurt my feelings."

"Perhaps it's only a momentary infatuation," I hazarded. "It may pass."

"Why should it? Barbara's young and pretty. She's quite nice. They're very well suited to one another. And besides, what good would it do if it did pass? They love each other now and the present in love is all that matters. I'm nineteen years older than Peter. If a man stops loving a woman old enough to be his mother do you think he'll ever come to love her again? You're a novelist, you must know more about human nature than that."

"Why should you make this sacrifice?"

"When he asked me to marry him ten years ago I promised him that when he wanted his release he should have it. You see, there was so great a disproportion between our ages I thought that was only fair."

"And are you going to keep a promise that he hasn't asked you to keep?"

She gave a little flutter of those long thin hands of hers and now I felt that there was something ominous in the dark glitter of that emerald.

"Oh, I must, you know. One must behave like a gentleman. To tell you the truth, that's why I'm lunching here to-day. It was at this table that he proposed to me; we were dining together, you know, and I was sitting just where I am now. The nuisance is that I'm just as much in love with him now as I was then." She paused for a minute and I could see that she clenched her teeth. "Well, I suppose I ought to go. Peter hates one to keep him waiting."

She gave me a sort of little helpless look and it struck me that she simply could not bring herself to rise from her chair. But she smiled and with an abrupt gesture sprang to her feet.

"Would you like me to come with you?"

"As far as the hotel door," she smiled.

We walked through the restaurant and the lounge and when we came to the entrance a porter swung round the revolving doors. I asked if she would like a taxi.

"No, I'd sooner walk, it's such a lovely day." She gave me her hand. "It's been so nice to see you. I shall go abroad to-morrow, but I expect to be in London all the autumn. Do ring me up."

She smiled and nodded and turned away. I watched her walk up Davies Street. The air was still bland and springlike and above the roofs little white clouds were sailing leisurely in a blue sky. She held herself very erect and the poise of her head was gallant. She was a slim and lovely figure so that people looked at her as they passed. I saw her bow graciously to some acquaintance who raised his hat, and I thought that never in a thousand years would it occur to him that she had a breaking heart. I repeat, she was a very honest woman.

THE VERGER

The Promise 573

was gallant. She was a liar and Lysle flung at her that people
worked as hard as they pleased had she been prosperously to come
impoverished.

THERE had been a christening that afternoon at St. Peter's,
Neville Square, and Albert Edward Foreman still wore his
verger's gown. He kept his new one, its folds as full and stiff as
though it were made not of alpaca but of perennial bronze, for
funerals and weddings (St. Peter's, Neville Square, was a
church much favoured by the fashionable for these ceremonies)
and now he wore only his second-best. He wore it with com-
placence, for it was the dignified symbol of his office, and without it (when he took it off to go home) he had the disconcerting
sensation of being somewhat insufficiently clad. He took pains
with it; he pressed it and ironed it himself. During the sixteen
years he had been verger of this church he had had a succession
of such gowns, but he had never been able to throw them away
when they were worn out and the complete series, neatly
wrapped up in brown paper, lay in the bottom drawers of the
wardrobe in his bedroom.

The verger busied himself quietly, replacing the painted
wooden cover on the marble font, taking away a chair that had
been brought for an infirm old lady, and waited for the vicar to
have finished in the vestry so that he could tidy up in there and
go home. Presently he saw him walk across the chancel, genuflect
in front of the high altar and come down the aisle; but he still
wore his cassock.

"What's he 'anging about for?" the verger said to himself.
"Don't 'e know I want my tea?"

The vicar had been but recently appointed, a red-faced ener-
getic man in the early forties, and Albert Edward still regretted
his predecessor, a clergyman of the old school who preached
leisurely sermons in a silvery voice and dined out a great deal
with his more aristocratic parishioners. He liked things in
church to be just so, but he never fussed; he was not like this
new man who wanted to have his finger in every pie. But Albert
Edward was tolerant. St. Peter's was in a very good neighbourhood and the parishioners were a very nice class of people. The
new vicar had come from the East End and he couldn't be expected to fall in all at once with the discreet ways of his fashionable congregation.

"All this 'ustle," said Albert Edward. "But give 'im time, he'll
learn."

When the vicar had walked down the aisle so far that he
could address the verger without raising his voice more than
was becoming in a place of worship he stopped.

"Foreman, will you come into the vestry for a minute. I have
something to say to you."

"Very good, sir."

The vicar waited for him to come up and they walked up the
church together.

"A very nice christening, I thought, sir. Funny 'ow the baby
stopped cryin' the moment you took him."

"I've noticed they very often do," said the vicar, with a little
smile. "After all I've had a good deal of practice with them."

It was a source of subdued pride to him that he could nearly
always quiet a whimpering infant by the manner in which he
held it and he was not unconscious of the amused admiration
with which mothers and nurses watched him settle the baby in
the crook of his surpliced arm. The verger knew that it pleased
him to be complimented on his talent.

The vicar preceded Albert Edward into the vestry. Albert
Edward was a trifle surprised to find the two churchwardens
there. He had not seen them come in. They gave him pleasant
nods.

"Good-afternoon, my lord. Good-afternoon, sir," he said to
one after the other.

They were elderly men, both of them, and they had been
churchwardens almost as long as Albert Edward had been
verger. They were sitting now at a handsome refectory table
that the old vicar had brought many years before from Italy

and the vicar sat down in the vacant chair between them. Albert Edward faced them, the table between him and them, and wondered with slight uneasiness what was the matter. He remembered still the occasion on which the organist had got into trouble and the bother they had all had to hush things up. In a church like St. Peter's, Neville Square, they couldn't afford a scandal. On the vicar's red face was a look of resolute benignity, but the others bore an expression that was slightly troubled.

"He's been naggin' them, he 'as," said the verger to himself. "He's jockeyed them into doin' something, but they don't 'alf like it. That's what it is, you mark my words."

But his thoughts did not appear on Albert Edward's clean-cut and distinguished features. He stood in a respectful but not obsequious attitude. He had been in service before he was appointed to his ecclesiastical office, but only in very good houses, and his deportment was irreproachable. Starting as a page-boy in the household of a merchant-prince, he had risen by due degrees from the position of fourth to first footman, for a year he had been single-handed butler to a widowed peeress and, till the vacancy occurred at St. Peter's, butler with two men under him in the house of a retired ambassador. He was tall, spare, grave and dignified. He looked, if not like a duke, at least like an actor of the old school who specialised in dukes' parts. He had tact, firmness and self-assurance. His character was unimpeachable.

The vicar began briskly.

"Foreman, we've got something rather unpleasant to say to you. You've been here a great many years and I think his lordship and the general agree with me that you've fulfilled the duties of your office to the satisfaction of everybody concerned."

The two churchwardens nodded.

"But a most extraordinary circumstance came to my knowledge the other day and I felt it my duty to impart it to the churchwardens. I discovered to my astonishment that you could neither read nor write."

The verger's face betrayed no sign of embarrassment.

"The last vicar knew that, sir," he replied. "He said it didn't make no difference. He always said there was a great deal too much education in the world for 'is taste."

"It's the most amazing thing I ever heard," cried the general. "Do you mean to say that you've been verger of this church for sixteen years and never learned to read or write?"

"I went into service when I was twelve, sir. The cook in the first place tried to teach me once, but I didn't seem to 'ave the knack for it, and then what with one thing and another I never seemed to 'ave the time. I've never really found the want of it. I think a lot of these young fellows waste a rare lot of time readin' when they might be doin' something useful."

"But don't you want to know the news?" said the other churchwarden. "Don't you ever want to write a letter?"

"No, me lord, I seem to manage very well without. And of late years now they've all these pictures in the papers I get to know what's goin' on pretty well. Me wife's quite a scholar and if I want to write a letter she writes it for me. It's not as if I was a bettin' man."

The two churchwardens gave the vicar a troubled glance and then looked down at the table.

"Well, Foreman, I've talked the matter over with these gentlemen and they quite agree with me that the situation is impossible. At a church like St. Peter's, Neville Square, we cannot have a verger who can neither read nor write."

Albert Edward's thin, sallow face reddened and he moved uneasily on his feet, but he made no reply.

"Understand me, Foreman, I have no complaint to make against you. You do your work quite satisfactorily; I have the highest opinion both of your character and of your capacity; but we haven't the right to take the risk of some accident that might happen owing to your lamentable ignorance. It's a matter of prudence as well as of principle."

"But couldn't you learn, Foreman?" asked the general.

"No, sir, I'm afraid I couldn't, not now. You see, I'm not as young as I was and if I couldn't seem able to get the letters in me 'ead when I was a nipper I don't think there's much chance of it now."

"We don't want to be harsh with you, Foreman," said the vicar. "But the churchwardens and I have quite made up our minds. We'll give you three months and if at the end of that time you cannot read and write I'm afraid you'll have to go."

Albert Edward had never liked the new vicar. He'd said from the beginning that they'd made a mistake when they gave him St. Peter's. He wasn't the type of man they wanted with a classy congregation like that. And now he straightened himself a little. He knew his value and he wasn't going to allow himself to be put upon.

"I'm very sorry, sir, I'm afraid it's no good. I'm too old a dog to learn new tricks. I've lived a good many years without knowin' 'ow to read and write, and without wishin' to praise myself, self-praise is no recommendation, I don't mind sayin' I've done my duty in that state of life in which it 'as pleased a merciful providence to place me, and if I *could* learn now I don't know as I'd want to."

"In that case, Foreman, I'm afraid you must go."

"Yes, sir, I quite understand. I shall be 'appy to 'and in my resignation as soon as you've found somebody to take my place."

But when Albert Edward with his usual politeness had closed the church door behind the vicar and the two churchwardens he could not sustain the air of unruffled dignity with which he had borne the blow inflicted upon him and his lips quivered. He walked slowly back to the vestry and hung up on its proper peg his verger's gown. He sighed as he thought of all the grand funerals and smart weddings it had seen. He tidied everything up, put on his coat, and hat in hand walked down the aisle. He locked the church door behind him. He strolled across the square, but deep in his sad thoughts he did not take the street that led him home, where a nice strong cup of tea awaited him; he took the wrong turning. He walked slowly along. His heart was heavy. He did not know what he should do with himself. He did not fancy the notion of going back to domestic service; after being his own master for so many years, for the vicar and churchwardens could say what they liked, it was he that had run St. Peter's, Neville Square, he could scarcely demean himself by accepting a situation. He had saved a tidy sum, but not enough to live on without doing something, and life seemed to cost more every year. He had never thought to be troubled with such questions. The vergers of St. Peter's, like the popes of Rome, were there for life. He had often thought of the pleasant reference the vicar would make in his sermon at evensong the first Sunday after his death to the long and faithful service, and the exemplary character of their late verger, Albert Edward Foreman. He sighed deeply. Albert Edward was a non-smoker and a total abstainer, but with a certain latitude; that is to say he liked a glass of beer with his dinner and when he was tired he enjoyed a cigarette. It occurred to him now that one would comfort him and since he did not carry them he looked about him for a shop where he could buy a packet of Gold Flakes. He did not at once see one and walked on a little. It was a long street, with all sorts of shops in it, but there was not a single one where you could buy cigarettes.

"That's strange," said Albert Edward.

To make sure he walked right up the street again. No, there was no doubt about it. He stopped and looked reflectively up and down.

"I can't be the only man as walks along this street and wants a fag," he said. "I shouldn't wonder but what a fellow might do very well with a little shop here. Tobacco and sweets, you know."

He gave a sudden start.

"That's an idea," he said. "Strange 'ow things come to you when you least expect it."

He turned, walked home, and had his tea.

"You're very silent this afternoon, Albert," his wife remarked.

"I'm thinkin'," he said.

He considered the matter from every point of view and next day he went along the street and by good luck found a little shop to let that looked as though it would exactly suit him. Twenty-four hours later he had taken it and when a month after that he left St. Peter's, Neville Square, for ever, Albert Edward Foreman set up in business as a tobacconist and newsagent. His wife said it was a dreadful come-down after being verger of St. Peter's, but he answered that you had to move with the times, the church wasn't what it was, and 'enceforward he was going to render unto Cæsar what was Cæsar's. Albert Edward did very well. He did so well that in a year or so it struck him that he might take a second shop and put a manager in. He looked for another long street that hadn't got a tobacconist in it and when he found it, and a shop to let, took it and stocked it. This was a success too. Then it occurred to him that if he could run two he could run half a dozen, so he began walking about London, and whenever he found a long street that had no tobacconist and a shop to let he took it. In the course of ten years he had acquired no less than ten shops and he was making money hand over fist. He went round to all of them himself every Monday, collected the week's takings and took them to the bank.

One morning when he was there paying in a bundle of notes and a heavy bag of silver the cashier told him that the manager would like to see him. He was shown into an office and the manager shook hands with him.

"Mr. Foreman, I wanted to have a talk to you about the money you've got on deposit with us. D'you know exactly how much it is?"

"Not within a pound or two, sir; but I've got a pretty rough idea."

"Apart from what you paid in this morning it's a little over thirty thousand pounds. That's a very large sum to have on deposit and I should have thought you'd do better to invest it."

"I wouldn't want to take no risk, sir. I know it's safe in the bank."

"You needn't have the least anxiety. We'll make you out a list of absolutely gilt-edged securities. They'll bring you in a better rate of interest than we can possibly afford to give you."

A troubled look settled on Mr. Foreman's distinguished face. "I've never 'ad anything to do with stocks and shares and I'd 'ave to leave it all in your 'ands," he said.

The manager smiled. "We'll do everything. All you'll have to do next time you come in is just to sign the transfers."

"I could do that all right," said Albert uncertainly. "But 'ow should I know what I was signin'?"

"I suppose you can read," said the manager a trifle sharply.

Mr. Foreman gave him a disarming smile.

"Well, sir, that's just it. I can't. I know it sounds funny-like, but there it is, I can't read or write, only me name, an' I only learnt to do that when I went into business."

The manager was so surprised that he jumped up from his chair.

"That's the most extraordinary thing I ever heard."

"You see, it's like this, sir, I never 'ad the opportunity until it was too late and then some'ow I wouldn't. I got obstinate-like."

The manager stared at him as though he were a prehistoric monster.

"And do you mean to say that you've built up this important business and amassed a fortune of thirty thousand pounds without being able to read or write? Good God, man, what would you be now if you had been able to?"

"I can tell you that, sir," said Mr. Foreman, a little smile on his still aristocratic features. "I'd be verger of St. Peter's, Neville Square."

THE SOCIAL SENSE

I DO NOT like long-standing engagements. How can you tell whether on a certain day three or four weeks ahead you will wish to dine with a certain person? The chances are that in the interval something will turn up that you would much sooner do and so long a notice presages a large and formal party. But what help is there? The date has been fixed thus far away so that the guests bidden may be certainly disengaged and it needs a very adequate excuse to prevent your refusal from seeming churlish. You accept, and for a month the engagement hangs over you with gloomy menace. It interferes with your cherished plans. It disorganises your life. There is really only one way to cope with the situation and that is to put yourself off at the last moment. But it is one that I have never had the courage or the want of scruple to adopt.

It was with a faint sense of resentment then that one June evening towards half-past eight I left my lodging in Half Moon Street to walk round the corner to dine with the Macdonalds. I liked them. Many years ago I made up my mind not to eat the food of persons I disliked or despised, and though I have on this account enjoyed the hospitality of far fewer people than I otherwise should have done I still think the rule a good one. The Macdonalds were nice, but their parties were a toss-up. They suffered from the delusion that if they asked six persons to dine with them who had nothing in the world to say to one another the party would be a failure, but if they multiplied it by three and

asked eighteen it must be a success. I arrived a little late, which
is almost inevitable when you live so near the house you are going to that it is not worth while to take a taxi, and the room
into which I was shown was filled with people. I knew few of
them and my heart sank as I saw myself laboriously making
conversation through a long dinner with two total strangers. It
was a relief to me when I saw Thomas and Mary Warton come
in and an unexpected pleasure when I found on going in to
dinner that I had been placed next to Mary.

Thomas Warton was a portrait-painter who at one time had
had considerable success, but he had never fulfilled the promise
of his youth and had long ceased to be taken seriously by the
critics. He made an adequate income, but at the Private View
of the Royal Academy no one gave more than a passing glance
at the dull but conscientious portraits of fox-hunting squires
and prosperous merchants which with unfailing regularity he
sent to the annual exhibition. One would have liked to admire
his work because he was an amiable and kindly man. If you
happened to be a writer he was so genuinely enthusiastic over
anything you had done, so charmed with any success you might
have had, that you wished your conscience would allow you to
speak with decent warmth of his own productions. It was impossible and you were driven to the last refuge of the portrait-
painter's friend.

"It looks as if it were a marvellous likeness," you said.

Mary Warton had been in her day a well-known concert
singer and she had still the remains of a lovely voice. She must
in her youth have been very handsome. Now, at fifty-three, she
had a haggard look. Her features were rather mannish and her
skin was weather-beaten; but her short grey hair was thick and
curly and her fine eyes were bright with intelligence. She dressed
picturesquely rather than fashionably and she had a weakness
for strings of beads and fantastic ear-rings. She had a blunt
manner, a quick sense of human folly and a sharp tongue, so that
many people did not like her. But no one could deny that she
was clever. She was not only an accomplished musician, but she
was a great reader and she was passionately interested in painting. She had a very rare feeling for art. She liked the modern,
not from pose but from natural inclination, and she had bought
for next to nothing the pictures of unknown painters who later
became famous. You heard at her house the most recent and
difficult music and no poet or novelist in Europe could offer the

world something new and strange without her being ready to
fight on his behalf the good fight against the philistines. You
might say she was a highbrow; she was; but her taste was almost
faultless, her judgment sound and her enthusiasm honest.

No one admired her more than Thomas Warton. He had fallen
in love with her when she was still a singer and had pestered her
to marry him. She had refused him half a dozen times and I had
a notion that she had married him in the end with hesitation.
She thought that he would become a great painter and when he
turned out to be no more than a decent craftsman, without
originality or imagination, she felt that she had been cheated.
She was mortified by the contempt with which the connoisseurs
regarded him. Thomas Warton loved his wife. He had the
greatest respect for her judgment and would sooner have had a
word of praise from her than columns of eulogy in all the papers
in London. She was too honest to say what she did not think.
It wounded him bitterly that she held his work in such poor
esteem, and though he pretended to make a joke of it you could
see that at heart he resented her outspoken comments. Sometimes his long, horse-like face grew red with the anger he tried
to control and his eyes dark with hatred. It was notorious among
their friends that the couple did not get on. They had the dis-
tressing habit of fripping in public. Warton never spoke to others
of Mary but with admiration, but she was less discreet and her
confidants knew how exasperating she found him. She admitted
his goodness, his generosity, his unselfishness; she admitted them
ungrudgingly; but his defects were of the sort that make a man
hard to live with, for he was narrow, argumentative and conceited. He was not an artist and Mary Warton cared more for
art than for anything in the world. It was a matter on which
she could not compromise. It blinded her to the fact that the
faults in Warton that maddened her were due in large part to his
hurt feelings. She wounded him continually and he was dogmatic
and intolerant in self-protection. There cannot be anything
much worse than to be despised by the one person whose approval is all in all to you; and though Thomas Warton was intolerable it was impossible not to feel sorry for him. But if I have
given the impression that Mary was a discontented, rather tiresome, pretentious woman I have been unjust to her. She was a
loyal friend and a delightful companion. You could talk to her
of any subject under the sun. Her conversation was humorous
and witty. Her vitality was immense.

She was sitting now on the left hand of her host and the talk around her was general. I was occupied with my next-door neighbour, but I guessed by the laughter with which Mary's sallies were greeted that she was at her brilliant best. When she was in the vein no one could approach her.

"You're in great form to-night," I remarked, when at last she turned to me.

"Does it surprise you?"

"No, it's what I expect of you. No wonder people tumble over one another to get you to their houses. You have the inestimable gift of making a party go."

"I do my little best to earn my dinner."

"By the way, how's Manson? Someone told me the other day that he was going into a nursing-home for an operation. I hope it's nothing serious."

Mary paused for a moment before answering, but she still smiled brightly.

"Haven't you seen the paper to-night?"

"No, I've been playing golf. I only got home in time to jump into a bath and change."

"He died at two o'clock this afternoon." I was about to make an exclamation of horrified surprise, but she stopped me. "Take care. Tom is watching me like a lynx. They're all watching me. They all know I adored him, but they none of them know for certain if he was my lover, even Tom doesn't know; they want to see how I'm taking it. Try to look as if you were talking of the Russian Ballet."

At that moment someone addressed her from the other side of the table, and throwing back her head a little with a gesture that was habitual with her, a smile on her large mouth, she flung at the speaker so quick and apt an answer that everyone round her burst out laughing. The talk once more became general and I was left to my consternation.

I knew, everyone knew, that for five and twenty years there had existed between Gerrard Manson and Mary Warton a passionate attachment. It had lasted so long that even the more strait-laced of their friends, if ever they had been shocked by it, had long since learnt to accept it with tolerance. They were middle-aged people, Manson was sixty and Mary not much younger, and it was absurd that at their age they should not do what they liked. You met them sometimes sitting in a retired corner of an obscure restaurant or walking together in the Zoo

and you wondered why they still took care to conceal an affair
that was nobody's business but their own. But of course there
was Thomas. He was insanely jealous of Mary. He made many
violent scenes and indeed, at the end of one tempestuous period,
not so very long ago, he forced her to promise never to see Manson again. Of course she broke the promise, and though she
knew that Thomas suspected this, she took precautions to prevent him from discovering it for a fact.

It was hard on Thomas. I think he and Mary would have
jogged on well enough together and she would have resigned herself to the fact that he was a second-rate painter if her intercourse with Manson had not embittered her judgment. The
contrast between her husband's mediocrity and her lover's
brilliance was too galling.

"With Tom I feel as if I were stifling in a closed room full of
dusty knick-knacks," she told me. "With Gerrard I breathe the
pure air of the mountain tops."

"Is it possible for a woman to fall in love with a man's mind?"
I asked in a pure spirit of enquiry.

"What else is there in Gerrard?"

That, I admit, was a poser. For my part I thought, nothing;
but the sex is extraordinary and I was quite ready to believe that
Mary saw in Gerrard Manson a charm and a physical attractive-
ness to which most people were blind. He was a shrivelled little
man, with a pale intellectual face, faded blue eyes behind his
spectacles, and a high dome of shiny bald head. He had none
of the appearance of a romantic lover. On the other hand he was
certainly a very subtle critic and a felicitous essayist. I resented
somewhat his contemptuous attitude towards English writers
unless they were safely dead and buried; but this was only to
his credit with the intelligentsia, who are ever ready to believe
that there can be no good in what is produced in their own
country, and with them his influence was great. On one occasion I told him that one had only to put a commonplace in
French for him to mistake it for an epigram and he had thought
well enough of the joke to use it as his own in one of his essays.
He reserved such praise as he was willing to accord his contemporaries to those who wrote in a foreign tongue. The exasperating thing was that no one could deny that he was himself a brilliant writer. His style was exquisite. His knowledge
was vast. He could be profound without pomposity, amusing
without frivolity, and polished without affectation. His slightest

article was readable. His essays were little masterpieces. For my part I did not find him a very agreeable companion. Perhaps I did not get the best out of him. Though I knew him a great many years I never heard him say an amusing thing. He was not talkative and when he made a remark it was oracular. The prospect of spending an evening alone with him would have filled me with dismay. It never ceased to puzzle me that this dull and mannered little man should be able to write with so much grace, wit and gaiety.

It puzzled me even more that a gallant and vivacious creature like Mary Warton should have cherished for him so consuming a passion. These things are inexplicable and there was evidently something in that odd, crabbed, irascible creature that appealed to women. His wife adored him. She was a fat, frowsy boring person. She had led Gerrard a dog's life, but had always refused to give him his freedom. She swore to kill herself if he left her and since she was unbalanced and hysterical he was never quite certain that she would not carry out her threat. One day, when I was having tea with Mary, I saw that she was distraught and nervous and when I asked her what was the matter she burst into tears. She had been lunching with Manson and had found him shattered after a terrific scene with his wife.

"We can't go on like this," Mary cried. "It's ruining his life. It's ruining all our lives."

"Why don't you take the plunge?"

"What do you mean?"

"You've been lovers so long, you know the best and the worst of one another by now; you're getting old and you can't count on many more years of life; it seems a pity to waste a love that has endured so long. What good are you doing to Mrs. Manson or to Tom? Are they happy because you two are making yourselves miserable?"

"No."

"Then why don't you chuck everything and just go off together and let come what may?"

Mary shook her head.

"We've talked that over endlessly. We've talked it over for a quarter of a century. It's impossible. For years Gerrard couldn't on account of his daughters. Mrs. Manson may have been a very fond mother, but she was a very bad one, and there was no one to see the girls were properly brought up but Gerrard. And now that they're married off he's set in his habits. What should we

do? Go to France or Italy? I couldn't tear Gerrard away from his
surroundings. He'd be wretched. He's too old to make a fresh
start. And besides, though Thomas nags me and makes scenes
and we frip and get on one another's nerves, he loves me. When
it came to the point I simply shouldn't have the heart to leave
him. He'd be lost without me."

"It's a situation without an issue. I'm dreadfully sorry for
you."

On a sudden Mary's haggard, weather-beaten face was lit by
a smile that broke on her large red mouth; and upon my word at
that moment she was beautiful.

"You need not be. I was rather low a little while ago, but now
I've had a good cry I feel better. Notwithstanding all the pain,
all the unhappiness this affair has caused me, I wouldn't have
missed it for all the world. For those few moments of ecstasy
my love has brought me I would be willing to live all my life
over again. And I think he'd tell you the same thing. Oh, it's
been so infinitely worth while."

I could not help but be moved.

"There's no doubt about it," I said. "That's love all right."

"Yes, it's love, and we've just got to go through with it.
There's no way out."

And now with this tragic suddenness the way out had come.
I turned a little to look at Mary and she, feeling my eyes upon
her, turned too. There was a smile on her lips.

"Why did you come here to-night? It must be awful for you."

She shrugged her shoulders.

"What could I do? I read the news in the evening paper while
I was dressing. He'd asked me not to ring up the nursing-home
on account of his wife. It's death to me. Death. I had to come.
We'd been engaged for a month. What excuse could I give Tom?
I'm not supposed to have seen Gerrard for two years. Do you
know that for twenty years we've written to one another every
day?" Her lower lip trembled a little, but she bit it and for a
moment her face was twisted to a strange grimace; then with a
smile she pulled herself together. "He was everything I had in
the world, but I couldn't let the party down, could I? He always
said I had a social sense."

"Happily we shall break up early and you can go home."

"I don't want to go home. I don't want to be alone. I daren't
cry because my eyes will get red and swollen, and we've got a
lot of people lunching with us to-morrow. Will you come, by the

way? I want an extra man. I must be in good form; Tom expects to get a commission for a portrait out of it."

"By George, you've got courage."

"D'you think so? I'm heartbroken, you know. I suppose that's what makes it easier for me. Gerrard would have liked me to put a good face on it. He would have appreciated the irony of the situation. It's the sort of thing he always thought the French novelists described so well."

THE COLONEL'S LADY

ALL this happened two or three years before the outbreak of the war.

The Peregrines were having breakfast. Though they were alone and the table was long they sat at opposite ends of it. From the walls George Peregrine's ancestors, painted by the fashionable painters of the day, looked down upon them. The butler brought in the morning post. There were several letters for the colonel, business letters, *The Times* and a small parcel for his wife Evie. He looked at his letters and then, opening *The Times*, began to read it. They finished breakfast and rose from the table. He noticed that his wife hadn't opened the parcel.

"What's that?" he asked.

"Only some books."

"Shall I open it for you?"

"If you like."

He hated to cut string and so with some difficulty untied the knots.

"But they're all the same," he said when he had unwrapped the parcel. "What on earth d'you want six copies of the same book for?" He opened one of them. "Poetry." Then he looked at the title page. *When Pyramids Decay,* he read, by E. K. Hamilton. Eva Katherine Hamilton: that was his wife's maiden name. He looked at her with smiling surprise. "Have you written a book, Evie? You are a slyboots."

"I didn't think it would interest you very much. Would you like a copy?"

"Well, you know poetry isn't much in my line, but—yes, I'd like a copy; I'll read it. I'll take it along to my study. I've got a lot to do this morning."

He gathered up *The Times*, his letters and the book, and went out. His study was a large and comfortable room, with a big desk, leather arm-chairs and what he called "trophies of the chase" on the walls. On the bookshelves were works of reference, books on farming, gardening, fishing and shooting, and books on the last war, in which he had won an M.C. and a D.S.O. For before his marriage he had been in the Welsh Guards. At the end of the war he retired and settled down to the life of a country gentleman in the spacious house, some twenty miles from Sheffield, which one of his forebears had built in the reign of George III. George Peregrine had an estate of some fifteen hundred acres which he managed with ability; he was a Justice of the Peace and performed his duties conscientiously. During the season he rode to hounds two days a week. He was a good shot, a golfer and though now a little over fifty could still play a hard game of tennis. He could describe himself with propriety as an all-round sportsman.

He had been putting on weight lately, but was still a fine figure of a man; tall, with grey curly hair, only just beginning to grow thin on the crown, frank blue eyes, good features and a high colour. He was a public-spirited man, chairman of any number of local organisations and, as became his class and station, a loyal member of the Conservative Party. He looked upon it as his duty to see to the welfare of the people on his estate and it was a satisfaction to him to know that Evie could be trusted to tend the sick and succour the poor. He had built a cottage hospital on the outskirts of the village and paid the wages of a nurse out of his own pocket. All he asked of the recipients of his bounty was that at elections, county or general, they should vote for his candidate. He was a friendly man, affable to his inferiors, considerate with his tenants and popular with the neighbouring gentry. He would have been pleased and at the same time slightly embarrassed if someone had told him he was a jolly good fellow. That was what he wanted to be. He desired no higher praise.

It was hard luck that he had no children. He would have been an excellent father, kindly but strict, and would have brought up his sons as gentlemen's sons should be brought up, sent them to Eton, you know, taught them to fish, shoot and ride. As it was, his heir was a nephew, son of his brother killed in a motor accident, not a bad boy, but not a chip off the old block, no, sir, far from it; and would you believe it, his fool of a mother was sending him to a co-educational school. Evie had been a sad disappointment to him. Of course she was a lady, and she had a bit of money of her own; she managed the house uncommonly well and she was a good hostess. The village people adored her. She had been a pretty little thing when he married her, with a creamy skin, light brown hair and a trim figure, healthy too and not a bad tennis player; he couldn't understand why she'd had no children; of course she was faded now, she must be getting on for five and forty; her skin was drab, her hair had lost its sheen and she was as thin as a rail. She was always neat and suitably dressed, but she didn't seem to bother how she looked, she wore no make-up and didn't even use lipstick; sometimes at night when she dolled herself up for a party you could tell that once she'd been quite attractive, but ordinarily she was—well, the sort of woman you simply didn't notice. A nice woman, of course, a good wife, and it wasn't her fault if she was barren, but it was tough on a fellow who wanted an heir of his own loins; she hadn't any vitality, that's what was the matter with her. He supposed he'd been in love with her when he asked her to marry him, as least sufficiently in love for a man who wanted to marry and settle down, but with time he discovered that they had nothing much in common. She didn't care about hunting, and fishing bored her. Naturally they'd drifted apart. He had to do her the justice to admit that she'd never bothered him. There'd been no scenes. They had no quarrels. She seemed to take it for granted that he should go his own way. When he went up to London now and then she never wanted to come with him. He had a girl there, well, she wasn't exactly a girl, she was thirty-five if she was a day, but she was blonde and luscious and he only had to wire ahead of time and they'd dine, do a show and spend the night together. Well, a man, a healthy normal man had to have some fun in his life. The thought crossed his mind that if Evie hadn't been such a good woman she'd have been a better wife; but it was not the sort of thought that he welcomed and he put it away from him.

George Peregrine finished his *Times* and being a considerate fellow rang the bell and told the butler to take it to Evie. Then he looked at his watch. It was half-past ten and at eleven he had an appointment with one of his tenants. He had half an hour to spare.

"I'd better have a look at Evie's book," he said to himself.

He took it up with a smile. Evie had a lot of highbrow books in her sitting-room, not the sort of books that interested him, but if they amused her he had no objection to her reading them. He noticed that the volume he now held in his hand contained no more than ninety pages. That was all to the good. He shared Edgar Allan Poe's opinion that poems should be short. But as he turned the pages he noticed that several of Evie's had long lines of irregular length and didn't rhyme. He didn't like that. At his first school, when he was a little boy, he remembered learning a poem that began: *The boy stood on the burning deck,* and later, at Eton, one that started: *Ruin seize thee, ruthless king;* and then there was Henry V; they'd had to take that, one half. He stared at Evie's pages with consternation.

"That's not what I call poetry," he said.

Fortunately it wasn't all like that. Interspersed with the pieces that looked so odd, lines of three or four words and then a line of ten or fifteen, there were little poems, quite short, that rhymed, thank God, with the lines all the same length. Several of the pages were just headed with the word *Sonnet,* and out of curiosity he counted the lines; there were fourteen of them. He read them. They seemed all right, but he didn't quite know what they were all about. He repeated to himself: *Ruin seize thee, ruthless king.*

"Poor Evie," he sighed.

At that moment the farmer he was expecting was ushered into the study, and putting the book down he made him welcome. They embarked on their business.

"I read your book, Evie," he said as they sat down to lunch. "Jolly good. Did it cost you a packet to have it printed?"

"No, I was lucky. I sent it to a publisher and he took it."

"Not much money in poetry, my dear," he said in his good-natured, hearty way.

"No, I don't suppose there is. What did Bannock want to see you about this morning?"

Bannock was the tenant who had interrupted his reading of Evie's poems.

"He's asked me to advance the money for a pedigree bull he wants to buy. He's a good man and I've half a mind to do it."

George Peregrine saw that Evie didn't want to talk about her book and he was not sorry to change the subject. He was glad she had used her maiden name on the title page; he didn't suppose anyone would ever hear about the book, but he was proud of his own unusual name and he wouldn't have liked it if some damned penny-a-liner had made fun of Evie's effort in one of the papers.

During the few weeks that followed he thought it tactful not to ask Evie any questions about her venture into verse, and she never referred to it. It might have been a discreditable incident that they had silently agreed not to mention. But then a strange thing happened. He had to go to London on business and he took Daphne out to dinner. That was the name of the girl with whom he was in the habit of passing a few agreeable hours whenever he went to town.

"Oh, George," she said, "is that your wife who's written a book they're all talking about?"

"What on earth d'you mean?"

"Well, there's a fellow I know who's a critic. He took me out to dinner the other night and he had a book with him. 'Got anything for me to read?' I said. 'What's that?' 'Oh, I don't think that's your cup of tea,' he said. 'It's poetry. I've just been reviewing it.' 'No poetry for me,' I said. 'It's about the hottest stuff I ever read,' he said. 'Selling like hot cakes. And it's damned good.' "

"Who's the book by?" asked George.

"A woman called Hamilton. My friend told me that wasn't her real name. He said her real name was Peregrine. 'Funny,' I said, 'I know a fellow called Peregrine.' 'Colonel in the army,' he said. 'Lives near Sheffield.' "

"I'd just as soon you didn't talk about me to your friends," said George with a frown of vexation.

"Keep your shirt on, dearie. Who d'you take me for? I just said: 'It's not the same one.' " Daphne giggled. "My friend said: 'They say he's a regular Colonel Blimp.' "

George had a keen sense of humour.

"You could tell them better than that," he laughed. "If my wife had written a book I'd be the first to know about it, wouldn't I?"

"I suppose you would."

Anyhow the matter didn't interest her and when the colonel began to talk of other things she forgot about it. He put it out of his mind too. There was nothing to it, he decided, and that silly fool of a critic had just been pulling Daphne's leg. He was amused at the thought of her tackling that book because she had been told it was hot stuff and then finding it just a lot of bosh cut up into unequal lines.

He was a member of several clubs and next day he thought he'd lunch at one in St. James's Street. He was catching a train back to Sheffield early in the afternoon. He was sitting in a comfortable arm-chair having a glass of sherry before going into the dining-room when an old friend came up to him.

"Well, old boy, how's life?" he said. "How d'you like being the husband of a celebrity?"

George Peregrine looked at his friend. He thought he saw an amused twinkle in his eyes.

"I don't know what you're talking about," he answered.

"Come off it, George. Everyone knows E. K. Hamilton is your wife. Not often a book of verse has a success like that. Look here, Henry Dashwood is lunching with me. He'd like to meet you."

"Who the devil is Henry Dashwood and why should he want to meet me?"

"Oh, my dear fellow, what do you do with yourself all the time in the country? Henry's about the best critic we've got. He wrote a wonderful review of Evie's book. D'you mean to say she didn't show it you?"

Before George could answer his friend had called a man over. A tall, thin man, with a high forehead, a beard, a long nose and a stoop, just the sort of man whom George was prepared to dislike at first sight. Introductions were effected. Henry Dashwood sat down.

"Is Mrs. Peregrine in London by any chance? I should very much like to meet her," he said.

"No, my wife doesn't like London. She prefers the country," said George stiffly.

"She wrote me a very nice letter about my review. I was pleased. You know, we critics get more kicks than halfpence. I was simply bowled over by her book. It's so fresh and original, very modern without being obscure. She seems to be as much at her ease in free verse as in the classical metres." Then because he was a critic he thought he should criticise. "Sometimes her ear is a trifle at fault, but you can say the same of Emily Dickinson. There are several of those short lyrics of hers that might have been written by Landor."

All this was gibberish to George Peregrine. The man was nothing but a disgusting highbrow. But the colonel had good manners and he answered with proper civility: Henry Dashwood went on as though he hadn't spoken.

"But what makes the book so outstanding is the passion that throbs in every line. So many of these young poets are so anaemic, cold, bloodless, dully intellectual, but here you have real naked, earthy passion; of course deep, sincere emotion like that is tragic—ah, my dear Colonel, how right Heine was when he said that the poet makes little songs out of his great sorrows. You know, now and then, as I read and re-read those heart-rending pages I thought of Sappho."

This was too much for George Peregrine and he got up.

"Well, it's jolly nice of you to say such nice things about my wife's little book. I'm sure she'll be delighted. But I must bolt, I've got to catch a train and I want to get a bite of lunch."

"Damned fool," he said irritably to himself as he walked up-stairs to the dining-room.

He got home in time for dinner and after Evie had gone to bed he went into his study and looked for her book. He thought he'd just glance through it again to see for himself what they were making such a fuss about, but he couldn't find it. Evie must have taken it away.

"Silly," he muttered.

He'd told her he thought it jolly good. What more could a fellow be expected to say? Well, it didn't matter. He lit his pipe and read the *Field* till he felt sleepy. But a week or so later it happened that he had to go into Sheffield for the day. He lunched there at his club. He had nearly finished when the Duke of Haverel came in. This was the great local magnate and of course the colonel knew him, but only to say how d'you do to; and he was surprised when the Duke stopped at his table.

"We're so sorry your wife couldn't come to us for the week-end," he said, with a sort of shy cordiality. "We're expecting rather a nice lot of people."

George was taken aback. He guessed that the Haverels had asked him and Evie over for the week-end and Evie, without saying a word to him about it, had refused. He had the presence of mind to say he was sorry too.

"Better luck next time," said the Duke pleasantly and moved on.

Colonel Peregrine was very angry and when he got home he said to his wife:

"Look here, what's this about our being asked over to Haverel? Why on earth did you say we couldn't go? We've never been asked before and it's the best shooting in the county."

"I didn't think of that. I thought it would only bore you."

"Damn it all, you might at least have asked me if I wanted to go."

"I'm sorry."

He looked at her closely. There was something in her expression that he didn't quite understand. He frowned.

"I suppose *I* was asked?" he barked.

Evie flushed a little.

"Well, in point of fact you weren't."

"I call it damned rude of them to ask you without asking me."

"I suppose they thought it wasn't your sort of party. The Duchess is rather fond of writers and people like that, you know. She's having Henry Dashwood, the critic, and for some reason he wants to meet me."

"It was damned nice of you to refuse, Evie."

"It's the least I could do," she smiled. She hesitated a moment. "George, my publishers want to give a little dinner party for me one day towards the end of the month and of course they want you to come too."

"Oh, I don't think that's quite my mark. I'll come up to London with you if you like. I'll find someone to dine with."

Daphne.

"I expect it'll be very dull, but they're making rather a point of it. And the day after, the American publisher who's taken my book is giving a cocktail party at Claridge's. I'd like you to come to that if you wouldn't mind."

"Sounds like a crashing bore, but if you really want me to come I'll come."

"It would be sweet of you."

George Peregrine was dazed by the cocktail party. There were a lot of people. Some of them didn't look so bad, a few of the women were decently turned out, but the men seemed to him pretty awful. He was introduced to everyone as Colonel Peregrine, E. K. Hamilton's husband, you know. The men didn't seem to have anything to say to him, but the women gushed.

"You *must* be proud of your wife. Isn't it *wonderful?* You know, I read it right through at a sitting, I simply couldn't put it down, and when I'd finished I started again at the beginning and read it right through a second time. I was simply *thrilled.*"

The English publisher said to him:

"We've not had a success like this with a book of verse for twenty years. I've never seen such reviews."

The American publisher said to him:

"It's swell. It'll be a smash hit in America. You wait and see."

The American publisher had sent Evie a great spray of orchids. Damned ridiculous, thought George. As they came in, people were taken up to Evie, and it was evident that they said flattering things to her, which she took with a pleasant smile and a word or two of thanks. She was a trifle flushed with the excitement, but seemed quite at her ease. Though he thought the whole thing a lot of stuff and nonsense George noted with approval that his wife was carrying it off in just the right way.

"Well, there's one thing," he said to himself, "you can see she's a lady and that's a damned sight more than you can say of anyone else here."

He drank a good many cocktails. But there was one thing that bothered him. He had a notion that some of the people he was introduced to looked at him in rather a funny sort of way, he couldn't quite make out what it meant, and once when he strolled by two women who were sitting together on a sofa he had the impression that they were talking about him and after he passed he was almost certain they tittered. He was very glad when the party came to an end.

In the taxi on their way back to their hotel Evie said to him:

"You were wonderful, dear. You made quite a hit. The girls simply raved about you: they thought you so handsome."

"Girls," he said bitterly. "Old hags."

"Were you bored, dear?"

"Stiff."

She pressed his hand in a gesture of sympathy.

"I hope you won't mind if we wait and go down by the afternoon train. I've got some things to do in the morning."

"No, that's all right. Shopping?"

"I do want to buy one or two things, but I've got to go and be photographed. I hate the idea, but they think I ought to be. For America, you know."

He said nothing. But he thought. He thought it would be a shock to the American public when they saw the portrait of the homely, desiccated little woman who was his wife. He'd always been under the impression that they liked glamour in America.

He went on thinking, and next morning when Evie had gone out he went to his club and up to the library. There he looked up recent numbers of *The Times Literary Supplement, The New Statesman* and *The Spectator*. Presently he found reviews of Evie's book. He didn't read them very carefully, but enough to see that they were extremely favourable. Then he went to the bookseller's in Piccadilly where he occasionally bought books. He'd made up his mind that he had to read this damned thing of Evie's properly, but he didn't want to ask her what she'd done with the copy she'd given him. He'd buy one for himself. Before going in he looked in the window and the first thing he saw was a display of *When Pyramids Decay*. Damned silly title! He went in. A young man came forward and asked if he could help him.

"No, I'm just having a look round." It embarrassed him to ask for Evie's book and he thought he'd find it for himself and then take it to the salesman. But he couldn't see it anywhere and at last, finding the young man near him, he said in a carefully casual tone: "By the way, have you got a book called *When Pyramids Decay?*"

"The new edition came in this morning. I'll get a copy."

In a moment the young man returned with it. He was a short, rather stout young man, with a shock of untidy carroty hair and spectacles. George Peregrine, tall, upstanding, very military, towered over him.

"Is this a new edition then?" he asked.

"Yes, sir. The fifth. It might be a novel the way it's selling."

George Peregrine hesitated a moment.

"Why d'you suppose it's such a success? I've always been told no one reads poetry."

"Well, it's good, you know. I've read it meself." The young man, though obviously cultured, had a slight Cockney accent, and George quite instinctively adopted a patronising attitude. "It's the story they like. Sexy, you know, but tragic."

George frowned a little. He was coming to the conclusion that the young man was rather impertinent. No one had told him anything about there being a story in the damned book and he

had not gathered that from reading the reviews. The young man
went on:

"Of course it's only a flash in the pan, if you know what I
mean. The way I look at it, she was sort of inspired like by a
personal experience, like Housman was with *The Shropshire
Lad*. She'll never write anything else."

"How much is the book?" said George coldly to stop his chatter. "You needn't wrap it up, I'll just slip it into my pocket."

The November morning was raw and he was wearing a greatcoat.

At the station he bought the evening papers and magazines
and he and Evie settled themselves comfortably in opposite
corners of a first-class carriage and read. At five o'clock they
went along to the restaurant car to have tea and chatted a little.
They arrived. They drove home in the car which was waiting for
them. They bathed, dressed for dinner, and after dinner Evie,
saying she was tired out, went to bed. She kissed him, as was her
habit, on the forehead. Then he went into the hall, took Evie's
book out of his greatcoat pocket and going into the study began
to read it. He didn't read verse very easily and though he read
with attention, every word of it, the impression he received was
far from clear. Then he began at the beginning again and read it
a second time. He read with increasing malaise, but he was not
a stupid man and when he had finished he had a distinct understanding of what it was all about. Part of the book was in free
verse, part in conventional metres, but the story it related was
coherent and plain to the meanest intelligence. It was the story
of a passionate love affair between an older woman, married,
and a young man. George Peregrine made out the steps of it as
easily as if he had been doing a sum in simple addition.

Written in the first person, it began with the tremulous surprise of the woman, past her youth, when it dawned upon her
that the young man was in love with her. She hesitated to believe it. She thought she must be deceiving herself. And she was
terrified when on a sudden she discovered that she was passionately in love with him. She told herself it was absurd; with the
disparity of age between them nothing but unhappiness could
come to her if she yielded to her emotion. She tried to prevent
him from speaking but the day came when he told her that he
loved her and forced her to tell him that she loved him too. He
begged her to run away with him. She couldn't leave her hus-

band, her home; and what life could they look forward to, she
an ageing woman, he so young? How could she expect his love
to last? She begged him to have mercy on her. But his love was
impetuous. He wanted her, he wanted her with all his heart, and
at last trembling, afraid, desirous, she yielded to him. Then
there was a period of ecstatic happiness. The world, the dull,
humdrum world of every day, blazed with glory. Love songs
flowed from her pen. The woman worshipped the young, virile
body of her lover. George flushed darkly when she praised his
broad chest and slim flanks, the beauty of his legs and the flat-
ness of his belly.

Hot stuff, Daphne's friend had said. It was that all right. Disgusting.

There were sad little pieces in which she lamented the empti-
ness of her life when as must happen he left her, but they ended
with a cry that all she had to suffer would be worth it for the
bliss that for a while had been hers. She wrote of the long, tremulous nights they passed together and the languor that lulled
them to sleep in one another's arms. She wrote of the rapture of
brief stolen moments when, braving all danger, their passion
overwhelmed them and they surrendered to its call.

She thought it would be an affair of a few weeks, but miraculously it lasted. One of the poems referred to three years having
gone by without lessening the love that filled their hearts. It
looked as though he continued to press her to go away with him,
far away, to a hill town in Italy, a Greek island, a walled city in
Tunisia, so that they could be together always, for in another
of the poems she besought him to let things be as they were.
Their happiness was precarious. Perhaps it was owing to the
difficulties they had to encounter and the rarity of their meetings that their love had retained for so long its first enchanting
ardour. Then on a sudden the young man died. How, when or
where George could not discover. There followed a long, heartbroken cry of bitter grief, grief she could not indulge in, grief
that had to be hidden. She had to be cheerful, give dinner-par-
ties and go out to dinner, behave as she had always behaved,
though the light had gone out of her life and she was bowed
down with anguish. The last poem of all was a set of four short
stanzas in which the writer, sadly resigned to her loss, thanked
the dark powers that rule man's destiny that she had been
privileged at least for a while to enjoy the greatest happiness
that we poor human beings can ever hope to know.

It was three o'clock in the morning when George Peregrine finally put the book down. It had seemed to him that he heard Evie's voice in every line, over and over again he came upon turns of phrase he had heard her use, there were details that were as familiar to him as to her: there was no doubt about it; it was her own story she had told, and it was as plain as anything could be that she had had a lover and her lover had died. It was not anger so much that he felt, nor horror or dismay, though he was dismayed and he was horrified, but amazement. It was as inconceivable that Evie should have had a love affair, and a wildly passionate one at that, as that the trout in a glass case over the chimney piece in his study, the finest he had ever caught, should suddenly wag its tail. He understood now the meaning of the amused look he had seen in the eyes of that man he had spoken to at the club, he understood why Daphne when she was talking about the book had seemed to be enjoying a private joke, and why those two women at the cocktail party had tittered when he strolled past them.

He broke out into a sweat. Then on a sudden he was seized with fury and he jumped up to go and awake Evie and ask her sternly for an explanation. But he stopped at the door. After all, what proof had he? A book. He remembered that he'd told Evie he thought it jolly good. True, he hadn't read it, but he'd pretended he had. He would look a perfect fool if he had to admit that.

"I must watch my step," he muttered.

He made up his mind to wait for two or three days and think it all over. Then he'd decide what to do. He went to bed, but he couldn't sleep for a long time.

"Evie," he kept on saying to himself. "Evie, of all people."

They met at breakfast next morning as usual. Evie was as she always was, quiet, demure and self-possessed, a middle-aged woman who made no effort to look younger than she was, a woman who had nothing of what he still called It. He looked at her as he hadn't looked at her for years. She had her usual placid serenity. Her pale blue eyes were untroubled. There was no sign of guilt on her candid brow. She made the same little casual remarks she always made.

"It's nice to get back to the country again after those two hectic days in London. What are you going to do this morning?"

It was incomprehensible.

Three days later he went to see his solicitor. Henry Blane was an old friend of George's as well as his lawyer. He had a place not far from Peregrine's and for years they had shot over one another's preserves. For two days a week he was a country gentleman and for the other five a busy lawyer in Sheffield. He was a tall, robust fellow, with a boisterous manner and a jovial laugh, which suggested that he liked to be looked upon essentially as a sportsman and a good fellow and only incidentally as a lawyer. But he was shrewd and worldly-wise.

"Well, George, what's brought you here today?" he boomed as the colonel was shown into his office. "Have a good time in London? I'm taking my missus up for a few days next week. How's Evie?"

"It's about Evie I've come to see you," said Peregrine, giving him a suspicious look. "Have you read her book?"

His sensitivity had been sharpened during those last days of troubled thought and he was conscious of a faint change in the lawyer's expression. It was as though he were suddenly on his guard.

"Yes, I've read it. Great success, isn't it? Fancy Evie breaking out into poetry. Wonders will never cease."

George Peregrine was inclined to lose his temper.

"It's made me look a perfect damned fool."

"Oh, what nonsense, George! There's no harm in Evie's writing a book. You ought to be jolly proud of her."

"Don't talk such rot. It's her own story. You know it and everyone else knows it. I suppose I'm the only one who doesn't know who her lover was."

"There is such a thing as imagination, old boy. There's no reason to suppose the whole thing isn't made up."

"Look here, Henry, we've known one another all our lives. We've had all sorts of good times together. Be honest with me. Can you look me in the face and tell me you believe it's a made-up story?"

Harry Blane moved uneasily in his chair. He was disturbed by the distress in old George's voice.

"You've got no right to ask me a question like that. Ask Evie."

"I daren't," George answered after an anguished pause. "I'm afraid she'd tell me the truth."

There was an uncomfortable silence.

"Who was the chap?"

Harry Blane looked at him straight in the eye.

"I don't know, and if I did I wouldn't tell you."

"You swine. Don't you see what a position I'm in? Do you think it's very pleasant to be made absolutely ridiculous?"

The lawyer lit a cigarette and for some moments silently puffed it.

"I don't see what I can do for you," he said at last.

"You've got private detectives you employ, I suppose. I want you to put them on the job and let them find everything out."

"It's not very pretty to put detectives on one's wife, old boy; and besides, taking for granted for a moment that Evie had an affair, it was a good many years ago and I don't suppose it would be possible to find out a thing. They seem to have covered their tracks pretty carefully."

"I don't care. You put the detectives on. I want to know the truth."

"I won't, George. If you're determined to do that you'd better consult someone else. And look here, even if you got evidence that Evie had been unfaithful to you what would you do with it? You'd look rather silly divorcing your wife because she'd committed adultery ten years ago."

"At all events I could have it out with her."

"You can do that now, but you know just as well as I do that if you do she'll leave you. D'you want her to do that?"

George gave him an unhappy look.

"I don't know. I always thought she'd been a damned good wife to me. She runs the house perfectly, we never have any servant trouble; she's done wonders with the garden and she's splendid with all the village people. But damn it, I have my self-respect to think of. How can I go on living with her when I know that she was grossly unfaithful to me?"

"Have you always been faithful to her?"

"More or less, you know. After all, we've been married for nearly twenty-four years and Evie was never much for bed."

The solicitor slightly raised his eyebrows, but George was too intent on what he was saying to notice.

"I don't deny that I've had a bit of fun now and then. A man wants it. Women are different."

"We only have men's word for that," said Harry Blane, with a faint smile.

"Evie's absolutely the last woman I'd have suspected of kicking over the traces. I mean, she's a very fastidious, reticent woman. What on earth made her write the damned book?"

"I suppose it was a very poignant experience and perhaps it was a relief to her to get it off her chest like that."

"Well, if she had to write it why the devil didn't she write it under an assumed name?"

"She used her maiden name. I suppose she thought that was enough, and it would have been if the book hadn't had this amazing boom."

George Peregrine and the lawyer were sitting opposite one another with a desk between them. George, his elbow on the desk, his cheek on his hand, frowned at his thought.

"It's so rotten not to know what sort of a chap he was. One can't even tell if he was by way of being a gentleman. I mean, for all I know he may have been a farm-hand or a clerk in a lawyer's office."

Harry Blane did not permit himself to smile and when he answered there was in his eyes a kindly, tolerant look.

"Knowing Evie so well I think the probabilities are that he was all right. Anyhow I'm sure he wasn't a clerk in my office."

"It's been a shock to me," the colonel sighed. "I thought she was fond of me. She couldn't have written that book unless she hated me."

"Oh, I don't believe that. I don't think she's capable of hatred."

"You're not going to pretend that she loves me."

"No."

"Well, what does she feel for me?"

Harry Blane leaned back in his swivel chair and looked at George reflectively.

"Indifference, I should say."

The colonel gave a little shudder and reddened.

"After all, you're not in love with her, are you?"

George Peregrine did not answer directly.

"It's been a great blow to me not to have any children, but I've never let her see that I think she's let me down. I've always been kind to her. Within reasonable limits I've tried to do my duty by her."

The lawyer passed a large hand over his mouth to conceal the smile that trembled on his lips.

"It's been such an awful shock to me," Peregrine went on. "Damn it all, even ten years ago Evie was no chicken and God knows, she wasn't much to look at. It's so ugly." He sighed deeply. "What would *you* do in my place?"

"Nothing."

George Peregrine drew himself bolt upright in his chair and he looked at Harry with the stern set face that he must have worn when he inspected his regiment.

"I can't overlook a thing like this. I've been made a laughing-stock. I can never hold up my head again."

"Nonsense," said the lawyer sharply, and then in a pleasant, kindly manner, "Listen, old boy: the man's dead; it all happened a long while back. Forget it. Talk to people about Evie's book, rave about it, tell 'em how proud you are of her. Behave as though you had so much confidence in her, you *knew* she could never have been unfaithful to you. The world moves so quickly and people's memories are so short. They'll forget."

"I shan't forget."

"You're both middle-aged people. She probably does a great deal more for you than you think and you'd be awfully lonely without her. I don't think it matters if you don't forget. It'll be all to the good if you can get it into that thick head of yours that there's a lot more in Evie than you ever had the gumption to see."

"Damn it all, you talk as if *I* was to blame."

"No, I don't think you were to blame, but I'm not so sure that Evie was either. I don't suppose she wanted to fall in love with this boy. D'you remember those verses right at the end? The impression they gave me was that though she was shattered by his death, in a strange sort of way she welcomed it. All through she'd been aware of the fragility of the tie that bound them. He died in the full flush of his first love and had never known that love so seldom endures; he'd only known its bliss and beauty. In her own bitter grief she found solace in the thought that he'd been spared all sorrow."

"All that's a bit above my head, old boy. I see more or less what you mean."

George Peregrine stared unhappily at the inkstand on the desk. He was silent and the lawyer looked at him with curious, yet sympathetic, eyes.

"Do you realise what courage she must have had never by a sign to show how dreadfully unhappy she was?" he said gently.

Colonel Peregrine sighed.

"I'm broken. I suppose you're right; it's no good crying over spilt milk and it would only make things worse if I made a fuss."

"Well?"

George Peregrine gave a pitiful little smile.

"I'll take your advice. I'll do nothing. Let them think me a damned fool and to hell with them. The truth is, I don't know what I'd do without Evie. But I'll tell you what, there's one thing I shall never understand till my dying day: What in the name of heaven did the fellow ever see in her?"

EPISODE

It was quite a small party, because our hostess liked general
conversation; we never sat down to dinner more than eight, and
generally only six, and after dinner when we went up to the
drawing-room the chairs were so arranged that it was impossible
for two persons to go into a huddle in a corner and so break
things up. I was glad on arriving to find that I knew everyone.
There were two nice clever women besides our hostess and two
men besides myself. One was my friend Ned Preston. Our
hostess made it a point never to ask wives with their husbands,
because she said each cramped the other's style and if they
didn't like to come separately they needn't come at all. But
since her food and her wine were good and the talk almost
always entertaining they generally came. People sometimes accused her of asking husbands more often than wives, but she
defended herself by saying that she couldn't possibly help it
because more men were husbands than women were wives.

Ned Preston was a Scot, a good-humoured, merry soul, with
a gift for telling a story, sometimes too lengthily, for he was
uncommonly loquacious, but with dramatic intensity. He was
a bachelor with a small income which sufficed for his modest
needs, and in this he was lucky since he suffered from that form
of chronic tuberculosis which may last for years without killing
you, but which prevents you from working for your living. Now
and then he would be ill enough to stay in bed for two or three

weeks, but then he would get better and be as gay, cheerful and talkative as ever. I doubt whether he had enough money to live in an expensive sanatorium and he certainly hadn't the temperament to suit himself to its life. He was worldly. When he was well he liked to go out, out to lunch, out to dinner, and he liked to sit up late into the night smoking his pipe and drinking a good deal of whisky. If he had been content to live the life of an invalid he might have been alive now, but he wasn't; and who can blame him? He died at the age of fifty-five of a haemorrhage which he had one night after coming home from some house where, he may well have flattered himself, he was the success of the party.

He had that febrile vitality that some consumptives have, and was always looking for an occupation to satisfy his desire for activity. I don't know how he heard that at Wormwood Scrubs they were in want of prison visitors, but the idea took his fancy so he went to the Home Office and saw the official in charge of prisons to offer his services. The job is unpaid, and though a number of persons are willing to undertake it, either from compassion or curiosity, they are apt to grow tired of it, or find it takes up too much time, and the prisoners whose problems, interests and future they have been concerned with are left somewhat in the lurch. The Home Office people consequently are wary of taking on anyone who does not look as if he would persevere, and they make careful inquiries into the applicant's antecedents, character and general suitability. Then he is given a trial, is discreetly watched, and if the impression is unfavourable is politely thanked and told that his services are no longer required. But Ned Preston satisfied the dour and shrewd official who interviewed him that he was in every way reliable, and from the beginning he got on well with the governor, the warders and the prisoners. He was entirely lacking in class-consciousness, so prisoners, whatever their station in life, felt as ease with him. He neither preached nor moralised. He had never done a criminal, or even a mean, thing in his life, but he treated the crime of the prisoners he had to deal with as though it were an illness like his own tuberculosis which was a nuisance you had to put up with, but which it did no good to talk about.

Wormwood Scrubs is a first offenders' prison and it is a building, grim and cold, of forbidding appearance. Ned took me over it once and I had goose-flesh as the gates were unlocked for us

and we went in. We passed through the halls in which the men
were working.

"If you see any pals of yours take no notice of them," Ned
said to me. "They don't like it."

"Am I likely to see any pals of mine?" I asked dryly.

"You never can tell. I shouldn't be surprised if you had had
friends who'd passed bad cheques once too often or were caught
in a compromising situation in one of the parks. You'd be surprised how often I run across chaps I've met out at dinner."

One of Ned's duties was to see prisoners through the first
difficult days of their confinement. They were often badly
shaken by their trial and sentence; and when, after the preliminary proceedings they had to go through on entering the jail,
the stripping, the bath, the medical examination and the questioning, the getting into prison clothes, they were led into a cell
and locked up, they were apt to break down. Sometimes they
cried hysterically; sometimes they could neither eat nor sleep.
Ned's business then was to cheer them, and his breezy manner,
his natural kindliness, often worked wonders. If they were anxious about their wives and children he would go to see them
and if they were destitute provide them with money. He
brought them news so that they might get over the awful feeling that they were shut away from the common interests of
their fellow-men. He read the sporting papers to be able to tell
them what horse had won an important race or whether the
champion had won his fight. He would advise them about their
future, and when the time approached for their release see what
jobs they were fitted for and then persuade employers to give
them a chance to make good.

Since everyone is interested in crime it was inevitable that
sooner or later, with Ned there, the conversation should turn
upon it. It was after dinner and we were sitting comfortably in
the drawing-room with drinks in our hands.

"Had any interesting cases at the Scrubs lately, Ned?" I
asked him.

"No, nothing much."

He had a high, rasping voice and his laugh was a raucous
cackle. He broke into it now.

"I went to see an old girl to-day who was a packet of fun. Her
husband's a burglar. The police have known about him for
years, but they've never been able to get him till just now. Before he did a job he and his wife concocted an alibi, and though

he's been arrested three or four times and sent up for trial, the police have never been able to break it and he's always got off. Well, he was arrested again a little while ago, but he wasn't upset, the alibi he and his wife had made up was perfect and he expected to be acquitted as he'd been before. His wife went into the witness-box and to his utter amazement she didn't give the alibi and he was convicted. I went to see him. He wasn't so much worried at being in gaol as puzzled by his wife not having spoken up, and he asked me to go and see her and ask what the game was. Well I went, and d'you know what she said to me? She said: 'Well, sir, it's like this; it was such a beautiful alibi I just couldn't bear to waste it.' "

Of course we all laughed. The story-teller likes an appreciative audience, and Ned Preston was never disinclined to hold the floor. He narrated two or three more anecdotes. They tended to prove a point he was fond of making, that in what till we all got democratic in England were called the lower orders there was more passion, more romance, more disregard of consequences than could ever be found in the well-to-do and presumably educated classes, whom prudence has made timid and convention inhibited.

"Because the working man doesn't read much," he said, "because he has no great gift for expressing himself, you think he has no imagination. You're wrong. He's extravagantly imaginative. Because he's a great husky brute you think he has no nerves. You're wrong again. He's a bundle of nerves."

Then he told us a story which I shall tell as best I can in my own words.

Fred Manson was a good-looking fellow, tall, well-made, with blue eyes, good features and a friendly, agreeable smile, but what made him remarkable so that people turned round in the streets to stare at him was that he had a thick head of hair, with a great wave in it, of a deep rich red. It was really a great beauty. Perhaps it was this that gave him so sensual a look. His maleness was like a heady perfume. His eyebrows were thick, only a little lighter than his hair, and he was lucky enough not to have the ugly skin that so often disfigures red-heads. His was a smooth olive. His eyes were bold, and when he smiled or laughed, which in the healthy vitality of his youth he did constantly, his expression was wonderfully alluring. He was twenty-two and he gave you the rather pleasant impression of just loving to be alive. It was inevitable that with such looks and above all with that troubling sexuality he should have success with women. He was charming, tender and passionate, but immensely promiscuous. He was not exactly callous or brazen, he had a kindly nature, but somehow or other he made it quite clear to the objects of his passing fancy that all he wanted was a little bit of fun and that it was impossible for him to remain faithful to anyone.

Fred was a postman. He worked in Brixton. It is a densely populated part of London, and has the curious reputation of harbouring more criminals than any other suburb because trams run to it from across the river all night long, so that when a man has done a job of housebreaking in the West End he can be sure of getting home without difficulty. Fred liked his job. Brixton is a district of innumerable streets lined with little houses inhabited by the people who work in the neighbourhood and also by clerks, shop-assistants, skilled workers of one sort or another whose jobs take them every day across the river. He was strong and healthy and it was a pleasure to him to walk from street to street delivering the letters. Sometimes there would be a postal packet to hand in or a registered letter that had to be signed for, and then he would have the opportunity of seeing people. He was a sociable creature. It was never long before he was well known on whatever round he was assigned to. After a time his job was changed. His duty then was to go to the red pillar-boxes into which the letters were put, empty them, and take the contents to the main post-office of the district. His bag would be pretty heavy sometimes by the time he was through, but he was proud of his strength and the weight only made him laugh.

One day he was emptying a box in one of the better streets, a street of semi-detached houses, and had just closed his bag when a girl came running along.

"Postman," she cried, "take this letter, will you. I want it to go by this post most particularly."

He gave her his good-natured smile.

"I never mind obliging a lady," he said, putting down his bag and opening it.

"I wouldn't trouble you, only it's urgent," she said as she handed him the letter she had in her hand.

"Who is it to—a feller?" he grinned.

"None of your business."

"All right, be haughty. But I tell you this, he's no good. Don't you trust him."

"You've got a nerve," she said.

"So they tell me."

He took off his cap and ran his hand through his mop of curling red hair. The sight of it made her gasp.

"Where d'you get your perm?" she asked with a giggle.

"I'll show you one of these days if you like."

He was looking down at her with his amused eyes, and there was something about him that gave her a funny little feeling in the pit of her stomach.

"Well, I must be on my way," he said. "If I don't get on with the job pretty damn quick I don't know what'll happen to the country."

"I'm not detaining you," she said coolly.

"That's where you make a mistake," he answered.

He gave her a look that made her heart beat nineteen to the dozen and she felt herself blushing all over. She turned away and ran back to the house. Fred noticed it was four doors away from the pillar-box. He had to pass it and as he did so he looked up. He saw the net curtains twitch and knew she was watching. He felt pleased with himself. During the next few days he looked at the house whenever he passed it, but never caught a glimpse of the girl. One afternoon he ran across her by chance just as he was entering the street in which she lived.

"Hulloa," he said, stopping.

"Hulloa."

She blushed scarlet.

"Haven't seen you about lately."

"You haven't missed much."

"That's what you think."

She was prettier than he remembered, dark-haired, dark-eyed, rather tall, slight, with a good figure, a pale skin and very white teeth.

"What about coming to the pictures with me one evening?"

"Taking a lot for granted, aren't you?"

"It pays," he said with his impudent, charming grin.

She couldn't help laughing.

"Not with me, it doesn't."

"Oh, come on. One's only young once."

There was something so attractive in him that she couldn't bring herself to give him a saucy answer.

"I couldn't really. My people wouldn't like me going out with a fellow I don't know. You see, I'm the only one they have and they think a rare lot of me. Why, I don't even know your name."

"Well, I can tell you, can't I? Fred. Fred Manson. Can't you say you're going to the pictures with a girl friend?"

She had never felt before what she was feeling then. She didn't know if it was pain or pleasure. She was strangely breathless.

"I suppose I could do that."

They fixed the night, the time and the place. Fred was waiting for her and they went in, but when the picture started and he put his arm round her waist, without a word, her eyes fixed on the screen, she quietly took it away. He took hold of her hand, but she withdrew it. He was surprised. That wasn't the way girls usually behaved. He didn't know what one went to the pictures for if it wasn't to have a bit of a cuddle. He walked home with her after the show. She told him her name. Grace Carter. Her father had a shop of his own in the Brixton Road, he was a draper and he had four assistants.

"He must be doing well," said Fred.

"He doesn't complain."

Gracie was a student at London University. When she got her degree she was going to be a school teacher.

"What d'you want to do that for when there's a good business waiting for you?"

"Pa doesn't want me to have anything to do with the shop— not after the education he's given me. He wants me to better myself, if you know what I mean."

Her father had started life as an errand boy, then become a draper's assistant and because he was hard-working, honest and intelligent was now owner of a prosperous little business. Success had given him grand ideas for his only child. He didn't want her to have anything to do with trade. He hoped she'd marry a professional man perhaps, or at least someone in the City. Then he'd sell the business and retire, and Gracie would be quite the lady.

When they reached the corner of her street Gracie held out her hand.

"You'd better not come to the door," she said.

"Aren't you going to kiss me good-night?"

"I am not."

"Why?"

"Because I don't want to."

"You'll come to the pictures again, won't you?"

"I think I'd better not."

"Oh, come on."

There was such a warm urgency in his voice that she felt as though her knees would give way.

"Will you behave if I do?" He nodded. "Promise?"

"Swop me bob."

He scratched his head when he left her. Funny girl. He'd never met anyone quite like her. Superior, there was no doubt about that. There was something in her voice that got you. It was warm and soft. He tried to think what it was like. It was like as if the words kissed you. Sounded silly, that did, but that's just what it was like.

From then on they went to the pictures once or twice a week. After a while she allowed him to put his arm round her waist and to hold her hand, but she never let him go farther than that.

"Have you ever been kissed by a fellow?" he asked her once.

"No, I haven't," she said simply. "My ma's funny, she says you've got to keep a man's respect."

"I'd give anything in the world just to kiss you, Gracie."

"Don't be so silly."

"Won't you let me just once?" She shook her head. "Why not?"

"Because I like you too much," she said hoarsely, and then walked quickly away from him.

It gave him quite a turn. He wanted her as he'd never wanted a woman before. What she'd said finished him. He'd been thinking of her a lot, and he'd looked forward to the evenings they spent together as he'd never looked forward to anything in his life. For the first time he was uncertain of himself. She was above him in every way, what with her father making money hand over fist and her education and everything, and him only a postman. They had made a date for the following Friday night and he was in a fever of anxiety lest she shouldn't come. He repeated to himself over and over again what she'd said: perhaps it meant that she'd made up her mind to drop him. When at last he saw her walking along the street he almost sobbed with relief. That evening he neither put his arm round her nor took her hand and when he walked her home he never said a word.

"You're very quiet to-night, Fred," she said at last. "What's the matter with you?"

He walked a few steps before he answered.

"I don't like to tell you."

She stopped suddenly and looked up at him. There was terror on her face.

"Tell me whatever it is," she said unsteadily.

"I'm gone, I can't help myself, I'm so stuck on you I can't see straight. I didn't know what it was to love like I love you."

"Oh, is that all? You gave me such a fright. I thought you were going to say you were going to be married."

"Me? Who d'you take me for? It's you I want to marry."

"Well, what's to prevent you, silly?"

"Gracie! D'you mean it?"

He flung his arms round her and kissed her full on the mouth. She didn't resist. She returned his kiss and he felt in her a passion as eager as his own.

They arranged that Gracie should tell her parents that she was engaged to him and that on the Sunday he should come and be introduced to them. Since the shop stayed open late on Saturday and by the time Mr. Carter got home he was tired out, it was not till after dinner on Sunday that Gracie broke her news. George Carter was a brisk, not very tall man, but sturdy, with a high colour, who with increasing prosperity had put on weight. He was more than rather bald and he had a bristle of grey moustache. Like many another employer who has risen from the working class he was a slave-driver and he got as much work out of his assistants for as little money as was possible. He had an eye for everything and he wouldn't put up with any nonsense, but he was reasonable and even kindly, so that they did not dislike him. Mrs. Carter was a quiet, nice woman, with a pleasant face and the remains of good looks. They were both in the early fifties, for they had married late after "walking out" for nearly ten years.

They were very much surprised when Gracie told them what she had to tell, but not displeased.

"You are a sly one," said her father. "Why, I never suspected for a minute you'd taken up with anyone. Well, I suppose it had to come sooner or later. What's his name?"

"Fred Manson."

"A fellow you met at college?"

"No. You must have seen him about. He clears our pillar-box. He's a postman."

"Oh, Gracie," cried Mrs. Carter, "you can't mean it. You

can't marry a common postman, not after all the education we've given you."

For an instant Mr. Carter was speechless. He got redder in the face than ever.

"Your ma's right, my girl," he burst out now. "You can't throw yourself away like that. Why, it's ridiculous."

"I'm not throwing myself away. You wait till you see him."

Mrs. Carter began to cry.

"It's such a come-down. It's such a humiliation. I shall never be able to hold up my head again."

"Oh, Ma, don't talk like that. He's a nice fellow and he's got a good job."

"You don't understand," she moaned.

"How d'you get to know him?" Mr. Carter interrupted. "What sort of a family's he got?"

"His pa drives one of the post-office vans," Gracie answered defiantly.

"Working-class people."

"Well, what of it? His pa's worked twenty-four years for the post-office and they think a lot of him."

Mrs. Carter was biting the corner of her handkerchief.

"Gracie, I want to tell you something. Before your pa and me got married I was in domestic service. He wouldn't ever let me tell you because he didn't want you to be ashamed of me. That's why we was engaged all those years. The lady I was with said she'd leave me something in her will if I stayed with her till she passed away."

"It was that money that gave me my start," Mr. Carter broke in. "Except for that I'd never have been where I am to-day. And I don't mind telling you your ma's the best wife a man ever had."

"I never had a proper education," Mrs. Carter went on, "but I always was ambitious. The proudest moment of my life was when your pa said we could afford a girl to help me and he said then: 'The time'll come when you have a cook *and* a house-maid,' and he's been as good as his word, and now you're going back to what I come from. I'd set my heart on your marrying a gentleman."

She began crying again. Gracie loved her parents and couldn't bear to see them so distressed.

"I'm sorry, Ma, I knew it would be a disappointment to you,

but I can't help it, I can't really. I love him so, I love him so
terribly. I'm sure you'll like him when you see him. We're going
for a walk on the Common this afternoon. Can't I bring him
back to supper?"

Mrs. Carter gave her husband a harassed look. He sighed.

"I don't like it and it's no good pretending I do, but I suppose
we'd better have a look at him."

Supper passed off better than might have been expected. Fred
wasn't shy, and he talked to Gracie's parents as though he had
known them all his life. If to be waited on by a maid, if to sup
in a dining-room furnished in solid mahogany and afterwards to
sit in a drawing-room that had a grand piano in it was new to
him, he showed no embarrassment. After he had gone and they
were alone in their bedroom Mr. and Mrs. Carter talked him
over.

"He is handsome, you can't deny that," she said.

"Handsome is as handsome does. D'you think he's after her
money?"

"Well, he must know that you've got a tidy little bit tucked
away somewhere, but he's in love with her all right."

"Oh, what makes you think that?"

"Why, you've only got to see the way he looks at her."

"Well, that's something at all events."

In the end the Carters withdrew their opposition on the condition that the young things shouldn't marry until Gracie had
taken her degree. That would give them a year, and at the back
of their minds was the hope that by then she would have
changed her mind. They saw a good deal of Fred after that. He
spent every Sunday with them. Little by little they began quite
to like him. He was so easy, so gay, so full of high spirits, and
above all so obviously head over ears in love with Gracie, that
Mrs. Carter soon succumbed to his charm, and after a while
even Mr. Carter was prepared to admit that he didn't seem a
bad fellow. Fred and Gracie were happy. She went to London
every day to attend lectures and worked hard. They spent blissful evenings together. He gave her a very nice engagement ring
and often took her out to dinner in the West End and to a play.
On fine Sundays he drove her out into the country in a car that
he said a friend had lent him. When she asked him if he could
afford all the money he spent on her he laughed, and said a chap
had given him a tip on an outsider and he'd made a packet.

They talked interminably of the little flat they would have when they were married and the fun it would be to furnish it. They were more in love with one another than ever.

Then the blow fell. Fred was arrested for stealing money from the letters he collected. Many people, to save themselves the trouble of buying postal orders, put notes in their envelopes, and it wasn't difficult to tell that they were there. Fred went up for trial, pleaded guilty, and was sentenced to two years' hard labour. Gracie went to the trial. Up to the last moment she had hoped that he would be able to prove his innocence. It was a dreadful shock to her when he pleaded guilty. She was not allowed to see him. He went straight from the dock to the prison van. She went home and, locking herself up in her bedroom, threw herself on the bed and wept. When Mr. Carter came back from the shop Gracie's mother went up to her room.

"Gracie, you're to come downstairs," she said. "Your father wants to speak to you."

Gracie got up and went down. She did not trouble to dry her eyes.

"Seen the paper?" he said, holding out to her the *Evening News*.

She didn't answer.

"Well, that's the end of that young man," he went on harshly.

They too, Gracie's parents, had been shocked when Fred was arrested, but she was so distressed, she was so convinced that everything could be explained, that they hadn't had the heart to tell her that she must have nothing more to do with him. But now they felt it time to have things out with her.

"So that's where the money came from for those dinners and theatres. And the car. I thought it funny he should have a friend who'd lend him a car on Sundays when he'd be wanting it himself. He hired it, didn't he?"

"I suppose so," she answered miserably. "I just believed what he told me."

"You've had a lucky escape, my girl, that's all I can say."

"He only did it because he wanted to give me a good time. He didn't want me to think I couldn't have everything as nice when I was with him as what I've been used to at home."

"You're not going to make excuses for him, I hope. He's a thief, that's what he is."

"I don't care," she said sullenly.

"You don't care? What d'you mean by that?"

"Exactly what I say. I'm going to wait for him and the moment he comes out I'm going to marry him."

Mrs. Carter gave a gasp of horror.

"Gracie, you can't do a think like that," she cried. "Think of the disgrace. And what about us? We've always held our heads high. He's a thief, and once a thief always a thief."

"Don't go on calling him a thief," Gracie shrieked, stamping her foot with rage. "What he did he did just because he loved me. I don't care if he is a thief. I love him more than ever I loved him. You don't know what love is. You waited ten years to marry Pa just so as an old woman should leave you some money. D'you call that love?"

"You leave your ma out of this," Mr. Carter shouted. Then an idea occurred to him and he gave her a piercing glance. "Have you *got* to marry the feller?"

Gracie blushed furiously.

"No. There's never been anything of that sort. And not through any fault of mine either. He loved me too much. He didn't want to do anything perhaps he'd regret afterwards."

Often on summer evenings in the country when they'd been lying in a field in one another's arms, mouth to mouth, her desire had been as intense as his. She knew how much he wanted her and she was ready to give him what he asked. But when things got too desperate he'd suddenly jump up and say:

"Come on, let's walk."

He'd drag her to her feet. She knew what was in his mind. He wanted to wait till they were married. His love had given him a delicacy of sentiment that he'd never known before. He couldn't make it out himself, but he had a funny sort of feeling about her, he felt that if he had her before marriage it would spoil things. Because she guessed what was in his heart she loved him all the more.

"I don't know what's come over you," moaned Mrs. Carter. "You was always such a good girl. You've never given us a day's uneasiness."

"Stop it, Ma," said Mr. Carter violently. "We've got to get this straight once and for all. You've got to give up this man, see? I've got me own position to think of and if you think I'm going to have a gaol-bird for a son-in-law you'd better think again. I've had enough of this nonsense. You've got to promise me that you'll have nothing more to do with the feller ever."

"D'you think I'm going to give him up now? How often d'you

want me to tell you I'm going to marry him the moment he gets out?"

"All right, then you can get out of my house and get out pretty damn quick. And stay out."

"Pa!" cried Mrs. Carter.

"Shut up."

"I'll be glad to go," said Gracie.

"Oh, will you? And how d'you think you're going to live?"

"I can work, can't I? I can get a job at Payne & Perkins. They'll be glad to have me."

"Oh, Gracie, you couldn't go and work in a shop. You can't demean yourself like that," said Mrs. Carter.

"Will you shut up, Ma," shouted Mr. Carter, beside himself now with rage. "Work, will you? You that's never done a stroke of work in your life except that tomfoolery at the college. Bright idea it was of your ma's to give you an education. Fat lot of good it'll be to you when you've got to stand on your feet for hours and got to be civil and pleasant to a lot of old trouts who just try and give you all the trouble they can just to show how superior they are. I bet you'll like it when you're bawled out by the manageress because you're not bright and snappy. All right, marry your gaol-bird. I suppose you know you'll have to keep him too. You don't think anyone's going to give him a job, do you, not with his record. Get out, get out, get out."

He had worked himself up to such a pitch of fury that he sank panting into a chair. Mrs. Carter, frightened, poured out a glass of water and gave him some to drink. Gracie slipped out of the room.

Next day, when her father had gone to work and her mother was out shopping, she left the house with such effects as she could get into a suit-case. Payne & Perkins was a large department store in the Brixton Road, and with her good appearance and pleasant manner she found no difficulty in getting taken on. She was put in the ladies' lingerie. For a few days she stayed at the Y.W.C.A. and then arranged to share a room with one of the girls who worked with her.

Ned Preston saw Fred in the evening of the day he went to gaol. He found him shattered, but only because of Gracie. He took his thieving very lightly.

"I had to do the right thing by her, didn't I? Her people, they didn't think I was good enough for her; I wanted to show them I was just as good as they were. When we went up to the West

End I couldn't give her a sandwich and half of bitter in a pub, why, she's never been in a pub in her life, I *had* to take her to a restaurant. If people are such fools as to put money in letters, well, they're just asking for it."

But he was frightened. He wasn't sure that Gracie would see it like that.

"I've got to know what she's going to do. If she chucks me now—well, it's the end of everything for me, see? I'll find some way of doing meself in, I swear to God I will."

He told Ned the whole story of his love for Gracie.

"I could have had her over and over again if I'd wanted to. And I did want to and so did she. I knew that. But I respected her, see? She's not like other girls. She's one in a thousand, I tell you."

He talked and talked. He stormed, he wept. From that confused torrent of words emerged one thing very clearly. A passionate, a frenzied love. Ned promised that he would see the girl.

"Tell her I love her, tell her that what I did I just did because I wanted her to have the best of everything, and tell her I just can't live without her."

As soon as he could find time Ned Preston went to the Carters' house, but when he asked for Gracie the maid who opened the door told him that she didn't live there any more. Then he asked to see her mother.

"I'll go and see if she's in."

He gave the maid his card, thinking the name of his club engraved in the corner would impress Mrs. Carter enough to make her willing to see him. The maid left him at the door, but in a minute or two asked him to come in. He was shown into the stiff and little-used sitting-room. Mrs. Carter kept him waiting for some time and when she came in, holding his card in the tips of her fingers, he guessed it was because she had thought fit to change her dress. The black silk she wore was evidently a dress for occasions. He told her his connection with Wormwood Scrubs and said that he had to do with a man named Frederick Manson. The moment he mentioned the name Mrs. Carter assumed a hostile attitude.

"Don't speak to me of that man," she cried. "A thief, that's what he is. The trouble he's caused us. They ought to have given him five years, they ought."

"I'm sorry he's caused you trouble," said Ned mildly. "Perhaps if you'd give me a few facts I might help to straighten things out."

Ned Preston certainly had a way with him. Perhaps Mrs. Carter was impressed because he was a gentleman. "Class he is," she probably said to herself. Anyhow it was not long before she was telling him the whole story. She grew upset as she told it and began to cry.

"And now she's gone and left us. Run away. I don't know how she could bring herself to do a thing like that. God knows, we love her. She's all we've got and we done everything in the world for her. Her pa never meant it when he told her to get out of the house. Only she was so obstinate. He got in a temper, he always was a quick-tempered man, he was just as upset as I was when we found she'd gone. And d'you know what's she's been and gone and done? Got herself a job at Payne & Perkins. Mr. Carter can't abide them. Cutting prices all the time they are. Unfair competition, he calls it. And to think of our Gracie working with a lot of shop-girls—oh, it's so humiliating."

Ned made a mental note of the store's name. He hadn't been at all sure of getting Gracie's address out of Mrs. Carter.

"Have you seen her since she left you?" he asked.

"Of course I have. I knew they'd jump at her at Payne & Perkins, a superior girl like that, and I went there, and there she was, sure enough—in the ladies' lingerie. I waited outside till closing time and then I spoke to her. I asked her to come home. I said her pa was willing to let bygones be bygones. And d'you know what she said? She said she'd come home if we never said a word against Fred and if we was prepared to have her marry him as soon as ever he got out. Of course I had to tell her pa. I never saw him in such a state, I thought he was going to have a fit, he said he'd rather see her dead at his feet than married to that gaol-bird."

Mrs. Carter again burst into tears and as soon as he could Ned Preston left her. He went to the department store, up to the ladies' lingerie, and asked for Grace Carter. She was pointed out to him and he went up to her.

"Can I speak to you for a minute? I've come from Fred Manson."

She went deathly white. For a moment it seemed that she could not utter a word.

"Follow me, please."

She took him into a passage smelling of disinfectants which

seemed to lead to the lavatories. They were alone. She stared at him anxiously.

"He sends you his love. He's worried about you. He's afraid you're awfully unhappy. What he wants to know really is if you're going to chuck him."

"Me?" Her eyes filled with tears, but on her face was a look of ecstasy. "Tell him that nothing matters to me as long as he loves me. Tell him I'd wait twenty years for him if I had to. Tell him I'm counting the days till he gets out so as we can get married."

For fear of the manageress she couldn't stay away from her work for more than a minute or two. She gave Ned all the loving messages she could get into the time to give Fred Manson. Ned didn't get to the Scrubs till nearly six. The prisoners are allowed to put down their tools at five-thirty and Fred had just put his down. When Ned entered the cell he turned pale and sank on to the bed as though his anxiety was such that he didn't trust his legs. But when Ned told him his news he gave a gasp of relief. For a while he couldn't trust himself to speak.

"I knew you'd seen her the moment you came in. I smelt her."

He sniffed as though the smell of her body were strong in his nostrils, and his face was as it were a mask of desire. His features on a sudden seemed strangely blurred.

"You know, it made me feel quite uncomfortable so that I had to look the other way," said Ned Preston when he told us this, with a cackle of his shrill laughter. "It was sex in its nakedness all right."

Fred was an exemplary prisoner. He worked well, he gave no trouble. Ned suggested books for him to read and he took them out of the library, but that was about as far as he got.

"I can't get on well with them somehow," he said. "I start reading and then I begin thinking of Gracie. You know, when she kisses you ordinary-like—oh, it's so sweet, but when she kisses you really, my God, it's lovely."

Fred was allowed to see Gracie once a month, but their meetings, with a glass screen between, under the eyes of a warder, were so painful that after several visits they agreed it would be better if she didn't come any more. A year passed. Owing to his good behaviour he could count on a remittance of his sentence and so would be free in another six months. Gracie had saved every penny she could out of her wages and now as the time approached for Fred's release she set about getting a home ready for him. She took two rooms in a house and furnished them on the hire purchase system. One room of course was to be their bedroom and the other the living-room and kitchen. There was an old-fashioned range in it and this she had taken out and replaced by a gas-stove. She wanted everything to be nice and new and clean and comfortable. She took pains to make the two little rooms bright and pretty. To do all this she had to go without all but the barest necessities of existence and she grew thin and pale. Ned suspected that she was starving herself and when he went to see her took a box of chocolates or a cake so that she should have at least something to eat. He brought the prisoner news of what Gracie was doing and she made him promise to give him accurate accounts of every article she bought. He took fond, more than fond, passionate messages from one to the other. He was convinced that Fred would go straight in future and he got him a job as commissionaire from a firm that had a chain of restaurants in London. The wages were good and by calling taxis or fetching cars he would be able to make money on the side. He was to start work as soon as he came out of gaol. Gracie took the necessary steps so that they could get married at once. The eighteen months of Fred's imprisonment were drawing to an end. Gracie was in a fever of excitement.

It happened then that Ned Preston had one of his periodical bouts of illness and was unable to go to the prison for three weeks. It bothered him, for he didn't like to abandon his prisoners, so as soon as he could get out of bed he went to the Scrubs. The chief warder told him that Manson had been asking for him.

"I think you'd better go and see him. I don't know what's the matter with him. He's been acting rather funny since you've been away."

It was just a fortnight before Fred was due to be released. Ned Preston went to his cell.

"Well, Fred, how are you?" he asked. "Sorry I haven't been able to come and see you. I've been ill, and I haven't been able to see Gracie either. She must be all of a dither by now."

"Well, I want you to go and see her."

His manner was so surly that Ned was taken aback. It was unlike him to be anything but pleasant and civil.

"Of course I will."

"I want you to tell her that I'm not going to marry her."

Ned was so astounded that for a minute he could only stare blankly at Fred Manson.

"What on earth d'you mean?"

"Exactly what I say."

"You can't let her down now. Her people have thrown her out. She's been working all this time to get a home ready for you. She's got the licence and everything."

"I don't care. I'm not going to marry her."

"But why, why, why?"

Ned was flabbergasted. Fred Manson was silent for a bit. His face was dark and sullen.

"I'll tell you. I've thought about her night and day for eighteen months and now I'm sick to death of her."

When Ned Preston reached this point of his story our hostess and our fellow guests broke into loud laughter. He was plainly taken aback. There was some little talk after that and the party broke up. Ned and I, having to go in the same direction, walked along Piccadilly together. For a time we walked in silence.

"I noticed you didn't laugh with the others," he said abruptly.

"I didn't think it funny."

"What d'you make of it?"

"Well, I can see his point, you know. Imagination's an odd thing, it dries up; I suppose, thinking of her incessantly all that time he'd exhausted every emotion she could give him, and I think it was quite literally true, he'd just got sick to death of her. He'd squeezed the lemon dry and there was nothing to do but throw away the rind."

"I didn't think it funny either. That's why I didn't tell them the rest of the story. I wouldn't accept it at first. I thought it was just hysteria or something. I went to see him two or three days running. I argued with him. I really did my damnedest. I thought if he'd only see her it would be all right, but he wouldn't even do that. He said he hated the sight of her. I couldn't move him. At last I had to go and tell her."

We walked on a little longer in silence.

"I saw her in that beastly, stinking corridor. She saw at once there was something the matter and she went awfully white. She wasn't a girl to show much emotion. There was something gracious and rather noble about her face. Tranquil. Her lips quivered a bit when I told her and she didn't say anything for a minute. When she spoke it was quite calmly, as though—well, as though she'd just missed a bus and would have to wait for another. As though it was a nuisance, you know, but nothing to make a song and dance about. 'There's nothing for me to do now but put my head in the gas-oven,' she said.

"And she did."

THE KITE

I KNOW this is an odd story. I don't understand it myself and if
I set it down in black and white it is only with a faint hope that
when I have written it I may get a clearer view of it, or rather
with the hope that some reader, better acquainted with the
complications of human nature than I am, may offer me an explanation that will make it comprehensible to me. Of course the
first thing that occurs to me is that there is something Freudian
about it. Now, I have read a good deal of Freud, and some
books by his followers, and intending to write this story I have
recently flipped through again the volume published by the
Modern Library which contains his basic writings. It was something of a task, for he is a dull and verbose writer, and the
acrimony with which he claims to have originated such and such
a theory shows a vanity and a jealousy of others working in the
same field which somewhat ill become the man of science. I believe, however, that he was a kindly and benign old party. As
we know, there is often a great difference between the man and
the writer. The writer may be bitter, harsh, and brutal, while
the man may be so meek and mild that he wouldn't say boo to a
goose. But that is neither here nor there. I found nothing in my
re-reading of Freud's works that cast any light on the subject I
had in mind. I can only relate the facts and leave it at that.

First of all I must make it plain that it is not my story and
that I knew none of the persons with whom it is concerned. It

was told me one evening by my friend Ned Preston, and he told it me because he didn't know how to deal with the circumstances and he thought, quite wrongly as it happened, that I might be able to give him some advice that would help him. In a previous story I have related what I thought the reader should know about Ned Preston, and so now I need only remind him that my friend was a prison visitor at Wormwood Scrubs. He took his duties very seriously and made the prisoners' troubles his own. We had been dining together at the Café Royal in that long, low room with its absurd and charming decoration which is all that remains of the old Café Royal that painters have loved to paint; and we were sitting over our coffee and liqueurs and, so far as Ned was concerned against his doctor's orders, smoking very long and very good Havanas.

"I've got a funny chap to deal with at the Scrubs just now," he said, after a pause, "and I'm blowed if I know how to deal with him."

"What's he in for?" I asked.

"He left his wife and the court ordered him to pay so much a week in alimony and he's absolutely refused to pay it. I've argued with him till I was blue in the face. I've told him he's only cutting off his nose to spite his face. He says he'll stay in jail all his life rather than pay her a penny. I tell him he can't let her starve, and all he says is: 'Why not?' He's perfectly well behaved, he's no trouble, he works well, he seems quite happy, he's just getting a lot of fun out of thinking what a devil of a time his wife is having."

"What's he got against her?"

"She smashed his kite."

"She did what?" I cried.

"Exactly that. She smashed his kite. He says he'll never forgive her for that till his dying day."

"He must be crazy."

"No, he isn't, he's a perfectly reasonable, quite intelligent, decent fellow."

Herbert Sunbury was his name, and his mother, who was very refined, never allowed him to be called Herb or Bertie, but always Herbert, just as she never called her husband Sam but only Samuel. Mrs. Sunbury's first name was Beatrice, and when she got engaged to Mr. Sunbury and he ventured to call her Bea she put her foot down firmly.

"Beatrice I was christened," she said, "and Beatrice I always have been and always shall be, to you and to my nearest and dearest."

She was a little woman, but strong, active and wiry, with a sallow skin, sharp, regular features and small, beady eyes. Her hair, suspiciously black for her age, was always very neat, and she wore it in the style of Queen Victoria's daughters, which she had adopted as soon as she was old enough to put it up and had never thought fit to change. The possibility that she did something to keep her hair its original colour was, if such was the case, her only concession to frivolity, for, far from using rouge or lipstick, she had never in her life so much as passed a powder-puff over her nose. She never wore anything but black dresses of good material, but made (by a little woman round the corner) regardless of fashion after a pattern that was both serviceable and decorous. Her only ornament was a thin gold chain from which hung a small gold cross.

Samuel Sunbury was a little man too. He was as thin and spare as his wife, but he had sandy hair, gone very thin now so that he had to wear it very long on one side and brush it carefully over the large bald patch. He had pale blue eyes and his complexion was pasty. He was a clerk in a lawyer's office and had worked his way up from office boy to a respectable position. His employer called him Mr. Sunbury and sometimes asked him to see an unimportant client. Every morning for twenty-four years Samuel Sunbury had taken the same train to the City, except of course on Sundays and during his fortnight's holiday at the seaside, and every evening he had taken the same train back to the suburb in which he lived. He was neat in his dress; he went to work in quiet grey trousers, a black coat and a bowler hat, and when he came home he put on his slippers and a black coat which was too old and shiny to wear at the office; but on Sundays when he went to the chapel he and Mrs. Sunbury attended he wore a morning coat with his bowler. Thus he showed his respect for the days of rest and at the same time registered a protest against the ungodly who went bicycling or lounged about the streets until the pubs opened. On principle the Sunburys were total abstainers, but on Sundays, when to make up for the frugal lunch, consisting of a scone and butter with a glass of milk, which Samuel had during the week, Beatrice gave him a good dinner of roast beef and Yorkshire pudding, for his health's sake she liked him to have a glass of beer. Since she wouldn't for the world have kept liquor in the house, he sneaked out with a jug after morning service and got a quart from the pub round the corner; but nothing would induce him to drink alone, so, just to be sociable-like, she had a glass too.

Herbert was the only child the Lord had vouchsafed to them, and this certainly through no precaution on their part. It just happened that way. They doted on him. He was a pretty baby and then a good-looking child. Mrs. Sunbury brought him up carefully. She taught him to sit up at table and not put his elbows on it, and she taught him how to use his knife and fork like a little gentleman. She taught him to stretch out his little finger when he took his tea-cup to drink out of it and when he asked why, she said:

"Never you mind. That's how it's done. It shows you know what's what."

In due course Herbert grew old enough to go to school. Mrs. Sunbury was anxious because she had never let him play with the children in the street.

"Evil communications corrupt good manners," she said. "I always have kept myself to myself and I always shall keep myself to myself."

Although they had lived in the same house ever since they were married she had taken care to keep her neighbours at a distance.

"You never know who people are in London," she said. "One thing leads to another, and before you know where you are you're mixed up with a lot of riff-raff and you can't get rid of them."

She didn't like the idea of Herbert being thrown into contact with a lot of rough boys at the County Council school and she said to him:

"Now, Herbert, do what I do; keep yourself to yourself and don't have anything more to do with them than you can help."

But Herbert got on very well at school. He was a good worker and far from stupid. His reports were excellent. It turned out that he had a good head for figures.

"If that's a fact," said Samuel Sunbury, "he'd better be an accountant. There's always a good job waiting for a good accountant."

So it was settled there and then that this was what Herbert was to be. He grew tall.

"Why, Herbert," said his mother, "soon you'll be as tall as your dad."

By the time he left school he was two inches taller, and by the time he stopped growing he was five feet ten.

"Just the right height," said his mother. "Not too tall and not too short."

He was a nice-looking boy, with his mother's regular features and dark hair, but he had inherited his father's blue eyes, and though he was rather pale his skin was smooth and clear. Samuel Sunbury had got him into the office of the accountants who came twice a year to do the accounts of his own firm and by the time he was twenty-one he was able to bring back to his mother every week quite a nice little sum. She gave him back three half-crowns for his lunches and ten shillings for pocket money, and the rest she put in the Savings Bank for him against a rainy day.

When Mr. and Mrs. Sunbury went to bed on the night of Herbert's twenty-first birthday, and in passing I may say that Mrs. Sunbury never went to bed, she retired, but Mr. Sunbury, who was not quite so refined as his wife, always said: "Me for Bedford,"—when then Mr. and Mrs. Sunbury went to bed, Mrs. Sunbury said:

"Some people don't know how lucky they are; thank the Lord, I do. No one's ever had a better son than our Herbert. Hardly a day's illness in his life and he's never given me a moment's worry. It just shows if you bring up somebody right they'll be a credit to you. Fancy him being twenty-one, I can hardly believe it."

"Yes, I suppose before we know where we are he'll be marrying and leaving us."

"What should he want to do that for?" asked Mrs. Sunbury with asperity. "He's got a good home here, hasn't he? Don't you go putting silly ideas into his head, Samuel, or you and me'll have words and you know that's the last thing I want. Marry indeed! He's got more sense than that. He knows when he's well off. He's got sense, Herbert has."

Mr. Sunbury was silent. He had long ago learnt that it didn't get him anywhere with Beatrice to answer back.

"I don't hold with a man marrying till he knows his own mind," she went on. "And a man doesn't know his own mind till he's thirty or thirty-five."

"He was pleased with his presents," said Mr. Sunbury to change the conversation.

"And so he ought to be," said Mrs. Sunbury still upset.

They had in fact been handsome. Mr. Sunbury had given him a silver wrist-watch, with hands that you could see in the dark, and Mrs. Sunbury had given him a kite. It wasn't by any means the first one she had given him. That was when he was seven years old, and it happened this way. There was a large common near where they lived and on Saturday afternoons when it was fine Mrs. Sunbury took her husband and son for a walk there. She said it was good for Samuel to get a breath of fresh air after being cooped up in a stuffy office all the week. There were always a lot of people on the common, but Mrs. Sunbury who liked to keep herself to herself kept out of their way as much as possible.

"Look at them kites, Mum," said Herbert suddenly one day.

There was a fresh breeze blowing and a number of kites, small and large, were sailing through the air.

"*Those*, Herbert, not them," said Mrs. Sunbury.

"Would you like to go and see where they start, Herbert?" asked his father.

"Oh, yes, Dad."

There was a slight elevation in the middle of the common and as they approached it they saw boys and girls and some men racing down it to give their kites a start and catch the wind. Sometimes they didn't and fell to the ground, but when they did they would rise, and as the owner unravelled his string go higher and higher. Herbert looked with ravishment.

"Mum, can I have a kite?" he cried.

He had already learnt that when he wanted anything it was better to ask his mother first.

"Whatever for?" she said.

"To fly it, Mum."

"If you're so sharp you'll cut yourself," she said.

Mr. and Mrs. Sunbury exchanged a smile over the little boy's head. Fancy him wanting a kite. Growing quite a little man he was.

"If you're a good boy and wash your teeth regular every morning without me telling you I shouldn't be surprised if Santa Claus didn't bring you a kite on Christmas Day."

Christmas wasn't far off and Santa Claus brought Herbert his first kite. At the beginning he wasn't very clever at managing it, and Mr. Sunbury had to run down the hill himself and start it for him. It was a very small kite, but when Herbert saw it swim through the air and felt the little tug it gave his hand he was thrilled; and then every Saturday afternoon, when his father got back from the City, he would pester his parents to hurry over to the common. He quickly learnt how to fly it, and Mr. and Mrs. Sunbury, their hearts swelling with pride, would watch him from the top of the knoll while he ran down and as the kite caught the breeze lengthened the cord in his hand.

It became a passion with Herbert, and as he grew older and bigger his mother bought him larger and larger kites. He grew very clever at gauging the winds and could do things with his kite you wouldn't have thought possible. There were other kite-flyers on the common, not only children, but men, and since nothing brings people together so naturally as a hobby they share it was not long before Mrs. Sunbury, notwithstanding her exclusiveness, found that she, her Samuel and her son were on speaking terms with all and sundry. They would compare their respective kites and boast of their accomplishments. Sometimes Herbert, a big boy of sixteen now, would challenge another kite-flyer. Then he would manoeuvre his kite to windward of the other fellow's, allow his cord to drift against his, and by a sudden jerk bring the enemy kite down. But long before this Mr. Sunbury had succumbed to his son's enthusiasm and he would often ask to have a go himself. It must have been a funny sight to see him running down the hill in his striped trousers, black coat and bowler hat. Mrs. Sunbury would trot sedately behind him and when the kite was sailing free would take the cord from him and watch it as it soared. Saturday afternoon became the great day of the week for them, and when Mr. Sunbury and Herbert left the house in the morning to catch their train to the City the first thing they did was to look up at the sky to see if it was flying weather. They liked best of all a gusty day, with uncertain winds, for that gave them the best chance to exercise their skill. All through the week, in the evenings, they talked about it. They were contemptuous of smaller kites than theirs and envious of bigger ones. They discussed the performances of other flyers as hotly, and as scornfully, as boxers or football-players discuss their rivals. Their ambition was to have a bigger kite than anyone else and a kite that would go higher. They had long given up a cord, for the kite they gave Herbert on his twenty-first birthday was seven feet high, and they used piano wire wound round a drum. But that did not satisfy Herbert. Somehow or other he had heard of a box-kite which had been invented by somebody, and the idea appealed to him at once.

He thought he could devise something of the sort himself and since he could draw a little he set about making designs of it. He got a small model made and tried it out one afternoon, but it wasn't a success. He was a stubborn boy and he wasn't going to be beaten. Something was wrong, and it was up to him to put it right.

Then an unfortunate thing happened. Herbert began to go out after supper. Mrs. Sunbury didn't like it much, but Mr. Sunbury reasoned with her. After all, the boy was twenty-two, and it must be dull for him to stay home all the time. If he wanted to go for a walk or see a movie there was no great harm. Herbert had fallen in love. One Saturday evening, after they'd had a wonderful time on the common, while they were at supper, out of a clear sky he said suddenly:

"Mum, I've asked a young lady to come in to tea to-morrow. Is that all right?"

"You done what?" said Mrs. Sunbury, for a moment forgetting her grammar.

"You heard, Mum."

"And may I ask who she is and how you got to know her?"

"Her name's Bevan, Betty Bevan, and I met her first at the pictures one Saturday afternoon when it was raining. It was an accident-like. She was sitting next me and she dropped her bag and I picked it up and she said thank you and so naturally we got talking."

"And d'you mean to tell me you fell for an old trick like that? Dropped her bag indeed!"

"You're making a mistake, Mum, she's a nice girl, she is really and well educated too."

"And when did all this happen?"

"About three months ago."

"Oh, you met her three months ago and you've asked her to come to tea to-morrow?"

"Well, I've seen her since of course. That first day, after the show, I asked her if she'd come to the pictures with me on the Tuesday evening, and she said she didn't know, perhaps she would and perhaps she wouldn't. But she came all right."

"She would. I could have told you that."

"And we've been going to the pictures about twice a week ever since."

"So that's why you've taken to going out so often?"

"That's right. But, look, I don't want to force her on you, if you don't want her to come to tea I'll say you've got a headache and take her out."

"Your mum will have her to tea all right," said Mr. Sunbury. "Won't you, dear? It's only that your mum can't abide strangers. She never has liked them."

"I keep myself to myself," said Mrs. Sunbury gloomily. "What does she do?"

"She works in a typewriting office in the City and she lives at home, if you call it home; you see, her mum died and her dad married again, and they've got three kids and she doesn't get on with her step-ma. Nag, nag, nag all the time, she says."

Mrs. Sunbury arranged the tea very stylishly. She took the knick-knacks off a little table in the sitting-room, which they never used, and put a tea-cloth on it. She got out the tea-service and the plated tea-kettle which they never used either, and she made scones, baked a cake, and cut thin bread-and-butter.

"I want her to see that we're not just nobody," she told her Samuel.

Herbert went to fetch Miss Bevan, and Mr. Sunbury intercepted them at the door in case Herbert should take her into the dining-room where normally they ate and sat. Herbert gave the tea-table a glance of surprise as he ushered the young woman into the sitting-room.

"This is Betty, Mum," he said.

"Miss Bevan, I presume," said Mrs. Sunbury.

"That's right, but call me Betty, won't you?"

"Perhaps the acquaintance is a bit short for that," said Mrs. Sunbury with a gracious smile. "Won't you sit down, Miss Bevan?"

Strangely enough, or perhaps not strangely at all, Betty Bevan looked very much as Mrs. Sunbury must have looked at her age. She had the same sharp features and the same rather small beady eyes, but her lips were scarlet with paint, her cheeks lightly rouged and her short black hair permanently waved. Mrs. Sunbury took in all this at a glance, and she reckoned to a penny how much her smart rayon dress had cost, her extravagantly high-heeled shoes and the saucy hat on her head. Her frock was very short and she showed a good deal of flesh-coloured stocking. Mrs. Sunbury, disapproving of her make-up and of her apparel, took an instant dislike to her, but she had made up her mind to behave like a lady, and if she didn't know how to behave like a lady nobody did, so that at first things went well. She poured out tea and asked Herbert to give a cup to his lady friend.

"Ask Miss Bevan if she'll have some bread-and-butter or a scone, Samuel, my dear."

"Have both," said Samuel, handing round the two plates, in his coarse way. "I like to see people eat hearty."

Betty insecurely perched a piece of bread-and-butter and a scone on her saucer and Mrs. Sunbury talked affably about the weather. She had the satisfaction of seeing that Betty was getting more and more ill-at-ease. Then she cut the cake and pressed a large piece on her guest. Betty took a bite at it and when she put it in her saucer it fell to the ground.

"Oh, I am sorry," said the girl, as she picked it up.

"It doesn't matter at all, I'll cut you another piece," said Mrs. Sunbury.

"Oh, don't bother, I'm not particular. The floor's clean."

"I hope so," said Mrs. Sunbury with an acid smile, "but I wouldn't dream of letting you eat a piece of cake that's been on the floor. Bring it here, Herbert, and I'll give Miss Bevan some more."

"I don't want any more, Mrs. Sunbury, I don't really."

"I'm sorry you don't like my cake. I made it specially for you." She took a bit. "It tastes all right to me."

"It's not that, Mrs. Sunbury, it's a beautiful cake, it's only that I'm not hungry."

She refused to have more tea and Mrs. Sunbury saw she was glad to get rid of the cup. "I expect they have their meals in the kitchen," she said to herself. Then Herbert lit a cigarette.

"Give us a fag, Herb," said Betty. "I'm simply dying for a smoke."

Mrs. Sunbury didn't approve of women smoking, but she only raised her eyebrows slightly.

"We prefer to call him Herbert, Miss Bevan," she said.

Betty wasn't such a fool as not to see that Mrs. Sunbury had been doing all she could to make her uncomfortable, and now she saw a chance to get back on her.

"I know," she said. "When he told me his name was Herbert I nearly burst out laughing. Fancy calling anyone Herbert. A scream, I call it."

"I'm sorry you don't like the name my son was given at his baptism. I think it's a very nice name. But I suppose it all depends on what sort of class of people one is."

Herbert stepped in to the rescue.

"At the office they call me Bertie, Mum."

"Then all I can say is, they're a lot of very common men."

Mrs. Sunbury lapsed into a dignified silence and the conversation, such as it was, was maintained by Mr. Sunbury and Herbert. It was not without satisfaction that Mrs. Sunbury perceived that Betty was offended. She also perceived that the girl wanted to go, but didn't quite know how to manage it. She was determined not to help her. Finally Herbert took the matter into his own hands.

"Well, Betty, I think it's about time we were getting along," he said. "I'll walk back with you."

"Must you go already?" said Mrs. Sunbury, rising to her feet. "It's been a pleasure, I'm sure."

"Pretty little thing," said Mr. Sunbury tentatively after the young things had left.

"Pretty my foot. All that paint and powder. You take my word for it, she'd look very different with her face washed and without a perm. Common, that's what she is, common as dirt."

An hour later Herbert came back. He was angry.

"Look here, Mum, what d'you mean by treating the poor girl like that? I was simply ashamed of you."

"Don't talk to your mother like that, Herbert," she flared up. "You didn't ought to have brought a woman like that into my house. Common, she is, common as dirt."

When Mrs. Sunbury got angry not only did her grammar grow shaky, but she wasn't quite safe on her aitches. Herbert took no notice of what she said.

"She said she'd never been so insulted in her life. I had a rare job pacifying her."

"Well, she's never coming here again, I tell you that straight."

"That's what you think. I'm engaged to her, so put that in your pipe and smoke it."

Mrs. Sunbury gasped.

"You're not?"

"Yes, I am. I've been thinking about it for a long time, and then she was so upset to-night I felt sorry for her, so I popped the question and I had a rare job persuading her, I can tell you."

"You fool," screamed Mrs. Sunbury. "You fool."

There was quite a scene then. Mrs. Sunbury and her son went at it hammer and tongs, and when poor Samuel tried to intervene they both told him roughly to shut up. At last Herbert flung out of the room and out of the house and Mrs. Sunbury burst into angry tears.

No reference was made next day to what had passed. Mrs. Sunbury was frigidly polite to Herbert and he was sullen and silent. After supper he went out. On Saturday he told his father and mother that he was engaged that afternoon and wouldn't be able to come to the common with them.

"I dare say we shall be able to do without you," said Mrs. Sunbury grimly.

It was getting on to the time for their usual fortnight at the seaside. They always went to Herne Bay, because Mrs. Sunbury said you had a nice class of people there, and for years they had taken the same lodgings. One evening, in as casual a way as he could, Herbert said:

"By the way, Mum, you'd better write and tell them I shan't be wanting my room this year. Betty and me are getting married and we're going to Southend for the honeymoon."

For a moment there was dead silence in the room.

"Bit sudden-like, isn't it, Herbert?" said Mr. Sunbury uneasily.

"Well, they're cutting down at Betty's office and she's out of a job, so we thought we'd better get married at once. We've taken two rooms in Dabney Street and we're furnishing out of my Savings Bank money."

Mrs. Sunbury didn't say a word. She went deathly pale and tears rolled down her thin cheeks.

"Oh, come on, Mum, don't take it so hard," said Herbert. "A fellow has to marry sometime. If Dad hadn't married you, I shouldn't be here now, should I?"

Mrs. Sunbury brushed her tears away with an impatient hand.

"Your dad didn't marry me; I married 'im. I knew he was steady and respectable. I knew he'd make a good 'usband and father. I've never 'ad cause to regret it and no more 'as your dad. That's right, Samuel, isn't it?"

"Right as rain, Beatrice," he said quickly.

"You know, you'll like Betty when you get to know her. She's a nice girl, she is really. I believe you'd find you had a lot in common. You must give her a chance, Mum."

"She's never going to set foot in this house only over my dead body."

"That's absurd, Mum. Why, everything'll be just the same if you'll only be reasonable. I mean, we can go flying on Saturday afternoons same as we always did. Just this time I've been engaged it's been difficult. You see, she can't see what there is in kite-flying, but she'll come round to it, and after I'm married it'll be different, I mean I can come and fly with you and Dad; that stands to reason."

"That's what you think. Well, let me tell you that if you marry that woman you're not going to fly my kite. I never gave it you, I bought it out of the housekeeping money, and it's mine, see."

"All right then, have it your own way. Betty says it's a kid's game anyway and I ought to be ashamed of myself, flying a kite at my age."

He got up and once more stalked angrily out of the house. A fortnight later he was married. Mrs. Sunbury refused to go to the wedding and wouldn't let Samuel go either. They went for their holiday and came back. They resumed their usual round. On Saturday afternoons they went to the common by themselves and flew their enormous kite. Mrs. Sunbury never mentioned her son. She was determined not to forgive him. But Mr. Sunbury used to meet him on the morning train they both took and they chatted a little when they managed to get into the same carriage. One morning Mr. Sunbury looked up at the sky.

"Good flying weather to-day," he said.

"D'you and Mum still fly?"

"What do you think? She's getting as clever as I am. You should see her with her skirts pinned up running down the hill. I give you my word, I never knew she had it in her. Run? Why, she can run better than what I can."

"Don't make me laugh, Dad!"

"I wonder you don't buy a kite of your own, Herbert. You've been always so keen on it."

"I know I was. I did suggest it once, but you know what women are, Betty said: 'Be your age,' and oh, I don't know what all. I don't want a kid's kite, of course, and them big kites cost money. When we started to furnish Betty said it was cheaper in the long run to buy the best and so we went to one of them hire purchase places and what with paying them every month and the rent, well, I haven't got any more money than just what we can manage on. They say it doesn't cost any more to keep two than one, well, that's not my experience so far."

"Isn't she working?"

"Well, no, she says after working for donkeys' years as you might say, now she's married she's going to take it easy, and of course someone's got to keep the place clean and do the cooking."

So it went on for six months, and then one Saturday afternoon when the Sunburys were as usual on the common Mrs. Sunbury said to her husband:

"Did you see what I saw, Samuel?"

"I saw Herbert, if that's what you mean. I didn't mention it because I thought it would only upset you."

"Don't speak to him. Pretend you haven't seen him."

Herbert was standing among the idle lookers-on. He made no attempt to speak to his parents, but it did not escape Mrs. Sunbury that he followed with all his eyes the flight of the big kite he had flown so often. It began to grow chilly and the Sunburys went home. Mrs. Sunbury's face was brisk with malice.

"I wonder if he'll come next Saturday," said Samuel.

"If I didn't think betting wrong I'd bet you sixpence he will, Samuel. I've been waiting for this all along."

"You have?"

"I knew from the beginning he wouldn't be able to keep away from it."

She was right. On the following Saturday and on every Saturday after that when the weather was fine Herbert turned up on the common. No intercourse passed. He just stood there for a while looking on and then strolled away. But after things had been going on like this for several weeks, the Sunburys had a surprise for him. They weren't flying the big kite which he was used to, but a new one, a box-kite, a small one, on the model for which he had made the designs himself. He saw it was creating a lot of interest among the other kite-flyers; they were standing round it and Mrs. Sunbury was talking volubly. The first time Samuel ran down the hill with it the thing didn't rise, but flopped miserably on the ground, and Herbert clenched his hands and ground his teeth. He couldn't bear to see it fall. Mr. Sunbury climbed up the little hill again, and the second time the box-kite took the air. There was a cheer among the bystanders. After a while Mr. Sunbury pulled it down and walked back with it to the hill. Mrs. Sunbury went up to her son.

"Like to have a try, Herbert?"

He caught his breath.

"Yes, Mum, I should."

"It's just a small one because they say you have to get the knack of it. It's not like the old-fashioned sort. But we've got specifications for a big one, and they say when you get to know about it and the wind's right you can go up to two miles with it."

Mr. Sunbury joined them.

"Samuel, Herbert wants to try the kite."

Mr. Sunbury handed it to him, a pleased smile on his face, and Herbert gave his mother his hat to hold. Then he raced down the hill, the kite took the air beautifully, and as he watched it rise his heart was filled with exultation. It was grand to see that little black thing soaring so sweetly, but even as he watched it he thought of the great big one they were having made. They'd never be able to manage that. Two miles in the air, mum had said. Whew!

"Why don't you come back and have a cup of tea, Herbert," said Mrs. Sunbury, "and we'll show you the designs for the new one they want to build for us. Perhaps you could make some suggestions."

He hesitated. He'd told Betty he was just going for a walk to stretch his legs, she didn't know he'd been coming to the common every week, and she'd be waiting for him. But the temptation was irresistible.

"I don't mind if I do," he said.

After tea they looked at the specifications. The kite was huge, with gadgets he had never seen before, and it would cost a lot of money.

"You'll never be able to fly it by yourselves," he said.

"We can try."

"I suppose you wouldn't like me to help you just at first?" he asked uncertainly.

"Mightn't be a bad idea," said Mrs. Sunbury.

It was late when he got home, much later than he thought, and Betty was vexed.

"Wherever have you been, Herb? I thought you were dead. Supper's waiting and everything."

"I met some fellows and got talking."

She gave him a sharp look, but didn't answer. She sulked.

After supper he suggested they should go to a movie, but she refused.

"You go if you want to," she said. "I don't care to."

On the following Saturday he went again to the common and again his mother let him fly the kite. They had ordered the new one and expected to get it in three weeks. Presently his mother said to him:

"Elizabeth is here."

"Betty?"

"Spying on you."

It gave him a nasty turn, but he put on a bold front.

"Let her spy. I don't care."

But he was nervous and wouldn't go back to tea with his parents. He went straight home. Betty was waiting for him.

"So that's the fellows you got talking to. I've been suspicious for some time, you going for a walk on Saturday afternoons, and all of a sudden I tumbled to it. Flying a kite, you, a grown man. Contemptible I call it."

"I don't care what you call it. I like it, and if you don't like it you can lump it."

"I won't have it and I tell you that straight. I'm not going to have you make a fool of yourself."

"I've flown a kite every Saturday afternoon ever since I was a kid, and I'm going to fly a kite as long as ever I want to."

"It's that old bitch, she's just trying to get you away from me. I know her. If you were a man you'd never speak to her again, not after the way she's treated me."

"I won't have you call her that. She's my mother and I've got the right to see her as often as ever I want to."

The quarrel went on hour after hour. Betty screamed at him and Herbert shouted at her. They had had trifling disagreements before, because they were both obstinate, but this was the first serious row they had had. They didn't speak to one another on the Sunday, and during the rest of the week, though outwardly there was peace between them, their ill-feeling rankled. It happened that the next two Saturdays it poured with rain. Betty smiled to herself when she saw the downpour, but if Herbert was disappointed he gave no sign of it. The recollection of their quarrel grew dim. Living in two rooms as they did, sleeping in the same bed, it was inevitable that they should agree to forget their differences. Betty went out of her way to be nice to her Herb, and she thought that now she had given him a taste of her tongue and he knew she wasn't going to be put upon by anyone, he'd be reasonable. He was a good husband in his way, generous with his money and steady. Give her time and she'd manage him all right.

But after a fortnight of bad weather it cleared.

"Looks as if we're going to have good flying weather to-morrow," said Mr. Sunbury as they met on the platform to await their morning train. "The new kite's come."

"It has?"

"Your mum says of course we'd like you to come and help us with it, but no one's got the right to come between a man and his wife, and if you're afraid of Betty, her kicking up a rumpus, I mean, you'd better not come. There's a young fellow we've got to know on the common who's just mad about it, and he says he'll get it to fly if anybody can."

Herbert was seized with a pang of jealousy.

"Don't you let any strangers touch our kite. I'll be there all right."

"Well, you think it over, Herbert, and if you don't come we shall quite understand."

"I'll come," said Herbert.

So next day when he got back from the City he changed from his business clothes into slacks and an old coat. Betty came into the bedroom.

"What are you doing?"

"Changing," he answered gaily. He was so excited, he couldn't keep the secret to himself. "Their new kite's come and I'm going to fly it."

"Oh no, you're not," she said. "I won't have it."

"Don't be a fool, Betty. I'm going, I tell you, and if you don't like it you can do the other thing."

"I'm not going to let you, so that's that."

She shut the door and stood in front of it. Her eyes flashed and her jaw was set. She was a little thing and he was a tall strong man. He took hold of her two arms to push her out of the way, but she kicked him violently on the shin.

"D'you want me to give you a sock on the jaw?"

"If you go you don't come back," she shouted.

He caught her up, though she struggled and kicked, threw her on to the bed and went out.

If the small box-kite had caused an excitement on the common it was nothing to what the new one caused. But it was difficult to manage, and though they ran and panted and other enthusiastic flyers helped them Herbert couldn't get it up.

"Never mind," he said, "we'll get the knack of it presently. The wind's not right to-day, that's all."

He went back to tea with his father and mother and they talked it over just as they had talked in the old days. He delayed going because he didn't fancy the scene Betty would make him, but when Mrs. Sunbury went into the kitchen to get supper ready he had to go home. Betty was reading the paper. She looked up.

"Your bag's packed," she said.

"My what?"

"You heard what I said. I said if you went you needn't come back. I forgot about your things. Everything's packed. It's in the bedroom."

He looked at her for a moment with surprise. She pretended to be reading again. He would have liked to give her a good hiding.

"All right, have it your own way," he said.

He went into the bedroom. His clothes were packed in a suitcase, and there was a brown-paper parcel in which Betty had put whatever was left over. He took the bag in one hand, the parcel in the other, walked through the sitting-room without a word and out of the house. He walked to his mother's and rang the bell. She opened the door.

"I've come home, Mum," he said.

"Have you, Herbert? Your room's ready for you. Put your things down and come in. We were just sitting down to supper." They went into the dining-room. "Samuel, Herbert's come home. Run out and get a quart of beer."

Over supper and during the rest of the evening he told them the trouble he had had with Betty.

"Well, you're well out of it, Herbert," said Mrs. Sunbury when he had finished. "I told you she was no wife for you. Common she is, common as dirt, and you who's always been brought up so nice."

He found it good to sleep in his own bed, the bed he'd been used to all his life, and to come down to breakfast on the Sunday morning, unshaved and unwashed, and read the *News of the World*.

"We won't go to chapel this morning," said Mrs. Sunbury. "It's been an upset to you, Herbert; we'll all take it easy to-day."

During the week they talked a lot about the kite, but they

also talked a lot about Betty. They discussed what she would do next.

"She'll try and get you back," said Mrs. Sunbury.

"A fat chance she's got of doing that," said Herbert.

"You'll have to provide for her," said his father.

"Why should he do that?" cried Mrs. Sunbury. "She trapped him into marrying her and now she's turned him out of the home he made for her."

"I'll give her what's right as long as she leaves me alone."

He was feeling more comfortable every day, in fact he was beginning to feel as if he'd never been away, he settled in like a dog in its own particular basket; it was nice having his mother to brush his clothes and mend his socks; she gave him the sort of things he'd always eaten and liked best; Betty was a scrappy sort of cook, it had been fun just at first, like picnicking, but it wasn't the sort of eating a man could get his teeth into, and he could never get over his mother's idea that fresh food was better than the stuff you bought in tins. He got sick of the sight of tinned salmon. Then it was nice to have space to move about in rather than be cooped up in two small rooms, one of which had to serve as a kitchen as well.

"I never made a bigger mistake in my life than when I left home, Mum," he said to her once.

"I know that, Herbert, but you're back now and you've got no cause to leave it again."

His salary was paid on Friday and in the evening when they had just finished supper the bell rang.

"That's her," they said with one voice.

Herbert went pale. His mother gave him a glance.

"You leave it to me," she said. "I'll see her."

She opened the door. Betty was standing on the threshold. She tried to push her way in, but Mrs. Sunbury prevented her.

"I want to see Herb."

"You can't. He's out."

"No, he isn't. I watched him go in with his dad and he hasn't come out again."

"Well, he doesn't want to see you, and if you start making a disturbance I'll call the police."

"I want my week's money."

"That's all you've ever wanted of him." She took out her purse. "There's thirty-five shillings for you."

"Thirty-five shillings? The rent's twelve shillings a week."

"That's all you're going to get. He's got to pay his board here, hasn't he?"

"And then there's the instalments on the furniture."

"We'll see about that when the time comes. D'you want the money or don't you?"

Confused, unhappy, browbeaten, Betty stood irresolutely. Mrs. Sunbury thrust the money in her hand and slammed the door in her face. She went back to the dining-room.

"I've settled her hash all right," she said.

The bell rang again, it rang repeatedly, but they did not answer it, and presently it stopped. They guessed that Betty had gone away.

It was fine next day, with just the right velocity in the wind, and Herbert, after failing two or three times, found he had got the knack of flying the big box-kite. It soared into the air and up and up as he unreeled the wire.

"Why, it's a mile up if it's a yard," he told his mother excitedly.

He had never had such a thrill in his life.

Several weeks passed by. They concocted a letter for Herbert to write in which he told Betty that so long as she didn't molest him or members of his family she would receive a postal order for thirty-five shillings every Saturday morning and he would pay the instalments on the furniture as they came due. Mrs. Sunbury had been much against this, but Mr. Sunbury, for once at variance with her, and Herbert agreed that it was the right thing to do. Herbert by then had learnt the ways of the new kite and was able to do great things with it. He no longer bothered to have contests with the other kite-flyers. He was out of their class. Saturday afternoons were his moments of glory. He revelled in the admiration he aroused in the bystanders and enjoyed the envy he knew he excited in the less fortunate flyers. Then one evening when he was walking back from the station with his father Betty waylaid him.

"Hulloa, Herb," she said.

"Hulloa."

"I want to talk to my husband alone, Mr. Sunbury."

"There's nothing you've got to say to me that my dad can't hear," said Herbert sullenly.

She hesitated. Mr. Sunbury fidgeted. He didn't know whether to stay or go.

"All right, then," she said. "I want you to come back home,

Herb. I didn't mean it that night when I packed your bag. I only did it to frighten you. I was in a temper. I'm sorry for what I did. It's all so silly, quarrelling about a kite."

"Well, I'm not coming back, see. When you turned me out you did me the best turn you ever did me."

Tears began to trickle down Betty's cheeks.

"But I love you, Herb. If you want to fly your silly old kite, you fly it, I don't care so long as you come back."

"Thank you very much, but it's not good enough. I know when I'm well off and I've had enough of married life to last me a lifetime. Come on, Dad."

They walked on quickly and Betty made no attempt to follow them. On the following Sunday they went to chapel and after dinner Herbert went to the coal-shed where they kept the kite to have a look at it. He just couldn't keep away from it. He doted on it. In a minute he rushed back, his face white, with a hatchet in his hand.

"She's smashed it up. She did it with this."

The Sunburys gave a cry of consternation and hurried to the coal-shed. What Herbert had said was true. The kite, the new, expensive kite, was in fragments. It had been savagely attacked with the hatchet, the woodwork was all in pieces, the reel was hacked to bits.

"She must have done it while we were at chapel. Watched us go out, that's what she did."

"But how did she get in?" asked Mr. Sunbury.

"I had two keys. When I came home I noticed one was missing, but I didn't think anything about it."

"You can't be sure she did it, some of them fellows on the common have been very snooty, I wouldn't put it past them to have done this."

"Well, we'll soon find out," said Herbert. "I'll go and ask her, and if she did it I'll kill her."

His rage was so terrible that Mrs. Sunbury was frightened.

"And get yourself hung for murder? No, Herbert, I won't let you go. Let your dad go, and when he comes back we'll decide what to do."

"That's right, Herbert, let me go."

They had a job to persuade him, but in the end Mr. Sunbury went. In half an hour he came back.

"She did it all right. She told me straight out. She's proud of it. I won't repeat her language, it fair startled me, but the long and short of it was she was jealous of the kite. She said Herbert loved the kite more than he loved her and so she smashed it up and if she had to do it again she'd do it again."

"Lucky she didn't tell me that. I'd have wrung her neck even if I'd had to swing for it. Well, she never gets another penny out of me, that's all."

"She'll sue you," said his father.

"Let her."

"The instalment on the furniture is due next week, Herbert," said Mrs. Sunbury quietly. "In your place I wouldn't pay it."

"Then they'll just take it away," said Samuel, "and all the money he's paid on it so far will be wasted."

"Well, what of it?" she answered. "He can afford it. He's rid of her for good and all and we've got him back and that's the chief thing."

"I don't care twopence about the money," said Herbert. "I can see her face when they come and take the furniture away. It meant a lot to her, it did, and the piano, she set a rare store on that piano."

So on the following Friday he did not send Betty her weekly money, and when she sent him on a letter from the furniture people to say that if he didn't pay the instalment due by such and such a date they would remove it, he wrote back and said he wasn't in a position to continue the payments and they could remove the furniture at their convenience. Betty took to waiting for him at the station, and when he wouldn't speak to her followed him down the street screaming curses at him. In the evenings she would come to the house and ring the bell till they thought they would go mad, and Mr. and Mrs. Sunbury had the greatest difficulty in preventing Herbert from going out and giving her a sound thrashing. Once she threw a stone and broke the sitting-room window. She wrote obscene and abusive post-cards to him at his office. At last she went to the magistrate's court and complained that her husband had left her and wasn't providing for her support. Herbert received a summons. They both told their story and if the magistrate thought it a strange one he didn't say so. He tried to effect a reconciliation between them, but Herbert resolutely refused to go back to his wife. The magistrate ordered him to pay Betty twenty-five shillings a week. He said he wouldn't pay it.

"Then you'll go to prison," said the magistrate. "Next case."

But Herbert meant what he said. On Betty's complaint he

was brought once more before the magistrate, who asked him what reason he had for not obeying the order.

"I said I wouldn't pay her and I won't, not after she smashed my kite. And if you send me to prison I'll go to prison."

The magistrate was stern with him this time.

"You're a very foolish young man," he said. "I'll give you a week to pay the arrears, and if I have any more nonsense from you you'll go to prison till you come to your senses."

Herbert didn't pay, and that is how my friend Ned Preston came to know him and I heard the story.

"What d'you make of it?" asked Ned as he finished. "You know, Betty isn't a bad girl. I've seen her several times, there's nothing wrong with her except her insane jealousy of Herbert's kite; and he isn't a fool by any means. In fact he's smarter than the average. What d'you suppose there is in kite-flying that makes the damned fool so mad about it?"

"I don't know," I answered. I took my time to think. "You see, I don't know a thing about flying a kite. Perhaps it gives him a sense of power as he watches it soaring towards the clouds and of mastery over the elements as he seems to bend the winds of heaven to his will. It may be that in some queer way he identifies himself with the kite flying so free and so high above him, and it's as it were an escape from the monotony of life. It may be that in some dim, confused way it represents an ideal of freedom and adventure. And you know, when a man once gets bitten with the virus of the ideal not all the King's doctors and not all the King's surgeons can rid him of it. But all this is very fanciful and I dare say it's just stuff and nonsense. I think you'd better put your problem before someone who knows a lot more about the psychology of the human animal than I do."

THE TREASURE

RICHARD HARENGER was a happy man. Notwithstanding what
the pessimists, from Ecclesiastes onwards, have said, this is not
so rare a thing to find in this unhappy world, but Richard
Harenger knew it, and that is a very rare thing indeed. The
golden mean which the ancients so highly prized is out of fashion, and those who follow it must put up with polite derision
from those who see no merit in self-restraint and no virtue in
common-sense. Richard Harenger shrugged a polite and amused
shoulder. Let others live dangerously, let others burn with a
hard gemlike flame, let others stake their fortunes on the turn
of a card, walk the tight-rope that leads to glory or the grave, or
hazard their lives for a cause, a passion or an adventure. He
neither envied the fame their exploits brought them nor wasted
his pity on them when their efforts ended in disaster.

But it must not be inferred from this that Richard Harenger
was a selfish or a callous man. He was neither. He was considerate and of a generous disposition. He was always ready to
oblige a friend and he was sufficiently well off to be able to indulge himself in the pleasure of helping others. He had some
money of his own and he occupied in the Home Office a position
that brought him an adequate stipend. The work suited him. It
was regular, responsible and pleasant. Every day when he left
the office he went to his club to play bridge for a couple of
hours, and on Saturdays and Sundays he played golf. He went

abroad for his holidays, staying at good hotels, and visited churches, galleries and museums. He was a regular first-nighter. He dined out a good deal. His friends liked him. He was easy to talk to. He was well-read, knowledgeable and amusing. He was besides of a personable exterior, not remarkably handsome, but tall, slim and erect of carriage, with a lean, intelligent face; his hair was growing thin, for he was now approaching the age of fifty, but his brown eyes retained their smile and his teeth were all his own. He had from nature a good constitution and he had always taken care of himself. There was no reason in the world why he should not be a happy man, and if there had been in him a trace of self-complacency he might have claimed that he deserved to be.

He had the good fortune even to sail safely through those perilous, unquiet straits of marriage in which so many wise and good men have made shipwreck. Married for love in the early twenties, his wife and he, after some years of almost perfect felicity, had drifted gradually apart. Neither of them wished to marry anyone else, so there was no question of divorce (which indeed Richard Harenger's situation in the government service made undesirable), but for convenience sake, with the help of the family lawyer, they arranged a separation which left them free to lead their lives as each one wished without interference from the other. They parted with mutual expressions of respect and good will.

Richard Harenger sold his house in St. John's Wood and took a flat within convenient walking distance of Whitehall. It had a sitting-room which he lined with his books, a dining-room into which his Chippendale furniture just fitted, a nice-sized bedroom for himself, and beyond the kitchen a couple of maids' rooms. He brought his cook, whom he had had for many years, from St. John's Wood, but needing no longer so large a staff dismissed the rest of the servants and applied at a registry office for a house-parlourmaid. He knew exactly what he wanted and he explained his needs to the superintendent of the agency with precision. He wanted a maid who was not too young, first because young women are flighty and secondly because, though he was of mature age and a man of principle, people would talk, the porter and the tradesmen if nobody else, and both for the sake of his own reputation and that of the young person he considered that the applicant should have reached years of discretion. Besides that he wanted a maid who could clean silver well.

He had always had a fancy for old silver, and it was reasonable to demand that the forks and spoons that had been used by a woman of quality under the reign of Queen Anne should be treated with tenderness and respect. He was of a hospitable nature and liked to give at least once a week little dinners of not less than four people and not more than eight. He could trust his cook to send in a meal that his guests would take pleasure in eating and he desired his parlourmaid to wait with neatness and dispatch. Then he needed a perfect valet. He dressed well, in a manner that suited his age and condition, and he liked his clothes to be properly looked after. The parlourmaid he was looking for must be able to press trousers and iron a tie, and he was very particular that his shoes should be well shone. He had small feet and he took a good deal of trouble to have well-cut shoes. He had a large supply and he insisted that they should be treed up the moment he took them off. Finally the flat must be kept clean and tidy. It was of course understood that any applicant for the post must be of irreproachable character, sober, honest, reliable and of a pleasing exterior. In return for this he was prepared to offer good wages, reasonable liberty and ample holidays. The superintendent listened without batting an eyelash and, telling him that she was quite sure she could suit him, sent him a string of candidates which proved that she had not paid the smallest attention to a word he said. He saw them all personally. Some were obviously inefficient, some looked fast, some were too old, others too young, some lacked the presence he thought essential; there was not one to whom he was inclined even to give a trial. He was a kindly, polite man and he declined their services with a smile and a pleasant expression of regret. He did not lose patience. He was prepared to interview house-parlourmaids till he found one who was suitable.

Now it is a funny thing about life, if you refuse to accept anything but the best you very often get it: if you utterly decline to make do with what you can get, then somehow or other you are very likely to get what you want. It is as though fate said, this man's a perfect fool, he's asking for perfection, and then just out of her feminine wilfulness flung it in his lap. One day the porter of the flats said to Richard Harenger out of a blue sky:

"I hear you're lookin' for a house-parlourmaid, sir. There's someone I know lookin' for a situation as might do."

"Can you recommend her personally?"

Richard Harenger had the sound opinion that one servant's

recommendation of another was worth much more than that of an employer.

"I can vouch for her respectability. She's been in some very good situations."

"I shall be coming in to dress about seven. If that's convenient to her I could see her then."

"Very good, sir. I'll see that she's told."

He had not been in more than five minutes when the cook, having answered a ring at the front door, came in and told him that the person the porter had spoken to him about had called.

"Show her in," he said.

He turned on some more light so that he could see what the applicant looked like and, getting up, stood with his back to the fireplace. A woman came in and stood just inside the door in a respectful attitude.

"Good-evening," he said. "What is your name?"

"Pritchard, sir."

"How old are you?"

"Thirty-five, sir."

"Well, that's a reasonable age."

He gave his cigarette a puff and looked at her reflectively. She was on the tall side, nearly as tall as he, but he guessed that she wore high heels. Her black dress fitted her station. She held herself well. She had good features and a rather high colour.

"Will you take off your hat?" he asked.

She did so and he saw that she had pale brown hair. It was neatly and becomingly dressed. She looked strong and healthy. She was neither fat nor thin. In a proper uniform she would look very presentable. She was not inconveniently handsome, but she was certainly a comely, in another class of life you might almost have said a handsome, woman. He proceeded to ask her a number of questions. Her answers were satisfactory. She had left her last place for an adequate reason. She had been trained under a butler and appeared to be well acquainted with her duties. In her last place she had been head parlourmaid of three, but she did not mind undertaking the work of the flat single-handed. She had valeted a gentleman before who had sent her to a tailor's to learn how to press clothes. She was a little shy, but neither timid nor ill-at-ease. Richard asked her his questions in his amiable, leisurely way and she answered them with modest composure. He was considerably impressed. He asked her what references she could give. They seemed extremely satisfactory.

"Now look here," he said, "I'm very much inclined to engage you. But I hate changes, I've had my cook for twelve years: if you suit me and the place suits you I hope you'll stay. I mean, I don't want you to come to me in three or four months and say that you're leaving to get married."

"There's not much fear of that, sir. I'm a widow. I don't believe marriage is much catch for anyone in my position, sir. My husband never did a stroke of work from the day I married him to the day he died, and I had to keep him. What I want now is a good home."

"I'm inclined to agree with you," he smiled. "Marriage is a very good thing, but I think it's a mistake to make a habit of it."

She very properly made no reply to this, but waited for him to announce his decision. She did not seem anxious about it. He reflected that if she was as competent as she appeared she must be well aware that she would have no difficulty in finding a place. He told her what wages he was offering and these seemed to be satisfactory to her. He gave her the necessary information about the place, but she gave him to understand that she was already apprised of this, and he received the impression, which amused rather than disconcerted him, that she had made certain enquiries about him before applying for the situation. It showed prudence on her part and good sense.

"When would you be able to come in if I engaged you? I haven't got anybody at the moment. The cook's managing as best she can with a char, but I should like to get settled as soon as possible."

"Well, sir, I was going to give myself a week's holiday, but if it's a matter of obliging a gentleman I don't mind giving that up. I could come in to-morrow if it was convenient."

Richard Harenger gave her his attractive smile.

"I shouldn't like you to do without a holiday that I dare say you've been looking forward to. I can very well go on like this for another week. Go and have your holiday and come to me when it's over."

"Thank you very much, sir. Would it do if I came in to-morrow week?"

"Quite well."

When she left, Richard Harenger felt he had done a good day's work. It looked as though he had found exactly what he was after. He rang for the cook and told her he had engaged a house-parlourmaid at last.

"I think you'll like her, sir," she said. "She came in and 'ad a talk with me this afternoon. I could see at once she knew her duties. And she's not one of them flighty ones."

"We can but try, Mrs. Jeddy. I hope you gave me a good character."

"Well, I said you was particular, sir. I said you was a gentleman as liked things just so."

"I admit that."

"She said she didn't mind that. She said she liked a gentleman as knew what was what. She said there's no satisfaction in doing things proper if nobody notices. I expect you'll find she'll take a rare lot of pride in her work."

"That's what I want her to do. I think we might go farther and fare worse."

"Well, sir, there is that to it, of course. And the proof of the pudding's the eating. But if you ask my opinion I think she's going to be a real treasure."

And that is precisely what Pritchard turned out. No man was ever better served. The way she shone shoes was marvellous, and he set out of a fine morning for his walk to the office with a more jaunty step because you could almost see yourself reflected in them. She looked after his clothes with such attention that his colleagues began to chaff him about being the best-dressed man in the Civil Service. One day, coming home unexpectedly, he found a line of socks and handkerchiefs hung up to dry in the bathroom. He called Pritchard.

"D'you wash my socks and handkerchiefs yourself, Pritchard? I should have thought you had enough to do without that."

"They do ruin them so at the laundry, sir. I prefer to do them at home if you have no objection."

She knew exactly what he should wear on every occasion, and without asking him was aware whether she should put out a dinner jacket and a black tie in the evening or a dress coat and a white one. When he was going to a party where decorations were to be worn he found his neat little row of medals automatically affixed to the lapel of his coat. He soon ceased to

choose every morning from his wardrobe the tie he wanted, for
he found that she put out for him without fail the one he would
have himself selected. Her taste was perfect. He supposed she
read his letters, for she always knew what his movements were,
and if he had forgotten at what hour he had an engagement he
had no need to look in his book, for Pritchard could tell him.
She knew exactly what tone to use with persons with whom she
conversed on the telephone. Except with tradesmen, with whom
she was apt to be peremptory, she was always polite, but there
was a distinct difference in her manner if she was addressing one
of Mr. Harenger's literary friends or the wife of a Cabinet
Minister. She knew by instinct with whom he wished to speak
and with whom he didn't. From his sitting-room he sometimes
heard her with placid sincerity assuring a caller that he was out,
and then she would come in and tell him that So-and-So had
rung up, but she thought he wouldn't wish to be disturbed.

"Quite right, Pritchard," he smiled.

"I knew she only wanted to bother you about that concert,"
said Pritchard.

His friends made appointments with him through her, and
she would tell him what she had done on his return in the evening.

"Mrs. Soames rang up, sir, and asked if you would lunch with
her on Thursday, the eighth, but I said you were very sorry but
you were lunching with Lady Versinder. Mr. Oakley rang up
and asked if you'd go to a cocktail party at the Savoy next
Tuesday at six. I said you would if you possibly could, but you
might have to go to the dentist's."

"Quite right."

"I thought you could see when the time came, sir."

She kept the flat like a new pin. On one occasion soon after
she entered his service, Richard coming back from a holiday
took out a book from his shelves and at once noticed that it had
been dusted. He rang the bell.

"I forgot to tell you when I went away under no circumstances ever to touch my books. When books are taken out to
be dusted they're never put back in the right place. I don't
mind my books being dirty, but I hate not being able to find
them."

"I'm very sorry, sir," said Pritchard. "I know some gentlemen
are very particular and I took care to put back every book exactly where I took it from."

Richard Harenger gave his books a glance. So far as he could see every one was in its accustomed place. He smiled.

"I apologise, Pritchard."

"They were in a muck, sir. I mean, you couldn't open one without getting your hands black with dust."

She certainly kept his silver as he had never had it kept before. He felt called upon to give her a special word of praise.

"Most of it's Queen Anne and George I, you know," he explained.

"Yes, I know, sir. When you've got something good like that to look after it's a pleasure to keep it like it should be."

"You certainly have a knack for it. I never knew a butler who kept his silver as well as you do."

"Men haven't the patience women have," she replied modestly.

As soon as he thought Pritchard had settled down in the place he resumed the little dinners he was fond of giving once a week. He had already discovered that she knew how to wait at table, but it was with a warm sense of complacency that he realised then how competently she could manage a party. She was quick, silent and watchful. A guest had hardly felt the need of something before Pritchard was at his elbow offering him what he wanted. She soon learned the tastes of his more intimate friends and remembered that one liked water instead of soda with his whisky and that another particularly fancied the knuckle end of a leg of lamb. She knew exactly how cold a hock should be not to ruin its taste and how long claret should have stood in the room to bring out its bouquet. It was a pleasure to see her pour out a bottle of burgundy in such a fashion as not to disturb the grounds. On one occasion she did not serve the wine Richard had ordered. He somewhat sharply pointed this out to her.

"I opened the bottle sir, and it was slightly corked. So I got the Chambertin, as I thought it was safer."

"Quite right, Pritchard."

Presently he left this matter entirely in her hands, for he discovered that she knew perfectly what wines his guests would like. Without orders from him she would provide the best in his cellar and his oldest brandy if she thought they were the sort of people who knew what they were drinking. She had no belief in the palate of women, and when they were of the party was apt to serve the champagne which had to be drunk before it went off. She had the English servant's instinctive knowledge of social differences and neither rank nor money blinded her to the fact that someone was not a gentleman, but she had favourites among his friends, and when someone she particularly liked was dining, with the air of a cat that has swallowed a canary she would pour out for him a bottle of a wine that Harenger kept for very special occasions. It amused him.

"You've got on the right side of Pritchard, old boy," he exclaimed. "There aren't many people she gives this wine to."

Pritchard became an institution. She was known very soon to be the perfect parlourmaid. People envied Harenger the possession of her as they envied nothing else that he had. She was worth her weight in gold. Her price was above rubies. Richard Harenger beamed with self-complacency when they praised her.

"Good masters make good servants," he said gaily.

One evening, when they were sitting over their port and she had left the room, they were talking about her.

"It'll be an awful blow when she leaves you."

"Why should she leave me? One or two people have tried to get her away from me, but she turned them down. She knows where she's well off."

"She'll get married one of these days."

"I don't think she's that sort."

"She's a good-looking woman."

"Yes, she has quite a decent presence."

"What are you talking about? She's a very handsome creature. In another class of life she'd be a well-known society beauty with her photograph in all the papers."

At that moment Pritchard came in with the coffee. Richard Harenger looked at her. After seeing her every day, off and on, for four years it was now—my word, how time flies—he had really forgotten what she looked like. She did not seem to have changed much since he had first seen her. She was no stouter than then, she still had the high colour, and her regular features bore the same expression which was at once intent and vacuous. The black uniform suited her. She left the room.

"She's a paragon and there's no doubt about it."

"I know she is," answered Harenger. "She's perfection. I should be lost without her. And the strange thing is that I don't very much like her."

"Why not?"

"I think she bores me a little. You see, she has no conversation. I've often tried to talk to her. She answers when I speak to her, but that's all. In four years she's never volunteered a remark of her own. I know absolutely nothing about her. I don't know if she likes me or if she's completely indifferent to me. She's an automaton. I respect her, I appreciate her, I trust her. She has every quality in the world and I've often wondered why it is that with all that I'm so completely indifferent to her. I think it must be that she is entirely devoid of charm."

They left it at that.

Two or three days after this, since it was Pritchard's night out and he had no engagement, Richard Harenger dined by himself at his club. A page-boy came to him and told him that they had just rung up from his flat to say that he had gone out without his keys and should they be brought along to him in a taxi? He put his hand to his pocket. It was a fact. By a singular chance he had forgotten to replace them when he had changed into a blue serge suit before coming out to dinner. His intention had been to play bridge, but it was an off-night at the club and there seemed little chance of a decent game; it occurred to him that it would be a good opportunity to see a picture that he had heard talked about, so he sent back the message by the page that he would call for the keys himself in half an hour.

He rang at the door of his flat and it was opened by Pritchard. She had the keys in her hand.

"What are you doing here, Pritchard?" he asked. "It's your night out, isn't it?"

"Yes, sir. But I didn't care about going, so I told Mrs. Jeddy she could go instead."

"You ought to get out when you have the chance," he said, with his usual thoughtfulness. "It's not good for you to be cooped up here all the time."

"I get out now and then on an errand, but I haven't been out in the evening for the last month."

"Why on earth not?"

"Well, it's not very cheerful going out by yourself, and somehow I don't know anyone just now that I'm particularly keen on going out with."

"You ought to have a bit of fun now and then. It's good for you."

"I've got out of the habit of it somehow."

"Look here, I'm just going to the cinema. Would you like to come along with me?"

He spoke in kindliness, on the spur of the moment, and the moment he had said the words half regretted them.

"Yes, sir, I'd like to," said Pritchard.

"Run along then and put on a hat."

"I shan't be a minute."

She disappeared and he went into the sitting-room and lit a cigarette. He was a little amused at what he was doing, and pleased too; it was nice to be able to make someone happy with so little trouble to himself. It was characteristic of Pritchard that she had shown neither surprise nor hesitation. She kept him waiting about five minutes, and when she came back he noticed that she had changed her dress. She wore a blue frock in what he supposed was artificial silk, a small black hat with a blue brooch on it, and a silver fox round her neck. He was a trifle relieved to see that she looked neither shabby nor showy. It would never occur to anyone who happened to see them that this was a distinguished official in the Home Office taking his housemaid to the pictures.

"I'm sorry to have kept you waiting, sir."

"It doesn't matter at all," he said graciously.

He opened the front door for her and she went out before him. He remembered the familiar anecdote of Louis XIV and the courtier and appreciated the fact that she had not hesitated to precede him. The cinema for which they were bound was at no great distance from Mr. Harenger's flat and they walked there. He talked about the weather and the state of the roads and Adolf Hitler. Pritchard made suitable replies. They arrived just as Mickey the Mouse was starting and this put them in a good humour. During the four years she had been in his service Richard Harenger had hardly ever seen Pritchard even smile, and now it diverted him vastly to hear her peal upon peal of joyous laughter. He enjoyed her pleasure. Then the principal attraction was thrown on the screen. It was a good picture and they both watched it with breathless excitement. Taking his cigarette-case out to help himself he automatically offered it to Pritchard.

"Thank you, sir," she said, taking one.

He lit it for her. Her eyes were on the screen and she was almost unconscious of his action. When the picture was finished they streamed out with the crowd into the street. They walked back towards the flat. It was a fine starry night.

"Did you like it?" he said.

"Like anything, sir. It was a real treat."

A thought occurred to him.

"By the way, did you have any supper to-night?"

"No, sir, I didn't have time."

"Aren't you starving?"

"I'll have a bit of bread and cheese when I get in and I'll make meself a cup of cocoa."

"That sounds rather grim." There was a feeling of gaiety in the air, and the people who poured past them, one way and another, seemed filled with a pleasant elation. In for a penny, in for a pound, he said to himself. "Look here, would you like to come and have a bit of supper with me somewhere?"

"If you'd like to, sir."

"Come on."

He hailed a cab. He was feeling very philanthropic and it was not a feeling that he disliked at all. He told the driver to go to a restaurant in Oxford Street which was gay, but at which he was confident there was no chance of meeting anyone he knew. There was an orchestra and people danced. It would amuse Pritchard to see them. When they sat down a waiter came up to them.

"They've got a set supper here," he said, thinking that was what she would like. "I suggest we have that. What would you like to drink? A little white wine?"

"What I really fancy is a glass of ginger beer," she said.

Richard Harenger ordered himself a whisky and soda. She ate the supper with hearty appetite, and though Harenger was not hungry, to put her at her ease he ate too. The picture they had just seen gave them something to talk about. It was quite true what they had said the other night, Pritchard was not a bad-looking woman, and even if someone had seen them together he would not have minded. It would make rather a good story for his friends when he told them how he had taken the incomparable Pritchard to the cinema and then afterwards to supper. Pritchard was looking at the dancers with a faint smile on her lips.

"Do you like dancing?" he said.

"I used to be a rare one for it when I was a girl. I never danced much after I was married. My husband was a bit shorter than me and somehow I never think it looks well unless the gentleman's taller, if you know what I mean. I suppose I shall be getting too old for it soon."

Richard was certainly taller than his parlourmaid. They would look all right. He was fond of dancing and he danced well. But he hesitated. He did not want to embarrass Pritchard by asking her to dance with him. It was better not to go too far perhaps. And yet what did it matter? It was a drab life she led. She was so sensible, if she thought it a mistake he was pretty sure she would find a decent excuse.

"Would you like to take a turn, Pritchard?" he said, as the band struck up again.

"I'm terribly out of practice, sir."

"What does that matter?"

"If you don't mind, sir," she answered coolly, rising from her seat.

She was not in the least shy. She was only afraid that she would not be able to follow his step. They moved on to the floor. He found she danced very well.

"Why, you dance perfectly, Pritchard," he said.

"It's coming back to me."

Although she was a big woman she was light on her feet and she had a natural sense of rhythm. She was very pleasant to dance with. He gave a glance at the mirrors that lined the walls and he could not help reflecting that they looked very well together. Their eyes met in the mirror; he wondered whether she was thinking that too. They had two more dances and then Richard Harenger suggested that they should go. He paid the bill and they walked out. He noticed that she threaded her way through the crowd without a trace of self-consciousness. They got into a taxi and in ten minutes were at home.

"I'll go up the back way, sir," said Pritchard.

"There's no need to do that. Come up in the lift with me."

He took her up, giving the night-porter an icy glance, so that he should not think it strange that he came back at that somewhat late hour with his parlourmaid, and with his latch-key let her into the flat.

"Well, good-night, sir," she said. "Thank you very much. It's been a real treat for me."

"Thank *you* Pritchard. I should have had a very dull evening by myself. I hope you've enjoyed your outing."

"That I have, sir, more than I can say."

It had been a success. Richard Harenger was satisfied with himself. It was a kindly thing for him to have done. It was a very agreeable sensation to give anyone so much real pleasure.

His benevolence warmed him and for a moment he felt a great love in his heart for the whole human race.

"Good-night, Pritchard," he said, and because he felt happy and good he put his arm round her waist and kissed her on the lips.

Her lips were very soft. They lingered on his and she returned his kiss. It was the warm, hearty embrace of a healthy woman in the prime of life. He found it very pleasant and he held her to him a little more closely. She put her arms round his neck.

As a general rule he did not wake till Pritchard came in with his letters, but next morning he woke at half-past seven. He had a curious sensation that he did not recognise. He was accustomed to sleep with two pillows under his head and he suddenly grew aware of the fact that he had only one. Then he remembered and with a start looked round. The other pillow was beside his own. Thank God, no sleeping head rested there, but it was plain that one had. His heart sank. He broke out into a cold sweat.

"My God, what a fool I've been!" he cried out loud.

How could he have done anything so stupid? What on earth had come over him? He was the last man to play about with servant girls. What a disgraceful thing to do! At his age and in his position. He had not heard Pritchard slip away. He must have been asleep. It wasn't even as if he'd liked her very much. She wasn't his type. And, as he had said the other night, she rather bored him. Even now he only knew her as Pritchard. He had no notion what her first name was. What madness! And what was to happen now? The position was impossible. It was obvious he couldn't keep her, and yet to send her away for what was his fault as much as hers seemed shockingly unfair. How idiotic to lose the best parlourmaid a man ever had just for an hour's folly!

"It's that damned kindness of heart of mine," he groaned.

He would never find anyone else to look after his clothes so admirably or clean the silver so well. She knew all his friends' telephone numbers and she understood wine. But of course she must go. She must see for herself that after what had happened things could never be the same. He would make her a handsome present and give her an excellent reference. At any minute she would be coming in now. Would she be arch, would she be familiar? Or would she put on airs? Perhaps even she wouldn't trouble to come in with his letters. It would be awful if he had to ring the bell and Mrs. Jeddy came in and said: Pritchard's not up yet, sir, she's having a lie in after last night.

"What a fool I've been! What a contemptible cad!"

There was a knock at the door. He was sick with anxiety.

"Come in."

Richard Harenger was a very unhappy man.

Pritchard came in as the clock struck. She wore the print dress she was in the habit of wearing during the early part of the day.

"Good-morning, sir," she said.

"Good-morning."

She drew the curtains and handed him his letters and the papers. Her face was impassive. She looked exactly as she always looked. Her movements had the same competent deliberation that they always had. She neither avoided Richard's glance nor sought it.

"Will you wear your grey, sir? It came back from the tailor's yesterday."

"Yes."

He pretended to read his letters, but he watched her from under his eyelashes. Her back was turned to him. She took his vest and drawers and folded them over a chair. She took the studs out of the shirt he had worn the day before and studded a clean one. She put out some clean socks for him and placed them on the seat of a chair with the suspenders to match by the side. Then she put out his grey suit and attached the braces to the back buttons of the trousers. She opened his wardrobe and after a moment's reflection chose a tie to go with the suit. She collected on her arm the suit of the day before and picked up the shoes.

"Will you have breakfast now, sir, or will you have your bath first?"

"I'll have breakfast now," he said.

"Very good, sir."

With her slow quiet movements, unruffled, she left the room. Her face bore that rather serious, deferential, vacuous look it always bore. What had happened might have been a dream. Nothing in Pritchard's demeanour suggested that she had the smallest recollection of the night before. He gave a sigh of relief. It was going to be all right. She need not go, she need not go.

Pritchard was the perfect parlourmaid. He knew that never by word nor gesture would she ever refer to the fact that for a moment their relations had been other than those of master and servant. Richard Harenger was a very happy man.

WINTER CRUISE

CAPTAIN ERDMANN knew Miss Reid very little till the *Friedrich Weber* reached Haiti. She came on board at Plymouth, but by then he had taken on a number of passengers, French, Belgian and Haitian, many of whom had travelled with him before, and she was placed at the chief engineer's table. The *Friedrich Weber* was a freighter sailing regularly from Hamburg to Cartagena on the Colombian coast and on the way touching at a number of islands in the West Indies. She carried phosphates and cement from Germany and took back coffee and timber; but her owners, the Brothers Weber, were always willing to send her out of her route if a cargo of any sort made it worth their while. The *Friedrich Weber* was prepared to take cattle, mules, potatoes or anything else that offered the chance of earning an honest penny. She carried passengers. There were six cabins on the upper deck and six below. The accommodation was not luxurious, but the food was good, plain and abundant, and the fares were cheap. The round trip took nine weeks and was not costing Miss Reid more than forty-five pounds. She looked forward not only to seeing many interesting places, with historical associations, but also to acquiring a great deal of information that would enrich her mind.

The agent had warned her that till the ship reached Port au Prince in Haiti she would have to share a cabin with another woman. Miss Reid did not mind that, she liked company, and when the steward told her that her companion was Madame Bollin she thought at once that it would be a very good opportunity to rub up her French. She was only very slightly disconcerted when she found that Madame Bollin was coal-black. She told herself that one had to accept the rough with the smooth and that it takes all sorts to make a world. Miss Reid was a good sailor, as indeed was only to be expected since her grandfather had been a naval officer, but after a couple of roughish days the weather was fine and in a very short while she knew all her fellow-passengers. She was a good mixer. That was one of the reasons why she had made a success of her business; she owned a tea-room at a celebrated beauty spot in the west of England and she always had a smile and a pleasant word for every customer who came in; she closed down in the winter and for the last four years had taken a cruise. You met such interesting people, she said, and you always learnt something. It was true that the passengers on the *Friedrich Weber* weren't of quite so good a class as those she had met the year before on her Mediterranean cruise, but Miss Reid was not a snob, and though the table manners of some of them shocked her somewhat, determined to look upon the bright side of things she decided to make the best of them. She was a great reader and she was glad, on looking at the ship's library, to find that there were a lot of books by Phillips Oppenheim, Edgar Wallace and Agatha Christie; but with so many people to talk to she had no time for reading and she made up her mind to leave them till the ship emptied herself at Haiti.

"After all," she said, "human nature is more important than literature."

Miss Reid had always had the reputation of being a good talker and she flattered herself that not once during the many days they were at sea had she allowed the conversation at table to languish. She knew how to draw people out, and whenever a topic seemed to be exhausted she had a remark ready to revive it or another topic waiting on the tip of her tongue to set the conversation off again. Her friend Miss Prince, daughter of the late Vicar of Campden, who had come to see her off at Plymouth, for she lived there, had often said to her:

"You know, Venetia, you have a mind like a man. You're never at a loss for something to say."

"Well, I think if you're interested in everyone, everyone will be interested in you," Miss Reid answered modestly. "Practice makes perfect, and I have the infinite capacity for taking pains which Dickens said was genius."

Miss Reid was not really called Venetia, her name was Alice, but disliking it she had, when still a girl, adopted the poetic name which she felt so much better suited to her personality.

Miss Reid had a great many interesting talks with her fellow-passengers and she was really sorry when the ship at length reached Port au Prince and the last of them disembarked. The *Friedrich Weber* stopped two days there, during which she visited the town and the neighbourhood. When they sailed she was the only passenger. The ship was skirting the coast of the island stopping off at a variety of ports to discharge or to take on cargo.

"I hope you will not feel embarrassed alone with so many men, Miss Reid," said the captain heartily as they sat down to midday dinner.

She was placed on his right hand and at table besides sat the first mate, the chief engineer and the doctor.

"I'm a woman of the world, Captain. I always think if a lady is a lady gentlemen will be gentlemen."

"We're only rough sailor men, madam, you mustn't expect too much."

"Kind hearts are more than coronets and simple faith than Norman blood, Captain," answered Miss Reid.

He was a short, thick-set man, with a clean-shaven head and a red, clean-shaven face. He wore a white stengah-shifter, but except at meal-times unbuttoned at the neck and showing his hairy chest. He was a jovial fellow. He could not speak without bellowing. Miss Reid thought him quite an eccentric, but she had a keen sense of humour and was prepared to make allow-ances for that. She took the conversation in hand. She had learnt a great deal about Haiti on the voyage out and more dur-ing the two days she had spent there, but she knew that men liked to talk rather than to listen, so she put them a number of questions to which she already knew the answers; oddly enough they didn't. In the end she found herself obliged to give quite a little lecture, and before dinner was over, *Mittag Essen* they called it in their funny way, she had imparted to them a great deal of interesting information about the history and economic situation of the Republic, the problems that confronted it and its prospects for the future. She talked rather slowly, in a refined voice, and her vocabulary was extensive.

At nightfall they put in at a small port where they were to load three hundred bags of coffee, and the agent came on board. The captain asked him to stay to supper and ordered cocktails. As the steward brought them Miss Reid swam into the saloon. Her movements were deliberate, elegant and self-assured. She always said that you could tell at once by the way she walked if a woman was a lady. The captain introduced the agent to her and she sat down.

"What is that you men are drinking?" she asked.

"A cocktail. Will you have one, Miss Reid?"

"I don't mind if I do."

She drank it and the captain somewhat doubtfully asked her if she would have another.

"Another? Well, just to be matey."

The agent, much whiter than some, but a good deal darker than many, was the son of a former minister of Haiti to the German court, and having lived for many years in Berlin spoke good German. It was indeed on this account that he had got a job with a German shipping firm. On the strength of this Miss Reid, during supper, told them all about a trip down the Rhine that she had once taken. Afterwards she and the agent, the skipper, the doctor and the mate sat round a table and drank beer. Miss Reid made it her business to draw the agent out. The fact that they were loading coffee suggested to her that he would be interested in learning how they grew tea in Ceylon, yes, she had been to Ceylon on a cruise, and the fact that his father was a diplomat made it certain that he would be interested in the royal family of England. She had a very pleasant evening. When she at last retired to rest, for she would never have thought of saying she was going to bed, she said to herself:

"There's no doubt that travel is a great education."

It was really an experience to find herself alone with all those men. How they would laugh when she told them all about it when she got home! They would say that things like that only happened to Venetia. She smiled when she heard the captain on deck singing with that great booming voice of his. Germans were so musical. He had a funny way of strutting up and down on his short legs singing Wagner tunes to words of his own invention. It was *Tannhaüser* he was singing now (that lovely thing about the evening star) but knowing no German Miss Reid could only wonder what absurd words he was putting to it. It was as well.

"Oh, what a bore that woman is, I shall certainly kill her if she goes on much longer." Then he broke into Siegfried's martial strain. "She's a bore, she's a bore, she's a bore. I shall throw her into the sea."

And that of course is what Miss Reid was. She was a crashing, she was a stupendous, she was an excruciating bore. She talked in a steady monotone, and it was no use to interrupt her because then she started again from the beginning. She had an insatiable thirst for information and no casual remark could be thrown across the table without her asking innumerable questions about it. She was a great dreamer and she narrated her dreams at intolerable length. There was no subject upon which she had not something prosy to say. She had a truism for every occasion. She hit on the commonplace like a hammer driving a nail into the wall. She plunged into the obvious like a clown in a circus jumping through a hoop. Silence did not abash her. Those poor men far away from their homes and the patter of little feet, and with Christmas coming on, no wonder they felt low; she redoubled her efforts to interest and amuse them. She was determined to bring a little gaiety into their dull lives. For that was the awful part of it: Miss Reid meant well. She was not only having a good time herself, but she was trying to give all of them a good time. She was convinced that they liked her as much as she liked them. She felt that she was doing her bit to make the party a success and she was naïvely happy to think that she was succeeding. She told them all about her friend Miss Price and how often she had said to her: Venetia, no one ever has a dull moment in your company. It was the captain's duty to be polite to a passenger and however much he would have liked to tell her to hold her silly tongue he could not, but even if he had been free to say what he liked, he knew that he could not have brought himself to hurt her feelings. Nothing stemmed the torrent of her loquacity. It was as irresistible as a force of nature. Once in desperation they began talking German, but Miss Reid stopped this at once.

"Now I won't have you saying things I don't understand. You ought all to make the most of your good luck in having me all to yourselves and practise your English."

"We were talking of technical matters that would only bore you, Miss Reid," said the captain.

"I'm never bored. That's why, if you won't think me a wee bit conceited to say so, I'm never boring. You see, I like to know

things. Everything interests me and you never know when a bit
of information won't come in useful."

The doctor smiled dryly.

"The captain was only saying that because he was embarrassed. In point of fact he was telling a story that was not fit
for the ears of a maiden lady."

"I may be a maiden lady but I'm also a woman of the world,
I don't expect sailors to be saints. You need never be afraid of
what you say before me, Captain, I shan't be shocked. I should
love to hear your story."

The doctor was a man of sixty with thin grey hair, a grey
moustache and small bright blue eyes. He was a silent, bitter
man, and however hard Miss Reid tried to bring him into the
conversation it was almost impossible to get a word out of him.
But she wasn't a woman who would give in without a struggle,
and one morning when they were at sea and she saw him sitting
on deck with a book, she brought her chair next to his and sat
down beside him.

"Are you fond of reading, Doctor?" she said brightly.

"Yes."

"So am I. And I suppose like all Germans you're musical."

"I'm fond of music."

"So am I. The moment I saw you I thought you looked
clever."

He gave her a brief look and pursing his lips went on reading.
Miss Reid was not disconcerted.

"But of course one can always read. I always prefer a good
talk to a good book. Don't you?"

"No."

"How very interesting. Now do tell me why?"

"I can't give you a reason."

"That's very strange, isn't it? But then I always think human
nature is strange. I'm terribly interested in people, you know.
I always like doctors, they know so much about human nature,
but I could tell you some things that would surprise even you.
You learn a great deal about people if you run a tea-shop like
I do, that's to say if you keep your eyes open."

The doctor got up.

"I must ask you to excuse me, Miss Reid. I have to go and see
a patient."

"Anyhow I've broken the ice now," she thought, as he walked
away. "I think he was only shy."

But a day or two later the doctor was not feeling at all well. He had an internal malady that troubled him now and then, but he was used to it and disinclined to talk about it. When he had one of his attacks he only wanted to be left alone. His cabin was small and stuffy, so he settled himself on a long chair on deck and lay with his eyes closed. Miss Reid was walking up and down to get the half-hour's exercise she took morning and evening. He thought that if he pretended to be asleep she would not disturb him. But when she had passed him half a dozen times she stopped in front of him and stood quite still. Though he kept his eyes closed he knew that she was looking at him.

"Is there anything I can do, Doctor?" she said.

He started.

"Why, what should there be?"

He gave her a glance and saw that her eyes were deeply troubled.

"You look dreadfully ill," she said.

"I'm in great pain."

"I know. I can see that. Can't something be done?"

"No, it'll pass off presently."

She hesitated for a moment then went away. Presently she returned.

"You look so uncomfortable with no cushions or anything. I've brought you my own pillow that I always travel with. Do let me put it behind your head."

He felt at that moment too ill to remonstrate. She lifted his head gently and put the soft pillow behind it. It really did make him feel more comfortable. She passed her hand across his forehead and it was cool and soft.

"Poor dear," she said. "I know what doctors are. They haven't the first idea how to take care of themselves."

She left him, but in a minute or two returned with a chair and a bag. The doctor when he saw her gave a twitch of anguish.

"Now I'm not going to let you talk, I'm just going to sit beside you and knit. I always think it's a comfort when one isn't feeling very well to have someone near."

She sat down and taking an unfinished muffler out of her bag began busily to ply her needles. She never said a word. And strangely enough the doctor found her company a solace. No one else on board had even noticed that he was ill, he had felt lonely, and the sympathy of that crashing bore was grateful to him. It soothed him to see her silently working and presently he fell asleep. When he awoke she was still working. She gave him a little smile, but did not speak. His pain had left him and he felt much better.

He did not go into the saloon till late in the afternoon. He found the captain and Hans Krause, the mate, having a glass of beer together.

"Sit down, Doctor," said the captain. "We're holding a council of war. You know that the day after to-morrow is Sylvester Abend."

"Of course."

Sylvester Abend, New Year's Eve, is an occasion that means a great deal to a German and they had all been looking forward to it. They had brought a Christmas tree all the way from Germany with them.

"At dinner to-day Miss Reid was more talkative than ever. Hans and I have decided that something must be done about it."

"She sat with me for two hours this morning in silence. I suppose she was making up for lost time."

"It's bad enough to be away from one's home and family just now anyway and all we can do is to make the best of a bad job. We want to enjoy our Sylvester Abend, and unless something is done about Miss Reid we haven't a chance."

"We can't have a good time if she's with us," said the mate. "She'll spoil it as sure as eggs is eggs."

"How do you propose to get rid of her, short of throwing her overboard?" smiled the doctor. "She's not a bad old soul; all she wants is a lover."

"At her age?" cried Hans Krause.

"Especially at her age. That inordinate loquacity, that passion for information, the innumerable questions she asks, her prosiness, the way she goes on and on—it is all a sign of her clamouring virginity. A lover would bring her peace. Those jangled nerves of hers would relax. At least for an hour she would have lived. The deep satisfaction which her being demands would travel through those exacerbated centres of speech, and we should have quiet."

It was always a little difficult to know how much the doctor meant what he said and when he was having a joke at your expense. The captain's blue eyes, however, twinkled mischievously.

"Well, Doctor, I have great confidence in your powers of

diagnosis. The remedy you suggest is evidently worth trying, and since you are a bachelor it is clear that it is up to you to apply it."

"Pardon me, Captain, it is my professional duty to prescribe remedies for the patients under my charge in this ship, but not to administer them personally. Besides, I am sixty."

"I am a married man with grown-up children," said the captain. "I am old and fat and asthmatic, it is obvious that I cannot be expected to undertake a task of this kind. Nature cut me out for the rôle of a husband and father, not for that of a lover."

"Youth in these matters is essential and good looks are advantageous," said the doctor gravely.

The captain gave a great bang on the table with his fist.

"You are thinking of Hans. You're quite right. Hans must do it."

The mate sprang to his feet.

"Me? Never."

"Hans, you are tall, handsome, strong as a lion, brave and young. We have twenty-three days more at sea before we reach Hamburg, you wouldn't desert your trusted old captain in an emergency or let down your good friend the doctor?"

"No, Captain, it's asking too much of me. I have been married less than a year and I love my wife. I can hardly wait to get back to Hamburg. She is yearning for me as I am yearning for her. I will not be unfaithful to her, especially with Miss Reid."

"Miss Reid's not so bad," said the doctor.

"Some people might call her even nice-looking," said the captain.

And indeed when you took Miss Reid feature by feature she was not in fact a plain woman. True, she had a long, stupid face, but her brown eyes were large and she had very thick lashes; her brown hair was cut short and curled rather prettily over her neck; she hadn't a bad skin, and she was neither too fat nor too thin. She was not old as people go nowadays, and if she had told you that she was forty you would have been quite willing to believe it. The only thing against her was that she was drab and dull.

"Must I then for twenty-three mortal days endure the prolixity of that tedious woman? Must I for twenty-three mortal days answer her inane questions and listen to her fatuous remarks? Must I, an old man, have my Sylvester Abend, the jolly evening I was looking forward to, ruined by the unwelcome company of that intolerable virgin? And all because no one can be found to show a little gallantry, a little human kindness, a spark of charity to a lonely woman. I shall wreck the ship."

"There's always the radio-operator," said Hans.

The captain gave a loud shout.

"Hans, let the ten thousand virgins of Cologne arise and call you blessed. Steward," he bellowed, "tell the radio-operator that I want him."

The radio-operator came into the saloon and smartly clicked his heels together. The three men looked at him in silence. He wondered uneasily whether he had done something for which he was to be hauled over the coals. He was above the middle height, with square shoulders and narrow hips, erect and slender, his tanned, smooth skin looked as though a razor had never touched it, he had large eyes of a startling blue and a mane of curling golden hair. He was a perfect specimen of young Teutonic manhood. He was so healthy, so vigorous, so much alive that even when he stood some way from you, you felt the glow of his vitality.

"Aryan, all right," said the captain. "No doubt about that. How old are you, my boy?"

"Twenty-one, sir."

"Married?"

"No, sir."

"Engaged?"

The radio-operator chuckled. There was an engaging boyishness in his laugh.

"No, sir."

"You know that we have a female passenger on board?"

"Yes, sir."

"Do you know her?"

"I've said good-morning to her when I've seen her on deck."

The captain assumed his most official manner. His eyes, which generally twinkled with fun, were stern and he got a sort of bark into his rich, fruity voice.

"Although this is a cargo-boat and we carry valuable freight, we also take such passengers as we can get, and this is a branch of our business that the company is anxious to encourage. My instructions are to do everything possible to promote the happiness and comfort of the passengers. Miss Reid needs a lover. The doctor and I have come to the conclusion that you are well suited to satisfy Miss Reid's requirements."

"Me, sir?"

The radio-operator blushed scarlet and then began to giggle, but quickly composed himself when he saw the set faces of the three men who confronted him.

"But she's old enough to be my mother."

"That at your age is a matter of no consequence. She is a woman of the highest distinction and allied to all the great families of England. If she were German she would be at least a countess. That you should have been chosen for this responsible position is an honour that you should greatly appreciate. Furthermore, your English is halting and this will give you an excellent opportunity to improve it."

"That of course is something to be thought of," said the radio-operator. "I know that I want practice."

"It is not often in this life that it is possible to combine pleasure with intellectual improvement, and you must congratulate yourself on your good fortune."

"But if I may be allowed to put the question, sir, why does Miss Reid want a lover?"

"It appears to be an old English custom for unmarried women of exalted rank to submit themselves to the embraces of a lover at this time of year. The company is anxious that Miss Reid should be treated exactly as she would be on an English ship, and we trust that if she is satisfied, with her aristocratic connections she will be able to persuade many of her friends to take cruises in the line's ships."

"Sir, I must ask to be excused."

"It is not a request that I am making, it is an order. You will present yourself to Miss Reid, in her cabin, at eleven o'clock to-night."

"What shall I do when I get there?"

"Do?" thundered the captain. "Do? Act naturally."

With a wave of the hand he dismissed him. The radio-operator clicked his heels, saluted and went out.

"Now let us have another glass of beer," said the captain.

At supper that evening Miss Reid was at her best. She was verbose. She was playful. She was refined. There was not a truism that she failed to utter. There was not a commonplace that she forebore to express. She bombarded them with foolish questions. The captain's face grew redder and redder as he sought to contain his fury; he felt that he could not go on being polite to her any longer and if the doctor's remedy did not help, one day he would forget himself and give her, not a piece, but the whole of his mind.

"I shall lose my job," he thought, "but I'm not sure that it wouldn't be worth it."

Next day they were already sitting at table when she came in to dinner.

"Sylvester Abend to-morrow," she said, brightly. That was the sort of thing she would say. She went on: "Well, what have you all been up to this morning?"

Since they did exactly the same thing every day, and she knew very well what that was, the question was enraging. The captain's heart sank. He briefly told the doctor what he thought of him.

"Now, no German, please," said Miss Reid archly. "You know I don't allow that, and why, Captain, did you give the poor doctor that sour look? It's Christmas time, you know; peace and good-will to all men. I'm so excited about to-morrow evening, and will there be candles on the Christmas tree?"

"Naturally."

"How thrilling! I always think a Christmas tree without candles isn't a Christmas tree. Oh, d'you know, I had such a funny experience last night. I can't understand it at all."

A startled pause. They all looked intently at Miss Reid. For once they hung on her lips.

"Yes," she went on in that monotonous, rather finicking way of hers, "I was just getting into bed last night when there was a knock at my door. 'Who is it?' I said. 'It's the radio-operator,' was the answer. 'What is it?' I said. 'Can I speak to you?' he said."

They listened with rapt attention.

" 'Well, I'll just pop on a dressing-gown,' I said, 'and open the door.' So I popped on a dressing-gown and opened the door. The radio-operator said: 'Excuse me, miss, but do you want to send a radio?' Well, I did think it was funny his coming at that hour to ask me if I wanted to send a radio, I just laughed in his face, it appealed to my sense of humour if you understand what I mean, but I didn't want to hurt his feelings so I said: 'Thank you so much, but I don't think I want to send a radio.' He stood there, looking so funny, as if he was quite embarrassed, so I said: 'Thank you all the same for asking me,' and then I said 'Good-night, pleasant dreams' and shut the door."

"The damned fool," cried the captain.

"He's young, Miss Reid," the doctor put in. "It was excess of zeal. I suppose he thought you would want to send a New Year's greeting to your friends and he wished you to get the advantage of the special rate."

"Oh, I didn't mind at all. I like these queer little things that happen to one when one's travelling. I just get a good laugh out of them."

As soon as dinner was over and Miss Reid had left them the captain sent for the radio-operator.

"You idiot, what in heaven's name made you ask Miss Reid last night whether she wanted to send a radio?"

"Sir, you told me to act naturally. I am a radio-operator. I thought it natural to ask her if she wanted to send a radio. I didn't know what else to say."

"God in heaven," shouted the captain, "when Siegfried saw Brunhilde lying on her rock and cried: *Das ist kein Mann,*" (the captain sang the words, and being pleased with the sound of his voice, repeated the phrase two or three times before he continued), "did Siegfried when she awoke ask her if she wished to send a radio, to announce to her papa, I suppose, that she was sitting up after her long sleep and taking notice?"

"I beg most respectfully to draw your attention to the fact that Brunhilde was Siegfried's aunt. Miss Reid is a total stranger to me."

"He did not reflect that she was his aunt. He knew only that she was a beautiful and defenceless woman of obviously good family and he acted as any gentleman would have done. You are young, handsome, Aryan to the tips of your fingers, the honour of Germany is in your hands."

"Very good, sir. I will do my best."

That night there was another knock on Miss Reid's door.

"Who is it?"

"The radio-operator. I have a radio for you, Miss Reid."

"For me?" She was surprised, but it at once occurred to her that one of her fellow-passengers who had got off at Haiti had sent her New Year's greetings. "How very kind people are," she thought. "I'm in bed. Leave it outside the door."

"It needs an answer. Ten words prepaid."

Then it couldn't be a New Year's greeting. Her heart stopped beating. It could only mean one thing; her shop had been burned to the ground. She jumped out of bed.

"Slip it under the door and I'll write the answer and slip it back to you."

The envelope was pushed under the door and as it appeared on the carpet it had really a sinister look. Miss Reid snatched it up and tore the envelope open. The words swam before her eyes and she couldn't for a moment find her spectacles. This is what she read:

"Happy New Year. Stop. Peace and goodwill to all men. Stop. You are very beautiful. Stop. I love you. Stop. I must speak to you. Stop. Signed: Radio Operator."

Miss Reid read this through twice. Then she slowly took off her spectacles and hid them under a scarf. She opened the door.

"Come in," she said.

Next day was New Year's Eve. The officers were cheerful and a little sentimental when they sat down to dinner. The stewards had decorated the saloon with tropical creepers to make up for holly and mistletoe, and the Christmas tree stood on a table with the candles ready to be lit at supper time. Miss Reid did not come in till the officers were seated, and when they bade her good-morning she did not speak but merely bowed. They looked at her curiously. She ate a good dinner, but uttered never a word. Her silence was uncanny. At last the captain could stand it no longer, and he said:

"You're very quiet to-day, Miss Reid."

"I'm thinking," she remarked.

"And will you not tell us your thoughts, Miss Reid?" the doctor asked playfully.

She gave him a cool, you might almost have called it a supercilious, look.

"I prefer to keep them to myself, Doctor. I will have a little more of that hash, I've got a very good appetite."

They finished the meal in a blessed silence. The captain heaved a sigh of relief. That was what meal-time was for, to eat, not to chatter. When they had finished he went up to the doctor and wrung his hand.

"Something has happened, Doctor."

"It has happened. She's a changed woman."

"But will it last?"

"One can only hope for the best."

Miss Reid put on an evening dress for the evening's celebration, a very quiet black dress, with artificial roses at her bosom and a long string of imitation jade round her neck. The lights were dimmed and the candles on the Christmas tree were lit. It felt a little like being in church. The junior officers were supping in the saloon that evening and they looked very smart in their white uniforms. Champagne was served at the company's expense and after supper they had a *Maibowle*. They pulled crackers. They sang songs to the gramophone, *Deutschland, Deutschland über Alles, Alt Heidelberg* and *Auld Lang Syne*. They shouted out the tunes lustily, the captain's voice rising loud above the others, and Miss Reid joining in with a pleasing contralto. The doctor noticed that Miss Reid's eyes from time to time rested on the radio-operator, and in them he read an expression of some bewilderment.

"He's a good-looking fellow, isn't he?" said the doctor.

Miss Reid turned round and looked at the doctor coolly.

"Who?"

"The radio-operator. I thought you were looking at him."

"Which is he?"

"The duplicity of women," the doctor muttered, but with a smile he answered: "He's sitting next to the chief engineer."

"Oh, of course, I recognise him now. You know, I never think it matters what a man looks like. I'm so much more interested in a man's brains than in his looks."

"Ah," said the doctor.

They all got a little tight, including Miss Reid, but she did not lose her dignity and when she bade them good-night it was in her best manner.

"I've had a very delightful evening. I shall never forget my New Year's Eve on a German boat. It's been very interesting. Quite an experience."

She walked steadily to the door, and this was something of a triumph, for she had drunk drink for drink with the rest of them through the evening.

They were all somewhat jaded next day. When the captain, the mate, the doctor and the chief engineer came down to dinner they found Miss Reid already seated. Before each place was a small parcel tied up in pink ribbon. On each was written: Happy New Year. They gave Miss Reid a questioning glance.

"You've all been so very kind to me I thought I'd like to give each of you a little present. There wasn't much choice at Port au Prince, so you mustn't expect too much."

There was pair of briar pipes for the captain, half a dozen silk handkerchiefs for the doctor, a cigar-case for the mate and a couple of ties for the chief engineer. They had dinner and Miss Reid retired to her cabin to rest. The officers looked at one another uncomfortably. The mate fiddled with the cigar-case she had given him.

"I'm a little ashamed of myself," he said at last.

The captain was pensive and it was plain that he too was a trifle uneasy.

"I wonder if we ought to have played that trick on Miss Reid," he said. "She's a good old soul and she's not rich; she's a woman who earns her own living. She must have spent the best part of a hundred marks on these presents. I almost wish we'd left her alone."

The doctor shrugged his shoulders.

"You wanted her silenced and I've silenced her."

"When all's said and done, it wouldn't have hurt us to listen to her chatter for three weeks more," said the mate.

"I'm not happy about her," added the captain. "I feel there's something ominous in her quietness."

She had spoken hardly a word during the meal they had just shared with her. She seemed hardly to listen to what they said.

"Don't you think you ought to ask her if she's feeling quite well, Doctor?" suggested the captain.

"Of course she's feeling quite well. She's eating like a wolf. If you want inquiries made you'd much better make them of the radio-operator."

"You may not be aware of it, Doctor, but I am a man of great delicacy."

"I am a man of heart myself," said the doctor.

For the rest of the journey those men spoilt Miss Reid outrageously. They treated her with the consideration they would have shown to someone who was convalescent after a long and dangerous illness. Though her appetite was excellent they sought to tempt her with new dishes. The doctor ordered wine and insisted on her sharing his bottle with him. They played dominoes with her. They played chess with her. They played bridge with her. They engaged her in conversation. But there was no doubt about it, though she responded to their advances with politeness, she kept herself to herself. She seemed to regard them with something very like disdain; you might almost have thought that she looked upon those men and their efforts to be amiable as pleasantly ridiculous. She seldom spoke unless spoken to. She read detective stories and at night sat on deck looking at the stars. She lived a life of her own.

At last the journey drew to its close. They sailed up the English Channel on a still grey day; they sighted land. Miss Reid packed her trunk. At two o'clock in the afternoon they docked at Plymouth. The captain, the mate and the doctor came along to say good-bye to her.

"Well, Miss Reid," said the captain in his jovial way, "we're sorry to lose you, but I suppose you're glad to be getting home."

"You've been very kind to me, you've all been very kind to me, I don't know what I've done to deserve it. I've been very happy with you. I shall never forget you."

She spoke rather shakily, she tried to smile, but her lips quivered, and tears ran down her cheeks. The captain got very red. He smiled awkwardly.

"May I kiss you, Miss Reid?"

She was taller than he by half a head. She bent down and he planted a fat kiss on one wet cheek and a fat kiss on the other. She turned to the mate and the doctor. They both kissed her.

"What an old fool I am," she said. "Everybody's so good."

She dried her eyes and slowly, in her graceful, rather absurd way, walked down the companion. The captain's eyes were wet. When she reached the quay she looked up and waved to someone on the boat deck.

"Who's she waving to?" asked the captain.

"The radio-operator."

Miss Price was waiting on the quay to welcome her. When they had passed the Customs and got rid of Miss Reid's heavy luggage they went to Miss Price's house and had an early cup of tea. Miss Reid's train did not start till five. Miss Price had much to tell Miss Reid.

"But it's too bad of me to go on like this when you've just come home. I've been looking forward to hearing all about your journey."

"I'm afraid there's not very much to tell."

"I can't believe that. Your trip was a success, wasn't it?"

"A distinct success. It was very nice."

"And you didn't mind being with all those Germans?"

"Of course they're not like English people. One has to get used to their ways. They sometimes do things that—well, that English people wouldn't do, you know. But I always think that one has to take things as they come."

"What sort of things do you mean?"

Miss Reid looked at her friend calmly. Her long, stupid face had a placid look, and Miss Price never noticed that in the eyes was a strangely mischievous twinkle.

"Things of no importance really. Just funny, unexpected, rather nice things. There's no doubt that travel is a wonderful education."